# THE THINGAMAJIG THAT DOES THE JOB

With a roar, four trolls charged into the clearing. They were huge and foul-smelling, clad in skins and leather and rags. One brandished a rusty two-handed sword in one hand and others carried clubs.

A troll closed in on Moira, arms extended and fanged mouth agape. Wiz grabbed a burning faggot from the fire and charged. With a casual, backhanded swipe, the creature sent Wiz sprawling through the fire.

Wiz rolled out as the beast got a hand on Moira. Without thinking, he reached back into the fire and grabbed a burning brand. He pointed it at the troll and yelled, "bippity, boppity, boo."

The troll was unfazed but the tree behind it exploded into flame with a crackle and roar. The astonished troll weakened its grip and Moira twisted free.

"Moira! Run!" Wiz yelled and ducked under the grasping arms of another troll. He twisted about and pointed the stick at it. "Bippity boppity boo!" Another tree blazed up and the troll cringed back.

Whirling in a circle, Wiz pointed the branch and yelled, "BippityboppitybooBippityboppitybooBippity-boppityboo." Trees all around the clearing turned to fiercely burning torches and the confused trolls cowered and whimpered in the ring of light and heat.

# BAEN BOOKS by RICK COOK

*The Wiz Biz*
*The Wizardry Cursed*
*The Wizardry Consulted*
*The Wizardry Quested*
*Mall Purchase Night*

# The Wiz Biz

# Rick Cook

THE WIZ BIZ

This is a work of fiction. All the characters and events portrayed in this book are fictional, and any resemblance to real people or incidents is purely coincidental.

A Baen Books Original

Baen Publishing Enterprises
P.O. Box 1403
Riverdale, NY 10471

ISBN: 0-671-87846-8

Cover art by Tom Kidd

First printing, October 1997

Distributed by Simon & Schuster
1230 Avenue of the Americas
New York, NY 10020

Typeset by Windhaven Press, Auburn, NH
Printed in the United States of America

# Table of Contents

## WIZARD'S BANE

## WIZARDRY COMPILED

### PART I: LOAD TIME

## PART II: Link Time

## PART III: Compile

## Part IV: Run Time

# BOOK ONE:

# WIZARD'S BANE

**For Pati.**
**Who has her own**
**special brand of magic.**

# *One*
## MEETING IN MIDSUMMER

It was a fine Mid-Summer's morning and Moira the hedge witch was out gathering herbs.

"Tansy to stop bleeding," she said to herself, examining the stand that grew on the bankside. Carefully she selected the largest, healthiest stems and, reciting the appropriate charm, she cut them off low with her silver knife. She inspected each stem closely before placing it in the straw basket beside her.

When she had finished, she brushed a strand of coppery hair from her green eyes and surveyed the forest with all her senses.

The day was sunny, the air was clear and the woods around her were calm and peaceful. The oaks and beeches spread their gray-green and green-gold leaves to the sun and breeze. In their branches birds sang and squirrels chattered as they dashed about on squirrelish errands. Their tiny minds were content, Moira saw. For them there was no danger on the Fringe of the Wild Wood, even on Mid-Summer's Day.

Moira knew better. Back in her village the fields were deserted and the animals locked in their barns. The villagers were huddled behind doors bolted with iron, bound with ropes of straw and sealed with such charms as Moira could provide. Only a foolhardy person or one

1

in great need would venture abroad on Mid-Summer's Day.

Moira was out for need, the needs of others. Mid-Summer's Day was pregnant with magic of all sorts, and herbs gathered by the light of the Mid-Summer sun were unusually potent. Her village would need the healing potions and the charms she could make from them.

That most of her fellow hedge witches were also behind bolted doors weighed not at all with her. Her duty was to help those who needed help, so she had taken her straw basket and consecrated silver knife and gone alone into the Fringe of the Wild Wood.

She was careful to stay in the quietest areas of the Fringe, however. She had planned her route days ago and she moved cautiously between her chosen stands of herbs. She probed the forest constantly, seeking the least sign of danger or heightened magic. There was need enough to draw her out this day, but no amount of need would make her careless.

Her next destination was a marshy corner of a nearby meadow where pink-flowered mallow grew in spiky profusion. It was barely half a mile by the road on whose bank she sat, but Moira would take a longer route. Between her and the meadow this road crossed another equally well-travelled lane. Moira had no intention of going near a crossroads on Mid-Summer's Day.

She was fully alert, so she was all the more startled when a dark shadow fell over her. Moira gasped and whirled to find herself facing a tall old man wearing a rough travelling cloak and leaning on a carved staff.

"Oh! Merry met, Lord," she scrambled up from the bank and dipped a curtsey. "You startled me."

"Merry met, child," the man responded, blinking at her with watery brown eyes. "Why it's the little hedge witch, Moira, isn't it?" He blinked again and stared down his aquiline nose. "Bless me!" he clucked. "How you have grown my girl. How you have grown."

Moira nodded respectfully and said nothing. Patrius was of the Mighty; perhaps the mightiest of the Mighty. It behooves one to be respectful no matter what style one of the Mighty chooses to take.

The wizard sighed. "But it's well met nonetheless. Yes, very well met. I have a little project afoot and perhaps you can help me with it."

"Of course Lord, if I can." She sighed to herself. It was never too healthy to become involved with the doings of the Mighty. Looking at Patrius she could see magic twist and shimmer around the old man like heat waves rising from a hot iron stove.

"Well, actually it's not such a little project," he said confidingly. "A rather large one, in fact. Yes, quite large." He beamed at her. "Oh, but I'm sure you'll be able to handle it. You were always such an adept pupil."

In fact Moira had been so far from adept she had barely survived the months she had spent studying with the old wizard. She knew Patrius remembered that time perfectly. But if one of the Mighty asks for aid he or she can not be gainsaid.

"Lord," suggested Moira timidly, "might not one of your apprentices . . . ?"

"What? My apprentices, oh no, no, no. They don't know, you see. They can't know yet. Besides," he added as an afterthought, "they're all male."

"Yes, Lord," Moira said as if that explained everything.

The wizard straightened. "Now come along, child. The place is near and we haven't much time. And you must tell me how you have been getting along. It's been such an age since I saw you last. You never come to the Capital, you know," he added in mild reproach.

"For those of us who cannot walk the Wizard's Way it is a long journey, Lord."

"Ah yes, you're right, of course," the old man chuckled. "But tell me, how do things go on in your village?"

Moira warmed. Studying under Patrius had nearly

killed her several times, but of all her teachers she liked him the best. His absentminded, grandfatherly manner might be assumed, but no one who knew him doubted his kindness. She remembered sitting in the wizard's study of an afternoon drinking mulled cider and talking of nothing that mattered while dust motes danced in the sunbeams.

If Patrius was perhaps not the mightiest of the Mighty, he was certainly the best, the nicest and far and away the most human of that fraternity of powerful wizards. Walking with him Moira felt warm and secure, as if she were out on a picnic with a favorite uncle instead of abroad on the Fringe of the Wild Wood on one of the most dangerous days of the year.

Patrius took her straight into the forest, ignoring the potential danger spots all around. At length they came to a grassy clearing marked only by a rock off to one side.

"Now my child," he said, easing himself down on the stone and resting his staff beside him, "you're probably wondering what I'm up to, eh?"

"Yes, Lord." Moira stood a respectful distance away.

"Oh, come here my girl," he motioned her over. "Come, come, come. Be comfortable." Moira smiled and sat on the grass at his feet, spreading her skirt around her.

"To business then. I intend to perform a Great Summoning and I want your help."

Moira gasped. She had never seen even a Lesser Summoning, the materializing of a person or object from elsewhere in the World. It was solely the province of the Mighty and so fraught with danger that they did it rarely. A Great Summoning brought something from beyond the World and was far riskier. Of all the Mighty living, only Patrius, Bal-Simba and perhaps one or two others had ever participated in a Great Summoning.

"But Lord, you need several of the Mighty for that!"

Patrius frowned. "Do you presume to teach me magic, girl?"

"No, Lord," Moira dropped her eyes to the grass.

The wizard's face softened. "It is true that a Great Summoning is usually done by several of us acting in consort, but there is no need, really. Not if the place of Summoning is quiet."

So that was why Patrius had come to the Fringe, Moira thought. Here, away from the bustle and disturbance of competing magics, it would be easier for him to bend the fundamental forces of the World to his will.

"Isn't it dangerous, Lord?"

Patrius sighed, looking suddenly like a careworn old man rather than a mighty wizard or someone's grandfather.

"Yes Moira, it is. But sometimes the dangerous road is the safest." He shook his head. "These are evil times, child. As well you know."

"Yes, Lord," said Moira, with a sudden pang.

"Evil times," Patrius repeated. "Desperate times. They call for desperate measures.

"You know our plight, Moira. None know better than the hedge witches and the other lesser orders. We of the Mighty are isolated in our keeps and cities, but you have to deal with the World every day. The Wild Wood presses ever closer and to the south the Dark League waxes strong to make chaos of what little order there is in the World."

Moira's hand moved in a warding gesture at the mention of the League, but Patrius caught her wrist and shook his head.

"Softly, softly," he admonished. "We must do nothing to attract attention, eh?

"We need help, Moira," he went on. "The people of the North need help badly and there are none in the World who can help us. So I must go beyond the World to find aid."

He sighed again. "It was a long search, my child, long and hard. But I have finally located someone of great power who can help us, both against the League and against the World. Now the time is ripe and I propose to Summon him."

"But won't this alien wizard be angry at being brought here so rudely?"

"I did not say he was a wizard," Patrius said with a little shake of his head. "No, I did not say that at all."

"Who but a wizard can deal in magic?"

"Who indeed? Patrius responded. "Who indeed?"

It was Moira's turn to sigh, inwardly at least. Patrius had obviously told her as much of this mad venture as he intended to.

"What will you of me, Lord?" asked Moira.

"Just your aid as lector," the old wizard said. "Your aid and a drop of your blood."

"Willingly, Lord." Moira was relieved it wasn't more. Often great spells required great sacrifices.

"Well then," said the Wizard, picking up his staff and rising. "Let us begin. You'll have to memorize the chant, of course."

Patrius cut a straight branch from a nearby tree, stripped it of its leaves and stuck it upright in the clearing. Its shadow stretched perhaps four handsbreadths from its base, shortening imperceptibly as the sun climbed higher.

"When the shadow disappears it will be time," he told her. "Now, here is what you must say. . . ."

The words Moira had to speak were simple, but they sent shivers down her spine. Patrius repeated them to her several times, speaking every other word on each repetition so magic would not be made prematurely. As a trained witch Moira easily put the words in the right order and fixed them in her mind.

While the hedge witch worked on the spells, Patrius walked the clearing, carefully aligning the positions where they both would stand and scratching runes into the earth.

Moira looked up from her memorization. "Lord," she said dubiously, "aren't you forgetting the pentagram?"

"Eh? No girl, I'm not forgetting. We only need a pentagram to contain the Summoned should it prove dangerous."

"And this one is not dangerous?" Moira frowned.

Patrius chuckled. "No, he is not dangerous."

Moira wanted to ask how someone could be powerful enough to aid the Mighty and still not be dangerous even when Summoned, but Patrius motioned her to silence, gestured her to her place and, as the stick's shadow shortened to nothing, began his part of the chant.

"*Aaagggh!*" William Irving Zumwalt growled at the screen. Without taking his eyes off the fragment of code, he grabbed the can of cola balanced precariously on the mound of printouts and hamburger wrappers littering his desk.

"Found something, Wiz?" his cubicle mate asked, looking up from his terminal.

"Only the bug that's been screwing up the sort module."

William Irving Zumwalt—Wiz to one and all—leaned back and took a healthy swig of cola. It was warm and flat from sitting for hours, but he barely noticed. "Here. Take a look at this."

Jerry Andrews shifted his whale-like bulk and swiveled his chair to look over Wiz's shoulder. "Yeah? So?"

Wiz ran a long, thin hand through his shock of dark hair. "Don't you see? This cretinous barfbag uses **sizeof** to return the size of the array."

"So how else do you get the size?"

"Right. But C doesn't have an array data type. When you call an array you're actually passing a pointer to the

array. That works fine from the main program, but
sometimes this thing uses **sizeof** from a subroutine. And
guess what it gets then?"

Jerry clapped a meaty hand to his forehead. "The size
of the pointer! Of course."

"Right," Wiz said smugly. "No matter how big the
array, the damn code returns a value of two."

"Jeez," Jerry shook his head as he shifted his chair
back to his desk. "How long will it take to fix it?"

Wiz drained his drink before answering. "Couple of
hours, I guess. I'll have to run a bunch of tests to make
sure nothing else is wrong." He stood up and stretched.
"But first I'm going to get another Coke—if the damn
machine isn't empty again. You want one?"

"Nah," Jerry said, typing rapidly and not looking up.
"I'm probably gonna knock off in a few minutes."

"Okay," said Wiz and sauntered out the office door.

Save for the clicking of Jerry's keyboard and the hiss
of the air conditioner the corridor was quiet. Wiz glanced
at his watch and realized it was nearly five A.M. Not that
it mattered much. Programmers set their own hours at
ZetaSoft and that was one of the reasons Will Zumwalt
was still with the company.

The drink machine was next to a side door and Wiz
decided to step out for a breath of dawn air. He loved this
time of day when everything was cool and quiet and even
the air was still, waiting. *As long as I don't have to get up
at this hour!* he thought as he pushed the door open.

*The magical lines of force gathered and curled about
the old wizard. They twisted and warped, clawing at the
very fabric of the Universe and bending it to a new shape.
Far to the South, across the Freshened Sea, a point of
light appeared in the watery depths of an enormous
copper bowl.*

"A hit," proclaimed the watcher, a lean shaven-skull
man in a brown robe.

"What is it?" asked Xind, Master of the Sea of Scrying. He descended heavily from his dais and waddled across the torch-lit chamber hewn of blackest basalt to peer over the acolyte's shoulder.

Looking deep into the murky water his eyes traced the map of the World in the lines cut deep into the bowl's bottom. There was indeed a spark there. Magic where no magic ought to be. Around the edge of the bowl the other three acolytes shifted nervously but kept their eyes fixed to their own sectors.

"I do not know, Master, but it's strong and growing stronger. It looks like a major spell."

Xind, sorcerer of the Third Circle as the Dark League counted such things, passed a fat hand over the water as if wiping away a smear. "Hmm, yes. Wait, there's something . . . By the heavens and hells! There are no wards. That's a great wizard without protection!" His head snapped up. "Let the word be passed quickly!" The gray-robed apprentice crouched at the foot of the dais jumped up and ran to do his bidding.

Xind stared back into the Sea of Scrying and his round, fat face creased into a particularly unattractive smile.

"Fool," he muttered to the spark in the bottom of the bowl.

The haze in the clearing turned from wispy gray to opaque white to rosy pink. It contracted and coalesced until it took the form of a dark red door with a silver knob, floating a yard off the meadow. The grass bent away from it in all directions as if pressed down by an invisible ball. Moira concentrated on her chanting and pushed harder with all the magic she possessed.

As if in slow motion the door opened and a man came through. He stepped out as if he expected solid ground and slowly toppled through when he found air. His eyes widened and his mouth formed a soundless O. Then everything was moving at normal speed and the man extended his arms.

Wiz took two steps and fell three feet onto grass in what should have been a level walk. He caught himself with his arms and then collapsed with his nose in the green grass, weak, sick and disoriented. The light was different, he was facing the wrong way and he was so dizzy he couldn't hold his head up. He squeezed his eyes shut and concentrated on keeping his stomach in its proper place. The grass tickled his nose and the blades poked at his tightly shut eyes, but he ignored them.

Patrius made a flicking gesture at the man and then returned to the business of completing the spell. Moira, absorbed in her chant, barely noticed the small drop of dark fluid fly from the Wizard's fingertips and strike the new arrival on the temple. It splattered, spread and sank into the flesh and hair, leaving no sign of its passing.

*In the great, high, vaulted chantry of the Dark League, four black-robed wizards huddled about a glowing crystal. They murmured and moved like a flock of uneasy crows, all the while peering into the depths of the stone. Around them forces twisted and gathered.*

The attack came with a rush of magic, dark and sour. Moira cried out in terror and gestured frantically but she was thrust aside ruthlessly as the bolt lanced into the clearing and struck Patrius full-on.

A crackling blue nimbus burst out around the old wizard. He raised his arms over his head as if to shield himself, but his clothes and beard burst into flame. In an instant he was a ghastly flaming scarecrow capering about the clearing and shrieking in mortal agony. He toppled over and the screams turned to a puling whimper. His flesh blackened and charred.

Finally there was nothing but a smouldering husk with knees and arms flexed up against the body. He was so badly burned that there wasn't even a smell in the air.

Moira cowered sobbing on the ground, the blazing after-image burning in her sight even through her eyelids. Wiz had gone flat on his face when the bolt hit.

*All right,* Wiz told himself. *Time to get up. On three. One, two . . .* He realized he wasn't going to make it, so he settled for rolling over on his back.

"Lord?" a small voice asked tentatively.

Wiz opened his eyes. Standing over him was the most beautiful girl he had ever seen. Her waist-length hair was the color of burnished copper. Her skin was pale and creamy under a dusting of freckles. Her eyes were deep sea green. She was wearing a long skirt of forest green in some rough-woven material and a white peasant blouse with a scoop neck. Wiz stared.

"Are you hurt, Lord?" the vision said in a lilting, musical voice. As she bent down to help Wiz up he was treated to an ample display of cleavage.

"N-n-n-no," Wiz managed to stammer, dizzy from the transformation and awed by her loveliness. He looked into her face. "You're beautiful," he said softly.

Moira saw the look in his eyes and swore under her breath. *Fortuna!* An infatuation spell! Patrius had bound this unknown wizard to her with an infatuation spell. Gently she helped the alien wizard to his feet and wondered if she should curtsey.

"How are you called, Lord?" Moira asked respectfully.

"Ah, Wiz. I'm Wiz Zumwalt, that is. Who are you?"

"I am called Moira, Lord, a hedge witch of this place." She ignored the discourtesy of his question. She reddened under his fixed gaze and wondered what to do next. She had already sent an urgent call for one of the Mighty to attend them, but even by the Wizard's Way that would take time. Wizards did not like to be bothered by idle chatter, but this one *stared* so.

"Lord, are you of the Mighty in your home?" she asked to make conversation.

"Say what?"

"Forgive me, Lord. The Mighty are the wizards of the first rank in our land."

"Wizards?" Between the transition and Moira, Wiz's brain wasn't working and he had never been much good at small talk with beautiful women.

"Magicians. Sorcerers," Moira said a little desperately. Wiz looked blank and a dreadful thought grew in the back of Moira's mind. "Forgive me Lord, but you *are* a wizard, are you not?"

"Huh. No, I'm not a wizard," Wiz said numbly, shaking his head to clear it.

Moira felt sick. This man was telling the trth! There was no sign or trace of magic about him, nothing save his odd clothing to distinguish him from any other mortal. She turned away from him and tears stung her eyes.

"Hey, what's wrong?" Wiz laid a hand on her shoulder.

"Everything," Moira sobbed. "You're not a wizard and Patrius is dead."

"Patrius . . . ?" Wiz trailed off. "Oh my God!" For the first time he saw the charred corpse at the edge of the clearing.

"I'm sorry," he said. "Is there anything I can do?"

"Yes," Moira said fiercely. "You can help me bury him."

"If you value your life," the black robe hissed, "keep your mouth shut and your eyes on the floor. Toth-Set-Ra has little patience with impertinence." Xind led the acolyte down the flagged corridor. Their sandals scuffed on the rough stone floor and guttering torches in iron brackets gave a dim and uncertain light to guide them. The guards at the door were hobgoblins, creatures somewhat larger than men and nearly twice as broad and bulky. Their laced armor shone blackly by the torchlight and the honed edges of their halberds glinted evilly. At the approach of the wizards they snapped to attention.

"Two with news for the Dread Master," Xind said with considerably more assurance than he felt. "We are expected." The hobgoblins nodded. One reached behind to swing open the great oaken door.

Both wizard and acolyte prostrated themselves on the threshold.

"Rise," croaked a voice from within. "Rise and speak."

The room was dark but a baleful green light played round a high-backed chair and the figure hunched in it.

Shakily, the pair rose and moved toward the light.

The man in the chair was wizened and shrunk in on himself until he was more a mummy than a living man. But his eyes burned red in the black pits of his hairless skull and he moved with the easy grace of a serpent coiling to strike. The light seemed to come from within him, playing on the chair and the amethyst goblet in his hand. The reflected greenish glow made Xind's complexion appear even more unhealthy than usual.

"We have slain a wizard, Dread Master, one of the Mighty of the North."

"Yes," Toth-Set-Ra hissed. "It was Patrius. May his soul rot forever. And you destroyed him. How nice."

The novice started and opened his mouth to ask how the wizard knew, but Xind trod on his foot in warning.

"He was performing a Great Summoning, Dread Master," Xind said, his head bowed respectfully.

"Indeed?" croaked Toth-Set-Ra. "Oh, indeed?" His reptilian gaze slid over his subordinates and settled back on the carved goblet. "And what was it that was Summoned?"

Xind licked his lips. "We do not know, Lord. The distance was too great and . . ."

"You do not know?" Toth-Set-Ra's voice grew harsher. "You disturb me with news I already know and you cannot tell me more than I can sense unaided?" His stare transfixed the black robe, steady, intent and pitiless. "What use are you, eh? Tell me why I shouldn't finish you now."

"Because you would lose our services," the acolyte said steadily. Xind blanched and trembled at the young man's audacity and Toth-Set-Ra shifted his basilisk stare to him. The acolyte stood with his eyes respectfully downcast but no hint of trepidation in his manner.

"Servants such as you I do not need," snapped the wizard. "Incompetents! Bunglers! Blind fools!" Without shifting his eyes, he threw the amethyst cup at them. It passed between the pair and shattered into priceless shards on the flags. Both men flinched away.

"Very well," he said finally. "Prove your worth. Find out what Patrius died to birth. If you are quick and if it is important I will give you your lives. If not, I have other uses for you."

The wizard sat glaring after them for several minutes. Finally he sealed the door with a gesture which raised a wall of blue fire across it. He went to a cabinet of age-blackened oak, opened it with curious and diverse gestures and removed an elaborately engraved box about the size of a man's head.

Carrying it gently he brought it back to the table. He set the box carefully in the center of the pentagram inlaid in silver in the dark onyx top and then, stepping back, made a gesture. The top flew open and a small red demon appeared in a puff of smoke. The demon flew toward him only to be brought up short by the pentagram. It dropped to its knees and pressed its clawed, misshapen hands against the invisible walls, seeking a way out.

"It is secure," croaked Toth-Set-Ra. "Now, by the spells which made you and the spells which bind you, I would have word of the world."

"There is pain and suffering," squeaked the demon.

"There is mortal misery and unhappiness, and boredom and ennui among the non-mortal."

"Specifically!" snapped the wizard and the demon fell back gibbering under the lash of his voice.

"What you will, Dread Master. What you will of me?"

"The Wizard Patrius."

"Dead, Dread Master. Struck down unprotected by your servants as he strove to weave a powerful spell. The Mighty in the midst of the mighty laid low."

"The spell?"

"A Great Summoning, Master. A Great Summoning."

"His assistants?"

"None, Master. None save a hedge witch."

Toth-Set-Ra frowned.

"And the Summoned?"

"A man, Master, only a man."

"A magician? A wizard?"

"I see no magic, Master. Save the hedge witch's and Bal-Simba, who comes after Patrius's burning."

"And what is his virtue? What is the special thing which made Patrius summon this one?"

"I do not know, Master. I see no answer."

"Then look ahead," commanded Toth-Set-Ra. "Look to the future."

"Aiii," gibbered the demon. "Aiii, destruction for us all! Pain and fire and the fall of towers. Magic of the strangest sort loosed upon the land! A plague, a pox, the bane of all wizards!" He capered about the pentagram as if the table had become red hot.

"How?" snapped the wizard. "Is he a wizard, then?"

"No wizard, Master. Magic without magic. Magic complex and subtle and strange. A plague upon all wizards, a bane. A bane! Aiii Good Master, let me leave him! Aiii!"

Toth-Set-Ra scowled. The demon was frightened! He knew from experience that it took a very great deal to frighten a demon and this one was so terrified it was almost incoherent.

"Leave then," he said and made the gesture of dismissal. The demon vanished in a puff of smoke and the lid of the box snapped down.

Toth-Set-Ra sat long scowling at the carven box while the heatless blue light from the flame at the door played across his leathery face and reflected from the sunken pits of his eyes. *A plague upon all wizards*. What could that be? And why would Patrius—may his soul rot!—risk his life to Summon such a one? The Northerners relied on magic fully as much as the League. Magic was as vital to life as air. More vital, he corrected himself. There were spells which allowed a man to live without air.

Might the demon have been mistaken? Toth-Set-Ra cocked his head to one side as he considered the notion. It was not unknown for demons to be wrong. They were, after all, no better than the spells that created them. But this scrying demon had never failed him. Not like this.

A trick by the Northerners? The scowl deepened. The wizard held out his hand to the side, fingers extended, and an amethyst goblet, twin to the one that lay in fragments on the floor, filled with wine from an unseen pitcher and flew to his clawlike grasp. Yes, it was possible the Northerners had staged the incident for the League's benefit, or even spoofed both the demon and the Sea of Scrying.

Toth-Set-Ra took a sip of the magically concocted vintage and shook his head. What possible advantage could the North have gained that was worth the death of their most powerful wizard?

Assuming Patrius *was* dead, of course. . . . Too many possibilities! He needed more information and quickly. He motioned toward the door and the curtain of fire vanished as suddenly as it had come. He struck a tiny gong and instantly one of his goblin guards was in the doorway.

"Atros, to me," he commanded. "At once!" The guard bowed and vanished in a single movement and Toth-Set-Ra scowled into the bottom of his wine. He would have an answer. If it took every wizard, every spell and every creature at his command, he would have an answer. And quickly!

They raised a mound over Patrius where he lay. Moira set Wiz to finding rocks while she used her silver knife to cut the green sward into turfs. The profanation rendered the knife useless for magical purposes, but she didn't care. She placed the turfs about the charred hulk who had been the greatest and best of wizards. From time to time she stopped to wipe away her tears with the sleeve of her blouse, unmindful of the dirt that it left streaked upon her cheeks. There was no proper shroud to be had, so Moira covered Patrius's face with her apron, tucking it in carefully around the body and murmuring a goodbye before she gently laid the bright green sod over him. The tiny flowers nodding in the grass made a fitting funeral bouquet.

Finally, she and Wiz piled the stones over the turf. They stuck the charred stump of the old wizard's staff upright in the top of the cairn.

"Dread Master?" The bear-like form of Atros blocked the door. Where the League's greatest wizard affected the robe of an anchorite, his subordinate wore a black bearskin, belted with studded leather and pinned with an intricately worked and bejeweled brooch. Toth-Set-Ra's pate was shaven and Atros wore his thick, dark hair to his shoulders, held in place with a golden filet. More, Atros was nearly as large as the hobgoblins and Toth-Set-Ra was tiny.

In spite of the contrast there was no question as to who held power.

"Patrius is dead," Toth-Set-Ra told his lieutenant without preamble. Atros said nothing. His spies had already told him that and he knew Toth-Set-Ra knew it.

"He attempted a Great Summoning, or so I am told,

and he brought someone from outside the World. A man."

Atros waited impassively.

"I want that man, Atros. I want him badly. See to it."

"It will take resources . . ." the great bear trailed off.

"You have them. Use them. Search the North. Scour the Capital if you must. But bring me that man!"

Atros bowed. "Thy will, Dread Master." And he was gone, leaving Toth-Set-Ra to brood.

Out in the corridor it was Atros's turn to scowl. The old crow had set him a pretty problem indeed! According to his spies the Sea of Scrying had failed to pick up any trace of the man. That scrying demon Toth-Set-Ra was so proud of must have failed or he would not have been given this mission—or the power to command so much of what his master controlled. Whoever he was, this man from without the World must have a very powerful masking spell to so effectively cloak his magic.

Well, magic wasn't the only way to find someone. That was the old crow's mistake, Atros thought. If he couldn't do it by magic he didn't think he could do it at all. But there were other ways. The Wild Wood was alive with creatures who were either allies, could be bribed to help, who were controlled or who could be enticed into helping. In the lands of Men there were spies, human and non-human. There were the Shadow Warriors. And then there were the massive and mighty magics of the City of Night. Here was power indeed to turn on finding a lone man.

That was the crux of it, he thought to himself as he strode along the dank, unevenly-flagged corridor. All that power, but only until he found this man. Oh, he would find him, never fear. That would be the easy part. And there were other things that could be done with the power he had just been given. Perhaps even concocting a nice little surprise for that scrawny excuse for a sorcerer who sat in the room down the hall.

Atros was intelligent but he was no more subtle than the bear whose name he had taken. It never occurred to him to wonder if perhaps Toth-Set-Ra might have considered that possibility as well.

Moira knelt weeping over Patrius's grave. Wiz stood by feeling clumsy and awkward. She was so beautiful he wanted to take her into his arms and comfort her. But when he put a hand on her shoulder she jerked away. He felt like a fool watching her cry, so he wandered around the edge of the clearing.

"Do not enter the woods," Moira said sharply through her tears. "It is not safe," she sniffed.

"You mean lions and tigers and bears?"

"And other things," Moira said grimly.

"You mean like . . . ULP!"

A huge black man stepped into the clearing directly in front of Wiz. He wore a leopard skin over his shoulders and a leather skirt around his huge middle. Around his neck was a necklace of bone with an eagle's skull as a pendant. In his right hand he carried an intricately carved staff nearly as tall as he was. He grinned and Wiz saw his teeth were filed to needle-sharp points.

He was so black his skin showed highlights of purple and he was the biggest man Wiz had ever seen. It wasn't just that he was more than six-and-a-half feet tall. His frame was huge, with shoulders twice as broad as a normal man's. He had a great black belly, arms thicker than Wiz's legs and legs like tree trunks.

Open-mouthed, Wiz backed away. Then Moira caught sight of him and let out a cry.

"Bal-Simba! Oh, Lord, you came." She ran across the clearing to meet him, checked herself suddenly and dropped him a respectful curtsey. "I mean, merry met, Lord."

The black giant nodded genially. "Merry met, child." He looked over to the freshly-raised mound and his face darkened. "Though I see it is not so merry."

"No, Lord," Moira looked up at him. "Patrius is dead, slain by sorcery."

Bal-Simba closed his eyes and his face contorted. "Evil news indeed."

Moira's eyes filled with tears. "I tried, Lord. I tried, but I could not . . ." She broke down completely. "Oh, Lord, I am so sorry," she sobbed.

Bal-Simba put a meaty arm around her shoulders and held her close. "I know, child. I know. No one will blame you for there was nothing you could have done." Moira cried helplessly into his barrel chest. Wiz stood by, wishing he could help and feeling like a complete jerk.

"Now child," Bal-Simba said as her sobs subsided. "Tell me how this came to pass. We sensed a great disturbance even before you called."

Moira drew away from him and sniffed. "He performed a Great Summoning without wards," she said as she wiped her eyes. "Just as he completed the spell he was struck down."

"What did he Summon?"

"Him," said Moira accusingly.

The black wizard looked down on Wiz in a way that reminded Wiz uncomfortably of a cat watching a mouse.

"How are you called?" Bal-Simba asked.

"I'm Wiz. Wiz Zumwalt." He waved hesitantly. "Hi."

The black giant nodded. "You are a wizard then. Of what rank?"

"Well no, I'm not a wizard," Wiz explained. "Wiz is just a nickname. My real name's William Irving . . ." He stopped as Bal-Simba held up a hand.

"I did not ask for your true name," he said sternly. "Never, *ever* tell anyone what you are truly named for that places you in the power of all who hear."

"You mean like knowing somebody's password? Ah, right."

"Like that," the wizard agreed. "I tell you again, Wiz. Never reveal your true name."

"Now," he went on in a somewhat gentler tone. "What is your special virtue?"

"Huh?"

"What is it that you do?"

"Oh, I'm a programmer. From Cupertino. Say, where are we, anyway?"

"We are in the North of World on the Fringe of the Wild Wood," Bal-Simba told him.

"Where's that in relation to California?"

"Far, far away I am afraid. You were Summoned from your own world to this one by he who is dead." He nodded in the direction of the freshly raised cairn.

"Oh," Wiz said blankly. "Okay." He paused. "Uh, how do I get back?"

"That may take some effort," Bal-Simba told him. The black giant suddenly became more intent.

"Again. What is your special virtue?"

"I told you, I'm a programmer. I work with computers."

"I do not think we have those here. What else do you do?"

"Well, ah. Nothing really. I just work with computers."

"Are you a warrior?"

"Huh? No!" Wiz was slightly shocked.

"Think," commanded Bal-Simba. "There must be something else."

"No, there really isn't," Wiz protested. "Well, I do watch a lot of old movies."

It was Bal-Simba's turn to look blank.

"That's all there is, honest." Wiz was facing the black wizard so he did not see Moira's face fall.

"There must be more here," said Bal-Simba. He paused for a minute.

"Now. I swear to you that I mean you no harm." He smote his breast over his heart. "I swear to you that I will neither willingly harm you nor allow you to come to harm." He struck his chest again. "That I may aid you, will you give me leave to look deeper into you?"

"Uh, yeah. Sure," Wiz said a little apprehensively.

"Then sit here where you may be more comfortable." Bal-Simba guided Wiz to the rock where Patrius had sat so recently. He reached into his pouch and drew out a small purple crystal. "Look at this." Wiz gazed at the tiny gem cupped in the great pink palm. "Look deeply. Fix your attention on it. Observe . . . observe."

Wiz's eyes glazed and his mouth went slack.

"To business then." Bal-Simba tucked the crystal back into his pouch and began the task of learning all he could about this visitor from so far away.

"Strange indeed," muttered Bal-Simba, turning from where Wiz dozed in a trance. "Very strange."

"How so, Lord?" Moira asked.

"There is no sign of magic."

"No magic! None at all?"

"None that I can detect. Despite his name, this Wiz is as lacking in manna as a newborn babe."

Moira crumpled. "Then it was all for nothing," she said bitterly. "Patrius died for nothing! Oh, Lord, I am so sorry."

"I do not know. There is something—strange—about him, but it is not magic."

"The effects of the Summoning?"

Bal-Simba frowned. "I do not think so. It goes beyond that, I believe." He kept silent for a moment.

"You say Patrius told you he was summoning a wizard?" he asked at last.

"Yes, Lord." Then Moira stopped. "Well . . . not exactly."

"What then exactly?"

Moira screwed up her face in an effort to remember. "Patrius said he was Summoning someone who could help us against the League." She made the warding gesture. "Someone with great magical power. When I asked him if the man was a wizard he evaded the question. But," she added thoughtfully, "he never called him a wizard."

"But he did say that this man had great power?"

"Yes, Lord. He said he looked long and hard to find him."

"That I can believe," Bal-Simba said absentmindedly. "Searching beyond the World is long and hard indeed. Hmm . . . but he did not call him a wizard, you say?"

"No, Lord."

"When I asked Patrius that he would not answer."

Bal-Simba's head sunk down on his chest.

"Lord," Moira interrupted timidly, "didn't Patrius tell the Council what he was doing?"

Bal-Simba grimaced. "Do you think we would have allowed this madness had we known? No, we knew Patrius was engaged in a great project of some sort, but he told no none, not even his apprentices, what he was about.

"He had spoken to me of the tide of our struggle with the Dark League and how it fared. He was not sanguine and I knew in a general way that he intended something beyond the common. But I had assumed he would lay the project before the Council when it came to fruition. I assumed rashly and it cost us dearly."

"But why, Lord? Why would he take such an awful risk?"

"Because with the League so strong not all of the Mighty together could have performed a Great Summoning."

He caught the look on Moira's face.

"You did not know that? Yes, it is true. All of us together are not enough to make magic of that sort against the League's opposition." He smiled ruefully. "Thus the Council wanes as the League grows greater."

"Then why . . . ?"

"Patrius obviously believed that by working alone and without the usual protections he might be able to complete the Summoning before the League realized what was happening. He was wrong and it cost him his life." He nodded toward Wiz. "Patrius risked his life to gain a man of great magical power. Instead he brought us someone who *seems* as common as dirt. It makes no sense."

Again the great Bal-Simba was silent, his head sank down on his necklace in contemplation.

"What do you think of this?" he asked finally.

"Lord, I am not qualified to pass on the actions of the Mighty."

Bal-Simba waved that aside. "You were here. You saw. What do you think?"

Moira took a deep breath. "I think Patrius made a mistake. I think he intended someone else and under the strain of the attack . . ." her green eyes misted and she swallowed hard as she relived those awful moments ". . . under the strain of the attack he Summoned the wrong person."

"Possible," Bal-Simba rumbled. "Just possible. But I wonder. Wizards who make mistakes do not live to become Mighty, still less as mighty as Patrius."

"Yes, Lord," said Moira meekly.

"I do not convince you, eh girl? Well, I am not sure I convince myself." He turned back and looked at Wiz, sitting dazed and uncomprehending on the stone. "In any event, the problem now is what to do with our visitor."

Moira snorted. "He is an expensive visitor, Lord. He cost us so much for so little."

"Perhaps, but we cannot leave him to wander. You can see for yourself that he is as helpless as a sparrow. Sparrow, hmm? A good world name for him, especially since the name he uses is too close to his true name. But no, he cannot be left to wander."

"Will you take him with you, Lord?"

Bal-Simba frowned. "That would not be wise, I think, and dangerous besides. The fewer who know of him the better. No, he needs to go someplace safe. A sanctuary with as little magic as possible. A place where he can remain while I consult the others of the Mighty."

"My village is . . ."

"Unsafe," the black giant said. "Already we are being probed. I suspect the League would like very much to get their hands on him."

"Would it matter so much? Since he has no magic, I mean."

"Hush, girl. You do not mean that."

Moira looked at Wiz with distaste but shook her head. Falling into the hands of the League was not a fate to be wished on anyone, even someone who had caused the death of Patrius.

"What then?"

"There is a place. A few days into the Wild Wood where he could find sanctuary. A place of very little magic."

Moira's eyes lit and she opened her mouth but Bal-Simba motioned her to silence. "Best not to say it. There might be others about to hear, eh? No, you will have to take him—there—and give him into the charge of the one who lives there."

"Me, Lord? But I have my work."

"I will see another is sent in your place. He must be guided and protected, do you not see?"

"But why me, Lord?"

Bal-Simba ticked off the reasons on his fingers. "First, you are here and already privy to this business. The less others know of it the better. Second, you know the way through the Wild Wood. Third, time is of the essence. This place grows increasingly dangerous. And fourth," he held up his pinky finger and his eyes twinkled, "he is in love with you."

Moira made a face. "An infatuation spell! But I am not in love with him."

"Nonetheless, he will follow at your heels like a puppy. No, you are the logical one to serve as the mother hen for our Sparrow."

"Forgive me, Lord, but I find his presence distasteful."

Bal-Simba sighed. "In this world, child, all of us must do things which are distasteful on occasion."

Moira bowed her head. "Yes, Lord." *But I don't have to like it!* she thought furiously.

"Very well, off with you then." He turned and gestured to Wiz. "Straight on and hurry." Wiz reeled and shook his head to clear it.

"I will need some things from the village, Lord."

"I will have someone meet you with food and your other needs at the bridge on the Forest Highway."

"Lord, cannot I at least go back to say goodbye? Just for a few minutes?"

Bal-Simba shook his head. "Too dangerous. Both for you and the villagers. No, you will have to move quickly and quietly and attract as little notice as possible."

"Yes, Lord," Moira sighed.

"Now go, girl, and quickly. I cannot shield this clearing for much longer. I will consult the Council and come to you at your destination."

Moira bowed her head. "Merry part, Lord."

"Merry meet again, Lady."

"Huh?" said Wiz groggily.

"Come on you," Moira said viciously and grabbed his hand. She jerked and Wiz staggered to his feet.

"Well, move, clumsy. Come on!" and she strode off with a lovesick Wiz stumbling along in tow.

Bal-Simba watched the ill-assorted pair disappear down the forest path. Then he sat on the rock just vacated by Wiz and turned his attention to weaving masking spells to buy the travellers as much time as he possibly could.

# Two

## PASSAGE IN PERIL

The afternoon was as fine as the morning, warm and sunny with just a bit of a breeze to stir the leaves and cool the traveller. The birds sang and the summer flowers perfumed the air. Here and there the early blackberries showed dark on their canes.

Wiz was in no mood to appreciate any of it. Before they had gone a mile he was huffing and blowing. In two miles his T-shirt was soaked and beads of sweat were running down his face, stinging his eyes and dripping from the tip of his nose. Still Moira hurried him along the twisting path, up wooded hills and down through leafy vales, ignoring his discomfort.

Finally Wiz threw himself down on a grassy spot in a clearing.

"No more," he gasped. "I've got to rest."

"Get out of the open, you crack-brained fool!" the red-haired witch snapped. Wiz crawled to his feet, staggered a few steps and collapsed against a tree trunk.

"Sorry," he panted. "I'm just not up to this. Got to rest."

"And what do you think the League is doing meantime?" Moira scolded. "Will they stop just because you're too soft to go on?"

"League?" asked Wiz blankly.

27

"The ones who pursue us. Don't you listen to anything?"

"I don't hear anyone chasing us. Maybe we've lost them."

"Lost them? *Lost them!* What do you think this is? A game of hide-and-seek? You idiot, by the time they get close enough for us to hear it will be too late. Do you want to end up like Patrius?"

Wiz looked slightly green. "Patrius? The old man back there?"

Moira cast her eyes skyward. "Yes, Patrius. Now come on!"

But Wiz made no move. "I'm sorry," he gasped. "I can't. Go on without me. I'll be all right."

Moira glared down at him, hands on hips. "You'll be dead before nightfall."

"I'll be all right." Wiz insisted. "Just go on."

Moira softened slightly. He was a nuisance, but he was a human being and as near helpless as made no difference.

"Very well," she said, sitting down. "We rest."

Wiz leaned forward and sank his head between his knees. Moira ignored him and stared back the way they had come.

"That old man," Wiz said at last. "What killed him?"

"Magic," Moira said over her shoulder.

"No really, what killed him?"

"I told you, a spell."

Wiz eyed her. "You really believe that, don't you? I mean it's not just a phrase. You mean real magic."

Moira twisted to face Wiz. "Of course I mean magic. What did you think? A bolt of lightning just happened to strike him while he was Summoning you?"

"You're telling me there really is magic?"

Moira looked annoyed. "How do you think you got here?"

"Oh," said Wiz. "Yeah. Well look, this magic. Can it get me home?"

"Patrius might have been able to do that, but I cannot," she said angrily. She got to her feet. "Now come along. If you have breath enough to talk you have breath enough to walk."

By paths and game trails they pushed on through the forest. Twice more they stopped to rest when Wiz would no further. Both times Moira fidgeted so impatiently that Wiz cut the stop short, barely getting his breath back. There were a thousand questions he wanted to ask, but Moira sternly forbade him to talk while they walked.

Once she stopped so suddenly that Wiz nearly trod on her skirt. She stared intently at a patch of woods before them. Besides a ring of bright orange mushrooms beside the trail, Wiz saw nothing unusual.

"This way," she whispered, grasping his arm and tugging him off the path. Carefully and on tiptoe, she led him well around that bit of forest, striking the trail again on the other side.

"What was the detour about?" Wiz asked at their next rest stop when he had breath enough to talk.

"The little folk danced there on last night to honor the Mid-Summer's Day. It is unchancy to go near such a place in the best of times and it would be very foolish to do so today."

"Oh come on! You mean you believe in fairies too?"

"I believe in what I see, Sparrow. I have seen those of Faerie."

"But dammit . . ." Moira cut him off with an imperious gesture.

"Do NOT curse, Sparrow. We do not need what that might attract."

That made sense, Wiz admitted. If magic really worked and there was the burned husk of a man lying under the sod back behind them to suggest that it did then curses might work too. Come to that, if magic worked there was nothing so odd about fairies dancing in the moonlight. He shook his head.

"Why do you call me Sparrow?" he asked, feeling for safer ground.

"Because Bal-Simba called you so. You needed a name to use before the World."

"I've got a name," Wiz protested.

"Bal-Simba told you never to speak your true name to anyone," Moira told him. "So we needed something to call you."

"My friends just call me Wiz."

"I will call you Sparrow," Moira said firmly. "Now come along."

Again she set off in an effortless stride. Wiz came huffing along behind, glumly admiring the swing of her hips and the easy sway of her body. He was used to being treated with contempt by beautiful women, but he had never been this taken with a woman and that made it hurt worse than usual.

*One thing you have to say about my luck,* he thought. *It's consistent.*

Finally they topped a small rise and Wiz could see a road through the trees ahead. Off to the left he could hear the sound of running water. Moira crouched behind a bush and pulled Wiz roughly down beside her.

"This is the Forest Highway," Moira whispered. "It leads over the Blackstone Brook and on into the Wild Wood."

"Where we're going?" said Wiz, enjoying Moira's closeness and the smell of her hair. Instinctively he moved closer, but the hedge witch drew away.

"Yes, but not by the road. I am to meet someone here. You wait in the woods. Do not make a sound and do not show yourself." She pulled back and continued down the trail, leaving Wiz with the memory of her closeness.

In spite of its grandiose title, the Forest Highway was a weedgrown lane with the trees pressing in on either side. The Blackstone Brook was perhaps ten yards wide and ran swift, deep and dark as its name under a rough log bridge.

As Moira predicted, there was a man waiting under the trees by the roadside. He was tall, lean, long-faced and as brown as the rough homespun of his tunic and breeches. When Moira stepped out of the trees he touched his forehead respectfully.

"I brought the things, Lady."

"Thank you, Alber," Moira replied kindly.

"Lady, is it true you are leaving us?"

"For a time, Alber. A short time, I hope."

"We will miss you," he said sadly.

Moira smiled and embraced him. Watching from behind his bush Wiz felt a pang of jealousy. "Oh, and I will miss you all as well. You have been like a family to me, the whole village." Then she smiled again. "But another will be along soon to take my place."

"It will not be the same, Lady," he said dejectedly. He turned and gestured to the small pile of objects under a bush by the roadside.

"The messenger said two packs. And two cloaks."

"Correct, Alber." Moira did not volunteer and he did not ask.

Quickly she began to sort through the items, checking them and re-stowing them into the packs.

"Shall I wait, Lady?"

"No." She smiled up at him. "Thank you again." The hedge witch made a sign with her right hand, first two fingers extended. "Go with my blessing. May your way home be short and safe and the journey uneventful."

"May you be safe as well, Lady." With that Alber turned and started down the road.

As soon as he had disappeared around a bend, Moira motioned Wiz out of hiding.

"A brave man," Moira said as she tied the drawstring on one of the packs and set it aside.

"Why?" asked Wiz, nettled. "For bringing us this stuff?"

"Don't sneer, Sparrow," she said sharply. "This 'stuff' will sustain us on our journey. Alber was willing to chance Mid-Summer's Day to see that we will eat and be warm in the Wild Wood."

"Nice of him. But brave?"

Moira finished loading the second pack and shook her head. "Sparrow, how did you survive so long?"

"I survived just fine up until this morning," Wiz retorted. "So what about Mid-Summer's Day?"

Moira sighed in exasperation. "Mid-Summer's Day is the longest day of the year. All magics associated with the sun and fire are at their most potent this day and magics of green and growing things are unusually potent as well.

"It is a day of power, Sparrow, and not a day for mortals to be about."

"We're out."

"Not by choice, Sparrow," Moira said grimly. "Now come." She slung a large leather pouch over her shoulder and shrugged one of the packs onto her back. Then she stood and watched as Wiz struggled into the other one. As soon as he was loaded, they started off across the bridge.

Well behind them, Alber stuck to the relative safety of the road. Thus he was easily seen by a soaring raven gyring and wheeling over the green and leafy land.

Alber saw the raven as it glided low over the road. He made a warding sign, for ravens are notoriously birds of ill omen, and hurried on his way.

Above him the raven cocked his glossy black head and considered. Like most of his kind he knew enough to count one and two and one person travelling alone was not what his master searched for. There were two, and the bird's keen eyes could see no sign of anyone else on the road.

But this was the only human he had seen today and this one was well away from the normal haunts of man.

The raven was not intelligent, but he had been well schooled. With a hoarse caw he abandoned the search to his fellows and broke away to the south to report.

The forest deepened after Wiz and Moira passed over the river. They left the road around the first bend past the bridge and toiled up a winding game trail that ran to the top of a steep ridge. By the time they reached the top even Moira was breathing heavily. She motioned Wiz to rest and the pair sank down thankfully under the trees.

Through a gap Wiz could look ahead. The valley was a mass of green treetops. Beyond the valley lay another green ridge and beyond that another ridge and then another fading off into the blue distance. There was no sign of habitation or any hint of animal life. Only endless, limitless forest.

This was no second-growth woodland or a carefully managed preserve. The oaks and beeches around them had never been logged. The big ones had stood for centuries, accumulating mosses and lichen on their hoary trunks, growing close and thrusting high to form a thick canopy overhead. Here and there was an open patch where one of those forest giants had succumbed to age, rot or lightning and the successors crowding in had not yet filled the place. There were snags and fallen limbs everywhere, green with moss and spotted with bright clumps of fungus.

*This is the forest primeval,* Wiz thought and shivered slightly. He had never thought that trees could make him nervous, but these huge moss-grown boles pressed in on him from all sides, their leaves shutting off the sun and casting everything into a greenish gloom. The breeze soughing through the treetops sounded as if the forest was muttering to itself or passing the news of invading strangers, like jungle drums.

"I see why they call it the Wild Wood," he said.

"This is not the Wild Wood," Moira told him. "We are still only on the Fringe of the Wild Wood."

"Does anyone live here?"

"None we would care to meet. Oh, a few cottagers and a small stead or two. But most who live on this side of the Blackstone have reason to shun their fellows. Or be shunned by them. We will best avoid company of any kind until we reach our destination."

"Where are we going anyway?" Wiz sidled closer to her.

"To a place of refuge. You need not know more. Now come. We have far to go."

It was late afternoon when they came over the second ridge and descended into another valley. Although the forest was as dense as ever, there was a water meadow through the center of this valley. The broad expanse of grass was a welcome sight to Wiz, oppressed as he was by the constant trees. Here and there trees hardly more than shrubs luxuriated in the warmth and openness. Also interspersed were small ponds and marshy patches marked by cattails, reeds and sweet blue iris.

They halted at the edge of the open and Moira surveyed the cloud-flecked sky uneasily.

"Nothing," she sighed. "Now listen, Sparrow. We cannot go around because there are bogs above and below. We must cross and do it quickly, lest we be seen. Once we start we must not stop." She looked him over critically. "We will rest now."

Moira knelt, scanning the meadow and the sky above it while Wiz caught his breath.

"Moira?"

"What?" She did not stop searching the meadow.

"We're being chased, right?"

"That *is* why we are running."

"Well then, can I ask a dumb question?"

"Of course," the hedge witch said in a tone that indicated he had been doing nothing else.

"Why are we being chased? What did we do?"

"*We* did nothing. It is *you* they want, Sparrow, and

they want you because Patrius Summoned you at the cost of his own life."

"Yeah, but why?"

"We do not know that, Sparrow."

"Do they know?"

"I doubt it."

Wiz shifted slightly. "Well, if you don't know and they don't know then why the bloody—heck—are they chasing us?"

"They hope to learn from you what Patrius's aim was."

"But I don't know either!"

Moira snorted. "I doubt they will take your unconstrained word for that, Sparrow."

"Look, I don't want any part of this, okay? Can't we talk to them? Isn't there some way I can prove I don't know anything and then they can leave me alone."

"Sparrow, listen to me," Moira turned to him. "The Dark League of the South is not interested in your innocence or guilt. The fact that Patrius Summoned you is enough to make them want you. Probably they want to squeeze you for the knowledge we both know you do not possess. Possibly they simply want you dead or worse."

Moira laid her hand on his. "But either way, Sparrow," she said gravely, "if you are given a choice between the worst death you can imagine and falling alive into the hands of the League, do everything in your power to die."

Wiz dropped his eyes from her intense stare. "I get the picture."

"Good." She turned back to the clearing and checked the ground and sky again. "Then make ready. We will not try to run because the ground is boggy, but walk quickly!"

Moira rose and moved into the clearing with Wiz on her heels. The thigh-high grass whisked against their legs as they walked and the soil squished beneath their feet. Unlike the forest, the meadow was rich with life. Insects buzzed and chirped, frogs croaked or plonked into puddles as they went by. Dragonflies flitted by and once a yellow-and-black butterfly circled their heads.

In spite of the sunshine and wildlife, Wiz wasn't cheered. Except for an occasional bush, the travellers were the tallest things in the meadow. He felt like a large and very conspicuous bug on a very flat rock, and the further they got from the suddenly friendly line of trees, the more nervous he became.

Moira was feeling it too. She pushed ahead faster, her head turning constantly. She dared not use active magic, but she listened as hard as she could for any sign of others' magic.

Suddenly Moira dropped in her tracks. She went down so quickly that Wiz thought she had tripped.

*"Get down!"* she hissed and Wiz sprawled in the wet dirt beside her.

"What?" Wiz whispered.

"Something in the air of to our left. No, don't look! The flash of your face might betray us." After a second she bobbed her head up for a quick look.

"Fortuna!" she breathed. "It is searching the area. All right, see that tree ahead of us?" She nodded towards a big bush a few yards up the trail. "When I give the signal, *crawl* to it. Understand?" Again her head bobbed up. *"Now!"*

On hands and knees they crawled for what seemed to Wiz to be an eternity. He dared not raise his head, so all he saw was a narrow strip of wet black earth and green grass stems on each side. By the time he pulled up under the bush he was panting, and not entirely from exertion.

They dragged themselves back far under the overhanging branches, heedless of the mud or the tiny crawling things in the litter of dead leaves. As soon as they were settled, Moira pulled her cloak off her pack and threw it over them, turning two people into one lumpy brown mass and leaving just a narrow crack to see out.

Even as frightened as he was, Wiz was exhilarated by Moira's closeness. Her warmth and the sweet, clean odor of her was wonderful and the danger added spice.

"What is it?" he whispered.

"Shhh."

Then a shadow passed over them and Wiz saw what they were hiding from.

The dragon glided noiselessly above the trail they had just left. Its hundred-foot batwings were stiff and unmoving as it let the warm air rising from the meadow bear it up. Its long flat tail twitched slightly as it steered its chosen course. The four legs with their great ripping talons were pressed close to its body and its sinuous neck was fully extended. It came so low and so close that Wiz could see the row of white fangs in its slightly open mouth.

Wiz's breath caught and he tried to sink into the dirt. Instinctively he grabbed Moira's hand and they clung together like frightened children while the nightmare beast swooped above trees and turned to cross the meadow from another direction.

Clearly the monster had seen something on the water meadow. Again it glided across and again it flew directly over the bush where Wiz and Moira cowered. Wiz felt as if the dragon's gaze had stripped him naked.

Four times the dragon flew over the meadow and four times Wiz trembled and shrank under Moira's cloak. Finally it pulled up and disappeared over the trees.

For long minutes after Wiz and Moira lay huddled and shaking. At last Moira threw the cloak back and sat up. Reluctantly, Wiz followed suit.

"Was that thing looking for us?" he breathed at last.

"Very likely," Moira said, scanning the skies warily.

"Are there more of them?"

"Dragons are usually solitary creatures and one so big would need a large hunting territory."

She frowned. "Still, I do not know of any like that who live nearby. Wild dragons make ill neighbors. It may be the one from the southern lake or it might be one of the ones who lair in the hills to the east. If it is coursing this far afield there may be others."

"Wonderful," Wiz muttered.

Moira sighed shakily. "I dislike playing hideabout with dragons, but we should be safe enough if we stay under the trees and are careful about crossing open spaces."

"Sounds good to me."

"There is risk, of course," Moira continued, half to herself. "The forested ways are not always the most free of magic. Besides, with the forest close around us we will not have as much warning of the approach of others."

"Others?"

"Trolls, wolves, evil men and others who do the League's work."

"Great," Wiz said.

Moira missed the irony entirely. "Not great, but our best chance, I think." She folded the cloak. "Now come. Quickly."

"Well?" Atros demanded.

"The searchers are out as you commanded, Master," said the new Master of the Sea of Scrying. "But so far nothing."

"With all the magic of the League you cannot find two insignificant mortals?" Atros rumbled.

The Master, only hours in his post, licked his lips and tried not to look past Atros's shoulder at the place where a newly flayed skin hung, still oozing blood, on the stone wall of the chamber. The skin of a very fat man.

"It is not easy Master. Bal-Simba—cursed be his name!—has been casting confusion spells, muddying the trail at the beginning. The Council's Watchers are on the alert and we cannot penetrate too deeply nor see too clearly." He paused. "We do know he has not taken the Wizard's Way."

Atros rubbed his chin. Walking the Wizard's Way was the preferred method of travel for those who had the magical skill to use it. But it was also easy to detect anyone upon it. Perhaps this strange wizard preferred stealth to speed.

"And those already in the North," he asked, "behind the Watchers' shield of spells?"

"Our best servants are creatures of the dark. On Mid-Summer's Day their power is at its weakest. Our dragon allies and our others seek as best they can, but there is so much magic upon the land that it is hard to scan." He gestured into the Sea of Scrying. Atros looked and saw sparks and patches of magic everywhere.

"Someone mighty enough to be worth the risk of a wizard like Patrius must leave a track even through that," the giant magician objected.

The newly made black robe lowered his head. "We have found no sign, Master."

Atros bit his lip thoughtfully. It was possible for a magician to hide his presence through cloaking spells, but such spells usually betrayed that something was being hidden. Either the League's servants were unusually inept or this magician from beyond the World was extremely powerful. Someone that powerful might indeed tip the balance against the League.

Unless . . .

"Is there sign of aught unusual in the cities of the North?"

"Nothing, Master, save what you know. Nothing unusual anywhere in the North's territories."

"Then perhaps he whom we seek is not within the North's territories," Atros said suddenly. "Patrius performed his Great Summoning on the Fringe of the Wild Wood? Then search the Fringe most carefully. And extend your search into the Wild Wood itself."

"Thy Will, Master," said the Watcher. "But there is no sign of anything unusual on the Fringe. Besides, it will mean weakening our search of the North's lands."

"If he was in the North's lands we would have some sign ere now," Atros said. "Perhaps he goes another way to mislead us."

It was the Master's turn to rub his chin thoughtfully. "If he pushes into the Wild Wood he brings himself closer to our servants and his magic will stand out even more strongly against the non-human magics of that place."

"Only if he uses magic," Atros said. "If he weaves little or none he will be much harder to find, will he not?"

"What kind of wizard travels without magical protection?"

"A most powerful and dangerous one. So search carefully." Atros paused for a moment, looking down into the Sea once more.

"But our alien wizard will not find it so easy to shield his travelling companion," he said. "Tell your searchers to look carefully for signs of a hedge witch in the Wild Wood. That should stand out strongly enough."

They camped where dusk found them, spreading their cloaks against a fallen log. Moira would not allow a fire, so their dinner consisted of some bits of jerked meat and a handful of leathery dried fruit. Normally Wiz didn't eat red meat, but things were decidedly not normal and he gnawed gratefully on the pieces Moira placed in his hand.

As the twilight faded Moira took a stick and drew a design around them and their resting place.

"The circle will offer us some small protection," she told him. "Do not leave it tonight for anything."

"Not even for . . . ?"

"Not for anything," she repeated firmly.

Without another word Moira rolled herself in her cloak and turned away from Wiz. He sat with his back to the log staring up at the unfamiliar stars.

"This is soooo weird," Wiz said, more to himself than Moira.

"Sleeping outdoors is not what I am used to either," she said.

"No, I mean this whole business. Dragons. The magic and all. It's just not like anything I'm used to."

Moira rolled over to face him. "You mean you really do not have magic where you come from?"

"The closest I ever came to magic was working with Unix wizards," said Wiz.

"Eunuchs wizards? Did they do that to themselves to gain power?"

"Huh? No. Not Eunuchs, Unix. Spelled . . ." Wiz realized he couldn't spell the word. He recognized the shapes of the letters, but they twisted and crawled in his mind and no meaning attached to them. When he tried to sound the word out only runes appeared in his head.

"Never mind, but it's not that at all. It's an operating system."

"Operating system?" Moira said frowning.

"An operating system is a program which organizes the resources of a computer and virtualizes their interfaces," Wiz quoted.

"A computer? One who thinks?"

For the thousandth time in his life, Wiz wished he were better at making explanations. "Well, kind of. But it is a machine, not alive."

"A machine is some kind of non-living thing then. But this machine thinks?"

"Well, it doesn't really think. It follows preprogrammed instructions. The programmer can make it act like it is thinking."

"Is it a demon of some kind?"

"Uh, no. A demon's something else. It's a program that does something automatically when called. Unless of course it's a daemon, then it's active all the time."

Moira wrinkled her brow. "Let us go back a bit. What do you have to do with these creatures?"

"They're not creatures, really."

"These demons, then."

"I told you, they're not demons. A demon is something else."

"Never mind all that," Moira said impatiently. "Just tell me what you do."

"Well, I do a lot of things, but basically I'm a systems-level programmer. That means I write programs that help applications programs—those are the things people want done—to run. "

"What is a program?"

Wiz sighed. "A program is a set of instructions that tells the computer what to do."

"You command these beings then?"

"I told you, they're not . . ."

"All right. These creatures, or not-demons or whatever they are. You command them?"

"Well, kind of."

"But you have no magic!"

Wiz grinned. "You don't need magic. Just training, skill, discipline and a mind that works in the right way."

"The qualities of a magician," Moira said firmly. "And with these qualities you master these—things."

"Well, you try to. Some days you get the bear and some days the bear gets you."

"There are bears involved too?"

"No, look, that's just an expression. What I mean is that sometimes it's easy to get the computer to do what you want and sometimes it isn't."

"Powerful entities are often hard to control," Moira nodded. "So you are the master of these—whatever they are."

"Well, not exactly the master. I work under a section chief, of course, and over him there's a department head. Then there's the DP Administrator . . ."

"These entities tell you what to do?"

"They aren't entities, they're people."

"But you do not master these, what did you call them?"

"The section chief, the department head . . ."

"No, I mean the other things, the non-living ones."

"Oh, the computers."

"You master the computers."

"Well, no. But I program them according to the tasks assigned me."

"So you are only a low-level servant," Moira concluded firmly.

"No, I'm not! It's an important job," Wiz said desperately.

"I'm sure it is," Moira said. "Even temple sweepers perform an important job."

"No, it's not like that at all! It's . . ." He realized it was hopeless. "Just forget it, okay? It was an important job and I was damn good at it."

"Do not curse, Sparrow," Moira snapped. "We are in enough danger as it is." With that she rolled over and settled down to sleep.

Wiz didn't follow suit. He sat there listening to the wind in the trees and the occasional cry of a night animal. Once he heard a wolf howl far off.

*Damn!,* he thought. *Here I am in the middle of a forest with a beautiful girl asleep at my side and I can't do anything about it. I didn't think it was supposed to work this way.*

Wiz had never read much fantasy, but he knew that the hero was supposed to get the girl. But then he didn't feel very heroic. He was cold, uncomfortable and most of all, he just felt ineffectual. The same old klutzy Wiz.

And lonesome. Oh my God, was he lonesome! He missed his apartment, the traffic-clogged streets, the movies, the all-night pizza joint on the corner. With a great inrushing pang, he felt utterly lost.

He even missed the goddamn buggy text editor at work. *Do you realize there probably isn't a computer anywhere on this world?* He thought. *I have probably written my last program.*

That hurt worse than anything. All his life Wiz had only been good at one thing. When he discovered computers in high school, he found he was as good with them as he was bad with people. He had put his life into being the best ever with computers and if he hadn't been the best ever, he had certainly been damn good. Only a lack of money and fascination with immediate problems had kept him from going to grad school and getting the Ph.D. that would have led him to the top rank of computer scientists.

So here he was in a world where none of that meant diddly. What was he supposed to do with himself? He couldn't earn a living. He wasn't really strong enough for physical labor and the only thing he knew how to do was useless.

*Goddamn that old wizard, anyway.* Then he started guiltily remembering Moira's admonition against cursing. *I wonder if it matters if you just do it in your head?*

If he was big and strong it might have helped. But he was skinny and gangly. The only difference between him and the classic pencil-necked geek was that he didn't wear glasses.

*Good thing too,* he thought. *If I did, I'd probably have broken them by now.*

It wasn't fair. It just wasn't fair.

Somehow he got to sleep and dreamed uneasily of home and his beloved computers.

The next morning Wiz was sore all over. His legs

ached from the unaccustomed exercise and the rest of him hurt from sleeping on the ground.

Moira was already up and seemingly none the worse for the night. Her copper hair was combed and hung down her back in a long braid. Her face was freshly scrubbed and she looked heart-stoppingly beautiful.

She was sitting cross-legged going through the contents of her worn leather shoulder bag. There was already a pile of things on the ground beside her.

"I do not think I can afford to keep all these things," she said in response to his unasked question. "I will have to discard them carefully as we go."

"I'll carry them for you."

Moira snorted. "The problem is not weight, you idiot. Magic calls to magic and these things," she gestured, "are magical. The League may be able to find us through them."

She looked down at the small pile and sighed. "They cost much time and no little effort to gain. All are useful and in a way they are all parts of me. But," she added with forced cheerfulness, "better to discard them now than to have them lead the League to us."

"Uh, right."

Moira gathered the items back into her pouch. "I will dispose of them one at a time as we go along," she said standing up. "It will make them harder to find, I hope."

Wiz scrambled to his feet, feeling the kinks in his muscles stretch.

"We can make better time today," the hedge witch said. "Mid-Summer's Day is past and the magic will be less strong. We do not have to move quite so cautiously."

"Great," Wiz muttered, appalled at the prospect.

True to her word, Moira set an even faster pace for the day's journey. Wiz struggled to keep up, but he didn't do any better than he had the day before. Several times they had to stop while he rested and Moira fidgeted.

From time to time Moira would take something from her pouch. Sometimes she flung the object as far as she could into the woods. A couple of times she buried it carefully. Once she hid a folded bit of cloth in a hollow log and once she dropped a piece of carved wood into a swiftly running stream.

Wiz could see the effort it took her to discard each of those items but he said nothing. There was nothing he could say.

The forest was more open than it had been the day before. The trees were smaller here. They were just as thick where they grew, but they were interspersed with clearings. Once they passed the ruins of a rock wall, running crazily through the woods.

They kept to the forest and stayed as deep among the trees as possible. Occasionally they had to skirt an open space and it was near one such clearing that Moira stopped suddenly and sniffed.

"Do you smell it?" she asked.

Wiz sniffed. "Something burnt, I think."

"Come on," Moira said, forging ahead and breasting through the undergrowth.

They were in the clearing before they recognized it. One minute they were pushing through bushes and brambles and the next they were standing on the fringe of a meadow, looking at the smoldering remains of a homestead.

There had been at least three buildings, now all were charred ruins. The central one, obviously a house, had stone walls which stood blackened and roofless. The soot was heaviest above the door and window lintels and a few charcoaled beams still spanned the structure. Of the nearer, larger building, a planked barn, there was almost nothing left. On the other side of the house was a log building with part of one wall standing.

"Something else," Wiz said, sniffing again. "Burned meat, I think."

But Moira was already running across the meadow. Wiz cast a nervous eye to the clear blue sky, then shifted his pack and followed.

When he caught up with her, Moira was standing in the space between the remains of the house and the smoldering heap of ashes that had been the barn, casting this way and that.

"What about dragons?" Wiz asked, looking up.

Moira's suggestion on what to do with dragons was unladylike, probably impractical and almost certainly no fun at all.

"Did a dragon do this?" Wiz asked as they walked around the remains of the house.

"Probably not," Moira said distractedly. "Dragons might attack cattle in the fields or swine in their pen, but they seldom burn whole farms. This was done from the ground, I think."

"Well, then who?"

"Who is not important, Sparrow. The important thing is what happened to the people."

"I don't see anyone," Wiz said dubiously.

"They may all have escaped. But perhaps some are lying hurt nearby and in need of aid. I *wish* I had not been so quick to discard parts of my kit this morning."

"There doesn't seem to be anyone here."

"Then search more closely."

Moira didn't call out and Wiz didn't suggest it. He felt conspicuous enough as it was.

While Moira searched near the house and log building, Wiz wandered around the remains of the barn. The heaps of ashes were unusually high there and from the remains he guessed the barn had been full of hay when it went up. He wondered what had happened to the animals.

Wiz stumbled over something in the debris. He looked down and saw it was an arm, roasted golden crisp and then obviously gnawed. A child's arm. Wiz opened his mouth to scream and vomited instead.

"What is it?" Moira came rushing up as he heaved his guts out. "What did you . . . Oh." She stopped short as she saw what lay on the ground between them.

"Oh my God," he moaned, retching the last bit of liquid from his stomach. "Oh my God."

"Trolls," Moira said, her face white and drawn, her freckles standing out vividly against the suddenly pale skin. "They burned this place and put the flames to use."

"They ate them," Wiz said

"Trolls are not choosy about their fare," Moira said looking out over the smoldering ruins.

"Hey! Do you think they're still around?"

"Possibly," Moira said abstractedly. "After a meal like this trolls would be disinclined to go far."

"Then let's get out of here before they come back for dessert."

"*No!*" Moira shouted. Wiz started and turned to see tears in her eyes. "We go nowhere until we bury these folk."

"But . . ."

"There was no one to do it for my family."

"Did your family end up . . . like that?" Wiz finally asked.

Moira's face clouded. "I do not know. We never found them."

"What happened?"

"It was a summer day, much like today only later in the year. I had gone into the wood to pick berries. I filled my apron with them that my mother might make preserves. My father had found a bee tree, you see.

"It took me all the afternoon to gather enough berries. I was away for hours. And when I returned . . . there was no one there.

"The door to the cottage stood open and the cream was still in the churn, but my parents and brother and sisters were gone. I looked and called and searched until after nightfall. For three days I looked, but I never found them."

"What happened to them?"

"I don't know. But there are worse things on the Fringe of the Wild Wood than being eaten by trolls."

Without thinking, Wiz clasped his arms around the hedge witch and hugged her to him. Without thinking she settled into his arms to be hugged and buried her head in his shoulder. They stood like that for a long minute and then Moira straightened suddenly and pulled away.

"Come on!" she said sharply. "Find something to dig with."

There was a charred spade leaning against the remains of the log building and Moira set Wiz to work digging a grave in what had been the kitchen garden. The tilled loam turned easily, but Wiz was red-faced and sweating before he had a hole large enough to suit Moira.

While he dug, Moira searched for pieces of bodies. Somewhere she found a smoke-stained old quilt to serve as a shroud. Wiz kept his head down and his back to her so he would not have to see what she was piling on the cloth spread among the heat-blasted cabbages.

With Wiz's help, she hauled the lumpy stinking burden to the hole and dumped it in. It weighed surprisingly little, Wiz thought.

They shoveled dirt onto the quilt as quickly as they could. Wiz wielded the spade uncomplainingly in spite of the aches in his arms and back and the blisters springing up on his hands.

"It will not stop wolves or others from digging down," Moira said frowning at their handiwork as Wiz scraped the last of the earth onto the mound. "It should be covered with stone that their rest may be more secure."

"You want rocks?" Wiz said warily.

She thought and then shook her head. "There is not time. We will leave them as they are and hope." Then she bowed her head and her lips moved as she recited a blessing over the pathetic mound of fresh earth. When that was done she turned abruptly and signaled Wiz to follow.

The hurried back to the shelter of the forest. For once Moira didn't have to urge Wiz on. He was more than eager to get away from that grisly farmstead and he was absolutely convinced of the reality of magic and their present danger.

"How did it go with the Council, Master?" Bal-Simba's apprentice asked as the giant wizard came into his study.

"Well enough, Arianne." He leaned his staff against the wall and loosened his leopard-skin cloak. "But it is very good to be away from them for a while." Bal-Simba settled into a carved chair with a sigh and leaned back.

The tower room was bright and sun-washed. The batik hangings spoke of animals, birds, flowers and cheerful things. The wide windows on both sides were thrown open and a soft summer breeze wafted through the room, stirring the hangings on the walls and ruffling the parchments on the large table in its center. Arianne, a tall thin woman with ash-blonde hair caught back in a single braid, brought him a cup of wine from the sideboard.

Bal-Simba drained the cup with another sigh and handed it back for a refill.

"Well, I have done all I can to protect our visitor. The Watchers are on the alert and they are confusing the search as best they may."

"And the other matter?" she asked, handing him a second cup of wine.

"The Council has not the faintest idea why Patrius brought this Sparrow among us." He shook his great head. "I had hoped that Patrius had confided in one of the Mighty, but it appears he did not. The Sparrow is as much a mystery to us as he is to the League."

"Why do you think Patrius Summoned this one?" Arianne asked.

"Our red-headed hedge witch thinks it was a mistake, that Patrius intended to Summon some great wizard, became confused under the attack and got this Wiz instead."

"And you, Lord?"

"I do not know. Certainly the Sparrow has no skill at magic, or ought else that I can find. But yet . . . Did I tell you that Patrius did not mark a pentagram to enclose the Summoned? That suggests he did not expect the Summoned to defend himself with magic."

Arianne frowned. "Which means that he either was certain the Summoned would not attack him or that he knew he had no magic. Yes. What did Patrius say to the hedge witch?"

"Apparently Patrius was being oracular. He said he sought help but when she asked him what kind he talked in riddles."

"That would be like Patrius," Arianne agreed. "He loved his little surprises.'

"This surprise cost him his life, Lady."

They were silent as Bal-Simba finished the second cup of wine. Arianne moved to refill it, but Bal-Simba shook his head.

"Lord, there are certain aspects of this business I do not understand."

"You are not alone, Lady."

"I mean your actions."

"Ask then." Arianne was Bal-Simba's apprentice not only for her skill in magic but because, like Bal-Simba, she had considerable administrative ability. One day she would sit on the Council of the North.

"Why did you leave the pair of them on the Fringe with no protection?"

"I could not bring them here by the Wizard's Way, so I sent them to a place of safety. Why alone? Because two can go in stealth where an army may not tread. This Moira is no woods ranger, but she grew up on the Fringe and she has the reputation for a sturdy head on her shoulders."

"Where did you send them?"

"Heart's Ease," Bal-Simba told her.

Arianne looked hard at the huge map on the wall. "Lord, that is deep within the Wild Wood itself! You set them a dangerous course."

"But the safest available under the circumstances," Bal-Simba replied. "The League will be searching for a magician. This Sparrow has not the slightest magic. The League will expect him to come to the Capital, or at least to the civilized lands. Instead they go in the opposite direction. If we keep interfering with the League's searchers we can further confuse the League."

"We know the League is searching for them with every resource at their command." She smiled thinly. "Old Toth-Set-Ra must be stirred indeed to mount such an effort."

"When he realized Patrius had performed a Great Summoning, he decided that the Summoned was a weapon of some kind. He means to have it." Bal-Simba smiled. "Perfectly logical if you know how Toth-Set-Ra's mind works."

"And we bend our efforts to frustrating him. Lord, is this Sparrow really worth so much of our effort?"

Bal-Simba considered for a moment. "Probably not. But while the League is engrossed in trying to find our Sparrow, they cannot make mischief elsewhere. That is worth some little effort on our part."

He stroked his eagle's skull pendant absently. "Besides, I think we owe this Sparrow something. He was snatched from his own world and dropped here by the efforts of one of the Mighty. It was no fault or choice of his own."

The blonde woman nodded. "But still, to send two people into the heart of the Wild Wood . . ."

"Would you have me bring them here by the Wizard's Way and all of us lost when the League saw and struck?" Bal-Simba said sharply. Arianne stiffened.

The wizard's face softened. "Forgive me, my Lady. Your are right about the dangers and I am uneasy about our fugitives." He heaved a great gust of a sigh. "I gave them the best chance I could, now let us hope they can make good use of it."

She smiled and placed her hand on his shoulder. "Apologies are not needed, Lord. I understand." He smiled back and put his bearlike paw over her hand.

"There are so few unconstrained choices, Arianne. So very few choices left to us."

"We do the best we can, Lord."

Bal-Simba sighed again. "Aye. That at least we do."

Moira allowed them a fire that night, which was a mixed blessing for Wiz. It meant warmth and hot food, but he had to gather firewood, and the sticks and branches rubbed his blistered hands raw.

"Now what's your problem?" she asked when she saw him wince as he dropped a load of wood by the stone hearth.

"Nothing," Wiz said, blowing on his hands.

Moira scrambled up and took one of his hands in hers. "You're hurt," she said with real concern. "I'll attend to those once the food is started."

When she had the mixture of dried meat, fruit and barley simmering in a small bronze pot, she pulled out her shoulder bag and motioned Wiz to sit down beside her in the firelight.

"You must not be used to work," she said as she rummaged in her kit.

"You don't get many blisters at a VT 220," he agreed.

Moira looked blank.

"It's a terminal. A, ah, thing that . . . oh, forget it."

Moira produced a tiny earthenware jar and smeared the raw and blistered places on Wiz's palms with the dark, pungent salve it contained.

"Your hands should be healed by morning," she told him, scraping salve from her finger back into the jar. "We should cover those, but I don't have anything to put over them."

"That's fine," Wiz said. "It doesn't hurt anymore. Whatever that stuff is, it works like a charm."

"Oh, it's not a charm," Moira said seriously. "Just a healing potion. With the proper charm I could heal your hands instantly, but that would take magic and it might attract attention." She moved away from him to check the contents of the pot.

"You're a magician, right?" he asked, trying to recapture the moment.

Moira shrugged. "In a small way. I am a hedge witch."

"That's interesting. What does a hedge witch do?"

"What do I do? Oh, herbs and simples. A little healing. Some weather magic. I try to warn of dangers, find lost objects and strayed animals." She lifted the pot off the fire and produced two wooden bowls and horn spoons from her pack.

"Eat now," she said. "You can use a spoon well enough even with your hands."

The mixture in the pot looked awful but tasted surprisingly good. The tartness of the fruit and the rich saltiness of the meat blended well with the bland barley.

"Is Bal-Simba a hedge witch too?"

Moira laughed, a delightful sound. "No, Bal-Simba is of the Mighty." Her face clouded. "Probably he is the Mightiest of the Mighty now that Patrius is dead." She returned to her eating.

"What do the Mighty do?" Wiz asked in an effort to keep the conversation going.

"They are our greatest wizards. They teach the other orders, they help wherever great magic is required, they study arcane lore and they try to protect us from the Dark League." She sighed. "These days mostly they try to protect us from the Dark League."

"Why aren't they protecting us then?"

Moira looked annoyed. "They are protecting us, Sparrow. Bal-Simba stayed behind to cast false trails to confuse the League's agents who sought to spy us out. The whole North is protected by the Watchers of the Council of the North who blunt the League's efforts to use their magic here. Even now the Watchers are doubtless holding off the League's efforts to search us out. Just because you cannot see the works of the Mighty, never doubt they protect you, Sparrow."

"Sorry."

"You should be sorry."

They sat in uncomfortable silence.

"What's magic like?" Wiz asked at last.

"Like?" Moira asked, puzzled. "'t's not like anything. It simply *is*. Magic is the basic stuff of the World. We swim in a sea of magic like fish in the ocean."

"And you can make it work for you?"

"A magician can make magic work for himself or herself. But there are very few magicians. Perhaps one person in one hundred has any talent at all for magic and far, far fewer ever become truly skilled."

Wiz studied the effect of the firelight on her hair and eyes. "How do you learn to do magic?"

"You find a magician to take you as an apprentice. Then you study and practice and learn as much as you can. Eventually you either cannot learn more or you must travel to find a more advanced teacher."

"But there aren't schools or anything?"

Moira snorted. "Magic is a craft, Sparrow. It cannot be learned by rote like sums or the days of the week."

"How did you learn?"

"There was a hedge witch in the village that took me in after . . . after I left home. He taught me what he could. Then I traveled to the Capital and studied under some of the wizards there." She sighed. "I did not have talent of a high order so I became hedge witch for the village of Blackbrook Bend."

"So, how do you work magic?"

"First you must know what you are doing," Moira said. "Then you must perform the appropriate actions with the proper phrases. If you do it correctly and if you make no mistakes, then you make magic work for you."

Wiz gestured with the stick he had used to poke up the fire. "You mean if I wave a magic wand and say— uh—'bippity bobbity boo' then . . . ?"

A lance of flame shot from the smouldering end of the stick into the heart of the campfire. The blaze exploded in a ball of incandescent white and an evil orange column soared above the tops of the trees. Wiz gasped for breath in the suffocating blast of heat. Through the haze and blinding glare he saw Moira, on her feet and gesturing frantically.

Suddenly it was quiet. The fire was a friendly little campfire again and the cool night air flowed into Wiz's lungs and soothed his scorched face. Moira stood across the fire from him, her hair singed, her cloak smouldering and her eyes blazing.

"Yes." She snapped. "That's *exactly* what I mean."

"I'm sorry," Wiz stammered. "I didn't mean to . . ." Then his jaw dropped. "Hey, wait a minute. That was magic!"

"That was stupid," the hedge witch countered, beating out an ember on her cloak.

"No, I mean I worked magic," Wiz said eagerly. "That means I *am* a magician. Bal-Simba was wrong." He grinned and shook his head. "Son of a gun."

"What you are is an idiot," Moira snapped. "Any fool can work magic, and far too many fools do."

"But . . ."

"Didn't you listen to anything I just told you? Magic is all around us. It is easy to make. Any child can do it. If you are careless you can make it by accident as you just did."

"Well, if it's so easy to make . . ."

"Sparrow, easy to make and useful are *not* the same thing. To be useful magic must be controlled. Could you have stopped what you just created just now? Of course not! If I had not been here you would have burned the forest down. A careless word, a thoughtless gesture and you loose magic on the world."

She stopped and looked around the clearing for signs of live coals. "And mark well, magic is not easy to learn. There are a hundred ways, perhaps a thousand of doing what you just did. And most of them are useless because they cannot be controlled. Without control magic is not just useless, it is hideously dangerous."

"But I still made magic," Wiz protested.

Moira snorted. "You made it once. By accident. What makes you think you could do it again?"

"What makes you think I couldn't?" Wiz countered, picking up the stick. "All I have to do is point at the fire and say . . ."

"*Don't*," Moira yelled. "Don't even *think* of trying it again."

Wiz lowered the stick and looked at her.

"Sparrow, heed me and heed me well. The chance that you could do that again is almost nil. The essence of success in magic is to repeat absolutely everything with not the tiniest variation every single time you recite a spell."

She gestured at him. "Look at you. You have shifted your stance, you are holding the stick at a different angle, you are facing southeast instead of North, you are . . . oh, different in a dozen ways. Could you say those words with exactly the same inflection? Could you give your wrist exactly the twist you used in the gesture? Could you clench your left hand in exactly the same way?"

"Is all that important?"

"All that is *vital*," Moira told him. "All that and much more. The phase of the moon, the angle of the sun. The hour of the day or night. All enter into magic and all must be considered.

"No matter what you have been told, magical talent does not consist of some special affinity for magic, some supernatural gift. Magical ability is the ability to control what you produce. And that turns on noticing the tiniest detail of what is done and being able to repeat it flawlessly."

*That makes a weird kind of sense*, Wiz admitted to himself. *Like programming. There's no redundancy in the language and the tiniest mistake can have major consequences. Look at all the time I've spent going over code trying to find the missing semicolon at the end of a statement, or a couple of transposed letters.* It also meant he probably was a magical klutz. He was the kind of guy who walked into doors and spent five minutes hunting for his car every time he went to the mall.

"Wait a minute, though," Wiz said. "If all it takes is a good memory, why can't most people learn to do magic?"

Moira flicked a strand of coppery hair away from her face with an exasperated gesture. "A good memory is the least part of what we call the talent."

"Sure, but with practice . . ."

"Practice!" Moira snorted. "Perform a spell incorrectly and you may not get the opportunity to do it again.

"Look you, when those without the talent attempt a spell, one of three things will happen. The first, and far away the most likely outcome is that nothing at all will happen. What comes out is so far removed from the true spell that is it completely void. That is the most favorable result because it does no harm and it discourages the practitioner.

"The second thing that can happen is that the spell

goes awry, usually disastrously so." She smiled grimly. "Every village has its trove of stories of fools who sought to make magic and paid for their presumption. Some villages exist no longer because of such fools.

"The third thing is that the spell is successful. That happens perhaps one out of every thousand attempts." She frowned. "In some ways that is the worst. It encourages the fool to try again, often on a grander scale."

"So what you're saying is that its easy to make magic by accident but hard to do on purpose."

"Say rather virtually impossible to do on purpose." Moira corrected. "Without the talent and proper training you cannot do it.

"But there is another level of complication beyond even that," Moira went on. "A magician must not only be able to recite spells successfully, he or she must thoroughly understand their effects and consequences." She settled by the fire and spread her cloak. "Do you know the tale of the Freshened Sea?"

Wiz shook his head.

"Then listen and learn.

"Long ago on a small island near the rim of the Southern Sea (for it was then so called) there lived a farmer named Einrich. His farm was small, but the soil was good and just over the horizon was the Eastern Shore where the people would pay good money for the fruits his island orchards produced. All he lacked was fresh water for his trees, for the rains are irregular there and he had but one tiny spring.

"Some years the rains were scant and so were his crops of apples and pears. Some years they came not at all and Einrich spent day after weary day carrying buckets of water so his trees would not perish.

"All around him was water, but he had not enough fresh to feed his groves. Daily he looked at the expanse of sea stretching away to the horizon on all sides and daily he cursed the lack.

"Now this Einrich, ill-fortune to him!, had some talent for magic. He dabbled in it, you see, and somehow he survived his dabblings. That gave him knowledge and a foolish pride in his own abilities.

"So Einrich conceived a plan to give him more water. He concocted and cast a spell to turn the water around his island fresh.

"He constructed a demon, bound it straitly, and ordered him to make fresh the water around his island."

"Wait a minute," Wiz said. "What do you mean he 'constructed' a demon?"

"Demons are the manifestations of spells, not natural creatures as the ignorant believe," Moira said. "They are the products of human or non-human magicians, although they may live long beyond their creators.

"To continue: In doing this, Einrich was foolhardy beyond belief. Great spells work against great forces and if they are not done properly the forces lash back. Einrich was not so fortunate as to die from the effects of his bungling. His house was blasted to ruin and a huge black burn still marks the spot on the island, but he survived and the water around his island turned to fresh.

"He spent all the long summer days working in his orchards while the fruit swelled and ripened on his trees. With plentiful water his fruit was the largest and finest ever. So when the time came he harvested all his boat could bear and set out for his markets on the east coast of the sea.

"He thought it odd that he saw no other vessels, for usually the waters inshore were the haunt of fishing vessels and merchantmen trading in the rich goods of the east. Einrich sailed on, finding nothing in the water save an occasional dead fish.

"When he sighted land his unease grew. For in place of the low green hills of the Eastern land he saw cliffs of dazzling white. As he drew closer he realized that the familiar hills had turned white, so white the reflections almost blinded him.

"He sought the familiar harbors but he could not find them. All was buried under drifts of white, as if huge dunes of sand had devoured the land.

"And instead of the sweet scent of growing things, the land breeze brought him the odor of rotting fish. All along the shoreline were windrows of dead sea creatures. Here and there a starving seabird tore eagerly at the decaying flesh.

"Finally, Einrich put ashore in a cove. When he stepped from his boat he stepped onto a beach of salt.

"Einrich had bound his demon to its task, but he had not limited it. The whole of the Southern Sea had been turned to fresh water. The fish within could not live in the fresh water, so they died.

"Worse, Einrich had not instructed the demon where to put the salt it winnowed. The creature simply dumped it on the nearest shoreline. In the space of a few days the greatest and most beautiful cities of the World disappeared under waves and rifts of salt. Their people perished or were doomed to roam the world as homeless wanderers—living testaments to the power of magic ill-used.

"And to this day the demon sits in the Freshened Sea, sifting salt from the water and dumping it on the land. The eastern shores are a desert of salt and the water is still fresh."

"What happened to Einrich?" Wiz asked, awed.

Moira smiled grimly. "A suitable punishment was arranged. If you travel to that cursed shore, and if you look long enough, you will find Einrich, ever hungry, ever thirsting and hard at work with a shovel, trying to shovel enough salt into the sea to render it salty again."

"Whew," Wiz breathed.

"The point, Sparrow, is that magic is not to be trifled with. Even successful magic can bring ruin in its wake and unsuccessful magic far outnumbers the successful."

"Could I have done something like that, by accident?"

"Unlikely," Moira sniffed. "You do not have a talent for magic and you have no training. You could easily kill yourself or burn down a forest, but you have not the ability to work great magic.

"The most dangerous magicians are the half-trained ones. Either the ones who are still being schooled or who think they are greater than they are. The evil they do often lives after them. They and the League, of course."

"What is the League, anyway? A bunch of black magicians?"

Moira frowned. "They are a dark league. Some of them are black, it is true. But so is Bal-Simba and many others of the North."

"No, I mean magicians who practice black magic. You know, evil spells and things like that."

"Evil magic depends partly on intent and partly on ignoring the consequences," Moira said. "Spells may help or harm but they are not of themselves good or evil."

"Not even a death spell?"

"Not if used to defend oneself, no. Such spells are dangerous and are best avoided, but they are not evil."

"All right, what separates you from this League?"

Moira was silent for a moment. "Responsibility," she said thoughtfully. "Magic is not evil in itself, but tends to affect many things at once. Often the unintended or unwanted effects of a spell are harmful. Like Einrich's means of getting water for his orchards."

"We called those side effects," Wiz said. "They're a pain in the neck in programming too."

"Be that as it may, the question a responsible magician must face is whether the goal is worth the consequences. All the consequences. Those who follow the Council of the North try to use magic in harmony with the World. Those of the League are not so bound."

Moira shifted and the fire caught and heightened the burnished copper highlights in her hair.

"Power is an easy prize for a magician, Sparrow—if

you can stay alive and if you are not too nice about the consequences. The ones who join the League see power as an end to itself. They magic against the World and scheme and intrigue among themselves to get it."

Wiz nodded. "I've known hackers like that. They didn't care what they screwed up as long as they got what they wanted."

"It may be so on all the worlds," Moira sighed. "There are always those whose talent and ambition are unchecked by concern for others. If they have no magical talent they may become thieves, robbers and cheats. With talent they are likely to travel south and join with the Dark League."

"Why go south. Why not just stay and make trouble?"

"Two reasons. First, the Council will not have them in the civilized lands. Second, they must still serve an apprenticeship no matter how much talent they have." She smiled tightly. "The tests for an apprentice are stringent and many of them are aimed at uncovering such people.

"Once they pass over the Freshened Sea they are beyond the Council's reach. They are free to work whatever magic they wish and that place shows the results. All of the Southern Shore is alight with mountains of fire and the earth trembles constantly from the League's magic. The land is so blasted that none can live there save by magic. The very World itself pays the price for the lusts of the League."

"Why put up with them at all? When we had problems like that we'd kick the troublemakers off the system. Or turn them over to the cops—ah, the authorities."

"You have an easier time than we do, Sparrow," Moira said ruefully. "There is no way to bar a magician from making magic, so we cannot 'kick them off the system.' As for the authorities, well, the Council exists in part to check the League but this is not a thing easily done.

"Individually the ones of the League are mighty

sorcerers. Toth-Set-Ra, their present leader," Moira made a warding sign, "is the mightiest wizard in all the World."

"If he's so powerful how come he hasn't taken the North?"

"Because the League contains the seeds of its own destruction," Moira said. "To conquer the North, the League would have to act in careful concert. This they cannot do because of the rivalries within. The Mighty are more constrained than the sorcerers of the League and so perhaps not so powerful individually. But they work easily together and can defeat any of the League's efforts.

"The League is like the Phoenix which renews itself by regular immolation. When it is sundered by contention and many strive for the Dark Throne, then we of the North have a time of peace. When a strong leader emerges and brings most of the wizards of the South under his sway, the League harries the North and magics are loosed upon the land." Moira sighed. "Twas ever so. And now we live in a time when the League is united as never before.

"Toth-Set-Ra," again the warding sign, "is a mighty sorcerer, skilled in magic and cunning in lore. And it is our age's woe that he has especially powerful tools at his command."

"It doesn't sound very secure to me," Wiz said dubiously.

"Little in life is secure," Moira replied. "But we contrive." She rose and moved to the other side of the fire.

"And now let us see if we can get some sleep, Sparrow. Morning comes early and we still have far to go."

# *Three*

## THE WATCHER AT THE WELL

The land was different here. The valleys were narrower, the ridges more numerous and the slopes steeper. But the trees were as tall and their leaves shut out the sun as fully as they had in the flatter country behind them.

The forest was making Wiz claustrophobic, but since the water meadow open spaces didn't appeal to him either.

They were following the valleys now, but Wiz wasn't sure it was an improvement. Moira seemed to become more nervous. When they walked they went as fast, but Moira stopped more often to listen intently. She spoke seldom and only in whispers and she glared fiercely at Wiz every time a branch cracked under his feet.

Finally they came up a gentle rise and looked down into a valley even steeper and narrower than the ones around them. From the disturbance of the treetops Wiz could make out the line of a road or a stream running through its center.

Moira placed her enchanting head next to Wiz's, so close he could count the freckles on her cheek and inhale the fragrance of her hair.

"The Forest Road," Moira whispered nodding at the line. "We must follow its track."

"I thought we needed to stay under cover," Wiz whispered back dubiously.

"I said we would follow the road, not walk it. If we keep to the wood we should be all right." She grasped his wrist and squeezed hard. "But make no sound. This place is a natural funnel and if the League realizes we are bound into the Wild Wood, this is where they will set their traps."

Cautiously then they went downhill until they struck a game trail that ran along the slope. As they moved with it, the land gradually grew steeper. Although he couldn't see, Wiz had the impression that the valley was narrowing as well.

"Hsst." Moira tugged at Wiz's sleeve. "Voices. Off the path." She looked left and right and then surprised Wiz by scrambling up the steep bank. They climbed like frightened squirrels until they were nearly thirty feet above the trail. They flattened themselves against the slope with a thin screen of bushes between them and the path below.

Two men came up the path. They were dressed in rough homespun. The taller one was lean and balding with a narrow rodent face and greasy stringy blond hair. The shorter one was also blond, but he was beefier, younger and his hair fuller. The tall one carried a machete-like sword that he swung idly with a practiced motion of the wrist. The other had a big knife or short sword thrust scabbardless through his belt. Wiz held his breath as they came close.

"What is it we're looking for anyway?" the younger man asked.

"Gold, me lad. Two bags of gold walking around in human skins." He swished the frond off a fern with a casual swing of his chopping sword. "There's a man and a woman as might be making for the Wild Wood and there's those who would pay steep for them."

*Don't look up*, Wiz prayed, *please don't look up!*

"What do they look like?" the young man asked as the pair passed the spot where Wiz and Moira lay.

"Like strangers, and strangers at the Gap are easy enough to find."

The man asked another question but they turned a corner in the path and the woods and distance made their speech unintelligible.

Wiz and Moira looked at each other.

"We don't have to ask who they're looking for, do we?" Wiz whispered.

Moira gestured him to silence and motioned for him to wait. He realized the pair who had just passed might be the vanguard of a larger party and clamped his mouth shut.

Minutes ticked by before Moira gestured him up and on. They climbed down from their perch and plunged downslope into the forest, breasting through thickets and thrusting past tangles of underbrush. The going was slower and noisier but somehow that seemed like a reasonable tradeoff.

At last Moira stopped them under a large clump of something multi-stemmed and leafy.

"Were those guys from the League?" Wiz asked in a whisper.

Moira shook her head. "Not they. They owe allegiance to naught but gold. There are robbers who haunt the Forest Road. Apparently the League offers rich reward for us and that has served to concentrate them."

"So what do we do now?"

"We must go on. The problem comes when we reach the Forest Gate ahead. That is a pass barely wider than the Forest Road itself. It marks the end of Fringe and the beginning of the Wild Wood and it will doubtless be guarded."

"Can we go around?"

Moira shook her head firmly. "We must go through the Gate itself."

"How do we get through?"

She smiled grimly. "Cautiously, Sparrow. Very cautiously indeed. Now move as quietly as you can, and no talking! That pair were not woodsmen, but a few of these rogues are skilled rangers indeed."

They went ahead even more slowly now. Wiz joined Moira in scanning the woods. After their encounter with the robbers the forest seemed even more oppressive. Every tree or bush became a potential hiding place until the woods seemed alive with bandits waiting to pounce. A burst of birdsong would make Wiz start and the scampering of a squirrel in a tree would reduce him to terror.

Finally Moira halted and pointed. Wiz followed her finger and saw the Forest Gate.

Ahead the canyon narrowed into a gorge. At the bottom it was only wide enough for the road and a rocky stream. The gray stone walls rose sheer for a hundred feet or more before the canyon widened out and the trees grew on the slope, which rose for hundreds of feet.

And the gate was guarded. Wiz saw four men on the road and one more sitting on the cliff edge. Their manner left no doubt there were more men on down the gorge or hidden by the trees.

"I don't suppose we could use magic to get through?" Wiz whispered.

Moira surveyed the scene and bit her lips. "It is a trap. Those men are out in the open in hope that we will try something like that. Make no doubt there are magicians waiting to pounce."

"What then?"

"We thread our way between them. I hope they are not too thick along the slopes. Now be quiet."

They were higher on the mountainside than the walls of the gorge, a good 200 feet above the place where the trees began. If most of the robbers were down on the road and there weren't too many sentinels on the heights and the robbers weren't too alert, they should be able to work their way along the slope without being seen.

*And if frogs had wings they wouldn't bump their asses every time they took a step,* Wiz thought sourly.

With agonizing caution they worked their way forward. In spite of their steepness the slopes were thickly wooded and well-grown with brush. Most of the time they could see only a few yards in any direction. Wiz kept his eyes on the ground, putting his feet down as carefully as he could. Every time he scuffed the leaves the sound rang in his ears. He was certain the noise they made echoed off the walls of the canyon. Every few yards they halted for a long minute to listen.

Luck seemed to be with them. It was a hard climb up to the slope from the road and few of the robbers were inclined to make it. Those that did were more interested in looking down the road than they were in checking the mountainside. Moving with exquisite care, Wiz and Moira passed the watchers, sometimes so close they could see them through the trees.

The mountainside grew steeper and the ground became more rocky. Trees were scarcer and the brush thicker. The terrain forced them closer and closer to the cliff edge. Below them they could see the gorge curve sharply in a hairpin bend and beyond that the land widened out again.

Finally, at the very point of the hairpin, the wood narrowed to a thin band. And at its narrowest point there was a man sitting on a rock.

He was at his ease, hands clasped around one knee and the other leg dangling. Like his fellows he was looking over the canyon. Obviously the last thing he expected was to find his quarry on the slopes. There was a leather patch over his right eye, the eye closest to Wiz and Moira.

But to get by him they would have to pass scant feet from him. *In the movies this is always where they jump the sentry,* Wiz thought. This wasn't a movie and Wiz wasn't a trained commando. The man was at least a head taller than he was and heavily muscled. He was wearing a broadsword, while their only weapon was Moira's eating knife. The last thing Wiz wanted to do was make like Bruce Lee.

Moira obviously agreed. Crouching low, she began to work her way forward, keeping as much brush as she could between her and the man on the rock. Crouching even lower, Wiz followed.

Moira was almost behind the man when Wiz stepped on a loose rock.

With a crunch and a clatter the stone went rolling down the slope, taking several others with it. The sentry's head whipped around and he saw Moira behind a bush not six feet from him.

"Hey!" he shouted and sprang to his feet, grabbing for his sword. Moira cringed and made ready to run.

Wiz stood up too. As the man took his first step toward Moira he literally blindsided him and shoved him with all his strength, away from his beloved and toward the cliff edge.

The man whooped, tottered on the brink and then went over the cliff backwards, screaming all the way down.

The scream was cut off by an enormous *splash* and a second later the gorge resounded with curses. When Wiz peeked over the edge he saw that the stream made a pool in the bend of the canyon and the man was in the middle of it, treading water and swearing at the top of his lungs.

A laughing voice called out to him.

"By the nine netherhells I was pushed! They're up there I tell you. Get after them!"

Again the laughing voice.

"Damn your mangy hide I am *not* drunk! There's someone up there and they're getting away."

"Better search along that cliff, lads," came a harsher, louder voice. "Who knows? There may actually be someone up there."

Wiz and Moira ducked in among the trees and ran for all they were worth, never slowing until they were past the Gate and out on the forest floor again.

There were no sounds of pursuit, but just to be safe Moira led them back and forth through the stream several times and doubled back on their trail twice. All the while she said nothing to Wiz and shushed him when he tried to speak.

By the time Moira was satisfied the sun was dipping toward the horizon. She paused as if considering, and abruptly she changed direction and started angling back almost the way they had come. Finally she struck a track like a sunken road and led Wiz up it.

The road was canopied over with trees and thickly covered with fallen leaves, but there was not so much as a blade of grass growing on it. Here and there were bare spots where he could see paving blocks of blue-gray marble dressed square and neatly fitted together. Occasionally there would be another stone sticking up to one side with a runic inscription on it.

Whatever this was, it wasn't the Forest Road. It was too wide and too well-built. More, there was a different—feel—about it, and Wiz wasn't sure he liked the feel at all.

They came over a crest and Wiz looked down on a ruin. Delicate fluted columns and graceful arches protruded here and there from the trees and bushes. Wiz could make out the remains of a wall of the same blue-gray marble running around the place.

It was big, Wiz saw as they trudged down the road toward the ruin. The wall had to enclose several hundred acres. It was hard to imagine what the ground plan could have been, but Wiz formed an impression of a palatial, spacious building that had stood in the midst of extensive gardens.

Moira turned off from the road before they got to what should have been the main gate and searched until she found a breach in the wall. Without a word to Wiz she scrambled over the broken stones and onto the grounds.

She led deeper into the ruin, passing dry fountains surmounted by statues weathered almost to shapelessness, elaborate porticos and paved courtyards which had apparently never been roofed. At last she found a spot that seemed to suit her.

"We will camp here."

"What was this place anyway?" Wiz asked, staring up at the ruined arches. The pillars were too tall and too thin and the arches themselves were too pointed. Like everything else about the ruin they were at once beautiful and unsettling.

"A castle," Moira said as she dropped her pack beside him. "They say it belonged to a wizard."

"I thought we were supposed to avoid magic."

"It was not my plan to come this way," the red-haired witch said tartly. "I hoped to be well beyond this part of the Wild Wood by nightfall, but we lost too much time playing hide and seek. This place still has the remnants of the owner's guard spells and they offer some protection. If it does not meet with your approval I am truly sorry."

"Hey, I didn't mean . . ."

"Oh, be quiet," Moira snapped and Wiz lapsed into abashed silence.

As the afternoon turned to twilight Moira sent Wiz to gather firewood. He came back with a good armload which she accepted wordlessly and with little grace. Then she set about kindling the fire. Wiz stood watching her.

"All right," he said grimly. "Let's have it."

"Have what?" She looked up as the fire sprang to life.

"Whatever's eating you. You've been mad ever since we got past the gate and I want to know why."

"Mad? Me? What have I to be angry about? Just because your clumsiness nearly got us both killed, that is no reason for me to be angry."

"Okay, my foot slipped. I'm sorry, all right? And in case you hadn't noticed, I saved your bacon back there."

"And that makes it right?"

"It sure as hell makes it better."

"Sparrow, curing a disease is no excuse for causing it. If you had not been so lead-footed there would have been no need for rescue.

"Bal-Simba has given me the job of saving your worthless carcass. That would be dangerous enough if you were an adult. But you have the mind and manners of a child and that makes it ten times worse. If you do not feel I truly appreciate you, then, again, I am indeed sorry!"

"All right, that's it!" Wiz shouted and reached over to pick up his pack.

"Just what do you think you're doing?" Moira demanded.

"Leaving. You don't want me around? Fine! I'll make my own way."

"Don't be a bigger fool than you already are. You wouldn't last one day out there by yourself."

"Maybe not," Wiz said bitterly, "but it would be better than putting up with you. Lady, I'm sick of you and I'm sick of listening to you run me down. I'm outta here."

"And just where do you plan to go tonight?"

"I don't care. I'll find a place." He turned and stalked off.

"Sparrow! Wiz . . ." Moira dropped her arm. "All right, make a fool of yourself!" she yelled after him. "See if I care," she muttered as she settled on a log by the fire. *He'll be back as soon as he gets over this temper tantrum,* she thought. *Meanwhile he should be safe enough inside the walls. Oh Bal-Simba, such a task you have given me!*

By the light of the rising moon Wiz pushed his way

through the brush and weeds that choked the ruined courts and overgrown gardens.

*Bitch!* He thought. *Arrogant, insufferable goddamn bitch! I didn't ask for all this and I sure as hell didn't ask for her. She's done nothing but insult me since I met her. Well, to hell with that, Lady. And the hell with you too!*

He went on, stumbling occasionally over loose bits of marble, heedless of the branches that whipped at him. He'd find someplace to camp and then figure out what to do in the morning. It would probably be better to stay inside the walls tonight, he decided. That damn red-headed bitch was probably right about the protective spells and he had had a bellyful of magic already.

At the bottom of a ruined garden someone was playing a flute. The thin, plaintive music caught all the longing and unfulfilled dreams that ever were.

Guided by the bright moonlight, Wiz made his way among the overgrown bushes over the cracked flag path to the sound.

There was a pool there, rank with cattails and dark with lilypads. A broken marble bench lay beside it. On a dark rock overhanging the water sat the flute player, clad only in a pair of rough trousers with long hair down to his shoulders. Wiz listened until he reached the end of his song.

"That was beautiful," Wiz said involuntarily into the silence.

"Did you enjoy it, mortal?" the player asked. As he turned, Wiz realized his mistake.

It was man-sized and man-like, but it was not a man. The face was utterly inhuman with a broad flat nose and huge eyes with no trace of pupil. The hair was a mane, starting low on the forehead and sweeping back to the shoulders. Large pointed ears peeked out of the mane on either side. The trousers were fur, fur that clad the body from the waist to the tiny hoofed feet.

"Uh, yes. I enjoyed it," said Wiz, startled by the creature's appearance.

"Oh, do not be afraid, mortal. I cannot harm you. I am bound to this well."

"You play beautifully."

"It is the song of heart's desire." said the creature.

Around the pool, frogs croaked and trilled in crescendo. There must be thousands of them, Wiz thought distractedly, but he could see none of them in the moonlight.

"When Ali Suliman held here . . . did you know Ali Suliman?" the creature asked. "No? Before your time I fear. A most refined gentleman and a truly great sorcerer. Such a delightful sense of humor. Well, when Ali Suliman had this place things were much different. The palace was ablaze with light and filled with guests. Often Ali Suliman would bring his—special—guests to this pond to hear me play and discourse with me."

The thing sighed gustily and shook its shaggy head. "All is changed, alas. Few mortals come here now and fewer still hear my music."

"I'm sorry," said Wiz, abstractedly.

The being waved its flute in a dismissing gesture.

"The music is not important. It is the desire it represents that matters. The longing, the yearning in the mortal breast." He gazed at Wiz with opalescent eyes. "I can fulfill that desire," it said with utter conviction. "I can give you the one thing you want most. That is what matters."

The hair prickled on the back of Wiz's neck. The creature was so compelling that Wiz did not doubt for an instant that it could do what it said. In the back of his mind he knew he shouldn't be here listening to this, but the promise held him.

"Your heart's desire, mortal," the creature crooned. "Your heart's desire." The frogs croaked louder.

Wiz licked his lips. "How do I know you can deliver?" he asked.

"Oh, by magic," cackled the being, its pupilless eyes like opals in the moonlight. "By magic."

"What is my heart's desire?"

"Why a woman, mortal. A woman not far from this very place."

"What do you want in return?"

"Merely a game, mortal. It grows lonely here and time must be passed."

"What kind of game?"

"Why any kind you chose. Would you have a race? Will you wrestle me?"

Neither one sounded like a good idea to Wiz. The furry haunches were powerfully muscled and the thing's chest was broad and deep.

"No, nothing physical."

"Then something magical?" The creature made a swipe with his hand and left a glittering trail through the night air.

"I—I don't practice magic," Wiz stammered.

The creature grinned disquietingly. "A pity. A true pity. Well then, what about a game of the mind? The riddle game? Yes, the riddle game."

Like a lot of programmers Wiz took inordinate pride in his problem-solving ability. He firmly believed that any riddle could be solved by a combination of logic and careful examination. Besides, by using truth tables it is possible to construct some mind-boggling riddles, and Wiz had a lot of experience with truth tables.

Wiz licked his lips and found they tasted metallic. The invisible frogs redoubled their croaking.

"All right. I'll play your riddle game. Who goes first?"

The thing on the rock chuckled, an eerie, burbling sound. "Oh, there is only one riddle in the riddle game, mortal. And I am the one who asks it."

"Oh." That wasn't the way the game was played as Wiz remembered it, but now he was committed. "Ask then."

The thing on the rock blew a thin airy phrase on its flute and began to sing:

> *"Black as night, white as snow*
> *Red as blood from the death-wound flow*
> *Precious as gold*
> *Worthless as dross*
> *Cold beyond cold*
> *Gained without loss*
> *Higher and deeper and wider than all*
> *At fingertips always, gone beyond call*
> *What am I?"*

The frogs fell silent in chorus. Wiz racked his brains trying to come up with something that fit. *Precious as gold, worthless as dross* . . . Something that was valuable only to one person? *Gained without loss?* Wiz's mind ran itself in tight little circles as he tried to imagine what cold possibly fit.

"The answer, mortal," the creature leaned forward, his yellow eyes glowing with unholy light. "I will have the answer or I will have thy soul."

"Give me a minute," Wiz muttered. "Just give me a minute, okay?"

"You do not have a minute, mortal, not even a second." The thing stretched its arms toward Wiz, its fingers spreading like talons. "Answer or you are mine, mortal. Now and forever!"

Panic crushed Wiz's chest. His mouth tasted like metal and his lips were dry. The thing's hypnotic eyes rooted him to the spot as firmly as one of the rushes. He could not run, he could not cry out. He could only tremble as the creature moved closer and closer in its mincing gait, hooves tapping on the rock.

"Leave him!" Moira's voice rang out. "You cannot have him."

The pressure released and with a great gasping sob

Wiz fell to the ground. He twisted his head and saw the hedge witch standing behind him.

"But he agreed," the creature howled, dancing up and down on the rock. "Of his own free will he agreed to the bargain!"

"The bargain is invalid. He is under an infatuation spell and has no free will on this."

Wiz simply gaped.

"He made a bargain. A bargain!"

"Trickster and cheat! There could be no bargain and well you know it. Now be off with you! Seek other prey."

Moira threw her arms wide and her cloak billowed behind her like wings in the moonlight. With an awful shriek the creature whirled and dove into the pond. The frogs cut off in mid-croak and waters parted soundlessly to receive him.

"Mortals, mortals, cursed mortals," the thing's words came faintly and wetly from the pool. "Doomed and dying mortals. One day soon the World will see no more of you. You will vanish like the dew on the grass. Doomed and dying mortals."

Wiz heard the words but he didn't look. He huddled in his cloak and dug his fingers into the sod as if he expected to be dragged into the pool at any second.

"Oh, get up," Moira said angrily. It's gone and you're safe enough for now.

"What in the World ever made you agree to play the riddle game with the likes of that?" she asked as Wiz picked himself up. "Don't you know you could never win?"

"He promised me my heart's desire," Wiz said numbly. "He said he could give it to me by magic."

"By magic!" Moira mocked. "You blithering, blundering fool, don't you know by now to stay away from magic? It's bad enough I have to leave people who need me to come on this idiot's errand, but I have to babysit you every second."

"I'm sorry," Wiz said.

"Sorry wouldn't have saved you if I had been a moment later. You blind fool!"

"Well, you said this place was safe," Wiz said sullenly.

"No, you ninny! I said the wards would keep out most of what was outside. They do nothing against things which already are within the grounds." She stopped, drew a deep breath and let it out in a sigh.

"Listen to me. There is no place in the Wild Wood that is safe. Do you understand me? No place! You cannot let down your guard for even an instant and if you see or hear anything that even vaguely *hints* of magic, run from it! Don't investigate, don't stay around it, just get away and let me know."

"I'll try," Wiz said.

"You'll do more than try if you want to live to reach our destination. Now come with me." She turned on her heel and stalked away with Wiz following.

Moira fumed all the way back to camp. She was furious with Wiz, and, she reluctantly admitted, furious with herself for letting him storm off. Her orders from Simba were to get him to a place of refuge and she had nearly failed because she let her dislike for him overmaster her judgment.

*He has spirit,* she admitted grudgingly, *even with that whipped-puppy air of his. Spell or no, he really would have gone off on his own.* Moira couldn't allow that. *I must be more civil to him.* The thought did absolutely nothing for her mood.

They ate dinner in uncomfortable silence. The food did little to lighten the atmosphere. The cakes were overbaked and the meat was almost raw on one side for lack of turning. The meal was over and they were settling down for the night before Wiz could summon up the courage to ask the question which had been gnawing at him ever since he recovered his wits.

"Moira, what did you mean when you said I was under a spell?" Wiz finally asked.

The hedge witch looked annoyed and uncomfortable. "Patrius placed you under an infatuation spell."

"Infatuation spell?" Wiz asked blankly.

"The spell that makes you love me," she said sharply.

"But I don't need a spell to love you," Wiz protested. "I just do."

"How do you think an infatuation spell works?" Moira snapped.

"But . . ."

"Oh, leave me alone and go to sleep!" She drew her cloak about her and rolled away from him.

# Four

## BEYOND THE FRINGE

Wiz woke from a dream of home to rain on his face.

Judging from the sodden state of the campfire, it had been raining for some time, but the water had only now filtered through the leaves of the tree they had slept under.

He spluttered, rolled over and wiped the water out of his eyes.

"Awake at last," Moira said. She was already up and had her pack on her back with her cloak on over everything. "Come on. We need to get going."

"I don't suppose there is any sense in suggesting we hole up someplace warm and dry?"

Moira cocked an eyebrow. "In the Wild Wood? Besides, we have a distance to travel."

Wiz pulled his cloak free of his pack. "How long is this likely to last?"

Moira studied the sky. "Not more than one day," she pronounced. "Summer storms are seldom longer than that."

"Great," Wiz grumbled.

"It will be uncomfortable," she agreed, "but it is a blessing too. The rain will deaden our trail to those things which track by scent." She looked up at the leaden, lowering sky.

81

"Also, dragons do not like flying through rain."

"Thank heaven for small favors."

Their breakfast was a handful of dried fruit, devoured as they walked. They picked their way through a gap in the ruined wall and struck off into the forest.

It rained all day. Sometimes it was just a fine soft mist wafting from the lowering gray skies. Sometimes it pelted down in huge face-stinging drops. When it was at its worst they sought shelter under a tree or overhanging rock. Mostly it just rained and they just walked.

At first it wasn't too bad. The rain was depressing but their wool cloaks kept out the water and the footing was. However as the downpour continued, water seeped through the tightly woven cloaks and gradually soaked them to the skin. The ground squished beneath their feet. The carpet of wet leaves turned as slippery and treacherous as ice. Where there were no leaves there was mud, or wet grass nearly as slippery as the leaves.

At every low spot they splashed through puddles or forded little streamlets. Wiz's running shoes became soaked and squelched at every step. Moira's boots weren't much better.

Wiz lost all sense of time and direction. His entire world narrowed down to Moira's feet in front of him, the rasp of his breath and the chill trickle down his back. He plodded doggedly along, locked in his own little sphere of misery. Unbalanced by the weight of his pack, he slipped and fell repeatedly on the uneven ground.

Moira wasn't immune. She was also thoroughly soaked and she slipped and slid almost as much as he did. By the time they stopped for a mid-afternoon rest they were drenched and muddy from falling.

Unmindful of the soggy ground, they threw themselves down under a huge pine tree and sprawled back against the dripping trunk. For once Moira seemed as out of breath as Wiz.

Under other circumstances—say as a picture on

someone's wall—the forest might have been beautiful. The big old trees towered around them, their leaves washed clean and brilliant green. The rain and mist added a soft gray backdrop and the landscape reminded Wiz of a Japanese garden. There was no sound but the gentle drip of water from the branches and, off in the distance, the rushing chuckle of a stream running over rocks.

Abstractly, Wiz could appreciate the beauty. But only very abstractly. Concretely, he was wet, chilled, miserable, exhausted and hungry.

"Fortuna!" Moira exclaimed. Wiz looked up and saw she had thrown back her cloak and pulled up her skirt, exposing her left leg and a considerable expanse of creamy thigh lightly dusted with freckles.

"Close your mouth and stop gaping," she said crossly. "I hurt my knee when I slipped crossing that last stream."

"How bad is it?" he asked as he scrambled over next to her.

Moira prodded the joint. "Bad enough. It is starting to swell."

"Does it hurt?"

"Of course it hurts!" she said in disgust. "But more importantly I will not be able to walk on it much longer."

"Maybe you should put some ice on it."

Moira glared at him.

"Sorry. I forgot."

"What I need is a healing poultice. I have the materials in my pouch, but they must be boiled and steeped." She looked around and sighed. "We are unlikely to find dry wood anywhere in the Wild Wood this day."

"There are ways of finding dry wood even in a rain."

Moira looked interested. "Do you know how?"

Wiz realized he hadn't the faintest idea. His apartment didn't even have a fireplace and his method of starting a barbeque involved liberal lashings of lighter fluid followed by the application of a propane torch.

"Well, no," he admitted. "But I know you can do it."

"That I know also," Moira snorted. "Were I a ranger or a woodsman I would doubtless know how it is done. But I am neither, nor are you."

"Can't you use magic?"

She shook her head. "I dare not. A spell to light wet wood is obvious and could well betray us. Besides, I threw away my fire lighter."

"What are you going to do?"

"I can walk for a while longer. As we came over the last rise I saw a clearing that looked man-made. We shall have to go in that direction and hope we can find someone who will grant us the use of his fire."

"That's dangerous."

"Less dangerous than using magic, if we are careful. We will approach cautiously and if aught seems amiss we will depart quietly. Now, give me your hand."

Wiz pulled the hedge witch to her feet and for a brief tingling instant their bodies touched down the whole length. Then Moira turned away and started off.

Mercifully, the going was easier in the new direction. There were no hills to climb and the rain gradually slacked off. Moira started to limp, but she refused Wiz's offer of assistance.

As afternoon faded to evening, they threaded their way through the dripping trees until at last Moira motioned Wiz to stop and eased forward carefully.

There, in a rude clearing hacked into the forest, stood a cottage. Some of the felled trees had gone to build the dwelling and some into the split-rail fences around the field. Knee-high stumps still stood among the crops. The cottage was roofed with shingles and the chimney was stone. A thin curl of smoke hung low over the field. It was crude and Spartan, but to Wiz it looked beautiful.

"Hallo the house!" Moira called without entering the clearing.

"Who calls?" came a man's voice from the cabin.

"Two travellers seeking a fire."

"Show yourselves then."

Moira limped into the clearing with Wiz following. Ostentatiously she reached up and threw back the hood of her cloak. She nudged Wiz and he did the same.

The householder stepped into the door of the cabin. He was a stocky middle-aged man with a full black beard shot with streaks of gray. Wiz noticed that one hand was out of sight, possibly holding a weapon.

"Advance then, the two of you," he called. Wiz and Moira picked their way across the field to the cabin door.

The man stood in the door, just inside the threshold. "I will not invite you in," he said stolidly. Moira nodded and stepped forward. He backed away to let her enter.

She turned and they both looked at Wiz, but neither Moira nor the householder bade him enter nor made any motion to him. They looked and Wiz looked. Finally he got tired of it and stepped inside.

"Welcome," said the peasant, smiling. "Welcome, Lady." He nodded to Wiz. "Sir."

The cottage was a single large room with a fireplace at one end. There was a ladder leading to the loft and at the loft trap Wiz saw three wide-eyed children peeking down.

The furniture was plain and obviously home-made, built to last rather than for comfort. A spinning wheel stood in the corner next to a bag of wool. The smell of smoke and wool oil filled the house.

"Seat yourselves, please." Their host gestured to a high-backed bench to one side of the fireplace.

"What was that all about?" Wiz asked as they sat down.

"What?"

"The business at the door."

"There are things which can take human form and deceive all save the most clever. But few of those can enter a house unbidden. In the Wild Wood only the foolish or very powerful invite a guest within."

"Umm," said Wiz.

The cottager settled himself on a similar bench across from them. "I am called Lothar," he said.

"I am called Moira, a hedge witch. He," she jerked a nod at Wiz, "is called Sparrow. We thank you for the use of your fire. I have injured my leg and wish to brew a healing poultice, if you will allow it. If you or any of yours have ills that I may treat I will be happy to do so."

"You're welcome to the fire, Lady, but none of us are in need of healing."

Moira looked skeptical but said nothing.

"You are also welcome to spend the night within if you so wish," Lothar said grandly.

"Thank you, Goodman. We would be most grateful."

Moira produced the small bronze kettle from her pack and Lothar called the children down from the loft. He sent the oldest, a boy of about ten, to fetch water. While Moira laid out her kit on the rough plank table the other two children, a boy and a girl about eight and six respectively, watched in awe.

When the water was fetched, Moira selected several leaves and roots from the packets in her pouch and put them to simmer over the fire. Meanwhile Lothar bustled about fixing a meal.

They dined on venison, tubers and vegetables and Lothar served up a pitcher of beer to wash it down. It was a delicious change from trail food and Wiz wolfed down his portion.

As they ate the twilight deepened to night. The only light came from the fire crackling on the hearth. The smell of pine smoke filled the room. Outside the crickets began to sing.

After dinner they retired to the fireside. Although Lothar had said little while they were eating, he began to pump them for news as soon as they were seated. Since he was mostly concerned with the happenings around his old village of Oakstorm Crossing, and since that village was fairly far from Moira's there was little she could tell him. She answered as best she could and Wiz and the children listened.

"How fare you, Goodman?" Moira asked when she had run out of information.

Lothar smiled and Wiz saw two of his front teeth were missing. "Well enough, Lady. Well enough."

"You are far from neighbors here."

"Aye, but I've good land. And more for the clearing."

"Did you not have a farm where you were before?"

"Well, you know how it is on the Fringe. Farms are small and the soil is worn thin. It's hard to make a living in the best of times, and when the crops aren't good, well . . ." He shrugged his massive shoulders.

"My grandsire talked of this land," Lothar told them. "His father's father lived near here. So when things got bad in our village, we came here."

"It is dangerous to lie this deep in the Wild Wood," Moira said noncommittally.

Lothar smiled. "Not if you keep your wits about you. Oh, it was hard enough at first. Our first two crops failed in a row and the cattle were stolen. Then my wife died and my daughter had to look after the little ones. But we stuck it out and here we are." His smile widened. "Secure on a farm the likes of which I could never have had back on the Fringe."

Moira smiled back tightly and the tension grew thick.

"It looks like a nice place," Wiz said.

"Wait another few years," Lothar told him. "Next year I will clear more land and erect a proper barn. Then we will expand the house and add storerooms. Oh, my grandsire did not lie when he called this land rich!"

"I wish you good fortune," Moira said neutrally.

"Thank you, Lady. But you make good fortune. It takes hard work and planning, but if you give it that, you will have all the good fortune you could desire."

Moira looked uncomfortable, but she nodded as if Lothar had said something wise.

"Well, it looks like you've done all right for yourself," Wiz said, trying to break the tension.

"Thank you sir. We have. It's not easy, running a farm and raising four children without help, but it's a good life none the less."

"Four children?" Wiz asked and then shut up when he caught Moira's glare.

"There's my oldest daughter, Lya," Lothar said hesitantly.

"She's gone to nurse an elf child," the youngest child piped up. Her older brother poked her sharply in the ribs and Moira and Lothar both looked embarrassed.

"They offered us their protection," the man said simply. "Since then things have been better."

Kar-Sher, late a brown robe of the League and now the Master of the Sea of Scrying, hurried down the corridor, his sandals padding softly on the uneven floor of black basalt. At every turning and each intersection he paused to listen and peer around corners.

*It had all been so easy when Xind had done it*, he thought as he strained to catch a sign that he might be followed. Now the North was stirred and the Watchers of the Council were blocking him at every turn. Clear sight of the North was hard to come by these days and the Dread Master grew ever more impatient. He wondered if he had been so wise to undermine Xind when he did.

Well, that is a deed done. It raised me high in the League and with a bit of fortune I may rise higher yet.

Satisfied there was no one behind him, he continued down the corridor. *I have power of my own now. I am no longer a brown robe, I am an ally to be courted.* A rough hand reached out of the darkness and clasped his shoulder in an iron grip. Kar-Sher jumped and squeaked.

"Quietly, you fool!" Atros whispered, dragging him back into a shadowed alcove.

"You, you startled me," he said looking up at the hulking form of the League's second most powerful wizard.

Atros grinned mirthlessly. "You should be more alert. Now, what have you?"

"Only this: The Dread Master . . ."

"The old crow," Atros interrupted.

"Eh?"

"He is an old crow. Soon to be no one's master, dread or otherwise. You should learn to call him so."

"Yes Master," said Kar-Sher. "Ah, as I said, the—old crow—stays close to the City. There is no sign of new magic further south."

"Cloaking spells?"

"They would show."

"Like the cloaking spell this new northern wizard shows?"

Kar-Sher made an annoyed gesture. "That is different. It would take a truly mighty wizard to cast a spell that effective."

"Toth-Set-Ra has that reputation."

"You don't think . . . ?"

"I think you should be very careful what you assume about the old crow. Now. Are you sure there is no sign of secret magic being made to the South?"

Kar-sher considered and then shook his head. "Nothing at all."

"Well, then. Keep your watch." He turned to go, but Kar-Sher plucked at his cloak.

"Master, will we strike soon? The old crow grows impatient. I do not know how much longer I will hold my position."

Atros regarded him coldly. "The old crow is impatient for one thing only; this strange wizard. Events are already in motion to snare him. In a day or two that will be accomplished. Meanwhile it keeps our master occupied."

"What if he finds out about us?"

"He does not even suspect. Keep your wits about you a few days longer and you are safe. Now wait here until I am out of sight." Atros stepped out into the corridor and strode on.

Kar-Sher waited until he had his nerve back and started up the corridor in the opposite direction.

Neither of them had noticed the fat black spider hanging motionless in her web above their heads.

"So," hissed Toth-Set-Ra as he broke contact with his spy. "So indeed." He leaned back and rubbed his forehead. Peering through a spider's eyes was disorienting. His brain kept trying to merge eight images with apparatus designed for two.

A spider's eyesight might be poor, but there was nothing wrong with a spider's hearing. He had heard exactly what he expected to hear.

*You run too fast, Atros. It is time you were taught another lesson.* He extended his hand and an amethyst goblet flew to his grasp.

He expected Atros to connive against him, just as he had connived against the Council of the League to win his present power. It was his good fortune that Atros was nearly as clumsy a plotter as he was as a wizard. Powerful enough, perhaps, but lacking the finesse, the last measure of ability that raised a plotter or wizard to true greatness.

He sipped the wine and reflected on the best way to check his subordinate. *Someday soon, Atros, I will send Bale-Zur to you.* But not yet. One does not discard a tool merely because it is flawed. One uses it, preferably to destruction, while a new tool is forged.

Still, this tool was showing signs of blunting. In spite of all the power he had been given, Atros had still not brought him the alien wizard. Toth-Set-Ra rotated the goblet in his hand and frowned at the purple sparks that glinted off its facets. That wizard was the immediate problem, the unknown. Once he had been found and neutralized there would be time to deal with Atros.

*A pity I cannot send Bale-Zur to that wizard.* He could, of course. Bale-Zur could find and destroy any mortal whose true name had ever been spoken. Unlike other demons he did not need to know the true name of his quarry. It was sufficient that the true name had been spoken just once somewhere in the World.

It was that special power which had raised Toth-Set-Ra from a minor wizard to the leadership of the Dark League in a single blood-red night of slaughter. But Bale-Zur could only destroy. Toth-Set-Ra wanted to take alive this wizard whom Patrius had died for. He wanted to squeeze him, to wring the secrets of his foreign magic from him. Killing him was an option, but only a last resort.

Bale-Zur was almost as crude a tool as Atros, but both were useful. This other one now, this Kar-Sher, was much less useful. Under his mastership the Sea of Scrying had been useless in the search and all he could do was whine about Northern interference with his magic.

*Yes,* the wizard thought. *This one is eminently dispensable.* He paused to admire the play of fire in the goblet again. *But not yet. Not quite yet.*

In his own way Toth-Set-Ra was a frugal man. He always wanted the maximum return from his actions.

They slept on straw ticks on the floor that night. Lothar offered them his bed in the loft, but Moira declined politely. Before retiring, she took the poultice, which had been simmering in the pot, wrapped it in a clean cloth, and tied it about her knee. She turned her back while she did so and Wiz tried not to look.

By the next morning the swelling had vanished. She did several deep knee bends and pronounced herself healed.

"Lady, if we could get you back to my world, you

could make a fortune as a team doctor for the NFL,"
Wiz told her. She cocked an eyebrow but did not ask
for an explanation.

Lothar insisted on feeding them a breakfast of flat-
bread, sausage and beer before they left. Both he and
Moira were obviously uncomfortable, but Moira thanked
him kindly and Lothar gave them some dried fruit and
parched grain to add to the supplies.

It had stopped raining and the sun was shining
brightly. As they left the clearing, Wiz noticed a detail
he had missed the night before. Four mounds of earth,
one large and three much smaller, neatly laid out next
to the cabin and enclosed by rude rail fence.

Moira saw him looking at the three small graves. "They
only count the children who live," she said.

Once out of the clearing, they angled away from the
path they had taken the day before. The woods were
still sodden, but there were no rivulets to cross and,
except in the shadiest places, things seemed to be
drying rapidly.

Whether because the footing was still somewhat
uncertain or to spare her knee, Moira did not walk as fast.

"What happened back there anyway?" Wiz asked when
the clearing was lost from sight.

"What do you mean?"

"Between you and Lothar. Everything started out all
right, then—boom—it was like you'd bumped into your
ex at a cocktail party."

"My ex at a . . . ?"

"I mean you both got real cold and distant," he
amended.

"Was it that obvious? Moira sighed. "I tried to conceal
it. He gave us shelter and aid when we needed it and
that is no small thing in the Wild Wood. I should have
tried harder to be gracious."

"Yeah, but why?"

"Because he is a fool!" Moira snapped. "There is no

place in the wild wood for mortals, Sparrow. Only fools try to live here and they fail."

"I guess it was rough at first, but he seems to be doing all right now."

"Yes. Because he bartered away his daughter."

"What?"

"You heard the child. His daughter has been given to the elves in trade for the safety of his miserable farm!"

"He traded his daughter to the elves?"

"Life in the Wild Wood is hard for those who have little magic." She smiled a little bitterly. "Call it a 'fostering.' That puts a better face upon it."

"What did they want with her?"

"As the little one said. She is a nursemaid to an elven infant." Moira's face softened. "Elves seldom have young. That must have been an event beneath the Elf Hill."

"Wait a minute," Wiz protested. "She wasn't . . . ah, I mean she wasn't married when she went, was she?"

"You mean was she unspoiled? Probably. Elves prefer virgin's milk when they can get it."

"But how . . . ? Oh, magic. Never mind."

They walked on a bit in silence. "What a fate. Locked under a hill forever."

"It has its compensations. The elves are kind enough in their unhuman fashion. They do not mistreat their servants."

"But to spend your whole life like that!"

"No," Moira said. "Time passes oddly under the hill. Someday, when the elf child needs her no longer, she will emerge as young as when she went in." She sobered. "Of course that stead will likely long be dust by then and there will be none who know her. That is the cruelest fate."

"Yeah," Wiz said, thinking of the graves. "I'm not sure living in safety is worth what it cost Lothar."

"The price has only been partly paid." Moira made a face. "Wait. As the children grow up they will go one by one to drudge for the elves. Plague, murrain, raids by trolls or others. There will always be another need and Lothar will always return to the elf hill to seek aid."

Wiz was shocked. "Doesn't Lothar realize that?"

"Not he," she said contemptuously. "I have seen his kind before. He hopes long and hard that something will happen. Like most mortals he lives for today and puts off the reckoning as long as he may." She increased her pace.

"It is an old, old story, Sparrow. As farms get smaller and the soil wears out within the Fringe there have always been those who sought to go beyond it to carve out new homes. But the Wild Wood is not for mortals. It is a place full of Magic, given to others, and mortals violate it at their peril."

"Well, why not? My whole country was a howling wilderness once and we settled it."

"Because the magic in the Wild Wood is too strong, Sparrow. Within the Fringe the hedge witches and other orders can stand between the World's magic and people. Beyond the Fringe there is too much powerful magic. If we were to make the attempt we would only be swept away and our people with us. Believe me Sparrow, it has been tried and it has never worked. The Fringe is this limit of lands where mortals can live."

"Umm," said Wiz again and shifted his pack.

"What did Lothar mean when he said his grandfather knew this place?" he said after they had walked a bit more.

Moira snorted. "He was probably making it up. I doubt his grandfather ever came within a weeks journey of that stead."

"But men did live in the Wild Wood once, didn't they?"

"Parts of it, yes."

"Why did they leave?"

"Because they were fools like that man," Moira

snapped. "Because they went where they should not and paid the penalty for it! Now save your breath for walking." She lengthened her stride and left him staring at her back.

*They're being pushed back*, Wiz thought as he struggled to keep up with the hedge witch. *This whole area was inhabited once and the people have been forced out.* The Wild Wood was creeping into the Fringe like the African desert creeps south in drought. And the results were the same. The people either moved or died.

Would the rains ever come to turn back the Wild Wood? Wiz wondered. Moira's reaction hinted she didn't think so. When magic became too strong people could no longer co-exist with it and they had to leave. The part of the world where humans could live was shrinking under the pressure of magic.

Wiz shook his head. All his life he had been taught that wilderness needed protection from encroaching humans. Here the humans were the ones who needed protecting.

Wiz wondered if the trolls, elves and other magical creatures would establish preserves for humans. Somehow he didn't think so.

# *Five*
## NIGHT FLIGHT

"Have you found them then?" The balefire nimbus played about Toth-Set-Ra as he hunched in his high-backed chair.

Atros grinned. "We know roughly where they are. We have only to summon our creatures for the final search." He shook his great shaggy head. "We have been closing in on them for the last three days. They evaded our ambush at the Forest Gate and fought their way through to the Wild Wood. Then they camped for the night within the ruins of the Rose Palace of Ali Suliman," (while the search swept past them, Atros did not add). "We lost them somewhat in the next day's rain, but we have them generally located."

"How have they avoided you for so long?"

Atros shrugged. "Bal-Simba—blast his eyes—is a clever foe. His Watchers have been working hard to muddy our Sight. The whole of the North is covered with blanking and false trails."

He hesitated. "There is another thing. The wizard has a most pussiant cloaking spell. We cannot find the least trace of his magic anywhere in the North."

"Indeed?" croaked Toth-Set-Ra. "Oh indeed? And the hedge witch?"

"That is the strangest thing of all. The hedge witch discarded most of her magical apparatus early on. Some trolls found parts of her magic kit strewn about." He neglected to mention that the trolls were sleeping off a feast and had not reported their finds for three days. That had cost the troll father his head. "Apparently the hedge witch is relying on the other one to protect her."

Toth-Set-Ra rubbed the line of his cheekbone with a leathery forefinger. "Strange," he agreed. "Either this one is a most powerful wizard or she is a most trusting witch."

"I would suggest he is a powerful wizard, Dread Master. Judging from their success at eluding us."

"But you have found them?"

"We have them penned in a small part of the forest. They are somewhat to the west of the elf duke's hold."

"But you have found them?" Toth-Set-Ra pressed.

Atros smiled. "Tonight, Lord. Since we cannot locate them by magic, we must search by eye and ear. I am flooding the area with our creatures and allies. At night they are at their most powerful." His smile grew broader. "Besides what weary travellers can refrain from lighting a fire to cook their dinner and warm their bones? And a fire in the Wild Wood can be seen for a long way away."

Toth-Set-Ra looked unimpressed. "And if our wizard chooses to use magic?"

"Our black robes will be watching, ready to pounce."

"*My* black robes," Toth-Set-Ra croaked softly. "They are mine and do not ever forget it."

*We shall see, old crow*, Atros thought. *After tonight we shall see.*

"In any event, it is results I want, not details. Bring me this strange wizard with the most perfect cloaking spell. And bring him to me alive, Atros. Do you understand? I want him alive."

"Thy will, Dread Master," said Atros and bowed out of his presence.

There were a few other details Atros forebore to mention. His searchers were mostly allies or those who wanted the reward promised. Worse, nearly half of the searchers were trolls. Trolls are none too bright and far too inclined to murder to be ideal for this task.

Beyond that, Atros knew he could not hold his army together much beyond one night. The creatures not sworn to the League were restless, chancy things who would not stay no matter how great the promised reward. Even the League's sworn servants could not stay long. Such a concentration would quickly attract the attention of the Council's Watchers.

Not that it mattered, Atros told itself. One night would be more than sufficient.

Where were they bound? he wondered. They seemed to have a destination. The elf duke's hill? That made no sense. Elves were badly disposed to mortals of all varieties. Besides, if they wanted shelter among the elves there were easier roads to take.

Whatever their destination, they would have to swing south shortly or they would blunder into the deadest dead zone in all the North, a place where the tiniest spark of magic would show instantly. By now Atros had a grudging respect for this alien wizard's masking spells, but no spell could be good enough to hide them in that.

Atros was well satisfied as he went down the corridor. Not only did he have things well in hand for the capture of the strange wizard, but his other plans were well in hand besides.

Soon. Very soon.

"Where are we going anyway?" Wiz asked, sitting on a stump by the fire.

Moira looked up from stirring the porridge. "Someplace safe."

"You said that before."

"I prefer not to name it. There is always the chance of being overheard."

"Well, what's it like? A farm?"

Moira laughed. "No, it is a very special place hidden away in the Wild Wood. A place built like no other in the World."

"You make it sound wonderful."

"It is that."

"Have you ever been there before?"

"This deep in the Wild Wood? Not likely. I have heard of it, though."

"Right now anyplace that put a roof over our heads would be wonderful."

"Patience, Sparrow. We are perhaps a day or two from our destination."

"Then what happens?"

"Then you will be safe and I can return to my village."

"Oh."

"I have work to do, Sparrow. There are people who need me."

"Yeah, I guess so. Only . . ." Moira held up her hand to silence him.

"Wait," she said. "There is something . . ."

With a roar four trolls charged into the clearing. They were huge and foul smelling, clad in skins and leathers and rags. One brandished a rusty two-handed sword in one hand and the others carried clubs.

A troll closed in on Moira, arms extended and fanged mouth agape. Wiz grabbed a faggot from the fire and charged. With a casual, backhanded swipe and without taking his eyes from his prize, the creature sent Wiz sprawling through the fire.

Wiz rolled out as the beast got a hand on Moira. Without thinking he reached back into the fire and grabbed a burning brand. He pointed it at the troll and yelled "Bippity boppity-boo."

The troll was unfazed but the tree behind it exploded

into flame with a crackle and a roar. The astonished troll weakened its grip and Moira twisted free.

"Moira! Run!" Wiz yelled and ducked under the grasping arms of another troll. He twisted about and pointed the stick at it.

"Bippity boppity boo!" he shouted and another tree blazed up. The troll cringed back.

Whirling in a circle, Wiz pointed the branch and yelled "BippityboppitybooBippityboppitybooBippityboppityboo." Trees all around the clearing turned to fiercely burning torches and the confused trolls cowered and whimpered in the ring of light and heat.

Wiz sprinted in the general direction Moira had taken. Behind him he could see the forms of the trolls black against the orange-yellow glow. The scent of burning pine filled his nostrils and he coughed from the smoke. One of the trolls groped after him. Wiz pointed the stick at a tree between them, shouted "Bippity boppity boo" and watched the tree turn to a lance of flame in the very face of the monster. Then he turned and ran as fast as he could.

As Wiz charged through the forest, a dim shape flitted from behind a tree into his path. He flinched until he saw it was Moira, her form distorted by her cloak. He clasped her hand and she gave a welcoming squeeze. His cloak was back in the clearing, he realized, as were both their packs. But Moira was safe and none of the rest mattered.

Behind them the reddish glow of the fires lightened the night. Also from behind them came a series of hooting roars.

"They hunt us," Moira whispered and released his hand. "Come quickly."

The forest sloped gently downhill and they followed the slope as best they could. Wiz silently blessed the open parklike nature of the Wild Wood here because they could move quickly and quietly through it.

Ahead he could hear the bubble and murmur of a running stream. Behind him came the sounds of the trolls. They seemed to have spread out along the ridge and were casting back and forth, calling to each other as they went. Once Wiz saw a misshapen form silhouetted on the ridgeline by the faint fireglow. He tried to shrink in on himself even though he knew night and distance made him invisible.

They paused on the rocky stream bank while Moira turned this way and that, seeking the best path. There were boulders to serve as stepping stones, but instead Moira led Wiz directly into the chill, swift waters.

"The water will mask our scent," she explained over the stream's clamor, "and some things cannot cross running water."

"You mean like trolls?"

"The trolls are the least of it," Moira said. "Listen."

Off in the distance came the sound of a horn and again the hunting roar of trolls echoed through the trees. *My God,* thought Wiz. *Is every nightmare in creation after us?*

The water was not deep, but the current was swift and the bottom rocky. By the time they left the stream, some little distance above the place they had entered, Wiz had fallen into holes twice and was soaked from head to foot. Moira had lost her balance once and was thoroughly wet down one side.

With Moira leading they sprinted over the wide pebble beach and into the sheltering dark of the trees. The forest was thicker here and the underbrush more profuse. Wiz and Moira crowded into it and peered back the way they had come.

"Which way?" Wiz panted.

Moira cast about indecisively. "Ahh," she breathed at last. "They throng to the south and east of us. To the west and north are areas rich in magic."

"So we go west and north?" Wiz suggested.

Moira shook her head. "To enter a powerful area with the hunt so close upon us would be our doom. With magic all about us we would stand out like ants on a griddle."

"Lay low?"

Moira didn't answer. Which was answer enough.

"Can't you use magic to get us out of this?"

Moira snorted. "If I used magic they would sniff us out at once. We avoid them only because they cannot sense magic upon us."

A weird, warbling howl pierced the night, chilling Wiz's blood. Across the stream, a huge wolf-like shape loomed on the ridge, outlined by the rising moon. Even in the moonlight its eyes burned red. It was the epitome of all the wolf nightmares of Wiz's childhood.

"Dire Beast," Moira breathed. She squeezed Wiz's hand even tighter and they crept away, clinging to the shadow and thickets. Behind them the wolf creature howled again but made no move to follow.

Once away from the stream bank they ran. They scrambled up another ridge and half-ran half-slid into a valley. The woods were thicker and darker, but that was no comfort. Still the sounds of their hunters rang and the trees seemed to close in about them to the point of suffocation.

There were brambles to catch at clothing and rip flesh. Once Wiz took a thorny branch full in the face and once they had to stop to disentangle Moira's cloak from a barbed bush. As they worked the fabric off the grasping thorns Wiz saw that Moira's hands had been cruelly lacerated by pushing through the spindly growth.

Finally, exhausted, Moira led Wiz into a thicket. There was a hollow in the center as if once long ago a tree had been uprooted there. Together they cowered and panted in the little crater beneath the bushes and listened to the sounds of pursuit echoing through the forest.

Dared they stay here? Wiz wanted to ask but he was afraid to make a sound. Besides, he didn't think he would like the answer. Unbidden, Moira's words on the first day came back to him. *If you have a choice between the worst death you can imagine and falling into the hands of the League, do everything in your power to die.* Had they really come to that? he thought, looking over at Moira.

Suddenly something hissed in Wiz's ear like a disturbed snake. Wiz jumped.

"Hsst," came the sound again. "Hsst, Lady, over here." He turned and stared but saw nothing. Then part of the bush seemed to twist and coalesce and a tiny man stood beckoning to them where a second before there had been only moonlight and branches. He was clad in a pointed cap, tunic and breeks with pointed shoes. Wiz could not tell the color in the dim light.

"Come this way. Quickly." The little being turned and skipped through the undergrowth. Moira started to follow but Wiz caught her arm. "Trap?" he panted.

Moira scowled and shook off his hand. She hurried after the little man, who was dancing with impatience.

Wiz was half-blown when they started, but he pushed ahead gamely. The trail led through glades and over ridges until at last they arrived at the base of a hill. As their guide approached, a rock rolled away and pale golden light flooded out into the dark.

"Enter and be welcome," said a melodious male voice from within.

Again Moira started forward and again Wiz caught her arm.

"Didn't you tell me to avoid places like this?"

"Would you rather the trolls and Dire Beasts?" she snapped. Wiz nodded and followed her into the hill.

"May there be peace upon you. May you leave the woes of the World behind," the voice said, as if reciting a formula.

"May there be confusion to our enemies and may we return to the world we know," Moira said firmly into the air.

"May it be so," responded the voice and their host seemed to step out of the wall of the tunnel to them.

He was tall, graceful and silver-haired. His eyes were so blue as to be almost purple and his skin was the color of milk. Wiz could see the blue veins underneath.

He wore a long tunic of scarlet, intricately worked, and a collar of beaten gold. His belt was dark leather decorated with bronze the length around.

"My Lady," he bowed to Moira. "My Lord," he nodded to Wiz.

"My Lord." Moira dropped a deep curtsey.

"My Lord," Repeated Wiz and made a clumsy bow. He barely noticed that the rock had slid silently back across the entrance, sealing them within.

Their host regarded them serenely. "I am called Aelric. I am duke of this place and I bid you welcome here."

"We thank you for your hospitality, Lord," Moira said. "I am called Moira and this one is called Sparrow."

Duke Aelric looked narrowly at Wiz. "Ahhh," he said simply, but with a world of meaning.

"You have heard of us then, Lord?"

"A mite." The elf duke made a languid gesture. "But there will be time for talk later. I hope you will do me the pleasure of dining with me this evening."

"We would be honored, Lord," Moira said.

"Let it be so then." Duke Aelric snapped his fingers and their guide capered out and bowed low to his master.

"Most dread Lord, most gracious Lady, if you will deign to follow me?" The little creature turned and moved down the tunnel. Duke Aelric touched his fingertips to his forehead and faded back into the rock. Wiz gaped until Moira jabbed him with her elbow. Then he followed her and their guide down the corridor.

Wiz's shoes squeaked on tessellated marble floors inlaid in fantastic patterns. Over his head columns of scarlet and gold soared upward until lost in the gloom. Here and there an elaborately carved lantern cast a gentle yellow glow through its alabaster panes, making the light more mellow rather than brighter. Occasionally the glint of gold added accent and unostentatious richness to their surroundings.

They passed down stately corridors, through tapestry-hung halls and up sweeping curving staircases, yet they saw no one. Not even a faint, distant footstep or the furtive motion of a curtain dropping into place showed that there was anyone in the huge underground palace but themselves and their tiny guide.

At last they came to a massive door, twice their height and finely carved. The elf placed his hand on the intricately worked handle and pushed gently.

The door swung open to reveal a spacious, richly appointed room. It was more brightly lit than the rest of the palace and the carved and gilded lanterns along the walls cast a warm light on the furnishings of pale brown wood and heavy silken hangings the color of chrysoberyl. The ceiling was painted the blue of a summer sky and spangled with glittering golden stars. Lines of silver traced out the shape of unfamiliar constellations. The air was heavy with the scent of roses and lilies.

"My master bids you be comfortable," the elven major-domo squeaked. "There will be time to rest and bathe before dinner. My Lady's chamber is to the right," he swept a bow in that direction, "and my Lord's is to the left. Peace and repose be unto you." With that he bowed out.

"Wow," said Wiz as he looked around at the splendor. "This is really something."

"Elves contrive to live well," Moira said, laying her cloak onto an elegantly proportioned table and sinking down onto a silken cushion of the palest blue in the chair next to it.

"All right!" Wiz said and dropped onto a couch nearby.

Moira removed the ribbon from her hair and shook out her flaming locks. Wiz watched, enthralled.

"It was brave of you to save me from the trolls," she told him. "You gave me my life at the risk of yours and I thank you for it."

The words were sweet, but her tone was used to thank a stranger for a service. Moira was sincere and grateful, but that was all. She had been warmer to the man from the village, Wiz thought.

"It was nothing, Lady," he said uncomfortably.

"It was, and again I thank you."

Wiz did not reply. "Lady," he said finally, "may I ask you a question?"

"Since you must."

"I mean we won't be overheard or anything will we?"

"We will almost certainly be overheard, although mayhap Duke Aelric is too noble to pry into the affairs of his guests. Question if you must, but guard your tongue."

"Where is everyone? I mean, does Aelric live here all alone?"

Moira shrugged. "I doubt it, for elves are social creatures. But the place cold be aswarm with elven folk and we might see none. All elves have the trick of not being seen when it pleases them."

"Why did Aelric help us? Are the elves allied against the League?"

Again the shrug. "Allied against the League? No. Elves ally with none and barely notice what mortals do to each other. His Grace acted for his own reasons and those are beyond conjecture. Barring war or murder, elves are deathless and they fill their years with contests and rivalries among themselves. They play deep and subtle games with their own kind and meddle seldom in the affairs of mortals. Perhaps we are part of such a game."

"Well, as long as he's willing to put us up, we can be whumpuses for all I care."

"What's a whumpus?"

"An imaginary animal." Wiz lay back on the couch and

started to put his feet up before looking at his muddy shoes and thinking better of it. "Now what?"

"Now we had best make ready for dinner." Moira rose from the chair. "This is your room, I believe."

The bedroom managed to be magnificent, simple and cozy all at once. The canopied bed was made of some rich dark wood crafted in sleek, almost modern, lines and polished until it glowed a warm reddish brown. The sheets were tan and the thick comforter was a pale russet. The lighting was soft and indirect, brighter than the twilight the elves seemed to prefer but not as bright as the sitting room. The bed looked so inviting Wiz nearly sank down onto it, but he knew if he got comfortable he'd never be ready for dinner. He had a strong feeling it would not do to keep Aelric waiting.

The bath beyond was walled in pink-veined marble set with gold. In the center of the room was a sunken tub of steaming water, fragrant with herbs.

Wiz moved toward it, pulling at his shirt.

He had the shirt over his head when soft warm hands touched his bare back.

"Hey!" Wiz tried to turn, but the hands restrained him gently and helped him get the shirt off. With his head free, Wiz turned, but the room was empty.

"What is this?"

The only answer was a very feminine giggle as someone started to undo his belt. He looked down and saw nothing, yet his belt was unhooked and fingers began to unzip his fly. Instinctively he reached down to knock the invisible hands away, but he met only air. Again someone or something giggled.

*Oh well,* Wiz thought and submitted.

Once his unseen companion had undressed him, he stepped into the just-too-warm water and sighed luxuriously.

Wiz was expertly soaped, scrubbed and rinsed. The water that came off him was black with dirt, but the

water in the tub remained so clear he could see his
toes.

Clean and glowing, he was assisted from the tub and
rubbed down with towels he could not see. It felt like
there were two or three pairs of hands working on him
at once. *Either there's a whole harem in here or she
doesn't look anything like what I imagined,* Wiz thought.

His clothes were gone, but when he reentered the
bedroom new clothes were laid out for him, a shirt with
enormous puffed sleeves, a russet doublet several shades
darker than the bedspread and a pair of tight buckskin
breeches. Soft calf-high boots of ox-blood leather completed the outfit.

This time there were no invisible hands to help him
so Wiz dressed himself, struggling with the unfamiliar
fastenings.

*Not bad,* he thought, surveying the result in a full-
length mirror. He looked like a real swashbuckler, lean
rather than skinny.

Moira was waiting for him when he emerged. If Wiz
looked good in his borrowed clothes, Moira was breathtaking. She wore a gown of emerald green velvet, cut
low and caught tight at the waist, with full-length sleeves
that flared sharply from elbow to wrist. Her hair was a
flaming mane about her face, held in place with silver
pins set with opals. Wiz could only stare.

"Do you like it?" she asked somewhat shyly. "I've never
had a dress like this."

"It's gorgeous," said Wiz when he finally got his lower
jaw under control. "You're gorgeous."

"Thank you, Sparrow," she dropped him a mock
curtsey. Then she became serious. "Now watch yourself.
Be respectful and above all, be courteous. Elves place
great store on courtesy and there are very few mortals
who have shared Duke Aelric's table."

Wiz nodded dumbly and moved toward her. She
moved away with fluid grace.

"Shall we go?"

"Is it time?"

Moira only smiled and opened the door. Their guide was waiting for them. He bowed so low his forehead almost touched the floor and led them off.

Again their way took them down empty corridors and magnificent halls, all bathed in the soft dim light. At length the little man brought them down a stair as subtly curved and carefully proportioned as a sea shell, to a great bronze door. The door swung open at their approach. The creature bowed to the floor and motioned them within.

Their host awaited them inside the door.

"My Lady. My Lord." He had changed his red tunic for a tight-fitting outfit of silver-gray velvet. Silver glinted at his neck and wrists and a silver band set with a fiery blue opal held back his white hair. He was fully as magnificent as he had been when they first saw him, but now the effect was less barbaric, more civilized.

He bowed to them and Wiz bowed back as best he could. Then the duke took Moira's arm in his and led them to the table.

The odd half-light made it impossible for Wiz to judge the size of the room. The far walls were lost in the dimness, but Wiz didn't feel dwarfed. The floor was elaborately patterned parquetry and the table was draped in snow-white linen. Softly glowing balls of light hung above the table. They danced gently in an unfelt breeze and the ripple and play of the light was like candlelight on the table and diners.

Invisible pipers played a high reedy tune in the background, at once medieval and modern, like soft progressive jazz performed on recorders.

The duke seated Wiz on his left and Moira on his right.

"You seemed to have created an uncommon stir among the mortals," Aelric observed to Moira as they sat down.

"It was not intentional, Lord."

"And you were the object of a Grand Summoning," he said to Wiz.

"Yes, Lord. Uh, it wasn't my idea."

"No doubt," Aelric said equitably.

The elf duke was a perfect host, charming, gracious and witty. He made Moira laugh and dimple without arousing more than a twinge of jealousy in Wiz and contrived to make Wiz feel more at ease than he had since he arrived on this world. Only once did Moira bring the talk back to the circumstances which led them beneath the elf hill this night.

"Lord, why did you aid us?"

Aelric smiled, just a hint of a smile. "Let us say we find your pursuers an annoyance. Trolls and such like are uneasy neighbors and were they to find that which they seek they might be encouraged to tarry."

"We thank you for your service."

"The pleasure was mine, Lady," he said with an easy smile and again changed the subject.

For all his charm, Wiz could not warm to their host. There was malice there, Wiz thought, as he listened to the flow of the elf duke's talk. The casual malice of a cat with a mouse. There was alien, and underneath it was boredom. Would it be boring to live forever? Yes, in the end it would be, no matter how rich, how powerful or how skilled you were.

The food was rich and varied. The portions were small but there were many dishes and each plate was brought forth as carefully arranged as if by a master designer. Most of it was unidentifiable. But it was all delicious.

Once Wiz had been taken to one of the fanciest restaurants in San Francisco as part of a dog-and-pony show for a client. The meal had been very much like this. Excellent food, beautifully presented in magnificent surroundings. Except this was better on all counts.

The girl who served them was human. Wiz wondered

if she was Lothar's daughter. But she was so quick and efficient and so quiet and downcast she was gone before he could ask the question. Probably not a good thing to ask anyway, he decided uncomfortably.

They had gone through a half a dozen courses of meats, vegetables, sweets and savories when the duke reached out to lay a gentle hand on Moira's wrist, interrupting the story she was telling.

Aelric frowned. "Your pardon Lady, Lord. But it seems we have a caller asking for you."

Wiz froze, his spoon halfway to his mouth.

Aelric listened and then said into the air. "You may speak."

A hazy shimmering began to congeal in the center of the hall but the elf prince raised his hand. "I said you may speak. None enters here unbidden." The half-shadow dissipated until only a little shimmer remained.

"You have two mortals here," wailed a voice, high, thin and reedy with all the despair in the universe.

"What is within this hill is not the business of out-siders."

"You have two mortals," the voice repeated. "We want them."

"Your wants are no concern of mine," Aelric said in a bored tone. "Now speak on matters of interest or begone."

"My master will reward you well," crooned the voice.

The elf duke cocked his head and arched his brows. "It might be of interest to know what your master has that he possibly believes I should want. But not tonight. Say you further?"

"My master offers double what the Council offers for the mortals."

Aelric frowned. "I have no part in mortal quarrels," he said sharply. "What I do, I do because it pleases me and for no other reason. Those who are here stay here and those outside stay outside."

"My master is powerful," the voice wailed. "He is powerful and determined. Give us the mortals."

"Your master is a mortal," Aelric responded. "That is limit enough on his power."

"Will you duel him by magic?" the voice asked.

"Perhaps some other time. Now I am at meat. And you grow tedious."

The voice changed. It deepened and became louder. "GIVE THEM TO US," it roared. "GIVE THEM OR WE SHALL KICK THIS HILL DOWN ABOUT YOUR EARS."

Aelric yawned elaborately. "Tedious indeed," he said. "Now be off with you." He lifted a hand languidly and gestured.

"GIVE US the mortaaalllls. . . ." The voice lessened and died like a train whistle down a tunnel.

Aelric turned to Wiz and Moira and smiled sweetly. "Uncouth creatures. Now, you were saying?"

"Forgive me, Lord," Wiz broke in, "but aren't you afraid he will do something?"

Aelric gave Wiz a look that froze his bones and cleaved his tongue to the roof of his mouth.

"Forgive him, Lord," said Moira quickly. "He is from far away and is unused to our ways. Please forgive him," she begged. "Please."

Aelric cocked his head and stared at Wiz. "Far away indeed, Lady. Very well, but teach him manners." Then his expression softened.

"Know, infant, that this place has stood for aeons and on. It was built by magic on a foundation of magic and it would take more magic than a mortal could learn in a puny lifetime to touch it or any of mine."

"Yes, Lord," said Wiz, very subdued.

The rest of dinner passed off without incident. Aelric was again the gracious host, diverting and ever attentive to his guests' needs. By the time the last sweets had been removed with nuts in golden bowls and the wine brought forth in crystal flagons, Wiz was almost relaxed.

Almost. He regarded the elf prince in the same light as a friendly lion—magnificent, unsettling and not at all someone you wanted to spend time with.

At last Moira yawned delicately behind her hand and Aelric took that as a sign that the dinner was over.

"I should not keep you," he said with a charming smile. "You have had a long day already and several—interesting—days before that. May you rest well."

"Thank you, Lord." Moira returned the smile. "And thank you again for your hospitality." She extended her hand and the elf lord raised it to his lips.

"You are more than welcome. Thank you for gracing my table." He turned to Wiz. "And thank you, Lord. It was a privilege to meet someone from so far away."

Wiz bowed as best he could.

"You do not know why you were Summoned then?" Aelric said suddenly.

"Beg pardon?" Wiz asked, confused by this turn of the conversation. "Ah, no Lord."

"Well then," said Duke Aelric with an odd, cold smile. "It will be interesting to see what becomes of you, Sparrow."

"Thank you, Lord," Wiz replied, not sure whether he should be thanking the elf or not.

"Then will we see you again, Lord?" Moira asked.

"I doubt it," Duke Aelric said. "But it will be interesting nonetheless." Again the alien smile, like a rather sleepy cat examining a newly discovered plaything.

"Lady, do you suppose he knows something about me?" Wiz asked as soon as they were back in their rooms.

"He knew who we were," Moira said, yawning and stretching in a way that made her dress swell alarmingly and Wiz's heart nearly stop.

"I mean do you think he knows why Patrius brought me here?"

"Who knows what an elf knows?"

"Shouldn't we ask him?"

"Sparrow, if he knew and if he wanted us to know, he would tell us. It might be he was making sport of us. Elves are prone to such tricks. But I do know this. If he did not tell us there is no point in asking him."

"But . . ."

"But I am going to bed," Moira said firmly. "You may sit up and attempt to fathom the unfathomable if you wish."

Wiz watched the door to Moira's room close after her and then turned toward his room. He dropped his clothes on a chair in the corner and headed groggily for his own bed.

*I wonder if he really does know. Or if he's just playing head games,* Wiz thought dreamily as he drifted off to sleep.

In the morning there were fresh packs in the main room. The clothes they had worn into the hill were waiting for them with all traces of travel stain gone. Somehow they had even restored the nap to the suede on Wiz's running shoes. Moira's cloak was clean and patched so expertly there was no sign it had ever been rent and tattered. There was a new cloak hanging next to Wiz's pack to replace the one he had lost.

Sitting on the table was a round loaf of brown bread, still warm from the oven, a slab of pale yellow cheese, a pitcher of brown ale and a bowl of white onions.

"It appears we are to break our fast alone this morning," Moira said, pulling her chair closer to the table. She poured herself a tankard of ale and used her knife to hack off a chunk of cheese and a thick slice of bread. With the knife point she speared one of the onions and took a healthy bite.

Although the idea of beer and onions for breakfast made Wiz a little queasy, he followed suit. In spite of his misgivings the combination was delicious. The cheese was sharp and tangy, the onions were mild and sweet and the ale refreshingly astringent on his tongue.

"Doesn't time run differently in these places?" Wiz asked Moira around a mouthful of bread and cheese.

"Not if the elf lord does not will it so," she said. "He promised me when we entered that it would not."

"So that's what that greeting was all about!"

"Just so. Albeit we had little enough choice should he have decided to make centuries pass like minutes."

"I take it we're going on this morning?"

"I doubt Duke Aelric's hospitality holds for more than a single night," said Moira, appropriating the heel of the loaf. "Besides, the sooner we reach our destination the better." She looked at the bread and sighed. "I wish we could carry bread like this on our journey. It is unusually good."

"It's baked by elves," Wiz said smiling.

"Their servants morelike. What's so funny?"

"Never mind," Wiz chuckled. "I'm not even going to try to explain it to you." Then he turned serious. "What are the chances someone is going to be waiting for us outside?"

"Small enough. Oh, they may watch the door we entered like cats at a mouse hole. But I do not think we will go out that same way. Not only time but space runs strangely in places the elves make their own."

Wiz picked up the last crumb of cheese and popped it into his mouth. He let it melt away on his tongue savoring the bite and flavor. "Well, when do we leave?"

"As soon as we gather our things," said Moira. She stood up from the table and fastened her cloak at her pale freckled throat with the turquoise and silver clasp. Wiz followed suit, throwing his cloak over his back.

"Don't we need to ring for someone to show us out?"

"I doubt it," said Moira as she reached for the door

handle. "If a guide is needed one will be waiting when we open the door."

The door swung outward at her touch and brilliant morning sunlight flooded in. Instead of a marble corridor lined with travertine pillars the door opened into a sunny forest glade. An orange and brown butterfly flitted lazily above the deep green grass that ran to their threshold.

Moira looked over at Wiz, smiled slightly and shrugged. Wiz shrugged back. Then they adjusted their packs and set out under the warm morning sun.

# Six

## HEARTS' EASE

The morning was bright and sunny. Instead of dark and sinister, the Wild Wood was fresh and green. There was almost nothing among the trees and ferns to remind them of the night before.

Their path led out of the glade and back up the heavily wooded hill above the door. There was no hint or scent of danger, but still they moved along quickly.

They climbed a series of forested ridges, each looking down on the tops of the trees in the valley below. At the top of the third ridge, Moira scanned the valley while Wiz sat puffing on a rocky outcrop.

"There!" the hedge witch said, pointing. Below and off to one side a square stone tower stood rough and grey above the trees of the forest. About its base clustered outbuildings enclosed by a stockade of peeled logs.

"Heart's Ease," said Moira. "Our journey's end." She shifted her pack as Wiz struggled to his feet and they headed off down the path.

"Will we be safe here?" Wiz asked as the trail flattened out in the valley and he found he had breath for more than walking.

"In daylight nothing dare come close," Moira told him. "Anything magic here would be immediately known to the Watchers. There are non-magic agents, of course, human and such, but . . ." she shrugged. "We are safe here as anywhere."

"Thank God!" Wiz said fervently.

Moira frowned. "Do not be so free with names of power."

"I'm sorry," Wiz said contritely.

The forest enclosed them until they were almost on top of the castle. The trees were as huge and hoary as anywhere in the Wild Wood, but they didn't seem as threatening here.

"It feels friendly," Wiz said wonderingly, aware for the first time how oppressive the Wild Wood had been at its most benign.

"It is friendlier," Moira agreed. "The forest folk hereabouts are kindly disposed toward the inhabitants of Heart's Ease. They watch over the place and those who live there." She shifted her pack with a swell and jiggle in her blouse that made Wiz's heart catch. "Besides, this is a quiet zone. There is almost no magic here, for good or ill."

Atros returned to his sleeping chamber fuming. It had been a long, frustrating evening. *Damn those elves and their impudence!* They had spirited his quarry out from his very grasp, humiliated him in front of the entire League and ruined his plans. His impromptu army disintegrated once they knew the elf duke guested the two they sought.

*So they had been making for the elf hill after all,* the wizard thought as he stripped off his bearskin cloak by the light of a single lamp glowing magically in one corner. He did not understand it and he was too tired to really think upon it. Perhaps the one who had been Summoned was some strange kind of elf and not a man at all? True, Toth-Set-Ra's scrying demon had called the Summoned a man, but demons could be wrong.

*Too many possibilities,* he thought as he pulled his silken tunic over his head. *For now sleep and in the morning . . .* He moved toward the great canopied bed and then stopped. There was something, or someone, making an untidy lump under the sheets. He stepped back cautiously and possessed himself of his staff. He muttered a protective spell and then moved to the bed again. Reaching out with his staff, he flipped back the fine woolen coverlet and recoiled at what lay beneath.

There on the gore-clotted sheets was a thing which had once been a man. His back was broken, his ribs were smashed, his arms and legs dislocated and cruelly contorted, and his head lay at an impossible angle. But worse, he had no skin. He had been so expertly flayed that even his nose remained in place. His pallid eyeballs stared up at the ceiling and his ivory white teeth seemed to smile out of the mass of bloody tissue that had been a face.

Even in its present state, Atros had no difficulty identifying the body as Kar-Sher, Keeper of the Sea of Scrying.

"Do you like my little present, Atros?" hissed a familiar, hateful voice. The dark-haired giant started and looked around. In the shadows behind the feebly glowing lamp a face took shape. The face of Toth-Set-Ra.

"I told one I know what he was called," the wizard's voice went on, soft and full of menace. "Not his true name, Atros, just what he was called. And you see the result."

The old wizard cackled. "Oh, I did take his skin afterwards. I needed it, you see. It is amazing what you can do with the skin of a wizard, even a wizard who set himself so much above his station. A wizard who was such an inexpert plotter as this one."

Atros looked around wildly, swinging his staff this way and that to try to ward off an attack.

"I tell you again Atros, the League is mine!" The skull-face image said. "You, all of you, exist to serve me. And serve me you shall—one way or the other. Meditate upon that, Atros. Meditate upon it while you sleep."

The image winked out, leaving Atros alone in the chamber cold and shaking. Did the old crow mean to spare his life? Or was this just some torture designed to shake his will before he too was killed?

Atros spent the rest of the night in sleepless suspense and confusion. Plots to replace Toth-Set-Ra were very far from his mind.

A woman waited to greet them at the stockade gate. She was beautiful, tall and stately as a ship under sail. She was not young, yet not as old as her long white hair proclaimed. As Wiz got closer he saw that the lines around her eyes and mouth were those of one who had lived hard, not long.

She wore a long gown of midnight blue velvet, caught with a silver cord at her waist. The dagged sleeves of her dress fitted her upper arms tightly and swept halfway to the ground at her wrists.

Her right hand rested on the shoulder of a bent, manlike creature with a long sharp nose and huge hairy ears. He was as ugly as she was beautiful, but the contrast was not incongruous.

"Merry met and well come," she said in a voice like ringing silver. "I am Shiara, the mistress of this place, and Heart's Ease is your home for as long as you care to stay."

"Thank you, Lady," said Moira, curtseying. Wiz hastened to bow.

"Not 'Lady,'" the woman told her. "Just plain Shiara."

"Not plain either," said Wiz, moved by her beauty.

Shiara smiled but did not look in his direction. *She's blind!*, he realized.

"Your companion is gallant," Shiara said to Moira.

"He has his moments," Moira sniffed.

"You are called Sparrow, are you not?"

"Yes, Lady. Ah, yes Shiara."

"Well, merry met at Heart's Ease, Sparrow," the lady said. "You must both be tired. Ugo will show you to your rooms."

The ugly little creature sniffed and shuffled through the stockade gate without a backwards glance.

The ground within covered perhaps two acres. There were six or eight small buildings, huts and storehouses and a large garden laid out behind. Attached to the base of the stone tower was a large building, also of peeled logs, roofed with shingles and chinked with moss.

"Is she a wizardess?" Wiz whispered to Moira as they came up the flagstone walkway.

"She was of the Mighty," Moira said and motioned him to silence.

Ugo led them into the building and Wiz saw it was a single large room, a great hall with a huge smoke-blackened fireplace in one side and a table big enough to seat twenty people down the center. In spite of its rude exterior, the hall was richly furnished with heavy velvet drapes on the walls and massively carved furniture placed carefully about. The whole effect reminded Wiz of a picture he had seen once of J.P. Morgan's hunting lodge.

Ugo took them down the hall without pausing and through a low stone door into the tower proper. There was a narrow stair twisting off to the right and climbing so steeply Wiz was afraid he would lose his balance. At the second floor landing Ugo opened a door for Moira and bowed her through. Wiz started to follow but Ugo blocked him with a rough hairy arm.

"Lady's room," he said gruffly. "Come." He led Wiz on up the stairs to the very top of the tower.

"Your room," Ugo grumbled as he opened the door.

The room was small and simply furnished with a narrow rope bed, a table and single chair. But there was a fire laid in the fireplace and a basin and pitcher of steaming water sat on the table. The bed was covered with a bright counterpane and a snow-white towel lay beside the basin. Against one wall, next to the fireplace, stood a full-length mirror.

"Dinner at sun's setting," the goblin told him. "Do not be late."

Dinner was simple but savory. Most of the dishes were vegetables and tubers from the castle garden, with wild mushrooms from the forest and forest fruits for dessert. There was very little meat, which suited Wiz.

"Moira has been telling me of your travels," Shiara said. She held a knife in one hand and extended the other hand, palm down and fingertips spread, over the table, finding her plate by the heat from the food.

"It was quite a trip," Wiz said. "Lady," he added hastily as Moira frowned.

"I understand you rescued Moira when you were beset by trolls."

"Well, kinda. Mostly she rescued me."

"Still, from what Moira tells me it was a bravely done deed." She smiled slightly. "Though perhaps charging a troll with a stick is not the wisest move."

"Thank you, Lady," said Wiz, ignoring the second sentence. "Uh, Lady, do you know if they are still looking for us?"

Shiara turned serious. "Somewhat, I understand. Although your guesting the night in an elf hill seems to have thrown them off the scent and dampened the ardor of many of the League's allies. There are few who would willingly try conclusions with any of the elven kind, much less an elf duke."

"Then are they likely to find us here?"

She considered. "Perchance. But in this quiet place it would be hard. We do not use magic at Heart's Ease, so they cannot find you directly. There is little magic here to reflect off us and show us those with the Sight. No, Sparrow, if they find you at all it will be by accident.

"Besides," she continued, "finding you and getting here are very different things. In a quiet zone such as this any attempt at magic would be seen instantly by the Watchers and countered. We are a hundred leagues or more from the shores of the Freshened Sea so they cannot come at us overland. The forest creatures are our friends, so they would find it difficult to sneak close.

"All things considered we are safe enough."

"That's a relief."

"Just do not get careless," Moira said sharply.

"True," their blind hostess said. "Safety is at best relative and we are deep in the Wild Wood. Do not wander off, and leave things you do not understand strictly alone."

There was silence for a bit while they ate.

"Lady, what do we do now?" Wiz asked at last.

"You remain here as my guests while the Mighty consider your situation."

"And Moira?" Wiz asked, dreading the answer.

"I am to remain as well," said the red-haired witch, in a tone that showed she didn't like it. "In their wisdom the Mighty have decreed that even here you need a keeper." She grimaced. "And I am chosen for the task."

"You don't have to stay on my account," Wiz protested.

"I stay because the Mighty would have it so."

"Peace, peace," said Shiara. "Lady, I think your quarrel is with those not present, not the Sparrow."

"True, Lady," Moira said contritely. She turned to Wiz. "I am sorry I spoke so."

They contrived to get through the rest of dinner without snapping at each other.

At first Wiz simply luxuriated in life at Heart's Ease. He had a bed to sleep in, a roof over his head, no one was chasing him and, best of all, he didn't have to walk all day.

But that palled quickly. There was nothing for him

to do. Moira made herself useful, cooking and helping to clean, but Wiz had no domestic skills.

"Is there anything I can do?" he asked Ugo one day as the goblin was sweeping out the great hall.

"Do?" Ugo grunted.

"To help."

Ugo bent to his sweeping. "Don't need help. Take care of Lady by myself."

It wasn't that he was interested in doing housework, Wiz admitted to himself; he was bored and he felt completely useless.

He wandered out into the garden where Moira was on her hands and knees weeding an herb border.

"Can I help?"

Moira looked up and did not rise.

"How?" she asked suspiciously.

Wiz spread his arms. "I just want to make myself useful."

Moira snorted skeptically, as if she felt his offer was a ruse to get close to her. Since that was partially true, Wiz reddened.

"Very well, weed that section over there." She nodded her head toward a part of the border on the other side of the garden.

The border contained tall fennel plants, their feathery pale green foliage smelling strongly of licorice. Sprouting thickly around them were broad-leafed seedlings, each with two or three yellow-green leaves.

Even though the smell of licorice made Wiz slightly nauseous, he set to work with a will, pulling up the tiny plants without damaging the fennel. The summer sun beat strongly on his back and before he had weeded five feet he was sweating heavily. The border was wide and he had to reach to get the weeds at the far side. In ten feet his shoulders were twinging from the reaching and by the time he had done twenty feet his back was sore as well. He took to stopping frequently to rest his aching muscles and to watch Moira at work on the other side of the garden.

Moira worked steadily and mechanically, flicking the weeds out of the bed with a practiced twist of her wrist. Her long red hair hung down beside her face and every so often she would reach up and brush it out of the way, but she never broke the rhythm of her work. There was a smudge of dirt on her cheek and her skirt and blouse were grimed and stained, but she still took Wiz's breath away.

At last Wiz reached the end of the fennel and went to Moira for further instructions.

"It took you long enough," she said as he approached.

"There were a lot of weeds," said Wiz, bending over backwards in an effort to get he kinks out of his back. "I don't think that patch had been weeded in some time."

Moira looked up at him sharply. "I weeded it myself not three days ago."

"Well, weeds must come up quickly here. They were all over the place."

Moira got to her feet and went over to examine Wiz's handywork. At the sight of the clean bare earth under the fennel plants she sucked in her breath and clenched her teeth.

"What's wrong?"

"Those," she said pointing to Wiz's piles of "weeds," "were lettuces. They were planted there so the fennel could shade them." She sighed and stooped to gather the wilted plants into her apron. "I hope you like salad, Sparrow, because there is going to be a lot of it tonight."

"I'm sorry," he mumbled.

"It is not your fault, Sparrow," she said in a resigned voice. "I should have known better than to trust you with such a task."

That made Wiz feel even worse.

"Go back inside. I will finish up here."

"Lady, I'm really sorry."

"I know you are, Sparrow. Now go."

Finally, by appealing to Shiara, Wiz got a regular job. Under a shed roof against the palisade was a woodpile and next to the woodpile stood an old tree stump with an axe in it. Wiz's job was to chop firewood for Hart's Ease.

The axe was shaped like a giant tomahawk with no poll and a perfectly round straight haft. The design made it hard to handle and it took Wiz two or three hours a day to chop enough wood for the hearths and kitchen fires. He didn't see how Ugo had been able to get the wood chopped with all his other work. *Except,* Wiz thought glumly, *he's probably a lot more efficient at it, than I am.*

The goblin servant came by the wood pile several times to check Wiz's progress and sniffed disapprovingly at what he saw. He also very ostentatiously examined the axe for damage each time and strictly forbade Wiz to sharpen it.

Worse than the boredom, Moira avoided him. She wasn't obvious about it and she was always distantly polite when they met, but she contrived to spend as little time in his company as she could. Wiz took to standing on the batlements of the keep and watching her as she worked in the garden far below. From the occasional glance she threw his way he knew she saw him, but she never asked him to stop.

He had been closer to her when they were on the run, Wiz thought miserably. About the only time he could count on seeing her was when they sat down to dinner.

But the worst thing of all was that there were no computers. Because of the magical changes that let him speak the local language, Wiz couldn't even write out programs. He took to running over algorithms mentally, or sitting and sorting piles of things algorithmatically. At night his dreams of Moira alternated with dreams of working at a keyboard again and watching the glowing golden lines of ASCII characters march across the screen.

One morning Moira found him sitting at the table in the hall practicing with broomstraws.

"What are you doing, Sparrow?" she asked, eyeing the row of different length straws on the table before him.

"I'm working a variation on the shell sort."

"Those aren't shells," Moira pointed out.

"No, the algorithm—the method—was named for the man who invented it. His name was Shell."

"Is this magic?" she demanded.

"No. It's just a procedure for sorting things. You see, you set up two empty piles . . ."

"How can piles be empty?"

"Well, actually you establish storage space for two empty piles. then you . . ."

"Wait a minute. Why don't you just put things in order?"

"This is a way of putting them in order."

"You don't need two piles to lay out straws in order."

"No, look. Suppose you needed to tell someone to lay out straws in order."

"Then I would just tell them to lay them out in order. I don't need two piles for that either."

"Yeah, but suppose the person didn't know how to order something."

"Sparrow, I don't think *anyone* is that stupid."

"Well, just suppose, okay?"

She sighed. "All right, I am working with someone who is very stupid. Now what?"

"Well, you want a method, a recipe, that you can give this person that will let them sort things no matter how many there are to be sorted. It should be simple, fast and infallible.

"Now suppose the person who is going to be doing the sorting can compare straws and say that one is longer than another one, okay?"

"Hold on," Moira cut in. "You want to do this as quickly as possible, correct?"

"Right."

"And your very-stupid person can tell when one straw is longer than another one, correct?"

"Right."

"Then why not just lay the straws down on the table one by one and put them in the right order as you do so? Look at the straws and put each one in its proper place."

"Because you can't always do that," Wiz said a little desperately. "You can only compare one pair of straws at a time."

"That's stupid! You can see all the straws on the table can't you?"

"You just don't understand," Wiz said despairingly.

"You're right," the red-headed witch agreed. "I don't understand why a grown man would waste his time on this foolishness. Or why you would want to sort straws at all." With that she turned away and went about her business.

"It's not foolishness," Wiz said to her back. "It's . . ." *Oh hell, maybe it is foolishness here.* He slumped back in the chair. After all, what good is an algorithm without a computer to execute it on?

But dammit, these people were so damn literal-minded! It wasn't that Moira didn't understand the algorithm—although that was a big part of it, he admitted. To Moira the method was just a way to sort straws. She didn't seem to generalize, to see the universality of the technique.

Come to that, most of the people here didn't generalize the way he did. They didn't think mathematically and they almost never went looking for underlying common factors or processes. This is what it must have been like back in the Middle Ages, before the rise of mathematics revolutionized Western thought.

*Well,* he thought, looking around the great hall with

its fireplace and tapestries, *this isn't exactly Cupertino. This is the Middle Ages, pretty much.*

*So here I am, a Connecticut Yankee in King Arthur's Court. Full of all kinds of modern knowledge. And that and a quarter—or whatever they use here for quarters—will get me a cup of coffee—or whatever they drink here for coffee.*

If he had been a civil engineer or something he could have put his knowledge to use. He might at least have shown people how to build better bridges or catapults or whatever. But he wasn't even a hardware type. Strictly software. And the only thing his knowledge was good for was sorting straws.

With a disgusted motion Wiz swept the half-sorted straws onto the floor. He dragged the heavy carved chair from the table to a place by the window and sat with his feet propped on the window ledge staring out.

Back home he could look out over the freeway and housetops to rolling golden hills marked with dark slashes where clumps of oaks and eucalyptus grew. Here all he could see was trees and off in the distance mountains covered with more trees. He missed that combination of open vistas and people close by. He even missed the rivers of automobiles that poured down the freeway.

He did a quick calculation and realized they were coming down to the wire on the project at work. Probably cursing him for disappearing at a critical point. *I wonder who they got to replace me?* The thought of a stranger working at his terminal, rearranging his carefully piled stacks of printouts made him ache. He got up and started to pace the length of the hall.

He had left half a box of fried chicken in his desk drawer, he remembered. *Will they find that before it starts to stink up the office? And what about my apartment? The rent should be due by now. The bills will be piling up in the mailbox. How do they handle stuff like that when someone disappears?* Wiz didn't have a cat because the apartment didn't allow pets. For the first time he was glad of it. *At least there was no one who was really dependent on me.*

Ugo came in with a load of wood for the evening's fire. As he dropped it by the fireplace, he saw the chair against the window.

"You move?" he demanded.

"Yes."

He scowled and pointed at the chair. "Do not move things. It would confuse the Lady." He shifted it back to its place by the table.

"I'm sorry," Wiz said contritely.

"Do not move things," the goblin said sternly and continued on his way.

"Damn!" Wiz said to the empty air.

"Do not curse, Sparrow."

Wiz turned and saw Moira had come back into the hall.

"Sorry," he muttered.

"Is something wrong?"

"No, just a little homesick."

"I am sorry, Sparrow. I, too, wish to go home."

"At least you can get there from here," he said sullenly.

Moira compressed her lips. "Not while the Mighty bid me here to watch over you."

"You don't do much watching. The only time I see you is at meals."

"Oh? Do you feel the need for a nursemaid, Sparrow?"

"I'm in love with you. I want to be close to you. Is that so hard to understand?"

Moira dropped her eyes. "That was none of my doing."

"All right, you don't love me," Wiz said bitterly. "Then take this damn spell off me!"

"Do not use language like that." Moira said sharply.

"Sorry," Wiz snapped, "but that's what it is."

The red-headed witch sighed. "Sparrow, if I had my way you never would have been bound to me in the first place. If it were in my power to remove the spell I would do so in an instant. But I cannot.

"*I* did not put the spell on you, Patrius did. It is not an infatuation spell I know and I do not have the faintest idea how to release you. Bal-Simba or one of the other Mighty could perhaps remove it. When Bal-Simba comes here I will ask him to take the spell off. More, I will *beg* him to take it off."

She softened. "I am sorry, Sparrow, but that is the best that I can do."

"Great," Wiz said. "In the meantime I've got a case of terminal puppy love combined with the moby hots for you. I've got to live under the same roof with you and have nothing to do with you. Da . . . darnit, before this happened you weren't even my type! I like willowy brunettes."

Moira reddened. "I suppose you think this is easy for me! To have you trailing after me like a puppy dog, or a bull and me a cow in season? To have to stay here when there are people elsewhere who need me? To have to tiptoe around avoiding you for both our sakes? *Do you think I enjoy any of it?*" she shouted, her freckles vivid against her flushed skin, her bosom heaving and her green eyes flashing like emeralds in candlelight. Wiz could only stare, but Moira didn't notice.

"Sparrow, believe me when I tell you I want nothing so much as to be rid of you and gone from this place." She turned on her heel and slammed out the door.

"*Damn* that old wizard anyway!" Wiz said viciously in his teeth. Then he went off to the woodpile to turn logs into kindling.

Moira didn't exactly apologize and neither did Wiz. But the outburst seemed to clear the air slightly and for a while things at Heart's Ease were a little less strained.

Other than that, life went on as before. Wiz chopped wood and moped about, Moira stayed out of his way, Shiara was as beautiful and gracious as ever and Ugo grumbled.

In addition to cutting firewood and sighing after Moira, Wiz did try to learn more about his new world and his new home.

"Ugo, why is Heart's Ease so special?" Wiz asked one morning when the little wood goblin came out to the wood pile to collect his work.

"Because the Lady live here," said Ugo in a tone that indicated only an idiot would ask such a question.

Wiz put the axe down and wiped his brow. "I mean besides that. Moira said there was something about the way it was built."

"No magic," Ugo told him. "Every stone raised by hand. Every board and beam felled by axe and shaped by adze. All joined with pegs and nails. No magic anywhere in the building."

"Why not?"

"The Lady does not like magic," the goblin servant said, gathering in an armload of wood. "It hurts her now." With that he turned away to his duties.

Pumping Ugo for information was never very satisfactory, Wiz thought as he washed and changed for dinner. *But then damn little around here is.*

Wiz pulled a clean shirt out of his chest and paused in front of the mirror before putting it on. The days at the woodpile had put muscle on his frame and the sun had darkened his normally pasty torso. He still wasn't going to win any bodybuilding contests, but he had to admit he looked a lot better than he normally did.

"Pretty good for someone who's totally useless," he told himself.

"Are you sure?" the mirror asked soundlessly.

Wiz jumped and gasped. Then he stared. The mirror was angled so it did not catch the full brightness of the sun. It's surface was dark and cloudy as always.

"Are you sure you're so useless?" the mirror repeated. The words formed in Wiz's mind.

"Well, yeah I'm sure," Wiz said aloud.

"You shouldn't be," the mirror said. "You were brought from a long way at the cost of a man's life. There are a lot of people who are looking very hard for you. I'd say that makes you pretty important."

*Great!* Wiz thought. *Now I'm getting a pep talk from a Goddamn mirror.*

"You need it from someone, bub. You've been sulking like a twelve-year-old ever since you got to Heart's Ease. You need to pull out of it."

"What's the use? I don't fit in here and I never will."

"With that attitude you're damn straight you never will," the mirror told him. "This isn't the first time you've been a fish out of water. You're the guy who spent two years doing software maintenance in a COBOL shop and managed to fit in pretty well."

"Well yeah, but that was different."

"Not that different. Wiz, old son, you've never exactly been a fount of social graces, but you've always gotten by. And you have never, *never*, given up before."

"So I should beat my head against a stone wall?"

"How do you know it's a stone wall? Face it, you haven't tried all that hard. There's got to be something here for you. All you have to do is find it."

"I'm not so sure."

"Patrius was. He must have had a reason to bring you here."

"Moira says Patrius made a mistake."

"Moira may be beautiful, but she's not always right."

"Well . . ."

"Moira is a consideration, though. If you were someone here, it might change her attitude."

"If you're going to offer to play me a game, I refuse," Wiz told the mirror.

"No offer," the mirror told him. "Only the observation."

"Okay, but what could make me special here?"

The mirror was silent.

"Well?" Wiz demanded.

"I don't know the answer to that."

"Great. Then why the hell bring it up?"

"Because you have two choices," the mirror bored on inexorably. "You can believe you will never amount to anything here, never fit in, and dissolve in your own bile. Or you can believe you have a place here and try to find it. Which do you prefer?"

"All right. But how? What do I have to do?"

"You'll think of something," the mirror told him.

"You'll think of something," Wiz mimicked. "Thanks a lot!"

"Sparrow?" Wiz turned and there was Shiara standing in the open door.

"Who are you talking to?" she asked. Wiz flushed and opened his mouth to deny it. Then he changed his mind. After all, magic worked here.

"I was talking to the mirror, Lady."

Shiara frowned. "The mirror?"

"Well, it talked to me first," he said defensively.

Frowning, the mistress of Hart's Ease swept into the room, her long black gown swishing on the uneven floor. "This mirror?" she asked, putting out a hand to brush her fingertips across its silvery surface.

"Yes, Lady. That mirror."

Shiara smiled and shook her head.

"I'm sorry, Lady, I know you don't allow magic in the castle, but . . ."

"Sparrow, I think you have been brooding overmuch," Shiara told him gently.

"Lady?"

"There is no magic here. This is an ordinary mirror."

"No magic?" Wiz repeated dumbly.

"No magic at all. Just a mirror."

Wiz felt himself turning crimson to his hair roots. "But it talked to me! I heard it."

"It talked to you or you talked to you?" she asked

gently. "Sometimes it is easier to hear things about ourselves if they appear to come from outside us."

Wiz looked back at the mirror, but the mirror remained mute.

Late one afternoon Wiz happened to pass Moira in the great hall.

"Moira," he asked, as she went by with a nod, "what happened to Shiara?"

The hedge witch stopped. "Eh?"

"She was a wizardess, wasn't she? But Ugo told me magic hurts her."

"It does. To be in the presence of even tiny magics causes her pain. That is why she lives here in the quietest of the Quiet Zones in a keep built without the least magic."

"How?"

"What happened?"

"By carpenters, masons and other workers who built without magic. Isn't that the way you build things in your world?"

"No, I mean how did it happen to her?"

Moira hesitated. "She lost her sight, her magic and her love all in one day. It is a famous tale, but of course you would never have heard it." She sighed. "Shiara the Silver they called her. With her warrior lover, Cormac the Gold, she ranged the World recovering dangerous magical objects that they might be held safely in the Council's vaults.

"Not only was she of the Mighty, but she was a picklock of unusual skill. No matter what wards and traps protected a thing, she could penetrate them. No matter how fierce the guards set over a thing, Cormac could defeat them. With him to guard her back, she removed magic from the grasp of the League itself."

"What happened?"

"We went to the well once too often," Shiara said drily from the doorway.

They both whirled and blushed. "Your pardon, Lady," Moira stammered. "I did not know . . ."

"Granted willingly." Shiara swept into the hall, moving unerringly to them. "So you have not heard my story, Sparrow?"

"No, Lady. I'm sorry. I didn't mean to talk about you behind your back."

"There is no need to be sorry." Her mouth quirked up at the corner. "The bards sing the tale in every tavern in the North, I understand. The price of fame is having your story told over and over by strangers."

"I'm sorry," Wiz said again.

"Perhaps you would like to hear the story as it happened?"

"We do not wish to pain you, Lady." Moira said.

Shiara chuckled, a harsh, brittle sound. "My child, the pain is in the loss. There is little enough ain in the telling." She seated herself in her chair by the fireplace. "Sometimes it even helps to repeat it."

Moira sat down on the bench. "Then yes, Lady, we would like to hear the story, if you do not mind."

"I've never heard it, Lady," Wiz said, sitting down as close to Moira as he could without being too obvious about it. Moira shifted slightly but did not get up.

"Well then," Shiara smoothed out the folds in her skirt and settled back. "We were powerful in those days," she said reminiscently. "My hair was white even then and Cormac, ah, Cormac's hair was as yellow as fine gold."

"And he was strong," Moira put in breathlessly. "The strongest man who ever lived and the best, bravest swordsman in all the North."

"Not as strong as the storytellers say," Shiara said. "But yes, he was strong."

"And handsome? As handsome as they say?"

Shiara smiled. "No one could be that handsome. But he was handsome. I called him my sun, you know."

Ugo entered unnoticed with a bundle of wood and set about kindling a fire.

# Seven
## SHIARA'S STORY

Shiara sensed the boy and girl looking up at her. Young, Shiara thought, so very young. Convinced the world is full of hope and possibilities and so blind to the truth. She felt the warmth of the fire on her face and turned her head to spread the heat. Then she sighed and began the old, old tale.

"Once upon a time, there was a thief who loved a rogue . . ."

Cormac, tall and strong with his corn-ripe hair caught back by a simple leather filet. He had doffed his leather breeks and linen shirt and stood only in his loin cloth. The fire turned his tan skin ruddy and highlighted the planes and hollows of his muscles. The scars stood out vividly on his torso and legs.

"Well, Light. Do we know what the thing is?"

Shiara shook her head and the motion made her tresses ripple. The highlights in her hair danced from the flames and the motion.

"Only that it is powerful—and evil. An evil that can shake the World."

"Mmmfph," Cormac grunted and turned back to his sword. Again he checked the leather cords on the hilt,

137

running his fingers over them for any sign of looseness or slickness that might make the sword slip in his hand. "And it lies above us, you say?"

Shiara nodded. "In a cave well above the tree line this thing sleeps." She bit her lip. "It sleeps uneasily and I do not like to think what it might become when it awakens."

"And we must either possess it or destroy it." He shook his head. "It's an awful way to make a living, Light."

"Terrible for two such honest tradesfolk," she agreed, falling into the well-worn game.

The thief had been very, very good. With skill, cunning, carefully arrayed magic and a good element of luck he had managed to penetrate the crypt beneath the Capital where the most dangerous treasures of the Council were stored.

In the end it had not been the Council that had caught him. When the vault's magic detectors screamed and guards and wizards came rushing to investigate, they found the thief already dead, his throat torn out by the guardian the original owner had set upon the thing he had come to steal.

The object of the daring raid had been a chest imprisoning a demon of the sixth order, a thing powerful enough but not so unusual as to attract the close scrutiny of the Mighty The real treasure was in the hidden drawer in the bottom of the chest. What the compartment contained was well worth scrutiny.

"I had heard of the thieving of course," Cormac told her as they toiled up the steep trail toward the foreboding summit, "but I had not known what was in the compartment."

"A parchment," Shiara said. "A map and a note that a very old and very great treasure of magic lay somewhere in a cave near the top of this mountain."

"So we come hotfoot deep into the Wild Wood to stir up something which has lain undisturbed for aeon and on," Cormac said. "Better, I think, to leave it lie. Sufficient unto the day are the evils thereof, Light."

Shiara smiled thinly. "This evil's day has come it seems. Someone knew of the map and we have strong reason to believe that that someone now knows at least generally what the map had to say. We think someone was looking through the eyes of our thief when he died."

Cormac grunted. "So it is a race then." He looked up at the summit with its wreath of grey-black clouds.

"A race," Shiara agreed. "Although we may have lost already."

"You sense something?"

"No, but I can use my head as well as my magic. Whoever sent that thief had more time to prepare than we did. If the League knew generally what was on that parchment they could easily have been ready to move."

"So that is why we were sent upon the Wizard's Way. I mislike this, Light. If the League are ahead of us it means a meeting battle. Those are always chancy and I have the feeling we would be outnumbered."

"I doubt any of the factions of the League Council would be left out of such an enterprise, so I cannot argue with you. But what would you? There were no others in the Capital fit for such a mission and we dared not delay." She looked up the trail. "We can only hope we are in time."

As they worked their way up the steep slopes the forest changed around them. The great oaks and beeches gave way to pine and firs and thick green rhododendrons. Here and there outcrops of dark rock poked through the thinning soil, more and more of it as they climbed.

The air changed about them as well, growing cooler and dank with the glacier's breath. There was a dampness in the air that hinted fog and even in full daylight the mists moved the horizons closer. The mountain loomed over them and they had to crane their necks further and further back to see the snow-clad summit.

They were almost to the treeline when Cormac pulled even with Shiara and spoke quietly in her ear. "We're being followed I think."

Not by look or action did Shiara show she had heard. "How many?"

Cormac shook his head. "Not many. Not creatures born to the woods either."

"The League? The ones who set the thief?"

"Possibly."

Shiara stopped and closed her eyes. With intangible eyes and ears she searched for signs of magic about them. She did not dare risk active magic so close to something so powerful.

"Ahhh," she breathed at last. "The League indeed. But one man only. Luck may be with us, my Sun. I think this is a private quest, not an expedition sent by the League Council."

"You know this man?"

"He is called Toth-Ra, a minor wizard."

"Is he dangerous?"

"Like an adder. Small and puffed with malice."

"And we seek a dragon yonder." Cormac jerked his head toward the snow-covered heights. "Well, Light, what say you?"

"I say leave him for now. He cannot do us much harm and I will need everything I have for lies above."

Well behind the pair Toth-Ra toiled up the slope. He puffed as he came and stopped to rest frequently both because he was unused to exertion and because he did not want to tread too closely on the heels of the two Northerners ahead of him.

A pretty train this, he thought, like ants following a scent trail.

Even further above, he knew, was the party sent by

the League to obtain the treasures of the mountain. A group of black robes and apprentices, carefully balanced to represent each faction of the League council. After them the two from the Council of the North. And finally, himself, representing naught but his own interests.

Like a jackal following lions. He smiled sourly. Well enough. For when lions fight, jackals win.

Toth-Ra had little doubt these lions would fight. Even without the Northerners, the very richness of what lay above guaranteed that.

And if perchance he was wrong? If the fragile coalition that governed the League could hold together under the pressure of the indescribable wealth and power from this hoard? Well, there would still be crumbs for a clever jackal to gather.

With his face set in an unaccustomed smile, Toth-Ra continued his climb.

Shiara and Cormac were almost to the tree line when they heard a noise. The trail paralleled a cliff here and a thin moan came from a clump of bushes off the trail off the cliff side.

Cormac drew his sword, but Shiara moved instinctively to the sound of a creature in pain. She thrust through the narrow band of bushes that lay between them and the cliff face.

"Cormac, come here."

As Cormac breasted through the brush he saw a twisted shape like a small man lying on the rocks. Obviously it had fallen from the cliff above them.

"It's a wood goblin," Cormac siad, looking over it. "Leave the poor creature."

Shiara shook her head. "He has a soul and so deserves succor."

"Have we time to do this?"

She looked up at him. "Have we time not to?"

Gently she moved the twisted broken body off the

blood-smeared rocks and placed it carefully on a patch of grass. Quickly the wizardess spread out a collection of healing implements and set to work.

Shiara labored the chance-found creature as if it were one of her own. She chanted and muttered, made passes with her silver wand and sprinkled the body with herbs and powders.

As Cormac watched the wounds scabbed over and began to close. The twisted limbs straightened and the bones within them knit. The little creature's breathing slowed and became more regular. At last it relaxed and began to snore sonorously.

"Now what?" Cormac asked as Shiara turned away fro the sleeping goblin.

"He needs rest and a chance to rebuild his strength. In another day or two he will be fine, but now . . ."

"We do not have a day or two to give over to nursing him. Have you forgotten what brought us here?"

"No, I have not forgotten. But he," she nodded to the creature, "will be awake soon and we can ask where his tribe is. I will have to rest a bit in any case." She finished packing her kit and sat down heavily beside her patient.

It was less than an hour later that the wood goblin stirred, moaned and opened his eyes. He started and tried to rise at the sight of the two humans, but Shiara placed a hand on his shoulder.

"Rest now," she told him. "We're friends." The goblin looked dubious but settled back. "I am Shiara and this is Cormac. What is your name?"

"Ugo. Me Ugo." The goblin's speech was creaky and slurred but he was understandable.

"Does your tribe live nearby?" Shiara asked.

"Tribe all dead," the little goblin said sadly. "Ugo all alone."

Cormac grunted in sympathy. Unlike their large cousins the hobgoblins, wood goblins lived in closely knit groups. A wood goblin whose tribe had perished had little to live for and scant chance of surviving.

"I am sorry," Shiara said. "Now rest here for a while and you will feel better." She rose and signaled Cormac that she was ready to move on.

"Wait, Lady," cried Ugo. The little creature scrambled painfully up and knelt in front of her. "Take me with you. I serve you, Lady," the goblin pleaded. "Let me stay and serve you."

Cormac looked at Shiara. The last thing they needed was a servant of any sort, much less an ailing wood goblin. But refusing would surely doom him. Without a substitute for his tribe the little creature had no will to live.

Shiara reached down and put a hand on the goblin's head. "Very well, Ugo. We accept your service." His ugly face glowed and he looked up adoringly at Shiara.

"Here is your first task, Ugo, and it is an important one. We go to the top of this mountain on a mission from the Council of the North. If we are not back in three sunsets," she held up three fingers for emphasis, "you must make your way to the Fringe and contact the Council. Tell them we have failed and others must be sent to complete the business. Do you understand?"

"Yes, lady. Wait three sunsets. If you not back, go tell Council."

"Then wait for us here, Ugo. Do not follow. Rest and stay out of sight. we should be back in three days and if not, the message must reach the Council."

"Yes, Lady. Ugo wait."

"Do you really think the wight can get through the Wild Wood if something happens to us?" Cormac asked once they were out of earshot.

Shiara shrugged. "Probably not. But it gives him a reason to live and a sense of his own worth. We will be done in less than three days."

"Much less, I hope," said Cormac, scowling at the mountain jutting above them.

Evening found them above the tree line, halfway across a jumbled field of boulders. There was no snow but the air was cold and the wind keen and sharp. They used the faggots they had gathered on their climb through the forest to build a fire in a place where two great boulders leaned together and provided shelter from the winds.

"Our follower?"

"Camped down in the trees. He apparently plans to gain the summit in a single push tomorrow."

"By which time, luck willing, we will have completed our business and be away."

"Luck willing," Shiara agreed.

Their evening meal was barley porridge flavored with dried meat. It was quickly eaten, but neither made a move to bed down. Instead they sat, staring into the fire and enjoying the warmth reflecting off the boulders.

"Light, would you have chosen this life," Cormac asked her. "Could you have chosen freely, I mean?"

Shiara stared into the flames. "I do not know," she said at last. "Being a wizardess is not a free choice. You are born gifted and you try to build your life around it." She lifted her head and looked at him. "And you? Did you choose freely?"

He laughed easily. "Oh, aye. Even as a child I had a taste for trouble. Mine was a free choice." He sobered. "As freely as any man can choose, at least. I had no hand for farming and I did not want to starve."

"Do you regret it?"

Cormac shook his head. "We've had a good run, lass. We've had some fine times and our fame will live after us. But there are times I miss the things I have not had."

"A home?" She asked with a little smile. "And children?"

"The rest, aye. And children, perhaps. I was an only child you know. My line dies with me."

Shiara laid her fingertips on his shoulder. "That could still be," she said softly.

"Perhaps. But I'm an old horse to break. I suppose it's a matter of making choices and then regretting that in making them we give up other things." He picked up a stick and poked the fire with it idly. "I chose the sword road because it promised honor and fame. I have had all that, so I cannot complain of a bargain unfulfilled."

"Did duty have no role in your choosing?"

Cormac grinned. "Oh, a mite. But I remember the day you came to the parade ground seeking a guardsman to cover your back while you burgled some trinkety bit of magic. I saw you and decided none other would be your quest companion." He shook his head. "There were one or two others who were minded to volunteer, but I convinced them otherwise."

"So you presented yourself to me the next day with knuckles bloody." Shiara smiled at the memory. "But was it only my beauty?"

"Well, I always have been a frippery fellow, Light. With never your fine, serious purpose."

"Mock me if you will, but we do important work." She sighed. "I do not know what I would have chosen had I been free to choose. But I had a talent for this and a head for the proper sort of spells. The job needed doing, desperately, so here I am."

"And you regret it?"

Shiara shook her head and the ends of her silvery hair danced in the firelight. "No. My bargain has been fulfilled as well." She smiled at him. "I have had all that and love as well."

Cormac reached over and squeezed her hand. "We've had more luck than any two mortals deserve, Light."

Shiara stared into the fire. "It cannot last, you know."

Cormac's brows arched. "A premonition?"

"A thought, rather. It is risky work we do and soon or late it will catch up with us."

A ghost of a cloud crossed Cormac's brow. "Mayhap," he said easily. "Or mayhap we will both die peacefully in bed." He leered at her. "The same bed, I hope." Shiara reached out and drew him to her.

They made love, desperately and with a bittersweet passion, as if their coupling could erase the whole World and any thought of the morrow.

They found the cave less than three hours after they broke camp the next morning. Above the boulder field ran a steep canyon, cleaving its way toward the mountain's top. There was a rushing glacial stream, chill and sharp, down the canyon, making the dark rocks slippery and hard to climb.

They came around a twist in the canyon and saw the cave mouth halfway up the cliff. There was a boulder-strewn ledge leading up from the canyon floor, making a natural pathway. The cave entrance itself was dark, jagged and about as inviting as the mouth of Hell.

"Wait," hissed Shiara and put her hand on Cormac's bicep. She pointed a little downslope from the mouth of the cave.

There was a flash of white against the dark rock, like the branches of a dead and barkless tree. Cormac squinted and caught his breath. They were bones, not branches and from their shape and size they could only be the bones of one thing.

"A dragon," Cormac said quietly. "A dragon died here, and not a small one, either."

"Dragons prefer caves as lairs," Shiara said. "It would appear that this one chose the wrong resting place."

"It did not die naturally." Cormac pointed with his blade. "Look at the way the ribs are smashed. But what could do that to a grown dragon?"

"The sort of creature which would be set to guard a great treasure," Shiara said gravely.

"And you think it is still there, Light?"

"A thing which could slay a dragon would not be expected to have a short life."

Cormac scanned the ledge and the cave mouth again. "There are no other bones. Surely other things would have tried to lair here from time to time."

"Perhaps they did not arouse the guardian. Dragons are more intelligent than most animals. And greedier than most men. Or perhaps whatever is within is careful to dispose of its refuse so as not to warn others."

"Hmm. A pretty problem then." Cormac backed warily out of sight of the cave mouth and settled on a rock. "Do you sense magic?"

Shiara wrinkled her nose. "Like smoke in a hut in wintertime. It is everywhere and strong. There is a blocking spell to confine the emanations, but this near I can feel it pressing. Whatever is within that mountain is powerful indeed." She shivered. "And malign!"

"But you cannot tell me what guards that door?"

"If I had to guess I would say a demon. But it would only be a guess."

"So what now?"

"Now," Shiara said, bending to her kit, "we need a stalking horse. Something to enter the cave in our stead and see what lies within." She looked up at him. "Plug your ears."

Cormac clapped hands to his ears while Shiara drew from her bag a gnarled brown root no longer than the length of her index finger. Looking more closely Cormac could see that the root was bifurcated and vaguely man-shaped.

Shiara blew upon the root and spoke softly to it. Instantly the valley was filled with a hideous inhuman screaming. The root writhed and screamed in Shiara's grasp until she completed the spell. Then she stood up and threw the root to the ground.

Cormac blinked. Standing before him was himself, an exact duplicate down to the scars on his arms and the creases in his worn leather swordbelt.

"How do you like our stalking horse?"

"A mandrake image." Cormac walked around the figure and nodded approvingly. "Lady, you outdo yourself."

"Let us hope the guard at that gate finds it satisfactory," Shiara said. She leaned close and whispered in the ear of the homunculus. Wordlessly the thing turned and strode up the path toward the cave.

"It even has my walk," Cormac said as the thing climbed to the cave mouth.

"It is your true double."

The homunculus went fearlessly to the cave mouth and stepped in without breaking stride. Shiara and Cormac held their breaths for three long heartbeats. Then there was a terrible bellowing roar from the cave and the sounds of swift combat. They saw movement in the darkness and then a tiny brown thing came flying out of the cave to bounce off the opposite wall of the valley.

"A demon in truth!" Cormac breathed. "How do you slay such a one?"

"With a more powerful demon," Shiara said, still transfixed by what they had seen.

"You don't have one of those in that bag of yours do you Light?"

"Not likely. But if it cannot be slain, then perhaps it can be immobilized." She set down her bag and rummaged around in it. "First we must know more about it."

"You're not going to send another homunuculus of me into that, are you? It does me no good to see myself slain."

"That was the only mandrake root I had. But let us see what happens with something different."

With her silver wand she sketched a quick design in the dirt and spoke a single phrase. Now another warrior stood before them, a tall lean man with dark hair, a lantern jaw and icy blue eyes. He was dressed in a mail hauberk and carried a two-handed sword over his shoulder.

"Donal to the flesh!" Cormac laughed. "He looks as if he just stepped off the drill ground at the Capital."

"No flesh, just an illusion. Now let us see what the demon makes of this one." She spoke to the thing and without a word it turned and started up the ledge.

At the mouth of the cave the false Donal halted and bellowed out a challenge that made the valley ring. There was no response. It approached the entrance and thrust over the threshold with its great sword. Again nothing. Finally it strode bodly into the cavern calling insults to whatever was within.

Once more Cormac and Shiara held their breaths. But this time there was no sound of battle from the cave.

After a minute the illusion returned to the cave mouth and waved to them.

"It didn't go for it."

"But that does not make sense," Shiara protested. "The illusion was indistinguishable from the homunculus."

"Not to the demon," Cormac observed.

"Yes, but I don't see why the demon would attack a homunculus and a dragon but not an illusion. It doesn't . . ." she stopped short. "Fortuna, a true name! The homunculus had a true name but the illusion did not." She turned to Cormac with her sapphire eyes wide. "That thing can sense a being's true name!"

"Dragons don't have true names," Cormac protested.

"Adult dragons do. Oh, not juveniles such as our cavalry ride, but when a dragon becomes a full adult it acquires a true name. The homunculus had a true name just as any demon does. That is how you control them. But the illusion did not."

Cormac eyed the cave mouth. "A very pretty problem then."

"Worse than that," Shiara said. "The demon did not know the true name of homunculus and I doubt the dragon stopped for conversation before entering the cave. Yet the demon killed them both."

"Meaning what?"

"Meaning it distinguishes beings with true names from beings without them. But that it does not have to know a thing's true name to find it and kill it. It is enough that a thing has a true name."

Cormac gave a low whistle. "No wonder it is tied so tight to that cave. With that power it could seek out and destroy anyone in the World. Light, do you suppose the demon itself is the treasure?"

"I doubt it. I think the demon merely guards the treasure."

"It must be treasure indeed to have such a guardian."

"Aye," Shiara said, studying the cave mouth. "Well, we will learn little more sitting here. I think it is time to take a closer look."

"Tread softly, Light."

She turned to smile at him. "I will, my Sun."

The pair approached the cave mouth cautiously. Cormac had his broadsword out and Shiara held her silver wand before her like a torch.

As they came closer Shiara stopped and pointed to a line carved in the living rock across the front of the cave.

"The ward line. The demon cannot cross it."

"Are you certain?"

"Certain enough. Give me a torch."

Cormac reached into his pack and pulled out one of the pine torches Shiara had prepared. The wizardess tapped the end with her wand and it burst into flame.

Shiara drew back and threw the torch across the line and they both ducked back out of sight of the cave mouth.

There was no sound or movement from the cave. When they peeked around the corner they could see the torch lying on the rough rock floor of the cavern, burning brightly.

The space revealed by the torchlight was perhaps three times Cormac's height and somewhat less than that wide, but it ran back into the mountain well beyond the circle of illumination. There was no sign of life or movement.

"The demon must only materialize when someone enters the cave," Shiara whispered.

"Well what now?" Cormac whispered back. "Are you satisfied with your view of the demon's empty home?"

"Wait," said Shiara, pointing inside the cavern. "What's that?"

Cormac followed her finger. There was something lodged in a crevice high on one wall of the cave. "A box, I think," he said.

Shiara eyed the thing speculatively. "I wonder . . . Cormac, have you a rope in your pack?"

"You know I do, Light. And a grapnel too."

Quickly Cormac retrieved the rope and hook from where they had dropped their packs.

"You want that box then?"

Shiara stood by him, her wand in hand. "I do. But be ready to run if we get more than we bargain for."

Cormac swung the grapnel and cast it expertly into the cave. There was a hollow "clang" as the hook connected with the box. Cormac tugged and it clattered out of the crevice and onto the cave floor.

In the torchlight Cormac saw that his prize was a bronze coffer, decorated in high relief and apparently bearing an inscription on the top. Another quick throw and Cormac dragged the box out of the cave and across the warding line.

"Don't touch it," Shiara warned. As Cormac recoiled his rope she bent to examine the coffer.

Shiara opened the box with a pass of her wand and a whispered incantation. Nestled inside was a smoky gray globe about six inches in diameter.

"The heart of the demon!" Shiara exclaimed triumphantly. "Now we can truly control this creature."

She removed the ball from the coffer and held it in her hand. Another muttered spell and a dense cloud of smoke began to form within the cavern. Through the smoke loomed a great black shape.

The huge horned head swivelled toward them, but before the creature could do more, Shiara raised her wand and spoke another spell. The demon froze as it was, the only sign of life the fire burning in its eyes.

Shiara sighed and sagged. "That should hold it," she said. Carefully, she replaced the sphere in the box and carried it back into the cave. The demon did not even twitch when she crossed the threshold.

The wizardess was still considering the coffer when Cormac came up to her.

"Do we take that with us?"

"I wish we dared. It is a dangerous thing to leave behind, but it would be a greater danger to carry it with us. There might be something above us which can undo what I have done and I do not wish to find a rampaging demon here when we return."

"Conceal it?"

"That is best." She cast about the cavern looking for a hiding place.

"Light, come look at this."

Cormac was standing over a head-high pile of bones.

"So our demon did clean the place deliberately."

"Not that. Look." Cormac shifted his torch and used his sword as a pointer. At one side of the bone pile lay the crushed and mutilated corpse of a man in a brown robe.

"An acolyte of the League! Then they are here before us."

"Yes, but why only one body? Surely they would not send a brown robe alone on such a mission?"

"Surely not. But they might use an acolyte as we used our mandrake homunculus."

Cormac nodded grimly. "Aye, that's just the kind of thing they would do. But then where are the rest? Did they scatter away at the sight of the demon?"

"Most likely they are somewhere up ahead of us. Once they knew the demon was here, they found a way to counteract it. I do not think they tampered with the box, so perhaps they had the password." She looked up the tunnel. "I think we face an interesting meeting."

"Best be on with it then," Cormac said, shifting his grip on his sword.

The passage sloped up, climbing steadily toward the summit. Cormac went first, naked sword in one hand and smoking torch in the other. Shiara followed with another torch.

"You're unusually pensive," Cormac told her when they had gone a small ways into the cavern. "What bothers you, Light?"

"That demon."

"Well, it is trouble past and overcome. I am more concerned about what we might find above us."

"Yes, but it is how we overcame it. Why was the box where we could reach it? A few feet further back in the cave and the demon would have been safe from our efforts."

Cormac shrugged. "So our sorcerer made an error. Even the best magician can err through overconfidence."

"I know," Shiara said. "That is what troubles me."

Their way climbed steeply upward but the path was smoothed and widened. Either this had never been a natural cavern or it had been extensively reworked. The smooth black rock seemed to soak up the light of their torches and the darknes pressed in on them from all sides. Shiara hurried slightly to stay within touching distance of Cormac.

There was a low, distant rumble and the earth beneath them moved slightly.

"Earth magic," Shiara said. "Very potent and barely held in check here." She looked around. "Left to its own, I think this mountain would have erupted hundreds of years ago."

"A fitting lair for a sorcerer."

"More than that, prehaps."

"Light, will you stop being so gloomy? You're beginning to make me nervous."

She smiled. "You're right, my Sun. This place is affecting me, I am afraid."

They climbed and climbed until it seemed they would emerge at the very top of the mountain. Finally their way leveled out and there before them was a door.

The portal was of the deepest black granite, polished so smooth the burning brand in Cormac's hand threw back distorted reflections of the two adventurers. A gilt tracery ran along the lintel and down the doorposts. Runes, Shiara saw as she moved closer. Runes of purest gold beaten into the oily black surface of the granite.

Shiara formed the runes in her mind, not daring to move her lips. "It is a treasure indeed," she said at last. "A trove of magic of the sort seldom witnessed. This is the tomb of Amon-Set."

Cormac wrinkled his nose. "The name is somewhat familiar. A boggart to frighten children, I think."

"More than that," she told her beloved. "Before he was a night-fright, Amon-Set was mortal. A sorcerer. So powerful his name has lived after him and so evil he is a figure of nightmare."

"Aye," Cormac breathed. "The great dark one from the beginning of the World. And he lies here?"

"I would not take oath he is dead."

"I mislike rifling the tombs of sorcerers," Cormac said apprehensively.

"I like it even less than that. Such places are mazes of traps and snares for the greedy or the careless." She sighed and straightened. "Fortunately we do not have to steal. Only keep what is here from being loosed upon the World."

"But before that we must enter."

"So we must, love." Shiara set down her pouch and knelt beside it. "Leave that to me."

The lock was a cunning blend of magic and mechanics. Slowly and deliberately, Shiara worked upon it, running her fingers over the surface to sense the mechanism within. Sometimes she operated upon it with cleverly constructed picks. Sometimes she used incantations. Finally she pushed against it gently and the door sung open. Motioning Cormac to remain outside, she entered cautiously.

The room was vast, so big the walls were lost in the gloom. The marble floor, tesselated in patterns of black and darkest green, stretched away in front of them. Shiara had the feeling that by stepping through the door she had become a piece on a gigantic game board.

The way was lit by witch-fires of pale yellow enclosed in great massively-carved lanterns, the light pouring out through the thin panels of alabaster or marble that formed their panes. The glow held an odd greenish tinge that gave an unhealthy pallor to everything it touched.

Here and there a censer smoked, emitting heavy fumes that curled and ran along the floor like snakes. The incense was pungent with hints of cinnamon and sandalwood, heady with the fumes of poppies and the sharp chemical tang of ether. It was neither pleasant nor offensive, just strange. It did not quite hide the musty odor of time long passed in a place undisturbed and the faint sweetish hint of corruption that hung in the air.

Worse than the incense to Shiara was the magic that

closed around her as soon as she stepped over the
threshold. It was as close and stifling as a heavy quilt
on a hot summer's day. It pressed against her flesh and
blocked her nostrils until she wanted to gasp for breath.
It twisted and moved around her in odd directions and
peculiar angles. She felt that if she stared into the air
long enough the magic would become visible. She did
not want to contemplate what might follow.

Shiara took one more step forward and did gasp.
There on the floor of the chamber, like a flock of crows
dropped in mid-flight, lay half a score of black-robed
bodies, already decomposing in the strange atmosphere
of the room. Obviously the League's sorcerers had found
a trap that guarded the treasure.

In spite of the dead, Shiara's gaze was drawn to the
objects scattered around the room. Each sat on its own
pedestal like exhibits in a museum—or pieces on a game
board—and each of the ones Shiara could see was
different. There was no obvious pattern or order to their
placement, but Shiara did not doubt there was some
subtle design there.

"What lies within?" Cormac asked from just over the
threshold.

"Danger and magic," Shiara told him. "Stay where you
are for a moment."

On the nearest pier of blue-white marble sat a jeweled
crown. The golden band was made to curl snake-like
around the wearer's brow. Gems covered its surface so
thickly the gold would be scarce visible when it was worn.
Blue sapphires, blood-red rubies, sea-green emeralds, and
lustrous pink pearls ran in twisted bands across the gold.
Over each temple sat a smoky yellow topaz, golden as the
eye of a dragon. In the center of the forehead was a blue-
white gem the likes of which Shiara had never seen. Over
all of it flashes of substanceless flame licked and leaped,
clear as the fire of burning alcohol. Truly this was a thing
designed to adorn the brow of a mighty sorcerer.

Awed, Shiara reached out to touch the crown. Reached and then drew back. Some sense warned her tht to touch it would be fatal.

"Cormac, come in," she called, not taking her eye off the glittering prize on the podium. "Move carefully and on your life, touch nothing!"

"Fortuna!" Cormac exclaimed when he saw the remains of the League's expedition. "What happened to them?"

"One of them touched something, I think. Help me search the room, but move carefully!"

As Shiara and Cormac passed from pedestal to pedestal the extent of the trove became apparent. Each pedestal held an item of magician's regalia. Here a great gold thumb ring with a strangely carved sardonyx cameo stood on a drape of leaf-green velvet. There a chest of scrolls stood open, each scroll bearing the name of the spell it recorded. Against one wall an elaborately embroidered robe, set with gems and so stiff with bullion it stood upright and ready to receive its wearer. Above another pedestal floated a pair of silken slippers decorated with pink-blushed pearls. There were flashing swords and black lacquered armor, chests of gold and heaps of jewels, amulets and talismans and silver-bound spellbooks galore. Every item reeked of powerful, subtle magic and ancient, ancient evil.

"Fortuna!" Cormac called from the shadows at the far end of the huge wall. "Light, come look at this."

Shiara followed the sound of Cormac's voice and gasped at what she saw. This was no mere treasure house or cenotaph. It was indeed the tomb of a mighty wizard!

The body lay beneath a clear crystal bell on a dais of milk-white crystal. Beneath the white silk shroud broidered round with blood red runes, the wizard's husk was as incorrupt and composed as if he were only sleeping. Amon-Set had been a man of no more than average height, Shiara saw, with pale skin given only a

semblance of color by the stark whiteness of the sheet.
The tracery of blue veins patterned his flesh in a manner
disturbingly like the scales of a venomous reptile. The
hands crossed on his chest were as long and slender as
the hands of an artist. His hair was dark and shiny as
polished jet and his brows were thin and dark, elegant
against his skin. His lashes were long and dark as well.
Shiara did not care to contemplate what the eyes beneath
them must have been like.

"Back away from it!" she called to Cormac. "Do not
get closer."

As Cormac edged off, Shiara approached. With shaking
hands she passed her wand over the bier. Then she
sighed and her shoulders slumped. Magic aplenty she
found there, but not the smallest spark of life. Amon-
Set was truly dead.

"The scroll did not lie," Cormac said awestruck. "There
is treasure indeed here."

"The life's work of one of the most powerful wizards
that ever lived," Shiara agreed grimly. "My Sun, can you
imagine the havoc all this could wreak if it were loosed
upon the World?"

"Well," said Cormac briskly, "that is what we are here
to prevent, is it not?"

Shiara nodded and passed her wand over the closest
pedestal. Then she frowned and drew back. She moved
to the next pedestal and repeated the pass. The expression on her face showed that what she found was no
more to her liking.

"Magic?" asked Cormac.

"Aye. What is on these stands is protected by the spells
around them and cannot be touched. I will have to
unravel this maze before we dare move any of it."

Again and again, Shiara tested the pedestals, until at
last she had tried each of them.

"I see how it is now," she said at last. "The spells
protecting these things are all interlocked like jackstraws.

If you move them at random than the whole mass comes down upon you."

"Jackstraws have a key," Cormac pointed out.

"And so does this riddle. One of these objects is the key. It can be moved first and then the next and then the next."

"How long will it take you to sort out the pile then?"

"Hours. Perhaps days. This is no simple puzzle and I dare not make a mistake." Her eyes went to the bodies on the floor.

"Should you summon more of the Mighty to help?"

Shiara considered and then shook her head. "There is nothing others could do here that I could not. Involving others only means risking them as well."

Cormac shrugged acceptance and Shiara set to work on unravelling the puzzle. Three times she passed round the great gloomy chamber, testing each object.

"It is no good," she said at last. "All of the spells are interlinked and apparently none of them are the key."

"I thought you said there had to be a key."

"I thought so, but I can find no sign of one."

"Well, Light. Where does that leave us?"

Shiara frowned and tapped the wand against her jaw. "I do not know. It seems beyond reason that all this exists merely as a death trap for the unwary. There must be a key. Else why not destroy everything in the beginning and be done with it?"

"Malice?" Cormac suggested.

"A poor motive for all this work. Those of Amon-Set's skill seldom did things for such simple reasons."

"Well then?"

"There is one alternative. Rather than remove all these objects we could destroy them here."

"Wouldn't that scar the land?"

"Most probably," Shiara agreed. "It also means the loss of all the knowledge here. I do not want to do that unless I have to. But Cormac, we cannot allow what is here

to fall to the wrong person. Even a hedge wizard could
rise to bestride the World with what is in this place."

Cormac sighed. "Do as you think best, Light."

She nodded. "I think with the right spell I can destroy
all of this at once."

"How do you propose to do that?"

"Earth magic. The forces are finely balanced here.
They can be upset with but little effort—well, little
enough in terms of the results. I believe I can fashion
a spell to turn the magic against itself and so unbalance
the flow."

"Earth magics are hardly a specialty of the Mighty,"
Cormac pointed out.

"Earth magics are uncontrollable. But all we want is
destruction. It should be an easy matter to take the top
of this mountain off."

"And take us up with it?"

"No. I will set the spell in motion through a counting
demon. We will have time to get away."

Again Shiara knelt with her bag and set to work. She
had nearly finished the spell when Cormac came over
to her. He waited at a respectful distance until she
paused.

"You know, Light, I have been thinking."

"And?"

"Well, curse my suspicious nature, but it occurs to me
there may be more here than we see. We know that none
of the visible things is the key to this pile of magical
jackstraws, but did it occur to you that there might be
something here that is not visible?"

"Cormac, you are brilliant! Of course the final key
would be hidden! Why did I not think of that?"

"Because you're an honest thief, lass," Cormac grinned.
"Now myself, I'm a bit of a rogue."

She leaned over and kissed him. "You are that."

He looked around the room. "Now if I were a master
sorcerer with a secret to hide, where would I hide it?"

"Someplace close, I think," Shiara said, looking around the great room. "Either in this room or in a room off it." She started toward one wall and then stopped.

"Cormac, I want you to examine the room carefully for anything strange or unusual."

"In this place? Fortuna! But what will you be doing?"

"I am going to finish my spell." She bit her lower lip. "Even once we find the key we may not want to use it. And I wish to finish this business and be away quickly."

"As you will, Light." He moved off.

"And Cormac, touch nothing!"

Again the grin. "Since it's you who ask, Light."

While Cormac searched, Shiara concentrated on completing her spell. She forced herself to think only of the technical aspects, blocking out the unease that almost stifled her. Only when the spell was complete and primed and her counting demon duly instructed did she look up.

"Have you found anything?" she called to Cormac across the gloomy expanse of the hall.

"Nothing I care to think overmuch on," he called, crossing the black-and-green floor. "The place is strangely proportioned, these pedestals seem strewn about at random and the pattern on this miserable floor makes my eyes ache." He looked down at the patterned marble at his feet.

"The floor," Shiara said reflectively. "Yes." She looked up. "There may be a message here." She stepped back to the entrance and looked out over the elaborate pattern formed by the squares of marble that floored the hall.

From the door the tiles made the floor seem to sweep away in a roller-coaster perspective, tilting and writhing off into the distance. There seemed to be no horizon line and no point of perspective save madness in the bizarre geometry of the tiles. And yet. . . .

"Cormac, walk out that way," she said pointing toward one corner of the hall. The swordsman followed her

pointing finger. "A little further. Now stop." Inexorably
the pattern seemed to pull him to the right. It was
somehow wrong to move to the left at that point.

"Now go left," she commanded. Cormac dubiously
obeyed. "Further left. No, don't look down at the floor!
Don't close your eyes. Just keep to your left." With his
gaze locked at the shoulder level Cormac moved more
to his left and off into the gloom.

"Now what do you see?"

"Nothing much," Cormac called back. "I just bumped
into a wall. Wait a moment, I seem to have company."

Shiara gasped.

"Nay, lass, he's not dangerous now. But I think you
will enjoy this."

"Stay where you are." Shiara moved away from the
door and toward Cormac who was invisible in the gloom.
"Talk to me. Anything, just so I can follow the sound
of your voice."

"Well, it's dark over here, darker than any other part
of the room. And our friend isn't much of a conver-
sationalist."

"Fine," said Shiara coming up to him. "Don't look at
that floor. It's both a trap and a hiding place. It is designed
to draw you away from this spot and perhaps ensnare you
if you are so foolish as to watch the floor as you walk."

She nodded to Cormac's silent companion. "I think
that's what happened to him."

Standing almost next to Cormac with his eyes fixed
on the floor was a black-robed wizard. He was obviously
alive but equally obviously caught fast in the grip of a
spell. He could neither move nor talk but his eyes burned
with venomous hatred as he looked at the floor.

"Why it's Jul-Akkan isn't it?" Shiara said pleasantly. "I
thought you might be along on this and of course you're
too old a fox to be caught by the death spells around
the hoard. What did you do, wait outside while the others
rushed to the pedestals?"

She turned to Cormac. "Note him well, Cormac. Jul-Akkan is high in the Council of the League. Indeed he bid fair to become a master of all the League, were he able to rid himself of one or two of his more troublesome colleagues. Now here he is, caught like a fly in a honey bowl."

Cormac shifted and raised his sword for the killing stroke.

"No," Shiara commanded. "I don't know what that would do to the spell and I doubt you could kill him so easily. No, best leave him while we attend to our main business." She stooped to examine the wall behind Cormac.

"Now let us see what is here."

A quick search of the wall revealed a thin narrow crack in the polished black stone of the wall. Carefully she ran her hand along it, feeling rather than seeing the unevenness that marked a panel in the otherwise solid stone.

She knelt down and pressed her hand against the panel. "It is locked and enchanted, but not guarded, I think."

"Don't bet your life on that, lass," Cormac warned. "This fellow was tricky enough for ten wizards."

"I will venture nothing on the chance. I merely make the observation."

Shiara looked up at him from where she knelt. "You do not have to be here for this."

Cormac shook his head. "You may need me." Then he laid his hand on hers. "Besides, a World without Light is not a World fit to live in."

"Thank you Cormac," she squeezed his hand. "Now stand out of my light while I unravel this puzzle."

Again working partly by magic and partly with her picks and other tools, Shiara carefully pried the secrets from the lock. Cormac stood by nervously, fingering his sword hilt, his head turning this way and that as he searched for tangible manifestation of the danger he sensed here. Finally there was a click and the panel swung smoothly back.

Behind the panel lay another smaller room lit with the same balefire glow as the great hall. It took only a single lantern to light it. The stink of incense and the reek of magic was fully as strong here as it was beyond. But there were fewer pedestals bearing treasures.

"A puzzle within a puzzle," Cormac said as he surveyed their latest find.

Shiara pointed to a pier off to one side of the chamber. "There, I think."

Cautiously she approached and then sucked in her breath at what she saw.

Laying atop the pedestal was a magician's staff. But it was like no magician's staff Shiara had ever seen. It was perhaps four feet long and as thick as her wrist, but it was not wood or even metal. Instead it was made of a crystalline substance that seemed to show flickers of an amethyst light deep within itself. Tiny crabbed characters ran inscribed in bands around its surface, save for a space about a hand's breadth wide near the top. There was no knob or finial on either end. It was more a sceptre than a staff, she realized. A symbol of rule as well as a tool of magical power.

The wizardess passed her wand over the pedestal and smiled at the result.

"This is the key. If I neutralize the spell and move this, we can remove all else in this place."

"Be careful, Light."

"I will my Sun."

Slowly and carefully Shiara began to unravel the spell binding the staff to the pedestal. She made a final sweeping gesture and the spell flickered and died.

In spite of removing the spell and in spite of her urgent desire to finish this business, Shiara was reluctant to touch the evilly-glinting object before her. She had handled such staffs of other wizards before, but there was something about this one that awed and dismayed her.

Finally she placed her hand upon it and felt the waves of magic flow through her. It seemed as if a dark and vastly deep space opened up around her, inhabited by huge shadow things that pressed close, whispering offers of power, the fulfillment of all dreams and the slaking of all lusts. She had but to wield the staff and . . .

Quivering, Shiara fought the temptation. She lifted the staff and carried it across the chamber at arm's length as if it were a poisonous serpent.

The waves of magic beat stronger against her, calling to her more and more clearly. In a fit of panic Shiara tried to drop the staff and found she could not. Now it was the staff which was holding her.

All too late Shiara saw the deadly nature of the trap. The demon at the gate, the spells upon the common items were sufficient to ward off an ordinary thief or hedge magician. To penetrate those and unravel the maze of spells within the cavern and ultimately to possess the key would take someone truly skilled in magic. One of the Mighty, or a black-robe wizard of the League.

The whole cavern and all the magics within it existed simply to sort the untalented or the incompetent from the powerful and to lure the powerful to the sceptre. The sceptre was the last and deadliest trap of them all.

No, Amon-Set was not dead, not truly. Within the smoky purple depths of the scepter he had waited out the ages, waiting for one whose body and skill he could use to live again. The snow-white corpse on the crystal bier was indeed dead. But his soul lived within the sceptre; lived, hungered and awaited its prey.

The wizard who was skilled enough to grasp the sceptre of Amon-Set was a suitable vehicle for his reincarnation. And that was the true purpose of everything here. To find such a one and put them in a position where Amon-Set could possess them and so live again.

Shiara could feel herself ebbing away as the alien presence intruded. She twisted and struggled in the grip of the long-dead sorcerer. She fought back with every bit of skill and knowledge at her command.

It was a hopelessly uneven fight. She felt the chamber's magics convulse and yield under her desperate thrusts, but the core of Amon-Set locked her in an ever tightening embrace.

"Now!" a strange creaking voice cried from the door of the chamber. Shiara realized vaguely that someone else had entered the fray.

Cormac whirled at the voice and saw Jul-Akkan stumble into the room. Shiara could not break Amon-Set's hold on her, but her struggles had loosed the grip of the guard spells.

Cormac's sword flickered at the wizard with the speed of a striking snake, but not fast enough; even weakened Jul-Akkan was faster still. His hand flicked out and Cormac screamed and dropped to the floor.

Without pausing, Jul-Akkan leaped across the room and grasped the sceptre with both hands.

For an instant three beings warred. Then with a final mighty effort Shiara was able to let go of the cursed thing. Jul-Akkan fell back with both hands planted on the sceptre and his eyes widening as Toth-Amon took him.

Shiara staggered and shook her head. Through pain-dimmed eyes she saw Cormac writhing in the final agonies of a death spell and the one who was Jul-Akkan writhing in the throes of rebirth. In seconds Cormac would be dead and Toth-Amon would be loosed upon the world again. Her Sun and her World both teetered on the brink of destruction.

Shiara's eyes locked with Cormac's as he pleaded silently with her to do something to release him from the awful pain.

Without bothering with the timing demon, Shiara

triggered the destruction spell. "Forgive me, love," she whispered as he slumped to the floor.

Magic after magic flared incandescent around the living, the dead and the reborn. The room shook under the force of the spells. The pedestals tottered and toppled. The lanterns crashed to the floor and went out.

Amon-Set struggled to rise, but he did not have full control. The sceptre slipped from his hands and dashed into pieces on the shaking floor. All around them the magic grew in violence as forces contained past their time burst free at last.

And then, in a mighty explosion of magic, the roof fell in. Shiara screamed as she saw Cormac's body crushed under a falling block. Waves of magic flayed her. Her last sight was of the brilliant blue glow. The after-image burned itself into her brain. Reflexively and in shock, she stumbled from the room.

Above her the top of the mountain blew off. A column of angry orange fire shot high into the smoke-stained sky and bombs of flaming lava arced down into the forest, setting fires where they fell.

Toth-Ra examined the great still demon carefully. Obviously the guardian had been neutralized in some manner. So far, so good he thought. He had the word and sign to pass the demon, stolen from the crypt of the League, but he was satisfied not to use them.

Let us see if anything of use remains here. He walked past the thing and inspected the cavern carefully. It did not take him long to find the coffer. When he opened it, he gasped. The heart of the demon lay within.

Toth-Amon smiled. Here was an auspicious beginning. Obviously the Council's agents had beaten him here, but they were unlikely to know all the secrets of this place. There were still treasures to be gleaned while they attempted to unravel the mysteries.

Then the ground began to move under him. Toth-Ra

ran to the mouth of the cave and reached it in time to see the mountain erupt, taking the treasures of Amon-Set with it.

Balked, he danced in fury. "Gone. Gone, ay, all gone," he shrieked.

No, he realized. Not all gone. There was still the guardian of the gate.

Heedless of the shaking earth or the erupting mountain he moved back across the magically marked threshold clutching the box tightly. Once safely outside, he released the demon.

"What is your name?" he asked sharply.

"Bale-Zur," the thing rumbled.

"And what is your virtue?" the wizard asked.

"To slay," the great deep voice boomed out again. "To rend and tear any whose true name has ever been spoken in the World."

Toth-Ra shivered. Here was power indeed! The treasure of Amon-Set might be consumed in fire, but at least one of his servants could be bound to his cause. He eyed the burning mountaintop carefully. Perhaps this one alone would be sufficient to make him the greatest in the League.

"And what is your desire?"

"To slay," the demon repeated. "To slay and slay again."

Toth-Ra placed both hands on the dusky globe. "Then I will bargain with you," the wizard said.

It was hours later when Ugo found Shiara wandering in the canyon above the boulder field.

"You live, Lady," the little wood goblin cried joyfully as he ran to her.

"Who?"

"Ugo, Lady. You set me to watch. Then bad things happen and I come to look." He stopped. "Where is other?"

"Gone," Shiara said dazedly. "Gone." Then she seemed to gather herself and held out her hand.

"Lead me, Ugo. Your senses are keen and between the night and the clouds I cannot see."

"Close to high noon, Lady," the little creature said sadly. "Sorry, Lady."

Shiara said nothing. Ugo approached her and gently took her hand in his.

"Famous victory," the wood-goblin said. "Bards will sing it long."

Shiara the Silver only laughed bitterly and let the goblin lead her down the smoldering mountain.

"And what happened afterwards?" Moira breathed at last.

Shiara the Silver raised her head from her breast and turned her blind, lined face to her questioner. "Afterwards?" She said simply. "There was no afterwards."

"Foolishness," grumbled Ugo, poking up the fire.

# *Eight*
## FORLORN HOPE

The long golden days of Indian Summer dragged by at Heart's Ease. Moira worked in the garden or the kitchen. Wiz chopped wood and mooned over Moira. If the tensions within the household did not ease, at least they did not to grow significantly worse.

There was always work to be done and the time rolled forward with everyone except Wiz fully occupied. But for all of them, except perhaps Ugo, there was a sense of being suspended. Greater plans and long-range decisions were set aside awaiting word from Bal-Simba and the Council on what was to be done with Wiz.

For Wiz everything depended on what the Council found. If he did have some special ability then perhaps he could redeem himself with Moira. At least he would be able to make himself useful and stop feeling like a parasite.

In his more realistic moments, Wiz admitted he couldn't possibly imagine what that ability might be. The image of him standing before a boiling cauldron in a long robe and a pointed cap with stars was simply silly and the thought of himself as a warrior was even worse.

"Lady, may I ask you a question?" Wiz said to Shiara one day when Moira wasn't around. The former wizardess was sitting on a wooden bench on the sunny side of the keep, enjoying the warmth from the sun before her and the sun-warmed stones behind.

"Of course, Sparrow," she said kindly, turning her face to his voice.

"Patrius was a great Wizard wasn't he?"

"One of the greatest the North has ever seen." She smiled reminiscently. "He was not only skilled in magic, he—well—he saw things. Not by magic, but because had the kind of mind that let him see what others' sight had passed over."

"But he didn't make mistakes very often?"

"Making mistakes is dangerous for a wizard, Sparrow. Magicians who are prone to them do not last."

Wiz took a deep breath and rushed on. "Then he couldn't have been wrong about me, could he?"

Shiara paused before answering. "I do not know, Sparrow. Certainly he was engaged in a dangerous, difficult business, performing a Great Summoning unaided. If he were to make a mistake it might be in a situation such as that.

"On the other hand," she went on as if she sensed Wiz's spirits fall, "Patrius could look deeper and see more subtly than anyone I ever knew. It may well be that we cannot fathom his purposes in bringing you here."

"Do you think the Council will figure out what he was up to?"

Again Shiara paused. "I do not know, Sparrow. Patrius apparently confided in no one. The members of the Council are the wisest of the Mighty. I would think they would discover his aim. But I simply do not know." She smiled at him. "When the Council knows something they will send word. Best to wait until then."

In the event it was less than a week later when word came to Heart's Ease.

It was another of the mild cloudless days that seemed to mark the end of summer in the North. Wiz was up

on the battlements, looking out over the Wild Wood—
and down at Moira who was busy in the garden.

"Sparrow," Shiara's voice called softly behind him, "we
have a visitor."

Wiz turned and there, standing next to Shiara was Bal-
Simba himself.

"Lord," Wiz gasped. "I didn't see you arrive."

"Such is the nature of the Wizard's Way," the huge
wizard said with a smile. "How are you, Sparrow?"

"I'm fine, Lord."

"I am happy to see that you made your journey here
safely. Although not without peril, I am told."

"Well, yes, Lord, that is . . ." Wiz trailed off, overawed
by the wizard's size and appearance.

"I will leave you now, Lord," Shiara put in. "Doubtless
you have things to discuss."

"Thank you, Lady," Bal-Simba rumbled.

"What did you find out?" Wiz demanded as soon as
Shiara had closed the door.

"Very little, I am afraid," Bal-Simba said regretfully.
"There is no trace of magic in you. You are not a wizard
and have not the talent to become one. There is a trace
of—something—but not the most cunning demons nor the
most clever of the Mighty can discern ought of what it is."

Wiz took a deep, shuddering breath. "Which means—
what?"

"It means," the wizard said gently, "that to all intents
and purposes you are an ordinary mortal with nothing
magic to make you special."

"Okay, so send me home then."

Bal-Simba shook his head. "I am truly sorry, Sparrow,
but that we cannot do."

"Oh crap! You brought me here, you can send me
home."

"It is not that simple, Sparrow."

"It is that simple! It is exactly that simple. If you can
bring me here you can send me back."

"No it is not!" Bal-Simba said sharply. "Now heed me. I will explain to you a little of the magic that brought you here.

"Did you ever wonder why Patrius chose to Summon you at a place far removed from the Capital? No, why would you? He did it because he hoped to do alone what he and all the Mighty could not accomplish acting together.

"Normally a Great Summoning is done by several of the Mighty together. But such a gathering of magic would be immediately visible to the magicians of the Dark League. They would strive to interfere and we would have to use magic to protect it. Soon there would be so much magical energy tied up in thrust and parry that the circle could not hope to make the Great Summoning.

"Of us all, only Patrius had the knowledge and ability to perform a Great Summoning unaided. He knew he could not completely escape the League's attention, but he apparently hoped that they would not realize what was happening until he had completed the spell." Bal-Simba looked grim. "As it happened he was wrong and the gamble cost Patrius his life.

"Simply put, Sparrow, there is no hope of returning you to your world unless we can perform a Great Summoning unhindered and there is no hope of that with the League growing in power."

Wiz's face twisted. "Damn."

"Even non-magicians should not swear, Sparrow," Bal-Simba said sternly.

"Well, what am I supposed to do? You've just told me I'm nothing and I'll always be nothing. I'm supposed to be happy about it?"

"I did not say you were nothing. I said you have nothing of magic about you. You have a life to live and can make of it what you will."

"Fine," Wiz said bitterly. "I don't suppose you could

use your magic to whip me up a VAX? Or even a crummy IBM PC?"

"I am afraid not, Sparrow. Besides, I do not think those things would work here."

Wiz leaned forward against the parapet and clasped his hands together. "So," he sighed. "What do I do now?"

"Survive," Bal-Simba said. "Live. That is the lot of most."

"That's not very enticing," Wiz growled. "I can't go home and there's nothing for me here."

Bal-Simba followed his gaze down into the garden where Moira was kneeling among the plants.

"Things change, Sparrow. Things change."

"Not much to hope for, is it?"

"Men have lived on the hope of less," Bal-Simba rumbled. "Do you have courage, Sparrow? The courage to hope?"

Wiz turned to face him and smiled bitterly. "I can't have much else, can I?"

They stood looking out over the battlements and to the forest beyond for a moment more.

"You can stay here for as long as you like," Bal-Simba said finally. "The Dark League still seeks you and it is not safe for you to wander abroad in the world."

"Thanks," Wiz mumbled. "I guess I can find some way to make myself useful."

"That will be your choice, Sparrow."

As he moved to go, Bal-Simba placed his left hand on Wiz's shoulder and made an odd gesture in front of his eyes with his right. A thrill ran though Wiz's body and he shivered involuntarily.

"What did you do?" he asked.

"A minor magic, Sparrow," the giant black wizard said. "It is for your own good, I assure you."

He left Wiz staring out over the forest and descended the stairs.

After Bal-Simba left, Wiz looked down at the flagged courtyard spread out below.

*It's a long way*, he thought. *It would take, what?, five, six seconds to fall that far.*

That was one out, anyway. Short and relatively painless. He could just swing a leg over and solve everyone's problems in an eyeblink. Moira could go back to her village, Shiara and Ugo would have peace again and him, well, he wouldn't care any more.

He drew back from the edge. No dammit! I'll be damned if I'll let this beat me like that! Besides, he thought wryly, with my luck I'd probably just cripple myself. Oh, to hell with it! He went back to staring out at the forest.

Moira met Bal-Simba in the great hall.

"Forgive me, Lord. I do not mean to pry into what is not my affair, but what did you find out about Sparrow?"

Bal-Simba shrugged. "As we suspected Lady. He has no magic and none of the Council can imagine what use he might be to us."

Moira closed her eyes and sighed. "I had hoped . . ."

"So had we all, Lady," Bal-Simba rumbled. "But do you care so much for him?"

"Care for him?" Moira blazed. "I can't stand him! Lord, he is not competent to weed a garden! He can barely be trusted within these walls by himself and he needs a keeper if he goes abroad."

"You should not be so hard on him," Bal-Simba said. "He cannot help it that he is as he is. Would you fare better in his world?"

"You are right, Lord," Moira sighed. "But it is so terribly hard when he is making eyes at me constantly. And when I look at him I'm reminded of what he cost us. He cost us so much and he is worth so little."

"Do not presume to judge his worth," Bal-Simba rumbled. "True worth is often hidden, even from the Mighty."

"I know, but . . . Oh, Lord, let me return to the

Fringe and my people," she pleaded. "They need me and Shiara can look after him."

Bal-Simba shook his head. "Your people are looked after, little one. As for letting you go—do you so relish the trip back across the Wild Wood and through the Fringe alone?"

Moira thrust out her chin. "I did it before, and with him in tow."

The black wizard shook his head. "And you made it only by luck and the grace of an elf duke. I do not think Aelric would be so accommodating a second time and you used more than your share of luck getting here."

"You mean I'm trapped here?"

"For a time, little one. When the League's interest has died somewhat more, we can bring both of you back to the Capital by the Wizard's Way. From there you may go as you will. In the meantime, try to be kind to our lost Sparrow."

Moira sighed. "I will try, Lord. But it is not easy."

"Very little in life is," the wizard said.

Wiz stood at the top of Heart's Ease and looked west over the Wild Wood. The sun was going down and already the shadows had stretched across the clearing below. The swallows swooped and wheeled over the keep and Wiz heard the whoosh of their passage more often than he saw one flit by.

"Is it a beautiful sunset, Sparrow?" asked a soft voice behind him. Wiz turned and saw Shiara standing by the door.

Wiz swallowed his misery. "Yes Lady, it is a very pretty sunset."

Shiara moved unerringly to the parapet. "Describe it for me if you would."

"Well, there are a lot of clouds and they're all red and orange. The sun's almost down on the horizon, but it's still too bright to look at directly. The sunlight's only on the very tops of the trees, so they're bright green and everything else is a real dark green."

They stood together in silence for a bit.

"Before—before I used to love to watch the sunset," Shiara said.

"I never had much time for sunsets," Wiz told her. "I was always too busy."

"Too busy for the sun?" Shiara's face clouded slightly. "Too busy for the sun, Sparrow?"

Wiz sighed. "Yeh. Too busy for the sun and a lot of other things. There was always so much to do, so much to learn." He grinned wryly. "You may not believe this, but computer programming really is a discipline. You have to work and study and slave over it to be any good. I did and I was good. One of the best."

"These things sound like hard taskmasters."

"Sure, sometimes. But it was rewarding too. There were always new things to discover and new ways to apply what you knew. Someone was always coming up with a new hack or a user would find some kind of obscure bug—ah, problem."

"And you devoted your life to this. To the exclusion of everything else?"

"Yeah, I guess I did. Oh, I had friends. I was even engaged to be married once. But mostly it was computers. From when I was fourteen years old and my school got its first time-sharing terminal." He smiled. "I used to spend hours with that thing, trying to make it do stuff the designers never thought of."

"This girl you were promised to, what happened?"

Wiz shrugged. "We broke up. She had kind of a bad temper and I think she resented the time I spent with the machines."

"I'm sorry."

"Hey, don't be. She married someone else and the last I heard they were happy together."

"I meant for you."

Wiz shrugged again. "Don't be," he repeated. "I wouldn't have been a very good husband and I had the computers." He turned to face her, away from the forest and the setting sun.

"You know the worst thing about this business? It's not being jerked out of my own world and plopped down here. It's not being chased by a bunch of monsters out of the Brothers Grimm's nightmares. It's that there are no computers. It's that I'll never again be able to do the thing I spent all my life learning to do. The thing I love most doesn't exist here at all. I can't have it ever again."

"I know, Sparrow," said Shiara the Silver softly, looking out toward the sunset with unseeing eyes. "Oh I know."

"I'm sorry Lady," said Wiz contritely. "I've been thinking of my own problems."

"We each of us dwell on our own lot," Shiara said briskly, "sometimes too much. The real question is what do we do to go beyond it."

They were silent for a bit as the clouds darkened from orange to purple and the shadows crept deeper across the yard below. The swallows were fewer now and a lone brave bat fluttered around the battlements, seeking the insects that had attracted the birds.

"Lady, may I ask you a kind of personal question?"

"You may ask," said Shiara in a tone that implied it might not be answered.

"How do you go about rebuilding a life? I mean I can't work with computers here and that's all I know. How do I become something else?"

"The same way you became a—ah, hacker? Yes, hacker. One day at a time. You learn and you try to grow." She smiled. "You will find compensation, I think."

Bal-Simba left them that evening, walking the Wizard's Wary back to the Capital. For several days Wiz remained sunk in black depression, dividing his time between the battlements and his room and only coming down to eat a hasty and silent evening meal. Ugo took over the woodcutting chores again.

Finally, on the fifth day, Shiara asked for his help.

"We have many things ripening in the garden," she explained. "Moira is busy in the kitchen preserving what she has picked, Ugo has so much else to do and I," she spread her hands helplessly, "I am not much good at harvesting, I am afraid."

Moira looked askance at Wiz when Shiara brought him to the kitchen for directions. But he had been so genuinely miserable since Bal-Simba's visit that she kept her reservations to herself. Anything to get him out of himself, she thought, even if it means ruining half the crop.

So Wiz took a large basket and set to work picking beans. He worked his way down the rows without thought, examining every vine methodically. The beans had been trained to tripods of sticks, making rows of leafy green tents. As instructed, he took only those pods which were tan and dry, meaning the beans within were fully ripe.

He filled the basket and two more like it before the afternoon was over. Then he sat down outside the kitchen and carefully shelled the beans he had picked.

He was nearly done with the shelling when Moira came out of the kitchen and saw him working.

"Why thank you, Sparrow," she said in genuine pleasure. "That is well done indeed."

Once it would have thrilled Wiz to hear her praise him like that. But that time was past. "Pretty good for someone who's worthless, huh?"

Moira sobered. "I'm sorry, Wiz. I should not have said that."

"Meaning it's all right to think it, but not to say it."

"It isn't right to hurt another person needlessly," she said earnestly. "I spoke in anger and loss. I hope you will forgive me."

The way she said it hurt Wiz even more. She was sincerely sorry, he realized, but she was sorry for hurting his feelings, not for the thought. She was a queen, graciously asking pardon of one of her subjects.

"You know I can't refuse you anything, Moira."

Moira closed her eyes and sighed. "I know, Wiz. And I'm sorry."

"Well, that's the way it is. Anyway, here are your beans."

Wordlessly Moira took the basket of shelled beans and went back into the kitchen.

That day in the garden was a turning point for Wiz. From then on he largely took over the job of harvesting the rapidly ripening crops. He spent several hours a day working outdoors while Moira divided her time between the kitchen, pantry and stillroom. Most of the time Wiz picked without supervision, although Moira occasionally came out to instruct him in the finer points of gathering herbs and some of the more delicate vegetables.

A few times he went out into the Wild Wood with Ugo to gather fruits and berries. There were several ancient orchards in the quiet zone, their trees long unpruned and loaded with apples, pears and other fruits. The sight of the trees, so obviously planted and long unattended, made Wiz sad. He wondered if some long-ago Lothar had planted those saplings, full of hope for the future.

Ugo forbade Wiz to gather more than half the fruit on any tree. "Leave for forest folk," he admonished. Still they brought back basket upon basket of crisp pears and small flavorful apples which Moira set about processing in the kitchen or storing in the cellars.

Three of the four "cellars" were not under the keep or hall at all. They were root cellars, small underground rooms a few steps from the kitchen door. One day Moira asked Wiz to help her move several barrels of apples packed in oak leaves from the kitchen out to the furthest cellar.

Huffing and puffing, they tilted the heavy barrels and rolled them out to the place where they would be stored. It took both of them to carry each barrel down the steps into the cool twilight of the root cellar.

"Whoo!" Wiz gasped, standing upright after the last of the barrels had been shifted into place. "I wonder how they did this before we got here?"

"Ugo doubtless did it," panted Moira. "Wood goblins are stronger than they look and they can be very ingenious when needs be."

"Do you think we've got enough food here for the winter?"

Moira ran a practiced housewife's eye over the cellar. "That and then some, if I am any judge. It is the flour, salt and other staples that are the concern. The Mighty bring those to Heart's Ease over the Wizard's Way and they have not increased the supply since we came."

"Why not?"

"First because the Wizard's Way was chancy when the Dark League was in full cry for us. Secondly, because they dared not increase the amount of supplies brought through lest it reveal to the League that there are extra mouths here."

Moira looked around the cellar again and breathed deeply to take in the scent of the apples and other good things stored in the earth. Then she sighed.

"Penny," Wiz said.

"What?"

"A penny for your thoughts. I was wondering what you were thinking."

"What I was thinking was none of your concern, Sparrow," Moira said coldly. "And if you are through prying into my private thoughts, we still have work to do. Come!"

"No, I don't think I am done," Wiz said slowly. He moved in to block her way out. "There's still something I want to know and I think you owe it to me to tell me."

Moira stopped, suddenly unsure of herself. She'd seen Wiz bewildered, sullen, lovesick, awestruck, depressed and in the throes of a temper tantrum, but she had never seen him coldly angry as he was now.

"What is it I must tell you then?"

"Why are you so mad at me?"

"Crave pardon?" she said haughtily.

Wiz plowed ahead. "From the moment I met you you've disliked me. Fine, I'm not a magician, I don't know my way around this place and I'm a first-class klutz. *But why are you so bleeding mad at me?*"

The question brought Moira up short. Wiz had never spoken to her like that before and she had never really examined her feelings toward him deeply.

True, he was inept and he had nearly gotten them both killed repeatedly on the journey. But it was more than that. She had disliked him from the first meeting in the clearing.

"I had to leave people who needed me to bring you here."

"Not guilty," Wiz said. "That was Bal-Simba's idea, not mine." He paused. "Besides, I think there's something more to it than that."

"There is," she said bitterly. "Patrius died to bring you here." Her eyes flashed. "We lost the best and most powerful of the Mighty and got you in return."

Wiz nodded. "Yeah, so you've told me. But I wasn't looking to come here and I've suffered more from what Patrius did than you or any of the others. Again, not guilty."

Moira drew herself up. "If my feelings do not meet with your approval I am truly sorry! It is perhaps unreasonable of me, but that is the way I do feel."

"I doubt it," Wiz bit out. "Bal-Simba's loss was greater than yours and he doesn't hold me responsible. There's something a whole lot more personal here. Now what?"

"I don't . . ."

"Lady, I think the least, the very least, you owe me is a straight answer."

Moira didn't reply for a long time. "I think," she said finally, "it is because you remind me of my failure."

"What failure?"

"The death of Patrius." Moira's eyes filled with tears. "Don't you see? I failed in my duty and Patrius died."

"What I see is you trying to take the whole bleeding world on your shoulders," Wiz snapped. "Look, I'm sorry for what happened to Patrius, all right? But I didn't make it happen. I was kidnapped. Remember?"

"You were involved," Moira shot back. "If he hadn't Summoned you, he wouldn't have died."

"Wrong. If he hadn't gotten me he would have gotten someone else—maybe the super-wizard he wanted, I don't know. But the point is, I had nothing to do with it. He made the choice of his own free will. He knew the risks. *I am not responsible.*"

"No," Moira admitted slowly, "you were not."

"And I'll tell you something else, lady. You weren't responsible either."

"Little you know about it! An acolyte's job is to protect the master."

"You're not an acolyte. You're a hedge-witch Patrius stumbled across and roped into his scheme. From what you and the others tell me, there is no way you could have protected him."

"Thank you," Moira said tightly. "All I needed was to be reminded of my weakness."

"Yes, you do need to be reminded of it!" Wiz flared. "You're not all-powerful and you cannot be held responsible for something utterly beyond your control."

"Ohhh!" Moira gasped, turning from him.

"I'll tell you something else you're not responsible for," he said to her back. "You're not responsible for what happened to your family. You didn't do it and you can't undo it and feeling guilty about it is only going to make you miserable."

Moira spun on her heel and slapped him with all the force of her body. Wiz's head snapped to the side and he staggered back. Their eyes locked. Then Moira's shoulders heaved and she began to sob silently, hugging herself and rocking back and forth on her heels.

Wiz took a step toward her and stopped. "Look, I'm sorry I said that. I shouldn't have, Okay?"

"But dammit," he added forcefully, "it's true!" and he turned and left the cellar.

Moira took her dinner in her room that night, making Ugo grumble and complain about the stairs he had to climb to take it to her. Shiara made a point of not noticing and Wiz picked at his food and muttered.

The argument marked a change in their relationship. Wiz still loved Moira, but he began to notice things about her he hadn't seen before. She had a temper, he realized, and a lot of the time the things she said to him weren't justified. She was beautiful but she wasn't really pretty by the conventional standard of either world. Most of all, he saw, she was terribly involved with her work. She was as married to being a hedge witch as Wiz had been to computers.

For her part, Moira seemed to warm slightly to Wiz. She never spoke of their fight in the cellar and Wiz could see she still resented the things he had said, but she started to unbend a little. They could hardly be called close, but Moira began to go a little beyond common civility and Wiz's dreams were no longer haunted by Moira.

# *Nine*
## MAGIC FOR IDIOTS AND
## ENGLISH MAJORS

Slowly summer came to an end. The air grew cooler and the trees began to change. Standing on the battlements Wiz could watch flocks of birds winging their way over the multicolor patchwork tapestry of the Wild Wood. The swallows no longer flitted about in the evenings and the nights bore a touch of frost.

The garden was harvested now and Moira and Shiara spent their days in the kitchen, salting, pickling, preserving and laying by. Wiz helped where he could in the kitchen or out in the garden where Ugo was preparing the earth for its winter's rest.

In some ways Wiz was more at home in the kitchen than Moira. The way of preserving that the hedge witch knew relied heavily on magic. But for Shiara's comfort there could be no magic in the kitchen at Heart's Ease.

"These will not be as good as if they were kept by a spell, but we will relish them in deep winter nonetheless," Moira said one afternoon as they chopped vegetables to be pickled in brine.

"Yeah," said Wiz, who had never particularly liked sauerkraut. "You know on my world we would can most of this stuff. Or freeze it."

"Freezing I understand, but what is canning?"

"We'd cook the vegetables in their containers in a boiling water bath and then seal them while they were still very hot. They'd keep for years like that."

"Why cook them before you sealed them?"

"To kill the bugs." He caught the look on her face. "Germs, bacteria, tiny animals that make food spoil."

"You know about those too?" Moira asked.

"Sure. But I'm surprised you don't think disease is caused by evil spells."

"I told you that there is no such thing as an evil spell," Moira said, nettled. "And some ills are caused by spells. But most of them are the result of tiny creatures which can infest larger living things. What I do not understand is how you can sense them without magic."

"We can see them with the aid of our instruments. We have optical and electron microscopes that let us watch even viruses—those are the really tiny ones."

"You actually see them?" Moira shook her head. "I do not know, Sparrow. Sometimes I think your people must be wizards."

"I'm not."

Moira bit her lip and turned back to her cutting.

As evenings lengthened the three of them took to sitting around the fireplace in the hall enjoying the heat from the wood Wiz had cut. Usually Moira would mend while Wiz and Shiara talked.

"Lady, could you tell me about magic?" Wiz asked one evening.

"I don't know many of the tales of wonders," Shiara said. She smiled ruefully. "The stories are the work of bards, not the people who lived them."

"I don't mean that. What I'm interested in is how magic works. How you get the effects you produce."

Moira looked up from her mending and glared. Shiara said nothing for a space.

"Why do you want to know?" She asked finally.

Wiz shrugged. "No reason. We don't have magic where I come from and I'm curious."

"Magic is not taught save to those duly apprenticed to the Craft," Moira scolded. "You are too old to become an apprentice."

"Hey, I don't want to make magic, I just want to know how it works, okay?" They both looked at Shiara.

"You do not intend to practice magic?" she asked.

"No, Lady." Wiz said. Then he added: "I don't have the talent for it anyway."

Shiara stroked the line of her jaw with her index finger, as she often did when she was thinking.

"Normally it is as Moira says," she said at last. "However there is nothing that forbids merely discussing magic in a general fashion with an outsider—so long as there is no attempt to use the knowledge. If you will promise me never to try to practice magic, I will attempt to answer your questions."

"Thank you, Lady. Yes, I will promise."

Shiara nodded. Moira sniffed and bent to her mending.

After that Wiz and Shiara talked almost every night. Moira usually went to bed earlier than they did and out of deference to her feelings they waited until she had retired. Then Wiz would try to explain his world and computers to Shiara and the former wizardess would tell Wiz about the ways of magic. While Shiara learned about video game-user operating systems, Wiz learned about initiation rites and spell weaving.

"You know, I still don't understand why that fire spell worked the second time," Wiz said one evening shortly after the first hard frost.

"Why is that, Sparrow?" Shiara asked.

"Well, according to what Moira told me I shouldn't have been able to reproduce it accurately enough to work. She said you needed to get everything from the angle of your hand to the phase of the moon just right and no one but a trained magician could do that."

Shiara smiled. "Our hedge witch exaggerates slightly. It is true that most spells are impossible for anyone but a trained magician to repeat, but there are some which are insensitive to most—variables?—yes, variables. The coarse outlines of word and gesture are sufficient to invoke them. Apparently you stumbled across such a spell. Although I doubt a spell to start forest fires would be generally useful."

Wiz laughed. "Probably not. But it saved our bacon."

"You know, Sparrow, sometimes I wonder if your talent isn't luck."

Wiz sobered. "I'm not all that lucky, Lady."

The former sorceress reached out and laid her hand on his. "Forgive me, Sparrow," she said gently.

Wiz moved to change the subject.

"I can see why it takes a magician to discover a spell, but why can't a non-magician use a spell once it's known?"

"That is not the way magic works, Sparrow."

"I know that. I just don't understand why."

"Well, some spells, the very simple ones, can be used by anyone—although the Mighty discourage it lest the ignorant be tempted. But Moira was basically correct. A major spell is too complex to be learned properly by a non-magician. A mispronounced word, an incorrect gesture and the spell becomes something else, often something deadly." Her brow wrinkled.

"Great spells often take months to learn. You must study them in parts so you can master them without invoking them. Even then it is hard. Many apprentices cannot master the great spells."

"What happens to them?"

"The wise ones, like Moira, settle for a lesser order. Those who are not so wise or perhaps more driven persevere until they make a serious mistake." She smiled slightly. "In magic that is usually fatal."

Wiz thought about what it would be like to work with a computer that killed the programmer every time it crashed and shuddered.

"But can't you teach people the insensitive spells?" he asked. "The ones that are safe to learn?"

Shiara shrugged. "We could, I suppose, but it would be pointless. Safe spells are almost always weak spells. They do little and not much of it is useful. Your forest fire spell was unusual in that it was apparently both insensitive and powerful.

"There are a very few exception but in general the spells that are easy to learn do so little that no one bothers to learn them, save by accident."

"Well, yeah, but couldn't you build on that? I mean start from the easy spells and work up to the harder ones that do something useful?"

Shiara shook her head. "Once again, magic does not work that way. Mark you, Sparrow, each spell is different. Learning one spell teaches you little about others. Wizardry is a life's work, not something one can practice as a side craft. You must start very young and train your memory and your body before you begin to learn the great magics."

"I see the problem," Wiz said.

"That is only the beginning. Even if ordinary folk could learn the great spells, we would be cautious about teaching them lest they be misused. A wizard has power, Sparrow. More power than any other mortal. By its very nature that power cannot be easily checked or controlled by others. Few have the kind of restraint required to do more good than harm."

"But more people are dying because only wizards can use the really powerful spells," Wiz protested, thinking of Lothar and his cottage in the Wild Wood.

"More would die if those who are not wizards tried to use them. Life is not fair, Sparrow. As you know."

Wiz didn't pursue the matter and their talk went on

to other things. But it troubled him for the rest of the evening.

*Shiara's right,* he thought as he drifted off to sleep that night. *You can't have just anyone working magic here. It would be like giving every user on the system supervisor privileges and making them all write their own programs in machine language. Not even assembler, just good old ones and zeroes.* He sleepily turned the notion over in his mind, imagining the chaos that would cause in a computer center. *You can't trust users with that kind of power. God, you don't even want most programmers writing in assembler. You make them use high-level languages.*

A vagrant thought tugged at the edge of Wiz's sleep-fogged brain. A computer language for magic?

*My God! I'll bet you could really do that!*

He sat bolt upright. Well why not? A computer language is simply a formalism for expressing algorithms and what's a magic spell but an algorithm?

If it did really work that way the possibilities were mind-boggling. You'd need the right language, of course, but God what you could do with it.

These people were the original unstructured programmers. They were so unstructured they didn't even know they were programming. They just blundered around until they found something that worked. It was like learning to program by pounding randomly on the keyboard.

They never seemed to generalize from one spell to another. They needed some kind of language, something to let them structure their magic.

It would have to be something simple, Wiz decided. A language and an operating system all in one. Probably a very simple internal compiler and a threaded interpreted structure. And modular, yes, very modular.

Forth with object-oriented features? Yep, that made sense. All thought of sleep vanished as Wiz got of bed. His mind was full of structural considerations.

He dug a chunk of charcoal out of the fireplace and started sketching on the hearth by the wan moonlight. Just a basic box diagram, but as he sketched, he became more and more excited.

A Forth-like language was about the simplest kind to write. Essentially it was nothing but a loop which would read a command, execute it and go on to read the next command. The thing that made such languages so powerful was that the command could be built up out of previously defined commands. MOBY could be defined as command FOO followed by command BAR. When you gave the loop, the interpreter, the command MOBY, it looked up the definition in its dictionary, found the command FOO, executed it, went on to the command BAR and executed it, thus executing the command MOBY.

At the top of a program was nothing but a single word, but that word was defined by other words, which were defined by other words, all the way back to the most basic definitions in terms of machine language—or whatever passed for machine language when the machine was the real world.

The more Wiz thought about that, the better he liked it. Forth, the best-known example of the genre, had been originally written to control telescopes and Forth was a common language in robotics. It had the kind of flexibility he needed and it was simple enough that one person could do the entire project.

That Forth is considered, at best, decidedly odd by most programmers didn't bother Wiz in the slightest.

The critical question was whether or not a spell could call other spells. The way Shiara had used a counting demon to trigger the destruction spell in her final adventure implied that it could, but the idea seemed foreign to her.

He sat on the hearth, sketching in the pale moonlight until the moon sank below the horizon and it became too dark to see. Reluctantly he made his way back to bed and crawled under the covers, his excitement fighting his body's insistence on sleep.

Nothing fancy, he told himself. He would have to limit his basic element to those safe, insensitive spells Shiara had mentioned. So what if they didn't do much on their own? Most assembler commands didn't do much either. The thing that made them powerful was you could string them together quickly and effectively under the structure of the language.

Oh yes, debugging features. It would need a moby debugger. Bugs in a magic program could crash more than the system.

*It's a pity the universe doesn't use segmented architecture with a protected mode,* Wiz thought to himself as he drifted off.

As he was slipping into unconsciousness, he remembered one of his friend Jerry's favorite bull session raps. He used to maintain that the world was nothing but an elaborate computer simulation. "All I want is a few minutes with the source code and a quick recompile," his friend used to tell him.

He fell asleep wondering if he would get what Jerry had wanted.

All through the next day Wiz's mind was boiling. As he chopped wood or worked in the kitchen he was mentally miles away with dictionaries and compiler/interpreters. He didn't tell Moira because he knew she wouldn't like the notion. For that matter, he wasn't sure Shiara would approve. So when they were sitting alone tht evening he broached the subject obliquely.

"Lady, do you have to construct a spell all at once?"

"I am not sure I know what you mean, Sparrow."

"Can't you put parts of simple spells together to make a bigger one?"

Shiara frowned. "Well, you can link some spells together, but . . ."

"No, I mean modularize your spells. Take a part of a spell that produces one effect and couple it to a part of a spell that has another effect and make a bigger spell."

"That is not the way spells work, Sparrow."

"Why not?" Wiz asked. "I mean couldn't they work that way?"

"I have never heard of a spell that did," the former wizardess said.

"Wouldn't it be easier that way?" he persisted.

"There are no shortcuts in magic. Spells must be won through hard work and discipline."

"But you said . . ."

"And what I said was true," Shiara cut him off. "But there are things which cannot be put into words. A spell is one, indivisible. You cannot break it apart and put it back together in a new guise any more than you can take a frog apart and turn it into a bird."

"In my world we used to do things like that all the time."

Shiara smiled. "Things work differently in this world, Sparrow."

"I don't see why," Wiz said stubbornly.

Shiara sighed. "Doubtless not, Sparrow. You are not a magician. You do not know what it is like to actually cast spells, much less weave them. If you did it would be obvious."

Wiz wasn't sure who had said "be sure you're right and then go ahead," but that had been his motto ever since childhood. The stubborn willingness to go against common opinion, and sometimes against direct orders, had gotten him the reputation for being hard to manage, but it had also made him an outstanding programmer. He was used to people telling him his ideas wouldn't work.

Most of the time they were wrong and Wiz had always enjoyed proving that. In this case he knew he was right and he was going to prove it.

All the same, he didn't want anyone to know what he was up to until he was sure he could make it work. The thought of Moira laughing at him was more than he could bear.

Just inside the Wild Wood, perhaps 200 yards from the keep of Heart's Ease, was a small log hut. From the stuff on the floor Wiz suspected it had been used to stable horses at one time. But there were no horses here now and the hut was long deserted. Wiz cleared out the debris and dragged a rude plank bench which lay in a corner under the window. There was a mouse nest in another corner, but he didn't disturb that.

The next problem was writing materials. This world apparently wasn't big on writing, at least there weren't any books in Heart's Ease. The usual material was parchment, but he didn't have any. Finally he settled on shakes of wood split from the logs in the woodpile and wrote on them with charcoal.

Fundamentally, a computer language depended on three things. It had to have some method for storing and recalling data and instructions, instructions had to be able to call other instructions and it had to be able to test conditions and shift the flow of control in response to the results. Given those three very simple requirements, Wiz knew he could create a language.

His first experiment would just be to store and recall numbers, he decided. He wanted something useful, but he also wanted something that would be small enough not to be noticed, even here in the quiet zone. Besides, if magic hurt Shiara he did not want to make detectable magic.

Drawing on what Shiara had told him, he put together something very simple, even simpler than the fire spell he had discovered by accident.

Although the spell was simple, he labored over it for an entire day, checking and rechecking like a first-year computer science student on his first day in the computer lab.

Late that afternoon he picked up a clean slab and a piece of charcoal. His hand was shaking as he wrote 1 2 3 in large irregular characters on the wood. Then he very carefully erased the numbers leaving only a black smear.

"Remember," he said and passed his hand over the board. There was a stirring shifting in the charcoal and the individual particles danced on the surface like an army of microscopic fleas. There, stark against the white of newly split wood, appeared 1 2 3.

"Son of a bitch!" Wiz breathed. "It worked."

He stared at the reconstituted numbers for a long time, not quite believing what he had done. He repeated the experiment twice more and each time the characters or designs he scrawled on the board and erased reappeared on command.

*Okay, the next step is a compare spell. In IF-THEN. For that I'll need . . .* Then he started as he realized how late it had gotten. He still hadn't cut wood for the next day and it was almost time for dinner.

For a moment the old fascination and new sense of responsibility warred in his breast. Then he reluctantly put down the board and started back to the keep. *If I don't show up soon someone is likely to come looking for me,* he thought. *Besides, they'll need wood for tomorrow.*

No one seemed to notice his absence or made any comment when he disappeared the next day after his stint at the woodpile. The comparison spell also proved to be straightforward. The final step was the calling spell, the spell that would call other spells. That was the key, Wiz knew. If it worked he had the beginnings of his language.

Again Wiz worked slowly and carefully, polishing his ideas until he was sure he had something that would work. It took nearly three days before he felt confident enough to try it.

Once more he wrote a series of numbers on a clean slab of wood. Then he erased them. Then he readied the new spell.

"Call remember," he commanded.

There was a faint "pop" and a tiny figure appeared on the work bench. He was about a foot high with dark slick hair parted in the middle and a silly waxed mustache. He wore white duck trousers, a ruffled shirt and a black bow tie. Without looking at Wiz, he passed his hand over the board and once again the bits of charcoal rearranged themselves into the numbers Wiz had written. Then with another "pop" the figure disappeared.

Wiz goggled. A *demon! I just created a demon.* Shiara had said that once a spell grew to a certain level of complexity it took the form of a demon but he had never expected to make one himself.

He had never considered what a command would look like from within the computer. *I never had to worry about that,* he thought, bemused.

This particular command looked darned familiar. Wiz didn't know for sure, but he doubted that bow ties and waxed mustaches were worn anywhere on this world. After wracking his brains for a couple of minutes he remembered where he had seen the little man before. He was the cartoon character used to represent the interpreter in *Starting Forth*, Leo Brodie's basic book on the Forth language.

That made a crazy kind of sense, Wiz told himself. What he had just written functionally was very close to a Forth interpreter. And he was basing his language in part on Forth. Apparently the shape of a demon was influenced by the mental image the magician has of the process.

*I wonder if he speaks with a lisp?*

Then he sobered. More to the point, how could he be sure that his language's commands would respond only to the explicit spells that defined them and not by some chance idea or mental image? Wiz made his way back to the castle in deep thought.

It wasn't at all as easy as that. The first thing Wiz discovered was that the universe was not orthogonal. The rules of magic were about as regular as the instruction set on a Z80. Some things worked in some combinations and not in others. Murphy said "constants aren't" and Murphy was apparently one of the gods of this universe.

He was uncomfortably aware that he didn't really understand the rules of magic. He deliberately limited his language to the simplest, most robust spells, counting on the power of the compiler to execute many of them in rapid succession to give him his power. But even that turned out to be not so simple.

There were some things which seemed to work and which were very useful, but which didn't work consistently or wouldn't work well when called from other spells. Wiz suspected the problem was that they were complex entities composed of several fundamental pieces. He deliberately left them out of the code. *After all*, he rationalized, *this is only version 1.0. I can go back and add them later.*

He benchmarked his compiler at about 300 MOPS (Magical Operations Per Second). Not at all fast for someone used to working on a 3 MIPS (Million instructions per Second) workstation, but he wanted reliability, not speed. *Besides, my benchmarks are for real*, he told himself, *not some vapor wafting out of the marketing department.*

There were other problems he hadn't anticipated. Once he tried to write down a simple definition using a combination of mathematical notation and the runes of this world's alphabet. He gave up when the characters started to glow blue and crawl off the board. After that he was careful never to put a full definition on a single piece of anything. He split his boards into strips and wrote parts of code on each board.

The clean, spare structure of his original began to disappear under a profusion of error checking and warning messages. To keep side effects to a minimum he adopted a packaging approach, hiding as much information as possible in each module and minimizing interfaces.

Wiz spent more and more time at the hut poring over his tablets and testing commands. Sometimes the mice would come out and watch him work at the rude plank bench under the window. Wiz took to eating his lunch in the hut and left crumbs for the mice. Winter was a hard time for the poor little things, he thought.

Moira noticed the change in Wiz, but said nothing at first. Part of her was relieved that he was no longer constantly underfoot, but part of her missed the ego boost that had given her. Deep down there was a part of her which missed seeing Wiz constantly, she finally admitted to herself.

If Shiara noticed, she said nothing. She and Wiz still talked magic, but now it was no longer an everyday occurrence.

What Ugo noticed was anyone's guess. Probably a great deal, but the goblin kept his counsel and grumbled about his chores as always.

Like a small boy with a guilty secret, Wiz went well beyond Heart's Ease for the first test of his new system. He found a sheltered glade surrounded on all sides by trees and bushes. There he set to work on his first real spell.

There was a jay's tail feather lying on the leaves, slate blue and barred with black. Wiz picked it up, held it by the quill and slowly and carefully recited his spell.

Nothing happened. The spell had failed! Wiz sighed in disappointment and dropped the feather. But instead of fluttering to the ground, the feather rose. It rotated and twisted, but it ever so gently fell upward from his hand.

Wiz watched transfixed as the feather wafted itself gently into the air.

It wasn't much of a spell, just enough to produce a gentle current of air which could barely be felt against the outstretched palm. But Wiz was elated by its success. He had actually commanded magic!

They marked Mid-Winter's Day with a feast and celebrations. Ugo cut a large log for the fire. They had mulled wine flavored with spices, nuts, dried fruits and delicacies. With the nuts, fruit and spices Moira whipped up what she called a Winter Bread. It reminded Wiz of a fruitcake.

"In my country it is the custom to give gifts at this time of the year," Wiz told them. "So I have some things for you."

Wiz was not very good with his hands, but from a long-ago summer at camp, he had dredged up the memory of how to whittle. He reached into his pouch and produced two packages, neatly tied in clean napkins for want of wrapping paper.

"Lady," he said, holding the first one out to Shiara. She took it and untied the knot by feel, fumbling slightly as she folded back the cloth. Inside lay a wooden heart carved from dark sapwood, laboriously scraped smooth and polished with beeswax until it glowed softly. A leather thong threaded through a painstakingly bored hole provided a way to wear it.

"Why, thank you Sparrow," Shiara said, running her fingertips over the surface of the wood.

"This is for you," he said holding the second package out to Moira. Inside was a wooden chain ending in a wooden ball in a cage.

"Thank you, Sparrow." Moira examined her present. Then her head snapped up "This is made from a single piece of wood," she said accusingly.

Wiz nodded. "Yep."

She stared at him gimlet-eyed. "Did you use magic to get the ball into the cage?"

"Huh? No! I carved it in there." Briefly he explained how the trick was done.

Moira softened. "Oh. I'm sorry, Sparrow. It's just that when I see something like that I naturally think of magic."

"It's a good thing I didn't make you a model ship in a bottle."

"No," she said contritely. "I'm sorry for believing you had gone back on yur promise not to practice magic."

"It's all right," he mumbled uncomfortably.

In spite of that, the holiday passed very well. For perhaps the first time since he had been summoned, Wiz enjoyed himself. Part of that was the holiday, part of it was that he now had real work to do and part of it— a big part of it—was that Moira seemed to be warming to him.


Wiz was chopping wood the next morning when Ugo came out to see him. "More wood!" the goblin commanded, eyeing the pile Wiz had already chopped.

"That's plenty for one day," Wiz told him.

"Not one day. Many day," the goblin said. "Big storm come soon. Need much, much wood."

Wiz looked up and saw the sky was a clear luminous blue without a cloud in sight. The air was cold, but no colder than it had been.

"Big storm. More wood!" Ugo repeated imperiously and went on his way.

*Well*, thought Wiz, *it's his world*. He turned back to the woodpile to lay in more.

All day the sky stayed fair and the winds calm, but during the night a heavy gray blanket of clouds rolled in. Dawn was rosy and sullen with the sun blushing the mass of dirty gray clouds with pink. By mid-morning the temperature had dropped ominously and the wind had picked up. Ugo, Moira and Wiz all scurried about last-minute tasks.

It started to snow that afternoon. Large white flakes swirled down out of the clouds, driven by an increasing wind. Thanks to the clouds and the weak winter sun, dusk came early. By full dark the wind was howling around Heart's Ease, whistling down the chimneys and tugging at the shutters and roof slates.

For three days and three nights the wind howled and the snow fell. The inhabitants warmed themselves with the wood Wiz had cut and amused themselves as they might in the pale grayish daylight that penetrated through the clouds and snow. They went to bed early and stayed abed late, for there was little else to do.

Then on the fourth day the storm was gone. They awoke to find the air still and the sky a brilliant Koda-chrome blue. Awakened by the bright light through the cracks in the shutters, Wiz jumped out of bed, ran to the window and threw the shutters wide.

Below everything was white. The snow sparkled in the mild winter's sun. Tree branches bore their load of white. Down in the courtyard of the keep, the outbuildings were shapeless mounds buried under the snowdrifts. The whole world looked clean and bright and new that morning from Wiz's window.

After a quick breakfast Wiz and Moira went outside.

"It appears no damage was done," Moira said as she looked over the buildings in the compound. "The roofs all seem to be secure and the snow does not lie too heavily on them." Her cheeks and the tip of her nose were rosy with the cold, almost hiding her freckles. "We will have to shovel paths, of course."

"Yeah, and make snowmen," Wiz said, sucking the cold crisp air deep into his lungs and exhaling in a huge cloud.

Moira turned to him. "What is a snowman?"

"You've never made a snowman?" Wiz asked in astonishment. "Hey, I'm a California boy, but even I know how to do that. Here, I'll show you."

Under Wiz's instruction, they rolled the snow into three large balls and stacked them carefully. There was no coal, so stones had to serve as eyes and buttons, while Moira procured a carrot from the kitchen to act as the nose.

"What does he do?" Moira asked when they finished building him.

"Do?" said Wiz blankly.

"Yes."

"It doesn't do anything. It's just fun to make."

"Oh," said Moira, somewhat disappointed. "I thought perhaps it came to life or something."

"That's not usually part of the game," Wiz told her remembering *Frosty the Snowman*. "It's something done only for enjoyment."

"I suppose I ought to do more things just for enjoyment," Moira sighed. "But there was never time, you see." She looked over at Wiz and smiled shyly. "Thank you for showing me how to make a snowman."

"My pleasure," Wiz told her. Suddenly life was very, very good.

He spent most of the rest of the day helping Ugo shovel paths through the drifts to reach the outbuildings. For part of the afternoon he cut firewood to replace the quantities that had been burned during the blizzard. But with that done, they were at loose ends again. The snow was still too deep to do much outside work and most of the inside work was completed. So Wiz suggested a walk in the woods to Moira.

"If it's not too dangerous, I mean."

"It should not be. The storm probably affected all kinds of beings equally." She smiled. "So yes, Wiz, I would like to walk in the woods."

They had to push through waist-high drifts to reach the gate, but once in the Wild Wood the going was easier.

The trees had caught and held much of the snow, so there was only a few inches on the ground in the forest.

Although the weak winter's sun was bright in the sky it was really too cold for walking. But it was too beautiful to go back. The snow from the storm lay fresh and white and fluffy all around them. Here and there icicles glittered like diamonds on the bare branches of the trees. Occasionally they would find a line of tracks like hieroglyphics traced across the whiteness where some bird or animal had made its way through the new snow.

"We had a song about walking in a winter wonderland," Wiz told Moira as they crunched their way along.

"It is a lovely phrase," Moira said. "Did they have storms like this in your world?"

"In some places worse," Wiz grinned. "But it never snowed in the place where I lived. People used to move there to get away from the snow."

Moira looked around the clean whiteness and cathedral stillness of the Wild Wood. "I'm not sure I'd want to be away from snow forever," she said.

"I had a friend who moved out from—well, from a place where it snowed a lot and I asked him if he moved because he didn't like snow. You know what he told me? I like snow just fine, he said, it's the slush I can't stand."

Moira chuckled, a wonderful bell-like sound. "There is that," she said.

They had come into a clearing where the sun played brighter on the new snow. Wiz moved to a stump in the center and wiped the cap of snow off with the sleeve of his tunic.

"Would my lady care to sit?" he asked, bowing low.

Moira returned the bow with a curtsey and sat on the cleared stump. "You have your moments, Sparrow," she said, unconsciously echoing the words she had said to Shiara on their arrival at the castle.

"I try, Lady," Wiz said lightly.

Sitting there with her cheeks rosy from the cold and

her hair hanging free she was beautiful, Wiz thought. So achingly beautiful. *I haven't felt this way about her since I first came to Heart's Ease.*

"But not as hard as you used to." She smiled. "I like you the better for that."

Wiz shrugged.

"Tell me, where do you go when you disappear all day?"

"I didn't think you'd noticed," he said, embarrassed.

"There have been one or two times when I have gone looking for you and you have been nowhere to be found."

"Well, it's kind of a secret."

"Oh? A tryst with a wood nymph perhaps?" she said archly.

"Nothing like that. I've been working on a project." He took a deep breath. *It's now or never, I guess.*

"Actually I've been working out some theories I have on magic. You see . . ."

Moira's mouth fell open. "Magic? You've been practicing *magic*?"

"No, not really. I've been developing a spell-writing language, like those computer languages I told you about."

"But you promised!" Moira said, aghast.

"Yes, but I've got it pretty well worked out now. Look," he said, "I'll show you." He reached into his pocket and pulled out the jay's feather he had used in his experiment. "I'll use a spell to make this feather rise."

"I want nothing to do with this!"

"Just hold up a minute will you? I know I can make this work. I've been doing it in secret for weeks."

"*Weeks?*" Moira screeched. "Fortuna! Haven't you listened to *anything* you've been told since you got here?"

"I'm telling you it works and I've been doing it for a long time," Wiz said heatedly. "You haven't seen any ill effects have you? In fact you didn't even know I was working magic until I told you."

Moira let out an exasperated sigh. "Listen. It is

possible, *just possible,* that you have been able to do parlor tricks without hurting anything. But that doesn't make you a magician! The first time you try something bigger there's going to be trouble."

"I tell you I *can* control it."

"Those words are carved on many an apprentice's tomb."

"All right. Here, give me your shawl."

"No. I'm going to tell Shiara."

"Moira, please."

Dubiously, Moira got off the stump and unwound the roughly woven square of cloth she wore around her neck under her cloak.

The shawl was bigger than anything Wiz had ever worked with, but he set it down on the stump confidently. Mentally he ran over the rising spell, making a couple of quick changes to adapt it for a heavier object. He muttered the alterations quickly and then thrust his hands upward dramatically.

"Rise!" he commanded.

The edges of the shawl rippled and stirred as a puff of air blew out from under the fabric. Then the cloth billowed and surged taut as the air pressure grew. Then the shawl leaped into the air borne on a stiff breeze rising from the stump. The wind began to gently ruffle Wiz's hair as the air around the stump pushed in to replace what was forced aloft by the spell.

"See," he said triumphantly. "I told you I could make it work."

"Shut it off!" Moira's green eyes were wide and her freckles stood out vividly against her suddenly pallid skin. "Please shut it off."

The wind was stronger now, a stiff force against Wiz's back. Wisps of snow and leaves on the forest floor began to stir and move toward the rising air. Even as Wiz started the spell and the wind rose even higher. Moira's shawl was long gone in the the uprising gale.

The wind grabbed leaves and twigs off the ground and hurled them into the sky. The trees around the clearing bowed inward and their branches clattered as they were forced toward the column of air rising out of the clearing.

"Do something!" Moira shouted over the force of the wind.

"I'm trying," Wiz shouted back. He recited the counter-spell, inaudible in the howling wind. Nothing happened. The gale grew stronger and Wiz backed up against a stout tree to keep from being pushed forward.

He realized he had made a mistake in the wording and swore under his breath Again he tried the counter spell. Again nothing.

In designing the spell Wiz had made a serious error. the only way to undo it was to reverse the process of creating it. There was no word which could shut the flow of air off quickly.

Meanwhile the wind was picking up, gaining even more force. Now the leaves and twigs were supplemented by small branches torn from the trees around them. With a tremendous CRACK and a thunderous CRASH, a nearby forest giant, rotten in its core, blew over and toppled halfway into the clearing.

The wind was so great Wiz was forced to cling to the tree trunk to keep from being swept up in the raging vortex of air. Moira was invisible through the mass of dirt, leaves, snow and debris being pulled into the air. Desperately Wiz tried the counterspell again. Again nothing.

The vertical hurricane carried denser ground air aloft. As it rose the pressure lessened and the water vapor in the air condensed out. Heart's Ease was marked by a boiling, towering mushroom cloud that could be seen for miles.

In the heart of a raging hurricane Wiz forced himself to think calmly. Again he reviewed the spell, going through it step by step as if he were back in front of his terminal. Taking a deep breath and ignoring the howling in his ears, he recited the spell again, slowly and deliberately.

The wind cut off as if by a switch.

The clearing was quiet save for the sound of branches falling back to earth and crashing through the trees around them. Moira was wet and disheveled, her red hair a tangled mess from the buffetting it had received from the wind.

"Of course there are still a few bugs in the system," Wiz said lamely.

"Ohhh," Moira hissed. "I don't want to talk to you." She spun away from him.

"All right. So it wasn't perfect. But it worked didn't it? And I shut it off didn't I?"

Moira shuddered with barely suppressed rage. But when she turned to face him she was icy calm.

"What you have done is less than any new-entered apprentice could do, were his master so foolish as to allow it," she said coldly. "Not only have you proved that you have no aptitude for the Craft, you have shown you have no honor as well."

"Now wait a minute . . ."

"No!" Moira held up a hand to silence him. "You gave your word that you would not attempt to reduce the things Shiara told you to practice. Now you boast of having violated that oath almost from the beginning and with no shred of excuse. You were not driven to forswear yourself by need. You did so only for your own amusement."

"Shiara didn't teach me . . ."

"Shiara taught you far more than was good for either of you," Moira snapped. "You have proven yourself unworthy of her teaching and of her trust." She paused and considered. "Normally a matter such as this would be handled by your master. But you," she sneered, "have no master."

The way she looked at him made Wiz feel as if he had crawled out from under some forest rock.

"Doubtless this matter will be placed before the Council and they will decide your fate. In the meantime you must be kept close and watched since it is obvious you cannot be trusted and your word cannot be relied upon."

She turned and stalked out of the clearing and back toward Heart's Ease. Wiz opened his mouth to call after her, then trudged up the path in her wake, fuming.

# Ten

## STORM STRIKE

"Moira, wait!" Wiz ran up the path after her. She kept walking, eyes straight ahead.

"Okay," Wiz said defensively, as he trotted along beside her. "So it got a little out of hand."

"A *little* out of hand?" Moira screamed. "A LITTLE out of hand. Ohhh . . . This is beyond all your stupidity. Not only do you learn nothing, you cannot even be trusted to keep your word."

"Now wait a minute . . ."

"Get back to the keep. You must be kept mewed for your own safety and ours as well." She threw him a contemptuous glance. "Tomorrow I will destroy your tools before they wreak more mischief."

"Destroy it? But I was right!"

"Go!" Moira commanded with a hefty shove in the small of his back. Wiz stumbled forward and gave his beloved a wounded look.

"Must I take you by the ear?" she demanded. "Now go!"

Shiara was collapsed in a chair with Ugo hovering about her. Her skin was ghastly pale and she was breathing in quick shallow pants.

"Magic," Ugo said. "Big magic and close pain her."

Wiz started guiltily. *Of course. That much magic must have hurt her terribly.* Seeing Shiara was even worse than Moira's anger.

"It seems that our Sparrow adds untrustworthiness to his other accomplishments," Moira said tightly. "He has been using your 'purely theoretical discussions' to learn to practice magic."

Ugo threw Wiz a look of poisonous hate.

Shiara clenched her fists on the chair arms so hard her knuckles turned white and levered herself erect. "Go to your room and remain there," she commanded. "We will decide what is to be done with you tomorrow."

"I'm getting damned tired of being ordered around," Wiz said.

"Your feelings and the state of your soul are of very little concern to me right now," Shiara said. "Now go. Or must Ugo escort you?"

"Look I'm sorry . . ."

"That too is of no concern to me. Ugo!"

"Okay, okay," Wiz backed off hastily as the wood goblin came toward him with fire in his eyes. "I'm going." He spun and started for the stairs.

*"What was that?"* The voice of Toth-Set-Ra boomed out in the head of the new master of the Sea of Scrying.

"I do not know, Dread Master. Something to the North . . ."

"Imbecile! I know that already." Toth-Set-Ra's mental "voice" settled back into normal tones.

"It appears to come from a quiet zone in the Wild Wood."

There was a thoughtful pause. "Yessss. I know of the place. Send word that it is to be investigated. I want to know what caused that."

Toth-Set Ra turned back to the grimore he had been perusing. His hand caressed the elaborately illuminated parchment made from human skin but his eyes would not focus on the glowing runes that squirmed wormlike across the page. *The end to you and all yours* the demon's voice echoed tinnily, mockingly, in his ears. *A bane, a curse a plague upon the race of wizards. Magic beyond magics.*

He slammed the book shut and stalked out of his chamber. "Send Atros to me by the Sea of Scrying" he flung over his shoulder to the goblin guards.

The watchers around the rim of the great copper bowl bowed low as he swept into the vaulted stone chamber and fell back respectfully as he approached the edge. Toth-Set-Ra ignored them and stared deep into the sea.

The waters within were stained the color of weak tea by the blood of virgin sacrifices but the map graved on the bottom was easy to read. Glowing gems marked the cities of the World. A blood-red ruby, pulsing fitfully with inner light, represented the City of Night on the southern shore of the Freshened Sea. To the north and inland was the blazing blue sapphire which represented the headquarters of the Council. Here and there other gems winked green or blue or red or orange, their depth of hue marking the strength of the magics to be found there.

The effect was breathtaking, like a handful of gemstones strewn carelessly across the bottom of a rocky pool. But Toth-Set-Ra paid no heed. His trained senses searched for bright spots not marked with precious stones. Those were places of new or unexpected magic.

There, well within the line setting the Wild Wood off from the Fringe was a glowing white pustule on the reddish copper surface. It was fading, the wizard saw as he bent his full attention to the spot, but it had been strong. Very strong and uncontrolled while it lasted. In the center of one of the quietest places in the Wild Wood, too.

He scowled again and reached out, weighing and savoring the magic that marked this place. It was powerful, that he knew almost without bothering to look. He sensed the disturbance in the weather, but he could see no purpose in it. There had been a mighty wind, but nothing seemed to have been accomplished.

His scowl deepened. Strange. Great spells were almost always supposed to accomplish great purposes. The spell itself was strange as well. It was as if a mass of minor spells had suddenly worked in the same direction.

Toth-Set-Ra was reminded of a marching column of army ants. Individually insignificant, they assumed enormous power because they all moved together. He savored the image and decided he didn't like it at all.

Behind the wizard, the door opened and Atros entered quietly. He spoke no word and Toth-Set-Ra paid him no heed. Heart's Ease. Yes. That was the place. Heart's Ease.

Then Toth-Set-Ra's fist smashed to the rim of the bowl, making the waters within quiver and the magical indications dissolve. He whirled to face his lieutenant. "Storm that place," he commanded, his brows dark and knit. "Bring me the magician responsible for that magic."

"Dread Master . . ." Atros began.

"Do it!" Toth-Set-Ra commanded. "Do not argue, do not scruple the cost. Do it!"

The big dark man bowed. "Thy will, Lord."

"Alive, Atros. I want that magician alive."

"Thy will, Lord."

Toth-Set-Ra turned back to the Sea of Scrying, searching it with his eyes, trying to pry more meaning from it. Atros bowed again and backed from the room, considering the ways and means of accomplishing the task.

A purely magical strike was clearly impossible. The Quiet Zone lay well beyond the barriers set up by the Northerners. Magical assault would be detected immediately and countered quickly. If he was willing to spend his strength recklessly he could undoubtedly penetrate the Northern defenses, but he might not have time to find and seize the magician before the counterassault.

*Fortunately,* thought the big wizard, *I have minions*

*in place.* The old crow thought always of magic, but there are other ways to accomplish things. This time magic would be the mask, the shield, the cloak flourished in the opponent's face. The dagger behind the cloak would use no magic at all.

Even as he strode down the corridor, he began issuing orders into a bit of crystal set in his cloak clasp. Before he had reached the end of the hall those orders were being carried out.

As Wiz was making his sullen way up the stairs at heart's Ease, the City of Night erupted into a hive of activity. Lines of slave porters toiled down the gloomy narrow streets, bent under the burden of provisions and weapons. Apprentices, wizards and artisans all jostled each other and the slaves as they rushed to carry out Toth-Set-Ra's commands.

In the bay, ships were hurriedly rigged and loaded. In the mountain caves where the dragons and flying beasts were kept, animals were groomed, harnesses checked and packs were loaded.

Within minutes of Toth-Set-Ra's order, the first flights of dragons were away from their cave aeries high on the mountain that loomed over the City of Night. They issued from their caverns like flights of huge, misshapen black bats. Their great dark wings beat the air as they climbed for altitude and sorted themselves into squadrons under the direction of their riders.

In a tower overlooking the bay, the busiest men of all were the black-robed master magicians who would coordinate the attack and make the magical thrusts. Down in the great chantry beneath the tower, brown-robed acolytes and gray-robed apprentices turned from their magical work and set to preparing the spells the black robes commanded. Astrologers updated and recast horoscopes to find the most propitious influences for the League and those which would be most detrimental to the Council.

Further below, in the reeking pits where the slaves were stabled, slavemasters moved among their charges, selecting this one and that to be dragged out struggling and screaming. Whatever the spells, they would require sacrifices.

Far to the North, a spark appeared in a crystal.

"Lord, we are getting something," the Watcher called out as the pinpoint of light caught his attention.

The Watch Master hurried to his side. "Can you make it out yet?"

The Watcher, a lean blonde young man stared deep into his scrying stone. "No Lord, there is too much background, or . . . Wait a minute! I think we're being jammed."

"A single source?" The Watch Master bent over to peer into the crystal.

The Watcher frowned. "No Lord, it is spread too wide." The Watch Master straightened up with a jerk.

"Sound the alarm. Quickly!"

On a cliff overlooking the Freshened Sea, the Captain of the Shadow Warriors reviewed his troops' dispositions and permitted himself a tiny smile of satisfaction.

For months he and his men had camped undetected on the enemy's doorstep. They used no magic in camp, save for the communications crystal the commander wore about his neck. Even their great flying beasts were controlled, cared for and fed without magic. Instead their magicians had spent their time listening intently to the world-murmurs of magic from the Northerners.

For months the men had subsisted mostly on cold food. Cooking was limited so the smoke might not betray them. In twos and threes they had penetrated miles inland, observing and sometimes reporting back to their masters in the City of Night.

Thinking on that, the Captain frowned. This was not

supposed to be an assault mission. But now his patrols had been hastily consolidated into a strike force and ordered to penetrate a Quiet Zone to assault a castle and capture the magicians laired there.

The message he received was as short as it could be so the Watchers of the North would not intercept it. *Burn the keep called Heart's Ease and bring the magicians there alive and unharmed to the City of Night.* That was all, but for his well-trained band that was enough.

He had no doubt his men could do it. The castle defenses were minimal and although his men did not normally use magic, they had it at their call.

In the forest clearing three flying beasts waited. Their gray wrinkled skin bore neither hair nor scales. Their long necks and huge blunt heads thrust aloft as their great nostrils quivered in the wind. The huge bat-like wings were unfurled to their full 300-foot span and the animals moved them gently up and down at the command of their mahouts. Unlike dragons, these creatures were cold-blooded. They must warm themselves up before they could fly. Even from this distance the captain could smell the carrion stench of the animals.

Ritually, the Captain checked his weapons. The long, single-edged slashing sword was over his back with the scabbard muffled with oiled leather at the mouth. His dagger and axe hung at his waist. The contents of the pouches and pockets scattered about his harness: poisons, powders of blindness, flash powders and pots of burning. A blowgun lay alongside his sword and the needles were sheathed in their special pouch. Everything was muffled and dull. There was nothing on him or his men to shine, clink or clatter and almost nothing of magic.

Their enemies might see the Shadow Warriors but even the Mightiest of the Mighty would be hard-put to sniff them out by magic.

The Captain moved to his flying beast and an aide formed a stirrup so he could mount. Behind him the five Warriors of his troop had settled themselves onto the beast's broad back, their feet firmly placed in the harness.

The animal shifted slightly as the Captain settled in and opened its gaping mouth to honk complaint. But without a sound. Its vocal cords had been cut long ago so it might not betray itself in the presence of the enemy.

The Captain looked over his shoulders. Three other beasts were visible with their warriors aboard and their mahouts holding the reins without slack. To the side one of his sergeants signaled that the beasts out of his sight were also ready. The Captain nodded and raised his arm in signal.

In unison great leathery wings beat the air, raising flurries of dead leaves and dust as the animals clawed for purchase in the sky. Once, twice, three times the animals' mighty wings smote the air and then they were away, rocking unsteadily at first as each animal adjusted its balance, and then climbing swiftly into a sky only touched by the rising moon. From other clearings on the forested top beasts rose by twos and threes to soar into the clouds. As they climbed they sorted themselves out into four formations of threes. They might have appeared to be on a mass mating flight, save that not even these creatures mated so deep in winter.

The long, snake-like necks stretched forth and the animals squinted to protect their eyes from the searing cold.

The cold bit sharp and fierce at the Captain despite his gloves and the muffler-like veil wound around his face. He flexed his fingers to keep them supple and otherwise ignored it. Cold, hunger and hardship were always the lot of the Shadow Warriors and they were trained from childhood to bear them. Again he considered the plan and nodded to himself.

A glance behind him showed the Captain that the

other warriors on his beast were flat against the animal's back, partly to cut the air resistance and partly to stay out of the wind.

As the gaggle of flying beasts scudded through the sky, the Captain kept a close watch for landmarks. With the force under a strict ban on magic, he could not use more reliable methods. His trained senses told him there was little magic below or around him to conceal any use of magic by the Shadow Warriors.

Far below a lone, lost woodsman caught a glimpse of the horde as it hunted across the sky. With a whimper he thrust himself back into a bramble thicket and hid his eyes from the sight.

As the Shadow Warriors flew east the other parts of the operation fell into place.

The stone hall was boiling with activity. All along the line Watchers called out as new magic appeared in their crystals. Reserve Watchers rushed to their stations. Magicians whispered into communications crystals. Wizards took their stations, ready to repel magical attacks and to add their abilities to those of the Watchers. Finally, from their laboratories and lodgings, the Mighty began to arrive. The room filled with the nose-burning tang of ozone and shimmers of magical force.

Bal-Simba entered with Arianne at his side. He stood in the doorway for a moment, surveying the organized chaos, and then moved to the great chair on the platform overlooking the room.

On the wall opposite a map sprang into existence showing the Lands of the North and much of the Freshened Sea. Already there were six arrowheads of red fire approaching the Southern Coast. Six strikes coming in at widely spaced points, two of them obviously directed at the Capital. Here and there nebulous patches of gray and dirty green glowed on the map where the Sight would not reach.

Bal-Simba leaned forward in the chair to study the pattern of the attack.

"What do you make of it?" he asked his apprentice.

"If half of that is real," she said, gesturing to the colors on the map, "it is the biggest attack the League has ever mounted. Do you suppose that has something to do with the great disturbance in the Wild Wood this afternoon?"

"No, that was something else."

"This is powerful, but it seems—disorganized—as if it was hastily put together. Also, we have had no reports from the South to suggest an attack was being readied."

Bal-Simba waved her to silence. "Let us watch and see if we can find the underlying pattern."

Down in the pit three sweating magicians worked to keep the map updated. To the right of Bal-Simba's great chair on the platform five of the Mighty sat in a tight ring around a glowing brazier, mumbling spells. Now and then one or the other of them would throw something on the fire and the smoke and the reek would rise up to fill the chamber. Down in the earth and up in the towers, others of the Mighty worked alone, weaving and casting their own spells to aid the defense.

"Seventh group coming in," sang out one of the Watchers. "Airborne. Probably dragons."

Bal-Simba studied the configuration written in lambent script on the wall.

"Launch dragons to intercept. Tell them not to stray over the water."

"Dragons away, Lord."

"Time to intercept seventeen minutes," another talker reported. Others huddled over crystals keeping contact with the dragon force.

"Porpoises report three krakens moving toward the Hook. Formation suggests they are screening something else."

Around the room crystals glowed green, red and yellow as the talkers contacted the forces of the North and prepared for the struggle. From the most battle-ready guard troops to the hedge-witches in the villages the word went out. All the North braced to receive the assault.

But no one thought to tell the inhabitants of a small keep hidden away in the Wild Wood.

High above the Capital the Dragon Leader climbed for altitude. Reflexively he checked the great bow carried in a quiver by his steed's neck. The fight was unlikely to close to a range where arrows would do any good, but it gave him a sense of security to know they were there. Outside the freezing wind tore and whistled about him, but inside his magically generated cocoon a warming spell kept him comfortable. He would have to turn that off as he approached intercept to present minimal magical signature and to make his detectors more sensitive, he knew, and he hated that more than he feared dying.

Echeloned out below and behind him were the seven other dragons of his squadron. He spared them a glance as he checked his communications with the other dragon flights and with the Watchers back in the high hall of the keep.

His dragon's wings beat air as the beast clawed for height. With each stroke the Dragon Leader felt muscles pulse and jump beneath his thighs. With gentle leg pressure he turned his mount south, toward the Fresh-ened Sea and the swiftly moving misty patch on the magic detectors that might indicate an air attack coming in. Reflexively his head swiveled, seeking any sign of his foes.

The moon was bright and just beginning to wane. The silvery light picked out the surface of the clouds, creating a wonderland of tops and towers, nubbly fields and high streaming pennons beneath him. Here and there the contorted fields of clouds were marked by pools of inky black where an opening let the light stream through to the ground below.

The Dragon Leader took it all in as he scanned the surface. He was less interested in the beauty than in what the clouds might conceal. As the first group off, his troop had drawn high cover—flying above the clouds to seek out the League's agents. Other troops were at work beneath the clouds while the clouds themselves were searched magically. Somewhere ahead of him was the enemy—or what appeared to be the enemy, he corrected himself. It was not unknown for the League to enhance a bat or a raven to make it look like a ridden dragon. The Dragon Leader bit his lips and kept scanning the cloud tops.

"Time to intercept twelve minutes," a voice said soundlessly inside his skull. He did not reply.

One of his men waved and pointed below. There silhouetted against the pale cloudtops, were four dragons skulking north. The Dragon Leader did not need to call the Capital to know they were not in the Council's service.

He rose in his stirrups and looked behind him. The rest of his troop had seen the enemy too and were waiting expectantly for his signal.

The Dragon Leader switched off his warming spell, gestured down at the other dragons and patted the top of his head in the time-honored signal to dive on the enemy. A gentle nudge with the knees, a slight pressure on the reins and his mount winged over to dive on the invading force.

The Dragon Leader was well into his dive when the four dragons below him winged over and scattered into the clouds. The leader swore under his breath and signalled his squadron to break off the attack. *We'll never find them in that*, he thought. *Sharp eyes in that patrol. It was almost as if they had been warned.*

*As if they had been warned . . . !*

"Break! Break!" he screamed into his communications crystal. But it was already too late. The hurtling shapes plummeting down from the moon-haze were upon them and two of his dragons had already fallen to the ambush.

Abstractedly, the Dragon Leader realized he had been suckered. A flight of enemy dragons had snuck in earlier, perhaps laying silent and magicless on the ground until it was time to climb high above the chosen ambush site. Then they had waited until the flight committed to the attack on the decoys. Another part of his mind told him that if they succeeded in eliminating the top cover the lower squadrons would be horribly vulnerable to dragons diving out of the clouds.

But that was all abstract. The reality was the twisting, plunging battle all about him. In the distance he saw the flare of dragon fire. Another circle and he saw a ball of guttering flame dropping into the clouds. A dragon and probably a rider gone. He could not tell whose.

The Dragon Leader leaned forward against the neck of his mount and pressed his body close to cut air resistance. His dragon was diving with wings folded for maximum velocity. Now it was a simple speed contest. If he could plummet fast enough he had a chance of reaching the dubious safety of the clouds. If not, man and beast would be incinerated in a blast of dragon fire or dashed to pieces on the cold earth below.

The clouds reached out for him, first in wisps and tendrils and then as a solid, gray mass. He was in them now and hidden from sight. Magic could find him, but unless the searcher was a wizard, he would need to scan the clouds actively. He doubted his enemies would try. Dragon riders had a saying: "he who lights up first gets smoked." The Dragon Leader had no intention of using active magic.

*Enough hiding,* he thought, and turned his mount in a wide, climbing arc. His attackers had not followed him into the cloud, which meant they had probably gone hunting other prey. Even if they had not, they would be loitering on the cloud tops, without speed or height advantage. Fine with him. The Dragon Leader had lost his wingman in the first stoop and he was spoiling for a fight.

His mount was tiring, but the Dragon Leader urged her up out of the clouds, trying for enough altitude to rejoin the battle.

His magic detector screamed in his ear and he jerked under the impact of the seraching spell. Too late he saw his mistake. The enemy dragon had been laying for him, not down on the clouds but well above with no magic showing. Now he was trapped. The other was too close and had too much maneuvering ability to lose in the clouds again and there was no time to turn into the attack.

In desperation the Dragon Leader threw his mount into a tight spiral dive and clawed his bow and a heavy iron arrow free from his quiver. Over his shoulder he could see his opponent hurtling down on him, with speed, altitude and position all on his side.

At the last instant he kneed his mount and jerked the reins hard over and down. The dragon dropped her inside wing and dived even more steeply. A brilliant burst of dragon-fire destroyed his night vision and bathed his face with heat. Then his first opponent hurtled past, so close they could almost have touched, and was lost in the pearly clouds.

His opponent's wing man had more time to react. He had slowed his dragon, great wings beating mightily to brake his dive and he had used the time to line up. Worse, the Dragon Leader was in the process of recovering from the sideslip and could not maneuver.

But shooting dragon fire is not an easy matter and the wing man was not as skilled as his leader. The blast of blinding, scorching heat only touched the Dragon Leader and his mount. He smelled burned hair and knew it was his. His dragon bucked and roared in pain, but both of them were still in the air. Meanwhile the wing man was diving past, still trying to slow and turn on his opponent.

It was a fatal combination. The Dragon Leader loosed a shaft as the enemy swept by. It was nearly a right-angle deflection shot and the mechanics worked against him as much as they did against the enemy. But he felt a tingle in his hands as the arrow leapt from the bow and he knew the arrow had seen its target.

The shaft sensed the enemy dragon and adjusted its trajectory accordingly. The tiny crystal eyes on either side of the broad barbed head both acquired the dragon and guided the arrow unerringly. The range was so close that the wing man's magic detector barely had time to begin to sound and he had no time at all to maneuver out of the way.

The shaft struck deep into the dragon's neck with force that drove it through scales and muscle until it struck bone. The beast arched its neck back and screamed in mortal agony while its rider clung desperately and despairingly to its back. Then the arrow's spell took hold and the dragon went limp.

Below him the Dragon Leader saw the shape of the other dragon twisting dark against the gray-white clouds. As it disappeared into the cloud bank there was a faint pinkish glow marking the dragon's last feeble gout of flame.

The Dragon Leader craned his neck, swiveling and searching for others in the night sky. There were none and no sign of battle anywhere. The moonlit cloud field was as quiet and serene as if nothing had happened here.

But it had happened, the Dragon Leader knew. His own scorched skin told him that. Soon there would be pain as the nerves started to complain of destroyed tissue. Now it was merely heat. The wheezy breathing and weary movements of his mount's great wings told him she too had suffered from the other dragon's fire. And worst, there would be at least three empty roosts back at the aerie tonight. That hurt more than the burns ever would.

"There will be other days," the Dragon Leader promised through cracked and blistered lips as he looked to the south. "There will be other days."

It was late and the fire in Wiz's chamber had long since burned to cold, gray ash. He sat by the fireside, now lit only by the silver moonlight pouring in through the window, watching cloud shadows make patterns on the pier glass.

*Damn fools,* he thought for the tenth time. *Can't they see how valuable all this is. All right, so I made a mistake. But don't they see its worth?*

"We've had this conversation before," the mirror told him.

"But they're wrong," Wiz said. "Damn it, they are wrong and I'm right. I know it."

All evening he had alternated between anger, chagrin and self-pity. Each cycle was less satisfying than the one before and by now he was just going through the motions.

"That's not really the issue, is it?" the mirror spoke quietly in Wiz's mind. "If it was you wouldn't be telling me all this again, would you?"

"Can't they see . . . ?"

"Can you? What is really eating at you?"

"They were wrong!" Wiz protested tiredly. They were wrong and he was right and that was all there was to it.

"Is it?" the mirror asked. "Is that all there is to it?"

Wiz didn't answer. Magic or no, the damn mirror was right. There was more than that.

He had been convinced he was right and he had done what he always did when he believed that: he went ahead without worrying about what others thought.

"And this time?" the mirror prompted him.

*This time others had been involved,* he realized. There was no way they could not be.

Working magic wasn't like sneaking some extra time on the computer to try a new hack. If this barfed, the results were a lot worse than crashing the system. It wasn't just his life he was messing with, but theirs as well, and not surprisingly they resented it bitterly.

"Well, wouldn't you?" the mirror asked. "Do you like having people mess with your life?"

"All right," Wiz said tiredly. "You're right. I was right too, but I was wrong in the way I went about it. I should have tried to work with them rather than ignoring them. Maybe I should have convinced them, won them over, before proceeding. But dammit! They didn't have to make such a big deal of it."

"But you promised," the mirror said soundlessly.

That stopped him. To these people promises were something important. You kept your promises here because they had a force more binding than contracts on his home world.

People were so much more *sincere,* so much more *real* here. Surrounded by magic and the stuff of fantasy the people were more intensely human than the people he had known at home.

Or was it just that he cared more about them? He did, he realized. Not just Moira, but Shiara and Ugo, too. Even the tiny unseen folk of the forest.

He'd hurt them by betraying their trust and that, in turn, had hurt him. He was unhappy here so he'd tried to do what he always did—take refuge in technical things, to bury himself in not-people. Only this time it had only involved him more closely with the people around him.

Slowly, slowly, William Irving Zumwalt began to think about what it meant to consider other people's feelings.

Perhaps he was right about the magic language. But that didn't make what he had done right. Magic wasn't a computer system where he had the expertise to follow up his idea.

What was it one of his professors used to say? *Always use the right tool for the job. The right tool to repair a television set is a television repairman.* The right tool for this job was a wizard. He should have talked to Bal-Simba or one of the other Mighty and let them follow through. But he had wanted to be somebody here so he had charged ahead like some damn user with a bright idea. And very predictably he had screwed things up and caused a lot of people trouble.

*Let's face it. I'm not a magician and I never will be. I can't be anything special here. I'm just me and I have to live with that and make the best of it.*

Bal-Simba had said that too. The black giant was wise in ways more than magic.

*So no more magic,* Wiz resolved firmly. *I'll explain my idea and that will be the end of it. Then I'll chop the wood and learn to live as best I can. Perhaps some day they'll forgive me for what I did. In the meantime. . . .*

He grinned. *In the meantime I accept being a sparrow and quit trying to be an eagle.*

He looked at the mirror. But all he saw was the dim reflection of a moonlit window and he heard nothing at all.

Wiz rose from his chair, drained, exhausted and his knees aching from sitting in one place too long. *Time for bed,* he thought. *Way past time. You've got a life to build tomorrow.*

There was a "whoosh" overhead followed by several bumps on the roof.

*A confused bat?* He hesitated, then picked his cloak off the chair and went into the hall. It was doubtful anyone else had heard and he wanted to see what the noise was.

His shoes padded lightly on the stone corridor. All the castle was deathly still. He heard no more thumps. At

the end of the corridor was a short flight of stone steps
to the roof door. Wiz put his foot on the first step up.

The door burst inward with a crash and black-clad
warriors poured down on him. Too stunned to shout, Wiz
flinched back from the black apparitions.

He found himself staring into merciless dark eyes and
felt the prick of a dagger at his throat. He was forced back
roughly against the wall and held as the rest of the
storming party rushed by, but otherwise he was unharmed.

The Shadow Warriors' orders were explicit: seize the
magicians and burn the castle. Whether the other
inhabitants lived or died was not in their orders and was
thus of little concern to them. Wiz was subdued and
silent, so he lived.

The Shadow Captain spared a long searching glance
for the prisoner as he went by. The man so expertly
pinned against the wall was peculiar, but he was clearly
not a magician. There was neither trace nor taint of
magic about him.

It never occurred to the Shadow Captain that someone
might be working magic second hand or that there was
no more reason to expect a magic sign on such a one
than to expect machine oil on the clothes of a programmer who wrote control software for industrial robots.
The notion was so utterly alien that Toth-Set-Ra himself
had not considered it. The captain's orders covered only
magicians.

Swiftly and silently, the assault force padded down the
stairs. In teams of two and three, warriors checked every
room on every level, but the vanguard never slowed. Wiz
was dragged along by a knot of Shadow Warriors to the
rear of the party.

They were down on the second level when they met
their first opposition. It was Ugo, coming up the stairs
with a tray balanced on one hand and a branch of candles
in a candelabra in the other.

The Shadow Warriors flattened against the wall as the

flickering light preceded the wood goblin onto the landing. When he reached the top of the stairs the warriors closed in.

Unlike the human, Ugo did not freeze when the black shapes came out at him out of the shadows. With a roar he threw the tray at the closest men and rushed the others brandishing the heavy brass candelabra. He made three steps before a blade lashed out. The wood goblin gasped, staggered and took two more steps toward the Shadow Warriors. This time three blades licked evilly in the candlelight and Ugo shuddered and fell. The candles flickered out on the cold stone floor.

The door on the landing flew open and Shiara and Moira appeared, outlined by the hearth fire in the room behind them.

"Ugo. What . . . ?" Moira gasped at the sight of armed men in the hall and tried to slam the door, but the warriors bounded forward, pushing the women back into the room.

Instinctively Wiz tried to break free of the warriors holding him.

"Wiz!" Moira screamed as she saw a knife flash high and then descend at his back, but the warrior had flipped the blade so he struck only with the heavy pommel. Wiz collapsed instantly, held up only by the warriors.

The captain's gaze flicked about the room. The one on the floor was not a magician. He knew of the white-haired one and confirmed that she was not practicing magic. That left the shorter red-haired woman and she was definitely a magician. He gestured and his men closed in on her.

If it had been in the shadow Captain's nature to question orders he might well have questioned this one. However Shadow Warriors exist to obey, not question.

"Sparrow? Wiz?" Shiara asked plaintively. "Moira what have they done to Sparrow?"

But Moira did not answer. Three warriors closed in

on her and Moira screamed and struggled in their grasp. Wiz lay like a sack on the floor and Shiara stood helpless, groping about her. Then one of the warriors broke a seed pod under Moira's nose. She inhaled the dark, flour-like dust and sagged unconscious.

At a gesture from their leader, the Shadow Warriors turned and filed out of the room. Two of them carried Moira and two more stood in the door menacing the unconscious man and the blind woman lest they should try to follow. Then they too turned and ran fleetly down the stairs.

As they passed through the great hall, the last of the Shadow Warriors tossed small earthen pots in behind them. The pots shattered against the walls and floor and burst into searing, blazing flame that clung and clawed its way up the wooden beams.

The wood was dry and well-seasoned. The flames ran across the painted rafters and leaped into the shingles. The hangings caught and flared up as well.

"Lord, they're pulling back!" the Watcher sang out. Bal-Simba scowled and shifted on his high seat. To his left the magicians continued their mumbling and gestures.

The runes of fire on the wall told the tale. The League forces were veering off, turning away to the south. Here and there the skirmishes continued as forces too closely engaged to break off fought it out. A few Northerners pursued, but cautiously, aware that every league to the south strengthened their opponents' magics and weakened their own.

Even the clouding magic was ebbing away.

"What damage?" Bal-Simba asked. Down in the pit a talker passed her hands over her crystal again and her lips moved silently.

"Three villages burned, Lord. Alton, Marshmere and Willow-by-the-Sea. A hard fight at Wildflower Meadows where a band of trolls gained the wall and torched some houses. There are others but I cannot see clearly yet. And the battle casualties, of course." She shrugged. The last were not her concern.

Bal-Simba frowned. "Little. Surprisingly little for such an effort."

Arianne looked up tiredly. "We were too strong for them," she said.

"Or they did not push too strongly," the High Lord said half to himself. He turned quickly to his talker. "Get reports from all the land. I want to know what else has happened."

"Isn't this enough Lord?" asked Arianne.

"No," Bal-Simba told his apprentice grimly. "It is not nearly enough. I would learn the rest of the price we paid this night."

"Sparrow? Sparrow." Dimly and faintly Wiz heard Moira's voice calling from a great distance. He stirred, but his head hurt terribly and he just wanted to sleep.

"Sparrow, wake up, please." Moira's voice? No. Shiara's. He was laying on the floor and there was smoke in the air. He pushed himself to his hands and knees. His head spun from the effort.

Shiara helped him stand. "Quickly," she said. "We must leave."

"Moira?" Wiz asked weakly.

"Outside! Hurry."

"I won't leave Moira."

"She's not here. Now outside." Wiz clasped her hand in his and started for the door.

As he led the way down the stairs he stumbled on a small limp form in front of the stairway.

"It's Ugo," he said, bending down. He gasped as he saw the horrible gaping wound that nearly severed the goblin's head from his shoulders.

Shiara knelt and moved between him and the body. She gently cradled it in her arms and the ends of her long silver hair turned dark and sodden where they touched the goblin's breast.

"Oh Ugo, Ugo," she crooned. "I brought you so far and for so little." By the flickering orange light Wiz could see the tears streak her face.

"He's dead, Lady." A fierce, hot gust brought choking gray strawsmoke and the pungent odor of burning pine up the stairwell. "Come, Lady," Wiz tugged at her sleeve. "Come on. We've got to get out of here."

Shiara raised her head. "Yes," she said. "Yes we must." She picked up Ugo's body, supporting the nearly severed head with one hand, cradling him as if he were a baby. For the first time Wiz realized how small the goblin had been.

With Wiz leading, they groped down the stairs, gasping in the heat and blinking from the thick smoke. Wiz guided Shiara through the blazing Great Hall, past the overturned furniture and patches where the floor burned fiercely. As they skirted along one wall, they passed the window seat. Wiz saw that the chair he had moved so long ago lay on its side roughly where he had dragged it.

They picked their way over the shattered remains of the door and out into the courtyard. The cold night air was like balm on their faces and they sucked great, gasping lungfuls, coughing and hacking up dark mucus that reeked of smoke.

Behind them the flames consumed Heart's Ease and shot high into the sky, grasping for the pitiless stars.

# *Eleven*
## HACKING BACK

Heart's Ease burned the whole night through. Far into the bleak winter morning sudden tongues of flame leapt from the ruins as the rubble shifted and the embers found fresh fuel. The walls stood, black and grim, but a little before dawn the roof crashed in, carrying with it what was left of the floors. There was nothing to do but stand aside and watch the flames. There was no help for Heart's Ease.

Shiara buried Ugo, refusing Wiz's offer of aid. Wiz didn't press. He sat alone, wrapped in Shiara's smoke-stained blue velvet cloak, utterly filled with pain and misery. Not even the chill of the stone beneath him penetrated.

It was mid-morning when Bal-Simba arrived. He came upon the Wizard's Way, accompanied by a party of armed and armored guardsmen who quickly spread out to search for any of the League's servants who might remain. The wizard closeted himself with Shiara for the rest of the day.

Wiz barely noticed. About noon he got up from his rock and returned to the tiny stable workroom in the clearing outside the palisade. It was almost evening when Bal-Simba found him there.

"You will be leaving Heart's Ease," he told Wiz gently.

"There is nothing left worth staying for. The Lady Shiara has agreed to accept accommodation closer to the Capital and you will live in the Wizard's Keep itself. There is no longer any point in trying to hide you, it seems."

Wiz just nodded mutely.

"Shiara has told me what happened yesterday," he went on. "I hope you learned from it." He paused. "I am sorry the lesson had to be taught at such great cost," he said more gently.

Wiz said nothing. There was nothing to say. Bal-Simba waited, as if expecting some reply.

"What about Moira?" Wiz asked at last.

"Most likely she was stolen away for questioning in the City of Night. The raid here was masked by a whole series of attacks all along our southern perimeter. It seems the League has a powerful interest in your kind of magic so I would expect she will be taken to their citadel for interrogation."

"Shiara said it was me they were after," Wiz said miserably.

"Most likely. The League has been tearing the North apart seeking knowledge of you ever since you were Summoned. When your actions drew their attention here they came looking for a magician and Moira was the only one they could find."

"What will they do with Moira?"

Bal-Simba hesitated. "For now, nothing. The Shadow Warriors are fierce and cruel, but they are disciplined. Doubtless their orders are to bring her alive and unhurt to their master."

"And then?"

Bal-Simba looked grave and sad. "Then they will find out what they wish to know. You do not want the details."

"We've got to get her back!"

"We are searching," Bal-Simba said. "The Watchers have been scouring the plenum for trace of her. Our dragon riders patrol as far south as they dare. We have sent word to all the villages of the North and searchers have gone out."

"Can they find her?"

Bal-Simba hesitated. "I will not lie to you, Sparrow. It will be difficult. The Shadow Warriors use little magic and they are masters of stealth. We are doing everything we can."

"But you don't think they'll find her." It was a statement not a question.

"I said it would be difficult," Bal-Simba sighed. "The Shadow Warriors may already be upon the Freshened Sea, or even back in the City of Night itself. If that is so, she is lost. We only know they did not transport her magically."

"We'll have to go get her! We can't let them have her."

Bal-Simba sighed again and for the first time since Wiz had known him he appeared mortal—tired and defeated.

"I'm sorry Sparrow. Even if she is already upon the sea there is nothing we can do."

Rage rose up in Wiz, burning away the guilt and grief. "Maybe there's nothing you can do, but there's something *I* can do."

"What is that?"

Wiz interlaced his fingers and cracked his knuckles. "I'm gonna hack the system," he said smiling in a manner that was not at all pleasant.

"Eh?"

"Those sons-of-bitches want magic? All right. I'll *give* them magic. I'll give them magic like they've never seen before!"

"It is a little late to start your apprenticeship, Sparrow," Bal-Simba said gravely.

"Apprenticeship be damned!" Said Wiz, taking slight satisfaction at the way the wizard started at the blasphemy. "I've spent the last five months building tools. I've got an interpreter, an editor, a cross-reference generator and even a syntax checker. They're kludgier than shit, but I can make them do what I need. The didn't call me Wiz for nothing!"

"Remember what happened the last time you tried."

Wiz's face twisted. "You think I'm likely to forget?" He shook his head. "No, I know now what I did wrong. I knew it then, really. The next time I call up a hurricane it will be on purpose."

"Will you then compound your folly?" Bal-Simba asked sternly. "Will you add fresh scars to the land just to satisfy your anger?"

"Will you get Moira back any other way?" Wiz countered.

The Wizard was silent and Wiz turned back to the wooden tablets scattered over the rude table.

"Hurting us further would be an ill way to repay our hospitality to you," Bal-Simba said.

Wiz whirled to face him. "Look," he snapped. "So far your 'hospitality' has consisted of kidnapping me, making me fall in love with someone who hates me, getting me chased by more damn monsters than I ever imagined and nearly getting me killed I don't know how many times. When you get right down to it I don't see that I owe you much of anything."

He glared at Bal-Simba, challenging him to deny it. But the giant black Wizard said nothing.

"There's another thing," he went on. "You're so damn worried about the effects of magic on your world. Well, your world is dying! Every year you're pushed further back. It's not just the League. There's Wild Wood too. How long do you think you have before the whole North is gone? Do you really have anything to lose?

"All right, maybe I'll screw it up again." He blinked back the tears that were welling up in his eyes. "I've done nothing but screw things up since I got here. Maybe I'll make that scar on the land you keep talking about. But Dammit! At least I'll go out trying."

"There's no maybe about it," Bal-Simba said sharply. "You will 'screw it up.' You have no magical aptitude and no training. At best you can destroy uncontrolled."

"Patrius didn't think so," Wiz shot back. He turned to his tablets again.

"I could forbid you," Bal-Simba said in a measuring tone.

"You could," Wiz said neutrally. "But you'd have to enforce it."

Bal-Simba looked at him and Wiz stayed hunched over the tablets.

"I will do this much," he said finally. "I will not forbid you. I will not commit the resources of the North to this madness but I will send word to watch and be ready. If by some chance you do discomfit the League, we will make what use of it seems appropriate."

Wiz didn't turn around. "Okay. Thanks."

"I will arrange for some protection for you in case the Shadow Warriors return. I will also pass word for everyone to avoid this place. I think you will scar the land and kill yourself unpleasantly in the process."

"Probably."

Bal-Simba sighed. "Losing a loved one is a terrible thing."

Wiz grinned mirthlessly, not looking up. "Even that wasn't a free choice."

"Love is always a free choice, Sparrow. Even where there's magic."

Wiz shrugged and Bal-Simba strode to the door of the hut. The black giant paused with his hand on the doorjamb.

"You've changed, Sparrow,"

"Yeah. Well, that happens."

Wiz did not see Bal-Simba leave. He stayed in the hut most of the day, scrawling on wooden tablets with bits of charcoal. Twice he had to go out to split logs into shingles for more tablets.

The second time he went to the woodpile Shiara approached him.

"They tell me you will make magic against the League," Shiara said.

Wiz selected a length of log and stood it upright on the chopping stump. "Yep."

"It is lunacy. You will only bring your ruin."

Wiz said nothing. He raised the axe and brought it down hard. The log cleaved smoothly under the blade's bite.

"Where will you work?"

Wiz rested the axe and turned to her. "Here, Lady. I figure it's safe enough and it seems appropriate."

"You will need help."

He hefted the axe and turned to the billet. "I can manage alone."

He raised the axe above his head and Shiara spoke again. "Would it go better if I were here for—ah—a core dump?"

Wiz started, the axe wobbled and the log went flying. "You'd do that? After what happened?"

"I would."

"Why? I mean, uh . . ."

"Why? Simple. You mean to strike at the League for what they did here when even Bal-Simba himself tells us we can do nothing. I owe the League much, and I would hazard much to repay a small part of that debt."

"It will be dangerous, Lady. Most of what you said about this thing is true. It's a kludge and it's full of bugs. I could kill us both."

For the first time since Wiz had known her, Shiara the Silver laughed. Not a smile or a chuckle, but a rich full-throated laugh, as bright and shining as her name.

"My innocent, I died a long time ago. My life passed with my magic, my sight and Cormac. The chance of dying against the chance of striking at the League is no hazard at all."

She glowed as bright and bold as the full moon on Mid-Sumemr Eve and held out her hand to Wiz. "Come Sparrow. We go to war."

Donal and Kenneth entered Bal-Simba's study quietly, respectfully and with not a little trepidation. It was not every day that the Mightiest of the North summoned two ordinary guardsmen and even Donal's naturally sanguine disposition didn't lead him to believe that the wizard wanted to discuss the weather.

"I have a service it would please me to have done," Bal-Simba rumbled.

"Command us, Lord," said Kenneth, mentally bracing for it.

"That I cannot do," Bal-Simba told them. "This service carries a risk I would not order assumed."

*Oh Fortuna, we're in for it now!* thought Kenneth. Out of the corner of his eye he saw that Donal looked unusually serious.

"May we ask the nature of this service?"

"There is a Sparrow whose nest needs guarding," Bal-Simba told them.

"Have you got any tea?" Wiz asked Shiara. They were sitting by the fire in the hut which had been the kitchen and was now their home. Both of them were hoarse from talking and Wiz was surrounded by a litter of wooden shingles with marks scrawled on them in charcoal.

"Herbs steeped in hot water? Are you ill?"

"No, I mean a drink that give you a lift, helps you stay awake."

Shiara's brow furrowed. "There is blackmoss tea. I used to use it when I was standing vigil. But it is vile stuff."

"Do you have any?"

"In the larder, if it was not burned," she told him.

The tea was in a round birchbark box which had been

scorched but not consumed. Wiz put a pot to boil on the hearth and watched as Shiara skillfully measured several spoonsful of the dried mixture into the hot water. The stuff looked like stable sweepings but he said nothing.

Shiara proffered the cup and Wiz took a gulp. It was brown as swamp water, so pungent it stung the nose and bitter enough to curl the tongue even with the honey Shiara had added.

"Gaaahhh" Wiz said, squinching his eyes tight shut and shaking his head.

"I told you it was vile," Shiara said sympathetically.

Wiz shook his head again, opened his eyes and exhaled a long breath. "Whooo! Now that's programmer fuel! Lady, if we could get this stuff back to my world, we'd make a fortune. Jolt Cola's for woosies!"

"That is what you wanted?" Shiara said in surprise.

"That's exactly what I wanted. Now let's let it steep some more and get back to work."

Bal-Simba's guardsmen showed up the next day. They were a matched set: Dark-haired, blue eyed and tough enough to bite the heads off nails for breakfast. Kenneth, the taller of the pair, carried a six-foot bow everywhere he went and Donal, the shorter, less morose one, was never far from his two-handed sword. In another world Wiz would have crossed the street to avoid either of them, but here they were very comforting to have around.

With their help Wiz moved his things out of the old stable and into one of the buildings in the compound. The accommodations were not much of an improvement, but it was closer to the huts where they now lived and Shiara could come to it more easily to advise him.

"What do you think of this Sparrow?" Donal asked Kenneth one night in the hut they shared. Kenneth looked up from the boot knife he was whetting. "I think he's going to get us all killed or worse."

"The Lady trusts him."

"The Lady, honor to her name, hasn't been right in the head since Cormac died," Kenneth said. "That's why she's been living out here. Even for a magician she's odd."

"Not half as odd as the sparrow," said Donal. "I don't think he's slept in three days. He sits in there swilling that foul brew and muttering to himself."

"He's a wizard," pronounced Kenneth as if that explained everything. "All wizards are cracked."

"They say he's not a wizard," said Donal. "They say he's something else."

"That's all the world needs," Kenneth said. "Something else that works magic. I say he's a wizard and I'll be damned surprised if we come out of this one whole."

"Well," said Donal as he stretched out on the straw tick. "At least he keeps things interesting."

"So does plague, pox and an infestation of trolls," said Kenneth, replacing the knife in his boot.

Toth-Set-Ra sat on his raised seat in the League's chantry and heard the reports of his underlings. The great mullioned windows let in the weak winter's light to puddle on the floor. Magical lanterns hung from the walls provided most of the light that glinted off apparatus on the workbenches. Seated at a long table at his feet were the dozen most powerful sorcerers of the Dark League. Atros sat at his right. The Keeper of the Sea of Scrying was just finishing his report.

"And what else?" asked Toth-Set-Ra.

"Lord, there are signs of magical activity at Heart's Ease. It is possible the Shadow Warriors missed the magician."

Atros scowled at the man. The Shadow Warriors were his special preserve.

"Our magic detectors are excellent," Toth-Set-Ra said. "If there was another magician there, we would have found him."

"As you will, Lord. But we still show signs of magic in what was once a dead zone."

"Strong magic? Like before?"

The black robe shrugged. "Not strong, Lord, but the taste is much like before. The magician is . . . odd."

A thrill went down Toth-Set-Ra's spine as he remembered the demon's words.

"Perhaps our magician had an apprentice who was absent when the attack came," Atros suggested.

"You say not as strong as before?" Toth-Set-Ra asked. The black-robed one nodded. "Then watch closely," he ordered. "I wish to know all which happens at that place."

"Thy will, Lord," the black robe replied. "But it will not be easy. The northerners are screening it and we cannot get clear readings."

"Keep trying," he snapped.

"Thy will, Lord. Perhaps however the Shadow Warriors should return."

Toth-Set-Ra shook his head. "No, that is a trick which only works once. Bal-Simba—may the fat melt from his miserable bones!—will not be caught napping again." He frowned and sunk his head to his chest for a moment. "But I am not without resources in this matter. I will see what my other servants can do."

Night and day, Wiz drove himself mercilessly. Writing, thinking, rewriting and conducting occasional experiments—usually in the forest with only Donal or Kenneth for company. He slept little and only when exhaustion forced him to. Twice he nearly slipped because of fatigue. After that he made a point of getting a little rest before trying an experiment.

The blackmoss tea numbed his tongue and made his bowels run, but it kept him awake, so he kept drinking it by the mugful.

Wiz wasn't the only one getting little or no sleep. Shiara wasn't sleeping much either and there was no blackmoss tea to ease her. Wiz passed her hut late at night and heard her sobbing softly from pain. The lines in her face etched themselves deep around her mouth and down her forehead, but she never complained.

"Lady, you are suffering from all this magic," Wiz said to her one afternoon as they waited for a spell to finish setting up.

"I have suffered for years, Sparrow."

"Do you need a rest?"

A haggard ghost of a smile flitted across her face. "Would *you* rest, Sparrow?"

"You know the answer to that, Lady."

"Well then," she said and returned to her work.

And the work seemed to go so slowly. Often Wiz would get well into a spell only to have to divert to build a new tool or modify the interpreter. It was like writing a C compiler from scratch, libraries and all, when all you wanted was an application. Once he had to stop work on the spells entirely for three precious days while he tore apart a goodly chunk of the interpreter and rewrote it from the ground up. He knew the result would be more efficient and faster, but he gritted his teeth and swore at the delay.

Wiz took to talking to the guards, one of whom was with him constantly when he worked. Neither Kenneth or Donal said much as he favored them with his stream of chatter. Donal just leaned on his two-handed sword and watched and Kenneth simply watched.

Worst of all, he had to be painstakingly careful in constructing his spells. A bug here wouldn't just crash a program, it could kill him.

There was no one to help him. Shiara had no aptitude for the sort of thinking programming demanded and there was no time to teach her. Besides, even being around this much magic was an agony for her. Actually trying to work some, even second-hand might kill her.

But somehow, slowly, agonizingly, the work got done.

✦          ✦          ✦

"Behold, my first project," Wiz said with a flourish. He had been without sleep so long he was giddy and the effects of the tea had his eyes propped open and his brain wired. Consciously he knew that he desperately needed sleep, but his body was reinforcing the tea with an adrenaline rush and it would be some time before he could make himself crash.

Shiara held out her hand toward the silky transparent thing on the table. It moved uneasily like a very fine handkerchief on a zephyr.

"What is it?"

"It's a detector. You can send it over an area and it will detect magic and report back what it, uh, senses. 'Sees' would be too strong a word. It doesn't really see, it just senses and it sends back a signal." He realized he was speed-rapping and shut up.

Shiara moved her fingers through the thing's substance, feeling for the magic. The detector continued to flutter undisturbed by the intrusion in to its body. "That is not much use," she said doubtfully. "It sees so little and can tell so little of what it sees." She drew her hand back sharply and the gesture reminded Wiz how much it cost her to have anything to do with magic.

"One of them is almost no good at all. But I'm going to produce them by the hundreds. I'll flood the Freshened Sea with them. I'll even send them over the League lands—who knows?—perhaps the City of Night itself."

Shiara frowned even more deeply. "How long did it take you to produce this 'detector'?"

"Separate from the tools? I don't know. Maybe three days."

"And you will make hundreds of them? In your spare time, perhaps. Impractical, Sparrow. Or do you plan to teach the craft to a corps of apprentices?"

"Oh, no. When I say three days, I mean the time it took me to write the program to make them. Once I run some tests and make sure it's up to spec, I'll start cranking them out automatically."

"You will not need to watch them made? Isn't that dangerous?"

Wiz shook his head. "Not if I do it right. That's the whole point of the interpreter, you see. It lets you spawn child processes and controls their output."

It was Shiara's turn to shake her head. "Magic without a magician. A true wonder, Sparrow."

"Yeah," said Wiz uncomfortably, "well, let's make sure it works."

Silent, dumb and near invisible as a smear of smoke, the thing floated above the Freshened Sea. Sunlight poured down upon it. Waves glittered and danced below. Occasionally birds and other flying creatures wheeled or dove above the tops of the waves within its view. Once a splash bloomed white as a sea creature leaped to snare a skimming seabird.

A human might have been entranced by the beauty, oppressed by the bleakness or bored to inattention by the unchanging panorama below. The wisp of near-nothingness was none of these things. It saw all and understood nothing. It soaked in the impressions and sent them to a bigger and more solid thing riding the air currents further north. That thing, a dirty brown blanket perhaps large enough for a child, flapped and quivered in the sea winds as it sucked up sense messages from the wisp and hundreds of its fellows. Mindlessly it concentrated them, sorted them by content and squirted them back to a crag overlooking the Freshened Sea where three gargoyles crouched, staring constantly south.

The gargoyles too soaked in the messages. But unlike the things lower in the hierarchy and further south, they understood what they saw. Or at least they were capable of interpreting the images, sounds and smells, sorting according to the criteria they had been given and acting on the results.

Most of what came their way, the sun on the waves, the fish-and-mud smell of the sea, the wheel of the seabirds, they simply discarded. Some, such as the splash and foam of a leaping predator, they stored for further correlation. A very few events they forwarded immediately to a glittering thing atop a ruined tower in a charred stockade deep in the Wild Wood.

Thus it was that a certain small fishing boat seemed bound to pass beneath the cloud of wisps which was gradually blanketing the Freshened Sea. But no net is perfect and no weave is perfectly fine. Scant hours before the last of the insubstantial detectors wafted into position in that area, the boat sailed placidly through the unseen gap in the unsensed net.

Her name was the *Tiger Moth*. Her sails and rigging were neat and well cared for but not new. Her hull was weathered but sturdy with lines of dark tar along the weatherbeaten planks where she had been caulked for the winter's work. In every way and to every appearance she was a typical small fisher, plying a risky trade on the stormy winter waters of the Freshened Sea. If you looked you could find perhaps a hundred such boats upon the length and breadth of the sea at this season.

On the deck of the *Tiger Moth*, the captain of the Shadow Warriors looked at the clouds and scowled. There was another storm in the offing and naturally it would come from the south, blowing the vessel and its precious cargo away from League waters and safety. One more delay in a long series of delays. The Shadow Captain swore to himself.

His orders were strict. Bring the captured magician back at all costs. Do not fly. Use no magic which might attract attention, not even the sort of simple weather spells a fisherman with a mite of magical ability could be reasonably expected to possess.

When the flying beasts brought the raiders back to
their seashore camp, he had bundled his captive aboard
the waiting boat and set out at once for the League's
citadel in the City of Night. The other raiders had rested
the day and then flown off on their great gray steeds
after sunset. They had been back at the City of Night
for days now, while the Shadow Captain and his crew
of disguised fishermen faced more days of sailing to reach
the same destination. It was much safer to sneak his prize
south like this at the pace of an arthritic snail, but it tried
even the legendary patience of a Shadow Warrior.

The sea was against them. That was to be expected
at this time of the year, when what winds there were
blew up from the south and the frequent storms came
from the south as well. It was not a time for swift travel
upon the Freshened Sea.

The Shadow Captain knew too that the Council was
searching strongly for him and his prisoner. Several
patrols of dragon riders had flapped overhead, gliding
down to mast-top height to check him and his boat. The
Shadow Captain had stood on the poop and waved to
them as any good Northerner would, never hinting that
what the dragon riders sought lay in a secret cubby in
the bow of his vessel.

For two days his ship had been trailed by an albatross
which floated lazily just off the wavetops as if searching
for fish in the *Tiger Moth's* wake. It had not escaped the
Shadow Captain's notice that the bird never came within
bowshot.

While the albatross was with them, the Shadow
Warriors had acted the part of fishermen, casting their
nets and pulling in a reasonable catch, which they gutted
and salted down on the deck. Thus they kept their cover,
but it slowed them even more.

*And now a storm,* the Shadow Captain thought,
*Fortuna!*

❖          ❖          ❖

The object quivered gossamer and insubstantial in the magic field which held it, fluttering weakly against the invisible walls.

"What is it?" Atros asked.

"We do not know, Lord," the apprentice told him. "One of our fliers found it in the air above the city."

"What does it do?"

"We do not know."

"Well, what do you know?" the magician snapped.

"Only that we have never seen its like before," the apprentice said hastily.

"Hmmm," Atros rubbed his chin. "Might it be neutral?"

The apprentice shrugged. "Quite possibly, Lord. Or perhaps the work of a hedge magician. No wizard would waste his substance making such a bagatelle."

The magician regarded the caged thing on the table again. He extended his senses and found only a slight magic—passive magic at that. "Very well. Return to your watch. Inform me if any more of these are found."

"Thy will, Lord. But they are very hard to find or see."

"Wretch! If I need instruction from apprentices I will ask for it. Now begone before I give you duty in the dung pits."

"What does this do?" Shiara asked, tracing the slick surface of Wiz's latest creation dubiously.

"It's a Rapid Reconnaissance Directional Demon—R-squared D-squared for short." He grinned.

"Eh?"

"It's an automatic searcher. It transports to a place, searches for objects which match the pattern it's been given and if it doesn't find such an object, it transports again. When it does find the object, it reports back. It has a tree-traversing algorithm to find the most efficient search pattern."

"I doubt you'll find what you want in a tree," Shiara said doubtfully.

"No, that's just an expression. It's a way of searching. You see, you pick a point as the root and . . ."

"Enough, Sparrow, enough," said Shiara holding up her hand. "I will trust you in this." She frowned. "But why did you make it in this shape?"

"To match its name," Wiz grinned.

"You see, Kenneth, names are very important," Wiz said seriously. "Picking the right ones is vital."

Wiz sucked another lungful of cold clear air and exhaled a breath that was almost visible. Overhead the sun shone wanly in a cloudless pale blue sky. The weak winter's light gave the unsullied snow a golden tinge.

"Yes, Lord," replied Kenneth noncomittally from where he lounged against a tree, his long bow beside him.

Wiz paid no heed to the response. He continued to pace the little clearing as he talked, not really looking at Kenneth at all. The crusted snow crunched under his boots as he circled the open space among the leafless trees yet again.

"The wizards are right," Wiz went on. "Names are critical. You need a name that you can remember, that you can pronounce easily and that you aren't likely to use in conversation." He smiled. "It wouldn't do to ask someone to pass the salt and summon up a demon, would it?"

"No, Lord," said Kenneth tonelessly

Wiz never stopped talking, even though Kenneth was behind him now. "And most importantly, Kenneth, most importantly I need names that easily distinguish the named routine, uh, demon. I can't afford to get mixed up."

"Yes, Lord."

"It's a common problem in programming. There's a trick to naming routines meaningfully without violating the conventions for the language or getting things confused." Wiz altered his stride slightly to avoid a spot where a dark rock had melted the snow into a dirty brown puddle. "Here I'm using a mixture of names of Unix utilities for routines that have cognates in Unix and made-up names for the entities that aren't similar to anything. So I have to pick the names carefully."

"Yes Lord." Kenneth shifted slightly against the tree and squinted at the pale sun, which was almost touching the treetops. Fingers of shadow were reaching into the clearing, throwing a tangled net of blue across the golden snow and dirty slush alike.

"It's especially important that I keep the difference in the similar routines straight," Wiz said. "I have to remember that **"find"** doesn't work like **"find"** in Unix. In Unix . . ."

"Lord . . ." said Kenneth craning his neck toward the lowering sun.

" . . . the way you search a file is completely different. You . . ."

"Lord, get . . ."

A harsh metallic screech stopped Wiz in his tracks. He looked over his shoulder and glimpsed something huge and spiky outlined against the sun.

"*Down!*" Wiz dropped into the dirty slush as the thing barrelled over him. The wind of its passing stirred his hair and one of its great hooked talons slashed the hem of his cloak.

Open-mouthed, he looked up from the freezing mud in time to see a scaly bat-winged form of glittering gold zooming up from the clearing, one wing dipping to turn again even as its momentum carried it upward.

From across the clearing Kenneth's bowstring sang and a tiny patch of pale blue daylight appeared in the membrane of the thing's left wing close to the body. The creature craned its snaky golden neck over its shoulder and hissed gape-fanged at its tormentor.

Then it was diving on them again.

Wiz rolled and rolled toward the edge of the clearing,

heedless of the snow and mud. Kenneth's bow thrummed again and Wiz heard the whine of the arrow as it passed close to his right. Then the beast shrieked and there was a heavy thud as it struck earth. Wiz looked up to see the golden dragon-thing on the ground not five yards from him. The wings were still spread and the animal was using a wickedly-taloned hind leg to claw at the arrow protruding from its breast. There was a spreading scarlet stain on the glowing golden scales and the creature roared again in rage and pain.

Suddenly a second arrow sprouted a hand's span from the first. The animal stopped pawing at the arrow in its chest and brought its head up to look across the clearing. There was a disquieting intelligence in its eyes. Its head snaked around and it caught sight of Wiz. Without hesitating the beast dropped its leg and started toward him.

Kenneth's great bow sang yet again and another arrow appeared in the thing, in the shoulder this time. But the beast paid it no heed. It advanced on Wiz with a terrible evil hunger in its eyes.

Wiz whimpered and scrambled backward, but his heavy cloak had wrapped itself around his legs and it tripped him as he tried to rise.

The creature craned its neck forward eagerly and the huge fanged mouth gaped shocking red against the golden body. The arrows in the chest wobbled in time with its labored breathing and the dark red blood ran in rivulets down its body to stain the snow carmine.

Again an arrow planted itself in the thing's body and again it jerked convulsively. But still it came on, neck craning forward and jaws slavering open as it struggled to reach Wiz.

The great eyes were golden, Wiz saw, with slit pupils closed down to mere lines. The fangs were white as fresh bone, so close Wiz could have reached out and touched them could he have freed an arm from the cloak.

Suddenly the beast's head jerked up and away from

its prey and it screamed a high wavering note like a steamwhistle gone berserk.

Wiz looked up and saw Kenneth, legs wide apart and his broadsword clasped in both hands as he raised it high for the second stroke against the long neck. The guardsman brought the blade down again and then again, slicing through the neck scales and into the corded muscle beneath with a meat ax thunk.

The beast twisted its neck almost into a loop, shuddered convulsively, as was suddenly still.

The silence of the clearing was absolute, save for the breathing of the two men, one of them panting in terror and the other breathing hard from exertion.

"Lord, are you all right?"

"Ye . . . yes," Wiz told him shakily. "I'll be . . ." He drew a deep breath of cold air and went into a coughing fit. "What was that thing?"

"One of the League's creatures," Kenneth said somberly. "Now you see why you must not walk alone, Lord."

Wiz goggled at the golden corpse pouring steaming scarlet blood from the rents in the neck. "That was for me?"

"I doubt it came here by accident," Kenneth said drily.

Wiz tried to stand, but the cloak still tangled him. He settled for rolling over onto his hands and knees and then working the entangling folds of cloth out of the way before rising.

"You saved my life. Thank you."

The guardsman shrugged. "It was Bal-Simba's command that you be protected," he said simply. "Can you walk, Lord?"

"Yes. I can walk."

"Then we had best get you back to the compound. You'll catch cold, wet as you are."

Wiz looked down at his soaked and muddy cloak and for the first time felt the icy chill of his wet garments. He shivered reflexively.

"Besides," Kenneth said thoughtfully, "it is beginning to get dark and mayhap there are more of the League's creatures about."

Wiz shivered again and this time it had nothing to do with the cold.

Back at the compound, Shiara was concerned but not surprised at the attack.

"We could hardly expect to keep ourselves secret forever," she sighed. "Still, it will be inconvenient to have to be much on our guard. I think it would be best if you discontinued your walks in the Woods, Sparrow."

"I was thinking the same thing myself, Lady," Wiz said fervently from the stool in front of the fire where he huddled. Save for a clean cloak he was naked and the fire beat ruddy and hot on his pale skin as he held the garment open to catch as much warmth as possible.

"Uh, Lady . . . I thought we were supposed to be protected against attacks like that."

Shiara frowned. "Sparrow, in the Wild Wood there is no absolute safety. Even with all the powers of the North arrayed about us we would not be completely safe. With Bal-Simba's protection we are fairly immune to magic attack and the forest folk will warn of any large non-magical party that approaches. But a single non-magical creature can slip through our watchers and wards all too easily."

"What about a single magical creature?" Wiz asked.

Shiara smiled thinly, her lips pressed together in a tight line. "Believe me, Sparrow, I would know instantly of the approach of any magic."

From the corner where he had been listening, Kenneth snorted. "If all they can send against us are single non-magical beings then they stand a poor chance of getting either of you." He tugged the string of his great bow significantly. "Lady, I own the fault today was mine. I was not properly alert. But rest assured it will not happen again!"

"It would be well if it were so," Shiara said. "But I am not certain they expected to get anyone in today's attack."

"They came darned close," Wiz said.

"Oh, had they killed or injured one of us the League would have been happy indeed, but I think they had little real expectation of it."

"Then what is the point?" asked Kenneth.

"In a duel of magics you seek at first to unbalance your opponent. To break his concentration and unsettle his mind and so lay him open to failure. I think the League's purpose in such attacks is to upset us and hinder our work."

"Then they failed twice over," Wiz said firmly and stood up. "I'm dry enough and I've got work to do tonight. Kenneth, will you hand me my tunic?"

Another day, near evening this time, and Wiz had another creation to demonstrate to Shiara.

"Here, let me show you." Wiz made a quick pass and a foot-tall homunculus popped into existence. It eyed Wiz speculatively and then started to gabble in a high, squeaky voice. "ABCDEFGHIJKLMNOPQRSTUVWXYZ1234567890," the creature got out before Wiz could raise his hand again. At the second gesture it froze, mouth open.

"What good is that thing?" Shiara asked.

"You told me wizards protect their inner secrets with passwords? Well, this is a password guesser. When it gets up to speed it can run through thousands of combinations a second." He frowned. "I'm going to have to do some code tweaking to get the speed up, I think."

"What makes you think you can guess a password even with such a thing as that?" Shiara said.

Wiz grinned. "Because humans are creatures of habit. That includes wizards. The thing doesn't guess at random. It uses the most likely words and syllables."

"Ricidulous," Shiara snorted. "A competent wizard chooses passwords to be hard to guess."

"I'll bet even good wizards get careless. You remember

I told you we used passwords on computer accounts back home? There was a list of about 100 of them which were so common they could get you into nearly any computer and the chances were at least one person had used one of them.

"Look, a password has to be remembered. I mean no one but an idiot writes one down, right?" Shiara nodded reluctantly. "And you have to be able to say them, don't you?" Again Shiara nodded.

"Well then, those are major limits right there. You need combinations of consonants and vowels that are pronounceable and easy to remember. You also can't make them too long and you probably don't want to make them too short. Right? Okay, this little baby," he gestured to the demon on the table, "has been given a bunch of rules that help guess passwords. It's not a random search."

"But even so, Sparrow, there are so many possible combinations."

"That's why he talks so fast, Lady."

They brought Moira on deck the day the *Tiger Moth* raised the southern coast.

With no one at her oars and no wind behind her, the *Tiger Moth* ghosted between the great black towers that guarded the harbor. From the headlands of the bay mighty breakwaters reached out to clasp the harbor in their grasp. Where the breakwaters almost touched, two towers of the black basalt rose to overlook the harbor entrance. Great walls of dark rhyolite enclosed the city with its tall towers and narrow stinking streets snaking up the sides of an ancient volcano.

Everywhere the southland was bleak and blasted. The earth had been ripped open repeatedly by magic and nature and had bled great flows of lava. Now it was dark and scabbed over as if the wounds had festered rather than healed. The sky was dark and lowering, lead gray and filled with a fine gritty ash that settled on everything.

In the distance dull red glows reflected off the clouds where still-active volcanoes rumbled and belched. The chill south wind brought the stink of sulfur with it. Nothing lived in this land save by magic.

Moira was hustled off the ship and hurried up the street by a dozen of the false fishermen. After days in the cramped cubby it was agony for her to walk. But her captors forced the pace cruelly even when she cried into her gag in pain.

The street ended suddenly in a great wall composed of massive blocks of dark red lava. The party turned right at the wall and there, in a shallow dead-end alley, was a tiny door sheathed in black iron. The Shadow Captain knocked a signal on the door and a peephole slid back, revealing a hideously tusked unhuman face. Quickly the door opened and Moira was thrust through into the midst of a group of heavily armored goblins. The goblins closed in and bore her off without a word or backward glance.

"Only one magician, you say?" Toth-Set-Ra asked the Shadow Captain harshly.

"Only the woman, Dread Master. There were two other humans within the walls, the former witch they call Shiara and a man called Sparrow. She called him Wiz."

"And they were not magicians?"

"I would stake my soul upon it."

Toth-Set-Ra eyed him. "You have, captain. Oh, you have."

The Shadow Captain blanched under the wizard's gaze. "I found no other sign of a magician there," he repeated as firmly as he could manage.

"There should have been at least one other magician, a man. You're sure this Wiz or Sparrow was not a magician?"

"He had not the faintest trace of magic about him," said the Shadow Captain. He was not about to tell Toth-Set-Ra there had been something strange about that man.

"We shall see," Toth-Set-Ra said and waved dismissal. "Now return to your ship and await my pleasure." The Shadow Captain abased himself and backed from the room.

Toth-Set-Ra watched him go and drummed his fingers on the inlaid table. He was frantically anxious to know what this new prisoner could tell him, but he was skilled enough in the ways of interrogation to know that a day or two of isolation in his dungeons would do much to break her spirit. Question a magician too soon and she was likely to resist to the point of death. First you must shake her, wear away her confidence. Then she would be more pliable to magical assaults and more susceptible to pain.

Tomorrow would be soon enough. Let her lie a while in the dungeons. Then let five or six of the goblins use her. And then, then it would be easy to find out what she knew.

He smiled and his face looked more like a skull than ever. Yes, it would take a little time. But then, he had the time.

"**(defun replace—variables (demon))**" Wiz muttered, sketching on a clean plank with a bit of charcoal. "**(let((!bindings nil)))**"

"Lord."

"**(replace—variables-with-bindings(demon))**"

Wiz turned from the spell he was constructing to see Donal standing in the door, near blocking out the light.

"You made me lose my place," he said accusingly.

"Sorry Lord, but it's Kenneth. He's asked for you and the Lady."

Reluctantly Wiz put down the stick of charcoal and stood up, feeling his back creak and his thighs ache from sitting in one position on the hard bench too long. "What is it?" he asked. "More trouble?"

Donal regarded Wiz seriously. "I think he wants to sing a song," he said.

"A song?" Wiz asked incredulously. "He takes me away from my work to sing a song?"

Donal's face did not change. "Please, Lord. It is important."

As they stepped out of the hut, Wiz realized it was midmorning. The air was still chill, but no longer iron-hard. The sun was warm even as the earth was cold. Spring was on its way, Wiz thought idly as Donal led him to the courtyard. Shiara was already there, sitting on the stump used to chop firewood, her stained and worn blue cloak wrapped firm around her, but the hood thrown back and her hair falling like a silver waterfall down her back.

Kenneth stood facing her. He was holding a small iron-stringed harp Wiz had never seen before. From time to time he would pick a string and listen distractedly to the tone.

*Music,* Wiz thought. *In all the time I've been here I've never heard human music.* His resentment dulled slightly and he pulled a small log next to Shiara for a seat.

Shiara reached a hand out of her cloak and clasped Wiz's hand briefly.

"You may begin Kenneth," she said.

Kenneth's expression did not change. He struck a chord and a silvery peal floated across the court and up to the smokestained peak of Heart's Ease.

> *"Now Heart's Ease it is fallen*
> *for all the North to weep*
> *And the hedge witch with the copper curls*
> *lies fast in prison deep"*

His voice was a clear pure tenor and the sound sent chills down Wiz's spine. There was loss and sadness in the music and the pain Wiz had felt since that terrible night Heart's Ease fell came rushing back with full vigor. Instinctively he moved closer to Shiara.

"And none can find or follow
for there's none to show the way
and magic might and wizards ranked
stand fast in grim array

There's neither hope nor succor
for the witch with copper hair
for the Mighty may not aid her plight
deep in the Dark League's lair

Where the Mighty dare not venture
the meek must go instead
for shattered hearth and stolen love
and companion's blood run red.

There's the Lady called Shiara
with blue, unseeing eyes
whose magic's but a memory
but still among the wise.

There's a Sparrow who's left nestless now
bereft by loss of love
whose land lies far beyond his reach
past even dreaming of

With neither might nor magic
their wit must serve in place
and wizard's lore and foreign forms
twine in a strange embrace

But the fruit of that embracing
is nothing to be scorned
and the hedge witch with the copper curls
may yet be kept from harm

And if there's no returning
the witch with flame-bright hair

> *the price of a Sparrow's mourning*
> *be more than the League can bear."*

Kenneth's voice belled up over the harp and the song was strong off the ruined stone walls behind.

> *"For there will be a weregeld*
> *for life and hearth and love*
> *though worlds may shake and wizards quake*
> *and skies crash down above.*
>
> *Aye, there will be a ransom*
> *and the ransom will be high*
> *for the blood-debt to a Sparrow*
> *the League cannot deny."*

He stopped then, lowered the harp and bowed his head.

"Thank you, Kenneth," said Shiara. And Wiz stepped forward to embrace the soldier roughly.

"The mood was upon me, Lady," Kenneth said simply. "When the mood is upon me, I must."

"And well done," said Shiara, standing up. "Thank you for the omen."

"So, Sparrow," she sighed. "We go soon. Do we go tomorrow?"

"I don't know Lady," Wiz protested. "I've still got some spells to tune and . . ." Unbidden a quotation from his other life rose in his mind. *There comes a time in the course of any project to shoot the engineers and put the damn thing into production.* He raised his chin firmly.

"Tomorrow, Lady. Tomorrow we strike."

# *Twelve*
## THE NAME IS DEATH

Moira didn't know how far they had come. The flagged corridors twisted and turned in a way that made her head spin. The floor was uneven and the tunnels that led off usually sloped up or down.

The trickle of water down the center of the tunnel made footing treacherous, but she stayed to the middle nonetheless. To step out of the trail of slime was to risk ramming into a rough stone or dirt wall.

Worst of all, she cold not see. There was no light and her magic senses were blocked everywhere by the coarse, suffocating pressure of counter-spells. The magic was almost as nauseating as the stink of her goblin guards.

The dark was no hinderance to the goblins. They took crude amusement from her plight, forcing her along at a pace that kept her on the verge of stumbling. Finally, after she had fallen or run into the walls too often, they grabbed her arms and half-pushed, half-dragged her along.

By the time the goblins threw her in a small, mean cell and slammed the door, Moira was bruised, filthy and scraped and bleeding in a dozen places. Her palms were raw from falling and there was a cut on her head which turned her hair damp with blood. Her knees and shins ached.

She pulled herself into a sitting position and dabbed

at the cut on her head with the least-dirty part of the hem of her skirt. She tried to ignore the small skittering sounds in the dark around her and refused to think about the future.

"Well, Sparrow?" Shiara asked as she ducked to enter the low door of Wiz's workroom.

"I think we're about there, Lady." For the first time in days the crude plank table was clear. The rough wooden tablets which had been piled on it to toppling were now stacked more or less neatly in the corners of the room. The table had been pushed away from the small window and a bench had been drawn underneath it. A brazier in the center of the room made a feeble attempt to take the late-winter chill out of the air but neither Wiz nor Shiara doffed their cloaks. The door was open to let in more light.

"Are you sure you want to be here?" Wiz asked. "I mean it isn't necessary and it may be dangerous."

The blind woman shrugged. "It is dangerous everywhere and I would rather be at the center of events."

Shiara came into the hut and almost bumped into the table in its new and unfamiliar position. With a quick apology, Wiz took her hand and guided her to the bench.

"When do you begin?"

"I'll let you know in a minute. Emac!"

"Yes, master?" A small brown creature scuttled out of the shadows. It was man-like, perhaps three feet tall, with a huge bald head and square wire-rimmed glasses balanced on its great beak of a nose. A green eyeshade was pushed back on its domed forehead and a quill pen was stuck behind one flap-like ear.

"Are we ready?"

"I'll check again, master." The gnome-like being disappeared with a faint "pop." Shiara winced involuntarily at the strong magic so close to her.

"I'm sorry, my Lady. I'll tell them to walk from now on."

"What was that?" Shiara asked.

"An Emac. A kind of magic clerk. They help me organize things and translate simple commands into complex sets of instructions. I have several of them now."

"Emacs," Shiara said, wrinkling her nose. "I see—so to speak."

There was another "pop" and the Emac was back before Wiz. "We are all ready, Master."

Wiz looked at Shiara, who sat with her head turned in his direction, beautiful and impassive. The pale, soft winter light caught her in profile, making her look more regal than ever.

Wiz took a deep, shuddering breath. "Very well," he said and raised his hands above his head. "**backslash**" he intoned.

"**$**" replied the Emac.

"**class drone grep moira**"

"**$**" said the Emac again.

"**exe**," Wiz said and the Emac's lips moved soundlessly as he transmitted the order, expanding it into a series of commands to each of the drones.

Far to the South, in a dozen places along the frozen shores of the Freshened Sea, stubby white shapes popped into existence, scanned their surroundings and disappeared again.

"**running**" said the Emac.

Wiz was silent for an instant. *Please God, let them find her.* "All right," he said briskly. "Now let's see how much Hell we can raise with the League. **backslash!**"

It started as a tiny spark deep in the Sea of Scrying, a pinpoint of light on the graven copper likeness of the World. The acolyte peered deeper into the Sea and rubbed his eyes. Was there something . . . ? Yes, there it was again, stronger and sharper. And another, equally sharp and growing stronger. He raised his hand to summon the black-robed Master. When he returned his attention to the murky water there were four bright spots apparently scattered at random through his sector. Then the four doubled and there were eight, and sixteen, and thirty-two.

In the time it took the black-robed wizard to cross the room over a thousand points of bright magic light had bloomed on the bottom of the bowl. By the time the word passed to Toth-Set-Ra, the Sea of Scrying glowed with a uniform milky luminescence and all sight of things magic in the world had been lost.

With a small "pop" an apparition materialized in Moira's cell.

She clenched her jaw until her teeth ached. *I will be brave* she told herself. *I will not scream.*

But her visitor was the most unlikely demon she had ever seen. It was a squat, white cylinder with a rounded, gray top and two stubby legs beneath.

The dome-shaped head rotated and Moira saw it had a single glowing blue eye. As the eye pointed at her, the thing emitted a series of squeaks and beeps. Then it vanished, leaving Moira awake and wondering.

Deep beneath the bowels of the City of Night three demons guarded the portal to the Pits of Fire. The first of the demons bore the form of an immense dragon who coiled in front of the gate. The second demon was shaped as a gigantic slug, whose skin oozed pungent acid and whose passage left smoking grooves burned into the rock. The third and mightiest of the demons appeared as an enormously fat old man with three faces seated on the back of a great black toad.

Ceaseless, tirelessly and sleeplessly the three watched, holding the sole entrance to the lake of boiling incandescent lava and the well of earth magic that was the League's greatest resource.

Their vigil was broken by a "pop" and a tiny brown manniken stood before the three awesome sentries. Three heads and four faces swiveled toward him but the little man-thing made no move to approach the gate. Instead he opened his mouth and began to gabble in a voice so fast and high as to be inaudible to human ears. The three demons watched impassively until the little brown creature spoke a certain word. Then the dragon demon rose and crept away from the door, the slug demon heaved its acid-slimed bulk to the side of the corridor and the main demon spoke.

"Pass on," it said in basso profundo three-part harmony.

Without another word the little creature skipped through the now unguarded gate.

Beyond the great iron portal other demons reached deep into the roiling white-hot lava to sift out the magic welling up from the center of the World and turn it to their masters' uses. Feeding like hogs at a trough, they ignored the little brown creature who pranced in among their mighty legs. They paid no attention when the newcomer drew a pallid wriggling little grub from his pouch and cast it into the blazing pit.

As soon as it touched the flow of magic the grub began to swell. It grew and grew until it was as large as the demons, soaking up magic like a dry sponge soaks up water. The demons shifted and jostled as magic was diverted away from them. They tried futilely to regain their share. But now there were two full-sized worms in the pit and a dozen more growing rapidly. Unable to shoulder the worms away, the demons milled about in frustration and the flow of magic from the Pit to the city above dwindled to nothing.

Bal-Simba paced the great stone hall like a restless bear. Now and again he paused to peer over the shoulder of one of the Watchers.

"Anything?" he asked the head of the Watch for the dozenth time that morning.

"Nothing, Lord. No sign of anything out of the ordinary."

"Thank you." The wizard resumed pacing. The watcher stared into the crystal again and then frowned.

"Wait, Lord! There is something now." Bal-Simba whirled and rushed to his side.

"It's faint. Very faint, but there is something around the edges . . . No, now it's getting stronger." The Watcher looked up at Bal-Simba, awed. "Lord, there are indications of new magic in the city of Night itself!"

"What is it?"

"I do not know, Lord. Considering the distance and the masking spells it's a wonder that we can pick up anything at all. Whatever is happening there must be extremely strong."

"Hai Sparrow!" Bal-Simba roared. "You spread your wings, eh? Well fly, Sparrow, fly. And we will do some flying of our own." He motioned to Arianne who was sitting nearby. "Sound the alert. We will make what use we can of the opportunity our Sparrow gives us."

Again the dragons rose from their roosts in the Capital, formed into echelons and climbed away to the south. Again the Dragon Leader reviewed his instructions. A reconnaissance in force over the Freshened Sea, they told him. Scout to the South until you meet resistance. *Well,* he thought. *We'll see just how far south we can go. And then perhaps we'll go a little further.* He tested his bowstring grimly.

In their dark towers above the City of Night, the magicians of the League flew to arms. Spells pushed upon them from a hundred directions, elemental and relentless. In the harbor ships stirred uneasily as the waters tossed them.

"Get underway immediately," the Shadow Captain ordered, scowling at the sky. Most of the crew was still aboard the *Tiger Moth* and a mooring is the worst place for a ship to be in a time of danger.

Under the lash of the captain's voice the crew rushed to their stations. Hawsers were quickly cast off and two hands scrambled for the rigging. The oars were broken out and fitted into the locks. The crew hastily arranged themselves with an even number on each side. The captain saw the result and scowled again. Half the benches were empty, but it would have to do. With the mate beating time and the Shadow Warriors pulling for all they were worth, the *Tiger Moth* threaded its way through the clutter of ships and made for the breakwater gate and the open sea.

High in the watchtower overlooking the sea gate, a brown-robed mage threw back his arms and began his incantation. As the spell took shape in the plenum beyond human senses, a certain configuration of forces appeared. It was only a small part of the spell, but a lurking worm sensed it and battened onto that configuration. The worm's own spell twisted the conjuration out of its intended shape and the wizard screamed as he felt the spell writhe away from him and into a new and dangerous direction. The last thing he saw was a blinding, searing flash as the room exploded around him. His fellows, those who were not too close, saw the top of a black tower disappear in an incandescent blast.

The rest of the tower slumped like a child's sand castle built over-high and toppled into the bay. A huge block of hewed basalt crashed through the *Tiger Moth* just aft of the mast, breaking her back and bringing a tangle of rigging down on the poop where the Shadow Captain stood.

Impelled by the force of the block the *Tiger Moth* plunged beneath the cold black water. Only a few pieces of wood and rigging floated up.

The worm fed on the new power and spawned several copies of itself to lurk in the unimaginable spaces of magic and feed in turn when the opportunity arose.

"Master, our spells weaken!" the sweating wizard cried. With a curse Toth-Set-Ra strode to the lectern where the man had been conjuring and shoved him roughly aside. Quickly he scanned the grimore's page, creating the spell anew, and scowled at the result. What should have been bright and shining was wan and gray. Angrily he reached out for more power, but instead of the expected strong, steady flow he found only a wavering rivulet.

"To the Pit!" he roared at the shaking wizard. "Something interferes with the flow."

As wizards and acolytes alike hurried to do his bidding, Toth-Set-Ra stared unseeing at the awful runes inscribed on human parchment before him.

Was the Council attacking in retaliation for the raid on the North? He dismissed the idea even as the thought formed. He knew Northern magic and there was none of it here. The Council might have a new spell or two, but everything the League faced was new. Besides, he knew the work of every one of the Mighty and this was unlike any of them.

An attack from within, aimed at himself? He considered that somewhat longer. It would explain how someone had gotten into the Pit to interfere with the flow of magic. Had he given Atros too much power? That too he discarded. If Atros or any of the others had half this much power they would have struck long before. And again, he knew the magics of the League even better than he knew those of the Council.

Then who? As the City of Night shook and towers toppled Toth-Set-Ra racked his brains trying to find the source of the attack.

*A doom. A plague. A bane upon all wizards.* The

demon's words came back to him and the mightiest wizard in the World shivered.

The alien wizard! The stranger from beyond the world. This mass of army-ant spells pressing in on them must be his work.

It was well for the Shadow Captain that he was already dead, for the wizard's next oath would have blasted him where he stood. *He had the wrong magician!* Somehow this other one, this Wiz, the one they called Sparrow, had fooled the Shadow Warriors. The hedge-witch was a pawn to be sacrificed to protect the Council's king.

And he had fallen for it. By all the demons in the nine netherhells, he had been duped!

For a moment chill panic shook Toth-Set-Ra. Then he stopped short and laughed aloud. The other wizards in the chantry paused involuntarily at the sound. The Master of the Dark League seldom laughed and when he did it boded something truly horrible for someone. They turned back to their spells and incantations with renewed vigor.

Toth-Set-Ra was still chuckling when he reached the door of the chantry. *Fool me, will you? We shall see who is the fool in the end. For I tell you Wiz, or Sparrow, or whatever your true name is, you are as much in my power as if it were you and not that red-haired bitch I hold fast.*

Far to the north on a crag above the shores of the Freshened Sea three gargoyles stared forever South, testing the wind, sifting the whispers borne to them and sending on what they heard.

"It goes well, Sparrow." It was not a question. Shiara sat on the bench, pale and calm as a winter's dawn while Wiz paced the room, muttering in a way that had nothing to do with magic. He paused to glance once more into the bowl of water on the rude table between them.

"We're shaking them good and proper," he confirmed. "I can't interpret everything, but there are fires and earthquakes all over the area. Part of the City of Night's wall is down and a couple of towers have already slid into the harbor." He smiled. "We've just about ruined their whole day. Now if only . . ."

Shiara nodded. "I know Sparrow. Fortuna grant us this one final boon."

The crystal contrivance atop the ruined tower sparkled and flashed with the magical force of the messages arriving from the south.

Deep in her cell, Moira didn't know what was going on, but she was increasingly certain it wasn't being done to frighten her. Even this far under the earth she could hear occasional explosions, faint and muffled but audible nonetheless. Twice, groups of goblin soldiers tore by her cell in clattering, shouting masses. Once something huge and foul and slithering whuffled up the corridor while she pressed against the slimy rock wall and prayed to the depths of her soul that the thing would not notice her. Even the vermin seemed to have gone into hiding in the crannies and under the piles of rotting straw.

First the demon with the glowing blue eye and now this. What could it possibly mean?

Moira didn't hope, for hope had long since burned out of her. But she felt a stirring. Whatever was going on couldn't be good for her captors and misfortune to them was as much as she dared wish for.

With a faint "pop" an Emac appeared in front of Wiz, so close he almost stumbled over the demon in his pacing.

"We have found her, Master! RDsquaresquare has found her."

"Thank God! Where?"

"Underground master, far and deep underground. The coordinates are . . ."

Wiz waved the small brown demon to silence. "Show me in the bowl!"

The demon removed the quill from behind his ear and dipped the point in the water. Ink flowed from the pen, turning the clear water black and then shimmering as the image formed. Wiz looked intently at it and breathed a sigh of relief.

"Have we got a good enough fix?"

The Emac cocked his bald brown head and his huge ears quivered as he listened to something unhearable. "Yes, Master. We can come within a few cubits of the place."

"Then come with me." Wiz strode to the door, grabbing his oak staff and wrapping his cloak tighter as he stepped into the outdoor chill.

"Wait, Lord."

Wiz turned and saw Donal and Kenneth arrayed for battle. Their mail hauberks hung to their knees and their greaves and vambraces were secure to their limbs. Donal's great sword was over his shoulder and Kenneth's bow was slung across his back. Both wore their open-faced helms and their mail coifs were laced tight.

"You're not going," Kenneth said. "Not alone."

"I have to." Wiz told him.

"Bal-Simba told us to guard you and guard you we shall," said Donal.

Wiz shook his head. "It's too dangerous. Look, I appreciate the idea, but you can't come."

"Stubborn," said Donal.

"Too stubborn," said Kenneth. "You look, Sparrow. Someone has to keep your back while you're making magic."

"My magic can do that for me."

"Unlikely," said Kenneth.

"Take them, Sparrow," Shiara put in from the hut's door. "You may need them."

"It's dangerous," Wiz warned again. "You might get . . ." He cast his eyes over their well-used armor and weapons and trailed off. Both men looked at him in grim amusement. "Uh . . . right."

"It is Bal-Simba's wish," said Kenneth simply.

Wiz sighed. "Very well. Stand close to me and I'll see if I can make this thing work."

Donal and Kenneth pressed in against his back and he shifted his grip on the staff.

Wiz drew a deep, shuddering breath, filling his lungs with the cold, sweet air of Heart's Ease. He looked around slowly at the place he had come to call home. Then he tightened his grip on the staff and began.

"**backslash**" he said to the Emac. "**$**" the Emac responded, now ready and waiting for orders. "**transport**" he said and the Emac began to gabble silently translating the predefined macro spell into the words of power. "**arg moira**" He raised the staff high over his head as the air began to waver and twist around him. "**EXE**" he shouted.

And the world went dark.

*Something's gone wrong!* Wiz thought frantically. *It's not supposed to be like this!* His arms quivered from the strain of holding the heavy staff high. He could feel Donal and Kenneth pressing hard against his back and hear their breathing, but still the darkness did not lift. Then he shifted slightly and his staff scraped against something overhead, showering him with noisome dirt. He nearly laughed aloud as he realized that this darkness was simply the absence of light.

He pointed with his staff. "**backslash light exe**" he said, and a blue glow lit the world around him. All three blinked and looked about.

They were in a tunnel so narrow they could not pass abreast. The rough flagged floor was slippery with condensation and the air was close and foul with the odors of earth and decay. About ten yards in either direction the tunnel twisted away, hiding what was beyond. Wiz could see four or five low wooden doors bound strongly with iron set into the walls along this section of the corridor.

"Moira!" Wiz called "Moira!" But ringing echoes and the distant sound of dripping water were the only replies. Donal and Kenneth quickly moved up and down the corridor, checking the cells.

"They are empty, Lord," Donal said, as they returned to where Wiz stood fidgeting. He forbore to mention that some of the cells were merely empty of life.

"Damn! She's got to be here someplace. The Emac said they had her located to within cubits."

The two guardsmen exchanged looks. They knew how unreliable magic could be, how susceptible to counter-spells or the blurring effects of other magics, and how magicians could use the magic to trap other magicians. What better place for a threat to the League than the dungeons under the League's own stronghold? As unobstrusively as they could they shifted their stances and loosened their weapons.

Unheeding, Wiz reached into his pouch and pulled out a shiny silver sphere. He cupped it in his palm. "backslash cd slash grep moira" he said to the marble. It pulsed with a golden glow, flashing brighter and fainter to acknowledge the order. "exe" Wiz said and the light from the sphere steadied into a warm yellow illumination that highlighted his face. The marble grew into a ball of light the size of his fist and floated to the top of the tunnel.

"She's above us," Wiz told the other two. "We'll have to go up to the next level."

"Carefully, Lord," Donal said in a near whisper. "These tunnels are chancy at best and there are enemies about."

Wiz nodded and stepped under the glowing ball bobbing against the ceiling. "backslash" he said softly. "in here Moira" Again the warm light pulsated. "exe" Wiz whispered and the ball drifted off to the left, glowing steadily as it traveled up the tunnel. Wiz moved to follow it and Donal stepped in front of him, his great sword at the ready. Kenneth fell in behind with his bow in hand and the flap open on his belt quiver.

There was no need to renew the light spell. The golden ball suffused the tunnel with an even glow, warmer and more natural than the weird blue light of the staff.

Donal and Kenneth were not comforted. The light would be a beacon to anyone or anything guarding the tunnels. Wiz didn't notice. His eyes were fixed on the glowing ball.

They saw no one as they moved up the tunnel, but twice they heard movement behind one of the stout, low doors set in the wall at irregular intervals. In neither case was the sound the sort that made them want to stop and investigate even if they had the time. Once there was an explosion that shook dirt down on them. Donal and Kenneth looked apprehensive, as if the passage might collapse, but Wiz only smiled and pressed forward.

The tunnel twisted and turned, it wandered and wobbled, it branched and joined, it doubled back and redoubled on itself and it dipped and it rose. But it rose more than it dipped and always the sphere of light led them on.

Kenneth and Donal kept swivelling their heads, their eyes scanning everywhere for signs of danger. Wiz kept his attention on the sphere, with just enough on his surroundings so he didn't trip on the miserable footing. Thus when Donal stopped dead at a corner, Wiz walked into him.

"Oh shit," Donal breathed silently.

"Oh shit!" Wiz whispered, peering over his shoulder.

"Oh shit?" mouthed Kenneth, bringing up the rear.

Around the corner the tunnel widened into a room, its stone floor worn smoother and more even than the corridor. The seeking ball was not the main source of light, for on one side of the room logs burned brightly in a cavernous fireplace. Along the other walls rush torches flared in wrought iron holders. Sturdy tables and benches were scattered about. And in the center, clustered around the glowing golden intruder, were twenty goblins, all armored, armed and very much on the alert.

They were staring up at the light and muttering among themselves in their coarse goblin speech. A very large goblin poked at the seeker with a halberd.

One of the goblins turned from the light to look back the way it had come. His piggy little eyes widened at the sight of the three human heads peeking around the corner and he opened his tusked mouth to yell to his comrades.

"Fortuna!" Donal said under his breath, making the word a curse. Then he brandished his great sword and leaped into the open shouting a war cry. Kenneth was instantly at his back and Wiz stumbled in behind them.

Now goblins are powerful creatures, crafty, patient and fierce. But they are also also excitable and given to panic if things go wrong. Goblin attacks are legendary, but so are goblin routs.

These goblins were already in a bad way. Their citadel was besieged by powerful magic. Their last orders were to stay on guard, but those had come hours ago and they had had no word from their officers or the wizards they served since. They were on edge from hours of waiting and when three screaming humans burst into their guardroom in the wake of a mysterious light, they did what came naturally to their goblin natures. They panicked and ran.

"Son of a bitch," Wiz breathed as the clatter and shouting of the departing goblins died away.

"I told you you would need us, Lord," Donal said as he looked up the tunnel after the goblins.

Kenneth merely scowled. "They will be back soon

enough. And others with them. Let us not be here when they return."

"Right," Wiz said. Already the golden ball was disappearing out the door the goblins had taken. "Come on then."

If the tunnel had been convoluted before, now it became positively mazy. Every few yards there was another branching and never were there fewer than four ways to go. At times even the seeker hesitated before plunging off down one or the other of the passages. Wiz's sense of direction, never his strong point, was completely befuddled. It seemed they had walked for a mile at least, all of it over rough, slippery ground that always sloped up, down or to the side, and sometimes several ways together.

Finally they came to a place where a fresh fall of dirt and rocks blocked most of the passage. The ball did not hesitate. It floated to the top of the tunnel and vanished in the crevice between the debris and the ceiling. That left Wiz and his companions in darkness except for the faint glow coming through the crack.

"It doesn't look very big," Donal said, eyeing the crack doubtfully.

"The spell does know enough not to go where a man may not follow?" Kenneth asked.

"Well, ah . . ." Wiz realized he hadn't thought of that. "Come on, let's see if we can get through."

He scrambled up the mound of loose earth and tried to wedge his body through. His arms and head went in easily enough, but his torso went only halfway. He tried to back out but with his arms extended in front, he couldn't get any purchase. He kicked his legs and tried to writhe his body from side to side, but only succeeded in getting a mouthful of the fetid dirt.

"Help me out of here," he called as he twisted his head to one side and spat out the foul-tasting earth.

Donal and Kenneth each grabbed a leg and tugged strongly. Wiz slid out, still spitting dirt.

"Gah!" He wiped his tongue on the inside of his tunic. "No good. We'll have to dig."

Kenneth muttered a comment about half-something spells. Wiz ignored him and picked up his staff. "**backslash** light **exe**" he commanded, pointing the staff down the corridor. At once everything let up with eerie blue light. Then Wiz turned to work on the blockage.

They had no shovel, so at first Wiz threw dirt back between his legs like a dog. Then Kenneth took off his helm and passed it up to use as a scoop. When they came to rocks too large for Wiz to move by himself, Donal squeezed into the tunnel beside him to help. All the while Kenneth stood guard with his bow at the ready, looking nervously down the way they had come.

"I think it's big enough," Wiz said at last, panting from the exercise. "Let me check."

As he moved to climb back up the dirt pile, Donal caught his arm and shook his head. "Bal-Simba said to take care of you, Lord. I'll go first."

"I wish you'd remembered that while I was digging," Wiz said as Kenneth knocked the dirt out of his helm and laced it tight to his mail coif.

"Bal-Simba did not say to do your work for you," Donal replied. Then he scrambled up the dirt pile and squeezed into the crack, dragging his great sword behind him.

"All clear," he called after a moment from the other side and Wiz slithered through after him with Kenneth close behind.

Amazingly, the seeker's golden light was still visible, reflected off the wall at the end of the corridor. Wiz and his companions hurried on, turned a corner and there, about twenty-five yards in front of them, was the seeker, bobbing up and down gently in front of a stout oaken door.

"Moira? Moira?" Wiz called as they came down the corridor.

A pale tear-stained face appeared in the tiny barred window set in the door.

"Wiz? Oh, Wiz!"

Wiz rushed ahead of his companions and pressed against the door. "Oh my God! Darling, are you all right?"

"Oh Wiz, Wiz. I've been so . . . Oh Wiz!" and Moira started to cry.

"Come on, we'll get you out of there. Stand away from the door, now."

Moira backed from the window, as if reluctant to lose sight of him.

"Get as far away as you can and cover yourself," Wiz instructed her. "Tell me when you're ready."

"I'm . . . I'm ready." Moira called tentatively from within the cell.

Wiz raised his staff.

"What was that?" Atros growled.

"Vig noiss. Egplhossion." The goblin commander's human speech was slurred by his great tusks.

"I know that, idiot! But what caused it?"

The goblin merely shrugged, which only increased the wizard's ire. For over two hours Atros had been searching the dungeons based on the report of a troop of goblins who had been attacked in their guardroom by a strong force of human warriors and wizards. At least that was *their* story, Atros thought sourly. So far he had seen nothing to prove it.

"Well, where did it come from?" he snapped.

"That way, Master. Where special prisoner is." Atros ears pricked up. What was the old crow hiding down here? "Well, let's check. Quickly."

With nearly fifty heavily armed and armored goblins behind them Atros and the goblin commander set off down the tunnel at a trot.

The dungeons were a difficult labyrinth in the best of times, but with the incredible attack going on above, the maze of twisty little passages was almost impenetrable. The magic which usually guided the knowledgeable wasn't working and Atros was forced to rely on the memory and navigating skill of the goblins. He had a sneaking suspicion they had spent most of their time down here lost and wandering in circles—if a circle wasn't too regular a figure to describe their movments.

But something had obviously happened to those guards and Atros was encouraged by the report of humans in the dungeons—apparently Northern guardsmen at that. What was going on over their heads was unbelievably powerful, but it was also strange. None of the familiar magic or non-magical forces of the North had been encountered. Atros had perforce learned a grudging respect for the Northerners, not only for developing so many mighty new spells but for keeping everything so secret that the League's spies had gotten only the vaguest of hints.

However that left the League's more conventional resources uncommitted and Atros had a shrewd suspicion that they would be thrown in at a critical point. When that happened, he vowed as he jogged along grimly, he would be there and there would be such a duel of wizards as the World had never seen.

Wiz charged through the smoldering ruins of the door and swept Moira into his arms. She was dazed and weeping. She was filthy and her long red hair was matted with dirt, but she was still the most beautiful woman Wiz had ever seen.

"Oh my God, Moira, I thought I had lost you forever."

"Wiz, oh Wiz," Moira sobbed into his chest. Then he reached down, lifted her chin and kissed her.

"Now what?" Atros demanded of his hulking companion as they came around the bend. Ahead of them was a faint golden glow, the likes of which Atros had never seen down here.

The head goblin only shrugged and signalled his men to advance cautiously. As they moved down the tunnel cautiously the light grew brighter and steadier. They came around another bend and there, at the end of the tunnel was a shattered door with a golden light emanating from it and the sound of voices. Human voices. Atros stepped aside as the goblin captain and his soldiers advanced.

At the cell door, Kenneth stared down the corridor and fretted. It was bad enough that the Sparrow hadn't turned off his seeker ball now that they had found the hedge-witch. Worse he was clinched with her and he wasn't making any effort to get them away. Kenneth's well-developed sense of danger had been nagging ever since they entered the dungeons and now the nagging had grown to a full scream. If they stayed here much longer they were going to run into something they could not handle. Kenneth had no doubt at all these passages were full of things like that.

He frowned and squinted down the way they had come, careful not to expose his body with the light behind him. Was it his imagination or had he just heard a scuffling sound, like something heavy trying to move quietly?

*Well, one way to find out,* he thought to himself. Silently he nocked the arrow he was carrying in his bow hand. Then he drew and loosed a shaft down the corridor.

He was rewarded with a shout and the sound of running feet.

"*Attackers!*" Kenneth yelled, and fired another arrow. Donal was at his side instantly, his sword at the ready. "Lord, light the corridor and douse that globe!"

Wiz jerked his head up at Kenneth's cry. "Right," he said and snatched up his staff. "**backslash** light **exe**" he yelled, pointing the staff down the corridor. Moira gaped at him. Instantly the whole corridor lit up blue, revealing a packed mass of goblins thundering down on them.

"For-tuna," Donal breathed and grasped his sword more tightly.

Kenneth's bowstring thrummed twice more and two more goblins fell. The last one to go down was the goblin commander who dropped kicking and writhing with an arrow in his eye. His momentum carried him nearly two paces further.

The combination of the light and the loss of their commander was too much for the goblins. They broke and fled back down the tunnel. Kenneth got one more as they rounded the bend.

"Magic, Master! We must have magic!" The goblin soldier was breathing hard and foam slavered down his chin as he knelt before Atros.

"Fools! Buffoons!" roared Atros. "Must I do your work for you? There is no magic here. Only two humans. Finish them. Now."

"Magic, Master!" the goblin soldier begged.

"Idiot!" Atros kicked the creature in the face, sending him sprawling. The other goblins shifted and muttered. Atros realized he was dangerously close to overplaying his hand with these servants.

"Attack again," he ordered. "Attack now. If they use magic *then* I will loose my powers against them."

The goblins muttered more but they began to sort themselves out for an attack.

Atros watched, frowning. He still wasn't sure the alien wizard was with this group and he didn't want to use his magic unnecessarily. Whatever was going on in the City of Night was nullifying or weakening spells. Demons were not responding reliably to his call, so he could not learn the identity of his adversary. He did not know his strengths or weaknesses and the feel of the magic was maddeningly unfamiliar. Worse, he could not establish contact with his fellow wizards. He was on his own and deprived of his most reliable weapons.

If the wizard was in that room, then he would crush him. But there was no sign of great power and if the wizard was not there, Atros would rather sacrifice this band of goblins than reveal and weaken himself.

He stood aside as the goblins formed up, ignoring their sidelong glances and their mutterings. One more attack and he would have those humans. Then he would know.

"Lord, we have to get out of here," Kenneth said over his shoulder. "They're reforming just around the bend."

"Uh? Oh, right. Let's get going. Gather round close everybody." He put an arm around Moira's waist and drew her to him. Donal stepped in close behind and at the last second Kenneth spun away from the door and raced to them. Wiz lifted his staff. **backslash** transport . . . he began and then stopped.

"Damn," Wiz said under his braeth.

"What is it?" Moira asked.

"I don't have enough power to make the transport. I can't make the spell work with all those worms active."

"I would suggest, Lord, that you come up with an alternative," said Kenneth quietly, nocking an arrow, "and do so quickly." He returned to the door and stared down the weirdly lit corridor.

"I'll have to shut down the worms. It'll just take a few minutes."

"We may not have them," Kenneth replied, drawing his bow and stepping quickly into the corridor to loose a shaft. There was a roar of pain and then other roars and yells as the attackers charged.

Again, Kenneth brought down two more before they closed. By the time he laid his bow aside and drew his sword, Donal's two-handed sword was cleaving a glittering arc of death in the air before them. The leading goblin charged unheeding and died twitching and flopping at the guardsman's feet, his arm and shoulder nearly shorn from his body.

The other goblins hesitated for a fraction. Experienced fighters all, they knew that their situation was not as favorable as it looked to Moira gaping from the doorway. True, they had the humans outnumbered 20 to 1, but the tunnel was so narrow they could only come on three abreast, and a tightly packed three abreast at that. Their armor was good, but their weapons were for guard work, not a battle with armored men at close quarters. They had no archers, only a few pole arms and no shields.

Still, they were seasoned warriors and if the effects of the magical assault on the City of Night had unnerved them, they had no doubt they could win *this* fight. They dressed their lines and advanced in a packed mass. Barbed spears and cruelly hooked halberds reached out from the back ranks toward the two men.

Donal skipped forward, beating the pole arms aside and down with an overhead sweep of his blade. The goblins to his right were tied up by the tangle of weapons but the one to his left raised his sword for a killing stroke.

Before the blow could land Kenneth thrust home into the creature's exposed armpit. The light mail under the arm popped and snapped and the goblin went down shrieking. Donal gave ground, parrying with his great sword as the weapons of the back ranks thrust at him. Donal took advantage of the gap created by the falling goblin to slash the face of his rank mate and then leapt away so that the swords of the goblins cut empty air.

The goblins pressed forward as the humans retreated, the ones on the left stumbling on the bodies of their fallen comrades. Kenneth reached to his belt and drew a small war axe with his left hand. Donal parried a spear thrust from the rear ranks and riposted with a quick thrust to the head of the right-most goblin. The blade slid off the creature's knobbed helmet, but the force of the blow jarred the goblin and made him break step. The middle goblin aimed a whistling low cut at Kenneth's leg and gave Donal the opening he had been waiting for.

Kenneth stepped in and thrust to the goblin's neck. At the same time he brought the hatchet up and caught the left-most goblin's sword stroke between the haft and bit. A twist of his wrist and the sword was levered out of its owner's grasp and flying across the tunnel. The creature gaped in tusked amazement and then his eyes glazed in death as Kenneth's sword found his vitals.

But before Kenneth could skip out of range, a halberd licked out from among the goblin's legs. With a vicious jerk the hook on the back of the blade sank into the unprotected rear of Kenneth's calf. The guardsman hissed in pain and dropped. Donal slashed mightily with his great sword to cover his fallen companion, but the goblins pressed forward inexorably. Goblin blades flashed out, three and four at once. Rings popped on Donal's mail and a bright red gash opened in his side.

Wiz turned from his half-built spell at Moira's gasp in time to see Donal reel backward from the blows.

"**cancel!**" he shouted and pointed his staff at the packed mass. "**for 1 to 10 flash do**" he shouted. "**exe!**"

Instantly the corridor went from a bluish gloom to a light more brilliant than the brightest summer noon. Then it went pitch dark and then the light again and again and again. The goblins howled in pain from the blasts of light. In the strobe of the bolts Wiz could see them weirdly frozen, trying to shield their eyes and ignoring the two helpless men on the floor.

Wiz pointed his staff at the goblins and muttered another command. "**Bibbity boppity boo!**"

A ravening lance of flame shot from the end of the staff and struck the foremost goblin squarely. The creature shrieked, a high, almost womanish sound, as the fire took it. Another bolt shot from Wiz's staff and another goblin turned into a living torch. Again and again Wiz's staff shot fire and more goblins burned.

That was too much. The goblins broke and fled, the

ones in the fore trampling their fellows behind them in their haste to escape.

Wiz closed his eyes and breathed a silent prayer. Moira dashed out into the corridor to the wounded men.

Kenneth had an ugly wound in his calf but he could limp back with only a little assistance. Donal was in a worse way, conscious but groggy and bleeding heavily from the wound in his side. Moira and Wiz got the two inside and laid them on the dirty straw.

"My bow," Kenneth commanded and Wiz rushed back to get it. When he returned he found the guardsman had dragged himself to the door and was standing propped against the jamb.

"Thank you, Lord," he said as Wiz handed him the bow. "I will keep watch from here. But we need to be gone quickly."

"I'm trying," Wiz told him, "but this is more complicated than I bargained for. I don't think those damned worms were such a hot idea after all."

"Make haste Lord," Kenneth panted. "They have not gone far and they will come again soon."

"Likely with others who are not so flighty," said Donal, who came limping up in spite of Moira's efforts to keep him lying down.

Wiz took a deep breath and returned to the job of shutting down a worm.

It was an intricate process. The worms were under the control of the Emacs back at Heart's Ease and Wiz had no direct communication with them. He could not simply neutralize the worms, he had to shut at least some of them off completely. The entities had been busy reproducing themselves since they first appeared, so that was difficult.

"**backslash**, class worm suspend . . ." He shook his head. No, that wouldn't work! "cancel" He tried again. "**backslash** . . ."

"Lord, you'd better get out of here quickly," Kenneth said quietly. "We have a new problem."

The dragons rose from their shaking caverns as their riders fought to keep them under control. They formed into a group of ragged Vs as they swept once around the peak and then turned toward the sea. There was no attack warning, no battle plan, not even any orders. It was simply better to sortie blindly than to wait.

High above, the Dragon Leader watched them come. He had barely two squadrons behind him and the entire dragon cavalry of the City of Night was on the wing below. But he had height and position and the climbing ranks were confused and hesitant. He raised his hand over his head and pointed down. Then he nudged his mount and the entire force hurtled earthward in formation.

In the midst of a hurricane of sorcery there was no magic to aid either side. Magic detectors screamed constantly, useless in the boil of spells. Even the psychic link between dragon and rider weakened and wavered in the maelstrom of magics that enveloped the City of Night.

Freed from close control, the dragons fought by instinct. Formations dissolved into whirling, flaming chaos as the two groups collided. Great winged bodies hurtled into each other, ripping and tearing and unseating riders. Dragon fire flew in all directions without discipline or guidance.

The Dragon Leader got one good pass out of his mount and saw his target go down smoking. Then he was through the League formation and the dragon was climbing on powerful beats of leathery wings. He tried to pull clear of the milling swarm to get altitude for another pass, but his dragon had other ideas. Still climbing, they charged into the thick of the fight.

The dragon caught one opponent by climbing underneath him and blasting him before the hapless beast even knew they were there. But now they were in the thick of the fight with hostile dragons on all sides.

True to its instinct the dragon raised her head and bellowed out a challenge. Answering roars came from all around them. The Dragon Leader gave up trying to control his mount. Instead, he drew his bow and swiveled, looking for the nearest opponent.

The attack came from behind. A League dragon swooped down on them before either dragon or rider knew he was there. The dragon must have exhausted its fire because it made no attempt to flame them as it went past. Instead the Dragon Leader had a glimpse of the figure on its back drawing his bow and twisting to track them as he swept by. The swarthy face, slitted eyes and scalplock of the enemy rider burned themselves into his brain.

There was no room to maneuver and no time to turn. The League rider fired and the iron shaft buried itself in his dragon's neck.

But the dragon barely noticed. She dropped one wing and flicked her tail to turn more tightly on her tormentor. Almost as an afterthought she reached up with a forelimb and plucked the shaft free.

*What the . . . ?* Somewhere in the back of his mind the Dragon Leader was amazed he wasn't plummeting out of the sky on a dead dragon. Meanwhile he was turning inside his foe and closing rapidly.

The Dragon Leader fitted an iron arrow to his own bow, but there was no tingle of recognition from the seeker head. The spells on death arrows were being overwhelmed by the competing magics. Swearing, he shifted his aim and fired. If magic would not work, perhaps skill would.

It did. The shaft flew straight and true and pierced the rider through the back. The man threw up his arms and crumpled into his saddle. The dragon turned to take on another opponent, still bearing the dead man on its back.

The Dragon Leader looked around and urged his mount forward for another foe.

Eventually it was all too much. The League dragons, outfought, disorganized and only under rudimentary control, broke and fled south in a confused gaggle. Some dove and dashed for safety scant feet off the earth. Others concentrated on making the best possible speed no matter what their altitude. A few fell to the flames of their attackers as they ran.

As soon as they were well clear of the City of Night, the Dragon Leader signaled his men to break off and re-form. The squadrons were tattered and several of the dragons were riderless, but his force was intact. There was no question who had won this day.

Counting his men, the Dragon Leader ordered one more sweep over the City of Night before they turned to the North and home.

With shaking hands, Toth-Set-Ra removed the globe from the cabinet and set it in the middle of the floor. There was a muffled roar and the palace shook, showering a sprinkle of mortar on the wizard's dark robe. He paid no attention.

Quickly but carefully he checked the pentagram, brushing away dust or debris that might breach it. Bale-Zur was not to be invoked lightly nor without scrupulous attention to the proper precautions. He could be counted upon to take advantage of any loophole in the bargain.

Toth-Set-Ra shook back the sleeves of his robe, picked up the silver wand off the lectern and began his chant.

A cloud of stinking, reeking sulphurous smoke billowed up, hiding the walls of the chamber and making Toth-Set-Ra's eyes water and his lungs burn. He paid no notice but continued chanting as a dull red glow coalesced and grew in the heart of the smoke cloud.

"Bale-Zur. Bale-Zur. Bale-Zur. By the power of your true name and the force of our bargain I call you, I summon you, I command you to make yourself manifest."

As the wizard gestured, the smoke billowed even

thicker and the glow grew fiercer and larger. And then the smoke wafted away as though on a breeze, leaving the mightiest of demons revealed.

The huge black creature squatted toadlike in the chamber, nearly filling the pentagram and almost brushing the stone vaulting of the ceiling. His horned and warty head swivelled slowly and continually from side to side, as if seeking prey. The great claws clenched and relaxed against the stone.

"My due," the demon's voice boomed out, so low that the undertones made the wizard's bones quiver. "I will have my due."

"I give you one," hissed Toth-Set-Ra. "I give you the one known to men as Sparrow, called Wiz. By the power of his true name I give him to you."

The monster paused and considered. The huge mouth opened, showing rows of teeth like daggers, and the beast ran a surprisingly pink tongue over its black scaly lips.

"Sparrow is not his true name," the creature rumbled. "Nor is Wiz."

"By the power of his true name I give him to you!" Toth-Set-Ra repeated, more shrilly.

Again the demon Bale-Zur considered. At last the massive head stopped moving and the glowing red eyes focused on the wizard.

"This one's true name is not written upon the wind," the demon said at last.

Toth-Set-Ra licked his lips, suddenly gone dry. "But he has a true name," he insisted desperately. "All men have a true name."

"Then it has never been spoken within the World," said the demon, hopping cumbersomely forward. "Our bargain is broken and I will have my due."

Toth-Set-Ra screamed and backed away as the demon crossed the now-useless pentagram. He scuttled toward the door, but the great creature was too quick for him.

A huge clawed foot caught him squarely in the back as his hand touched the door handle.

In the riot and confusion of the shuddering palace no one noticed the screams. But they went on for a long, long time.

Blinded, burned and screeching, the goblins fell back around the bend in the tunnel. Atros paid them no heed.

*So,* breathed the wizard, now unknowingly the Mightiest in the League. *So he is here after all.* He spared a quick glance for his companions. Of the fifty or so who had accompanied Atros into the dungeons perhaps a dozen remained. No soldiers here, this would be a duel of wizardry.

The auspices were not ideal, but Atros meant to have this wizard and if his goblin soldiers could not take him, then he would do so himself. He flipped back his great fur cloak, baring his thickly muscled arms, and muttered a protective incantation before he stepped around the corner.

"What is it?" Wiz asked as the hulking skin-clad figure strode down the tunnel toward them.

"A wizard," Kenneth told him. "I'm sorry, Lord, but we cannot help you now. You must meet magic with magic in a duel of wizards."

Wiz licked his lips and took a deep, shuddering breath. Then he stepped into the blue-lit corridor, staff in hand.

Atros did not check his stride as Wiz came through the broken door. Stepping around the broken burned bodies of his goblin bodyguard he bored straight toward the slight dark-haired figure holding his oak staff as if it were a baseball bat.

As Atros came on Wiz pointed his staff at him. **"bippity boppity boo,"** he said and again the roaring lance of flame shot from the staff's tip. But the big wizard made a dismissing gesture with a flip of his wrist and the flame veered to one side, splashing off the wall and dissipating harmlessly.

Atros raised his hand and balls of fire flew from his fingertips; one after the other they caroomed down the hall at Wiz. Wiz reached into his pouch and threw a tiny, pallid grub at his attacker. Grub and fireballs met in mid-tunnel and the flames were sucked away, leaving only a medium-sized worm behind.

Quickly Wiz muttered another spell. Suddenly Atros found his progress slowed, as if he were walking through molasses. The more he pushed, the slower he moved until by exerting all his mighty strength he was barely able to move at all.

Atros paused for a second, examining the spell, tasting it. Experimentally he tried moving a hand slowly and found it moved normally. The resistance built higher the faster he tried to move. The southern wizard smiled slightly and spoke a counter-incantation. Then he strode on unhindered.

His next step was nearly his last. His foot landed on a patch of something as slippery as the slickest ice over polished marble. He could get no purchase and his feet shot out from under him. Instinctively Atros used a spell to stay upright. Again a pause while he analyzed the magic and again Wiz's best effort was nullified by a counterspell.

Atros assayed a transformation spell. But Wiz just stood there, unchanged and unharmed. A disorientation spell, a sleep spell and an earthquake spell followed in quick succession. Still his slender opponent stood unscathed.

Atros was baffled. He had never seen its like before. Normally a barrage of spells had some effect, but this was as if they weren't even reaching their target. A bit tentatively, Atros hurled a bolt of lightning down the corridor. It reached the worm and vanished.

*Aha!* The worm had grown noticeably larger. The thing

was actually soaking up magic. Again Atros smiled and shaped a spell carefully.

The Southern wizard raised his staff, an inky blob of darkness formed on the end of it and wobbled down the corridor. It was black beyond black, blacker than night and it floated toward Wiz like a balloon wafted on a breeze.

Wiz watched as the sphere of darkness passed over the now-fattened worm. The worm reached out greedily for the magic just as the sphere bobbed to the floor of the corridor to meet it, bending toward the worm like a lover bending toward a kiss.

The pair touched. Suddenly the worm faded and shrunk as the black sphere of negation drained the magic it had hoarded. As the worm grew smaller so did the sphere, until at last there was again a tiny writhing grub and the sphere closed in on itself and vanished.

Atros ground the worm under his heel as he stepped forward to confront Wiz.

Wiz hit Atros with everything but the kitchen sink. A hundred lightning bolts flashed toward him so fast the corridor was lit by a constant blinding glare and the air reeked of ozone. The tunnel roof caved in with a roar and a huge cloud of dust. Thirty sharp knives flew at Atros from all directions. His bearskin tried to crawl off his back. A hurricane swept down the corridor blowing with a force no man could withstand.

Still Atros came on. The lightning struck all about him but never touched him. The falling rocks bounced off an invisible shield over his head. His skin garment convulsed and lay still. The wind did not move a hair on his head.

Wiz's spells had raw power, but they lacked the carefully crafted subtlety of a truly great wizard. And Atros, for all his braggadocio, was one of the great wizards of the World. More, he had the hard-won experience that comes from fighting and winning a score of magical duels. But most of all, Atros was a killer. Wiz simply was not.

Now Atros raised his staff and it was Wiz's turn to endure.

"New magic in the City of Night, Lord. Strong and strange."

Bal-Simba rushed to the Watcher's side. "Is it Sparrow? Can you locate him?"

"It appears to be and, yes Lord, we have it very precisely. He is in the dungeons beneath the city." The Watcher peered deeply into the crystal again. "There is other magic close by, Lord. Very strong and . . . Atros! Lord, your Sparrow is locked in a magical duel with Atros!"

"Fortuna!" Bal-Simba swore. "How is the Sparrow doing?"

"I can't tell, Lord. His spells are so peculiar. But there is a lot of magic loose in those tunnels." Another pause and the Watcher tore his eyes from the crystal to face Bal-Simba. "He seems to be holding his own, but I don't think he is winning, Lord."

"A Sparrow against a bear. That is not an even match."

"I fear not, Lord."

Bal-Simba bowed his mighty head and frowned into the crystal. Then he snapped his head up and slapped his palm on his thigh with a crack like a pistol shot.

"A circle!" he bellowed to the assembled Mighty. "Quickly to me! I must have a circle!"

Magic constricted around Wiz like a vise. As quickly as he erected a barrier against the onrushing spells, it was torn away and magic wound ever tighter around him. Again and again Atros thrust with his staff and Wiz was driven back toward the door of the cell where Moira and the two wounded guardsmen cowered, blinded and deafened by the effects of the duel and choked by the dust and magic thick in the air.

Suddenly Atros took his staff in both hands, raised it high over his head and brought it down with a vicious chopping motion. Wiz raised his staff to ward it off, but he was driven to his knees by the force of the blow. Blindly he raised his staff and gestured again. But the stroke was weak and ill-judged and Atros thrust it aside contemptuously. He stepped forward again and raised his staff for a final, killing spell.

From the cell door a blazing ball flew over Wiz's head and straight at Atros's face. The wizard dropped his staff and flinched aside from the burning sphere. He gestured and it swerved off to splatter in a flaming gout on the tunnel wall behind him.

Atros looked over Wiz and saw Moira standing in the door with her eyes blazing and her hands extended clawlike.

"Witch!" he said contemptuously and made a shooing motion with both hands. Moira screamed and flew back into the cell as if pushed by an unseen hand. Then the skin-clad giant stooped to pick up his staff. Inside the cell an explosion blasted out. A choking cloud of dirt billowed from the shattered door and a reddish light like a new-kindled fire burned within. Atros frowned and made a warding move with his staff. Wiz shook his head and climbed half to his feet.

Within the cell, obscured by the dust and lighted by the fire behind, a huge misshapen thing moved. Atros took a step back and a firmer grasp on his staff. What new sort of demon was this?

The light grew brighter as the fire took hold of the straw. Through the smoke and reddish backlight the thing resolved itself into a vaguely man-like figure. It groped through the smoke and dust, narrowing and resolving as it moved toward the door as though coalescing into something solid. Atros shifted uneasily. There was something familiar about that figure . . .

Then it came through the door and out of the smoke.

"So," it rumbled in a familiar voice. "A bear chasing a sparrow, eh? Not very edifying Atros. Not very edifying at all."

"Bal-Simba!" Atros spat the name like a curse.

"Bal-Simba indeed," the great wizard agreed. He was disheveled and his hair and skin were powdered gray with dirt and dust, but his teeth showed white as milk and sharp as daggers as he smiled. "A worthier opponent than yon sparrow, mayhap?"

"Sparrow," Bal-Simba said without taking his eyes off the southern wizard, "please put out the fire in the cell. Atros and I have wizards' business to discuss."

"We discuss it on my ground, Northerner," Atros said with an evil smile.

"Oh, I think no one's ground." Bal-Simba's smile was no less evil. "Your protective spells are neutralized, your brother wizards are, ah, occupied elsewhere and Toth-Set-Ra is dead." He raised his eyebrows. "What? You did not know? Demon trouble I believe. Troublesome things, demons. Almost as much trouble as sparrows."

Their eyes locked and neither moved while Wiz scrambled on his hands and knees behind Bal-Simba's trunk-like legs and through the cell door. Moira was waiting and they clung together like frightened children, heedless of the smoldering straw.

Finally Atros snarled and thrust his staff at the black giant. Wiz saw the air between them twist and contort into a half-sensed shape that flew straight at Bal-Simba's chest. Bal-Simba turned his staff sideways and the thing disappeared in a shimmer of air.

He took a step forward. Atros gestured again and the bloody green slime in the center of the corridor massed and grew and rose up in a foul dripping wave in front of Bal-Simba.

Again Bal-simba gestured and the slime hung back. It recoiled, gathered itself and thrust forward like a striking snake. With an easy grace Bal-simba pirouetted to one side. The slime thing missed and fell into the center of the corridor with a hollow "splat." Before it could gather itself again the Northerner pressed his staff into the slime's "back." It quivered for a moment and then lay still.

The giant turned to face his giant assailant. Atros's lips were working as he prepared another spell. But Bal-simba didn't give him the chance to use it.

"And now." Bal-simba tapped his staff on the flagging and stepped forward. Atros gave ground, pawing the air frantically with his staff.

"And now." Bial-Simba stepped and struck the pavement with a ringing blow as Atros blanched and flinched.

"*And now,*" he bellowed and smote the floor so hard his staff shattered into three pieces. Atros screamed as a great chasm opened beneath him. He teetered on the crumbling brink for an instant and then toppled forward. He was still screaming ever fainter and further away when the earth closed with a clap of thunder, cutting off his screams forever.

The black giant sagged and put a hand on the tunnel wall to stay upright. "Whoo," he gasped and shook his head. "Whoo."

"Lord, am I glad to see you!" Wiz stepped out of the cell, leaning on Moira for support.

"Sparrow," Bal-Simba rumbled, "you are a great deal of trouble."

Wiz just laughed and hugged him.

"Lord," Moira hugged him from the other side. "Lord, I had lost hope."

"Always unwise, Lady," said Bal-Simba. He frowned. "My two guardsmen? Donal and Kenneth?"

"Here, Lord," croaked Kenneth, pulling himself erect on the frame of the cell door. "Donal is with me, but he is in a sore way."

"Then I suggest we take him someplace more comfortable," Bal-Simba said. "Sparrow, will you do the honors? I'm not sure I am up to walking the Wizard's Way just yet."

"With pleasure," Wiz grinned. "Uh, it may take me four or five tries to get the spell right."

It actually took six.

# *Thirteen*
# THE BEGINNING

Spring was returning to Heart's Ease.

Except for the spots in deepest shade the snow was
melting, exposing the wet black earth beneath. Here and
there the hardiest plants thrust forth brave green shoots
and the branches of the trees swelled with the promise
of buds. The ground was soggy and chill, and there was
still a skin of ice on the puddles in the morning, but the
afternoon air was soft and the sun shone more brightly
onto the warming land.

Wiz and Moira stood together in the door of his hut,
sharing a cloak and looking out over the Wild Wood.

Heart's Ease was still a gaunt blackened thumb against
the blue sky, but the burned parts of the stockade were
already down, removed by the forest folk. As soon as the
paths through the Wild Wood dried out men would
arrive, masons and carpenters who would begin rebuilding Heart's Ease. As before there would be no magic in
its construction.

"We don't have to stay here, love," Wiz told Moira.
"It will take time to make the place habitable and there's
no reason you should live in a log cabin. We could go
someplace more civilized. Even the Capital if you prefer."

"I want to stay here, I think," Moira said, snuggling
to him under the cloak. "Oh, I'd like to go visit my village

after things thaw and dry. But I like it here." She turned her face to his for a kiss and Wiz responded enthusiastically.

"Besides," she went on after a bit, "I think Shiara likes having us." She turned to him. "But where do you want to live?"

"Anywhere you are," Wiz told her. "I'd be happy anywhere with you."

Moira bit her lip and dropped her gaze. "We need to talk about that."

"Fine," Wiz agreed, "but not now. We've got company."

Moira looked up and saw Bal-Simba picking his way across the muddy court.

"Merry met, Lord," Moira said as he came up to them.

"Merry met, Lady, Lord," the great black wizard replied as he came puffing up, his bone necklace jangling. "Merry met indeed."

"What's happening at the Capital?" Wiz asked once they were seated around the log table in the tiny cabin. Wiz and Moira sat holding hands on one side and Bal-Simba seemed to fill the rest of the dwelling.

Bal-Simba smiled "Ah, they are still as roiled as ants whose hill has been kicked over. From the ditherings of the Council you would think it was the Capital which had been destroyed, not the City of Night." Then he sobered.

"But that is not why I am here, Lord. I came to tell you that with the Dark League's power broken, we may be able to send you home again."

Wiz frowned. "I thought that was impossible."

"With the League in ruins many things are possible. Their wizards are scattered and cannot interfere if the Mighty band together for a Great Summoning. I have consulted the Council and we are willing to perform a Great Summoning to return you to your world."

Wiz felt Moira's hand tighten in his and caught his breath.

*Home!* A place with pizza, books, movies, records and music. A place where someone or something wasn't trying to kill him all the time. A place where he didn't have to be dirty or cold or frightened. And computers again.

But a place with no Moira. He saw she was staring intently at the table top. Was all the rest of it worth that?

There was something else too. He could help people here. Back home it didn't matter if he worked on a project or not, not really anyway. There were other programmers who could do what he did, although maybe not as well. Here he *did* matter. He could make a big difference. And that was worth a lot.

"I will not lie to you, Sparrow," Bal-Simba said. "There will be an element of danger. It will be hard to locate your world out of the multitude and even with all of us working together we are not sure we can send you back. But we believe the chances are very good."

"I don't think I want to go," he said firmly and drew Moira to him. "Not now." The hedge-witch came close, but he could still feel the tension in her body.

Bal-Simba grinned. "I thought that would be your answer. But I had to make the offer. And remember Sparrow, you can change your mind. The North owes you a great debt."

"You owe a greater debt to Patrius," Wiz said. "It was his idea."

The wizard nodded. "I wish Patrius had been here to see it."

"I wish he had too," Wiz said gravely. "He should have been here to see it. It really was his victory. Besides, I would liked to have known him."

"But you made it happen," Moira insisted. "You did the work. And Patrius made a mistake. He said you were not a wizard."

Wiz sighed. "You still don't get it, do you? I'm *not* a wizard. Most likely I never will be."

"There are those among the League who would

dispute that—were they still alive to do so," Bal-Simba said, showing all his pointed teeth.

"They'd be wrong." Wiz sighed again. "As wrong as you are. Look, you still don't appreciate what Patrius did. It wasn't that he found me and brought me here—and I'm not unique, by the way. In fact I was probably a poor choice if things had gone as Partrius intended them. But he wasn't looking for a wizard at all."

"I did not know you had added necromancy to your talents, Sparrow."

"No magic, just logic. Although I didn't work it out until everything was all over." Wiz took his arm from around Moira's waist and leaned both elbows on the table.

"Your real problem was that you had a magical problem that couldn't be solved by magic. Every great spell was vulnerable to an even greater counterspell and as the League waxed you inevitably waned. Individually, the League's magicians were stronger than the Council's, they *had* to be because they didn't care about the consequences of their actions. Patrius knew that a conventional solution, a bigger magician, would only make matters worse in a generation or so when the League learned the techniques."

"That is common knowledge in the council," Bal-Simba rumbled. "Indeed one of the reasons it was so easy to get agreement to attempt to return you is there is a strong faction which wishes to be rid of you. Go on, Sparrow."

"Okay, take it one step further. Patrius must have. He realized what you needed was a completely new approach. He had the genius to see that despite everything you believed, everything your experience showed you, somewhere behind all your magic there had to be some kind of regular structure. He realized that if he could find that formalism you could control magic."

"Eh?" said Bal-Simba. "Forgive a fat old wizard, but I was under the impression that we do control magic."

"No," Wiz said emphatically and then caught himself. "Forgive me Lord, but it is true. Each magician can use the spells or demons he or she stumbles upon and masters, but none of you—Council or League—controls magic. You don't deal with magic as a whole. You have no coherent theory of magic and you usually can't generalize from what you do know to what you don't. That was the root of your problem. The League and the Wild Wood were just symptoms."

Wiz could see Bal-Simba rolling that idea around in his mind. Obviously he didn't like it, but he was not going to reject it out of hand. "Go on," he said neutrally.

"In my world we have a saying that Man is a creature who controls his environment. You're in trouble because there's an important part of your environment you can't control: magic. Patrius didn't go looking for a wizard to beat the League. He wanted someone who understood abstract formalisms and how to apply them to complex problems in the hope he *could* learn to control magic. He needed a computer programmer or a mathematician. Magical ability wasn't in the job description."

"It appears that he got more than he bargained for," Bal-Simba said.

Wiz shook his head. "No. He got exactly what he bargained for. I'm not a magician in the way you mean.

"I've told you about computers, the non-living thinking machines I used to work with? Well, back when they were very new we worked with them the way you work your spells. Every new program was written by cut-and-try and every program was unique. Anyone who wanted to use a computer had to be an expert and it took years of work and study to master a machine.

"Later we realized it didn't have to be that way. We found the computer could do a lot of the work. We could write programs that would take care of the tiresome, repetitive parts and we could design programs whose parts could be used over and over in many different programs.

"Finally we figured out that you didn't even have to have a programmer for every computer. You could write programs that anyone could use to do common jobs like word processing or accounting.

"So today anyone can use a computer. Even children use them regularly. You still need programmers, but we work at a higher level, on more difficult or unusual problems—or on writing the programs that those children use."

Bal-Simba frowned. "Well and good for your world, Sparrow, but I am not sure I see what use it is to us."

"Patrius did," Wiz told him. "He hoped he could do the same thing with magic we do with computers. And he was right.

"In the long run the important thing wasn't that I beat the League with magic. It wasn't even that I was able to rescue Moira." *Although I'll be damned if I'll take that long a view,* he thought. "The important thing was programs—ah, the 'structure'—I had to build to do it." He leaned forward intensely.

"Don't you see? With my system you don't need to be a wizard to work spells. You need programmer-wizards to create the spells, but once they are set up anyone can use them. All you have to do is understand how those spells work and anyone can make magic. Good, controllable magic."

"Magic in the wrong hands is dangerous," Bal-Simba said dubiously.

Wiz smiled. "Don't worry. Where I come from we have a lot of experience in keeping our systems secure and users' fingers out of the gears. If the spells are properly designed just about anyone can use them safely.

"And it goes beyond that. I can teach someone to do what I do. It's not hard, really. It takes an organized mind and a knack for thinking logically, but jut about anyone can learn it. If your magicians have the knack I can show them the tools and teach them how to use them.

"Don't you see?" he repeated. "It means humans don't have to walk in fear any more." He thought of a small cabin deep in the Wild Wood and the four carefully tended graves behind it. Of a burned farm near the Fringe and the mound of raw earth among the cabbages. "People don't have to be afraid."

Bal-Simba sat silent for a long time. "This will require thought," he said at last. "The Council must consider it carefully. No doubt you will be asked to come to the Capital to explain to them." He chuckled. "Oh, we're in for some rare debates in the Council chantry, I can see that."

The wizard pushed away from the table and rose. "But it will be soonest over if it is soonest started. And I should carry the news to them quickly. For that I will leave you now." He turned toward the door.

"No, wait!" Moira rose from the table. "There is one more thing you must do."

Bal-Simba cocked an eyebrow and waited.

Moira clasped her hands in front of her, took a deep breath and closed her eyes.

"Lord, I want you to remove the infatuation spell from Wiz," she said in a trembling voice.

"Eh?"

"Uh, never mind," Wiz told him. "I'm not sure I want it removed. Not now." He put his hands on Moira's shoulders but she shook them off with an angry gesture.

"Please, Lord. It is not fair to Wiz that I hold him in thrall thus."

"Now wait a minute . . ." Wiz began, but Moira cut him off. "It is his right, Lord."

"Now how is this?" asked Bal-Simba with a twinkle in his eye. "You wish to be rid of this troublesome Sparrow?"

"No, Lord, I do not. But I love him and I cannot . . ." she took a deep ragged breath and rushed on. "I cannot accept what is constrained from him. I love him too much to hold him by magic."

"Don't I have anything to say in this?" Wiz interjected.

Moira turned to him. "No, Wiz you do not. Not now. After the spell is removed, perhaps then. But don't you see? You feel what you must because of the spell."

"He may not love you once the spell is removed," Bal-Simba said gravely.

"Yes, I will!" Wiz shouted but neither paid any attention to him.

"I know that, Lord." Moira looked as if she would cry. "I know that. But I cannot take by magic what is not mine by right."

"You have treated him very badly, you know."

"Lord, please."

Bal-Simba steepled his hands and rested them on his great belly. "Lady, you ask a thing which is impossible."

"Lord!" Moira gasped, her face white. "But you said . . ."

"I know, but there have been changes since then. Your Sparrow is now the mightiest of the Mighty. His method of magic will likely spread throughout the World and he bids fair to outshine us all from hedge-witch to master sorcerer. And he does not want the spell removed.

"You on the other hand bid to become the Lady to the mightiest of the Mighty and that raises you high indeed. A poor old fat wizard who wishes to live out his days in peace would be well advised to stay in your good graces."

The black giant smiled, showing all his filed, pointed teeth, looking for all the world like an avuncular shark.

"More to the point Lady, I cannot remove what is not there."

"Huh?" said Wiz brilliantly.

"Lord, I saw Patrius cast the spell."

"And I removed it on my visit some months back," Bal-Simba said, still smiling. "It no longer seemed necessary."

Moira dropped her hand to her sides. "Then . . ."

"Oh yes, your Sparrow has been free for some little time." He cocked his head and eyed Wiz. "Although he seems to show no great interest in leaving his cage."

In response William Irving Zumwalt, the Sparrow grown large as a roc, spun Moira the hedge witch around and clasped her to him. She melted into his arms and their lips met again.

Over her shoulder and through a haze of coppery red hair, Wiz saw the Mightiest of the Mighty ease through the door and close it softly after him.

He moved amazingly quietly for one so large.

# Book Two:

# The Wizardry Compiled

For the Bixen of course
and for the Sunday Morning Breakfast Club
—because they all had a hand in it.

# PART I:
# LOAD TIME

# One

## POLITICS AND STRANGE BEDFELLOWS

*You can always tell a really good Idea by the enemies it makes.*

*—programmers' axiom*

Pelus the wizard paused for dramatic effect. " . . . and so, My Lords, we must act quickly," he concluded ringingly.

For the sixth time that morning.

"Not so quickly, not so quickly," old Honorious said testily from the end of the table. He cleared his throat and prepared to restate his position for the eighth time.

The traceried windows along the south wall of the council chamber had been thrown open and the fitful summer breeze rustled the brightly colored tapestries hung along the buff sandstone walls. Outside trellised roses climbed the walls and peeked in the windows, perfuming the air. The stained glass in the window panes threw patches of brilliant color on the walls, the table and the men and women in the chamber.

Sitting at the long wooden table was the Council of the North. Fifteen of the mightiest wizards in the World—and one programmer from Cupertino, California who was bored out of his skull.

William Irving Zumwalt, "Wiz" to his friends,

"Sparrow" to most, tried to shut out the bickering and concentrate on the latest improvement to his magic compiler. It wasn't easy, especially since every so often he would be called on to say something and he had to keep at least one ear cocked to the conversation.

The Council had been arguing over the same point for the entire morning. Everyone knew that eventually they would do it, just as everyone knew the idea was good as soon as it had been proposed. But Agricolus had to get his opinions on record, Juvian saw an opportunity to snipe at Pelus and Honorious was constitutionally opposed to anything that looked like action. The result was a three-hour wrangle over nothing much.

For Wiz, who had made a career out of avoiding bureaucracy in all forms, it was sheer torture.

*And I thought ANSI standards committee meetings were bad.* He tried to shut out the incessant droning and concentrate on the idea he was developing.

A shimmering green shape began to form in the air in front of him. Wiz realized he had been moving his lips and that was enough to start the spell up. The wizards on either side of him glared and he quickly wiped out his unintentional handiwork, flushing under their eyes.

"Come, My Lords," rumbled Bal-Simba from the head of the table. The enormous black wizard was clad in his usual leopard skin and bone necklace. Somehow he had managed to seem interested through the entire morning. "The hour draws nigh. Let us decide." He gestured to a ray of light moving along a design inlaid in light wood in the darker wood top of the table. The spot of light was almost at the end of the design.

That was one merciful feature of the Council meetings. By custom and for arcane magical reasons they lasted no longer than it took the sun to traverse a certain arc in the sky. That meant about four hours.

So Honorious grumbled, Juvian sniped and Agricolus had one more thing he wanted to make clear, but they voted nonetheless and of course they decided to act.

Wiz stood with the others while Bal-Simba led them through the closing ritual. *Another morning shot to pieces,* he thought as they filed out of the council chamber. He sighed to himself. *It could have been worse. All the Council members could have been present.*

"Wiz."

He turned and saw Moira waiting for him. The redheaded hedge witch was wearing a gown of sea green that matched her eyes and set off her milk-white freckled skin. Its cut showed off her figure as well. Wiz thoroughly approved.

"Darling, have I told you you look lovely?" he said hugging her.

She gave him a look that made him catch his breath. "Why no, My Lord," she said, with her green eyes wide. "Not for, oh, at least five minutes."

"Too long." Ignoring the Council members who were knotted about talking, he kissed her.

In a vague way he knew he had improved in the two years since he had been kidnapped to this world. A more active life had put muscle on his slender frame. He had let his dark hair grow shoulder length in the local fashion. Tight breeches and puffy-sleeved shirts had replaced jeans and short-sleeved white shirts. Over-all he now looked more like a romantic's idea of a pirate than a pencil-necked computer geek.

But Moira had been beautiful the first day he saw her and she had only gotten more beautiful. Well, he admitted, maybe that was subjective. They had been married for less than a year and brides were always beautiful. Then he looked at her again. Nope, she was definitely more beautiful.

"I wanted to see you and perhaps have lunch with you."

"Is something wrong?"

She shook her head. "Nothing, I just wanted to be with you."

"I wish I could darling, but I hadn't planned on having lunch. I've got a special tutoring session scheduled and I'm trying to get the module for the spell compiler done by the end of the week."

Moira sighed. "Of course. I understand."

"I'm glad to see you though."

"Probably the only chance I'll get," she muttered.

"What?"

"Nothing, my love. Nothing."

"Look, I'll try to get home early tonight, okay?"

"I'll have dinner waiting."

Wiz sighed. "No, you better go ahead and eat. You know how this works."

"I know," she said softly.

The man in the blue wizard's robe looked around carefully before stepping into the clearing. A lesser man might have shivered, but he was of the Mighty and he knew well how to hold his emotions in check.

There was no sign of life or movement in the open space. The summer grasses lay pristine and untrampled. Here and there small red and yellow flowers nodded above them. The trees surrounding the clearing rustled and sighed as the breeze played through their tops. The air at ground level was still and smelled of leaves and sun-warmed grass.

The blue-robed man knew better than to trust ordinary senses. This was the time and the place appointed for the meeting and his higher senses told him magic of a lofty order lurked in that glade.

*It is for the good of the entire World,* he told himself firmly.

Still, if any of his fellow wizards found out . . .

Little enough chance of that. No one kept watch on

the Mighty and with the Dark League defeated, watch of all sorts was lax in the North.

Even so, he had taken good care that the others would not find out. He had traveled the Wizard's Way only part of the distance to this place and come the final league on foot. He left the Capital with a plausible story about a real errand near here, an errand he had accomplished. If no one inquired too closely into these few hours, there was no way they could find out where he had gone or what he had done. If the other had taken similar precautions, they were both safe.

In the center of the clearing he stopped, extended his staff and traced a design in the air. The sigil glowed bright red and then began to fade imperceptibly toward crimson.

"Welcome magician," a voice hissed out behind him. Whirling, he saw the person he had come to meet.

The man was almost as tall as the blue-robed wizard and cadaverously lean. His skull was shaven, but showed black stubble from lack of recent attention. A wizard's staff was clasped firmly in his right hand. But most striking was his clothing.

In contrast to the blue of the first wizard's robe, the other wore the black robe of a wizard of the Dark League.

Wiz Zumwalt plopped down in the carved oak chair, poured a cup of wine from the carafe on the inlaid table and sighed deeply.

Bal-Simba looked up from the corner of the Wizards' Day Room where he was studying a scroll. "I take it it did not go well?" the giant black wizard asked mildly.

"You might say that." Wiz took a pull on the cup. Then he snorted with laughter.

"May I ask what is so funny?"

Wiz shook his head. "I was just thinking. Two years ago today I was being chased through the Wild Wood by trolls, bandits, Dire Beasts and the sorcerers of the Dark League."

"I remember."

"Now here I am, safe in the Capital of the North, the Dark League is in ruins and," he gestured mock grandly, "I'm supposed to be the greatest magician in the whole World."

"Your point, Sparrow?" Bal-Simba rumbled.

Wiz sighed deeply. "Just that right about now trolls, bandits and evil sorcerers look awfully good."

"I am Seklos," the black-robed one said. "I speak for the Dark League."

"Where is your master?" the northern wizard demanded.

"He is—indisposed," Seklos said. "I serve as his deputy with full authority to act in this matter."

The first one nodded. Since the great battle between the Sparrow and the Dark League, the conclave of sorcerers had been reduced to a pitiful few remnants. Their City of Night on the southern continent lay ruined and deserted and the black-robed ones who had once threatened to engulf the entire North were fugitives everywhere. The leaders of the Dark League, including Toth Set Ra, their chief, had died in the battle and the new leader was much less powerful. There were also disturbing rumors about him. The northern wizard was not surprised he had sent a deputy.

He advanced a step and then stopped. Crouching watchfully next to the wizard was a Shadow Warrior in the tight-fitting black of his kind. A slashing sword hung down his back and his eyes were hard and merciless through the slits in his hood.

"Foolish to bring such to a wizard's meeting," the blue-robed wizard said.

The other shrugged. "It seemed a simple enough precaution."

"We meet under a sign of truce. You need fear nothing from me so long as the sign glows."

Seklos regarded him with amused contempt. "I know

the usage. But we did not come here to discuss custom. What is your proposal?"

"My proposal?"

"The sign changes color," the wizard pointed at the glowing character, which was now definitely orange. "Let us not waste time."

He hesitated, thrown off his carefully prepared approach. "Very well. It concerns the Sparrow, this Wiz."

"Ahhh," said Seklos in a way that made the other think that he had known very well what the subject would be.

"You mean you are not—what was that phrase you used?—'living happily ever after'?" Bal-Simba smiled gently. "Few people do, Sparrow."

"Yeah, I know, but I didn't expect it would be anything like what it's turned out to be. I thought I'd be able to finish my magic compiler and teach a few people how to use it. Then I could go on to more advanced magic programs."

Bal-Simba nodded. More than most of this world's wizards, he understood that Wiz's magical power came not from innate talent—Wiz had no talent for magic in the conventional sense. Rather, his abilities rested on his discovery that it was possible to write a magic "language," like the computer languages he had used back in Silicon Valley. Wiz might be spectacularly untalented as a magician, but where computers were concerned he was about as talented as they come.

Wiz shook his head. "I never saw myself sitting in meetings or in a classroom, trying to pound programming into a bunch of apprentices."

"Power makes its own demands, Sparrow," Bal-Simba said gently, laying the scroll aside. "Your new magic makes you powerful indeed."

❖     ❖     ❖

"You know this Sparrow," the northern wizard hissed. "You know his power. He broke you utterly in a single day."

"And you are cast down from your former high estate in the North," the black robe retorted. "Do you wish our aid in restoring you? A trifle chancy, I fear. As you say, we are not so great as we once were."

"I desire no such thing," the blue robe said with dignity.

"Oh, the presidency of the Council then? To replace Bal-Simba?"

"I desire what we of the north have always sought. Balance, the preservation of the World."

"I fear your Sparrow is proving as dangerous to your precious balance as ever he did to our League," Seklos said. "Well, what did you expect when you Summoned someone so powerful?"

"We did not agree to the Summoning," the other said testily. "That was Patrius's idea and he did not share it with the Council. And as for danger, he went on fiercely, "he is a greater danger than you know. With his out-landish magic he upsets the very balance of the World. Mortals attract attention from those who have ignored us ere now. They are likely to act against us, Council and League both."

Seklos nodded, saying nothing.

"There is still time. He can be stopped before matters come to a head, but to do it I must have your magic behind me."

Seklos laughed. "You propose to become an initiate of the Dark League?"

The blue-robed one gestured angrily. "Do not mock me, wizard. And understand this. We are mortal enemies, you and I. Under other circumstances I would crush you as I would kill a poisonous serpent."

Seklos smiled unpleasantly and cocked his head, but he did not interrupt.

"But," the first man went on, "the Sparrow is a threat

to every human magic user in the World. For this once and on this one matter I suggest that we have common cause and propose that we act in concert to rid ourselves of this menace."

"You put the matter succinctly," said the black robe. "Let us therefore consider the destruction of this Sparrow."

"No!"

The other cocked an eyebrow. "Does our new alliance flounder so soon?"

"The Sparrow is to be neutralized, not destroyed."

"Why not?"

"Two reasons. First, I forbid it." Seklos smiled again, but the blue robe ignored him. "Second, if you had a modicum of mother wit you would know his death is your destruction. Kill the Sparrow, harm one hair of him, and every wizard in the North will descend upon you. They will grub you out of your burrows and exterminate you all."

"And doubtless in the inquiry your part in the business would be discovered."

"Doubtless," the blue robe agreed, making a brushing motion as if to shoo off an annoying insect. "No, we cannot kill him. But if he were to disappear there would be many to mourn aloud him and few to lament his passing in private."

"And you suggest . . . ?"

"A Great Summoning to send the Sparrow back where he belongs. Him and his alien magics."

"Such a thing would not be easy to do."

"It would take a number of wizards, but it would not be impossible."

"Patrius did it alone."

"I am not as great a magician as Patrius," the northerner said with dignity. "Nor do I wish to end as he did." He remembered how the Dark League had cut the mighty wizard down as he performed unaided the Great

Summoning which brought the Sparrow to this world. "This requires more than I can accomplish alone and the others on the Council who feel as I do will not act."

"And you think we will?"

The northerner shrugged. "You have more reason and less to lose. It cannot be pleasant to be reduced to lording it over field mice and birds."

Seklos' eyes glittered and the other knew his shaft had gone home.

"We can do nothing while he remains in the Capital," Seklos said at last. "He must be brought to us."

"He can he maneuvered out of the Capital."

"He must be brought to—a place. It would be best if it were done while he treads the Wizard's Way. Then it is a matter of a simple spell."

The blue robe shrugged. Any wizard of the Mighty could be counted on to use that magical means for transport for any journey of over a few leagues.

"How long would it take you to be ready? The next full moon is on . . ."

"I did not say I would do it," Seklos cut him off. "I said we would consider it." He nodded toward the sign hanging in the air, now a deep violet fading to black. "The sigil darkens. Our meeting is at an end." He turned and walked toward the opposite edge of the clearing. Wordlessly the Shadow Warrior followed, moving crabwise to keep his enemy always in sight.

Behind them the blue-robed wizard nodded. He knew full well that the remnants of the Dark League would join him in this. What other choice had they?

# *Two*

# NAILING JELLY TO A TREE

*Everything always takes twice as long and costs four times as much as you planned.*

—programmer's axiom

"I dunno," Wiz sighed again and drained his wine cup. "This isn't working out anything like I thought it would." He set the cup down and leaned toward Bal-Simba, elbows on knees.

"Look, I took the seat on the Council because you wanted me to. I'm not a wizard, I've never been a politician and those meetings are torture."

"Your position and power entitle you to a seat."

"Yeah, but I've got important work to do."

It was Bal-Simba's turn to sigh. He did so gustily and the bones of his necklace clattered with the movement of his barrel chest. "Sparrow, listen to a poor fat old wizard for a moment.

"You talk of finishing your spell engine. But that is only half your task. The other half is teaching others to use it and the largest part of that is getting them to accept it."

Wiz toyed with the cup, running his finger along the rim. "I suppose you're right. I never was any good at teaching. I guess I need to try harder."

321

"Perhaps it would be more to the point if you tried to understand how others feel. Your task is difficult. But you make it more so. Your attitude does not make you friends, either on the Council of among the other wizards and that adds to the hostility against your methods. Specifically, you do yourself no good at all when you belittle the Council."

"I don't belittle the Council!"

Bal-Simba arched a brow. "No? But your work is more important."

"Well . . ."

"Sparrow, the Council of the North has stood for centuries as the shield of humans against malevolent magic, both from the Dark League and from the World at large. It is the closest thing to a ruler this land has."

Wiz nodded. "Look, I'd be the last person to deny you and the other wizards have done a heck of a job. But magical programming changes things. As soon as I get the compiler perfected and get to work on the spells, anyone will be able to use magic. There won't be a need for a Council of wizards to guard and protect humans."

Bal-Simba shook his head. "Sparrow, much as I admire your directness I think it leads you astray. But even if what you say is so, we must still get from where we are to where you wish to be. To do that you need the cooperation of all wizards, especially the Mighty and most especially the Council. You do not get someone's cooperation by telling him he is obsolete and his life's work is outworn."

"It would be easier if some of the Mighty would learn to use the compiler. But they're all so *dense*."

"Wizards do not have the reputation for being stupid," Bal-Simba said with deceptive mildness.

Wiz sighed and rubbed his eyes. "You're right. Stupid isn't the word for it. But they don't generalize. You guys learn one thing at a time and you can't seem to work from a bunch of specifies to a general proposition." He shook his head. "And a lot of programming is general-ization."

"Nonsense!" came a firm voice from the doorway. Wiz and Bal-Simba turned to the sound and saw a tall theatrically handsome man in wizard's blue. His silver hair swept over his ears in carefully arranged waves to perfectly set off his aristocratic features and evenly tanned skin.

Bal-Simba nodded. "My Lord Ebrion."

Wiz stiffened, but he also nodded politely. *Dammit, I will not lose my temp*er.

"The essence of magic is in the particular," Ebrion said in his beautifully modulated voice as he came into the room. "To control magic we must understand *this* tree or *this* fire, not these 'classes' you keep on about. All trees are not alike, Sparrow, and it is only by deeply perceiving an object that we may control it magically."

Wiz kept quiet. He had enough trouble with Ebrion and his traditionalist friends already. Like all the tradi-tionalists, Ebrion didn't like Wiz. Unlike most of them he made no secret of his dislike beyond a certain cold civility. Worse, he was a theoretician, or the closest thing to a theoretician of magic this world had ever produced. Wiz's success had thrown him into the shade in his own specialty and that made him dislike Wiz all the more.

"Magic is both organic and particular, Sparrow," Ebrion went on as if lecturing an apprentice. "The best magic cannot be built up from bits and pieces like a jackdaw's nest. It must be conceived of whole."

"Wiz's method seemed effective enough against the Dark League," Bal-Simba said quietly.

"Lord, I have never denied that the Sparrow ranks among the Mighty, but sheer talent does not make his theories correct."

He waved a hand dismissingly. "Oh, I will admit the trick of constructing a demon to recite his spells for him is useful—albeit it was not unknown to us before. But his notion of how magic works?" He shook his head.

"The compiler is a lot more than a spell-reciting demon," Wiz interjected.

"So you have told us repeatedly. But at bottom that is all it does, is it not?"

"No, it's a compiler written in a threaded interpreted language that . . ."

Ebrion touched his fingertips to his forehead, as if stricken with a sudden headache. "Please Sparrow, spare us one of your explanations. You have told us this 'compiler' demon recites the spells you create and that much, at least, is comprehensible."

Wiz started to protest and then clamped his jaw. Ebrion wasn't interested in explanations and he wasn't any good at making them.

"Anyway, you're wrong," he said sullenly. "I don't have any talent for magic. Any one of the Mighty can sense that."

"We can all sense that you do not have our kind of talent. But you have shown us that you have enormous magical ability. What you have not shown us is that your system works. To do that you would have to teach others to make magic with it, by your own admission."

"So I'm a lousy teacher," Wiz said, nettled.

"For over a year you have dwelt here and tried to teach this marvelous system of yours. Have any of us mastered it? Has anyone but yourself learned it?"

"Programming takes time to learn. You didn't learn magic overnight did you?"

"No, but with a few-months study I was able to perform certain useful spells. Your pupils work and work and can do little—and that poorly."

"You've got to learn the basics and work up."

"No Sparrow, this 'general theory of magic' of yours is an illusion. You must learn one spell at a time. You must practice every gesture, every word, understand every influence. One spell at a time, Sparrow." He looked down at Wiz and smiled mockingly.

"*That* is how magic is made."

Wiz ground his teeth. He remembered one of the first classes, back when he was still trying to teach wizards in groups. The lesson was to construct a simple apparition spell, the rough equivalent of the "hello world" program in the C computer language.

Of course, the point was no more making a form appear than the point in C program was to put the words "hello world" on a computer screen. It was to familiarize the magicians with the basic workings of the magic compiler. Slowly and carefully, Wiz led his class through the fundamentals of his program for constructing magic spells. Then he asked each of them to make the spell with the compiler.

With a disdainful flick of his wand, Ebrion had created a shape that was ten times as real as the shadowy blobby forms the other students were struggling to make through the program.

"*That* is how magic is made," he said in a condescending tone as Wiz and the students stared at his result.

"The theory works," Wiz ground out. "Or did I just imagine taking on the Dark League?"

"Once again, I have never denied you were powerful," Ebrion said, as if repeating a simple lesson to a very slow pupil. "You attacked them with the completely alien magic of your world and overwhelmed them with spells they had never seen before. Thus you established your power. Surprise is ever an important weapon, Sparrow. As for the rest of your power, it would be a simple matter to put it to the test."

Ebrion meant a contest of wizards. Superficially it was a fair way of determining who was the better magician. But there were tricks to such contests, just as there were subtleties to any kind of competition. From apprentices to wizards of the Mighty, all magicians practiced against each other for sport. The only experience Wiz had in such a contest was when he had inadvertently gotten into a duel to the death with the second most powerful wizard of the Dark League. Only Bal-Simba's intervention had saved him.

When he saw Wiz would ignore the implied challenge, Ebrion went on. "You have taught us some new tricks and given us some important insights and for that we must thank you. But they do not amount to revolutionizing the practice of magic, nor do they sweep away all we have done here for hundreds of years. Magic is as it ever was, Sparrow."

"Except that the Wild Wood isn't pushing into human lands any more," Wiz snapped. "The Dark League isn't one step from throttling the entire North and the common people have a defense against hostile magic. You and all your *traditions* couldn't do any of that!"

As soon as the words were out of his mouth, Wiz was sorry. Ebrion's head jerked back as if he had been slapped and he blanched under his tan. He turned his back on Wiz and addressed Bal-Simba.

"My Lord I came merely to tell you that I will be leaving the Capital for Mountainhame on the morn and to inquire if there was some service I could perform there for you."

"No, nothing." Bal-Simba said.

"Then I will take my leave of you, Lord." And with that he bowed and left the room, ignoring Wiz completely.

"That was ill-done, Sparrow," Bal-Simba said as soon as the door had closed behind Ebrion.

"I know, Lord," Wiz said uncomfortably. "Do you think I should go apologize to him?"

Bal-Simba shook his head. "Leave him for now," he rumbled. "Perhaps when he returns you should speak to him."

"He was trying to get under my skin."

Bal-Simba frowned. "Get under . . . ah, I see what you mean. So he was, but you let him and that gave him the advantage of the encounter. You must learn to control yourself better."

"I'll try, Lord," Wiz said uncomfortably.

"Let us hope you succeed," Bal-Simba said. "You have students soon, do you not?"

"Yipe. I'm already late!"

"Go then, Sparrow. But remember what we have discussed."

# *Three*
## STIRRING THE POT

*It's never the technical stuff that gets you in trouble. It's the
personalties and the politics.*

—programmer's saying

*Presumptuous puppy!* Ebrion fumed as he made his
way down the stairs and out into the main courtyard.

He did not return to his tower or to any of his other
usual haunts. Instead he crossed the yard and made for
the main gate of the keep. Just inside the gate was a
much less plushly appointed day room used by off-duty
guardsmen, minor merchants, castle servants, apprentices
and others.

The big, low-ceilinged room was several steps down
from the yard. Light flooded in through the windows up
next to the whitewashed ceiling and reflected down onto
the worn plank tables and rough benches and stools.

Heads turned as he came in and then turned back.
This was hardly a place for the Mighty, much less a
member of the Council, but Ebrion was known for his
common touch. Two or three times in every turning of
the moon he could be expected to drop by and exchange
a few words with the habitués.

It was a time when apprentices should be at their
studies or serving their masters. Still, Ebrion expected

to find the one he sought here and he was not disappointed. Sitting by himself in a corner was a lank man with smoldering brown eyes and bowl-cut brown hair. Arms flat on the table and legs thrust straight out into the aisle, he was scowling into a mug of small beer as if he expected it to rise up and challenge him.

"Well met, Pryddian," Ebrion said pleasantly.

The young man looked up and nodded, but he did not rise as befitted an apprentice in the presence of one of the Mighty.

"My Lord."

Ebrion eased himself down upon the bench and studied the man. Pryddian was the oldest of the Keep's apprentices and now he was an apprentice without a master.

Pryddian seemed oblivious to the scrutiny. He kept his eyes fixed on his mug.

"I would speak with you on a matter of some import," Ebrion said. He made a show of looking around the room and lowered his voice. "What I say must stay between us."

Pryddian looked at him narrowly and nodded. Ebrion did not ask for a binding oath and the apprentice did not offer one.

"I had heard that Juvian released you."

"Arrogant old fool," Pryddian muttered. That earned him a sharp look from the wizard.

"I am sorry, Lord," he said sullenly. "But you know my story. I started my training here in the Capital instead of in some hedge witch's hovel. I am widely acknowledged to have more talent than any of the other apprentices." Ebrion nodded, acknowledging a plain fact and Pryddian took another swallow of beer.

"Yet after two years I am turned off over a trifle. Juvian assured me I would have no trouble finding another master. But no other wizard will take me on and no one will tell me honestly why."

Ebrion nodded sympathetically. That was not the story Juvian told, but it did not serve his purpose to say so.

"I know. I sought you out because I thought you should know there was more to the matter than a disagreement between you and Juvian." He paused, picking his words.

"Naturally I cannot violate the confidences of my fellow wizards, but I can tell you that today there is more to being a successful apprentice than magical talent and a willingness to work hard. It is also necessary to master the Sparrow's new magic."

Pryddian snorted. He had attended one or two classes and had not done well. Ever since he had made no secret of his contempt for Wiz's method's.

"I know. And between the two of us, I agree." He shrugged and spread his hands. "But who am I? The Sparrow sits on the Council of the North and has Bal-Simba's ear. He can see to it that apprentices either learn the new magic or are no longer apprentices."

"How is this? I thought apprenticeship was a matter between the wizard and pupil alone."

"And so it is," Ebrion assured him. "But a wizard must consider relations with his fellows. You understand these things, surely."

Pryddian nodded. "I suspected there was a favor involved, in spite of what everyone says."

"Oh, not *favor*," Ebrion said hurriedly. "We prefer to think of it as maintaining harmonious relations."

"Call it what you will, I am blackballed by the Sparrow."

"Well," the wizard admitted, "it would be—hmm—difficult for any wizard to take you as an apprentice."

"And my ability counts for nothing?"

"Times have changed. It seems the Sparrow's new magic is more important than talent for the old."

"So I am forever barred from becoming a wizard. Unless you . . . ?" He trailed off hopefully.

"The Sparrow knows how I feel about him and his new magic. I would do you little good, I fear."

Pryddian nodded knowingly. "And doubtless it would do you little good to have me."

Ebrion shrugged.

Pryddian finished his beer in a single long pull. "This Sparrow rises above himself," he said darkly.

"Perhaps, but he is of the Mighty." The wizard rose. "In any event, I felt you should know. I cannot speak openly, of course."

"Of course." The would-be apprentice looked up. "I thank you for the information, Lord. And as to this Sparrow, perhaps he needs his feathers plucked." He dropped his eyes to scowl at the now-empty mug as Ebrion left.

Outside the door of the day room, Ebrion allowed himself a smile.

Under any circumstances Pryddian would never have become a wizard. Talent he had, and stubbornness to persist in the face of gentle hints and not-so-gentle discouragement, but he was undisciplined and he had a vindictive streak that ran both broad and deep. If he had started his training in the villages he probably never would have been sent to the Capital. But Ebrion was very glad he was here. His combination of talent, frustration and a viperish tongue made him ideal. *Yes,* the wizard thought, *he is the perfect choice to bait the Sparrow into some heedless action.*

# Four

## FENCEPOSTS AND FALLING ROCKS

*Those who can't do, teach.*
                                    —article of faith among students
*And vice-versa.*
                                    —programmers' addendum to students' article of faith

Malus was waiting impatiently when Wiz arrived, obviously fuming.

To salve wizardly pride, Wiz did most of his teaching of actual wizards in private sessions. Malus was one of his least-favorite pupils. As a person, the pudgy little wizard was nice enough, always merry and joking. But he had particular trouble in grasping concepts and the thought that he was a slow learner made him even more resistant to the new magic.

Malus didn't even let Wiz finish his apology for being late.

"This spell you showed me," he said accusingly. "It does not work."

Wiz sighed inwardly. "Well, let me see your code."

Grudgingly, the plump little sorcerer produced several strips of wood from the sleeve of his robe. Laid in the proper order the characters on them would list out the spell. Putting them on separate pieces of wood was a safety precaution against activating the spell by writing it down.

Wiz arranged the wood strips on the table and frowned briefly at what was written there.

"Oh, you've got a fence post error."

"Fence post?" the wizard asked.

"Yeah. Look, say you've got a hundred feet of fence to put up and you need to put a post every ten feet. How many posts do you need?"

"I am a wizard, not a farmer!" Malus said, drawing himself up to his entire five-foot-four.

"Well, just suppose," Wiz said half-desperately.

Malus thought hard for a minute. "Ten, of course."

"Nope," Wiz said triumphantly. "Eleven. Unless you strung your fence in a circle."

"But one hundred taken as tens is ten."

"Yeah, but if you've got a hundred feet of fence and only ten posts in a straight line, you leave one end of the fence hanging free. If you put the posts in a closed figure, you only need nine because you start and end on the same post."

"And how am I to know such things? I told you I am not a farmer."

"Well, just keep it in mind, okay? Boundary conditions are always likely to give you trouble."

"Borders are always unchancy places," Malus agreed.

"Uh, yeah. Let's leave that for a minute. Do you have any other problems?"

"There is this business of names."

For about the fiftieth time, Wiz wished he hadn't been so cavalier in choosing names for the standard routines in his library. To wizards, a thing's name was vitally important and they took the name to be the thing.

"I told you that the names I used aren't necessarily representative."

Malus looked at him like he was crazy. "Very well. But even granting that, why must the names change haphazardly? That is what I do not understand."

"They don't change at random. They don't really

change at all. It's just that an object can be a member of more than one class."

"Classes again!"

"Look at this," Wiz said, dragging out a couple of sheets of parchment and laying them out side by side so all the spell was visible. "Okay, here this variable is called 'elfshot,' right?"

"Why is it named that?"

"It's not named that. That's only what it's called in this routine. Its name is **'dragons_tail'**."

"Well," demanded the wizard, "if it is **'dragons_tail'**, why do you call it 'elfshot'? And how do you add a **'dragons_tail'** to this, this loop variable."

"No, no," Wiz said desperately. "It is actually seven at this point in the program and that's what gets added to the loop variable."

"Well, if it's seven then why don't you just say so?" roared the wizard.

"Because it isn't always seven."

The wizard growled in disgust.

"Look, I think I'm getting a headache. Why don't we leave this for right now, okay? Just try working the program through again and we'll go over it in our next session."

The early end to the tutorial with Malus left Wiz with time to spare and a completely ruined temper. He wanted someplace quiet where he could be alone to think. Leaving his workroom door unlocked he left the central keep, threaded his way through two courtyards and climbed a set of stairs to the top of the wall surrounding the entire complex.

The parapet was one of his favorite places. It was usually deserted and the view was spectacular. The Capital perched on a spine of rock where two rivers met. From the north the ridge sloped gently up to drop off precipitously in cliffs hundreds of feet high to the south and along the east and west where the rivers ran.

On the highest part of the ridge stood the great castle of the Council of the North, its towers thrusting skyward above the cliffs. Here the Council and most of the rest of the Mighty had their homes and workshops. Behind the castle and trailing down the spine came the town. In the cliffs below the castle were the caverns that served as aeries for the dragon cavalry. As Wiz stood and watched, a single dragon launched itself from below and climbed out over the valley with a thunder of wings.

The parapet was nearly fifteen feet wide. It sloped gently toward the outer wall so that rainwater and liquid fire thrown by enemies would both drain over the sides and down the cliff. The outer edge was marked by crenellations, waist-high blocks of stone that would protect the defenders from enemy arrows. It always reminded Wiz of the witch's castle in *The Wizard of Oz*, except that this was much grander.

Wiz walked along, guilty about taking the time away from his work and yet happy to be away. The swallows whipped by him as they swooped and dove along the cliff edge to catch the insects borne aloft by the rising current of air.

The day was bright and cloudless and the air soft and warm enough that he appreciated the breeze blowing up from the river. Faintly and in the distance he could hear the sounds of the castle and town. Somewhere a blacksmith was beating iron on an anvil. From this distance it sounded like tiny bells.

There was a place he favored when he wanted to get away, a spot where a bend in the wall and a watch tower combined to shut out all sight and most sound of the Capital. From there he could look out over the green and yellow patchwork of the fields and woods and into the misty blue distance.

He leaned forward, resting his elbows in one of the crenellations. *If only . . .*

He felt the stone shift under his weight but by that

time it was too late. The block gave way and he was pitched headlong out over the abyss.

Frantically he lashed out with his arms and miraculously his fingers met stone. His arm was nearly yanked out of its socket as he twisted around and slammed face first into the wall. But his grip held and he was left dangling by one hand against the sheer wall.

The crenellation had taken part of the stone facing with it, leaving the rough inner masonry beneath. Wiz was hanging by his fingertips from the edge of the facing, just below where the stone block had been.

Far below him, between his dangling legs, he saw the dislodged block bouncing and tumbling off the cliff. It hit the water with a splash that looked no bigger than a match head. Wiz sucked in his breath and clinched his eyes tight to ward off the dizziness.

Frantically he scrabbled for a hold for his left hand. First his fingers slipped over the smooth surface of the facing. Then at last they caught on another place where the facing blocks had pulled loose. With both hands secure, Wiz opened his eyes and stared at the stone in front of his nose, breathing heavily.

At last he managed to look up. Bracing his feet against the wall, he levered his way up and snatched another handhold slightly higher up the wall. Then another and another and at last he was able to put his feet on the lip where the facing had pulled away. One more heave and he flopped back on the parapet. Bruised and shaken, he pulled himself back through the space where the crenellation had been.

He moved away from the edge and sank down with his head between his knees, breathing in great shaking gasps. Gradually he got himself back under control and looked around him.

The parapet was deserted. Not even the guards could be seen from this spot and there were no other strollers along the walls. He was completely isolated, but . . . .

Was it his imagination or had he seen a figure flit behind a tower as he pulled himself back onto the parapet?

The rest of the day passed uneventfully. He gave two more private lessons, tried to teach a class of apprentices what the concept of zero was all about and spent nearly half an hour listening to Pelus, who was trying to get him to vote against Juvian at the next Council meeting. The sun had set over the towers of the Capital by the time he left his work room and trudged down the winding stairs to the suite he and Moira shared. Lanterns along the walls cast a warm mellow light on the wide corridors.

Wiz was so tired he barely noticed.

As he came down the hall a young man came toward him. Wiz stepped slightly to the side but instead of moving out of his way the man seemed to step in front of Wiz so he jostled him as they passed.

"Clumsy Sparrow," the young man hissed.

Wiz started to say something, thought better of it, and swept past the sneering young man.

*What the hell is his problem?* Wiz thought.

He knew the man more or less by sight. An apprentice with a vaguely Welsh name. They had never exchanged more than a half a dozen words and now the man was going out of his way to be insulting.

*One more thing to worry about.* This place was getting to him. He was trying to do a job he wasn't very good at, a lot of the people here seemed to hate him, he couldn't concentrate on the parts he *could* do and even the simplest thing seemed to take forever. He was stretched tauter than a violin string and the fatigue and tension was telling on him.

The door to their apartment was open and he saw Moira sitting in the light of a magical lantern. The light caught her hair and glints of brushed copper played through it. Her mouth was twisted up in a little moue as she bent over the mending in her lap.

*Still*, Wiz thought, *there are compensations*.

As he came into the room he saw there was someone else there. A painfully thin girl with flyaway brown hair was sitting at Moira's feet working on a piece of embroidery.

Without a word the girl got up and left.

"Hi June," Wiz said to her back as she brushed by.

"What have you been doing?" he said as he came to her.

"Sewing." Moira laughed. "I fear I will never be skilled with a needle."

He leaned over and kissed her. "That's all right. You're good at plenty of other things."

She arched one of her coppery eyebrows. "And how am I to take that, My Lord?"

"As a compliment." He bent down and kissed her again. "And how has your day been?"

*Well, let's see. I insulted one of the most powerful members of the Council, botched a tutoring session and nearly killed myself by falling off the parapet.* "Oh, okay," he mumbled.

Moira looked at him sharply. "What did you do to your nose?"

"I ran into a door. How is June?" He asked quickly to change the subject.

Moira gave him an odd look, but she took the bait. "She improves, I think."

Like Moira, June had been found wandering as a child in the Fringe of the Wild Wood. Unlike Moira, no one knew where she came from or who her parents were. She was quiet, as shy and skittish as a woodland animal. She worked as a maid and servant around Wizard's Lodge—when anyone could find her.

Wiz had never heard her speak, although Moira said she occasionally talked.

"Can't you do something to heal her?" Wiz asked.

"Bronwyn, the chief healer, says she is not ill in her mind," Moira said. "That it is merely her way."

"If she's not ill, she's sure peculiar."

"That is odd coming from you, Sparrow," Moira said.

"Hey, I'm alien. I admit it. But she," he jerked his head toward the door, "is about three sigma west of strange."

Moira ignored the comment, something she often did when she didn't understand her husband. "She seems fascinated by your desk," she said.

Wiz looked at the disorderly pile of manuscripts, strips of wood, slates and books on the desk under the window. "Did she touch anything?"

"You know better than that. I would never allow it."

A wizard's working equipment was dangerous. Even Moira would not touch Wiz's desk, though having such a mess in their sitting room pained her.

"Hmm. Do you suppose she has a talent for magic?"

Moira shook her head. "I think it is your guardian that attracts her."

Like any wizard, Wiz had created a demon to guard his paraphernalia. His took the form of a foot-long scarlet dragon, now curled peacefully asleep atop Wiz's big leather-bound "notebook."

Wiz sat down and reached for the notebook. The dragon demon woke and slithered over to a corner of the desk where it resumed its nap.

For the next quarter hour neither of them said anything. The only sound in the room was the scritching of Wiz's pen and the rustle of fabric as Moira turned the piece in her lap this way and that.

"Oh, I have some news as well," Moira said, putting down her mending.

"That's nice," Wiz said without looking up.

"Bronwyn says she will teach me the rudiments of the healer's art. I am too old for an apprentice, of course.

In the village of Blackbrook Bend I often did simple healing and Bronwyn says we can build on that."

Wiz grunted.

"And then I'll sprout wings and grow two extra heads," she said sharply.

Wiz raised his head. "What?"

"You have not heard a word I said, have you?" Moira threw her mending on the floor and stood up.

"It is bad enough that you are always gone, but when you are here the least you can do is admit that I am alive!"

"I'm sorry, I was just . . ."

"I will *not* be ignored." Moira burst into tears.

Wiz came to her and took her in his arms.

"Oh, darling. I didn't mean to upset you."

"Hold me."

"Moira, I'm sorry I . . ."

"Don't talk, just hold me." She clung to him fiercely as if he were about to be swept away from her.

They made love that night. Afterward they lay in each other's arms without speaking. Wiz didn't fall asleep until long afterward and he didn't think Moira did either.

The next day Wiz stumbled through his classes, groggy from lack of sleep. By the time he got home that evening he was ready to drop, but when Moira suggested they walk out to the drill yard he didn't object.

In the early evenings the guardsmen held free-form practice on the drill ground. Because there was a gathering of young men there, the young ladies of the castle naturally congregated, to sit in the shade or walk along the colonnaded porch that surrounded the beaten earth of the practice court. And where the young ladies congregated naturally became a gathering place for everyone in the keep. From the highest of the Mighty to the workers in the scullery, it had become the traditional place for an evening stroll.

Wiz and Moira joined the promenade with Moira clinging tightly to his arm. They exchanged small talk with their acquaintances, received respectful bows Wiz's station entitled them to and spent a few minutes talking with Shamus, the Captain of the Guard and a friend of Moira's from her time at the Capital learning to be a hedge witch.

From a window above the practice yard Ebrion watched them pass. It would go hard on the hedge witch when the Sparrow disappeared and looking at them walk arm-in-arm that thought troubled him. With an effort he shook it off. The good of the many was much more important than the feelings of one hedge witch. Besides, there were rumors that the two were not getting along.

*She'll get over it quickly enough,* he told himself. Then he concentrated on what he knew was about to happen in the courtyard below.

"Look, there's Donal," Moira pointed to a tall dark-haired guardsman who was using a short spear—actually a padded pole—against a man with a sword and shield.

Donal was one of the guardsmen who had accompanied Wiz on his foray into the dungeons beneath the City of Night to rescue Moira. He was skillfully using the length of his weapon to keep his opponent at a distance and flicking the spear out in quick thrusts, searching for a weakness in the man's guard. As they watched he executed a fast double thrust and parry that swept his opponent's sword to the side and finished with a solid thrust to the face.

"Oh, well done!" Moira said, laughing and clapping.

Wiz smiled. In the back of his head a small voice was nagging him about all the work he had to do, but the evening was lovely, the place was pretty, and it was pleasant to walk with a beautiful woman, especially when she was your wife.

As they ambled along, a man stepped out from behind

one of the pillars and ran into Wiz, nearly knocking him down.

"Hey, watch it." He saw it was the apprentice who had nearly run into him in the hall the night before.

Pryddian curled his lip. "Clumsy Sparrow. Why not use your magic to fly out of the way?"

Moira gasped. Wiz wanted to smash his sneering face. Instead he stepped around Pryddian and walked toward the opposite side of the drill field.

"Wiz, you shouldn't let him talk to you like that," Moira hissed once they were out of earshot.

"What should I do? Turn him to stone?"

"Oh, don't be silly," she said angrily. "But at the very least you should put him in his place."

"How?"

Moira considered. Wiz did not have the wizard's manner that came with years of practicing magic. He could not freeze an apprentice with a look the way a real wizard could. Short of using magic on him—a thing unthinkable—there really was nothing he could do.

"I will speak to Bal-Simba about him."

"I wish you wouldn't. It will be all right, really."

Moira pressed her lips together and kept walking.

"Ah, Sparrow, My Lord." They turned and saw Juvian coming toward them, a fussy, balding little man who was always in a hurry.

Wiz nodded respectfully. "My Lord."

"Ah yes," Juvian came panting up. "My Lady, I wonder if you could excuse us for a moment. There is a matter of Council business we must discuss." He took Wiz by the elbow and led him off to the reviewing stand that stood on poles at one side of the field. Wiz threw Moira a helpless look over his shoulder, but he did not try to break the Wizard's hold on his arm.

"He's a lucky man," said a voice behind her.

Moira turned and saw Shamus.

"I doubt he would agree with you at this instant."

"Nonetheless, lucky." He smiled with an infectious warmth Moira remembered from her student days and extended his arm. "While he is occupied would you do me the honor of accompanying me?"

Moira smiled back. "Gladly."

Shamus was a lithe, compact man whose shock of sandy hair was thinning with the approach of middle age. His face was deeply tanned and a little windburned with tiny crinkles of laugh lines at the corners of his eyes and mouth. Moira had had a minor crush on him when last she stayed at the Capital, but her studies left her little time to pursue such things.

"We do not see you out here often enough."

"Wiz's work keeps him busy," Moira said with a trace more acid than she intended.

"True, but a wife does not have to walk only with her husband."

"I suppose so," Moira sighed and looked around at the strolling, chatting people. "It would be pleasant to be out more."

"It could be pleasant indeed," Shamus said with a smile. "I would be happy to show you."

Moira understood exactly what he was offering. Such things were accepted in the Capital and as long as the affair was carried on discreetly no censure attached to any of the parties.

Moira glanced over to where Wiz was finishing his conversation with Juvian. *It would serve him right!* She thought. Then she buried the notion with a guilty start.

"I am sorry, My Lord, but I must decline."

"Ah," said Shamus, looking across the drill yard. "A very lucky man indeed." He sighed. "You've broken my heart, you know."

Moira followed his eyes to Wiz standing beneath the reviewing stand. "I feel it will mend by the time the next pretty face comes along."

❖          ❖          ❖

The object of this by-play leaned back against one of
the posts, oblivious to the things being said about him.

In the rings the guardsmen whirled and dodged in
mock combat.

As Wiz put his weight against the post it shifted and
the entire marshal's stand teetered.

*"Look out!"* Moira screamed.

It all seemed to happen in slow motion. The guardsmen and strollers froze. Wiz looked up, mouth open, to
see the entire mass toppling down on him. He started
to move out of the way, but he was obviously too late.

An armored body hurtled into him, knocking him
sideways and slamming him into the earth. Behind them
the stand crashed to earth, raising a cloud of dust off the
practice field. A few boards fell across the pair, but the
guardsman was on top and his armor protected them both.

"Are you all right, Lord?" Wiz opened his eyes and
realized that the man on top of him was Donal.

"Fine," he gasped. "I'm fine."

Donal rolled off Wiz and climbed to his feet. Wiz
started to rise and fell back, gasping in pain..

"My shoulder. I've done something to my shoulder."

Moira came running across the drill yard, skirts flying.
"Are you all right?"

"I've hurt my shoulder."

Moira knelt beside him and ran her fingers lightly over
the injured joint. "It is separated." She looked up at
Donal. "Help me get his tunic off and I will fix it."

"It would be better if we let the healers handle it."

Moira's green eyes flashed. "Are you saying I cannot
heal a shoulder separation?"

Donal met her gaze levelly. "No Lady, only that
Bronwyn or one of the others can do it better."

Moira started to snap back, then with a visible effort,
she relaxed. "You are right, of course. Send one of your
men for her, and quickly."

"Already done, My Lady."

"Oh shit," Wiz muttered, "this hurts."

Moira rested her hand gently on the injured shoulder. "I know, my love. But Bronwyn will be here quickly enough. Try to relax and do not move."

Behind them Shamus was examining the post where it had snapped off. "Rotten wood," he said, wrinkling his nose. He broke a piece off and crumbled it in his fingers. "This needed replacing months ago, and probably all the rest besides."

Arianne knelt by the post, her brown eyes fixed on the break. "Yes," she said and reached up with slender fingers to caress the broken spot. "Yes, they should all be examined most carefully."

Bal-Simba was in his private study when Arianne found him a few hours later.

"You heard that Wiz nearly brought the marshal's stand down on himself on the drill field this afternoon?" she said without preamble.

Bal-Simba grunted. "I heard. Besides all else, our Sparrow is clumsy."

"He is that," she said tonelessly.

Bal-Simba looked up and gave his lieutenant his full attention.

"Meaning?"

"Meaning I examined that post just after the accident. The wood was old and beetle-bored, waiting to fail. So I went back and looked at the place on the parapet where he slipped the other day. It was damp and somewhat slick. There was nothing obviously unusual about either the post or the place on the parapet."

Bal-Simba waited.

"I could find no definite trace of magic about either the post or the damp spot. There seemed to be a hint of—something—about the post, but if it was indeed there it was so faint I could not be sure."

"You obviously think there is more to this than simple accidents," Bal-Simba said. "What?"

Arianne paused, choosing her words carefully. "Lord, I think someone is trying to kill Wiz by magic."

When Bronwyn finally released him, Wiz went looking for Donal. He found him alone in the armory, replacing a strap on his chain mail hauberk by the light of a magic globe.

"I wanted to thank you for this evening," Wiz told him. "You saved my life, I think."

"So clumsily you needed the attention of a healer to put your shoulder right," Donal said wryly.

"I'm alive and that's the important thing. Thank you."

Donal stared down at the new strap. "As you saved mine beneath the City of Night."

"Still . . ."

"Lord, if you wish think of it as payment of a debt." He turned back to the job of threading the strap into place.

"You know, I think about the time we spent at Heart's Ease. You, I, Kenneth and Shiara." His mouth twisted into a half-smile. "Back when there was a clear, simple job to do and all we had to do was do it."

"Yes, Lord," Donal said without looking up from tying the strap into the chain mail.

"Now everything's so complicated and there's so much more to it." He sighed. "What do you do when you're overwhelmed?"

"You do the best you can for as long as you can, Lord."

"And then?"

Donal jerked the strap tight and looked up. "Then, My Lord, you put your back to something and go down fighting."

"I don't think that really applies here," Wiz said.

Donal fixed him with his icy blue eyes. "Lord, I hope you are never in a situation where it does apply."

❖         ❖         ❖

"Subtle," Bal-Simba said at last. "Subtle indeed. But so subtle it is not sure."

Arianne smiled nervously. "If you mean to make me doubt my suspicions, Lord, you may spare yourself the effort. I do not know if I believe this or not."

"Oh, it is believable," Bal-Simba rumbled. "Overt magic in this place would be too easy to detect—and to trace back to its source. Wiz is known to be clumsy and an accident would be easy to accept. An attack using just the tiniest of magics to set up a mischance could perhaps pass unnoticed. And if the first one did not succeed, the next one might, or the next after that."

"That is my thinking, Lord."

He shook his head. "We have grown lax, Lady. With the Dark League broken we have let down our guard."

"You suspect the Dark League?"

"Who else? They are not all gone, after all, and those who are left would have ample reason for harming our Sparrow."

"There is one other thing, Lord."

"Eh?"

"I did not come by this on my own. Another first suggested the idea to me—before today."

"Who?"

"June, the orphan servant girl. She is convinced Wiz is in danger."

"How is your shoulder?" Moira asked as soon as Wiz came in.

"Fine now." He windmilled the arm. "See?"

"I am glad," she said quietly.

"What's the mater?" he asked, dreading the answer.

Moira bit hr lip. "Wiz, we have to talk."

"All right." *I'm losing her,* he thought. *I'm blowing it and I'm going to lose her.*

"I am sorry, I cannot go on like this."

"I know. I've got to stop ignoring you."

"Wiz, you are killing yourself," Moira said desperately. "Your ignoring me, that I could live with—I think. It is in a good cause. But you are burning yourself out trying to do too much."

"I've got to do it. Bal-Simba won't let me off the Council and we've got to have a version of the spell compiler anyone can use."

Moira bit her lip and considered. This wasn't just about her needs. As a hedge witch she had been inculcated with the idea that service to the community came before personal needs. The whole World needed Wiz and what he could do. She pushed her feelings to the back and tried to look at the situation as the helper of one of the Mighty with an important task to perform.

Wiz, lost in his thoughts, missed the shift completely. "I dunno," he sighed. "Sometimes I think it's getting worse instead of better."

"Worse than you know," the redheaded witch said. "There are some who claim you hide your secrets from us behind a veil of deliberate obscurity. That in this way your power among us grows."

"Oh, bullshit! Look, I'm doing the best I can, all right? But I'm a rotten teacher and these people are so *dense*."

"Some of the wisest and most powerful of our wizards have placed themselves under your tutelage," Moira said sharply. "Are you so superior that they cannot learn the most elementary matters?"

"Of course not! But you people don't think the way we do. I know they're trying but they just don't pick up the concepts."

"I understand that," Moira said more gently. "I remember what it was like when you tried to teach me this new magic. But Wiz, it makes problems for everyone."

"At least the ordinary people seem to appreciate what I'm doing. We've already got a few spells out there that anyone can use. **ddt**, the magic repellent spell, is everywhere and that's solved a lot of problems. But I can't do many more of those until I get the tools built. Meanwhile, I'm trying to teach the system to people who hate it and wasting time sitting in Council meetings listening to endless debates on nothing much."

Moira nodded sympathetically. Wiz was like a black-smith with a good supply of iron and charcoal but no tools. Given time he could make his own tools, but until he got them made, there was very little else he could do. She wasn't used to thinking of a spell as a thing built up of parts like a wagon, but by analogy she could understand the situation.

"If I could just get the other wizards to see that and take me seriously, I'd be a lot further along. Instead I have Ebrion claiming the spell compiler doesn't work at all!"

"But doesn't **ddt** show Ebrion and the others that your way of magic works?"

"It doesn't penetrate. They see it as a clever hack and claim it's like a non-magician using an enchanted item."

"But you *created* it!"

He shrugged. "So I'm a great magician. Any great magician could come up with something like that, they say. It's all an accident."

"They should have been in the dungeons beneath the City of Night when you broke the Dark League single-handed!"

"They weren't. Most of them didn't find out about the attack until the day it happened and they never had a really clear picture of what was going on. Besides, they claim it only proves my magic was so alien the Dark League didn't know what to expect."

Moira said something very unladylike under her breath.

Wiz made a face. "Look, the truth is they don't see it because they don't want to see it. I can't fight that—at least not until I've got better tools and can teach some more people to use them."

He sighed. "I don't know. I feel as if I'm being nibbled to death by ducks. If I could just put everything else aside and concentrate on writing code I could get this done. But the way it is now," he waved his hand helplessly over the books. "The way it is now I've got so many other things happening I just can't stay with anything long enough to accomplish anything."

"Perhaps you could."

"Yeah, but I've got to have trained helpers. Until I get some people who understand this kind of magic I can't do half the critical stuff."

Suddenly Moira brightened. "I have it!" She turned to Wiz excitedly. "You need help, do you not?"

"Yeah," Wiz sighed, running a hand through his hair. "I need help."

"And there are many in your land who can do what you do?"

"More or less."

"Then the thing to do is to have the Council bring others to your aid. With the Dark League broken they can do a Great Summoning easily enough and . . ."

*"No!"* Wiz snapped around, shaking her arm off his shoulders.

Moira turned white and flinched back as if he had struck her.

"I'm sorry," Wiz said. "I didn't mean to scare you. But no, I'm not going to have that on my conscience."

"Look, what Patrius did to me was a damn dirty trick." He took one of her hands in both of his. "I'll admit it worked out well in the end, but it was still a terrible thing to do. Even with you and all the rest I still get homesick sometimes." He grinned lopsidedly. "There are times I'd trade almost everything for a sausage, pepperoni and mushroom pizza."

He took her in his arms. "Look darling, I know you mean well, but I can't let you do that to someone else. Promise me you won't try to yank someone else through."

Moira blinked back tears. "Very well." She tapped herself on the chest with her fist. "I swear I will not use a Great Summoning to bring someone else here from your world."

"And that you won't influence anyone else to do it either."

She glared at him, but she swore.

"I'll have to ask Bal-Simba to swear that oath tomorrow," he said, releasing her arms.

She stood up straight. "Very well then. What *will* you do?"

"It'll work out," Wiz mumbled. "I'll think of something."

"What? What will you do?"

"Something! Look, leave me alone, will you?" He shook her arm from his shoulder angrily.

Moira stood stiff and straight. "Very well, My lord." She turned and ran from the room.

Wiz half rose to follow her and then thought better of it. He sank back to the bench and turned his attention to the book in front of him.

*Let her work it off,* he told himself. *She'll come back when she's calmed down some.* It wasn't a very attractive solution but it was the best he could think of at the moment.

Moira slammed the door behind her and stormed down the hall, the cloak she had hastily grabbed slung over her arm. By the time she reached the stairs she was crying openly. She paused at the landing to throw the cloak about her and raise the hood to hide her tears, then swept out into the main court.

She did not see the figure in the shadows at the foot of the stairs.

*Well, well,* Pryddian thought as Moira went past. *Trouble in the Sparrow's nest.* He smiled to himself and continued down the corridor.

# *Five*
## SHIARRA AGAIN

*Living with a programmer is easy. All you need is the patience of a saint.*

—programmers' wives' saying

Like the original Heart's Ease, the new one was a stone tower with an attached hall. The stones of the tower still bore traces of the fire which had destroyed the original and the hewn logs of the halls shone white and new. The freshly raised building exuded the odor of woods; the faint sweet smell of oak from the floors and paneling, the resiny tang of pine from the walls and rafters and the perfume of cedar wafting down from the shingles that roofed the hall.

Gliding through the hall like a swan, Shiara the Silver absorbed it all. She could not see, but she could smell and she could touch. What she sensed pleased her very much.

The warmth streaming in through the diamond-paned windows told her the day was bright and sunny. Perfect for sitting outside and enjoying the feel of the summer breezes.

She smiled. It was somewhat lonely here without Ugo, her goblin companion killed in the raid that destroyed Heart's Ease. Then Wiz and Moira had gone. But the forest folk took good care of her and Heart's Ease was still well named. It would be pleasant to sit in the sun, feel the breeze and smell the growing things.

Suddenly she stiffened as the presence of magic sent a sharp pain through her.

Either very near and very weak, or not too near and stronger. She considered again. The Forest Folk were careful of her and would not allow magic to approach Heart's Ease without warning her. Further away, then.

She heard the light pit-pat of tiny feet on the floor. "A visitor, Lady," the little creature said. "She is asking for you."

Shiara nodded, stately and graceful. "Make her welcome then. I will receive her here."

As the sound of tiny feet faded into the distance Shiara smiled once more. She had company. Obviously one of the Mighty since she had come on the Wizard's Way. It would be pleasant to talk magic and lore once more. Shiara was no longer of the Mighty. The accident that had deprived her of her sight left her hypersensitive to magic. Living as she did in the deadest Dead Zone in the North, Shiara was spared the pain of magic, but it also meant she was isolated from the World. Still, she enjoyed sitting and talking about what had once been so central to her life. Besides, it was a chance to catch up on the news from the Capital.

"Lady?" came a tremulous voice from the door.

"Moira?" The voice was so strained it was hard to recognize. "Merry met indeed."

"Merry met." Then a pause.

"Lady, I need help and I did not know where else to turn," Moira said miserably.

". . . and there you have it, Lady. I could not stand it, so I went away."

Moira and her hostess sat on a log bench outside the rebuilt keep of Heart's Ease. The night was mild and the moon near full above them. Both had cloaks, but they were only sitting on them rather than wrapping up in them. The moonlight picked out the glistening tear streaks down Moira's cheeks.

"Lady, I do not know what to do. There is no living with him and I'm miserable without him."

Shiara could not see the tears, but she heard them in Moira's voice.

"Do you love him?" she asked gently.

Moira sniffed. "You know I do, Lady. And I know he loves me. But that doesn't solve everything."

"It never does," Shiara said with a sigh.

Moira hesitated and Shiara heard her skirt rustle against her cloak as she turned toward her.

"Lady did you and Cormac . . ."

Shiara paused at the mention of her dead lover and quest companion, killed in the same accident that took her sight and magic. " . . . ever fight?" Shiara finished the question. "Oh, aye. Often and fiercely. He would stamp and bellow and bang his fist and I would scream like a fishwife and throw things. Crockery mostly." She smiled at the memory.

"That is not part of the legends, is it? Still, it is true. I think a necessary part of loving someone—loving them enough to share your life with them—is being able to have it out with them when needs be."

She put her hand on Moira's shoulder. "You are strong willed, both of you, and neither is easy. I would be surprised if you did not fight."

"But it doesn't seem to settle anything," Moira said despairingly. "We argue and nothing gets any better."

"Now that is another matter," Shiara said.

Shiara turned her sightless eyes to her guest. "I do not know that I am the person to advise you. I had little experience in such matters."

"You and Cormac were as famous for your love as for your deeds." She saw the look that crossed Shiara's face. "I'm sorry, Lady, I did not mean to pain you."

"Little enough pain in remembering the times you were happy, child." She shook herself.

"Since you want my advice," she went on practically, "the first thing I suggest is that you start with yourself."

"I have done all I can, Lady."

"Forgive me, that is not quite what I meant. From what you say, it sounds as if you have submerged yourself in the Sparrow and his work. You have told me much of him and his problems, but near nothing about you and what you do. It seems that as Wiz has risen in the World you have come down."

"It is no small thing to be the wife of a member of the Council of the North and the mightiest wizard in the land," Moira said.

"Aye, but that is reflected glory. What do you do yourself?" Shiara asked gently.

Moira stiffened.

"It is no small thing to be hedge witch of a village and have everyone look up to you," Shiara went on. "You are someone in your own right and you do important work. At the Capital you have no such work and your place is less clear, is it not?"

"There is something in that," she admitted grudgingly.

"One of the reasons Cormac and I were so in love was that we both had important work. Neither of us was identified by what the other did."

Moira considered that. "So you are saying I should change?"

"It is easier and more certain to change yourself than to change another person."

"And Wiz?"

"He must change too, in his own way." Shiara frowned. "This may not work. You cannot do all the changing, nor will he change simply because you nag at him. You must both strive, and hard, to succeed."

"I will try, Lady. I think he will also. But he is so weighted down with his work it will be difficult."

"It sounds as if the Sparrow is trying to take all the weight of the world upon his shoulders," Shiara said. "Like a certain hedge witch I once knew."

Moira blushed.

"But Lady, there are none in the World who can help him and he has forbidden us to Summon another from his world."

"Then you must give him the help he needs," Shiara told her.

"But how, Lady? I have no talent at all for this new magic."

"You are resourceful. You will find a way, I think. But that is not the worst of it, is it?"

"No," Moira sighed. "He gets lost in his work and it is as if his soul were stolen away. His body is there, but Wiz is gone."

"Then finally, you will have to train him to stop ignoring you. You must make him take time away from his work to spend with you."

"But how do I do that?"

"Seduction is one way," Shiara said judiciously. "More commonly, you simply must tell him when you feel slighted."

Moira sniffed. "I would think that anyone would recognize the signs."

Shiara sighed. "Anyone but a man."

Wiz sleepwalked through the whole day. He couldn't concentrate, he couldn't work and he knew his teaching was worse than usual. Even Malus noticed and approached him diffidently to ask what was wrong.

Bal-Simba hinted delicately that he was available if Wiz wanted to talk, but Wiz wasn't in the mood. He liked the giant black wizard as much as he respected him, but for the first time since coming to the Capital it was borne on him that he really had no close friends here. He thought about Jerry Andrews, his old cubicle mate, and some of the other people he had known in Silicon Valley and missed them for the first time in months.

He broke off in mid-afternoon and raced back to the apartment, his mind full of all the things he wanted to say to Moira. But there was no one there when he arrived.

Wiz sat down heavily at his desk and tried to work. After shuffling things around for half an hour or so, he gave up even the pretense.

Then he moped about the apartment, trying to think and take his mind off things at the same time. With no stereo, television or movies, it was hard to kill time, he discovered. There weren't even any books to read except a couple of grimores he had borrowed from the wizard's library.

*And they don't have much of a plot,* he thought sourly.

Finally he opened the sideboard and poured himself a large cup of mead from the small cask Moira kept there. Moira preferred the mead of the villages to the wines of the Capital and she liked to have a cup after supper. Wiz hadn't eaten yet, but it looked to be about supper time to him.

Normally he didn't care for mead, finding its sweetness cloying. But tonight it wasn't half bad. He had a second cup and that wasn't bad at all. The mead didn't exactly make his thinking clearer, but it did seem to narrow down the problem and focus him on the major outlines.

"Priorities," he said, hoisting his third cup to the dragon demon sitting atop his books. "I've got to start setting priorities." He drained the cup in a single long draught and went to the cask to refill it again.

"Moira's priority one," he said waving the cup in the general direction of the demon. "I've gotta get Moira back." He slopped a little mead from the cup and giggled. "Screw the wizards, scroo'm all. Moira's what's important."

He poured half the contents of the cup down his throat in a single swallow.

"Then the compiler. Never mind the Council. They're not important anyway. I finish the compiler and where's the Council, hey? Poof. All gone. Don't need them no more."

It took him a while, but sometime early in the morning he finished the cask of mead.

*Well*, he thought muzzily as he staggered into the bedroom, *it's one way to pass the time.*

The morning was death with birdsong.

Wiz's head was pounding, his eyeballs felt like they had been sandpapered and his mouth felt as if something small and furry had crawled in there and died.

*Now I understand why they invented television,* he thought as he splashed cold water on his face and neck. *No hangover.*

There was no food in the apartment and the only things to drink were water and a bottle of mead. The thought of the mead nearly made Wiz lose his stomach and the water wasn't very satisfying.

Somewhere in the back of his head, buried under several layers of pain, he remembered that the wizards had a spell that cured hangovers. He needed that more than he needed anything else right now, *except Moira*. Afterwards he could get breakfast in the refectory with the inhabitants of the castle who chose not to cook for themselves.

He groped his way toward the Wizards' Day Room where he expected to find someone who could put him out of his misery.

Naturally the first person he met was Pryddian.

The ex-apprentice took in Wiz's condition in a single glance. "A good day to you, My Lord," he said, much too loudly.

Wiz mumbled a greeting and tried to step by the man.

"What is the matter this morning, Sparrow?" Pryddian boomed, moving in front of him again. "Suffering from an empty nest?"

"Leave me alone, will you?" Wiz mumbled.

Pryddian was almost shouting now. "Poor Sparrow, his magic fails him this morning. All his mighty spells cannot even cure a simple hangover." Again Wiz tried to move around him and again the man blocked his way.

"You need the help of a real wizard, Sparrow. Maybe he could make you a love philtre while he's at it, eh? Something to keep your wife home at nights."

Suddenly it was all too much.

Wiz whirled on his tormentor. Pryddian caught his look and stepped back, hands up as if warding off a blow.

"**backslash**," he shouted.

The lines of magical force twisted and shimmered.

Wiz froze with his arm extended and his mouth open.

Pryddian shrank back, his face white.

Wiz dropped his arms. "**cancel**."

"I'm sorry," he mumbled. I didn't mean to . . ."

Pryddian gathered himself and beat a hasty retreat.

Wiz became aware that a dozen people were watching him from doors along the corridor. His face burning, he turned and fled.

Wiz had little less than an hour to contemplate the enormity of what he had almost done before Bal-Simba came calling. The giant black wizard was obviously not in a good mood.

"I must ask you this and I compel you to answer me truthfully," he said as soon as he had closed the door. "Did you threaten to use magic on Pryddian?"

"Yes, Lord," Wiz said miserably.

"And he did not threaten you first?"

"Well, he got in my face."

"But he offered you no threat?"

"No, Lord."

Bal-Simba looked as if he would explode.

"Lord, with the problems with the project and Moira gone and then him . . . Lord, I am sorry."

Bal-Simba scowled like a thundercloud. "No doubt you are. But that would not have saved Pryddian if you had followed through with your intent. Magic is much too powerful to be loosed in anger. You above all others should know that."

"Yes, Lord. But he has been riding me for days."

"Is that an excuse?" Bal-Simba asked sharply. "Do you hold power so lightly that you will loose magic on any person who annoys you? If so, which of us are safe from you?"

"No, Lord," Wiz mumbled, "it isn't an excuse."

The huge wizard relaxed slightly. "Pryddian's behavior has not gone unnoticed. He will be dealt with. The question is what to do with you."

He looked at Wiz speculatively until Wiz fidgeted under his gaze.

"It would be best if you were to absent yourself a while," Bal-Simba said finally. "I believe matters can be smoothed over but it will be easier to do if you are not here."

"Yes, Lord," said Wiz miserably.

"In fact, this would accomplish two things," he said absently. "I have received a request from the village of Leafmarsh Meadow. They have asked for one of the Mighty to assist them. That is sufficient reason for you to be gone, I think.

"Also, we have many reports that this new magic of yours is already at work on the Fringe of the Wild Wood."

"That would be **ddt**, the magic protection spell I hacked up," Wiz told him.

"The reports of the hedge witches and other wizards are somewhat confusing. I want to see what is going on through your eyes."

"Yes, Lord. Uh, what about Moira?"

"I am sure she is safe. If she returns while you are gone, I will tell her where you are.

"I will send a journeyman wizard with you. You will leave tomorrow morning. Meanwhile, it would be best if you were to stay out of sight." He looked down at Wiz. "And take something for that hangover."

This close to the Capital, the woods were carefully tended tree lots rather than the raw forest of the Wild Wood. But the trees still shut out prying eyes and the relative isolation made prying magic easy to sense. That was the important thing.

Ebrion made his way to the middle of the grove. He looked around cautiously, extended his magical senses for any hint of watcher and then extended his arm, finger pointing south.

As if on cue, a tiny bird flickered through the trees and landed on his outstretched finger. To the eye it was an ordinary wren, speckled brown on brown. A magician would have sensed instantly that it was no ordinary bird, but part of the reason for meeting in the woods was to keep the bird away from other magicians.

The bird cocked its head to one side and regarded the wizard with a beady eye.

*The Sparrow has left the Capital,* Ebrion thought at the bird. *He is to be gone perhaps four days and then he will return along the Wizard's Way. Be ready for him.*

He paused and then continued.

*One thing more. Your attempts to arrange an accident for the Sparrow have been discovered. I told you I would not have him harmed. Persist and our bargain is broken.*

The wren took wing and flashed through the trees. The wizard waited until it rose above the treetops and turned straight south. Then he nodded and started back to the Capital.

# Six

# APPLICATIONS MAGIC

*Applications programming is a race between software
engineers, who strive to produce idiot-proof programs, and
the Universe which strives to produce bigger idiots.*
— software engineers' saying
*So far the Universe is winning.*
— applications programmers' saying

Wiz's travelling companion was a wizard named
Philomen, a slender young man with an aristocratic
bearing and a reserved manner. Wiz had met him briefly,
but he didn't know him and he couldn't remember seeing
him in any of his classes.

As was custom, they did not walk the Wizard's Way
straight into the village. Instead they arrived on a hill
where the road topped the rise to look down at Leafmarsh Meadow. From here the village looked neat and
peaceful, spread out along the road that ran to the
Leafmarsh Brook and crossed to run deeper into the
fringe. This side of the river was a neat pattern of fields
and pastureland. The Fringe started on the other side
of the water and there the land was mostly forest,
although Wiz noted a number of fields, obviously freshly
hacked in the ancient woodland.

Towering over the village was a hill of naked gray

granite. It seemed to be a single enormous boulder, placed as if a careless giant had dropped it next to the river. Even to Wiz's relatively untrained senses there was something about the huge rock that hinted of magic.

"This will be my first real trip out of the Capital in almost a year," Wiz said in an effort to make conversation as they started down the hill toward the village.

"Indeed?" Philomen said. "You will find much changed, I think."

Wiz didn't have any good answer to that, so they walked along in a silence for a bit.

"Do you have any idea why they wanted help from the Council?"

"None, Lord. If they did not tell one of the Mighty, do you think they would tell one barely raised from apprentice?"

"No, I guess not," Wiz said. "Well, we'll know soon enough. That's the hedge witch's cottage there."

The place was on the outskirts of the village, a single-story house of whitewashed wattle and daub with thatched roof. The whitewash needed renewing and the thatch was turning black in spots. It was surrounded by a rather weedy garden and all enclosed by a ramshackle fence. The cottage wasn't exactly run down, Wiz decided, but it looked very much like the owner had other things on her mind than the condition of her property.

They came up the flagstone pathway to the door and Philomen rapped sharply upon it with his staff.

"Keep your britches on, I'm coming," came a cracked voice from inside. Then the door was flung open in their faces.

"What the . . ." She stopped dead when she saw her visitors in wizard's cloaks with staffs in their hands. She blinked once and her whole manner changed.

"Merry met, Lords," she said, bobbing a curtsey. "I am Alaina, hedge witch of this place."

She was older than Moira, but how much Wiz couldn't

tell because people aged so fast here on the Fringe. Her hair was gray and a greasy wisp had escaped the bun on the back of her head. She was shaped like a sack of potatoes. Her skin was coarse and her teeth, what were left of them, were yellow. From this distance it was obvious she hadn't bathed recently.

On the whole, she didn't look much worse than the average middle-aged peasant woman, but to Wiz the contrast with the hedge witch he knew best was striking.

*Well*, Wiz thought, *it would be too much to expect all hedge witches to be like Moira*.

"Merry met, Lady," Wiz and Philomen chorused.

"What brings you to Leafmarsh Meadow?"

"We were sent by the Council in answer to your request," Philomen said.

The hedge witch looked blank. "Request? Oh, yes, the request. Well, what can I be thinking of to keep such guests standing in my garden? Come in, Lords, come in and be welcome."

The place was even more run down and messier on the inside, but it managed to be homey at the same time. The cottage was a single large room with a fireplace at one end and an unmade bed in the corner. At the opposite end was a low work table with rows of shelves above it. Dried herbs and other less identifiable things hung from the rafters, giving the place an odor like hay with anise overtones.

"Please excuse the clutter," Alaina said and she moved piles of things off chairs to give them places to sit. "The girl only comes in three days a week and things do pile up in between times.

"Can I offer you refreshment? I have some very good mead. But of course gentlemen such as yourselves from the Capital do not drink mead."

There was an undercurrent of resentment, Wiz realized. As if she didn't want them here.

"Mead would be most satisfactory," Philomen said.

"None for me, thanks," Wiz said and from the way they both looked at him he realized he had committed some kind of social error in refusing the hospitality.

"I can't drink just now," he said quickly.

Alaina's expression smoothed. "Ah, a vow. I understand those things, of course. You are saving power for a special spell."

"More like doing penance," Wiz said wryly.

Once they were settled into the somewhat dusty chairs and Philomen and Alaina were clutching cups of mead Wiz decided it was time for serious talk. Alaina was keeping up a steady flow of conversation on inconsequential topics, as if she was trying to ward off discussion. Philomen was responding to her with bored civility, but making no move to come to the point.

"Your pardon, Lady," Wiz said, cutting off an anecdote about the profusion of dragon weed this year, "could you tell us about your problem?"

"My problem, ah yes," Alaina said, draining the rest of her mead in a single gulp. "It is nothing, really. Nothing at all." She reached over for the pitcher and refilled her cup.

"I am honored that you have come to us, do not misunderstand me," she waved an admonitory hand. "But it really was not necessary. Not necessary at all to send two such great wizards from the Capital for this."

"I thought you had asked for help," Wiz said.

Alaina made a dismissing motion, as if shooing off an insect. "That was Andrew, the mayor. He wouldn't give me a minute's peace until I sent off to the Council for aid." She smiled at her visitors. "You know how non-magicians are, My Lords, always frightened around magic and such. But I never dreamed they would send someone so soon. And two of you!"

*Meaning you expected to have this all wrapped up before the council took notice,* Wiz thought sourly. *Now*

*here we are and you won't get the additional prestige
out of this you thought you would.*

"I am sure your skill is up to the task, Lady," Philomen
said soothingly. "It just happened we were coming this
way on other business so the Council asked that we come
to assess the situation. Consider us merely observers."

That seemed to mollify the hedge witch.

"Well," she said. "Well indeed. I was going to wait until
the next full moon to lay this creature. But since your
lordships are here, I suppose I can do the job tomorrow."

"Very well then," Philomen said. "I presume there is
a place we can get dinner and stay the night."

"Oh, there is no inn in the village," Alaina said. "Much
too small, you know." She hesitated.

"I would ask you to sleep here, but . . ." She swept
out her arm, indicating the clutter and the single bed.
"In any event, I am sure you would be much more
comfortable staying at the mayor's house. No, I am sure
he will insist that you stay with him as soon as he knows
you are here."

"I am sure you know best, Lady," Philomen said.

"He is out on the brook gathering reeds for thatching,"
the hedge witch told them. "I will have someone send
for him immediately." She stood up. "Will you excuse
me, Lords?" She bobbed a curtsey and went out.

"Political, huh?" Wiz said once he was sure their
hostess was out of earshot.

"Such matters usually are, Lord. At least to some
extent. I would suggest that we let her lay this creature."
He looked at Wiz. "Unless you have reason to do
otherwise."

The man's tone made Wiz uncomfortable. "No, none
at all," he said, looking down at his boots.

"Might I further suggest, Lord, that we stand ready
to aid her should the need arise? Her style does not give
me confidence in her abilities."

Wiz and Philomen sat in uncomfortable silence for a

few minute more. Wiz still wasn't sure whether Philomen's coldness grew out of his nature or a dislike for him. A mixture of both, he suspected increasingly.

Alaina came rushing back breathless with the news that mayor Andrew had been summoned from the reed marsh and his wife was preparing to receive them at their house. It would take a few minutes, she told them, but they would receive a proper reception.

Wiz was becoming increasingly uncomfortable with both of them, so he excused himself.

"I want to stretch my legs a bit," he explained.

Philomen nodded. "As you will," and he turned his attention back to Alaina's latest story.

There wasn't much to the village, just a gaggle of houses spread out along a narrow lane. Most of them were timber or wattle and daub, but a few of the larger ones clustered around the place where the lane widened into a village square were made of native stone.

There weren't many people about, or if there were they were keeping out of sight. Once or twice Wiz passed someone in the street who bowed or curtseyed and then moved on quickly. He saw children peering at him from windows and doors, but very few adults.

Either people hereabouts were afraid of strangers or they knew who he was and they were nervous around wizards. Judging from the reactions he got, Wiz suspected the latter.

At the end of the village, where the stream made a looping bend, there was a grove of poplars on a bank overlooking a water meadow. As Wiz approached he smelled smoke and the smell drew him on toward the trees.

*Maybe there will be someone here to talk to*, he thought.

There was a wagon, hardly more than a cart, and an ox grazing in the meadow nearby. A man in rough brown breeches and a coarse linen shirt was busy building up a small campfire. He was burly with a greying beard and a seamed, weatherbeaten face. He looked up and smiled a gap-toothed smile as Wiz approached.

"Well met, My Lord."

"Uh, hi. Just passing through, are you?"

"Aye, My Lord," the man chuckled. "Passing through on my way to a better life. I am called Einrich."

"Wiz Zumwalt. Pleased to meet you. But why are you camped out here? I thought the villagers put travellers up where there are no inns."

The man shrugged. "I know no one here and I have no claim to guest right. Doubtless a place could be made for me, but the weather is fair. The people are willing to let me pasture my ox in their meadow and gather wood for my fire. That is sufficient.

"Besides," he added, "they have seen many like me recently. Better to save their hospitality for those who are travelling with their wives and children."

Wiz looked around and realized there were three or four other campfire rings under the trees. No one was using them now, but most of them looked as if they hadn't been long out of use.

"Where is everyone going?"

Einrich grinned, showing the place where his front teeth had been. "Why for land, young Lord. They go into the Wild Wood for land."

"You too?"

Einrich nodded. "I tarry here for a day or so to rest and feed up my ox. Then I am also on my way east for new land."

"All by yourself?"

"My sons and their families stay behind on the old farm to gather in the harvest." He grinned. "They can spare a dotard such as me and this way we can get an early start on our new farm."

Looking at Einrich's powerful frame, Wiz would not have called him a dotard. Old perhaps, by the standards of the peasantry, but he looked like he could still work Wiz into the ground.

"How far are you going?"

"As deep into the Wild Wood as I can. That way when my sons follow we will all be able to claim as much land as my sons and my sons' sons will ever need."

"Aren't you worried about magic?"

"No more!" Einrich said triumphantly. "With the new spell I can defeat any magic in the Wild Wood. Trolls, even elves, I can destroy them all."

Wiz frowned. **ddt**, his magic-protection spell, wouldn't destroy anything. It would only ward off magic and tend to drive magical influences away.

Wiz opened his mouth to say something, but Einrich interrupted him. "Oh, it is a grand time to be alive!" His eyes shone like a child's at Christmas. "Truly grand and I thank fortune that I lived to see this day. No longer must mortals cower at the threat of magic. Now we can walk free beneath the sun!"

"Wonderful," Wiz said uncomfortably.

"Will you join me for dinner, Lord? Plain fare, I fear, but plenty of it."

"No thanks. I think I am expected back at the village for dinner."

Wiz walked slowly back toward the village square, scowling and scuffing his boot toe in the dust of the road. This was what he had fought for, wasn't it? That people like Einrich could live their lives without having to fear magic constantly. Most of the Fringe and part of the Wild Wood had been human at one time, before the pressures of magic had driven the people back. Wasn't it just that they were reclaiming their own?

*Then why do I feel so damn uncomfortable with Einrich and what he's doing?*

The mayor met Wiz partway back to the village square. He was a stout, balding man with a face red from exertion. He was wearing a red velvet tunic trimmed with black martin fur obviously thrown hastily over his everyday clothes. He had washed the muck off, but the odor of the reed marsh still clung to him.

Mayor Andrew turned out to be almost as garrulous as Alaina. This time it suited Wiz because it meant that aside from complimenting the mayor on the village and making agreeable noises, he did not have to talk.

Dinner that evening was a formal affair. All the important people of the village turned out in their holiday best to honor the visitors. The villagers' manners were strained as they tried to follow what they thought was polite custom in the Capital. It reminded Wiz of a dinner he had attended once where the principals of an American software company were doing their best to entertain and avoid offending a group of powerful Japanese computer executives. That one turned into a rousing success after both sides discovered they shared a strong taste for single-malt scotch consumed in large quantities. For a moment Wiz considered trying to conjure up a bottle of Glenlivet, but he realized it would take more than booze to help this party.

"What is this thing that threatens you anyway?" Wiz asked Andrew during a particularly strained pause in the conversation as the mountainous platter of boiled beef was being removed and replaced with an an equally mountainous plate of roast pork.

Andrew twisted in his chair and pointed. "That!"

Wiz followed the mayor's finger out the window. Hulking against the night sky was the huge granite hill, its mass and shape cutting off the stars near the horizon.

"The hill?"

"Aye, the hill. We have lived in its shadow too long."

Wiz realized everyone was looking at him and the mayor.

"Is it dangerous?"

"Dangerous enough," the mayor said grimly.

"What does it do?"

"It mazes people. Those who climb it are overcome by its power and stricken dumb. For days or even weeks they wander as if simple."

"Young John fell off it and broke his back," a slat-thin woman halfway down the table put in. "The healer said it was a wonder that he ever walked again."

Wiz toyed with the pork that had been heaped on his plate. "Uh, maybe this is a dumb question, but why don't people just stay off the hill?"

There was stony silence all down the table. Philomen concentrated on his plate and everyone else glared at Wiz.

"Okay, so it was a dumb question," Wiz muttered.

"The thing is magic and I will not have magic so close to my village," Andrew said fiercely.

"Look, don't worry. I'm sure that we can take care of this thing tomorrow so it will never bother you again."

Somehow the rest of the meal passed off without incident.

Deep in the Wild Wood a wren perched on a finger and trilled out its message. Seklos, now second in command of the Dark League, considered carefully the news the bird had brought.

So, he thought, *our Sparrow leaves its nest. Very well, we will be ready when he seeks to return.* He dismissed the wren with a flick of his finger and turned to his work. In concert with the others of the Dark League, he had a demon to create. A most powerful and special demon.

As he reached for a spell book Seklos wondered idly what that fool in the Capital meant about attempts on the Sparrow's life. The Dark League would make only one such attempt. And when it came it would be crushingly, overwhelmingly successful.

# *Seven*
# DEMON DEBUG

*The three most dangerous things in the world are a
programmer with a soldering iron, a hardware type with a
program patch and a user with an idea.*

—computer saying

The morning was bright and clear. The day promised
to be hot, but by the time Wiz and Philomen emerged
from the mayor's house the whole village was astir.

"Oh, this is a great day," Mayor Andrew told them,
rubbing his palms together. "A great day indeed."

"I am sure it is," Philomen said soothingly. "We are
honored to be here to observe. Now, if you will excuse
us, we must consult with your hedge witch before the
ceremony."

As the villagers drifted in the direction of the mono-
lith, Wiz, Philomen and Alaina retired to one corner of
the meadow for some shop talk.

"Okay," Wiz said, looking over his shoulder at the
enormous mass of granite. "Probably the best tool for
this job is the Demon Deterrent Trap, **ddt**."

"Why not **demon_debug**?" asked Alaina.

"What's that?" "A wonderful cure for magic of all
sorts," the slatternly hedge witch told him. "It wipes it
right out."

"Where did you get it?"

Alaina gestured vaguely. "It is being passed through the villages. Much better than **ddt**, I assure you."

"Well, let's see it."

Alaina nodded and raised her staff.

"**demon—debug exe!**" she bawled at the top of her cracked voice.

There was a shimmering and shifting in the air in front of them and a squat demon perhaps three feet high and nearly as broad appeared on the grass before them.

Wiz looked the thing over and frowned. "This isn't one of my spells."

"Of course not, My Lord," the hedge witch said. "This is better."

The warty green demon leered up at him, showing saw-like rows of teeth in a cavernous mouth. The thing looked singularly unpleasant, even for a demon.

"How does it work?"

Alaina shrugged. "It is magic of course. How else does a spell work?"

"No, I mean how does it function? Haven't you listed it out to examine the code?"

"List?" Alaina said, puzzled. "Forgive me, Lord, but how do you make a spell lean? And what good would it do."

Wiz shot her a dirty look. Then he realized she was sincere. She didn't have the faintest idea how a spell worked or how to find out.

He shook his head. "Well, let's see then."

Philomen and the hedge witch hung back to watch the master work.

"**Emac.**"

"Yes, master?" A small brown mannikin popped up at his feet. It was perhaps three feet high with a head almost grotesquely large for its body. It wore a green eyeshade on its bald brown head and carried a quill pen stuck behind one flaplike ear.

The Emacs were one of the first classes of demons Wiz had created when he declared his one-man war on the Dark League. They were translators and recorders of spells in Wiz's magic language, magical clerks.

"**backslash**." Wiz commanded.

"**$**," said the Emac.

"**list demon_debug**," Wiz said.

The Emac pulled the pen from behind his ear and began to scribble furiously on the air in front of him. A mixture of runes, numbers, and mathematical symbols appeared in glowing green fire.

Wiz frowned as he studied the symbols.

"It's based on **ddt**, but it's been changed." He turned to the Emac again.

"**backslash**."

"**$**."

"**dif demondebug/ddt**."

Again the Emac scribbled and again the lambent characters hung in the air. But one section of spell stood out in violent magenta against the neon green.

Wiz bent forward over the Emac's shoulder to study the magenta section. It represented the changes between the original **ddt** and this new version. He traced his finger along the lines and his lips moved as he worked out what the changes did.

"Jesus H. Christ," he breathed at last. "What a nasty piece of work!" He straightened up and glared at the other two magicians.

"Who's responsible for this?"

"Ah, responsible for what, Lord?" Philomen asked.

"This!" Wiz shouted. "It isn't a defensive spell. It's offensive, a magic killer. You turn this loose on any kind of magical creature and it won't just protect you, it will destroy the thing."

"So much the better," the hedge witch said firmly. "That way it will never come around to bother us again."

"But why kill it?"

Alaina set her jaw firmly and her eyes glittered. "Because it is magic and because it threatens us. Perhaps the Mighty do things differently in the Capital, but we are simple folk out here on the Fringe. We treat harmful magic the way we treat poisonous serpents."

Before Wiz could reply Philomen placed a hand on his arm. "Forgive me, My Lord, but perhaps we should discuss this. Will you excuse us, My Lady?"

Alaina curtseyed stiffly and withdrew to the other end of the meadow.

"My Lord, it is unwise to give an order you cannot enforce," Philomen said as soon as the hedge witch was out of earshot. "Were you to forbid this, she could simply wait until we are gone and use **demon_debug** herself."

"This is too much. That thing doesn't hurt anyone permanently. From what they say it doesn't even affect anyone who doesn't climb it."

"Still, it is strong magic and that makes it an unchancy neighbor. The villagers' desire to rid themselves of the thing is understandable."

"Great. But where will it all end? Are these people going to go around destroying anything just because it's magic?"

"If they have the opportunity."

"That's crazy!"

"No, it is understandable. It is the people in the villages, especially along the Fringe, who have suffered the most from magic. To you in your pale tower in the Capital magic may be a thing to be learned and applied. Here it is a thing to be hated and feared. Is it any wonder that as soon as they were given an opportunity to practice magic safely, they should go looking for a weapon?"

"I gave them a defense," Wiz protested. "I didn't expect them to turn it into something so dangerous!"

"You did say you wanted even common folk to learn your new way of magic," Philomen said mildly.

"Yes, but not like this!"

"Are you now complaining because someone took you at your word?"

"I'm complaining because this spell is fucking magical napalm!" Wiz yelled. "I expected people to have more sense than this."

"Sense?" Philomen asked with a trace of malice. "My Lord, forgive me, but when have the folk of the villages ever shown such sense?

"Once it was the Council's job to maintain the balance of the World. But as you have said, the Council is outworn and lives beyond its usefulness. Or did you expect the folk along the Fringe to learn restraint and balance overnight?"

"I never said the Council was useless."

"You never put it in words," Philomen retorted. "But you said it with every act, every gesture, every roll of the eyes or yawn in Council meeting. Oh, your message got through, right enough. Even to the villages on the Fringe of the Wild Wood.

"Then you compound your actions by giving villagers a powerful spell they can use freely and telling everyone who would listen that you do not have to be a wizard to practice magic." Philomen's lip curled in contempt. "No, My Lord, you are getting exactly what you strived for."

Wiz couldn't think of anything to say.

"So come, My Lord, let us attend the laying of this thing. And for the sake of what little order remains in the World, let us put a good face on it." With that he turned and walked back across the meadow to where Alaina was waiting. Wiz hesitated for an instant and then followed.

The entire village was gathered before the stone by the time the three magicians arrived. All of them were wearing their holiday best. The adults were clumped together talking excitedly and the children were running around laughing and shrieking at play.

They parted like a wave for the three magicians. Andrew was standing at the front of a few of the other people from the feast last night.

Alaina looked over the crowd, eyes shining and her coarse face split in a huge smile.

"Well," she said briskly, "shall we begin?"

She motioned with her staff and the villagers fell back, Wiz and Philomen with them. Then she turned to face the rock, struck a dramatic pose and thrust her staff skyward.

"**demon_debug BEGONE exe!**" she bawled.

At first nothing seemed to happen. Wiz could feel the tension rising in the crowd and knotting up in his stomach. He took a firmer grip on his staff and began to review the spells he might use if this only roused the creature.

*Maybe it won't work,* he thought to himself, half-afraid and half-hopeful. *Maybe the spell will crash.*

Then the rock moaned.

The sound was so low it sent shivers through Wiz's bones, as if someone was playing the lowest possible note on the biggest bass fiddle in the world. It started low and then built and rose until it threatened to drown out all other sound.

There was something else there besides sound, Wiz realized. Some sort of mental influence, as if . . .

Wiz went white. "That thing's alive," he shouted to Philomen. "It's alive and intelligent!"

"Such things often are in their own way," the wizard agreed, keeping his eyes on the mass before them.

"But you can't kill it, it's intelligent!"

"Can we not? Watch."

Still groaning, the stone reared above them, heaving itself free of the earth and towering above them as if it would slam down on them and crush them like bugs. The villagers gasped and shrank back, but the thing slammed to earth in its own bed. The ground shook so

hard Wiz nearly lost his balance. The creature reared
again, not so high this time, and pounded to the earth
once more. It tried to rear a third time, but could only
quiver.

"Stop it!" Wiz yelled. "*Stop it!* Can't you see it can't
hurt you?"

" 'Tis magic," Andrew replied. " 'Tis magic and must
be burned from the land.

"Too long we trembled under the magical ones. Now
let them tremble." His voice rose to a shout over the
windy moans of the dying stone. "Let *them* know fear!"

The crowd behind him growled agreement.

The thing thinned, its stony gray turning opalescent
and gradually lightening until Wiz could dimly see the
outline of the hills through it. Then the creature's body
went foggy and he could see that the hills were cloaked
in summer's green. The outline blurred and became
indistinct and finally, at last, the mist dissipated, leaving
nothing but a hole in the ground with tendrils of smoke
rising from it.

Wiz stood shocked and numb, oblivious to the cheers
of the villagers. Someone was pounding him on the back
and shouting in his ear, but he couldn't make out the
words.

Alaina left in the midst of an excited knot of villagers,
talking and cheering and doing everything but hoisting
her on their shoulders in triumph. Some of the others
remained behind to gape at the huge pit where the rock
creature had stood. Then by ones and twos they began
to drift back toward the village square.

"A waste, I calls it," one old gaffer said to his younger
companion as they passed by where Wiz stood. "They
should have pounded it into gravel stead of just making
it disappear. We needs gravel for our roads, we does."

Finally only Wiz remained, standing at the edge of
the pit and looking down.

He didn't know what the thing was that had died here

today. He had never heard of such a creature and it may well have been the only one of its kind. But whatever it was it didn't deserve what had been done to it.

His cheeks were wet and he realized he was crying.

There was a footstep behind him. Wiz didn't turn around.

"Are you coming, My Lord?" Philomen asked. "There will be a feast tonight in honor of slaying the monster."

Wiz turned to face the wizard. "No thanks. Right now I don't think my stomach could stand a feast."

"Our presence is expected."

"Vomiting on your hosts is probably bad form, even in this bunch."

Philomen's face froze and he bowed formally. "As you will, My Lord. I will see you at the mayor's house then."

"Maybe." Wiz strode off toward Leafmarsh Brook and the bridge into the Fringe beyond.

"My Lord, where are you going?"

"Into the Wild Wood," Wiz flung back over his shoulder. "Right now I want some civilized company. Weasels maybe, or snakes."

# *Eight*
## SIDE EFFECTS

*You can't do just one thing.*

—Campbell's Law of everything

Sitting under a flowering bush on a hillside, Wiz called up an Emac and studied the code for **demon_debug** again.

It was obvious what had happened, he thought as he traced the glowing lines. Somewhere out in one of the villages, some bright person with a knack for magic and a little knowledge of his programming language had taken **ddt** apart and found a way to make it more effective. What he or she had done was related to the magic-absorbing worms Wiz had invented for his attack on the City of Night. The new spell, **demon_debug**, sucked the magical energy right out of its victim. It was crude, it was dangerous and it was absolutely deadly.

Without one hell of a protection spell there was no way that anything magical could survive **demon_debug**. Idly he picked up a water-worn pebble and ran his thumb across it while he thought about the implications.

This must be what Einrich meant when he said he could destroy any magic he met in the Wild Wood. That, and the way Alaina talked, made Wiz pretty sure the spell was spread far and wide through the Fringe.

Wiz flung the stone into the weeds. He had screwed this up more thoroughly than he had ever messed up anything in his life. Before he had just affected himself, and perhaps the lives of a few people around him. Now he had managed to meddle in the lives of an entire world; to meddle destructively.

He wasn't sorry he had invented the magic compiler. He thought of the last time he had come this way. He and Moira had stumbled over the burned ruins of a farm shortly after the trolls had raided it. He had dug the grave in the cabbage patch to bury the remains of the people the trolls hadn't eaten after roasting them in the flames of their own homestead. He still had nightmares about that.

He didn't want to go back to the way things had been. But looking down at the village and the scar where the rock creature had stood for time out of mind, he wasn't at all sure what was replacing it was much better.

He stood up and looked down on the village. The evening breeze bore the faint sounds of drunken revelry up the hill to him. In the center of the village people were piling wood head high for a bonfire. *Ding dong the witch is dead!* Never mind that the "witch" had stood harmlessly for longer than the village had been there. Never mind that the people who killed it behaved like a wolf pack with the blood lust up. The witch was dead so let's have a party. And if it's a good party, maybe we can go out tomorrow and find some more witches to murder.

He couldn't go back there. But he didn't want to go back to the Capital with its packs of wizards and no Moira. All he really wanted was to be alone for a while. Say a couple of centuries.

Well, he decided, there really wasn't any reason to go back. He had come to the village with only his cloak, staff, and a pouch containing a few magical necessities. He had his staff and pouch and the weather was warm enough that he doubted he would miss his cloak.

Turning his back on the village, Wiz headed down the other side of the hill, toward the Wild Wood.

He very quickly lost any sense of where he was. He might be wandering in circles for all he knew—or cared. If he wanted to go somewhere he could take the Wizard's Way. What he needed was to be alone and to try to sort out the mess.

Once he stopped to munch handfuls of blackberries plucked from a stand of thorny canes. Another time he stopped to drink from a clear rivulet. Most of the time he just walked.

The evening deepened and the shadows grew denser but Wiz barely noticed. Finally, the second time he almost ran into a tree he sat down to think some more. As he sat the dusk darkened to full night. The last vestiges of light faded from the sky and the moon rose over the treetops. The night insects took up their chorus and the night blooming plants of the Wild Wood opened their blossoms, adding just a hint of perfume to the earth-and-grass smell of the night. Wiz fell asleep under the tree that night. He dreamed uneasily of Moira.

"You step more spritely this morning," Shiara observed as her guest came into the great hall.

"Thank you, Lady, I feel better." She joined Shiara at the trestle table beneath the diamond-paned window and began to help herself to the breakfast spread out there.

"You found a solution then?"

Moira frowned. "Part of a solution, I think."

She heaped berries into an earthenware bowl and poured cream over them. She took an oat cake from the platter and drizzled honey on it. "Wiz always said that when you could not meet a problem straight forward you should come at it straight backwards."

Shiara nibbled reflectively on an oat cake. "That sounds like the kind of thing the Sparrow would say."

Moira nodded. "Once he told me something about a mountain that could move but wouldn't and a wizard named Mohammed." She wrinkled her nose. "I never understood that, but it gave me an idea."

Shiara chuckled. "Now that truly sounds like our Sparrow. And from this obstinate mountain and a straight backwards approach, you have discovered something to help you?"

"To help Wiz. But Lady, I need your advice."

"I know nothing about going straight backwards or moving mountains."

"No, but you know Bal-Simba. He will have to aid me in this."

The sun was high in the sky before it worked its way under the tree where Wiz lay. Twice he wrinkled his nose and shifted his position to keep the beams out of his eyes, but still he slept on.

Wiz was about to shift for the third time when something ran across his chest.

"Wha . . ." Wiz made a brushing motion with his arm. Something small and manlike hurdled his legs, squealing like a frightened rabbit. Wiz sat upright and shook his head to clear the sleep fog. He heard something else moving through the brush. Something—no, several somethings—large and heavy. He clambered to his feet and faced the noise just as a troll crashed through the undergrowth and into the clearing.

*Fortuna!*

Behind the first came two more, and then a fourth. All of them were more than eight feet high, hairy, filthy and stinking. They wore skins and rags and carried clubs the size of Wiz's leg.

He threw back his arms and raised his staff. Frantically he sought a spell he could use against four trolls.

The trolls stopped short, bunched up in a tight clump.

Wiz braced himself for their charge, but there was no charge. There was fear in their eyes. As one they turned and vanished into the forest.

Wiz let out his breath in a long sigh.

"Okay," he called over his shoulder, keeping his eyes on the place where the trolls had disappeared, "you can come out now."

"Thank you, Lord," said a small voice behind him.

There were five of them, all formed as humans and none of them more than a foot high. One of the women had a child no longer than Wiz's forefinger in her arms.

As soon as they came into the open Wiz knew what they were. Moira called them Little Folk. Wiz always thought of them as brownies.

"Thank you, Lord," the one in the lead said again. "We owe you our lives. I am called Lannach." He turned to his companions. "These are called Fleagh, Laoghaire, Breachean and she Meoan." At the mention of their names each bowed or curtsied in turn.

"Glad I could help," he said uncomfortably. Then he frowned. "You're a little far from home aren't you? I thought you always lived with humans?"

"No more, Lord," the little man said sadly. "Mortals will not have us."

"We lived in the place mortals call Leafmarsh Meadow," Lannach explained. "We were always the friends of mortals. We helped them as best we could, especially with the animals and the household work."

"We asked little enough," the small creature said. "A bowl of milk now and again. A bit of bread on Midsummer's Day as a sign of respect."

"But now mortals have their own magic and they need us no more."

"Need us no more," the little one crooned. "Need us no more. Need us no more. Need us no more." His mother hushed him and he trailed off into babbling.

"You mean they chased you out?" Wiz asked

incredulously. Dangerous magic was one thing, but he'd never heard anyone accuse brownies of anything worse than mischief. People were supposed to be glad for the help brownies provided with the chores.

"Chased us out?" Meoan hissed. "They kill us if they can." The little woman was white and shaking with fury. "Look at us, mortal! We are all that are left of the Little Folk of our village."

"She was handfast to one who is no more," Lannach said. "The father of the child."

"They laid in wait for my Dairmuirgh," she said. "When he came to the stable to groom their horses, they set their demon upon him and made him no more." She was crying openly, the tears trickling down her tiny cheeks, and rocking back and forth. "Ay, they murdered him as he sought to help them."

Back in Silicon Valley Wiz had known a few programmers who refused to work on weapons systems or any other kind of military job. He'd always thought that was a little peculiar. The programmer's job was to deliver software on time, in spec and functional. It was the job of the designers and managers to worry about what would be done with it. Now he was confronted by the results of his work and those people didn't seem peculiar at all.

"Oh shit. Look, I'm really sorry." He stopped. "I'm, well I'm responsible in a way," he confessed miserably. "It was my spell they took and hacked up to make that thing."

"We know," Lannach said. "We also heard what happened when that bitch from the village destroyed the Stone." He placed a tiny hand on Wiz's forearm. "Lord, you cannot be responsible for the uses mortals choose to make of your magic."

That made him feel even worse. "Thanks, Lannach. Where will you go now?"

The brownie shrugged. "We do not know. Unlike dryads and some other creatures, we are not tied to one place. But it was our home." He looked up and his limpid brown eyes gazed into Wiz's. "It is hard to lose the place which has been your home for so long."

"I know," Wiz said miserably, thinking of smoggy sunsets over Silicon Valley.

"We would not leave even now save for the little one," he nodded to Meoan's baby. "He must be protected."

Wiz understood. Children were rare among the manlike immortals. An infant was a cause for great rejoicing and such children as there were were carefully protected. The adults might be willing to stay and die in a place they loved, but they would not risk the baby.

"Lord," said the little man tentatively, "Lord, could we impose upon you further and travel with you?"

"I'm not really sure where I'm going."

The brownie shrugged. "Neither are we, Lord."

The Wild Wood was still a tangle of ancient forest that abounded with dangerous magic, but Wiz wasn't afraid. His own magic was potent and very frankly he wasn't sure how much he cared.

"Sure," he said, "come on."

They spent the rest of the morning travelling. In spite of their size, the brownies moved quickly and had no trouble keeping up with Wiz. They found berries to eat along the way and once the brownies located a tree bearing small wild plums, just going ripe.

It was shortly after noon when they topped a rise and looked down into the heavily forested valley beyond. Six or eight thin curls of smoke arose from scattered locations on the valley's floor and merged to form a thin haze over the whole valley.

Wiz remembered the last time he had come into the Wild wood. The forest valleys had been an unbroken sea of green. Mortals were not welcome in the Wild Wood and the few who came were not gently treated.

"I didn't know there were so many people out here," Wiz said, looking down on the scene.

"Mortals, spread quickly," Lannach observed.

"Aye," agreed Breachean in a rusty voice. "Give them a few harvests and they'll carpet this valley like flies on meat."

"I don't think we want to go that way," Wiz said. "Let's follow the ridge and skirt that place."

It was harder going along the ridge and they used game trails rather than the well-trod footpath that led down into the valley, but it was more pleasant for all of them. The trees here were huge and old, unscarred by woodsman's axe. The birds sang and the squirrels dashed about as they had for centuries. Most of the time there was neither sight of a clearing nor smell of wood smoke to remind them of what was going on in the valley.

Still, it was slower going. It was almost evening when they came down off the ridge and into the next valley.

They made their way down the trail in the deepening twilight, looking for a place to camp.

"What's that?" Wiz asked pointing to a strange glow moving though the woods ahead of them.

"Off the trail," Lannach whispered. "Quickly!"

Wiz took a firmer grip on his staff. "Hide?"

"No, just do not stand in their way."

The light came clearer and brighter through the wood, like sky glow at dawn. Then the first of the procession rounded the bend and Wiz saw the light emanated from figures on horseback.

*Elves*, he thought, *a trooping of elves*.

They came by ones and twos, riding immaculately groomed horses of chestnut, roan and blood bay. They were tall and fair of skin, as all elven kind, and dressed with the kind of subdued magnificence Wiz had come to associate with elves.

They passed Wiz and the brownies by as if they were not there, looking straight ahead toward a distant goal or talking softly among themselves in their own liquid tongue.

Last of all came the lord and the lady of the hold.

The man wore green and blue satin with an embroidered white undertunic. Instead of a simple filet to hold his long cornsilk hair, he wore a silver coronet. He had a hawk on his wrist, unhooded.

The woman was as fair and near as tall as her lord, with hair the same cornsilk color flowing free of her coronet and down her back to almost touch her saddle. She wore a long gown of deep, deep purple with a train that flowed over her saddle and her horse's rump.

The woman turned her head to look at Wiz where he stood beside the trail. The combination of beauty and sadness clutched at his heart.

Wiz stood open-mouthed in awe long after the party had disappeared.

"They go East," Lannach said. "Beyond the lands of men."

"I didn't think the elves would be bothered," Wiz said numbly. "They're too powerful."

"Not all the Fair Folk are as powerful as your friend Duke Aelric. Oh, doubtless they could protect their hills and a few other spots most dear to them. But what then? The lands they called their own would be changed utterly by the mortals.

"As all the land changes," he added sadly.

Pryddian came into the room a trifle uncertainly.

"You sent for me, Lord?"

Bal-Simba ignored him for a moment and then looked up from the scroll on his desk.

"I did," the great black wizard said. "We have no further need of you here. You are released from your apprenticeship."

Pryddian started. "What?"

"Your presence here is no longer required," Bal-Simba said blandly. "You may go."

"That is a decision for my master!"

"You have no master, nor will any of the wizards here have you." He turned his attention back to the scroll.

Pryddian stood pale and shaking with rage, his lips pressed into a bloodless line.

"So. Because I am the victim of an attack by magic I am to be punished."

"You are not being punished, you are being released."

"And what of the Sparrow, the one who attacked me? What happens to him?"

The giant wizard regarded Pryddian as if he had just crawled out from beneath a damp log. "The affairs of the Mighty are none of your concern, boy. You have until the sun's setting to be gone from this place." He turned his attention back to the scroll.

"Ebrion will have something to say of this."

"Ebrion is not here."

Pryddian frowned. "Well, when he comes back then."

Bal-Simba looked up. "If Ebrion or any of the other wizards wish to speak for you they may do so. But until they do you are no longer required here."

"I will wait then."

"You may wait. Outside the walls of the Keep."

"I . . ."

"Do you wish to provoke me now?" Bal-Simba rumbled. "I warn you, you would find me harder sport than the Sparrow and perhaps not as forebearing." He smiled, showing off his pointed teeth.

Pryddian snapped his mouth shut, spun on his heel and stalked from the room.

*What would Ebrion have to do with that one?* Bal-Simba wondered as he listened to the ex-apprentice slam down the corridor. He made a mental note to ask him when he returned.

The clouds rolled in during the morning, light and fleecy at first, but growing grayer and more threatening as the day wore on. Wiz and his companions trudged onward.

At last, just as the threat of rain became overwhelming, they found a rock shelter, a place beneath an overhanging cliff where the rain could not reach. They were barely inside when the skies opened and the summer rain poured down in torrents.

It was still so warm they did not need a fire and Wiz didn't feel like dashing in to the rain without a cloak to gather the wood for one. He and the brownies settled down with their backs to the cliff and watched the rain drape traceries of gray over the forest and the hills beyond.

Scant comfort," Lannach said as they settled themselves among the rocks.

"At least we're dry," Wiz told the brownie. "The last time I came this way I got soaked in one of these storms." He thought of the trek through the dripping forest and the peasant who had sheltered them that night. The one who had gained a farm in the Wild Wood at the cost of his wife and three children dead and a daughter given as a servant to the elves.

Meoan plopped herself down on one of the rocks and yanked at the ties of her bodice.

"We must be grateful for small comforts," she said bitterly. "Those who are driven from their homes had best take what they can find and be happy with it." She pulled down her bodice and offered a breast no larger than the first joint of Wiz's thumb to her baby.

"I'm sorry for what happened to you," he said tentatively.

The little woman looked up at him. "I know you are, Lord. But sorry does not heal what it hurts." Then she sighed deeply. "And I apologize to you. Since we met you have shown us nothing but kindness. I should not blame you for what those others did."

"We're not all like that, you know. Where I come from we learned the hard way that you've got to protect non-human things, to try to live with them."

"Would that the mortals of this world were so wise," Meoan said.

"Maybe they can be. It's just that they've been oppressed by magic for so long they're afraid of it and they want to exterminate it."

"Whether it hurts them or not," the brownie woman sniffed.

"When you're afraid of something it's hard to make fine distinctions. Humans suffered a lot because they had no protection against magic."

Meoan nodded. "I have heard the mothers lamenting for their children, struck down or stolen away by magic." She held her infant to her breast. "Life has been hard for mortals."

Wiz looked out at the rain. The sun had broken through at the horizon to paint the bottom of the clouds red and purple with its dying rays. The trees of the forest were tinged a glowing gold above, shading to deeper green out of the light. Already the shadows were beginning to thicken and take on substance.

"It's going to be too dark to travel soon," Wiz said. "It looks like we stay here tonight."

He looked around ruefully. The ground was hard and full of sharp rocks fallen from the ceiling with almost no drifted leaves which could be used to make a bed. There were leaves aplenty out on the slope, but they were soaked.

"Well, it won't be our most comfortable night, that's for certain."

"Unless you would care to share other quarters," said a musical voice behind them. "Welcome, Sparrow."

# Nine
## MEETING BY MOONLIGHT

*Friends come and go, but enemies accumulate.*
—Murphy's law #1024

*. . . and sometimes the real trick is telling the difference.*
—Murphy's law #1024a

Wiz whirled and saw an elf standing in the gloaming at the edge of the overhang.

He was tall and straight as a forest pine. His skin was the color of fresh milk. His white long hair was caught back in a circlet of silver set with pale blue opals. Although the forest was dripping and the rain still fell in a light mist, he was completely dry.

"Duke Aelric?"

The elf duke nodded. "The same." Then he smiled and stepped aside to reveal another elf standing behind him.

"And this is Lisella."

She was nearly as tall as Aelric and her skin as milk-fair. But her hair was black and glossy as a raven's wing where Aelric's was snow white and her eyes were green as emeralds rather than icy blue. Her gown was old rose with a subtle embroidery of deeper red. Her figure was slender and elegant.

Wiz gulped and bowed clumsily.

"I discovered you were in the area and thought you might do us the honor of dining with us this evening," Aelric said. He looked around the rock shelter. "Perhaps you would care to guest the night with me as well."

"Why, uh, yes," Wiz said, managing to tear his eyes away from the elf duke's companion. "Thank you, Lord."

"Well, then," Aelric said. "If you would care to accompany us. And your friends, of course."

The brownies had dived for cover as soon as Aelric appeared. Now they poked their heads out from behind rocks or from the crevices where they had gone to earth.

"Come on," Wiz said. "He won't hurt you."

Reluctantly the brownies came out and gathered tight around Wiz. Lannach wasn't clinging to his pant leg, but Wiz got the feeling he wanted to.

"Shall we go?"

Aelric and Lisella strode to the back of the shelter and the elf duke made a gesture to the blank stone. Soundlessly the rock dissolved and there was an oak door, magnificently carved and bound with silver. The door swung open and warm golden light flooded out.

Wiz had no idea where he was in the Wild Wood, but he was pretty sure he was a long way from where he and Moira had entered the elf duke's hold the first time they met.

*Time and space run strangely in places the elves make their own,* Moira had told him then. He shrugged and followed Aelric and Lisella into the hill with a gaggle of brownies close on his heels.

Once again Wiz sat in Aelric's great dining hall. The magical globes floating above the table cast the same warm light onto the scene. The food was as superb as it had been before and the soft music in the background was as enchanting.

But there were differences. The last time he and Moira had been fugitives, snatched from the pursuing army of the Dark League by Aelric's whim. Now Moira was somewhere else and Wiz was . . . what?

And beyond that there was Lisella.

In the warm glow of the magic lights she was even more beautiful than she had been beneath the moon. Her presence reminded Wiz that before he met Moira he had been attracted to tall slender brunettes.

From time to time their eyes met across the table. Lisella looked at Wiz with a kind of intent interest that both stirred him and reminded him uncomfortably of the way a cat regards a baby bird it can't decide if it wants to play with or eat immediately.

Although Aelric and Lisella were careful to include Wiz in the conversation, he had the distinct feeling that he was missing most of what was actually being said. They were playing some kind of game, he decided, some elaborate elven game with malice at its heart. Whatever these two were they were definitely not lovers.

Throughout dinner Aelric had kept up an easy conversation on inconsequential topics. Wiz had sensed that his host did not want to discuss serious matters, and still in awe of the elf duke, he had likewise avoided them. Finally, as light-footed servants placed bowls of nuts and decanters of wine on the damask-covered table, Lisella rose.

"Alas, My Lords, the hour grows late." She curtseyed to Aelric. "If you will excuse me?"

Aelric stood up and Wiz followed suit. "Of course, My Lady." He bowed and kissed her extended hand.

Then she turned to Wiz and fixed her green eyes on his. "Perhaps we shall meet again," she said softly and with a rustle of her brocaded gown she was gone.

"Remarkable, is she not?" Duke Aelric said. Wiz realized he was gaping and made a determined effort to shut his mouth. Aelric sat down and Wiz followed suit. "I thought it would amuse you to meet her." He picked up his wine glass and again Wiz followed his lead.

"Uh, why? I mean aside from the fact that she's beautiful."

Aelric cocked an eyebrow. "My dear boy, she *has* been trying to kill you for months."

Wiz choked, spewing wine across Duke Aelric's fine damask table cloth.

The elf duke dabbed the wine drops from his sleeve. "You mean you did not know? Dear me, and I was about to comment you for your insouciance."

"How . . . I mean why? I mean I've never seen her before."

"That is immaterial, Sparrow. As to the how, she has been arranging little accidents' for you for some time. So far you have been lucky enough to avoid them."

Wiz remembered the falling stone and the toppled viewing stand and felt sick. Then he looked closely at the elf duke. "Somehow I don't think it's been entirely luck."

Aelric smiled. "Your escapes were at least as much luck as your accidents were mischance."

Wiz absorbed that in silence. All of a sudden he felt like a piece on someone else's chess board. He didn't like it much.

"Thanks, I think. But why is she trying to kill me?"

"Oh, many reasons, I expect. The technical challenge for one. Penetrating a place so thick with magic as your Capital undetected and laying such subtle traps. That required superb skill, I can assure you."

He smiled reminiscently. "So did countering them. You've provided quite a diverting experience."

"And if I had missed that handhold on the parapet? Or hadn't jumped the right way when the stand collapsed?"

Aelric looked at him levelly. "Then the game would have been over."

Wiz was silent again. "You said there were many reasons Lisella wanted to kill me," he said at last. "What are some of the others?"

Duke Aelric poured more of the ruby wine into a crystal glass with an elaborately wrought and delicately tinted stem. "Surely you can guess. When last we met, I said I would follow your career with interest, Sparrow." He smiled wryly. "I admit I did not expect it to be quite this interesting."

"I didn't either, Lord."

"It is not often a mortal is sufficiently interesting to hold the attention of one of us. You have become interesting enough to fix the attention of quite a number of the never-dying."

The elf duke looked at his guest speculatively. "You have made yourself much hated, you know."

"Yeah," said Wiz miserably. "It wasn't supposed to work this way. Things kind of got out of hand."

"Not unusual when mortals dabble in magic," Aelric said. "Lisella is a minor difficulty. You would do well to dismiss her from your mind—after taking proper precautions, of course. What you have done has deeper consequences."

"You mean the destruction of magic along the Fringe?"

"I mean the destruction of mortals everywhere," the elf duke said. "You mortals make this new magic and in the process you raise forces against yourselves you do not understand. For the first time in memory there is talk of a grand coalition of magic wielders, a coalition aimed at the mortals."

"That's crazy!"

"That is mortal logic, Sparrow. None of these are mortals and many of them are not logical in any sense."

"But, I mean a war."

"They would not think of it as a war. Rather the extermination of a particularly repulsive class of vermin who have made themselves too obvious."

Wiz stared straight into the depths of the elf duke's eyes. "Do you think you could beat us?"

Aelric shrugged gracefully. "I really do not know."

Then he caught and held Wiz's gaze. "But I tell you this, Sparrow. Whoever wins, the outcome is likely to be the utter destruction of the World."

Wiz dropped his eyes. "Yeah. But does it have to happen? I mean, can't we prevent it?"

"It would be difficult at best," Aelric said. "That is not a consequence all of us wish to avoid. There are some who hunger for death and destruction on the widest possible scale. There are some who by their very natures cannot comprehend or appreciate the threat. And there are some who would find the end of the World merely diverting. A new experience, so to speak."

"What can I do?"

Aelric shrugged. "Remove the cause. The magical forces of the world make uneasy allies. If the threat were gone, the coalition would dissolve in an eye blink."

Wiz thought about that, long and hard. Aelric sipped his wine and said nothing more.

He didn't know what the chances of heading this thing off were, but he didn't think they were very good. Given the feelings of the people of the Fringe about magic, and given the power of the tools he had put in their hands, it wasn't going to be easy to get them to quit wiping out magic wherever they found it. Keeping them from pushing into the Wild Wood in search of land would be harder yet.

And he was going to have to have a hand in finding a solution. Not only because he helped create the problem, but because he was the only one who really understood the new kind of magic that lay at the root of it.

Wiz was even less confident of his ability to solve those problems than he was of his capacity as a politician or a teacher, but dammit! he had to try.

"I'm going back to the Capital," he announced. "Maybe I can undo some of this mess."

"A wise decision," Aelric said. "When do you propose to return?"

"I should go back tonight, but I'm beat and there's not much I could do there. First thing in the morning, then."

The elf duke nodded.

Wiz reached for his wine goblet. Then he froze in horror.

"Wait a minute! If Lisella wanted to kill me, she just had the perfect opportunity to poison me or something!" He stared at his goblet as if it had sprouted poison fangs and tried desperately to remember if Lisella's hands had ever been near it.

Duke Aelric chuckled. "Oh no. Murdering you while you sat together at dinner would be gauche. The fair Lisella is never gauche."

Wiz considered that and decided the elf duke was probably right. But he didn't drink any more wine.

"Oh, one other thing. The Little Folk who came with me. Could you, well, could you take care of them for me?"

Aelric looked startled.

"Are they so important?"

"Not important, no. But I kind of feel responsible for them and I can't take them with me."

The elf duke's brow creased and for a second Wiz was afraid he was angry. Then he relaxed and rubbed his chin.

"I doubt they would be happy within my hold," Aelric said finally. "But I could send them on to Heart's Ease under my protection. I do not think those who dwell there would mind their presence."

"Thank you, Lord. I really appreciate it."

Aelric made a throw-away gesture. "You are most welcome." Then he smiled wryly. "Sparrow, it is always a pleasure to share your company. One never knows what you will do next." He sighed. "Or what one is likely to do under your influence."

Lisella was not in evidence the next morning when Wiz bade Aelric farewell. The elf duke and the brownies accompanied him to a clearing outside one of the elf hill's many doors. It seemed impolite to walk the Wizard's Way from inside the hill—something like parking your motorcycle in your host's living room.

"Good luck, Sparrow," Aelric said as Wiz faced in his chosen direction.

"Merry part, Lord."

Aelric looked at him and Wiz flushed, remembering that the elves did not use the human formula.

"Merry meet again," Aelric said finally.

Wiz raised his staff to begin the spell that would take him home.

**"backslash."**

# Ten

# THE CITY OF NIGHT

*Whenever you use a jump, be sure of your destination address.*

—programmer's saying

Something had gone wrong! Wiz felt as if he had been spun around and tackled by a lineman. He was dizzy, pointing in the wrong direction and everything was wrong. His vision blurred, his head hurt and he was on the verge of throwing up.

As his sight cleared, Wiz saw he was in a low stone room. It was cold and lit by torches, not magic globes.

Ebrion stood before him.

"Merry met, my Lord," Wiz said instinctively. Ebrion looked uncomfortable.

"Merry met, Sparrow," came a cackling voice from behind him. "Merry met indeed."

Wiz turned and saw a bent man in the black robe of a wizard of the Dark League. He hobbled forward, leaning heavily on his staff.

The black-robed one smiled, not at all pleasantly. "Welcome, Sparrow. Welcome to your final resting place."

"Stayed behind?" Bal-Simba demanded. "What do you mean he stayed behind?"

"He departed into the Wild Wood when we had finished," Philomen told him.

"And you let him?"

Philomen hesitated. "We had words earlier that morning. I fear he was not well-disposed toward me. Then it turned out this rock creature was in some way sentient and that disturbed him even more. The Sparrow has an unusually tender regard for magical creatures of all sorts. He seems to feel that even the useless ones should be protected."

"So he went off into the Wild Wood. Alone."

"Lord, I tried to reason with him, but he would not listen. I am sorry, Lord."

"No need for that," Bal-Simba said flipping his hand dismissingly. "Perhaps our Sparrow needs some time by himself. And in any event, the longer he stays away the better for the situation here." He sighed. "I only wish he had gone through the settled lands rather than into the Wild Wood. But, no, you did nothing wrong."

"Thank you, Lord," said Philomen and withdrew with a bow.

Bal-Simba stood at the window looking out over the rooftops of the Capital toward the east as the shadows groped their way toward the horizon. Then he sighed again, shook himself and turned away to his desk.

*At least he will be in no danger,* Bal-Simba told himself. *As long as he stays away from elves he is certainly more powerful than anything he is likely to meet on this wandering.*

Wiz looked around desperately. The chamber was low but wide and long, with rough stone for the walls and floors and a couple of smoking torches to light it. Standing back in the shadows he saw even more black-robed wizards of the Dark League.

"We are going to send you back where you came from, Sparrow," Ebrion said finally. "Back to where you belong."

"But I don't want to go."

"Then you shall not," the other, black robe, said as he hobbled more fully into the light.

Wiz gasped.

The man's eyes glinted like chips of obsidian in a pink hairless mass of scar tissue. His nose was a slit and his ears shriveled like dried apricots. The hand clutching the staff was reduced to a claw, with only the thumb and forefinger remaining. Like the face, the hand was pink with scars.

"That was not the agreement," Ebrion protested.

"The agreement has changed," the other flung over his shoulder as he closed in on Wiz, thrusting his face so close Wiz could see where his eyebrows had been.

"Look upon me, Sparrow. I am called Dzhir Kar and I am your death." His breath stank in Wiz's face.

"My form does not please you?" he said, looking up at his captive. "A pity, Sparrow. For you caused it. A ceiling fell on me when you attacked the City of Night. There was a fire as well and I lay within the flames, slowly roasting and unable to move."

His face split into a hideous grin. "But I do not hold that against you, Sparrow. Oh no, not at all. For as I lay there and burned I discovered new strength within me. As I struggled to recover, I honed that strength. It made me Master of the Dark League, Sparrow."

He grasped Wiz's chin with a claw-like hand and pulled his face close.

"Look at me, little one! For I am your creation."

Wiz twisted his chin from the other's grasp and flinched away.

"Then look at *my* creation, Sparrow. My creation and your doom."

He gestured and two of the black-robed wizards moved forward into the fitful light. Each of them held a heavy chain and on that chain was a thing that made Wiz catch his breath.

It was long and lean, with a body made for coursing. The legs were a hound's legs, although the three ripping talons on each paw were like no dog that ever lived. The head was narrow with ivory fangs protruding from the heavily muscled jaws. Dzhir Kar made a gesture toward Wiz with his staff and the thing lunged and snapped at Wiz. The sound rang like a rifle shot in the gloomy chamber.

"Do you like my pet?" the black-robed wizard crooned, laying a gnarled hand upon the scaly head. "I made him especially for you, Sparrow."

The demon remained impassive under the caress, its yellow eyes fixed hungrily on Wiz.

"Not nearly as powerful as Toth-Set-Ra's demon, but he has seen you and that is enough.

"He is attuned to your magic, Sparrow. Make magic. Oh yes, please make magic. He will be upon you and your end will be truly wonderful to watch."

Wiz started to form a spell mentally. Instantly the creature's yellow eyes flicked open and its ears pricked forward.

"Go ahead," the wizard was almost dancing in anticipation. "Oh my yes, go ahead. We *want* to see this new Northern magic up close, don't we?"

The man was insane, Wiz realized. Crazy and full of spite and malice at the same time.

"No?" said the wizard in a disappointed tone. "Well, we will have to persuade you then. Flaying alive for a start. With salt rubbed well into the flesh to preserve it as the skin is peeled off. Toth-Set-Ra was right, there is *so* much one can do with a wizard's skin."

"*No!*" Ebrion bellowed.

Dzhir Kar stopped and regarded him as if he were an insect.

"I told you I would not have him harmed! We are to return him to his place only. That was our bargain."

"Bargains are made to be broken," Dzhir Kar said. He gestured to the surrounding wizards. "Take this one away."

"Fools," Ebrion shouted. "You seal your own doom."

"We will see who is doomed when the Council is deprived of its most powerful member," Dzhir Kar retorted. "And when it becomes known that one of the most powerful wizards in the North had a hand in the deed."

As the wizards of the Dark League closed in on him Ebrion stepped back and raised his arms. With a crash and a roar a dozen bolts of lightning struck him where he stood. Wiz flinched from the noise and the light.

So did the two wizards holding him. Instinctively, Wiz twisted in their slackened grips and broke free. Before anyone could react he was across the room and out the door.

*"Get him!"* screamed Dzhir Kar and the others leapt past the still smoldering corpse of Ebrion to comply. But Wiz was halfway down the rough flagged passageway and running for his life.

He turned the corner so fast he slipped and a bolt of lightning exploded on the stone behind him. He scrambled to his feet and ran on as the wizards came clattering out behind him.

He ran on at random, turning this way and that on panicked whim. The place seemed to be a maze of low stone passages with rough flagged floors. Behind him always he heard the sound of pursuit, sometimes close at hand and sometimes further away, but always there.

He ran out into a rotunda where five or six corridors came together and dashed down one to his left. Down another corridor he saw the bobbing gleam of torches.

The corridor was long and straight and Wiz ran down it full tilt. He was going so fast he almost ran straight into the wall ahead. Blind alley! He whirled and pounded back the way he had come, ribs aching and breath burning in his throat.

Again out into the rotunda and down another corridor. No sign of the lights now, but he was sure they were not far behind. Halfway down the corridor there was a place where the wall had collapsed. He slowed to avoid the pile of stones and saw lights before him and behind him, distant but coming his way. Without a thought he darted up the rubble pile and through the hole in the wall.

Suddenly he was outside on a narrow street between two- and three-story buildings of rough black stone. It was night, he realized and the moon was hidden by clouds. There was little enough light, but Wiz didn't slow down. He turned right and pounded down the street, heedless of the stitch in his side.

The empty windows of the upper stories gaped down at him like accusing eyes. Here and there an open doorway yawned like a devouring mouth. He ran without purpose or direction, on and on until a red mist fogged his vision. Finally, chest heaving and staggering with exhaustion, he turned into one of those open doorways in search of a place to hide and catch his breath.

Once through the door he sidled to the right, hugging the wall. After a dozen steps he stumbled over the bottom landing of a stone staircase. Still gasping for breath, he picked his way up the stairs.

The narrow twisting staircase had no railing and the steps were uneven and slick with wear. Wiz hugged the wall and made as much speed as he dared. At last he came to the top of the tower—or what was now the top. The entire upper section was missing, the walls bulged outward and the stonework was disrupted as if someone had set off an explosion inside it. Wiz looked out over the blasted, fire-blackened stone and for the first time he knew where he was.

The harbor with its encircling jetty, the ruined towers and the volcano bulking up behind him told him. The City of Night! The capital and base of the Dark League before their power had been broken.

A gibbous moon cast a sullen, fitful light over the

landscape, picking out the tops of the ruined towers and the acres of rooftops below him. Wiz looked out over desolation and shivered.

Puffing and blowing, he sank down to sit on the stair, his back against the ruined wall and his feet dangling over emptiness. He tried to remember what he knew about the geography of this place.

Almost none of it was first-hand. He had been here only once before, when he mounted his great attack to free Moira from the League's dungeons deep beneath the city. He had come along the Wizard's Way and departed in the same fashion. In the hours he had been here he had never seen the surface.

The City of Night was on the Southern Continent, he remembered, separated from his home by the Freshened Sea. It was a bleak, barren land, locked in the grip of eternal winter.

Supposedly the city had been deserted after the Dark League had been defeated. Large parts had been destroyed by the forces unleashed in the final battle. The League wizards who had survived had been hunted from their lairs, their slaves had been freed and returned to their homes and the goblins and most of their other creatures had departed as well.

But the land itself was ruined beyond reclamation by decades of exercise of power with no thought to the consequences. For the people of the North the city was a place of fell reputation where no one but would-be apprentices of the Dark League went willingly. There was nothing to attract anyone to the place and even maintaining a watchpost on the Southern Continent had been considered too difficult and not worth the effort. The City of Night had been left unrestored and uninhabited.

If there was anyone here besides the League wizards they were unlikely to help Wiz.

Wiz ground his teeth in frustration. All he had to do

to get help or to go home was to use magic. One single simple spell and it was done.

Of course before he could ever finish that spell the monster in the dungeon would be on him. He remembered the eagerness and ferocity burning in the thing's evil red eyes and he shuddered. He had no doubt at all the wizard had been telling him the truth.

He listened to the wind whistle through the broken tower and tried to decide what to do next.

A clattering in the street below drew his attention. Peering out through the shattered wall, Wiz saw a dark shape cross a silvery patch of moonlight. Then another and another.

"He came this way." The voice floated up to him from the street nearly a hundred feet below.

"He must be near here," the other wizard called out from the shadows. "Down this way."

Wiz could not see which way he pointed, but several pairs of feet pattered off away from his hiding place.

So they weren't waiting for him to use magic! Those searchers were as dangerous to him as the monster. They knew the city and he did not. How many of them were there? Wiz wracked his brain trying to remember how many wizards had been in the room when he appeared. A dozen? Certainly that. And more besides.

And Ebrion. A traitor to the Council and now dead at the hands of his erstwise allies.

*Well,* Wiz thought grimly, *you brought this on yourself. If you hadn't been so high-handed with the Council, Ebrion never would have gone to the Dark League.*

Somehow the thought didn't make him feel any better.

The wind gusted and Wiz shivered harder. He didn't remember any part of the city being this cold. Perhaps the Dark League had warmed it by magic when they held it. Now there was slick black ice in patches on the streets and occasional piles and drifts of snow in the corners and sheltered spots.

Wiz shifted position and listened again. Save for the moan of the wind down the deserted streets and about the ruined tower, there was no sound. Slowly and cautiously, he rose and started back down the steps. He couldn't stay here and if he didn't find some kind of shelter soon the wind would do what the Dark League and their pet monster hadn't yet been able to.

The moon cast a pale light on the steep, narrow street below when it was not obscured by scudding clouds. The City of Night was built on the flank of a volcano and the whole town sloped up from the harbor. Wiz hugged the side of the buildings and headed downhill. Not only was it easier walking, it was away from the underground room where he had appeared and where the wizards and his demon waited for him.

At every corner he paused and listened. The streets were narrow and the hard black basalt of the buildings turned them into echo chambers. His own footsteps rang so loudly on the pavement he was certain that any pursuer could track him by sound alone. He hoped that he could pick up a trace of anyone in the area the same way.

At the third cross street he paused an especially long time to catch his breath. Up ahead there was the tiniest scuffling sound, as if something was dragging stealthily along the building ahead of him.

Wiz froze and then dropped back into the shadows. Across the narrow street on the other side of the intersection he saw a stealthy movement in the shadows. At first it was just a flicker here and there, then it looked as if the entire shadow on that side of the street had come to life. Then the shadow took form and substance and Wiz held his breath as he realized what it was.

The huge head was man-high off the ground as the serpent glided along. Its tongue flickered in and out constantly as it tested the air for scent of prey. Even in the moonlight Wiz could see the diamond patterns of its scales.

Then it turned and soundlessly whipped down the side street. Wiz caught his breath, but he stayed in hiding for a long time.

"Alone?" Arianne asked wide-eyed. "Alone into the Wild Wood?"

"So it would seem," Bal-Simba told her. He had spent the last two hours trying to control his unease and finally told his deputy what had happened. "Philomen did not stop him."

"He could not very well forbid him," Arianne pointed out. "Wiz is a member of the Council, Lord."

"Yes, but he knows less of the Wild Wood than a child," Bal-Simba said. "Remember the stories Moira told about the troubles she had with him on their last journey."

"The Dark League is not seeking him now."

"True, else I would have every magician and dragon rider in the realm searching for him. But he has barely been out of the city in the last two years and he still has little understanding of the World's dangers."

They were both silent for a moment.

"Lord," Arianne said finally, "what do you think is troubling Sparrow now?"

"If I had to guess, I would say he is discovering the price of power." Bal-Simba made a face. "I do not think he likes it overmuch."

Then it turned and soundlessly whipped down the side street. Wiz caught his breath, but he stayed in hiding for a long time.

"Alone?" Arianne asked wide-eyed. "Alone into the Wild Wood?"

"So it would seem." Bal-Simba told her. He had spent the last two hours trying to control his unease and finally told his deputy what had happened. Philomen did not stop him.

"He could not very well forbid him," Arianne pointed out. "Wiz is a member of the Council, Lord."

"Yes, but he knows less of the Wild Wood than a child," Bal-Simba said. "Remember the stories Moira told about the troubles she had with him on their last journey."

"The Dark League is not seeking him, surely?"

"True, else I would have every magician and dragon rider in the realm searching for him. But he has barely been out of the city in the last two years and he still has little understanding of the World's dangers."

They were both silent for a moment.

"Lord," Arianne said finally, "what do you think is troubling Sparrow now?"

"If I had to guess, I would say he is discovering the price of power," Bal-Simba made a face. "I do not think he likes it overmuch."

# PART II:
# LINK TIME

# *Eleven*
## A BIT OF BURGLARY

*Always secure your files. You never know who's lurking
about.*

—programmer's saying

Pryddian, once apprentice wizard, closed the door
softly and looked around the sitting room. He saw no
signs of traps or warning devices anywhere. Once the
apartment's door had been breached there seemed to be
nothing to protect the contents.

There was no reason why there should be. Ordinary
theft was virtually unknown in the Wizards' Keep because
it was so easy to find thieves by magic. The wizards'
workrooms were carefully protected by multiple spells, but
there was no reason to extend that protection to living
quarters. After all, no one worked in his or her apartment.

With one very important exception.

Pryddian moved cautiously across the sitting room
toward the desk piled high with books and papers. With
the hedge witch fled and the Sparrow sent away there
should be no one here, but the enormity of what he was
doing made Pryddian careful nonetheless.

*Well,* Pryddian thought, *the Sparrow had it coming.*
This was a way to avenge himself and perhaps profit as
well.

As he approached the desk beneath, the red dragon demon reared up from among the clutter and hissed at him. Pryddian stopped and studied the creature carefully. He had expected something like this. Not even the Sparrow would be so careless as to leave his secrets completely unguarded.

However, Pryddian had come prepared, just as he had come armed with an unlocking spell for the door. The fact that it was a thing of the Sparrow's made it all the more delicious.

"**ddt exe!**" he whispered, pointing at the guardian demon.

The little red dragon paused in mid-hiss and scampered off the table. Pryddian watched in satisfaction as it ran whimpering for the bedroom.

Eagerly he bent over the desk and began to riffle through the material piled there. The large leatherbound book in the center of the table seemed most important, so he opened it first. But what was inside was the confused mishmash of the nonsense the Sparrow foisted off upon the wizards. Not a true spell in the lot. He slammed the book in disgust and turned to the piles of parchment, slates and tablets stacked around.

Quickly he sorted them, putting aside everything that was too arcane or too fragmentary to be useful. He was left with a sizable amount of material. Stacking the pile on top of the book, he reached into his cloak and produced a pen, a travelling inkwell and a sheaf of parchment. He dipped his pen into the ink and began to copy as fast as he could write, cursing when he blotted something in haste.

This was what he wanted. Not the inane babblings the Sparrow expounded in his classes, but his spells. His real power. Frantically he copied the crabbed smudged characters, taking care to put alternate lines on different sheets of parchment to prevent activating the spells. He added the marginal notes as he went, even though most of them meant nothing to him. With time perhaps he could puzzle out their meanings.

He was perhaps halfway down the pile when he came to the real prize. A powerful searching spell that would show the user anything that went on in the world. Flipping through the parchments he saw the spell commanded three separate sets of demons.

Pryddian licked his lips and his hand trembled. This must be the spell the Sparrow had used to track the Dark League. Like any magician, he believed that knowledge was power and this was a spell that would give him knowledge of the entire world.

The dragon demon peered around the corner at him and occasionally ventured a half-hiss. That Pryddian ignored. Every so often he glanced over his shoulder at the door, gripped by a mixture of elation and terror. If he was caught the consequences did not bear thinking about, but if he got away with this he would possess the essence of the Sparrow's magic.

Throw him out, would they? They would see who was the better wizard before he was through.

As he bent to copy the sheets he looked out between the drawn curtains and saw Moira coming across the courtyard, still wearing her travelling cloak.

*Fortuna!* The most powerful spell in the Sparrow's arsenal and he did not have time to copy it. Without thinking he thrust the originals inside his jerkin with the wad of copies. Hastily he gathered up his pen and ink and tried to put everything back where he found it.

Moira paused at the branching of the corridor and summoned up her courage.

*Well,* she thought, *soonest stated soonest done.* She took a deep breath, squared her shoulders and strode off down the hall toward the apartment she shared with Wiz.

As she made her way down the hall, a figure in a hooded cloak hurried by her. She nodded and half-voiced a greeting out of habit, but the hooded one ignored her. As he twisted to pass her she saw that it was the apprentice who had insulted Wiz on the drill ground.

If she had been less distracted, Moira might have wondered what an apprentice was doing in a wing reserved for wizards. Or why he was wearing a cloak with the hood up indoors. But she had more important things on her mind. She paused outside the door to their apartment, took a deep breath, wiped a sweaty palm on her skirt and opened the door.

The room was deserted. The little red dragon raised its head inquiringly as she came in, but there was no sign of Wiz.

*Just like him!* Moira thought. She was all steeled for what must be said and he wasn't here. She plopped down in her chair, determined to wait for him to come back.

Around the corner, Pryddian leaned against the wall, shaking and cursing inwardly. *She saw me!* He ground his teeth. *The bitch saw me!* True, she had not seen him come out of their apartment, but she had seen him in a hall where he had no business being. Once the Sparrow returned and missed the searching spell, it would take no great leap to trace the deed to him.

Even if the Sparrow noticed nothing amiss, it meant his foray was useless. As soon as he started using the knowledge he had stolen, the hedge witch would remember his presence and it would be obvious to everyone what he must have done. For all his daring and cunning, he was blocked before he could even begin. Pryddian turned his face to the wall and beat his fist against he stone in frustration.

Then he dropped his hand and gained control of himself. Perhaps he was not so blocked after all. If he used the Sparrow's magic anywhere in the North he would be detected as a thief. But there were other magics—and other places.

He let out a long, deep breath and straightened up.

It was not the path he would have chosen, but there was a way still open to him.

Bal-Simba looked up at the knock upon his study door. He wasn't surprised to see Moira standing there.

"Merry met, Lady," he said, leaning back in his oversize chair. "Come in."

"Merry met, Lord. Where is Wiz?" The words tumbled out almost as a single sentence.

"I sent him on an errand," Bal-Simba told her. "It seemed expedient."

"I heard something . . . Lord, did he really threaten magic against someone?"

Bal-Simba nodded and Moira closed her eyes in pain. "Lord, we have got to help him. We *must!*"

The giant wizard shook his head. "Neither of us has the skill, Lady. We are mere novices at this new magic and Wiz needs the help of the Mighty of his own world to do what needs to be done."

"Lord," she said formally. "I ask it of you and the Council that you do whatever is within your power to aid Wiz."

Bal-Simba smiled, showing his pointed teeth. "Willingly granted Lady, but what would you of us?"

"I have been thinking about this," Moira said. She stopped, gathering herself. Bal-Simba waited. The candles gave a bayberry tang to the air and the evening breeze made them flicker and the shadows dance on the wall.

"Lord," the redhaired witch said slowly, "we promised we would not Summon anyone hither, did we not?"

Bal-Simba looked at her narrowly. "That we did. A most solemn promise."

"So it was," Moira agreed. "But I do not recall ever promising not to *ask* others to help us."

"Eh?"

"Suppose we did not Summon another to us," she went on. "Suppose instead we used a Great Summoning to *send* someone to Wiz's people to appeal for their aid? Would the Council approve, do you think?"

The black giant's face split in an enormous grin. "Brilliant, Lady!" His laughter pealed off the ceiling. "You will wind up on the Council yet."

Then he sobered. "But it would be a dangerous journey."

"True, but think of what we could do if I brought Wiz back one of the Mighty of his world!"

"If *you* brought back . . . Oh no! No, My Lady! Wiz would have my head if I let you go haring off on such a scheme. And he would be richly entitled to it."

"But Lord . . ." Moira began.

"No! Not you. Someone else, but not you. And that's final!"

Wiz leaned back against the stone wall and shivered. He was so tired he could not keep his eyes open, but the least little movement or sound brought him awake with a start.

He was terribly hungry. His last meal had been at Duke Aelric's—how long ago? More than that, he was cold. Desperately, numbingly, bone-chillingly cold. He exhaled and watched his breath puff white.

It would be so simple to be warm again. But with that *thing* around he dared not use magic of any sort. He had only to begin forming a spell in his head and he could feel the quiver of the demon's anticipation. No matter how careful he was, he would be dead before he could ever complete the first line.

In theory he could write the spell out and then summon a demon to execute the code. But that wouldn't buy him much. In the first place, just the act of putting the spell down might be enough to send the demon arrowing after him. In the second place, even if the demon did finish the spell he wouldn't live to see it. He might come up with something that would finish the demon, but he wouldn't be there to see it.

*Besides*, he thought, *I've got a war to stop. I've got to get back to the Capital.*

He had been stupid to travel unprotected, he saw now. Moira had told him that wizards kept one or more defense spells primed and ready against sudden danger. He'd laughed and told her he didn't need such precautions. With his new magic he could launch a spell in an instant. He remembered that Moira hadn't looked happy, but she hadn't said anything.

If only he had time to prepare he knew he could take the beast, or at least get beyond its grasp. But he had come unsuspecting and unprotected and now it was too late.

He leaned back and thought of Moira. *At least she's safe*, he told himself as he drifted off into a restless half-sleep.

# *Twelve*

## STRANGER IN A STRANGE LAND

*Never argue with a redhaired witch. It wastes your breath and only delays the inevitable.*

—the collected sayings of Wiz Zumwalt

"I still think this is too dangerous," Bal-Simba grumbled for the twentieth time.

"Hush, Lord," Moira placed her hand gently on his massive ebony arm. "It is less dangerous for me than for any other. Who else knows as much about Wiz's world?"

"Will you not at least take a couple of guardsmen? Donal and Kenneth . . ."

"No, Lord. From what Wiz has told me they would only attract notice. And perhaps trouble."

"I suppose so." He sighed and looked around the room. Six other wizards were already at their places and the shadow on the sun dial crept ever closer to noon. "Best you take your place then, Lady. Remember, we will search for your signal every day two day-tenths after sunrise and two day-tenths before sunset. When we sense your signal we will perform the Grand Summoning. Do you have the cord?"

"Yes, Lord," Moira said, touching the pouch at her waist, "and thank you." She stretched up to kiss him on the cheek. "Please when Wiz returns tell him not to worry." Then she turned and strode to her place in the center of the circle of wizards.

Bal-Simba frowned slightly at that. He did not tell her he had expected Wiz back days ago. The great black wizard was beginning to get worried.

"Merry part, Lady."

Moira dropped him a slight curtsey from her position in the center of the floor. "Merry meet again, Lord."

The chant swelled up in six-part harmony as the wizards sought to bend the forces of the Universe to their will. Moira stood straight-backed at her place in the growing maelstrom of magical energies. As the grayness swirled up about her Bal-Simba thought he saw her lip quiver.

Jerry Andrews rattled off the sequence to start compiling the program. Then he leaned back and the chair creaked. He sucked a lungful of the chill, air-conditioned air and rubbed his eyes. The after image of the screen was burned into his vision.

The fix he had just installed was a fairly elegant piece of work. He would have liked to show it to someone, but he was alone. His new cubicle mate was a day person and they seldom met unless Jerry was going home late while he was coming in early.

*Whole damn company's going to hell,* he thought sourly. *Next thing you know we'll be doing weekly project reviews with input from marketing.* When that happened Jerry intended to bail out. He was an old hand and he knew the signs.

*Besides,* he thought, *this place hasn't been the same since Wiz Zumwalt went away.*

Wiz's disappearance had shaken people up plenty. There were lights in the parking lot at ZetaSoft now and security guards patrolled the grounds and the buildings.

It wasn't unknown for a late-working programmer to be robbed or killed in company parking lot, but it still struck hard when it happened close to home. Especially since they never found the body.

Besides, Wiz had been his friend. If it hadn't been for his taste for truly rotten puns, he would have been the perfect work companion.

*Well,* he thought, *just link this module in and . . .*

There was a sudden blurring of the world and Jerry Andrews realized he had a girl in his lap.

Since most of Jerry's lap was already taken up by his rather ample stomach, she promptly rolled off and landed on the floor.

She shook her mane of red hair and looked up at him, her green eyes wide. "Oh! Crave pardon, My Lord."

Jerry stared at her, stunned.

Moira rose quickly and clutched at the edge of the desk as the room spun around her. Even with Bal-Simba's improved technique she was still dizzy and weak from the aftereffects of the Summoning.

"Uh, hi," Jerry said for want of anything better to say. Not only was this totally unexpected, but she was gorgeous—if you liked busty redheads. Jerry liked busty anything.

"Greetings, My Lord," Moira said, still clutching the edge of the desk. "I am called Moira."

"I'm Jerry Andrews."

Her eyes widened again. "Oh, well met! Wiz has told me a great deal about you."

"Wiz? Wiz Zumwalt?"

"Yes. He is in trouble and he needs help."

"Wiz is alive?"

"Oh yes, but he is not here. There was a Great Summoning and Wiz . . ." she trailed off. "It is a rather long story, I fear, and perhaps a complicated one."

Jerry nodded. "That sounds like Wiz."

They couldn't stay here, he decided. Moira didn't have a badge and sooner or later the guard would come by. But it was early in the morning and there wasn't any place to sit and talk.

Jerry decided to fall back on his first instinct whenever he had a problem. "Let's get something to eat."

The Capital of the North did not so much end as it trailed off in a dispirited gaggle of buildings, set ever further apart along the high street as the rocky promontory slanted down to the surrounding plain. At the upper end of the town, the Front, the houses and shops of the well-to-do crowded close to the walls of the Wizards' Keep. The further you moved down the spine of rock, the meaner and poorer the town became.

Pryddian was no stranger to the Back of the Capital, but this was an area he had little occasion to visit. Down a twisting side street, so narrow the overhanging houses almost blocked the sun, there was a stable. So small and dark was the entrance Pryddian nearly passed the place before he realized it was what he sought. He kept the hood of his cloak up and looked up and down the street before ducking through the low door.

Inside the place smelt of moldy straw and horses ill-kept. The ex-apprentice wrinkled his nose at the odor and wondered what kind of person would keep a horse in such foul quarters.

"You want something?"

He whirled and saw a man standing beside one of the stalls, leaning on a pitchfork.

"I am looking for something."

The other advanced, still holding the pitchfork. Pryddian saw the man was short and powerfully built, with a permanent squint and lank dark hair. As he came closer Pryddian's nose told him he was as ill-kempt as his stable.

"If it's a horse we got 'em. If not, be on your way."

Pryddian licked his lips. If the rumors were wrong about this place he could be in a lot of trouble. But if they were true . . .

"I wish to meet—some people."

"Well, there's none here but myself. Now be off with you!" The man gestured threateningly with the pitchfork.

Pryddian almost turned and ran. But he was desperate, so he stood his ground.

"I need to reach the Dark League."

The man stopped. "You're an apprentice from the castle."

"Former apprentice. I seek a different master and I bring something with me that will be valued in other quarters."

"The way to the Dark League lies south and over the Freshened Sea, as everyone knows," the man said sullenly.

"No more. The City of Night is in ruins and the old roads are closed."

"That's nothing to me. I have no truck with the likes of those."

"A pity," said Pryddian, fingering his pouch. "I am prepared to pay for information." He reached in and pulled out a silver coin. "I pay well." He turned the coin around in his fingers so it flashed in the dim light.

"Well," said the stableman, lowering the pitchfork. "I don't say I know anything and I don't say I don't. But there are those that say that if you take the road west to the Wild Wood there is a place where you might be met, sometimes."

Pryddian held out the coin to the man's grasp. "Tell me more."

*Damn!* Jerry muttered as he peered around the corner into the lobby. The guard was at the desk reading a supermarket tabloid.

He pulled his head back and stopped to think. Moira had no business being in the building, of course, and right now Jerry didn't think he was up to inventing a good excuse for her presence. He had hoped the guard would be off making a round, but they did rounds at irregular intervals and in this case it looked like the next interval would come when the guard finished his reading.

"Okay," he whispered, "just stay close to me and don't

say anything." Moira nodded and they both sauntered around the corner.

As they came into the lobby the guard glanced up briefly and went back to his reading. Moira was behind and to one side of Jerry's bulk and the man obviously missed her.

Jerry leaned over to sign out on the sheet. The guard kept his nose buried in the tabloid.

"Good night," he said. The guard mumbled a response without looking up from his magazine. As they went by, Jerry got a glimpse of the headline.

## Americans Falling Down
## On the Job, Prof Warns

Wiz took a deep breath and examined the scene in front of him carefully, weighing the odds. There was a faint reptilian scent in the air he didn't like at all, but he was hungry enough and desperate enough to ignore it.

Most of the buildings in this district were utilitarian; warehouses, barracks, workshops and the like. This one was different. It was made of glossy dark marble instead of rough hewn basalt. The slanting late afternoon sun picked out the fine carving on the window and door frames. The courtyard itself was paved in an elaborate pattern of black and white and dark green blocks, laid in a way that made the surface appear to swoop and undulate wildly even though it was perfectly flat. Around the court was a colonnade and extending off the colonnade at close intervals were open doors like gaping black mouths. Wiz stood in a niche in the gateway for a moment and studied the place.

He could edge around the courtyard under the colonnade, but that would expose him to anything that might be hidden in the deepening shadows or lurking in one of those rooms. The main entrance was directly across from the gate and in this case the better part of valor seemed to be a dash across the center of the court.

*Place like this ought to have a lot more in it than a barracks,* he thought as he looked around carefully for the last time. *Then again, maybe not.* A place like this would attract looters.

He was halfway across the courtyard when he had another thought. *A place like this would have been guarded, too.*

Then the ground opened up beneath him.

Jerry and Moira stepped out the door into a world Moira found completely unsettling. The sky was gray but the night was not foggy. She wrinkled her nose. The air stank—an odd pungent reek like nothing she had ever smelled before.

In front of them was a large flat area whose black surface was marked with white lines. Here and there curiously shaped and brightly painted metal boxes or sheds stood on the dark surface. Lights on tall metal poles cast an orangish-pink glare over the scene. In the background she heard a continuous whooshing roar.

All in all, it was an unsettling place, stranger than she had imagined. Yet Wiz had come from here so it must be all right.

"Okay," Jerry told her, "the next question is where do we go to eat."

"My Lord, could we get pizza?"

"Right. Pizza it is. Little Italy's just around the corner. Come on, we'll walk." He set off toward the gate with Moira trailing behind.

The Little Italy was the sort of place that develops both regular clients and an idiosyncratic style over the years.

It was four o'clock on Saturday morning, but Mario, the owner, was behind the counter, baking loaves of bread to be used in the day's sandwiches. Jerry knew that at seven Mario's son would relieve him so the old man could go home and get a few hours sleep. Then he would be back for the lunch rush, take a nap in the afternoon and come back for the dinner crowd.

"Well, what do you want?" Jerry said as they came up to the counter. Mario stopped shaping loaves of dough and came up to wait on them.

"Pizza," Moira told him.

"Yeah, but what do you want on your pizza? What toppings?"

"Toppings?"

"Those things listed on the board."

Moira frowned. "Lord, I cannot read your language," she confessed.

"Look in the bins then." He pointed at the row of stainless steel containers lining the rear of the counter.

"What are you having?" she asked Jerry.

"I'll have my usual. Sausage, ham, salami, pepperoni, hamburger and extra cheese. Medium, to eat here."

Mario nodded and got to work, swabbing the dough with spicy red tomato sauce redolent with basil and oregano. Next he scooped up handfuls of coarsely grated cheese and sprinkled them lavishly over the pizza. He didn't stop until the cheese hid nearly every trace of the sauce.

"Do you want the same thing?" Jerry asked.

"That is a great deal of meat," Moira said dubiously as the old man piled on the toppings. "I think I would prefer something else." She looked at Jerry. "I can have any of those I want?"

"Or any combination. If you come up with an unusual combination Mario names it after you." He nodded toward the board. "Wiz had one up there for a while. Something with jalapeños and pepperoni."

"I want Wiz's pizza."

Mario shook his head. "Don't got no jalapeños."

The hedge witch's brow furrowed and she went back to frowning at the bins, absently brushing back her coppery hair as it fell forward.

"Made up your mind yet, lady?" Mario asked, setting Jerry's pizza aside.

"What are those?" she asked, pointing to one of the bins.

"Anchovies," Jerry told her. "Highly salted fillets of tiny fish."

"I want some of those on mine," Moira said, looking over the bins. "And onions. Lots of onions. Oh, and is that garlic? Can I have some of that as well?

"And what is that on the end, floating in water?"

"That's feta. Goes on the gyros."

"It looks wonderful. I would have that on my pizza as well."

Jerry and Mario exchanged looks, but the counterman marked the order down.

"By the way lady, what's your name?"

"Why do you wish to know?"

"Because," Mario said, "if you eat that, I'm gonna put it on the menu and name it after you."

Even deathtraps need regular maintenance. This one had not been touched since the City of Night fell and it might have been damaged by the earthquakes touched off by the attack. That, and an instinct to keep his feet together, saved Wiz.

Wiz shook his head and climbed slowly to his feet. He was bruised, stunned and his ankles ached from the shock of landing, but he was alive and basically unhurt. He looked up and saw a strip of daylight disappearing as the trap door swung slowly closed with a creaking of unoiled hinges. The door didn't close all the way and by the dim light coming though the remaining crack, Wiz took stock of his surroundings.

On either side of the pit was a contrivance of rotting wood and rusty iron spikes as long as his arm. Wiz wasn't at all sure what it was supposed to do and he didn't want to think about it too closely. Whatever it was, it wasn't working and that had saved him.

Still, his position was precarious enough. The trap was shaped like a bottle, narrow above where the trap door was and wider down at the bottom. Even if the pit had not been twenty feet deep It would have been impossible to climb back out.

Wiz looked around. He didn't think he was going to get out of this without help and right now he didn't have the faintest idea where he could find help.

" . . . so you see, My Lord," Moira said, "Wiz needs help."

They had taken a booth in the back while they waited for their pizza and Moira filled Jerry in on his cubicle-mate's adventures and current plight.

Jerry considered. The more he considered, the less likely the whole thing became. There was no way that Wiz Zumwalt could ever have landed someone like the redheaded dish sitting across from him. The rest of her story didn't sound too plausible either.

Still . . . When a beautiful woman drops into your lap out of thin air, the event demands some explanation. Hers was no more outrageous than any other theory Jerry could come up with.

"Okay, I believe you," Jerry said. "But it's not going to be as simple as you think."

"Pizza's ready," Mario called from the counter.

"Excuse me, I'll get them."

Moira fidgeted until he returned with the two steaming pizzas and paraphernalia. He set them down and shook a dash of red pepper flakes onto his.

"Want some?"

Moira looked at the shaker and liberally lashed her pizza with them.

"Careful, those are hot."

The hedge witch frowned and shook some flakes into her palm and popped a hefty pinch into her mouth.

"So they are," she agreed and added some more to her pizza.

Jerry sighed and took a bite of his own pizza. A couple of slices of pepperoni fell off the heaped toppings and onto the table.

"What is that?" Moira asked, pointing and wrinkling her nose.

"That's pepperoni," Jerry said. Here," he picked a slice off his pizza, "taste it."

The hedge witch drew away. "Thank you, no. It smells spoiled. I do not mean to be discourteous, My Lord, but I do not see how you can eat that."

Jerry eyed Moira's anchovy, onion, garlic and feta cheese pizza and said nothing.

They ate in silence for a few minutes, Jerry devouring about half his pie and Moira finishing her first slice.

"My Lord," Moira asked finally, "would you be willing to help us?"

"Oh sure. My deal with ZetaSoft is about through. But it isn't that simple."

He took another enormous bite of pizza and dribbled sausage crumbs and a piece of mushroom back onto his plate.

"If what you say is true you're going to need a lot more than me," Jerry said around the mouthful of pizza. "You're talking about taking a one-man program and turning it into full production software, with documentation, a bullet-proof user interface and probably a suite of programmers' tools as well."

Moira regarded him seriously but uncomprehending.

"Now, I presume there's some sort of deadline on this thing?"

"We need it as quickly as possible."

"Okay, that's do-able, but not with just one more programmer. We've got to have more people. We need a full team."

Moira helped herself to another slice of pizza. "Can we get them?"

Jerry considered. "There are some problems. For one thing it will be expensive."

Moira set down her slice of pizza. From the folds of her skirt, she produced a leather pouch. She opened the drawstring and tipped it up. A ringing cascade of golden coins rained out between the hot pepper flakes, grated parmesan and napkin dispenser. One or two of them rang tinnily against the pizza pans.

Behind the counter, Mario continued with his baking, oblivious to the fortune that had just been poured onto one of his Formica table tops.

Jerry stared and licked his lips, tasting pizza grease. Conservatively this redhaired space cadet had just put about $25,000 on the table—literally.

"Will that be enough?" Moira asked innocently. "I can get more, but it would mean another Summoning."

"Lady, for that kind of money we could buy a couple of software startups, programmers and all!" Jerry said fervently.

Then he stopped and frowned. "But that's only half of it. We'll have to recruit them and that's not going to be easy. You need the people fast, right?"

Moira nodded.

"You also need them good. They're going to have to pick up on a new language and a whole new operating environment and charge right into work. This is not gonna be a job for BASIC bozos or COBOL drones."

Moira nodded vigorously. She didn't know what BASIC or COBOL were, except that Wiz said they caused brain damage in those who used them.

"Now there's another thing. This has to be done secretly, correct?"

"We have no objection to telling those of your world how you aided us. Bal-Simba and the Council would not be so mean as to deny them credit."

"The Council?"

"The Council of the North. The wizards who oversee our land. They would gladly provide testimonial."

Jerry thought about what a letter of recommendation from a council of wizards would look like in his resume file.

"Totally secret," he said firmly. "And we need to find the people in a hurry."

"Is there some guild hall or chantry where we might go to find people?"

Jerry considered while he polished off another slice.

"Well, the headhunters are out, that's for sure."

"I should hope so! We need these people alive."

"That's not what I meant—although with the kind of candidates headhunters turn up it can be hard to tell if they are alive."

"You make sport of me."

"A little, maybe. But it's going to complicate things." He reached for the last slice of pizza on his plate.

"So what we need," he summed up, "are people who are good enough to do the job, who are available and who can be made to believe you." *And*, he added silently, *who are crazy enough to come along on something this dangerous.* "That's not a common combination."

Jerry's eyes fell on one of the handbills tacked to the bulletin board. Even from this distance he could see the picture of the man in full armor and the woman in a long dress.

"I think," he said slowly, "I know just the place."

Jerry took Moira home with him for the night. "There are no motels close by and I live near enough to walk," he explained as they trudged the deserted streets.

Moira simply nodded, unconcerned by the proprieties.

She was yawning behind her hand by the time they reached his apartment. He offered her his bed but she would not hear of it. So he settled her on the couch in his cluttered living room with a blanket and pillow.

"Tomorrow we'll get an early start," he told her. "The place is about an hour and a half from here and it may take us all day to find the people we need."

"Good night, My Lord," Moira said, drawing the blanket over her.

Jerry left her and headed into the bedroom. *If she's not here in the morning I'm not going to believe any of this!* he vowed to himself.

# *Thirteen*
## Recruiting Drive

*If you eat a live toad first thing in the morning, nothing worse will happen all day long.*

—California saying

*To you or the toad.*

—Niven's restatement of California saying

*—well, most of the time anyway . . .*

—programmer's caveat to Niven's restatement of California saying

Wiz spent a cold, miserable night in the freezing pit. With the dawn his prospects didn't look any brighter. If he didn't get out of here he was going to die of hunger and thirst. Actually, he'd probably die of the cold before he could die of hunger or thirst.

*Face it*, he told himself as he looked around for the hundredth time, *the only way this could get worse would be for the sorcerers to find you.*

Up above there was a scraping, as if something was clawing at the cover of the pit. With a groaning of hinges the cover moved aside and a shaft of sunlight streamed down into the depths.

Wiz looked up and saw a huge scaled head peering down at him. The dragon cocked its head to one side and ran its forked pink tongue over its ivory fangs.

*Okay,* Wiz thought, *so I was wrong.*

The dragon was a late adolescent, not yet grown to the point of acquiring true intelligence, but not far short of it. It was obviously one of the mounts for the Dark League's dragon cavalry, gone feral.

That meant the animal had all the ferocity native to dragonkind and not the least fear of man.

Again the forked tongue licked out, tasting the air in the pit. Then its lips curled back revealing even more of ripping fangs and the animal growled.

Wiz shrank back against the wall as the dragon inhaled deeply. Instinctively he crouched and turned his back even through he knew it wouldn't help him.

With a *whoosh* the dragon blasted a gout of flame down into the hole.

It was the shape of the trap that saved him. The dragon aimed his fire at Wiz, but Wiz was back out of sight under the overhang. That meant the full force of the dragon fire struck the rock walls of the neck.

The rock was wet, soaked from the eternal damp and the dragon's fire converted a good portion of the moisture into steam. The overhang protected Wiz, but the dragon got a burst of live steam square in the face.

Dragons are not immune to dragon fire, and still less to steam. The beast snapped its head back and roared a high whistling scream like a tea kettle gone berserk. It jerked back from the pit, whipped around and galloped off, roaring and screaming at the top of its lungs.

*Son of a bitch!* Wiz thought as the dragon's screams faded into the distance. He drew a deep lungful of moist warm air that stank of sulfur and dragon and looked around the pit in wonder.

*I'm alive. Son of a bitch!* He was still trapped in the pit and he was still hunted, but he was alive.

Wiz threw back his head and laughed at the wonder of it all.

"Rise and shine," Jerry said as he came out of the bedroom. "We need to get an early start today."

It was mid-morning, which didn't strike Moira as particularly early, but she didn't comment. She watched fascinated as Jerry pulled a couple of packages out of the refrigerator's freezer compartment and popped them into the microwave oven.

"Breakfast will be ready in a couple of minutes. The bathroom's over there if you need to freshen up." Moira nodded and went through the door. Most of the fixtures were strange to her, but fortunately Wiz had told her enough about his world that she was able to figure things out.

"Hope you like country breakfast," Jerry said. "I wasn't expecting company and it's all I've got."

The microwave oven beeped and Jerry removed the boxes. Moira opened hers and poked the contents dubiously with her fork. The eggs were tough, the sausage patty tougher and had an odd metallic taste besides. The biscuit and gravy were steaming hot on the surface and icy in the interior. If this was the "fast food" Wiz had raved about there was something seriously wrong with the man's taste buds.

She looked over at Jerry, who was busy shovelling the contents of his box into his mouth.

*Well, I have eaten worse,* she thought. Wordlessly she began eating what was in front of her.

Jerry drank coffee with his meal. Moira, who had wanted to taste this beverage Wiz had talked about, took one sip and stuck with water.

The day was bright but overcast. Except for the odd stink in the air, it was very pleasant.

"It will take us about an hour and a half to get there," Jerry said as he unlocked the door of his Toyota. "Depending on traffic, of course."

He held the door open for Moira and then went around and slid behind the wheel. Once in he reached back behind himself and pulled a dark cloth strap diagonally across his body. Then he looked at her.

"Strap in."

Moira looked at him, puzzled.

"Reach behind you and pull the belt out, bring it across and buckle it over beside the seat. No, you've got to pull it out smoothly or it won't come all the way."

With much tugging and contortions, Moira got the lap and shoulder belts fastened.

"It's for your own good," Jerry told the hedge witch. "It will protect you in case of a crash."

"A crash?" Moira echoed faintly.

"Yeah, a wreck. Oh, but that almost never happens," he said, catching sight of her face.

Moira barely had the belt fastened when Jerry started the car and pulled out in traffic. Moira found herself speeding along at an incredible clip bare inches from another car moving in the same direction. She looked up and saw other vehicles charging toward them, only to whiz by close enough to touch.

Moira gulped and turned white. Jerry, nonchalant and oblivious, kept his eyes on the road.

They came to an intersection and Jerry whipped the car through a right angle turn in the face of oncoming traffic. To Moira it appeared they had missed the truck bearing down on them by a hair's breadth. She stared at the dashboard and tried to ignore the outside world.

There was a tremendous roar in her right ear. Moira jumped at the sound and looked up involuntarily. To her right, barely an arm's length away sat a man who was going faster than they were. His arms were extended to the front and his beard and long hair were whipped into a wild tangle by the wind. The hedge witch caught a glimpse of the complicated black-and-silver contrivance he was sitting on before he flicked away around another car.

Jerry reached a place where the road narrowed, and

climbed gently. Instead of slowing on the hill, he speeded up. Moira moaned softly and concentrated hard on her lap. Her hand grasped the door handle until the freckles stood out stark against the white knuckles.

Jerry glanced over at her. "Don't pull on that!" he said sharply. "If the door comes open in traffic we could be in real trouble." Moira jerked her hand off the handle as if it had turned into a snake. She reached forward with both hands to grab the dashboard tightly.

Jerry wasn't a very good driver, but he had been driving the California freeways for almost twenty years. He speeded up smoothly and edged left to merge into the center lane of traffic.

Out the right window Moira saw trees and greenery whizzing by so fast they were a blur. She looked left just in time to see Jerry jerk the wheel and slip the car into a space barely longer than the automobile.

They were sandwiched between two semis—roaring, bellowing monsters that threatened to spread Moira and the car between them like butter on a sandwich. She moaned again and closed her eyes.

"It's not bad today," Jerry said conversationally. "You should see it when the traffic's heavy."

Moira mumbled something and kept her eyes on her lap.

"I beg your pardon?"

"I said I hope I never do see that," Moira said more loudly. But she didn't lift her eyes.

Jerry looked at her sympathetically. He was a white knuckle flier himself. "Okay. If there's anything you need, just let me know."

"My Lord," Moira said fiercely, "the only thing I need is for this trip to be over as soon as possible."

Wiz ran his hand over the surface of the stone one more time. There had to be a way out of this. After all, the Dark League would need to retrieve anyone captured in the pit, wouldn't they?

He looked over at the spike-and-wood contraption in the pit. *Then again, maybe not.* It would be perfectly in character for the Dark League to leave a captive to rot in a place like this. Well, he wouldn't get anywhere brooding on that. He would have to see what he could find.

Wiz put both his palms against the wall and pushed. His left hand met unyielding resistance, but the stone under his right hand seemed to shift. He pushed again. Yes, the stone had moved!

*A secret door.* Wiz didn't know much about dungeons and mantraps, but that fitted perfectly with his conception of them. There must be a passage behind this wall.

He pushed again. The block shifted a little, but nothing else happened. He pushed the stones around it. Some of them also moved but no door opened. He put his fingers on the edge of the block and tugged hard. The stone moved slightly, but that was all.

He dropped his arms. Either he hadn't found the right stones to push or the door was broken. Either way, it seemed like the best thing to do was force the door rather than rely on the mechanism. For that he needed something to pry with.

He looked at the iron spikes of the trap reflectively. The metal was dark and pitted with rust, but it looked strong. Each spike was about three feet long and perhaps two inches around, crudely forged to a point on one end.

He grabbed the end of a spike and tugged. The spike moved ever so slightly. He dug his heels into the stone floor and wrenched back on the spike with all his strength. The spike moved some more.

Eventually he was able to work the spike free of damp and somewhat rotten wood. It was heavier than he expected and his biceps ached from the pulling, but he ignored that and attacked the loose stone in the wall.

The tool was clumsy and there wasn't much of a joint around the stone, but Wiz set to with a will, heedless of the noise he made. His technique was crude and it took a long time before he was able to pry the block part way out of the wall. With hands trembling from eagerness and fatigue, he jammed the bar into the joint and heaved one final time. The block clattered out onto the floor and Wiz thrust his hand into the opening.

Behind the stone was nothing but dirt and rock.

With a groan he threw the iron bar across the trap and slumped to the floor. It wasn't a doorway at all, just a loose stone in the wall. He looked up at the hole in the ceiling. The only way out of here had to be through that hole. That meant he was trapped unless he could climb the overhanging walls or build a ladder.

There was wood in the spiked device, but not nearly enough to reach the surface, even if it were all combined into a single long pole. Stick the spikes into the wall and climb them like a ladder? Not enough spikes. Besides, how would he get past the overhang?"

Magic? With that demon on the loose he'd never live to complete the first spell.

And that was it, some half-rotten wood, a few pieces of iron and a block of stone levered from the wall.

*A block of stone? Just one?*

Wiz stood up and began to try the wall again. He found another loose stone, and then another and another. Most of the wall seemed to be loose, almost every other block could be pried free.

It was the cold, Wiz realized, the cold and the damp working at the stones. When this place was built the City of Night was kept magically warm. But with the fall of the League the magic had vanished and the stones had been subjected to alternate freezing and thawing. The walls of the trap had not been mortared and the working of the water had shifted the stones. The fact that most of the courtyard was paved in dark stone probably helped warm things up.

He picked up the spike and eyed the wall. This wasn't

as elegant as a hidden passage and it was sure going to take a lot longer, but it would work. *Besides,* he thought as he attacked the first stone, *I don't have anything better to do.*

The real problem was going to be to get out enough of the blocks to do some good without bringing the whole place down on his head, but he had some ideas on that and it would be a while before he really had to worry.

Moira did not look up when they turned off the freeway and headed up a poorly paved road. She did not know how long they rocked along before they turned again onto a dirt road and rattled over a cattle crossing. The dust tickled her nose and made her cough, but she still didn't look up.

"Well, here we are," Jerry said. You can look now." Moira kept staring at the dashboard, as if she intended to memorize every wrinkle and crack in the vinyl.

"Come on, end of the line. Are you all right?"

"I think," Moira said judiciously, "that Wiz was far braver than I ever knew."

She tore her eyes away from the dashboard and looked around. They were in a small valley. The brown hills above them were crowned with the gray-green of live oak trees. There was dust everywhere. The stink was still in the air, but not as strong here as in the city.

The field before them was crammed with vehicles standing cheek-by-jowl and all covered with a thin film of dust. A steady stream of people filtered out of the field, stopped at a table by the path and then headed over a low hill. Most of them were weighted down with bags, boxes, bundles and long poles of some light-colored wood.

"What is this place?"

"It's a war. These people come here to pretend to be living in ancient times. Um, something like your place but with no magic."

Moira looked around, bemused. "They come here to pretend to be peasants?"

"Well, ah, not exactly."

"And why would the Mighty of your world wish to pretend there is no magic?"

"Actually," Jerry explained, "some of them are pretending there is magic."

Moira opened her mouth to ask another question and then thought better of it. This was remarkably similar to conversations she had sometimes with Wiz.

"It gets a little complicated. But we've got a better chance of finding what we need here than anyplace else I can think of."

Moira nodded and followed him across the field toward the table. She wondered what awaited them at the end of that path.

Wiz leaned back against the wall and examined his handiwork. Even with the iron bar and the frost-loosened stones it had been a rough job to pry the blocks loose. His knuckles were scraped, his palms were blistered and his shoulders and arms ached from pulling on the prybar.

He had taken the stones in more or less checker-board around the walls and piled them in the center of the pit directly under the trap door. Standing on the pile, he could reach up to the narrow neck of the pit. He still had a long way to go before he would have enough blocks to reach the top of the trap.

*This is going to take forever,* he thought, rubbing his shoulders and looking up. But the sooner he got to it the quicker it would be done. Anyway, it took his mind off how cold and hungry he was.

Sighing, Wiz picked up the bar again and went back to work.

"Morning, My Lord, My Lady," said one of the three large young men sitting at the table. "Site fee's five bucks."

While Jerry peeled off several gray-green paper

oblongs, Moira studied him, trying to make sense out of what she was seeing.

He was not a guardsman, of that Moira was sure. He had the body of a man but the face was still that of a child. He was dressed in a simple tunic over the sort of blue trousers Wiz called "jeans." He wore a red leather belt with a cheap, gaudy sword thrust scabberdless through it. Like a boy pretending to be a warrior, she thought, but with more self-importance, as if he expected people to take him seriously.

"Okay," the man said. "Medievals are required on site. You'll have to stop by the hospitaller and get a loaner costume." He looked over at Moira in her long green wool skirt and scoop-neck blouse. "Your friend's fine."

Jerry was fitted with a slightly-too-small tunic in purplish gray, trimmed with a darker purple zig-zags and tied about the middle with a piece of brown cord. The color made him look ill, but the woman with the trunk of clothing had nothing else that would fit someone of his girth.

As they topped the rise Moira gawked at what was spread out in the small valley below.

Nestled in among the live oaks and chaparral was an encampment of hundreds of tents of different shapes, sizes and colors. What seemed like thousands of people in clothing of every shade and hue milled about the valley like ants in an anthill.

In the center of the valley was a cleared space with perhaps two hundred men whaling away at each other with wooden weapons. The smack of wood on wood, the clank and clatter of steel and the shouts echoed off the hillsides.

For an instant she thought they were actually hurting each other. Then she saw a warrior who had dropped like a sack of sand under the blow of a pole-ax roll out of the fight, stand up and walk off the field. As the fighter came away from the battle, he took off his helm

and shook out a mane of long blond hair. Moira realized
with a shock it was a woman.

"Excuse me, My Lord, My Lady," came a voice behind
them, "but you're blocking the trail."

As they stepped aside a boy of perhaps fourteen
struggled past them loaded down with several bundles
and a half-dozen pole weapons. When he passed, Moira
saw the heads were padding wrapped with some kind
of silvery material.

At the bottom of the hill was a market. There were
booths along the trail, and tables with cloths spread over
them. The smell of roasting meat rose from the food
stands and people milled and jostled through the throng,
admiring wares, talking, eating and sometimes buying.

Most of the people seemed to be dressed in rags and
patches, although here and there a man or a woman
might be more substantially dressed. Everyone and
everything was covered with fine brownish dust.

Many of the men and a few of the women were
wearing what she recognized as armor, mostly concoctions
of padded cloth, leather and light metal that looked as
if it would come apart at the first serious blow.

Moira looked around eagerly, but missed the thing she
had expected to see.

"Where is the hiring block, My lord?"

"The what?"

"The hiring block. This is a hiring fair, is it not?"

"No, not exactly. In fact most people come here to
forget their jobs."

"Then how are we to find the ones we need?"

"We'll have to ask. I think we need to find a herald first."

A man in a green cloak with crossed trumpets
approached them. "Excuse me, My Lord, but did I hear
you say you needed a herald?"

"Uh, yeah, I have an announcement I'd like you to
make. We're looking to hire a number of programmers
and other computer specialists for a rather special job."

"And so you came here?" The herald nodded. "Smart move. I think there are more computer types per square foot at one of these wars than at anything this side of an ACM meeting."

"ACM?" Moira asked.

"Association for Computing Machinery, a professional group," Jerry told her. "Anyway," he said turning back to the herald, "we're looking for systems-level programmers, systems analysts, documentation specialists, people with real-time or process control experience—if we can find them—and compiler writers."

"No machine operators?" the herald asked. "Employment or contract?"

"Contract. Probably three to six months."

"Well, normally they frown on even mentioning computers at these events," the said. "King Alfonso is a particular stickler for authenticity so you're not going to get it announced at court. But I don't think there'd be any real objection if I announced it in the merchant's area and the non-medieval camping area."

"Great. Uh, is there any place I can sit and talk to people?"

"You can borrow my pavilion," the herald said. "I want to talk to you about this anyway. I'm looking for a change myself."

The herald's pavilion turned out to be an aluminum-framed camping tent hung with banners and set well off to the side of the encampment.

Moira sat at a folding table under an awning, sipping lemonade from a wooden goblet and watching the knot of people who had gathered in response to the herald's announcement.

They didn't look like the Mighty Moira was used to. There wasn't a full gray beard among them and none of them showed the stately bearing and serene self-control she associated with powerful magicians.

The first one into the tent was a dumpy dark-haired woman in a blue-and-silver gown whose long dagged sleeves nearly trailed in the dust. Far too elaborate for such a place, Moira thought, especially since these people did not have cleaning spells.

Behind her were a tall dark-haired woman with piercing dark eyes and a shorter, sandy haired man with a neat spade beard who seemed to be her husband.

Next to them was a lean man going bald on top with his remaining hair pulled back into a pony tail.

She wondered how Jerry was explaining her world's needs to them.

"You certainly seem qualified, Ms. Connally," Jerry said to the woman sitting across from him. "I can't tell you the nature of the job until you sign the nondisclosure agreement."

"Judith, please," the dark-haired woman in the blue-and-silver brocade gown corrected.

"I can tell you it is a short-term contract, probably about six months. The assignment requires that you live on-site until it is completed. The site is remote and rugged and contact with the outside world is very limited."

"A black site?"

Jerry recognized the reference to an ultra-secret project where the programmers were kept totally isolated.

"Kind of dark gray, actually."

Her eyebrows went up. "SDI, right?"

Jerry smiled, as he had seen so many recruiters do. "I am really not at liberty to say.

"Now," he went on, "I should also warn you that there is an element of physical risk in this."

The other's eyes narrowed. "This is legal, isn't it?"

"Yes," Jerry said, "That is, there is absolutely no law against what we are doing." *At least not in California,* he added mentally. *I think Massachusetts still has a law against practicing witchcraft.*

"Now, tell me a little bit more about your background."

The interviews went quickly. Jerry wasn't interested in playing interviewer games, there was no application to fill out and no one had brought a resume to an SCA war. Besides, Jerry was a programmer himself, not some personnel bozo who only had the vaguest notion of what the job entailed.

*And nobody is going to ask me to fill out an EEOC report on this one.*

He had just talked to the eighth candidate when the herald, who went by the name of Ali Ahkan, stuck his head into the tent with a peculiar expression on his face.

"His Majesty, King Alfonso of Seville," the herald announced.

Jerry wasn't up on the etiquette, but he stood up as the king entered.

"Your Majesty."

King Alfonso turned out to be a tall, rather lean man in his mid-twenties with an olive complexion and dark unruly hair. He was wearing a crown of sheet brass set with agates, dark hose, a black velvet doublet and riding boots. A broadsword hung from his hip on a white belt. His clothes were powdered with the brownish dust from the site.

The king stuck out his hand. "Karl Dershowitz," said the king with a distinctly Texas drawl.

"Jerry Andrews."

"So tell me," said the king, pulling up the stool, "what's this super-secret job you're recruiting for?"

"How did you find out?"

He shrugged. "It's all over camp. Did you know you're with the CIA and you're recruiting programmers who are expert swordsmen to fight their way into Afghanistan so they can tap into the Russians' SDI computer network?"

"It's nothing like that," Jerry said uncomfortably.

"Of course not." The king smiled. "If anyone in this

bunch has a choice between a good story and the truth, the good story will win out every time."

"Look, I'm sorry if we're interfering with your event, but we needed some people with special talents in a hurry."

The king waved that off. "What interference? You're off in a corner in someone's pavilion talking to people one at a time. Oh, a couple of people did come to me to complain about the announcement you had the heralds make." He snorted. "Down in Texas we called them piss ants."

"Then why are you here?"

"Because my current contract just ran out and the job sounds interesting—Afghanistan or no. Could you tell me about it?"

The next candidate was as unimpressive as the king— Karl, Jerry corrected himself—had been impressive.

At first he thought the kid had wandered in by mistake. He was slightly plump in the face. A downy blond beard decorated his cheeks. His eyes were brown, dark in contrast to his skin and hair. He was wearing a pair of blue jeans and a satin tunic that had probably once been purple but was now faded and stained to something resembling blue. A cheap hunting knife was clipped to his belt and a wooden goblet hung from a leather thong.

Without waiting for an invitation he sat down. "Thorkil du Libre Dragonwatcher. I understand you're looking for programmers."

Jerry eyed him without enthusiasm. "We are. Are you a programmer?"

"Yeah," he said flushing, "and I'm damn good."

"Do you have a degree?"

"I attended Cal Tech."

"Yes, but do you have a degree?"

The kid fidgeted under Jerry's stare.

"Okay, so maybe I don't, but I'm *good*."

Jerry sighed to himself. Well, if you wanted to find

frogs you had to kiss a few toads—or however that saying went.

"We need people with experience."

"I've got experience," he protested. "I've worked in TOS 1.4, AmigaDOS and ProDOS."

Jerry, who didn't consider a computer a computer unless it ran at least BSD Unix, winced. "Those are game machines."

"The Amiga's no game machine," the kid flared. "Neither is the ST. Besides, I've done real-time programming in Forth on a Trash 80 Model I."

That was slightly more interesting. From Moira's confused recitation of what Wiz had done, Jerry knew he had used the Forth language for some of the programming. Besides, anyone who could do anything useful in real time on something as limited as a Model I clearly had talent.

"Okay," he said, making a mark on the clipboard, "I'll let you know later."

Panting, Wiz jammed his pry bar into the joint and leaned on it with all his strength again. The stone shifted more. He dropped the bar, got his fingers on the edge and tugged at the stone. The rock moved slightly and its neighbors shifted with it. Instinctively Wiz jumped backwards, lost his balance and went tumbling down the side of the rock pile. With a crash and a roar a whole section of the neck gave way. Stones cascaded down into the pit and went bouncing in every direction.

Coughing from the dust, Wiz looked up. The side of the neck had slumped in on itself. Half the pit was full of blocks and rubble and the vertical wall had collapsed into a steep incline that led out of the trap and into the courtyard.

Wiz shook his head to clear it. *Well, that works too.* Slowly and carefully, he climbed up the pile of rubble and out of the pit.

"Better than I expected," Jerry told Moira at the end of three hours. "We've got systems programmers, documentation specialists, real-time programmers and people with control and simulation experience here."

"Are they of the Mighty?"

"Well, they're a pretty high-powered bunch, especially considering we had to put together the team at such short notice. That first one, Judith Connally, has done real-time programming on military projects. Mike and Nancy Sutton, the husband and wife team, are a process control programmer and a documentation specialist respectively."

He made a face. "If I know Wiz, we're gonna *need* a documentation specialist. Anyway, we've got some good potential here."

"How will you select them?"

"Well, Moira, it's your show. You've got the ultimate say in who we choose."

"I will be guided by you in this, Lord," Moira said. "I know little of such matters. But there is one I would like included. The young one. Thorkil du Libre Dragonwatcher."

Jerry raised his eyebrows. "That kid? He's not in the same league with most of the rest of the people and I think he's a pirate to boot."

"I thought he said he was a programer."

"A pirate is a kind of programmer. He steals other people's software."

"Nonetheless, I would have him."

Jerry shrugged. "I think he's going to be more trouble than he's worth, but okay. I'll add him to the list." He made a note on the pad and looked up.

"Why do you want him, anyway?"

"A feeling," Moira said. "Just a feeling."

"A premonition?"

Moira smiled. "In this place? No, I just feel that he

has something to offer. I do not know, perhaps he reminded me of Wiz."

Jerry made a face. "Now that you mention it, there is a certain resemblance." He scribbled another note on the list. "Okay, then. That's our team."

"Now what?" Moira asked.

"Now we call them back, explain the terms and give them the contract to sign." He made another face. "This is where it is going to get *real* interesting."

There was food in the black and white palace after all. Wandering what had been the kitchen, Wiz found half a flat round loaf of bread and several strips of dried meat that had fallen behind a counter

The meat was probably tough before it had been dried and it was certainly stringy. The bread was heavy, and full of what seemed to be sawdust, but after two days and a night in the pit Wiz was in no mood to complain. He wolfed down his find and then curled up in a corner.

*Maybe there is justice in the world after all,* he thought drowsily as he drifted off.

" . . . and you receive a signing bonus of two point three ounces of gold and a rate of pay of two point three ounces of gold per week for the duration of the contract," Jerry told the selected group of programmers gathered under the awning.

"Gold?" asked Ali Akhan, the herald.

Jerry shrugged. "Simplifies matters for the employer."

"This guy's either a libertarian or a drug smuggler," Karl Dershowitz said. Jerry did not reply.

Moira smiled. "We really are . . ."

" . . . not at liberty to say," Nancy Sutton finished for her. "We know the drill."

"Okay," said Cindy Naismith, a short, slender woman with close-cropped brown hair. "What about performance penalties?"

"None. We can tell you so little about the project until you get on-site that it wouldn't be fair. However there is a bonus if the contract is completed on time to the client's satisfaction."

He pushed the clipboard out into the middle of the table. "If you accept the terms, sign this agreement."

Ali Akhan sat down and began to read through the six-page document. Jerry waited to see what happened when he got to the non-disclosure clause. The contract was something they had whipped together out of the pieces of contracts Jerry had in his computer at home. It was pretty much the standard verbiage—except for the non-disclosure agreement.

" . . . if this agreement is breached, employee will immediately be struck by lightning and hereby agrees to forfeit his immortal soul . . ." Ali Akhan read out. He looked up angrily. "What kind of shit is this? I mean it's very funny, but who's gonna believe that nonsense?"

Moira smiled sweetly. "Oh, I think we can contrive to convince, My Lord."

"This is weird," he muttered, reaching for a pen. Then he looked up and grinned. "You don't want me to sign in blood do you?"

"Oh no, that will not be necessary," Moira told him seriously.

Ali Akhan gave her a funny look and then signed his name. Taking the contract back, Jerry saw that his real name was Larry Fox.

Several other people looked at them strangely after they finished reading the contract, but none of them refused to sign it—much to Jerry's surprise. Either things were slow in the Valley or these people were stranger than most computer types.

*Considering the milieu . . .*

"Fine then," he told the assembled group. "We will meet at the back parking lot of Los Alamitos Mall at seven o'clock Wednesday morning. Have someone drive you or leave your cars at home. Transportation will be provided from the meeting point to our destination.

"Come packed and ready to leave. Oh yeah. Don't have anyone wait for you. Security, you know."

Several people looked at him strangely.

"Gotta be SDI," someone muttered.

"I wish we could leave sooner," Moira said as the newly formed team dispersed.

"I know, but we've got to give people time to get their affairs in order. Three days is really pushing it."

"Oh, I know, but I just wish . . ." She looked up at him. "Besides, I miss Wiz terribly."

Jerry studied her expression. "I'm getting kind of anxious to see him myself."

Wiz stayed at the black and white palace for as long as he dared. But there wasn't any more food to be found in the kitchen or the palace storerooms. Besides, the Dark League's search was working its way down into the waterfront neighborhood. He could hear the wizards calling to each other as they searched the streets and warehouses.

With the search moving to the waterfront, he decided the best thing he could do was to head back to the top of the town. Maybe there would be places up there heated by the volcano.

"Is there aught else to do here?" Moira asked after the last of their new employees had signed and left.

"Well, we could head back tonight, but there are a couple of more people here I'd like to talk to. The king has offered us space in his motorhome. Would you mind spending the night?"

"If we left now we would have to drive back the way we came in darkness?"

"Yes."

"Then let us stay the night," Moira said firmly. She wasn't looking forward to the return trip in daylight and the idea of doing it at night was more than she could stand.

While none of the city of Night was warm, there were definitely some parts that were colder than others. Whether because of the natural microclimate or magic, Wiz didn't know. But this street was especially cold.

Water had trickled down the street and frozen into a layer of glare ice, dark, shiny and unbelievably slick. Wiz picked his way up the edge of the street carefully. The last thing he needed now was a broken leg.

He was so busy watching his step that he forgot to watch where he was going. He turned the corner and literally collided with a black-robe wizard.

They were both knocked flat, but Wiz recovered quicker. He spun onto his hands and knees and took off like a sprinter around the corner.

The wizard pounded around the corner hot on his heels and shouting at the top of his lungs. "*I have found him. To me! To me! I have found HHHHIIIIIIIIIIMMMMMMMM . . .*"

Wiz ducked into a doorway and looked back to see the wizard go sliding by, flat on his back with his arms and legs waving in the air like a big black beetle. He almost laughed. Then he thought better of it and took off running as fast as he could.

When he stopped running he was more than a half a mile from the icy street. He sank to his heels with his head between his knees while he gasped in great lungfuls of the frigid air. Gradually his breath came back and he began to study his surroundings.

Behind him was a gate big enough to lead an elephant through. Through it he could see a courtyard with rooms opening onto it.

*One place is as good as another*, he thought. Keeping a wary eye for traps, he started exploring the building.

Nearly three hours later, Wiz stepped through the last

smashed door and wrinkled his nose. The storeroom had been thoroughly ransacked, more than once from the looks of it. Besides, it smelled as if something had been lairing here.

But there was nothing here now and a storeroom seemed like the best place to find food. The buildings around this courtyard had apparently been barracks, with the workrooms, armories and storerooms that supported the soldiers. The armories had been stripped to the walls and the barracks were deserted, but there was a chance there might be something left in the storerooms.

This one didn't look promising, he admitted as he poked among the rubble. There were bolts of cloth that had been pulled off the shelves, torn and trampled. Boxes of iron rivets had been broken open and the rivets scattered across the floor. Bundles of leather thongs, cracked and rotted hung from pegs on one wall. It didn't seem like the kind of place where food had been kept.

Still, he was here and a quick check of the other buildings showed nothing more promising. The barracks kitchen had been easy to locate, but there was nothing to eat there. What hadn't been carried off had been consumed by rats or larger animals.

The City of Night was more complex than he had ever imagined, Wiz thought vaguely as he poked the piles of rubbish in the corners and turned over debris on the floor. Somewhere there had to be food storehouses to feed the people who had lived here. But he didn't have the faintest notion where.

Wiz stopped short. There, on the very top shelf was a pottery jar with a familiar shape.

*Pickled fish*, he realized. There were some districts along the Freshened Sea where salted fish was packed in vinegar with garlic, onions, vegetables, and spices and sealed in crocks to age and ferment. To the people of those districts pickled fish was a delicacy. Everyone else made jokes about it, especially about its tendency to produce gas.

Apparently the jokes about pickled fish were universal and whoever used this room had kept a personal cache here rather than listen to them.

With shaking hands he took the jar off the shelf. It was full and the clay seal around the lid was unbroken. Quickly he smashed the lid with a piece of wood from the floor.

The contents were dark brown, definitely past their prime and Wiz had made his share of jokes about pickled fish. But this was the most delicious thing he had ever eaten. Heedless of the promissory rumblings of his stomach, he finished the entire crock.

At 7:00 A.M. the group gathered in the back parking lot of the shopping center.

They were carrying everything from designer luggage to backpacks. One or two of them had laptop computers under their arms. Jerry wondered how well those would work where they were going. A couple more had apparently believed the Afghanistan story enough to bring cases of liquor with them. That, at least, would be useful, he decided.

"Okay, people," he called out. "Moira here, will . . ." he looked around. "Where's Moira?"

"Here, Lord." Moira came trotting up with a large flat box under her arm.

"What's in the box?" Jerry asked her.

"A present." She handed it to him. "Will you hold it for me? Be careful not to tip it." Then she looked up and frowned at the sky.

"The haze will make it hard to tell the time," she said. "That complicates matters. Perhaps it would be best to wait for the afternoon time."

"That's smog and it's not going to clear today," Jerry told her. "If you need to tell the time, use my watch."

He stripped it off his meaty wrist and handed it to her.

Moira shook her head. I must know the time in day-tenths after sunrise," she said. "Not the time by your local system."

"Day-tenths?"

"One tenth of the time between sunrise and set."

"Wait a minute," said a small man with the face of an intelligent mouse and a mop of brown hair. He stripped off his own wristwatch, and began punching the tiny buttons beneath the face.

"There you go," he said handing the watch. "I haven't set it against the Naval Observatory in a couple of months so it may be a tenth of a second off, but I hope it will do."

Moira studied the madly spinning numbers on the display. They looked something like the numbers Wiz used, but she didn't know them well enough to use them.

She handed the watch to Jerry. "Here, My Lord. Tell me when it is two day-tenths."

"Coming up on it now."

"Hey, guys!"

Thorkil du Libre Dragonwatcher—Danny Gavin, Jerry reminded himself—came running across the parking lot with a backpack slung over one shoulder and bouncing against his hip.

"You are late," Moira said severely.

"Hey, I'm sorry. I had to hitch, okay?"

Moira opened her mouth to say something else, but Jerry interrupted her.

"Time in thirty seconds."

Moira handed her box to Jerry and gestured them all into a tight group. Then she drew out the golden cord Bal-Simba had given her and laid a circle perhaps fifteen feet in diameter in the dusty surface of the parking lot, muttering as she did so.

"Now," she said, turning to the programmers. "You

must all stand close together and above all, stay within the circle. Do not step outside it or break it in any way."

Checking the watch Jerry had given her, she raised her wand and began to chant.

At first no one said anything. Then the astonishment began to wear off and the cracks started.

"Is this where the flying saucer shows up?" someone asked.

"Scotty, beam me up," someone else called out.

Moira ignored them and went on with the chant.

"Next stop Oz," Judith chimed in.

And then the world dissolved.

# PART III:
# COMPILE

# *Fourteen*

## EMPLOYEE ORIENTATION

*You never find out the whole story until after you've signed the contract.*

—programmer's saying

They were crowded together on a smooth flagged floor. Looming over them on a dais at one end of the room was an enormous black man in a leopard skin loincloth and a necklace of bones. To his right was a blonde woman in a long gown.

The sun streamed in through narrow windows in the stone walls and struck shafts of gold through the dusty air.

At the points of the compass stood eight men and women in long blue robes, each holding a silver or ebony wand and each surrounded by glowing runes inscribed on the stone floor. Further back stood grim men in chain mail armed with swords and spears.

The programmers goggled.

Finally a female voice from the back of the group broke the silence. "Toto," she whispered hoarsely. "I don't think we're in Kansas any more."

"Merry met," the black man boomed out. "I am called Bal-Simba. I am speaker for the Council of the North and of the Mighty of this place. We are your employers."

"Did anyone bring a copy of that contract?" someone muttered.

Moira curtseyed. "Merry met, Lord. This one is called Jerry Andrews, of whom Wiz spoke often." She gestured to the rest of the group. "These others are also of the Mighty of their place. Jerry enlisted their aid."

Bal-Simba smiled, showing his teeth filed to points. "Excellent. Excellent. My Lords, Ladies, if you will come with me I will show you to your accommodations." The wizards at the compass points moved out of the way as he descended the dais and the guards stepped back. With a dozen thoroughly bewildered programmers trailing in a clump, the giant wizard left the chantry through the carved oak doors and down the stone steps into the flagged courtyard.

The morning sun made the stone walls glow warmly and cast glints of light off the windows. Banners floated from staffs at tower tops, peacock blue and brilliant green against the sky and clouds. Around them men and women stopped to stare at the newcomers and the newcomers slowed to stare back.

"Look!" one of the group pointed off to the east. A gaggle of six dark shapes stood out against the high white clouds, shapes with far too much neck and tail to be birds.

The entire group stopped dead in the courtyard. The programmers craned their necks and shielded their eyes in an effort to see better.

"Are those . . . ?"

"Jesus, they're dragons"

"How the hell would you know? You've never seen a dragon."

"I have now."

The dragons came closer, dropping lower and making it easier to pick out the details. Their guides made as if to move on but the programmers stood rooted in place.

"Hey, there are people on them!"

The Californians watched awestruck as the dragons glided around the tallest tower in tight V formation, wingtips almost touching as their riders pulled them into the turn. Then as one, the beasts winged over and fell away toward their aerie in the cliff beneath the castle.

And then they were gone. The newcomers let out a sigh with a single breath and everyone started across the courtyard again.

The programmer standing next to Bal-Simba, a heavy-set dark-haired woman wearing a faded unicorn T-shirt, touched his arm.

"Thank you," she said.

"For what, My Lady?"

She nodded toward where the flight of dragons had disappeared, her eyes shining. "For that. For letting me see that."

Bal-Simba looked at her closely. To him dragons were simply part of the World, sometimes useful, often dangerous, but nothing extraordinary. He had never stopped to think about what dragons on the wing meant. Now, confronted with her wonder, he saw them in a new light.

"Thank you, My Lady," he said gravely.

Not everyone was impressed with the dragons' performance. One who wasn't at all impressed was the leader of the flight.

"Where were you on that last turn?" he demanded of his wingman as they crossed the cavern that served as roost and aerie for the dragon cavalry.

"There's a turbulence on the west side of the tower at this time of day," his wingman explained. "I figured it would be safer to open it up a little."

"Turbulence, nothing! That was sloppy. What did you think you were doing hanging out there?"

Behind them the riders and grooms were leading the dragons to their stalls, the rider at the head, holding the bridle and talking gently to his mount and a groom at each wingtip and two at the tail to see that the dragons did not accidently bump and perhaps begin to fight.

Other teams of grooms hurried about, removing saddles and unfastening harnesses. The armorers removed the quivers of magic arrows from the harness and counted each arrow, carefully checking the numbers against the tally sticks before returning them to the armory.

In spite of the lanterns along the walls the aerie was gloomy after the bright morning. The entrance was a rectangle of squintingly bright white. It was noisy as well. The rock walls magnified sound and the shuffle of beasts, the shouts of the men and the occasional snort or hiss of a dragon reverberated through the chamber.

Both dragon riders ignored the noise and the bustle, intent on their conversation. The other members of the troop avoided them until the chewing out was done.

"Playing it safe, sir."

"Safe my ass! Mister, in combat that kind of safety will get you killed."

The wingman bridled. "Sir, there is no one left to fight."

The Dragon Leader grinned nastily. "Want to bet? Do you think the Council keeps us around because we look pretty?"

The wingman didn't answer.

"Well," the Dragon Leader demanded. "Why do you think we exist?"

"To fight, sir."

"Too right we exist to fight. And how much good do you think you're going to be in a melee if you've trained your mount to open wide on the turns? Mister, in my squadron if you are going to do something, you are going to do it right. We exist to fight, and war or no war, you will by damn be ready to fight. Is that clear?"

"Yes sir," the wingman said woodenly, eyes straight ahead.

"Every maneuver, every patrol, you will treat like the real thing. Remember those checklists they drilled into you in school? Well mister, you will live by those checklists. As long as you're in my squadron you will do *everything* by the checklist. Is that clear?"

"Yes, sir."

"Then see to it. And if you float out like that on a turn again you'll spend the next two weeks on stable duty! Now see to your mount."

The Dragon Leader watched the man go and frowned. With the Dark League crushed there were no enemy dragons to face. It was hard to keep an edge on his men. The kid was good, one of the best of the crop of new riders that had come along since the defeat of the Dark League, but he didn't have the same attitude as the men and women who had fought through the long, bitter years of the League's ascendancy.

He could have made it easy on himself and insisted on an experienced second. But somebody had to work these young ones up and if it wasn't done right they wouldn't be worth having if they had to fight.

Meanwhile his muscles were stiff, his flying leathers soaked with sweat and he stank of dragon and exertion. He turned and walked out of the aerie toward the riders' baths.

At the door the Dragon Leader looked back and sighed. *In some ways it was easier when we were at war.*

" . . . and there you have it, My Lords," Bal-Simba said finally. "That is our situation and that is what we need."

Jerry, Karl, Bal-Simba and Moira sat around the table. They had talked the day away and a good part of the night. Moira was hoarse, so Bal-Simba had taken over filling in the background while Jerry and Karl shot questions.

The remains of dinner, bread, fruit and cheese, sat

on the sideboard and a glowing globe on a wrought iron
stand beside the table gave them light.

The soft evening breeze ruffled through the room and
stars spangled the velvety blackness outside. Idly Jerry
wondered what time it was. Their watches had stopped
working at the moment of transition. After midnight, he
decided.

The rest of the programmers were bedded down
somewhere but Bal-Simba was eager to get started and
Jerry was too keyed up to sleep anyway.

"Well, it's hard to say until we've gone over the work
that's already been done," Jerry said. If the libraries and
tool kit are sufficiently developed . . ."

"I think it would be best if we left the technical details
until Wiz returns," Moira said. Out of the corner of her
eye she saw Bal-Simba shift uneasily. "He is the only one
among us who really understands them."

"Anyway, the outlines are clear enough," Jerry said. "As
I told Moira back in Cupertino I think this is do-able,
especially given the work Wiz has already put into it."

"How soon do you need all this?" Karl asked.

"As soon as possible," Bal-Simba told him. "Perhaps
a fortnight at most."

Jerry and Karl looked at each other.

"Well," Karl said, "no matter where you go, some
things don't change."

Bal-Simba frowned. "Is there a problem?"

Jerry sighed. This was the point where you usually
started lying to the client. But this was a very unusual
situation and an even more unusual client. Besides, there
was no one on this world to undercut them and steal
the contract by overpromising.

"Look," he said, leaning forward to rest his elbows on
the table, "the truth is, it will take us months to do this
job right."

"But Wiz put together his attack on the Dark League
in a matter of days!" Bal-Simba protested.

"Right," Jerry nodded. "What Wiz did was create a set of tools and build some simple programs, uh, spells with them. But there's a big difference between something that an expert hacks together for his own use and a production system."

"You need something anyone can use, right?" Karl asked.

"Any wizard," Bal-Simba amended. "But yes, basically."

"Okay, that means you need a lot more support, error checking and utilities and libraries. And it's all got to be wrapped up in a neat package with no loose ends."

The huge wizard thought about that for a minute. "How long will all this take?"

"We won't know that until after we've examined what's been done already and had a chance to talk to Wiz."

"You can begin the examination tomorrow," Bal-Simba said, rising. "There is no need to wait until Sparrow returns." He turned to Moira. "My Lady, will you escort them to their chambers?"

"If you please, My Lord, there is another matter I wish to discuss with you. I will ring for a servant."

The serving man was yawning when he arrived, but he came quickly and ushered the visitors out of Bal-Simba's study.

"Now," Moira said as the door closed behind them, "where is Wiz?"

"Well, as to that, My Lady . . ."

Her face darkened. "Something has happened to him, has it not?"

"Well . . ."

*"Has it not?"* She tried to shout but her strained vocal cords could only produce a whisper.

"We do not know," Bal-Simba told her. "He went off into the Wild Wood and no one has seen him since."

"Fortuna!" Moira stared. "You let him wander into the Wild Wood alone?" The she laughed bitterly. "And you were concerned about *my* safety?"

Wiz tiptoed down the corridor, stopping every few feet to listen. Outside the bright daylight promised warmth the sun failed to deliver.

He was desperately hungry, but he was past feeling the pangs. In the last two days he had turned up nothing that looked edible. He wasn't the only scavenger going through the rubble. Rat droppings abounded, as did signs of larger, less identifiable creatures.

He stopped to listen again, pressing himself flat against the wall as he did so. He had learned caution the hard way. Twice more since he left the palace with the trap he had barely avoided blundering into searching wizards of the League. Once he ducked into an open doorway just as two of them came around a corner not ten feet in front of him. Another time one of them caught a glimpse of him from one street over. The wizard made the mistake of calling for help and Wiz scampered away before he could get close.

He was surprised that no one had used magic to locate him. Even with the competing magical remnants in the City of Night it should have been easy for wizards who had stood in his presence to track him down, especially since he dared not leave the city. The land beyond the walls was as frozen and barren as Antarctica. Away from the shelter of these buildings he'd be dead in a day and he was sure the wizards knew it.

Perhaps Dzhir Kar was playing with him, stretching out the agony. Through his exhaustion, Wiz realized he could not win. Sooner or later, he had to use magic or fall to the searching wizards or the danger of this place.

Well, not yet. He was still alive and still free. At this minute finding food and warmth were more important to him than his ultimate fate. Moving as quietly as he could he moved down the corridor to the next door.

This place must have been pleasant once, or as pleasant as any in this benighted city ever had been. The building itself was mostly underground, a gloomy mass of tunnels and small rooms dimly lit by slowly fading magic globes. But this wing was built into the face of a cliff. The rooms on the outside had long narrow windows that looked out over the city. Judging by the shattered, soaked junk that remained they had been richly furnished as well.

But shattered, soaked junk was all that remained. What had once been rich fabric lay in sodden rotting piles. Scattered about were pieces of furniture, all hacked, broken and upended.

He looked at the wood regretfully. There were the makings there for a warming fire—if he could figure out how to light one without bringing the demon down on him and if he didn't mind attracting every wizard in the city.

Aside from that, there was no sign of anything useful. No food, no clothing, nothing. He turned to leave when something caught his eye. He bent and plucked it from the litter.

It was a halberd, its head red with rust and its shaft broken to about three feet long. Looking at the end of the shaft, Wiz could see it had been cut halfway through before it snapped, as if the owner had warded a stroke.

Wiz hefted it dubiously. He knew nothing about halberd fighting and this one was broken, useless for its original purpose. But it could still serve as a tool to pry open chests and boxes. Perhaps with it he would have a better chance of finding food.

Clutching his prize, Wiz crept back out into the corridor.

"Wiz kept notes on how his spell compiler worked," Moira explained to the gaggle of programmers who followed her into her apartment the next morning. "He did most of that here rather than in his workroom. I think it would be best if you removed them yourselves, lest I miss something."

"Thanks," Jerry said as he went over to the desk, "we'll get some boxes and . . ."

Then he saw the dragon sitting on top of the leather-bound book. A small, but very alert and obviously upset dragon. The dragon hissed and Jerry realized he, Karl and Moira were suddenly two paces ahead of everyone else in the group.

"What's that?"

"That is the demon guardian Wiz created to protect his spells, especially the book holding most of his secrets. He called it the Dragon Book," Moira explained.

Karl looked at Moira, Jerry looked at Karl and the dragon eyed them both.

"That *had* to be deliberate," Karl said finally.

Jerry made a face as if he had bitten into something sour. "Believe me, it was."

"Crave pardon?"

"There's a standard text on writing compilers called the dragon book." Jerry explained. "It's got a picture of a dragon on the cover. A red dragon."

"It was orange on my edition."

"As protection of the contents?" Moira asked.

"More like a warning of what the course is like. It's a real bear."

"Then why not put a bear on the cover?"

"Bears aren't red," Karl put in before Jerry could answer. "They're not orange either."

Moira frowned. "Oh," she said in a small voice.

"Anyway, how do we get rid of him?"

"Easily enough. Wiz taught me the dismissal spell." She stepped to the edge of the desk and spoke to the demon.

"**puff at ease exe.**"

The dragon crawled off the book and retired to the corner of the desk.

"That is a spell in Wiz's magic language," she explained, turning back to the programmers. "The word

**exe** is the command to start the spell, **at ease** is the spell and **puff** is the name of this demon."

"Well, it is a *magic* dragon," Karl said. A couple of the programmers groaned and Jerry winced again.

"Okay," Jerry said. "We'll get this stuff out of your way and moved to our office as soon as possible. Uh, do you know where we are going to be?"

"The under-seneschal is waiting to show you to your workrooms," Moira said. "He is in the courtyard, I believe."

"Great. Let's go then." Everyone moved back toward the door, except Danny Gavin who was lounging in a chair.

"Are you coming?" Jerry asked.

"No, I think I'll stay here," Danny said. "Unless you need me?"

Jerry looked at Moira and Moira shrugged.

"Just don't wander off."

Almost as soon as the door was closed Danny was out of his chair and over to the Dragon Book. The guardian demon raised its head when he opened it but made no protest.

*Now let's see what this magic stuff is like.* Danny scanned the first few pages quickly, picking up the basics of the syntax as he went. Then he flipped further back and looked at a few of the commands.

*Shit, this is a piece of cake.* He went back and re-read the first part of the book more carefully, already mentally framing his first spell.

"We had to prepare workspace for you on short notice," the under-seneschal said apologetically as he led the group across another courtyard. "I'm afraid all the towers are taken and Lord Bal-Simba doubted you would prefer caves. So to give you a place where you can all work together, we ah, well, we cleaned out an existing building."

He was a small, fussy man who seemed to bob as he walked and kept rubbing his hands together nervously. He had been given an impossible job on very short notice and he was very much afraid his solution would insult some very important people. As they moved across the courtyard he became more and more nervous.

"We weren't expecting so many of you, you see and we are so terribly crowded here . . ." His voice trailed off as they approached the building.

It was sturdily built of stone below and timber above. As they drew nearer, a distinctive aroma gave a hint of its original purpose and once they stepped through the large double doors there was no doubt at all as to what it was.

"A stable?" Jerry said dubiously.

"Well, ah, a cow barn actually," the man almost cringed as he said it.

"Wonderful," Cindy said, "back in the bullpen."

"Oh wow, man," said one of the group, a graying man with his hair pulled back into a pony tail, "like rustic."

"Hell, I've worked in worse," one of the programmers said as he looked around. "I used to be at Boeing."

The room was good-sized, but as cold as every other place in the City of Night. A mullioned window, its tracery in ruins, let in the sharp outside air. Piles of sodden trash and pieces of broken furniture lay here and there. On one wall stood a tall black cabinet, tilting on a broken leg but its doors still shut.

Wiz came into the room eagerly. Maybe there was something in the closed cabinet he could use.

Cold and hunger dulled his caution and he was halfway across the room before a skittering sound behind him told him he had made a mistake.

Wiz whirled at the sound, but it was too late. There, blocking the only way out, was a giant black rat. It was perhaps five feet long in the body and its shoulder reached to Wiz's waist. Its beady eyes glared at Wiz. It lifted its muzzle to sniff the human, showing long yellow teeth. Wiz stepped back again and the rat sniffed once more, whiskers quivering.

Wiz licked his lips and took a firmer grip on the broken halberd shaft. The rat eyed him hungrily and moved all the way into the room, its naked tail still trailing out into the corridor.

Wiz stepped to one side, hoping the rat would follow and leave him room for a dash to the door. But the rat wasn't fooled. It lowered its head and squealed like a piglet caught in a fence. Then it charged.

In spite of his disinclination to exercise, Wiz had naturally fast reflexes. Moreover, his two years in the World had hardened his muscles and increased his wind. He was far from being the self-described "pencil-necked geek" he had been when he had arrived here, but he was even further from being a warrior.

The monster closed in squealing. Wiz swung wildly with his rusty axe. The giant rat ducked under the blade and leaped for his throat.

Against a halfway competent swordsman the tactic would have worked. But Wiz wasn't even halfway competent. He had swung blindly and he brought his weapon back equally blindly, backhand along the same path.

The spike on the back of the axe caught the rat just below the ear. Any guardsman on the drill field would have winced at such a puny blow, but the spike concentrated the force on a single spot. Wiz felt a "crunch" as the spike penetrated bone. The rat squealed, jerked convulsively and fell in a twitching heap at Wiz's feet.

Wiz's first instinct was to turn and run. But he checked himself. *Think* he told himself sternly, *you've got to think.* Running wouldn't solve anything. There was nowhere to run to and running burned calories he could ill-afford to lose. Panic wouldn't get him the food he so desperately needed.

*Well,* he thought, looking down at the gray-furred corpse, *maybe I can use one problem to solve another.*

Kneeling over the body, he set to work with his halberd.

Wiz emerged from the room a while later wiping his mouth on a bit of more or less clean rag.

Rat sashimi, Wiz decided, wasn't half bad—if you used lots of wasabe. He didn't have any wasabe, but it still wasn't half bad.

While the rest of the team broke for lunch, Jerry, Karl and Moira went back to the apartment to start sorting through Wiz's papers.

"A barn!" Moira said angrily. "I cannot believe they would do that to you."

"Hey, it's dry and it looks like it can be made fairly comfortable," Karl said. "Besides, it's already divided up into cubicles."

"Well, I can assure you, My Lords . . ." Moira began as she started to open the door.

There was a low moan and the sound of scuffling from the apartment.

Moira threw open the door.

"Danny!" Jerry yelled.

The young programmer was rocking back and forth, his body slamming first forward almost to the desk and then back so forcefully the chair teetered.

"Something's wrong! He's having a stroke or something."

"Stay away from him!" Moira ordered. "He is caught in a spell."

"Stop it."

"I do not know how. The command should be in the book.

Jerry edged around the still-thrashing Danny and hooked the Dragon Book off the desk. The dragon demon ignored him, watching Danny the way a cat watches a new and particularly interesting toy.

"Damn, no index!"

"Try the table of contents," Karl suggested.

"No table of contents, either!" He paged frantically through the book and muttered something about hackers under his breath.

"Here it is." He read hurriedly. **"reset!"** he commanded.

Danny continued to jerk back and forward.

"Exe, My Lord," Moira said frantically. "You must end with exe."

"Oh, right. **reset exe!"**

Suddenly Danny flopped forward and hit the table with a thump.

Moira and Jerry gently raised him up and leaned him back in the chair.

"Are you okay?" Jerry asked as the teenaged programmer gasped for breath.

"'s alright," he slurred as he lifted his head off his chest. "I'll be alright." Jerry saw he was white and shaking but he was breathing more normally.

"What happened?" Danny mumbled.

Moira pressed a cup of wine into his hands.

"You were entrapped by the spell you created, My Lord," she told him. "The spell repeated endlessly and you could not get out."

"In other words you were stuck in a DO loop," Jerry explained.

Danny raised the cup in both hands and drained it in a gulp.

"Jesus. I was in there and it started and it just kept going over and over. Like a live wire you can't let go." He lowered the cup and it slipped from his numbed grasp to clatter on the table. "Jesus!"

"Tell us what happened."

"Well, I was flipping through the manual and I figured I'd try it out. So I set up a simple little hack, only when it started it just kept going. I didn't think I'd ever get out."

"That was a dumb-ass stunt," Jerry told him. "You're lucky it wasn't worse."

"How the hell was I supposed to know?" Danny snapped. "I didn't think . . ."

"You sure as hell didn't," Jerry cut him off. "And you'd better start thinking before you do a damn fool thing like that again!"

Danny muttered something but Jerry ignored him.

"Okay," Jerry said. "From now on nobody practices this stuff alone."

Wiz was feeling almost jaunty as he made his way up the street with the broken halberd over his shoulder. He was still cold, but on a day as bright as this he could almost ignore that. Besides, the cold was easier to bear when you weren't hungry all the time.

The halberd made a big difference in Wiz's standard of living. There turned out to be a lot more food left in the City of Night than he had realized. But almost all of what remained was locked behind doors or in cupboards or chests. In the last few days he had gotten very good at using the halberd's axe blade and the heavy spike behind to pry, chop and smash things open. Finding food was a full-time job, but it wasn't quite the hopeless one it had been.

Today he was well-fed on magically preserved meat and bread so dry and brick-like he had to soak it in water before he could eat it. The meat had an odd taste and the water he soaked the bread in hadn't been very clean, but his stomach was still pleasantly full.

And now this neighborhood looked promising. The street was lined with smaller buildings, two and three stories. A number of small buildings, shops or houses, were more likely to yield food than a few big ones. Best of all, the doors and window shutters on nearly every house on the street were intact. That meant they had not been systematically looted and larger scavengers had been kept out.

The weather added to his mood. There was not a trace of the clouds that usually hung low and gray over the Southern Lands. The only thing in the pale-blue sky was the sun and it was almost at its zenith. There wasn't a lot of warmth in it, but there was a certain amount of cheer.

A motion above the buildings caught his eye. Wiz turned his head just in time to see a black-robed wizard drift lazily over the rooftops. The man's robe fluttered about his ankles and his head moved constantly as he scanned the city.

Wiz shrank back against the wall. But he knew he stood out sharply against the dark volcanic rock of the street and buildings. There wasn't even a shadow to hide in and the wizard was floating in his direction. He was as exposed as an ant on a griddle and he would be fried like one as soon as the wizard spotted him.

Wiz bit his lip and silently cursed the bright sun and the shuttered houses. He looked up and down the street frantically, but there was not an open door or window to be seen.

There was a storm sewer opposite. It didn't look big enough to take him and it was covered with an iron grate, but it was the only chance he had. Wiz dashed across the street and levered up the grate with a quick jerk of his halberd. Then heedless of how deep the hole might be he thrust himself through.

It was perhaps eight feet from the street to the trickle of freezing slime that ran through the bottom of the sewer. The shock and the slippery bottom forced him to his hands and knees before he regained his balance. He looked up just in time to see the wizard float down the street housetop high.

Wiz dared not breathe as the man passed over the grating. The sorcerer looked directly down at his hiding place, but floated on by majestically. Apparently the shadows in the hole hid Wiz from him.

Once the man passed out of Wiz's field of vision, he breathed a sigh of relief. Then he froze again. There was something moving in the tunnel behind him. Something big.

The tunnel was as black as the inside of midnight, but Wiz heard a splash-scrape sound as if something too large to move quietly was trying to do so. He listened more intently. Again the splash-scrape, nearer this time.

Wiz realized he was trapped. He couldn't see the flying wizard, but he could not have gone far. Leaving the shelter of the sewer meant exposing himself to his enemies. On the other hand, whatever he was sharing this tunnel with was getting closer by the second.

For some reason it stuck in his mind that he had found no bodies in the ruins. Not even bones.

He listened again. There was no further sound from the tunnel except the drip, drip of water. The lack of sound reminded him of a cat getting ready to pounce.

With one motion he twisted around and lashed upward with the halberd. The spike caught on the edge of the hole and he swung himself up to grab the coping with his other hand.

Behind him came a furious splashing. He swung his leg up and rolled free of the sewer just as a huge pair of jaws snapped shut where he had been. Wiz had a confused impression of a mouth full of ripping teeth and a single evil eye before he rolled away from the opening.

Gasping, Wiz gained his feet and flattened against the building. There was no sign of the flying wizard and the creature in the sewer showed no sign of coming after him.

Muddy, chilled and thoroughly frightened, Wiz ran off down the street, looking for a place to hide.

"Well," said Jerry Andrews, "what have we got?"

The team was crowded into the Wizard's Day Room, which they were using as a temporary office while the last renovations were completed on the cow barn.

For the last two days the programmers had torn into Wiz's spell compiler and the material he had left behind. By ones and twos they had pored over the Dragon Book, Wiz's notes and conducted small and carefully controlled experiments.

Now Jerry had called a meeting to sum up, compare notes and plan strategy. He had set it for late afternoon, so most of the programmers were awake and functional. They had pushed the tables in the Day Room together to make a long table in the middle of the room and, heedless of tradition, pulled chairs from their accustomed spots up around it.

"Does the phrase 'bloody mess' do anything for you?" a lean woman with short black hair and piercing dark eyes asked from halfway down the table. "This thing is written in something that looks like a bastard version of Forth crossed with LISP and some features from C and Modula 2 thrown in for grins."

"When do we get to meet this guy, anyway?" someone else asked. "I'd like to shake him warmly by the throat."

"There may be a problem with that, My Lord," Moira said from her place next to Jerry. "He went off alone into the Wild Wood and we have not yet found him."

"We're going to need him," Nancy said. "Someone has got to explain this mess. Some of this code is literally crawling with bugs."

"You mean figuratively," Jerry corrected.

"I said literally and I mean literally," she retorted. "I tried to run one routine and I got a swarm of electric blue cockroaches." She made a face. *"Four-inch-long* electric blue cockroaches."

"Actually the basic concept of the system is rather elegant and seems to be surprisingly powerful," Karl said.

Nancy snorted.

"No, really. The basic structure is solid. There are a lot of kludges and some real squinky hacks, but at bottom this thing is very good."

"I'll give you another piece of good news," Jerry told them. "Besides the Dragon Book, Wiz left notes with a lot of systems analysis and design. Apparently he had a pretty good handle on what he needed to do, he just didn't have the time to do it. I think we can use most of what he left us with only a minimal review."

"Okay, so far we've just been nibbling around the edges to get the taste of the thing. Now we've got to get down to serious work."

"There's one issue we've got to settle first," Nancy said. "Catching errors."

"What's the matter, don't you like electric blue cockroaches?" Danny asked.

"Cockroaches I can live with. They glow in the dark and that makes them easy to squash. I'm more concerned about HMC or EOI-type errors."

"HMC and EOI?"

"Halt, Melt and Catch fire or Execute Operator Immediately."

"One thing this system has is a heck of an error trapping system," said Jerry.

"That is because the consequences of a mistake in a spell can be terrible," Moira told him. "Remember, a spell is not a computer which will simply crash if you make an error."

The people up and down the table looked serious, even Danny.

"Desk check your programs, people," Jerry said.

"That's not going to be good enough. There are always bugs, and bugs in this stuff can bite—hard. We need a better system for catching major errors."

"There is one way," Judith said thoughtfully.

"How?"

"Redundancy with voting. We use three different processors—demons—and they have to all agree. If they don't the spell is aborted."

"Fine, so suppose there's a bug in your algorithm?"

"You use three different algorithms. Then you code each primitive three different ways. Say one demon acts like a RISC processor, another is a CISC processor and the third is something like a stack machine. We split up into three teams and each team designs its own demon without talking to any of the others."

"That just tripled the work," someone said.

"Yeah, but it gives us some margin for error."

"I think we've got to go for the maximum safety," Jerry Andrews said finally. "I don't know about the rest of you, but I have no desire to see what a crash looks like from inside the system."

"My Lord, you seem to have made remarkable progress," Moira said as Jerry showed her through the programmers' new quarters.

The team had settled in quickly. Each programmer got his or her own stall and trestle tables filled the center aisle. The stalls were full of men and women hunched over their trestle table desks or leafing through stacks of material. At the far end of the room Judith and another programmer were sketching a diagram in charcoal on the whitewashed barn wall.

"Once you get used to giving verbal commands to an Emac instead of using a keyboard and reading the result in glowing letters in the air, programming spells isn't all that different from programming computers," Jerry told her. "We'd be a lot further along if Wiz were available, but we're not doing badly."

Moira's brow wrinkled. "I wish he was here too. But we cannot even get a message to him, try as we might." She shook the mood off. "It must be very hard to work with spells without having the magician who made them to guide you."

"It's not as bad as it might be," Jerry told her. "Probably our biggest advantage is that we know all the code

was written by one person and I'm very familiar with
Wiz's programming style.

"Look, a lot of this business is like playing a guessing
game with someone. The more you know about the
person and the way that person thinks, the more successful you are likely to be."

He sighed. "Still, it would be nice not to have to guess
at all. Besides, Wiz is good. He'd be a real asset."

"We are doing everything we can to locate him," Moira
said. "Meanwhile, is there anything else you need?"

"A couple of things. First, is there any way to get cold
cuts and sandwich fixings brought in? My people tend
to miss meals."

"Certainly. Anything else?"

"Well, you don't have coffee, tea or cola here, so I
guess not."

"Wiz used to drink blackmoss tea," Moira told him,
"but that is terrible stuff."

"Can we try some?" Jerry asked.

Moira rang for a servant and while they waited for
the tea, she and Jerry chatted about the work.

"We call the new operating system 'WIZ-DOS'—that's
the Wiz Zumwalt Demon Operating System."

"If this thing has a 640K memory limit, I quit!"
someone put in from one of the stalls.

"As far as we know there's no limit at all on memory,"
Jerry said. It's just that addressing it is kind of convoluted."

Moira didn't understand the last part, but her experience with Wiz had taught her the best thing to do was
to ignore the parts she didn't understand. To do otherwise
invited an even more incomprehensible "explanation."

"I'm sure Wiz would be honored to have this named
after him," she said.

The tea arrived already brewed. Moira, who had used
it when she was standing vigil as part of her training,
thought it smelled nasty. Jerry didn't seem to notice.

Moira poured out a small amount of the swamp-water-brown brew. Dubiously, she extended the cup. Jerry sniffed it, then sipped. Then he drained the cup and smacked his lips. "Not bad," he said appraisingly. "A little weak, but not bad. Can we arrange to have a big pot of this stuff in the Bull Pen while we're working?"

"Of course, My Lord, I'll have the kitchen send up a pot."

"I mean a big pot," Jerry said. "Say thirty or sixty cups."

Moira, remembering the effect that even a cup of blackmoss tea had on her, stared at him.

"Well, there are more than a dozen of us," he said apologetically.

Moira nodded, wondering if there was enough black-moss in the castle to supply this crew for even a week.

*Fifteen*

# WAR WARNING

*A jump gone awry is one of the hardest bugs to locate.*
                                                    —programmers' saying

Bal-Simba was walking in the castle garden when his deputy found him.

"Lord," Arianne said strangely. "Someone wishes to speak to you."

"Who?" the black wizard asked, catching her mood.

"Aelric, the elf duke."

Duke Aelric, or rather his image, was waiting for him in the

Watcher's room. The Watchers, who kept magical watch on the entire world, shifted uneasily at their communications crystals in the elf's presence.

Bal-Simba studied the apparition as he mounted the dais overlooking the sunken floor where the Watchers worked. The elf duke was wearing a simple tunic of dark-brown velvet that set off his milk-white complexion. His long hair was caught back in a golden filet set with small yellow gems at his temples. His face was serene and untroubled, not that that meant anything. Elves were inhumanly good at hiding their feelings and in any event their emotions were not those of mortals.

Bal-Simba had heard Wiz and Moira's story of their

rescue by Duke Aelric and their dinner with him, but this was the first time Bal-Simba had ever seen him. *Come to that, it is the first time I have ever seen any elf this close,* he thought as he seated himself in his chair.

Duke Aelric seemed not to notice Bal-Simba until he was properly settled to receive his guest.

"I seek the Sparrow, but I am told he is not available," Aelric said.

"He is not here."

"Do you know when he will return?"

Bal-Simba considered the question before answering. "I do not. He is off in the Wild Wood, I believe."

Aelric raised a silver eyebrow. "Indeed? Forgive me if I pry, but when did he leave?"

"Forgive my curiosity, but why do you wish to know?"

"Because he was on business of some urgency when he left my hold to return to your city a fortnight hence," Aelric said.

Bal-Simba frowned mightily. "He was coming straight back?"

Aelric waved a hand. "That was his plan. He left upon the Wizard's Way to return here immediately." He looked sharply at the black Wizard.

"I swear to you he did not arrive here," Bal-Simba told him. He struck his chest. "Upon my life I swear it."

"I believe you, oath or no," the image said.

"I will also tell you that we have been trying to contact him for several days without success. Frankly, we are becoming worried."

Elf and mortal fell silent, contemplating the implications.

"It occurs to me," the elf duke said slowly, "that someone may have transgressed upon my hospitality. I do not appreciate interference with those traveling to and from my abode."

"It occurs to me that Wiz may be in dire danger," Bal-Simba said, a trifle sharply.

"I hope not," Aelric told him. "For all our sakes."

It was Bal-Simba's turn to raise an eyebrow.

"A matter of forestalling a war between humans and other users of magic, I think," Duke Aelric explained.

"War?"

"Did you expect your drive to exterminate magical creatures along the Fringe would go unremarked? Or that your expansion deep into the Wild Wood would pass unnoticed?"

"I think that there is a great deal going on out on the Fringe that I and the Council are unaware of."

Aelric waved a languid hand. "That is as it may be. The Sparrow seemed to feel he could turn this human tide before it came to that." Then he sobered and power seemed to radiate out of him like a nimbus.

"But I tell you this, wizard. If you cannot find your Sparrow—and soon—then you may have lost your only chance to forestall a war which would rend the World asunder."

He nodded gravely. "Merry part."

Bal-Simba's eyes widened at the usage, but he nodded in reply. "Merry meet again." And the elf duke's image was gone.

Bal-Simba heaved a great sigh. "When an elf uses human courtesies you know you are in trouble," he remarked to no one in particular. Then the giant black wizard turned to the gaping Watchers in the pit.

"I want every Watcher we have scanning the World for our Sparrow." He turned to Arianne. "Set up a schedule so we may search day and night." Then to one of the wizards with a communication crystal. "Send the word out to all the villages and habitations at once. Wiz must be found. And order the dragon cavalry out to search as well."

"Lord, do you think he meant what he said about war?" Arianne asked.

"Have you ever known an elf to joke?" Bal-Simba said. "He was concerned enough to come to us. That is more than sufficient proof that something very dangerous is in the air."

"Jerry, I think you'd better look at this."

Judith was standing at the entrance to Jerry's stall with an odd look on her face.

"We got the voting module working and, well, I think you'd better see the result."

Jerry followed her over to her own stall where Karl was looking bemused at three small demons standing together on the table.

"We know that any spell above a certain level of complexity generates a demon as its physical manifestation," Judith explained. "So we expected this thing would produce demons. But watch what happens when we feed it correct code.

"**emac.**" An Emac popped up on the desk next to the trio of demons.

"**backslash test1 exe.**" Judith said and the Emac gabbled at the demons. The demons stood motionless and then the one on the left hummed.

"Okayyy," it sang in a vibrant bass.

"Okayyy," the middle one chimed in a rich baritone.

"Okayyyy," said the third demon in a fine clear tenor.

"Okaayyyyyy," the three demon voices blended in perfect harmony. Then the sound died away and they fell silent.

For a moment none of the programmers said anything.

"The question is, is that a bug or a feature?" Karl asked.

"I guess that depends on how you feel about music," Jerry said. "Anyway, we don't have time to fix it, so we'll call it a feature."

Judith looked at the demons and shook her head. "I'm glad we didn't build four processors. I'm not sure I could take a barbershop quartet."

"I don't thing you'd get a barbershop quartet," Jerry said judiciously. "A gospel group seems more likely."

"Worse."

By nature and training Danny needed a lot of time to himself. It had always been his refuge in times of trouble and his joy in times of special happiness.

The castle was too crowded for him to be really alone. But he had found a place on the rooftops where he could look down on the Bull Pen and the courtyards. From here he was hidden from view by any of the wizard's towers and could see out beyond the Wizards' Lodge, over the tile and slate rooftops of the town and off into the rolling blue distance.

Nearly every morning before he settled down to work, Danny would climb the narrow stairs to the attic and then go up the wooden ladder and out through the trap door that took him to his favorite place on the roof. He was not experienced enough in the ways of this World to know that the scuff-marks on the slates meant someone else came here too.

Today Danny had changed his pattern. It was late afternoon, normally a time when he would be settled in the Bull Pen and hard at work. But today his code had turned to shit and Cindy Naismith got on his case for something he said. So he left and came back up here for a while.

He wouldn't be missed, he knew. Not for some little time. Programmers set their own hours and besides, the rest of the team didn't like him very much.

Well, fuck 'em. That wasn't anything new to Danny.

Besides, he told himself, it wasn't like he was goofing off. He was still thinking about the problem, and he needed to clear his head, didn't he?

There was a soft scrabbling noise on the slate roof behind him.

Danny turned and there was a thin brown-haired girl with enormous doe eyes.

"Hi," Danny said, half-resenting the interruption.

The girl moved back up the roof, away from him.

"Don't worry, I won't hurt you." The girl froze.

"You okay?"

No response. If he moved toward her she would have fled, but he kept his place. She sat down on the roof behind and above him and looked out over the city.

Well, if she didn't want to talk . . . Danny turned back to watch the clouds himself. It wasn't as good as being completely alone, but it wasn't bad either.

Danny had taken to computers as a way to shut out the endless arguments that raged through his home. Later, after the divorce, the computer had become a way out of the loneliness, a friend who never turned its back on you or put you down.

At first he hadn't cared for programming, just racking up scores on video games. He had taken out his frustrations destroying aliens and monsters by the thousands and scoring points by the millions. Then he found out you could gimmick some of the games by editing character files. From that it was one small step to cracking copy protection to get games he couldn't afford to buy and one thing led to another. By the time he was sixteen, Danny was a very competent, if unsystematic, programmer.

He was also very, very lonely.

Now here he was in a world something like the one those games were based on. Full of monsters and where magic worked. And he was still just as alone and just as cut off as he ever had been. Well, fuck 'em. He'd get by, just like he always had.

Without thinking, he reached into his pocket and pulled out the sandwich he had stashed there—smoked meat and sharp cheese on a long roll.

Danny heard the girl shift on the roof behind him.

"Want some?" She obviously did, but she was afraid to approach him.

"Here." He broke off half the sandwich and held it out to her. She looked at him intently but didn't move. He considered tossing the sandwich up to her, but realized it would probably come apart in the air. He settled for reaching back and stretching out his hand.

"Come on, I won't hurt you."

Slowly, cautiously, the girl crept down the roof toward him. Finally she was close enough to stretch out and snatch the sandwich from him. Then she scrabbled quickly back up the roof. The entire performance reminded Danny feeding a particularly shy squirrel.

"What's your name?" he asked.

"June," the girl said around a mouthful of sandwich. "I am June."

"This is just like being at fighter practice."

Karl, Judith and several of the other team members were sitting on a low wall by the drill field watching the guardsmen practice. Under the arches of the colonnade Jerry was sitting on a bench watching girls.

Just then a flight of dragon cavalry swept over the castle.

"Okay," Karl amended, "it's almost like being at fighter practice."

Out on the field Donal was practicing spear work against multiple opponents.

"Tricky move with the spear," Karl said to no one in particular as Donal dodged and spun between two opposing swordsmen.

"Why does he keep the butt low like that?" Judith asked.

"He is trying to keep the point directed at his opponent's eyes," a guardsman who was lounging nearby said. "That makes it hard to judge the length of the spear."

Karl nodded. "And it sets him up to make a quick jab to the face, which will make almost anyone flinch."

The guardsman, a sandy-haired older man, looked

closely at Karl. "You sound as if you know something of the art, My Lord."

"I'm a fighter. Well, an SCA fighter," he amended quickly. "We used to fight with rattan weapons. For sport."

"Would not your magic gain you more than weapons skill in war?"

"We don't use swords and spears in war any more," Karl told him. "No, we do it strictly for fun."

The guardsman's seamed face crinkled into a frown. "A most peculiar sport, if you do not mind my saying so, Lord."

"That's what a lot of people in my world thought," Karl sighed. "By the way, I'm Karl Dershowitz." He extended his hand and the other man clasped it.

"I am called Shamus MacMurragh. I command the guardsmen of the castle."

"Pleased to meet you."

"Tell me," Shamus said, "how does our weapons play compare to your world?"

"Very well. We do some things a lot differently and I think we've spent more time on the theory than you have, but on the whole you compare very well with our methods."

"I am very glad to hear it, My Lord," Shamus said mildly. "Could you perhaps show us how you do these things."

Karl wasn't quite sure, but he suspected he had just been trapped. "Be glad to," he said with a casualness he did not feel.

It took a few minutes to outfit Karl in the padded cloth hauberk, greaves, vambraces and helm the guardsmen used for practice. The shield they brought him was a target somewhat over two feet in diameter. Karl whose SCA fighting style depended in large part on using the points of a heater shield, felt he was at a disadvantage, but he didn't say anything.

The sword they gave him was wood, not rattan, and a good deal heavier than what Karl was used to. Still, the balance was very good and it moved comfortably as he took practice swings.

"Remember to pull your blows, Lord," Shamus said as they faced off. "I do not want to be injured."

Karl nodded and licked his lips. Shamus moved with a catlike grace that suggested the guardsman wasn't the one who should be worried.

Karl came in in his standard fighting stance, shield in front, sword hilt over his head with the blade forward and down, resting on his shield.

Shamus looked at him quizzically for a moment and then stepped in with two cuts to the head. Karl was strong, but his wrist could not absorb or stop the blows. His blade was knocked casually aside and Shamus's sword rang off his helmet. Karl staggered back and nearly dropped the sword.

Shamus grasped his elbow to help support him. "Are you all right, My Lord?"

"Yeah, fine. Uh, in our system if you hit the other guy's sword, the blow is considered blocked."

"Matters are somewhat different in our world," Shamus said dryly. "But tell me, how can you strike anyone with your sword in that position?"

"You mean down in front of the head like that? Easy. You twist your hips, drive your elbow down and throw the forearm out." He demonstrated. "Like that."

"Interesting, but is it strong enough?"

"Well, I can make someone's helm ring pretty good with it."

"Try it on the pell," Shamus invited.

At the far end of the drill field was a row of head-high posts set in the earth. Each was about six inches thick and the dirt around them was freshly dug.

Karl stepped up to the nearest post, assumed his position and struck, overhead and slanting down and into the post. The blade turned in his hand, so the first cut only skimmed the post, scraping along the surface and taking a shaving with it. The second cut drove the sword edge perhaps two inches into the pine.

"Surprisingly strong, My Lord," Shamus commented as Karl stepped back, massaging his wrist from the shock. Then he stepped up, assumed his guard stance and sheared the post off cleanly with a single mighty swing.

"Such blows win battles," he said, stepping back.

"How did you do that?"

"Years of practice," Shamus said with a smile. "Of course there are one or two small tricks. But mostly an hour or two practice every day for, oh, six or seven years and you would be a creditable swordsman." He laughed and clapped the younger man on the shoulder.

"I think I just made a raging fool of myself," Karl muttered to Judith as he came off the field.

"I think it's called hubris,'" Judith told him. "How's your head?"

Karl rubbed his wrist. "It's my arm more than any my head and it will heal quicker than my pride." He looked back out at the practicing guardsmen. "You know what the worst of it is? I can't use any of this stuff in our combat back home. Our rules are so unrealistic that the techniques that really work won't work for us."

" . . . so anyway, we're working on a user interface. It's going to be really neat when we get it done."

June watched Danny and said nothing.

They sat side by side on the roof, looking out over the Capital to where the late afternoon sun turned puffy clouds into a symphony of pale golds and blush pinks.

They had met up on the roof nearly every day since their first encounter. Sometimes one or both of them brought food and they had an impromptu picnic. Sometimes they just sat and talked. Or rather Danny talked and June listened. June hadn't said a dozen words since that first day, but now they sat together on the slates. Sometimes they held hands.

"You ought to come and see the place sometime. It's really pretty interesting."

June smiled and shook her head.

"Well, look, I gotta get down there or they're gonna start asking questions. I'll see you tomorrow, okay?"

Danny started to rise, but June took hold of his arm and pulled him close. She kissed him full on the mouth and before Danny could respond she skittered away over the roof ridge.

Danny sat there for a moment longer, tasting her on his lips and trying to understand what had happened. One thing he was sure of. He liked it.

Even by the standards of the City of Night, this place was strange. The windows about the tower gave good light, else he never would have dared to approach the eerie blue glow issuing through the open doorway.

At this level the tower was divided into two rooms. The one beyond the carved black portal must be by far the larger, but the one was substantial as well. Looking at the layout, Wiz had the odd feeling that this level was larger inside than it was on the outside.

This was obviously a wizard's tower and judging by the effects a very powerful wizard at that. Through the inner door Wiz could see forms writhing in the smoky red dark. It might just be fumes from the ever-burning braziers, but he had no intention of crossing the threshold to find out.

This room must have been an adjunct to the workroom. There were shelves along one wall which had obviously held scrolls. Pegs and hooks on another wall had perhaps held ceremonial robes and other magical apparatus.

But none of that was left. The small room had been

thoroughly ransacked. Hangings had been pulled off the walls and lay rotting in a heap on the floor. The shelves were empty and broken. The floor was littered with broken glass, smashed crockery and bits of less savory items that might once have been in pots and jars. In one corner an armoire leaned crazily against the wall, its doors torn half off their hinges and showing the scars where someone had hastily chopped them open.

Wiz walked over to the cabinet and looked inside. The shelves were askew and the drawers were ripped apart. Like the room itself the armoire had been looted.

On an impulse, he stuck his hand into the cabinet. He struck the back much sooner than he expected and jammed his fingers painfully.

That wasn't right, he thought as he flexed the aching digits. The back was closer than it should be. He put his hand back in the cabinet and reached around to feel the back from the outside. Yes, there was definitely a space there. There was a good eight-inch difference between the inside and outside back.

A careful examination of the inside back and the sides showed him nothing. The wood was plain and the grain straight and simple. He pressed and twisted, but the back remained in place.

*Well,* he thought hefting his halberd, *there's always the field engineering approach.*

Three quick blows from the halberd splintered the thin wood of the back. On the third blow the armoire gave a despairing "sproing" and the remains of the back fell toward him. Eagerly Wiz reached inside.

At first he thought the compartment was empty. But when he thrust his hand into the dark recess, his fingers touched cloth. He lifted the garment off the peg on the side of the recess and brought it out into the light.

It wasn't much, just a brown wool travelling cloak, frayed and slightly moth eaten. The kind of thing a wizard might wear for a disguise, or because he was too engrossed in his magic to worry about appearances. *It doesn't even look very warm,* Wiz thought as he fingered the thin cloth. For the hundredth time Wiz thought of the fine gray and red cloak with the fur trim he had left in the village.

*Well, anything was better than nothing and that's what I've got now.* He threw the cloak over his shoulders and pulled it tightly about him. He was right, it wasn't very warm. Still it was comforting to have something to wrap around himself.

"I saw Moira today, My Lord," Arianne said as she and Bal-Simba finished the day's business in his study. "She asked if there was any news of Wiz."

"If there was news, she would be the first to know," the giant wizard told his deputy. "No, so far our search has turned up nothing." He frowned. "We know an accident did not befall him in the Wild Wood. If he started out on the Wizard's Way and did not return to the Capital, we may assume some magical agency intervened."

"Human?" Arianne asked.

"Perhaps. Although it appears that Sparrow has an unusual number of non-human enemies as well. Powerful ones." He paused for a second and frowned.

"And Lady . . ."

Arianne bent close at his gesture. "Yes, Lord?"

"Inquire—discreetly—into the activities of our own wizards over the last fourteen days. Especially any who have absented themselves from the Capital."

Arianne looked shocked. "Do you think . . ."

"I think," Bal-Simba said, cutting her off, "that we would be remiss if we did not explore every possibility to get our Sparrow back here as quickly as we can."

Arianne turned away to execute his command. "Oh, and Lady . . ."

Arianne turned back. "Yes, Lord?"

"Find that ex-apprentice, Pryddian, and ask him what he knows about this."

"Pryddian?"

"Just a thought. A direct attack on Wiz in the Capital would be difficult. It would be easier if he were outside our walls. Pryddian was the cause of our Sparrow's journey." He shrugged his mountainous shoulders. "Unlikely, but we have to start somewhere."

Pryddian was sweating as he came over the last rise before his destination and not just from the noon sun. Before him the road curved to the left around the base of a hill, actually a large limestone outcropping. To the right, away from the road and along the outcropping, was a wild jumble of small trees, laurel bushes and boulders. The former apprentice started down the road, his feet kicking up powdery white dust fine as flour as he walked.

When he reached the place where the road curved away he paused for an instant and scanned the bushes on the roadside. The dusty weeds beside the road showed no sign of disturbance, but there was a path there, leading off the road and in among the undergrowth. Pryddian patted the breast of his tunic for reassurance and then stepped off the road and onto the little-used path.

He breasted his way through the bushes, dodged around trees and boulders and followed the meandering path deeper into the woodland. The thick brush and second-growth trees showed that once this place had been logged. But that had obviously been long ago. Getting felled trees out of such a place would be backbreaking and not worth it so close to the Fringe of the Wild Wood. It had been done once and then the wilderness had been allowed to reclaim this place.

Finally the trail took a sharp turn and a dip and Pryddian stumbled through into an opening. He was against the flank of the hill now, in a little hollow hard against sheer rock face. All around him like grotesque sentries stood boulders twice as high as he was. Directly in front of him was a single table-high stone in the midst of a patch of beaten earth. There were dark splotches on the stone, as if something had been spilled there and allowed to dry.

Pryddian walked hesitatingly into the place. Suddenly an arm like iron clamped across his windpipe and he felt cold steel against his neck.

Instinctively he twisted his head and out of the corner of his eye saw that his captor was clad in the close fitting black of the Dark League's dread Shadow Warriors.

The Shadow Warrior pressed the edge to his throat and Pryddian ceased struggling.

"No move, no sound if you value your life," a voice grated behind him.

Pryddian licked his lips and remained silent.

"Better," the voice said at last. "Now, why are you here?"

"I am called Pryddian. I am . . . . URK." The Shadow Warrior's grip tightened on his windpipe.

"I did not ask who you were, but why you had come," his unseen questioner said sharply. "Answer only those questions I ask you, apprentice, or you will wish you had never been born."

"I came seeking the Dark League," Pryddian said when the pressure on his throat relaxed.

"And why should the dark League be interested in the likes of you?"

"I have talent. I desire to become a wizard and I bring you something." He reached toward his tunic, but the Shadow Warrior drew the blade perhaps a quarter of an inch along his skin. He felt the burning sting of the cut and then the warm wetness of blood trickling down his throat.

Pryddian froze, but the Shadow Warrior, reacting to an unseen signal, slackened his grip and moved the knife

away from his throat. Slowly he extended his trembling
hand and reached into his tunic. Equally slowly he
withdrew his hand, holding a roll of parchment.

"I give you the Sparrow's magic," he said.

"Lord, Moira asked again today about Sparrow,"
Arianne said.

Bal-Simba turned away from his window to face his
deputy.

"Today as every day, eh?" He shook his head. "The
answer is still the same. We can find no trace of him,
in all the World."

"Is he dead then?" Arianne asked.

Bal-Simba shook his head. "Moira does not think so.
I trust her judgment in this."

"Moira was away in his world when he left Aelric's
hold," Arianne pointed out.

"Still, I think she would know if he had died."

"Then where could he be?"

"There are many possibilities. He might be in a place
where he is shielded by magic. He might have been sent
beyond the World. He might be held in a state of
undeath.

"One thing I think we can safely venture. He is not
where he is voluntarily and wherever he is, he needs any
aid we can give him." He returned to his desk an sat
down again. "On that subject, have you learned more
in the matter you were pursuing?"

"You mean the actions of the Mighty? There is one
thing new. Ebrion is missing for near three weeks."

"Ebrion?"

Arianne nodded. "There is more. We cannot be sure,
but it appears that he may well be dead."

"Dead? How?"

Arianne shrugged. "We do not know. We are not even
certain that he is dead."

Bal-Simba sucked his lip against his sharpened teeth
thoughtfully. "Ebrion, eh?"

He twisted in his chair to face her. "This should be explored. Investigate closely."

"But discreetly," Arianne agreed. "I am already doing so, Lord."

*Just like all the rest,* Wiz thought as he surveyed the room in the failing light. Nothing to eat, just more piles of junk. The wind whistled through the broken windows and he shivered as he pulled the worn brown cloak tighter around himself.

Outside the setting sun poked fitfully through the layer of lead-gray clouds. By now Wiz knew the signs of a storm moving in, perhaps with snow. It was going to be another cold, miserable night. Too cold for foraging.

Since his encounter with the flying wizard, Wiz had stayed out of the open, at least in daylight. Every day, unless the winds were too high, one or more wizards of the Dark League floated over the ruined city looking for a sign of him. Now he tried to move from building to building only at night.

Well, none of that this evening. Storms in the Southern Land were nothing to take lightly. He needed a place to hole up. And food, of course.

He made one more survey of the room. Broken furniture, bits of smashed crockery and junk, and piles of what had probably once been wall hangings or drapes.

He poked at the largest pile, over against the far wall with his broken halberd. Nothing but cloth.

Then he stopped in mid-poke. Maybe he could use this after all. There was a lot more of it here than normal and it was pretty dry. More than enough to make a nest for a human.

Wiz burrowed into the pile of cloth and rolled himself in the rags. He pulled up the hood of his cloak and drew another layer of cloth over him. The material was none too clean. It had been soaked repeatedly and Wiz was not the first creature to nest in it, but it kept out the chill and as his body heat warmed the cloth, Wiz stopped being cold for the first time since he had arrived. As the wind whistled and howled outside, his breathing steadied and he fell deeply asleep for the first time in days.

Voices woke him the next morning. Human voices in the same room.

Beneath the hood of the cloak he could see two men had entered the chamber—men who wore the black robes of the Dark League.

"He is here," the older one protested, "I can smell him!" He cast about like a hunting dog, his head turning this way and that as if he actually was smelling Wiz out.

"He was here," the other one corrected. "Do you see him in the room? Or do you think he has acquired a cloak of invisibility?"

Wiz dared not breathe.

The balding wizard straightened up. "This is foolishness anyway. Why not use spells to find this Sparrow? I have stood in his presence and I could locate him in minutes, even if Dzhir Kar could not."

The other waved a hand airily. "Oh, but that would not be sporting. Our Dread Master desires to have his amusement with this alien wizard before he dies. Think of it as a little something to pay him back for all that he has cost us." He smacked his lips and his eyes sparkled. "And would it not be delicious to have this one slain by magic, unable to use magic in his own defense? You have to admit, Seklos, it has a certain piquancy to it."

"Piquancy be damned! That—creature is dangerous and should be destroyed immediately. Do you play with a louse before you crack it between your fingers?" He looked narrowly at his companion. "Well, you might. And so might he. But it is still foolishness."

The younger wizard shook his head. "No sporting

blood. That's your problem, Seklos, you've got no sporting blood at all."

"What I've got," the older wizard said, "is a cold from tramping all over this pest-bedamned city. If it weren't for that, I could smell him even more sharply. Now come on. Let's see if we can track him down and end this charade."

He strode out through the other door with his companion still trailing behind, smiling tolerantly.

It was several minutes after they left that Wiz could even shiver.

*Thank God I don't snore!* Wiz thought numbly.

For a long time after they left, Wiz stayed huddled in the rags. His bladder was full to bursting, but he did not abandon his shelter for nearly an hour after the wizards left.

*They still should have seen me,* he thought as he wiggled out of his cocoon. He had been snuggled into the pile of cloth, but he hadn't been completely hidden. The storm had passed during the night and light in the room had been bright enough. But still the wizards had missed him completely.

He paused and listened at the door. The hall was empty and there was no sign or sound of the wizards who had come so close to him. It was full daylight now so he looked around one more time. The only thing he had missed was a cracked and broken mirror hanging askew on the wall. Most of the glass was missing, but the piece that remained reflected back the empty room.

*Only it's not empty! I'm here.* He looked closely at the mirror. The mirror fragment showed the room, but there was no sign of Wiz. It was as if he was not there.

A cloak of invisibility! That was why the magicians hadn't seen him. He looked in the mirror again, turning this way and that and admiring his lack of reflection.

He'd heard about cloaks of invisibility, but he had never seen one. What was it Moira called it? A tarncape.

That was what he had found. He laughed aloud and spun in a full circle, the cloak standing out from his body from the speed.

Then he froze. *Magic!* Wiz thought, his heart pounding, *I've been using magic!* But the demon hadn't come for him. He hadn't even felt the quiver he felt when he tried to frame a spell.

Wiz slumped into the corner, his back against the cold stone wall, and tried to think. What was it the wizard had said?

Of course! The demon wasn't looking for him, it was looking for the kind of magic he made. He knew that the output of his spell compiler "felt" different from normal magic, probably because each of his large spells was built up on many smaller spells—the "words" in his magic language.

But the tarncape wasn't magic he had made. It was someone else's magic he had found. It didn't register with the demon even when he used it. And that meant that he could use magic after all! Provided it was magic not of his making.

Wiz thought about it, but he didn't see how that helped much. Obviously most of the magical items in the City of Night had been carried off in the chaos that followed the Dark League's defeat. There were undoubtedly some things left, but he didn't know how to use them and magical implements did not come with users manuals. Worse, he wasn't a wizard in the conventional sense. He had no training in the usual forms of magic so he probably wouldn't recognize a magical object unless it bit him on the ankle.

*Still,* he thought, fingering the cloak, *there ought to be something I can do with this.*

The garden was beautiful this early, Moira thought. The sun painted the towers of the Wizards' Keep golden and made the colors of the pennons leap out against the blue of the sky. The dew still filmed the plants and made diamond sparkles on the grass and the occasional spider web. The air was cool and perfumed with the fragrance of roses.

Moira plucked a yellow one off the bush. Wiz had liked yellow roses on her. He thought they looked good against her red hair and fair skin and he especially liked her to wear them in her hair.

What was it he had told her? Some custom in his world where a woman wore a rose over the left ear to show she was taken and the right ear to show she was available. Or was it the other way around?

Moira smiled at the memory and bit her lip to keep from crying.

A shadow fell over her. She gasped and whirled to see Bal-Simba.

"Oh, Lord, you startled me. Merry met."

"Merry met, Lady."

"Is there any news?"

"None, I am afraid, but it is a related errand that brings me to you. Do you recall the three-demon searching spell Wiz created to seek news of you? I mentioned it to Jerry today and he says they have found no trace of such a spell in Wiz's notes."

Moira frowned. "None? I could have sworn he had something, at least the copies on parchment of the wooden slabs he wrote on at Heart's Ease when he created the spell."

"Jerry says there is nothing in the material he has. Is there anything they missed?"

The hedge witch shook her head.

"Nothing." Then she brightened. "But Lord, what about the searching system Wiz set up to find me? Could we not direct the searching demons to seek out Wiz?"

"We thought of that," Bal-Simba told her. "But it appears that the spell requires constant attention. The small searchers, the ones like wisps of dirty fog, are easily blown about by the wind. The larger ones drift as well, given time. A year's storms have scattered the demons beyond recall."

"And without the spell we cannot recreate the work." Unconsciously she crushed the rose in her grasp.

"Wait a minute! Lord, what about the spell Wiz used to find me in the dungeon?" Moira asked. "The Rapid Reconnaissance Direction Demon?"

Bal-Simba slapped his thigh and the sound rang off the walls. "Of course! It could search the entire World in hours."

A quick survey of the notes in the Bull Pen turned up the spell. With Jerry and several of the other programmers who hadn't yet turned in at their heels, Moira and Bal-Simba went out into the courtyard to put the spell in operation.

"Now then," Bal-Simba said to himself as he flipped between the pages where the spell was written, alternate lines on each page to prevent activating the spell by writing it down. "Hmmm, ah. Yes, very well." He faced into the courtyard, squinted into the morning sun and raised one hand.

"**class drone grep wiz**," he commanded in a ringing voice. There was soft "pop" and a squat demon appeared in the courtyard. Its cylindrical body was white, its domed top was blue and it supported itself on three stubby legs. "**exe!**" commanded Bal-Simba.

The demon emitted a despairing honk and fell forward on its face. A thin trickle of smoke curled out of its innards.

"Let me see that spell again," Bal-Simba said to Moira.

Three repetitions produced no better results. Once the demon simply froze, once it flashed off never to return and once it ran around in tight little circles emitting little beeps and squawks. At last Jerry listed out the spell to see if he could discover the difficulty.

"I think I see what's wrong," Jerry said finally. "But it's not going to be easy to fix."

"What is the problem?" Bal-Simba asked.

"The problem is that this code wasn't written for anyone else to use."

"You mean this spell is protected by magic?" Moira frowned. Such protections were not unknown on powerful spells.

"Worse," Jerry said glumly. "This code is protected by being write-only."

"Eh?" said Bal-Simba.

"Wiz hacked this thing together to do a specific job, right? From the looks of it he was in a tremendous hurry when he did it."

"I was a prisoner of the Dark League," Moira said in a small voice. "He wrote the spell to find me."

"Okay, he needed it fast. He never expected that anyone else would use it, he used the quickest, dirtiest methods he could find, he didn't worry about conforming to his language specification and he didn't bother commenting on it at all." Jerry looked at the glowing letters again and shook his head. "I don't think *he* could have understood this stuff a month after he wrote it and I don't have the faintest idea what is going on here."

"This," he said pointing to a single line of half a dozen symbols, "apparently does about four different things. Either that or it's some kind of weird jump instruction." He scowled at the code for a minute. "Anyway, the whole program is like that. I don't see three lines in a row any place in this that I understand."

"We do not need to understand the spell," Bal-Simba rumbled. "We only need to use it this once."

Jerry shook his head. "It's not that simple. What are the commands? What are the options you can use? How is it all supposed to work? You already tried this and it failed. Until we understand it we won't know why it failed."

"How long will it take you to find out?"

Jerry shrugged.

"I don't know. The hardest part of a job like this is always getting your head cranked around to see the other guy's way of doing things. Once you do that, sometimes it just falls right into place." He frowned. "And sometimes not. Anyway, I'll put a couple of people on it. I wouldn't count on being able to use this any time soon, though."

"Hopes raised and dashed before breakfast," Bal-Simba said as they walked across the courtyard. "I am sorry, My Lady. I thought surely we had found the answer."

Moira clenched her jaw and held her head high. Bal-Simba saw she was crying. "There is still one thing we may try," she said tightly. "I will go to Duke Aelric and plead for his help."

Bal-Simba stopped dead. "What?"

"Elven magic is much more powerful than human. Surely they can find him."

"I was under the impression that duke Aelric was already looking for Wiz."

"Then we can share what we know."

"Dealing with elves is dangerous," Bal-Simba said neutrally.

Moira flicked a grim little smile. "Madness, you mean. But Aelric seems to have a fondness for Wiz and I think he might listen to me."

"I ought to forbid you to do this."

Moira resumed walked. "Forbid away. But do not expect me to heed you."

The hill managed to be peaceful and foreboding at the same time. The moonlight played down on the wooded knoll, silvering the leaves of the trees and the grassy clearing before them.

But the moon also caught the megalith standing at the base of the hill where woods met grass. Three great stones, two upright and one laid across them like the lintel of a door. Was it only a trick of the moonlight that made the shadows within stir?

Moira licked her lips and pressed them firmly together. In spite of her cloak she was chill and she did not think the warm summer night had much to do with it. She took a firmer grip on her staff and strode boldly into the clearing.

"I wish to speak to Duke Aelric," she said loudly.

There was no response, no movement. The hill lay in the moonlight exactly as it had. Moira thought of repeating her request and decided against it. Elves were a touchy breed and much consumed with politeness. A human thought pushy or demanding would be in dire trouble.

"My Lady."

Moira jumped. Duke Aelric was standing in the moonlight in front of her. He wore a white doublet and hose embroidered with silver that glinted in the moonlight and a hip-length cloak of pale blue.

He regarded her with interest but without the warmth he had showed the last time they had met. Nor did it escape her notice that the elf duke had not welcomed her, merely acknowledged her presence.

She licked her lips. "My Lord, we need your help in finding Wiz."

Aelric arched a silver brow. "An elf helping mortals? An odd notion, Lady."

"It has been known to happen."

He gestured languidly. "So it has, when it is sufficiently amusing. I fail to see the amusement here."

That was the end of it then, Moira acknowledged as a cold lump congealed in her stomach. When Wiz and Moira had first met Aelric, she had told him that elves acted for their own reasons and no mortal was ever likely to untangle them. Standing here in the moonlight with the elf duke she began to appreciate how true that was.

Moira took a deep breath and gathered all her courage. "Lord, forgive me for mentioning this, but is it not true that your honor is involved as well? Wiz *did* disappear while travelling from your hold."

Aelric gave her a look that made her go weak in the knees. For a horrible instant she thought she had offended the elf.

"My honor is my own concern," he said coldly, "and not a matter for discussion with mortals. I know who kidnapped him and at the proper time they will feel the weight of my displeasure."

"But you will not help us find Wiz."

Again the chilling, haughty gaze. "Child, do you presume to instruct me?"

"No, Lord."

"Then guard your tongue more carefully." Duke Aelric softened slightly. "Besides, I cannot find him."

He smiled frostily. "That surprises you? It surprises me as well—and tells me that others besides mortals had a hand in this." He motioned fluidly, as if brushing away a fly. "However that is my concern, not yours."

"But you know who kidnapped him?"

"That too is my concern. Little one, among the ever-living revenge is artifice most carefully constructed and sprung only at the proper moment. These ones have offended me and they shall feel the weight of my displeasure at the proper time."

With a sinking feeling Moira realized that to an elf, "the proper time" could mean years—or centuries.

"Now if you will excuse me." He sketched a bow and Moira dropped a curtsey. When she looked up she was alone in the clearing.

Dzhir Kar eyed the man in front of him skeptically. "So you bring us the Sparrow's magic?" he said coldly.

"Yes, Lord," Pryddian said. One of the wizards holding him jabbed him sharply in the kidney with his staff. Pryddian gasped and jerked under the influence of the pain spell.

"Yes, master," he corrected himself. "I stole it from the Sparrow himself."

Pryddian was very much the worse for wear. Once he had been passed on to the Dark League's hidden lair he had been questioned. Since the questioning had been merely "rigorous" rather than "severe" he still had all his body parts and could still function. But his back was bruised and bloody, one eye was swollen shut and he was missing a few teeth. It had taken nearly three days before the wizards who had remained behind were convinced he was worth passing on to their master. His trip south had been expeditious rather than comfortable. Now he waited in the arms of his captors for the misshapen creature before him to decide his fate.

Dzhir Kar considered. It was not unknown for apprentices to decide the Dark League offered them more scope than the Northern wizards—rare, but not unheard of. Still, this was neither the time nor the place to add apprentices, especially ones so recently allied with the North. A quiet dagger between the ribs would have been the normal response to such presumption.

But still, a spell of the Sparrow's . . .

"What is this thing?" he asked, flipping through the parchments.

"It is a searching spell. The Sparrow used it to scan the world. It involves three kinds of demons, you see, and . . ." Pryddian gasped again as the wizard prodded him with the pain spell.

"Confine yourself to answering my questions," Dzhir Kar said.

"A searching spell," Pryddian gasped out. "It can search the whole World in a single day."

Dzhir Kar thought quickly. This just might be the answer to his problem. A host of demons could search the City of Night far better than his wizards could. He had a limited ability to train his demon to ignore specific instances of Sparrow's magic. If it could be trained to ignore these demons, then the combination of the

Sparrow's own magic and his demon could do in a single day what his wizards had been unable to do in a matter of weeks.

He waved his hands and the guards released Pryddian and stood away. The ex-apprentice slumped to the floor, his legs unable to support him.

"Very well," Dzhir Kar said. "It amuses me to use the Sparrow's magic to track him down. If you can produce these demons as you say then I will give you your life. Moreover, if they can find the Sparrow, you will be accepted as a novice by the Dark League.

"If you cannot do these things, I will see to it that you suffer for your presumption." He looked up at the wizards. "Take him away."

He nodded to the guards and they half-carried, half-dragged Pryddian out.

They gave Pryddian a cell just off the main workroom and he set out to duplicate Wiz's searching system. It was not a simple matter for an untutored ex-apprentice to unravel the notes he had stolen. Nor was it easy to cast the spells once he learned them. The Sparrow seemed to delight in alternate choices at every step of the spell and the wrong choices did little or nothing. But Pryddian worked until he dropped. His black-robed jailers saw to that with their pain spells.

It might have amused him to know he was not the only person having trouble with the Sparrow's spells.

"This guy was a real hacker," Mike said, leaning over his wife's shoulder to study their latest task.

Nancy nodded and looked back at the code above her desk. "You don't have to tell me that. Jesus! I've seen better commented programs in BASIC." She took another look at the runes glowing blue before her. "And I've seen clearer comments in the London Times crossword puzzle!" She jabbed her finger at one line.

"What the hell is this monstrosity? And why the hell did he name it **corned__beef**?"

"Jerry says the name is probably some kind of rotten pun. What does it do?"

"Basically it takes the value of the characters of a demon's name, multiplies them by a number, adds another number and then divides the result by 65,353. Then it uses that result as a subscript in some kind of an array." She shook her head again. "Why 65,353? Jesus! You know, if this guy doesn't come back we may never understand some of this stuff."

The man sighed. "Well, let's get to it. This is going to take a while." He nodded to Wiz's book of notes on his magic compiler. "Hand me the Dragon Book, will you?"

Ghost-gray and insubstantial, the searching demons began to pour from the ruined tower and blanket the City of Night.

Each demon had very little power. It could only absorb impressions from the world around it and forward them to a larger demon which would catalog them. The final step in the process was a demon formed like a weird crystal construct that perched atop the tower. It did the final sorting and alerted the wizards if it found anything that looked worthwhile.

Wiz had endowed the demons with all the mortal senses, but no magical ones. Of those senses, sight was the most important to an airborne creature. Since Wiz wore his tarncape constantly there was little visible sign of him. Demons by the thousands searched every nook and cranny of the city, but they saw nothing of Wiz.

Dzhir Kar ground his teeth in fury at the news and ordered Pryddian beaten to make him fix the spell. But Pryddian could not repair what he did not understand and in spite of the demons Wiz eluded the Dark League.

# Sixteen
## TROUBLE IN THE NORTH

*You can't unscramble an egg.*

—old saying

*You can if you're powerful enough.*

—the collected sayings of Wiz Zumwalt

Dragon Leader looked back over the flight in satisfaction. They weren't parade-perfect, but their spacing was good. Even his wingman was keeping his proper distance and holding position on the turns.

As he moved in easy rhythm with his mount's wing beats, he surveyed the forest below. The trees were dark green in their late summer foliage and the pattern was broken here and there by the lighter green of a natural meadow or the twisting channel of a brown stream wandering among the trees. This far north there were a lot of streams because the land got a lot of rain.

Today's patrol had had good weather all day, thank goodness, and if he was any judge of weather, tomorrow would be fair as well. Only a few clouds, all of them high enough still to be tinted golden by the setting sun—and scattered enough not to provide shelter for possible ambushers, Dragon Leader thought.

No likelihood of that, of course. There were no more enemy dragons. This was simply a routine patrol over

511

the northernmost reaches of the human lands—a pleasant summer's excursion for men and dragons alike.

Dragon Leader gave a hand signal and applied gentle knee pressure to his mount's neck. As his dragon swept around to the right the three other dragons in the flight followed, speeding up to hold their relative position. He noticed that his wingman held almost exactly the right distance and speed.

*The kid's shaping up,* he thought as the dragons swept over a heavily wooded ridge, so low they startled a flock of brightly colored birds out of one of the taller trees. *He'll have his own squadron yet.*

But that was for the future. Just over the next ridge was the Green River and on a bluff above a wide looping bend sat Whitewood Grove, the northernmost of the settlements and their destination for the night.

It didn't have a full aerie, but there was a covered roosting ground for the dragons and snug quarters with their own bath for the riders. Right about now, Dragon Leader reflected, that sounded pretty good.

Again the dragons swept up over a ridge, buoyed by the upwelling currents of air. Dragon Leader started to signal another wide turn to line up on the village. Then he froze in mid-gesture.

*What in the . . .*

There was the river and a bluff, but there was no village there. Instead the rise was crowned by a grove of large trees.

Could they be that far off course? Unlikely. Although the people of the World did not use maps as the term is commonly understood—the Law of Similarity made any map a magical instrument—they did have lists of landmarks. Dragon Leader had been checking them automatically and they had hit each landmark in turn. Besides, he had been to Whitewood Grove many times. He recognized the shape of the bluff, the bend in the river and the rapids just downstream. He even saw a snag near shore he recalled from his last visit. Everything was exactly as it should be except the village was missing.

The hairs on the back of his neck prickled and his mouth tasted of metal. Suddenly Dragon Leader was very, very alert.

Without using his communications crystal he signaled his flight to break into pairs. A wave of his arm sent the second pair climbing and circling wide around the area. Then with his wingman following he bored straight in to pass over the place where the village should be.

Splitting his forces like this was bad tactics and Dragon Leader didn't like it at all. But if he hadn't made a stupid mistake, then whatever had caused this was probably more than a match for four dragons. Splitting into pairs increased the chances that someone would get word back to the Council. For the first time since the patrol began, Dragon Leader wished he had an entire squadron of a dozen dragons behind him instead of a single flight of four.

They came in low and fast over the bluff, nearly brushing the tops of the trees. It appeared a perfectly ordinary grove of Whitewood trees. This was definitely the spot, but there was no sign of a village. No buildings, no ruins, not even any footpaths. He signaled his wingman and they swept back over the spot, quartering the site.

The village of Whitewood Grove was simply gone. The wharf was gone from the river and even the path that led from the wharf to the village was missing.

They circled the site while Dragon Leader considered. There was nothing on any checklist that applied to a situation like this. Looking over his shoulder at the place where the village of Whitewood Grove should have been, he made a decision.

"Second element, run for the patrol base," he said into his communications crystal. "Fly all night if you have to and as soon as you are over the ridge start reporting to

the Capital. Wingman, stay on perimeter patrol. I am
going to land and inspect the site on foot. If I am not
back in the air in one half of a day-tenth, run for the
patrol base. Now go!"

To his right and high above he saw the second element
break off and scoot for the ridge. He waited until they
were across before he turned his dragon inward toward
the bluff.

There was barely room to land a dragon on the very
tip of the bluff. The air currents off the river made it
tricky and his dragon didn't like the place at all. She
bridled and growled and tried to break off the approach
twice. He had to force her down and once on the ground
she would not settle. She kept her wings half-spread and
her neck extended high in the classic fighting posture.
The way she was breathing told Dragon Leader she was
building up for an enormous gout of flames.

Which was fine with Dragon Leader. An aroused
dragon is far from the worst thing to have at your back
in a tight spot.

Sword in hand, he scanned the trees while keeping
close to the dragon's bulk. The grove of Whitewoods
looked peaceful and quite unremarkable. The early
evening sun tinged their glossy green leaves with gold.
A slight breeze gently rustled through the branches.
Somewhere a bird sang and close to the grove's edge a
red squirrel jumped from branch to branch. The grove
exuded the faint, sweet aroma of Whitewood blossoms.

None of which made Dragon Leader or his dragon
feel any more secure. The dragon stayed poised for
combat and on cat feet Dragon Leader moved into the
wood.

The Whitewoods were fully mature, large enough that
he could not have put his arms around them at their
base. The litter on the forest floor was deep with dead
leaves and rotting vegetation. There were ferns and there
were many apples and here and there a purple forest

orchid. But there was not the least little sign of anything
that might possibly have once marked human habitation.

Warily Dragon Leader moved out of the grove,
keeping watch over his shoulder as if he expected
something to pounce on him at any minute. As quickly
as he could he mounted, wheeled his dragon and
launched her off the bluff. The dragon dived for the river
to gain air speed and Dragon Leader finished securing
himself to the saddle on the fly. As his wingman came
up to join him and the pair ran south for the patrol base,
he realized his jerkin was soaked with sweat.

For the first time since the war with the Dark League
ended, Dragon Leader was very, very frightened.

Arianne gasped when Bal-Simba told her of the dragon
rider's report.

"Lord, what could have caused this?"

"I have not the slightest idea," Bal-Simba told her. "I
have never heard of such a thing."

The blonde witch thought hard for a moment. "How
many others know of this?"

"In the Capital? So far just two Watchers, you and
I."

"Then if I may suggest Lord, perhaps it would be best
if we kept it a secret for now."

Bal-Simba nodded. "The Watchers are already sworn
to secrecy. But that does not help us get our people
back—if they can be gotten back. Nor will it prevent such
things in the future."

"Such an attack must have been provoked by the
changes on the Fringe," Arianne said slowly. "Else this
would have happened before."

"Once again, my thinking. But what provoked it? And
what was provoked?"

"Perhaps the elves could tell us."

Bal-Simba snorted like a bull. "You grasp at straws."
Then his expression softened. "Besides, I have climbed

all over that notion and can find no way in. The elves will have nothing to do with any mortal except Wiz. And even if they would, I doubt I could convince them of our sincerity."

"Will not your word suffice as president of the Council of the North?" Arianne asked him.

"You know the answer to that, Lady," Bal-Simba rumbled. "I am not the mightiest magician among us, and the Council's power ebbs as people realize they do not stand in constant need of us. Wiz may be the most junior member of the Council, but he is our most powerful magician and our best hope for correcting what is wrong."

Arianne shuddered. "So if we do not find him, we face war."

"We must do more than find him, Lady," Bal-Simba said. "We must find him alive and sound."

# Seventeen

# EVERYTHING WILD

*Magic is real—unless declared integer.*
       *—from the collected sayings of Wiz Zumwalt*

"Okay, deal."

Karl, Judith, Mike and Nancy were seated around
the table in the Wizard's Day Room, settling in for a
quiet session of bridge. Ignoring the glares of the half-
dozen or so wizards present, they had pulled a table
from its accustomed place and brought chairs in around
it.

Mike opened a fresh pack of cards and dealt the first
hand with his wife Nancy as the dummy.

Nancy organized her hand and frowned. Every card
she held was a heart. By some weird happenstance, she
had drawn the entire suite of hearts!

"Damn, what a time to be dummy!"

Then she looked up and saw the strange expressions
on the other players' faces.

"What's wrong?"

Wordlessly, Mike laid down his hand, face up. Karl
and Judith followed suit. Mike had gotten every club,
Judith had all the diamonds and Karl had all the spades.

"Jesus!" Nancy breathed. "Are you sure you shuffled
those cards?"

"You saw me," Karl said. "My lord! I wonder what the odds are on that happening?"

"Astronomical," Judith said softly. "Simply astronomical."

They all looked at the cards for a minute.

"Well," Mike said finally. "Let's shuffle and get down to play."

He raked in the four hands and took great care to shuffle the deck thoroughly. Then he dealt them out again.

Nancy picked up her hand, looked at them, and threw them down. "Shit," she said informatively.

The others followed suit. This time Nancy had gotten all the clubs, Karl had the diamonds, Mike had the hearts and Judith had the spades.

"This isn't working," Karl said finally. "Somehow the magic in this place is interfering with the shuffle." He looked at the four piles of cards on the table and made a face. "Do you still want to play?"

"If we can find something that we can play," Judith said. "I don't think bridge is going to do it."

"How about poker?" Mike asked. "We could play for matches or something."

"I don't really know how to play poker," Judith protested.

"We'll make it easy," Mike told her. "Five-card draw."

This time Karl shuffled the cards and dealt the first hand. Then he picked up his cards and looked at them.

The hand was assorted, but it was a dog. Not even a pair and no card higher than a five. Well, that was okay too. Karl played poker for the long haul and the first hand of the game was a good place to find out how the other players would react to a bluff.

Suddenly the top of his head felt wet.

Karl looked up and saw that a tiny thundercloud, no bigger than his hand, had formed above his head. A miniature bolt of lightning flashed from peak to fluffy gray peak and a fine mist of rain settled on him.

"Let me guess," Nancy said. "You got the low hand."

Karl threw down his cards in disgust. "I don't think this universe is designed for card playing."

"Wait a minute," Mike said. "Let's try something that's more strategy and less pure luck of the draw. You ever played Texas Hold 'em?"

"That's a version of seven-card stud isn't it?" Karl asked.

"I don't know," Judith said. "I've never played stud poker."

"It's easy," Nancy told her. "You deal three cards to each player and four face down in the middle of the table. You try to make the best hand with the cards in your hand and the four on the table. You bet after the deal and then again after each card is turned. I'll help you with the first hand, if you like."

"And," Mike continued, "it's got the advantage that the outcome depends on the cards on the table more than the cards in your hand. That and your betting skill."

They had no chips, and matchsticks were not a part of this world, but they appropriated a bowl of unshelled nuts from the sideboard by the port, ignoring the audible sniffs of the wizards.

Again Mike shuffled the cards and dealt.

"Three filberts."

"I'll see your filberts and raise you a brazil nut," Judith said. She looked at the zebra-striped nut in her hand. "At least I think it's a brazil nut."

"What did we say, five pecans to a brazil nut?" asked Nancy, shoving into the pile of squirrel fodder.

"Ace," Mike said, flipping the card. "Place your bets."

They went around the table with everyone betting moderately. Mike reached out and flipped the second card.

"Ace again."

Nancy made a strangled sound.

"What's wrong?" her husband asked.

"Just keep going," Nancy said, staring at the cards.

Again everyone bet and again Mike flipped a card.

"Another ace . . . wait a minute!"

There on the table face up were an ace of clubs and ace of diamonds. The last card was the ace of spades.

"What the hell . . ."

He pulled a card from his hand and threw it face up on the table. An ace of spades.

"That makes seven aces," Nancy said, throwing down her and Judith's hands.

"No, nine," Karl said, adding his cards to the pile.

"Ten," Mike said bitterly, adding another ace from his hand. "Come on guys, let's go watch the sunset or something."

Over in the corner Malus and Honorious watched them leave.

"What do you suppose that was all about?"

"Obviously a divination of some sort." He shook his head. "I do not think they like the outcome."

"I wonder what it portends?" said Agricolus coming over to join them.

"Nothing good, I warrant you," said Juvian from his seat near the window. "I thought the Sparrow was bad with his strange magics and alien ways. Now we have near a score of them and they are all more fey than the Sparrow ever was."

"And they left the table and chairs out of place," Honorious snapped, ringing a silver bell to summon a servant to put them back. "Encroaching mushrooms. No manners at all."

"It is a plague! A veritable plague," Agricolus said.

Juvian, Malus and Honorious all nodded in glum agreement.

"Worse than that, perhaps," said Petronus, a wizard with thinning hair and a pronounced widow's peak, sitting apart from the others. "How much do we know of what these strangers do?"

"They have explained . . ." Agricolus started.

"Did you understand the explanation?"

"Well . . ."

"Just so. They labor endlessly in the very citadel of the North and foist us off with explanations none can understand. Meanwhile non-mortals everywhere prepare against us."

"Do you think something is amiss?" asked Malus.

"And you do not? We stand on the brink of a war of extermination that is somehow bound up with the Sparrow and we let his cohorts work in our very midst doing things they will not explain." He slapped his hand on his knee with a sharp crack. "If these strangers are so powerful, let them give us clear proof and reasonable explanations. As members of the Council of the North we should demand it of them."

"That would be a task for the president of the Council," Agricolus said.

"And I mean to talk to him about it. Now." He rose and bowed to his fellows. "My Lords." With that he swept out of the room.

"He does have a point," Honorious said, lowering his voice as the servant came into the Day Room and started moving the furniture back. "They should not hide what they are doing from us."

"I am not sure they are hiding from us," Malus said slowly.

"Do you mean you believe that rubbish, that, that 'spell compiler'?" Honorious snorted. "If so, I have an elixir of Immortality I wish to discuss with you."

The pudgy little wizard frowned. "I did not believe it when there was just the Sparrow and his wild talk. But now? All these newcomers can work magic, all their magic feels like the Sparrow's."

"They are all from his land," Agricolus pointed out.

"And they all claim that anyone can learn this magic," Malus countered. "Perhaps they are telling the truth."

"If they are telling the truth then why can not any of us grasp the essence of this thing?" Agricolus demanded.

"Perhaps we have not tried hard enough," Malus said. "We can hardly be said to have approached the Sparrow's magic with the same openness we would apply to learning a new spell from one of the Mighty."

Honorious snorted again.

"Well," the little wizard said, "I do not put it forward as fact, only as speculation." He put both hands on the arms of his chair and levered himself erect. "My Lords, I must return to my own work."

"There may be something in what he says," Agricolus said after a moment.

"Fortuna!" exclaimed Honorious. "Not you too?"

Agricolus shrugged. "I pride myself on having an open mind."

"And I find myself in a world gone mad!" Honorious retorted, ostentatiously picking up the scroll he had laid aside when the conversation began.

"My Lord, I think we have a problem," Moira told Karl when she found him in the Bull Pen the next morning.

"You mean another problem," he said looking up from the stack of wood strips he was pawing through. "What now? Can't you get us more parchment?"

"No, not that—although that will be a problem if your people don't start using slates for simple notes. This is more serious, I think."

"Won't it wait until Jerry gets in, eh? Well, lay it on me."

"Some members of the Council have formally petitioned to have your work stopped until they are satisfied that what you do is safe and effective." She made a face. "Forever, in other words."

"But why?"

"Oh, many reasons. Jealousy is one of them. Some of the Council fears any change. But mostly I think because none of them understand what you do."

"But they must have some idea. I thought Wiz had been teaching classes all along."

"Oh, he was. That is part of the problem. Your magic is so complicated and your ways of thinking so alien none of our wizards were able to learn what Wiz tried to teach them.

"Some of them claim his teaching was a smoke screen, designed to hide the real secret of his magic. But I know that is not so. He struggled hard to teach us and none of us could learn."

Jerry tapped a scroll thoughtfully against his cheek. "Well, programming sure isn't the easiest thing around, but it's not near that hard."

"For you perhaps. For us even the simplest things dissolve into confusion."

"Give me an example."

Moira paused and frowned. Very prettily, Karl thought. For the hundredth time he regretted she was taken.

"Well, there are these variables that are named one thing, called another thing and have a value of something else. Wiz must have explained that to me once a moon and I still don't think I understand it."

"Oh boy, I'm not surprised at that one," Karl told her. "It's near the trickiest notion in programming and it's something that confuses a lot of people. But it's still not that hard for someone who's got what it takes to be a wizard."

"Very well then," Moira said. "Can you explain it to me?"

Karl sighed. The clearest explanation he had ever seen n the subject started with a quotation from Tweedledee and Tweedledum in *Alice in Wonderland*—and the quotation was very apt.

He thought for a minute.

"Okay, look," he said. "You have a true name, right? A name that is uniquely yours and must be kept secret because it identifies you exactly?"

Moira thought for a moment and decided to ignore the rude and prying nature of the question. "I do," she admitted.

"But your true name isn't 'Moira,' is it? Moira's just what people call you?"

"Yes."

"And most people address you as 'Lady' because you're a witch. That is, you belong to the class of witches, right?"

"Yes," said Moira, who was beginning to see where this led.

"All right then," Karl said. "You are named one thing, you are called something else and you're an instantiation of a class called yet another thing." He grinned. "Then you get someone like Wiz, who is Sparrow to most people, Wiz to his friends, is an instantiation of the class of magicians and has a true name. Each of them is different and each of them applies in slightly different circumstances.

"It's the same in programming. A variable is an instantiation of a class, like integers, and it has its own name that uniquely identifies it, like a true name. At any given time it also has a value, which is what it actually *is* just then, but which can change with circumstances. Finally, it can also be known by other names in other circumstances and it can be referred to by a pointer, the way 'Moira' points to you without using your true name. See?"

Moira stood open-mouthed. "You mean *that's* what Wiz was trying to show me?" she asked incredulously. "That's all there is to it?"

Karl shrugged. "Pretty much."

"But that's so *simple*. Why didn't he just say that?"

"Probably because he never thought of it that way. From what everyone says Wiz was a master class hacker and hackers just don't think in those terms." He grinned. "We have a saying about people like your Wiz. Ask them what time it is and they'll tell you how to build a clock." Jerry put the scroll back on the pile.

"Now I'd like to ask you something. What did you mean just now when you said you don't think the way we do?"

"We do not generalize the way your people do."

"Who says so?"

"Why, Wiz."

"I think Wiz is wrong. You don't generalize the way Wiz does, but then most people don't. You're oriented to language, not mathematics. One of the things that confuses it is you're very careful in your speech. You don't use metaphors and similes in the way we do, probably because your language can directly affect the world around you. You can make magic by accident."

Moira thought hard.

"Then you think we can learn this new magic?"

"I'm sure of it. Oh, you'll probably struggle like an English major in a calculus class, but you can get it if you're willing to work at it."

"How is it you are so much more skilled at explaining all this?" Moira asked.

"Oh, that. I was a high school teacher for a while."

"A teacher? Then why did you become—whatever you are?"

Karl grinned ruefully. "Kind of a long story. Seems I started out to be an engineer and in my junior year I decided I'd rather be a teacher. So I switched majors and got my degree in education."

He looked out the window and sighed. "Well, after I had taught math for a couple of years, our high school got an inspection by the accreditation commission. I had more than enough math courses to teach math, but most of them were taken as engineering courses. So the accreditation commission decided they didn't count. I could either go back to college and take twenty-four hours of math courses I'd already had or I wouldn't be certified to teach math and that would count against the school's rating."

"You mean you were not a good teacher?" Moira asked.

"Oh no. I was a very good teacher. The accreditation commission rated my classroom performance 'superior'. But I had taken all my math courses with an ENG prefix instead of a MA prefix."

The hedge witch frowned. "Forgive me, My Lord, but I do not understand."

Karl sighed. "Neither did I. That's why I took a job as a software engineer—for twice as much money."

Moira thought hard for a moment.

"My Lord would you be willing to take on an additional duty? Would you be willing to teach this to others?"

Karl's mouth quirked. "In my copious spare time?"

"It would do much to ease the suspicion and mistrust."

Karl thought about it for a moment. "I guess I can spare an hour or so a day."

"Thank you, My Lord. In the meantime, you can expect a formal visit from representatives of the Council sometime very soon."

"Ducky," Karl said with a noticeable lack of enthusiasm. "Just what we need. A project review."

# *Eighteen*
## PLAYING IN THE BULLPEN

*Any sufficiently advanced technology is indistinguishable
from magic.*

—Clarke's law

*Any sufficiently advanced magic is indistinguishable
from technology.*

—Murphy's reformulation of Clarke's law

*Any sufficiently advanced magic is indistinguishable
from a rigged demonstration.*

—programmers' restatement of Murphy's
reformulation of Clarke

"We've got a good team," Jerry told the wizards as
they walked toward the converted cow barn, now known
universally as the Bullpen.

The late afternoon sun slanted golden across the court
and the air smelled of warm flagstones and dust, with
just a tinge of manure to remind them of the Bullpen's
original purpose.

Jerry kept up a flow of half-defensive small talk, Bal-
Simba was soothing and the other two, Malus and
Petronus, were distinctly cold.

"Have you had trouble adapting?" Bal-Simba asked.

"Some. It turns out that there's a strong psychological
component here. What a piece of code—a spell—does

527

is constrained by its structure, but its manifestation, the demon it creates, is strongly influenced by the outlook and attitude of the programmer." He sighed. "It's tough, but we're making good progress."

"We have confidence in you, of course," the giant black magician told him. "But the Council has a responsibility to oversee any use of magic in the North."

"And to see that magic is used wisely and safely," Malus said pointedly.

"Naturally we're glad to have you, but there probably won't be much to see," Jerry told him. *I hope,* he added to himself.

Bal-Simba nodded amicably. Actually the visit was about as casual as a surprise inspection by a team of Defense Department auditors, but part of the game was to pretend otherwise.

"There have been certain questions about your performance," Bal-Simba said as they approached the door. "I fear you have not made the best possible impression."

"With all due respect, Lord, we didn't choose our programmers to make a good impression. You need a difficult job done on a very tight schedule and we got the best people we could. I'm sorry that we aren't more presentable, but the most talented people are often a little eccentric."

Bal-Simba nodded, thinking of some of the peculiarities of his fellow wizards.

"Some say your people are as flighty as the Little Folk," Petronus said as they reached the door to the barn.

"That's because they don't know them," Jerry said, reaching out to open the small door set in the larger one. "People who do what we do tend to be very concentrated on their work. They may seem a little strange to anyone on the outside, but their main goal is always to get the job done. We've got a good team here and they're a pretty serious bunch."

He motioned Bal-Simba and the others ahead of him. The black giant ducked his head and stepped over the sill.

They stood together at the threshold to let their eyes adjust to the dim light. The barn still smelled of hay, grain and cattle, a dusty odor that tickled the back of the nose but not unpleasantly.

"Welcome to the . . ." Jerry's head jerked back as something zoomed past his nose, climbing almost straight up.

It was a Mirage jet fighter no bigger than his thumb. As it topped out of its climb it fired two toothpick-sized missiles toward the ceiling. There above them a half-dozen tiny airplanes were mixing it up in an aerial melee. One of the Mirage's missiles caught a miniature Mig-21 and blew its tail away. A tiny ejection seat popped out of the plane as it spiraled helplessly toward the flagstone floor and an equally tiny parachute blossomed carrying the pilot down to safety.

Jerry and the wizards gaped.

A two-inch-long F-16 peeled off from the dogfight and dove at Jerry's head.

*"Now cut that out!"* Jerry roared. The fighters vanished with soft pops and there was a snickering from one corner of the Bullpen.

Bal-Simba stared off at the wall and carefully avoided saying anything.

"Ah, yes," Jerry said. "Well, ah, this is where we work."

The central aisle of the barn was taken up by a plank-and-sawhorse table piled high with books, scrolls, blank sheets of parchment, inkpots, quills and wooden tablets marked and unmarked. At the far end of the barn the whitewashed wall was streaked and smudged from being used as an impromptu whiteboard. Next to the wall sat a waist-high brazier warming an enormous pot of blackmoss tea.

The stalls were on either side of the aisles and each stall held a littered trestle table and a chair. Most of them also held at least one programmer.

"All these ones are working on one great spell?" the giant magician asked dubiously.

"Yes, Lord. We divide the work so each of us has a specific part. Our first week here was spent doing systems analysis and producing a design document so we'd all know what we were doing."

Jerry gestured at the long table. "This is our central library. We keep the project documentation and specs here where we can all consult them."

Petronus reached out to examine a large book on top of the pile. Just as his fingers touched it, the pile shifted and hissed at him. He yanked his hand back as a scaly head on a long neck rose out of the mass and slitted yellow eyes transfixed him. Sinuously a small dragon flowed out of its lair among the books. It was bigger than the beast which had guarded Wiz's original book, perhaps two feet long. Its scales were the same vivid red, but they were tinged with blue along the edges. It eyed Bal-Simba with suspicious disapproval.

"Another demon?" the wizard asked.

"No, that's a real dragon. Wandered in here one day and decided it liked it."

"Hunts mice real good," Danny volunteered.

Petronus sniffed and the group moved on. The dragon whuffed suspiciously, decided these people bore watching, and trailed after them, eyeing the hem of Petronus's robe speculatively.

Jerry scanned the cubicles desperately for someone to show off. Cindy Naismith's feminist manner was likely to offend them, Larry Fox hadn't had a bath since they arrived and Danny was too big a risk to even consider. Finally he saw Karl was in his cubicle and steered the group, dragon and all, in there.

"This is Karl Dershowitz, one of our programmers. Karl, you know Bal-Simba and these are, ah, Malus and Petronius."

"Petronus," the wizard corrected, stonefaced.

"Ah, yes. Petronus. Anyway, they're here observing today and I wanted to show them what you were doing."

Bal-Simba pushed into the stall until he stood directly behind Karl. "What have you there?" he asked.

"I'm working on a sequencing module," Karl told them, slightly awed by Bal-Simba's bulk and pointed teeth. "This is the part that reports conflicts between the different processors."

"And this is the—ah—sequencer?" Bal-Simba gestured at what sat on the desk.

"No, this is a debugging tool. Each of these demons monitors one of the versions of the code and reports any destructive interactions."

Sitting on Karl's desk were three monkeys. One had his paws clasped tightly over its ears, another had its eyes clinched shut and the third was covering its mouth. "Hear-no-see-no-speak-no-evil," Karl said. "That means everything's running fine."

"There's something familiar about those three," Jerry said. "Something in their faces."

Karl looked sheepish. "Well, yeah. That kinda just happened."

The monkey demon in the middle suddenly opened his eyes and glared at the one to his left. He reached out and poked his fingers in the other's eyes. The demon recoiled and then grabbed his tormentor by the nose, twisting it sideways and leading him around the desk. The third monkey broke up laughing at the sight and the first two turned on him.

"Okay," Karl said, "we've got a conflict here. One of the processors jumped the queue and grabbed a resource intended for another one. When they got locked in contention the third processor got more than his share of resources."

He looked down at the orgy of eye-poking, nose-twisting and noggin-bopping going on on his desk.

"*Now* I recognize them," Jerry said.

"Uh huh," Karl said. "I've got the sound turned off. Otherwise it gets kinda noisy in here."

They watched the byplay between the monkey demons for a while longer.

"I know I'm going to regret asking this," Jerry said at last, "but what's the name of that module?"

"That's the Scheduling Transport Operating-system Object Generator and Editing System."

Jerry's lips moved as he worked out the acronym. Then closed his eyes. "I *knew* I was going to be sorry I asked."

The group backed out of the stall and moved down to the end of the aisle. Several benches had been arranged about the section used as a whiteboard. Jerry gestured for them to sit.

The dragon had decided Jerry and Bal-Simba were all right. He crowded close to Jerry's legs and bumped his head insistently on his calf. Absently, Jerry reached down and scratched him on the scales behind his pointed ears.

"Have some tea?"

Bal-Simba's nose wrinkled. I thank you, no." The others also shook their heads and the wizards started to sit down.

The dragon sighed luxuriously and pressed harder against Jerry's legs, forcing him to shift his stance or be knocked off balance. Jerry sat down on the bench harder than he intended, causing the other end to jump up and smack Petronus on the bottom as he sat down. The wizard glared, Jerry reddened and the dragon wuffed insistently, demanding more scratching.

"I want to apologize. Things aren't usually this lively."

"I should hope not," Petronus said.

"Quite a display," Malus said. "Attacked by a swarm of miniature demons as soon as we entered."

"Oh, they weren't attacking us," Jerry assured him. "They were playing a game. The idea is to shoot down your opponent's fighter."

"Your *opponent's* fighter?" asked Bal-Simba. "You mean those demons were not self-motivated?"

"Oh no. What would be the fun of that? The idea is to outfly the other guy."

"So each of those—fighters?—was directly controlled by a magician."

"Sure. At least most of them are. A few were probably drones thrown in to improve the dogfight simulation, but . . ."

"Dogs?" asked Malus. "You call those dogs?"

"Well, no, but it's called a dogfight you see, and . . ."

"If the creatures who are fighting are not dogs, why call it a dogfight?" The pudgy wizard waggled his finger at Jerry. "Confusion. That's what this new magic of yours does, it sows confusion everywhere."

"No, you see . . ." But he was interrupted before he could get any further.

"Fox," a female voice proclaimed from the other end of the Bull Pen, "that's disgusting!"

Cindy Naismith came striding down the aisle, eyes blazing, with Larry Fox trailing behind her.

"Jerry, I want you to do something about this right now!"

"Cindy, can't you see we're having a meeting?"

"Now!" Cindy demanded.

Jerry turned to the wizards. "Ah, excuse me, Lords." Then he faced Cindy and Larry. "Let's go talk, shall we?" and he herded them down to the opposite end of the Bull Pen.

"What the hell is this all about?" Jerry hissed as soon as they were safely away from the inspection party.

"It's about the so-called user interface this cretin wrote for the front end."

"The code's in spec," Larry said sullenly.

"Spec my ass!" Cindy blazed. "That routine is pornographic and demeaning to women!"

"Pornographic code?" Jerry asked, totally bewildered.

"Here," Cindy said. "See for yourself!" She turned and gestured to call up the demon. There was a small billow of pinkish smoke above the central table. It writhed and coalesced into solid flesh. Very solid and very pink.

Jerry gaped. "Holy shit!"

The demon was gorgeous, voluptuous and totally nude. A mass of blue-black hair spilled down over her shoulders, her blue eyes were alight with amusement and promise. She smiled at her watchers and ran a pink tongue tip over her blood-red lips in a way that was blatant invitation. Then she stretched and reclined on the table in a way that made her enormous breasts ride even higher on her ribcage and her dark nipples stick out like strawberries.

In the small part of his mind that was not totally occupied by the vision stretched out on the table, Jerry realized that all three wizards could see what was going on. In fact Malus was standing on the bench and craning his neck to get a better view.

"It gets worse," Cindy said. "You should *see* the things she does!"

"Yeah," breathed Jerry. "I mean, no. Of course not!" The demon shifted her shoulders and pointed her delicate toes at him, still smiling.

"Well, it's supposed to be user-friendly," Larry said in an aggrieved tone. "Hey, I offered to do a male version. Tom Selleck or something. But noooo, she wants to spoil everyone's fun."

"If that's your idea of fun . . ."

The demon smiled again and scissored her legs in a way that showed off her dark pubic patch.

"That's enough!" Jerry said sharply, tearing his eyes away from the demon.

"Look," Jerry mumbled, examining his shoelaces, "this module is supposed to help the user, not distract him. Do some work on that interface, all right?"

As Jerry walked away he heard Danny whisper urgently. "Hey Larry, give me that code, will you?"

"Sorry about the interruption," Jerry said as he came back to the wizards. "Now, let me show you what you came to see."

"I think we have seen enough of this—this circus!" Petronus said.

"Quite enough," Bal-Simba agreed amicably. "My Lord, could you create a demon so obedient to your commands as the ones we saw when we first came in?"

Petronus froze. "I would not demean myself . . ."

"But if you wished to, could you?" he shook his head. "I could not, I know. Have you ever seen a demon so instantly responsive?"

"No," Petronus finally admitted. "No, I have not."

Bal-Simba turned to Jerry. "And how long did it take to create that swarm of demons?"

"Hey Danny," Jerry called out, "how long did it take you to write that air combat game?"

Danny stuck his head around the corner of his cubicle. "Jeez, Jerry, you always assume . . ."

"How long, Danny?" Jerry said inexorably.

The young programmer shrugged. "Oh, maybe four hours."

"You see," Bal-Simba said to his fellow wizards. "In less time than it takes us to frame a moderately complex spell, this young one created a dozen demons whose subtlety we cannot match. This shows the worth of the effort, I think."

Petronus snorted. "Trinkets. A handful of magical trinkets."

Bal-Simba shifted his bulk and the bench teetered alarmingly. "You would rather they write their spells large for practice? Or released them outside the confines of this building? No, I think their wisdom in making trinkets is manifest."

"Well," said Malus, looking longingly down the table

toward the spot where the "user interface" had been, "they are certainly accomplishing *something*."

"It is obvious they are accomplishing a great deal," Bal-Simba said. "I think their work should continue unhindered."

Petronus looked from Bal-Simba to Malus. "Oh very well," he said at last. "I only hope we do not regret this afternoon's work." He rose and bowed to his colleagues. "My Lords, if you will forgive me, my own work presses." He turned and stalked the length of the Bull Pen without a backward glance.

"I too must be gone," said Malus. "Unless you have another demonstration?" he asked hopefully.

"No," Jerry said firmly. "Thank you for coming, Lord." Malus bowed and followed his colleague out.

"Thanks, Lord," Jerry said to Bal-Simba as the dumpy wizard pulled the door shut behind him.

"Petronus is firm in resolution, but not subtle in debate," Bal-Simba said, smiling to show off his filed teeth. "He gave me an opportunity and I took it." Then he sobered. "Besides, I was afraid of what might happen if we stayed within a moment longer."

"You and me both, Lord," Jerry agreed fervently.

Bal-Simba rose and Jerry rose with him. "I admit I had some misgivings, but it did not go badly, I think."

"I had a few misgivings myself. Uh, we really are making progress. I can show you if you want."

Bal-Simba chuckled. "Oh, I believe you, Lord. And no, it is not necessary to show me. I trust you and I doubt I would understand half of it."

Jerry followed the huge wizard to the door lost in thought.

"You look as if you have something pressing upon your mind," Bal-Simba said as he held the door for him.

"Well, yes Lord," Jerry said as they stepped out into the courtyard. He sighed. "Look, I know this is a new environment and it's a completely different culture and all, and I know that even the laws of nature are different here." He stopped and for an instant looked as if he might cry. "But Lord, this place gets weirder every day!"

Bal-Simba nodded and looked back at the Bull Pen. "My thought precisely," he said in a bemused tone.

Wiz eased his way down the corridor, hugging the wall and keeping a tight grip on his rusty halberd head. Somewhere off in the distance he could hear the faint drip, drip, drip of water. Dripping water meant running water and running water was likely to be cleaner than the foul musty slop he had found so far. So in spite of his misgivings, Wiz pressed on. It was so cold his breath hung in puffs before him. Short, sharp puffs because Wiz was panting from fear.

The corridor was utterly still and completely empty. Save for the soft dripping and the even softer pad of his own feet there was no sound at all. When he stopped the quiet pressed in around him like a smothering cloak.

Most of the lanterns in the stretch still worked, albeit dimly, holding the dark at bay and leaving the shadows as patches in the corners, to writhe threateningly each time the lamps flickered.

At first Wiz thought the patch ahead of him was another shadow. But it did not shift or vanish as he approached. In the dim light he was almost on top of it before he realized what it was.

In the center of the corridor lay a bloody heap of dark robes wrapped about a thing which might have been a wizard. The head had been smashed like a melon and there was a smear of blood and yellowish brains on the wall beside the corpse. The arms and legs stuck out at impossible angles and the torso was bent backwards as if it had been broken like a dry stick over a giant knee.

Wiz gasped and shrank back against the wall. There were killers aplenty in the ruins, he knew, but nothing

he had seen or heard that had the power to take a
wizard—or the sheer ferocity to do this.

Then Wiz looked more closely. There was steam rising
from the sundered torso, steam from the shattered skull
as the corpse gave up its body heat to the surrounding
cold. There were even faint wisps of steam coming from
the pools of blood surrounding the remains. The wizard
had been dead for only minutes. Whatever had done this
had to be nearby.

Wiz turned and ran, all thoughts of fresh water
forgotten.

# *Nineteen*
## HALF-FAST STANDARD TIME

*Putting twice as many programmers on a project that is late
will make it twice as late.*

*—Brooks' law of programming projects*

"Good morning," Karl said as he walked into his
makeshift classroom.

The faces of his pupils showed they didn't think there
was anything good about it. Their expressions ranged
from grim determination to equally grim disapproval. He
didn't know what methods Moira and Bal-Simba had used
to round up the dozen or so blue-robed wizards who
were sitting at the rows of tables in front of him, but
he had heard hints of everything from cajolery to
blackmail.

*Well,* Karl thought as he turned back to the black-
board. *At least I don't have to worry about this bunch
throwing spitballs.* He turned around to face the grim-
looking men and women in their magician's robes.
*Lightning bolts maybe, but no spitballs.*

"Okay," he said. "Let's go back and review some
basics."

"You sent for me, Lord?" Jerry Andrews asked as he
knocked on the door of Bal-Simba's study.

The black wizard looked up. "I did. Please come in and close the door."

*Uh-oh, one of those meetings!* Jerry thought as he complied.

"I wanted to find out if there was any way you can speed up your project," Bal-Simba said as soon as Jerry sat down.

"Lord, as I told you at our first meeting, this will take time. We have accomplished an amazing amount, largely because you have been willing to let us alone to get on with it. We're way ahead of any reasonable schedule on this project, but we're still only about forty percent done. It just takes time, Lord."

"I know," Bal-Simba said. "But there have been some, ah, changes since our first meeting. You know that we face the possibility of war with the elves and others?"

Jerry nodded.

"What I tell you now is not common knowledge and I would keep it so. In the past three days we have lost two northern villages."

Jerry's eyes widened. "You mean they were invaded?"

Bal-Simba smiled mirthlessly. "I mean we lost them. They are not there any more. Where they stood is virgin forest once again."

"That's scary."

"Perhaps more frightening than you know. Our watchers and other magicians had not the slightest hint that anything was amiss. There was not the least quiver, not a sign that magic was at work."

"That's *real* scary."

"That is also why I wish to keep it quiet for the time being. But you see why we must have your new magic, and have it soon.

"If we had this we could use it as evidence to help us bargain. Or as a weapon should the bargaining fail. In either event, we *must* have it quickly."

Jerry thought hard. Pressure to complete a project

early was nothing new and he had been in a few situations where the fate of the company depended on it. But this was the first time being late with a project meant war.

"How fast do you need it?"

"We need it today," Bal-Simba said. "But the need will be critical in a moon or less."

"We'll try," he said finally. "We'll try like hell, but there's no way we can have a working project in that amount of time."

"I understand," Bal-Simba said heavily. "Be assured that if it comes to open war we will return you and the others to your World before matters come to a head."

"Thanks," Jerry said uncomfortably. "Lord, you do understand that we're working as fast as we can? There's just not much more we can do."

"I do understand that and I thank you for your efforts. Meanwhile, is there anything we can do to make your job easier?"

Jerry made a wry face. "I don't suppose you could come up with a forty-eight-hour day, could you?"

"Would that help?" Bal-Simba asked.

Jerry froze. "You mean you *can* come up with a forty-eight-hour day?"

"No," the huge wizard said sadly. "Only a spell makes a night stretch to twice its normal length. The great wizard Oblius created it for his wedding night. It did not help him for he discovered that his reach exceeded his grasp—so to speak." He shrugged. "I do not think it would aid us for you to sleep twice as long.

"Or would it?" he asked as he caught the look on Jerry's face.

"Do you mean," Jerry said carefully, "that you have a spell that makes time pass half as fast?"

"We do," Bal-Simba said, "but it does not mean that time actually slows down. The people inside think so, but to outsiders they seem to speed up. Besides, it only works from sunset to sunrise."

Jerry whooped and pounded Bal-Simba on the back. "Fire up that spell! We just may be able to beat this sucker yet."

"People do not work at night," Bal-Simba protested.

"You're not dealing with people," Jerry told him. "These are programmers, boy. Programmers!"

Seklos announced his presence to his master by sniffling and wiping his nose on the sleeve of his robe. He had been showing Dzhir Kar progressively less respect as the hunt for the Sparrow dragged on interminably. Besides, his cold had gotten worse.

"We have lost another one," Seklos said without preamble.

Dzhir Kar raised his head. "Where? How?" he demanded.

"In the south tunnels. Isk-Nor. Killed like the others."

Dzhir Kar nodded. So far half a dozen of the Dark League's wizards had disappeared in the City of Night. Two of the bodies had been found, torn to pieces. Privately Dzhir Kar suspected that most or all of the others had deserted.

"I gave instructions that none were to hunt alone."

"He was not hunting. He was returning from a trip to a warehouse when he became separated from his companion."

"You mean he was out looting and found more than he bargained for," Dzhir Kar said sharply. "I warned you all that it is dangerous to go poking about. The City of Night is no longer ours."

Seklos sniffed and wiped his reddened nose on the sleeve of his robe. "And I warned you we must be done with your notion and sport and use magic to find him quickly."

"No! No detection spells. I forbid it."

"This is absurd! If you wish the Sparrow dead, then let us find him and kill him. "But this constant chasing about wastes our time and disperses our energies."

"Do you question my authority?" Dzhir Kar said dangerously.

"No master, only your judgment."

Dzhir Kar glared at his second in command. Under Toth-Set-Ra it would have been unthinkable for one of the Dark League, even the second, to use such language to the leader. But Toth-Set-Ra was dead. Dzhir Kar did not have his predecessor's power.

"I will consider what you say," he said at last.

"Consider this also. There are those who grow restive. The deaths and disappearances of their fellows upset them. All are cold and hungry and many wonder if the prize is worth the effort. Today they grumble quietly. But soon they will do more than that. We must either find the Sparrow or call this off and do one or the other quickly."

Dzhir Kar nodded and waved dismissal. The wizard bowed and, still sniffling, backed from the room.

After Seklos left, Dzhir Kar sat for a long time with his head bowed and his hood pulled up around his face. His lieutenant was right, the deaths and disappearances had made the other wizards nervous. If something was not done, he would have a mutiny on his hands— probably led by Seklos.

His position was anything but secure and he and Seklos both knew it. Unlike Toth-Set-Ra, who had a powerful slaying demon at his beck, or the councils which had ruled the Dark League by playing off the shifting factions, Dzhir Kar ruled by the force of his personality alone. As long as he led the Dark League to success, or at least kept it out of major trouble, he would remain in power. But this business had occupied far too many of his wizards far too long in something both boring and dangerous. If that did not change quickly, the Dark League would have a new leader.

He had promised the Dark League that this would be a simple task. Use the turncoat northern wizard to lure out the Sparrow, rely on the homing demon to neutralize the Sparrow's alien magic and then kill him quickly. On the strength of the League's hatred for the Sparrow and the demonstration of his demon, the League wizards had agreed to his plan.

He raised his head and looked over to where his creation sprawled, eyes slitted and tendrils quivering as it sought a trace of the Sparrow's magic. Dzhir Kar frowned. He hadn't told them the whole truth about his demon. A wizard never did, of course, for knowledge was power. But in this case he had concealed a crucial fact and now that concealment was coming back to haunt him.

It was not a desire for sport that kept him from using detection spells, it was necessity. Detection spells would interfere with the demon's senses. If anyone tried to use a detection spell to find the Sparrow, the demon would not be able to sense his magic in time to stop him from casting a spell. The League knew all too well what the Sparrow's magic was like if he were free to employ it.

Dzhir Kar's head dropped back on his chest and his claw hand tightened on the arm of his chair. Close. So very close to success and now time was running out.

"Two no-trump."

Karl, Nancy, Mike and Larry Fox were sitting at the table in the Wizard's Day Room, all hunched over their cards.

"I thought you'd given up on cards," Jerry said as he came over to them.

"We did, but we figured out a way to make it work," Nancy told him.

"Yeah. It turns out that in this universe a shuffled

deck of cards is in something like a Schroediger-indeterminate state," Mike explained. "The cards don't have a value until you—ah—'collapse the state vector' by revealing them."

"Which means you can't play a game if no one has seen the order of the cards," Nancy said. "Even Canfield solitaire, you go through the whole pack the first time."

"Anyway, the key to playing is to collapse the state vector after the cards are shuffled and before they're dealt."

"But if you have to look at the cards what's the point of playing?"

"Oh, the players don't have to know the values," Karl said. "It's enough if someone or something else does. So," he gestured at the head of the table, "meet Moe the Dealer."

Sitting there was a small demon wearing a green eyeshade, a violently patterned vest and garters to hold his shirtsleeves up. His skin was a particularly pale and unhealthy shade of green and a large cigar stuck out of the corner of his mouth.

"So youse gonna bid or youse gonna talk?" Moe demanded in a raspy voice.

"He looks at the cards after he shuffles and before he deals," Larry explained.

"Come on, come on, play cards," Moe said.

Jerry shook his head. "Amazing. Well, finish your game. Starting tonight we go on overtime."

Dark purple shadows were already creeping across the landscape when Danny climbed through the trap door and out onto the roof. June was already there, looking out over the World.

"I guess you heard there's a war brewing," he said without preamble as he sat down next to her. June nodded without taking her eyes off the horizon.

"They've got to have the project even faster, so they've

worked out something special," he said eagerly. "They're going to use magic to stretch the nights in the Bull Pen so we can get more work done."

June gasped and turned to him, her face chalk white. "*No!*"

"Hey, take it easy, it's not that big a thing."

June grabbed Danny's hand and held it tight in both of hers.

"Do not go! If you go you will never come out again."

"Hey now . . ." Danny said, but June started to cry silently.

He put his arm about her and patted her shoulder. "Look, it will be all right, I promise. It's only for a night."

"A night in such a place lasts an eon," June said. "I will be dead and dust ere you return."

"No you won't," Danny said and reached forward to pat her shoulder.

June released her hand and locked her arms about him fiercely. She pressed her lips to his and her tongue was like a living thing in his mouth.

Wordlessly she drew him down onto the roof slates, fumbling with his shirt as they went.

Half numb and half exhilarated, Danny followed where she led.

The moon peeking over the gabled roof caught the two naked bodies stretched on the slates. Danny rolled over on his side and admired the play of moonlight and shadow on the curve of June's hip.

"You're really something, you know that?" He ran his hand up over her hip and pressed her small breast, feeling her nipple harden in the center of his palm. June smiled contentedly and turned toward him, lifting her mouth up for a kiss,.

Danny kissed her long and gently. Then he broke away with a sigh and reached behind him for his clothes.

"You know I'm gonna get in a lot of trouble for this."

June didn't say anything; she just looked at him.

Danny got to his knees and picked up his pants. "I gotta see if I can get in."

June grasped his wrist hard. "You will not go."

Danny fidgeted. "I've got to," he said. "Look, this is important. For everybody, okay? They need me. I've got to go, okay?"

This time June seemed to accept it. She dropped her hands to her side and nodded dumbly.

He pulled his shirt over his head. "I'm gonna have to apologize all over the place, tell 'em how sorry I am." He stopped talking while he tucked his shirt into his pants. Then he leaned over and kissed her. "But I'm not sorry."

June smiled but her gaze was troubled.

Danny was in a daze as he made his way down the stairs and out into the courtyard. He wasn't sure what, but something had changed up there on that rooftop and somehow he knew the world would never be the same.

He approached the Bull Pen cautiously. It didn't look any different tonight than it had on any other night. The whitewashed sides shone silver in the moonlight and warm yellow light leaked out of the cracks around the door. But as he got closer he felt a tingling on his skin and the hairs on his arms and legs rose.

The feeling got stronger as he got closer. When he reached for the door there was a resistance like moving his hand through water. The latch was hard to work and the door was very hard to open. When he stepped through something pressed against his face and he couldn't breathe. Then he was through the door and everything was normal again.

"Where the hell have you been?" Jerry demanded as Danny came in.

"Just out."

He looked at him suspiciously.

"You were out screwing around, weren't you?"

Danny just grinned.

"Dammit, we're here to do a job, not get laid by the locals. If you can't keep your mind on what you're doing, then you don't belong here. Is that clear?"

Around them the other programmers were bent to their work, studiously ignoring Jerry and Danny.

"Yes, sir." Danny said meekly.

"I don't care what you do between sunrise and sunset or who you do it with. Men, women or underage goats, it doesn't matter. But between sunset and sunrise your ass belongs to me and you'll have it in here working. Do you understand me?"

"Yes, sir."

"Then get the hell over there and get it to work."

Danny's ears burned, but somehow the dressing down didn't sting as much. For perhaps the first time in his life, Danny knew that somebody really cared what happened to him.

As Danny took his seat Jerry shook his head and muttered under his breath before turning back to the routine he had been analyzing with Cindy Naismith.

"Are you sure that little punk's nineteen?" she asked. "He acts more like thirteen."

"He has a California driver's license that says he's nineteen." He looked at her. "He been bothering you?"

"No, nothing like that. At least not me any more than everyone else. But what the hell is he doing here?"

"Moira wanted him. Not my idea. Wouldn't be the first time the customer stuck a dud on a project team."

"Yeah, but usually they're the project manager's girlfriend or something."

"His work's not bad."

"No," Cindy admitted. "He likes to hack an easy out and he hates doing grunt work, but he's bright and he seems to take to this kind of programming."

"Let's just hope his love life lets him get some work

done," Jerry grumbled. "We've just doubled our number of programmer hours and we still can't afford to waste any of them."

The sun was just breaking over the distant mountains when the spell quit and the world jerked back to normal for the team. Most of them took it as a signal to stretch, yawn and head for bed. Mike and Larry stayed at their desks, deep in their work even after so many hours. Judith left with the rest, but she wasn't ready for bed yet. Every day at dawn dragon riders left the Capital on patrol. This was the perfect opportunity to see the dragons.

The aeries were in the cliff beneath the castle. Judith was nearly trembling with excitement as she made her way down the long flights of stairs cut into the rock. All her life she had dreamed about dragons, unicorns and other magical creatures and now she could see them close up. Maybe she could even get one of the dragon riders to take her for a ride. A handsome dragon rider.

In her mind's eye she was already soaring over the castle on dragon back when she reached the portal into the aerie. The two guardsmen on duty recognized her as one of the foreign wizards, which meant she was of the Mighty, after a fashion, and thus allowed to go nearly anywhere. It never occurred to them that she did not know what she was doing when she nodded to them and strode out onto the floor of the aerie.

The aerie was clangor, noise and barely organized confusion. Dragons were being harnessed, armed and carefully guided to their places. Swarms of men and women worked around them, grooming them, tending them and carefully moving the ones ready to fly to their assigned places.

The dragons themselves were fit and eager. They pranced and tried to flex their wings in anticipation. It took careful work by their handlers and a lot of attention from their riders to keep them calm.

As Judith watched, another dragon came up to the mark, spread its huge leathery wings and charged straight at the rectangle of sunlight that was the gate to the outside. It plunged through the portal, disappeared from sight for an instant below the sill and then rose into view again, wings beating as it climbed to join its fellows circling above.

Judith was so enchanted she didn't see the dragon being brought up behind her until she stepped right in front of it.

The dragon snorted explosively, jerked its head back and lashed its tail in surprise. The whipping tail missed another dragon by inches and slammed into a food cart, knocking it over and spilling chunks of beef and cow intestines everywhere.

The second dragon saw the food laid out before it and lunged for the meat in spite of the efforts of its crew. The first smelled the meat and turned, drawing a warning roar from the other dragon. The first one roared back a challenge and both beasts tried to rear and spread their wings in threat.

What had been organized confusion dissolved into chaos, with dragon roars reverberating from one end of the aerie to the other and men running everywhere trying frantically to get the animals under control.

The Master of Dragons, a gray-haired man with the light, compact build of a dragon rider and an empty sleeve from the accident that had ended his riding days came charging down from his platform.

*"You fornicating moron,"* he yelled at Judith over the roars of the dragons and the shouts of the men, *"Get the fornicating shit off the floor!"*

While the crews fought to control the dragons, rough hands grabbed Judith and hustled her out the door.

She stumbled through the portal and stood white and shaking under the disapproving eye of the guards for a moment. Then she burst into tears and dashed up the stairs.

With the coming of the programming team Moira had blossomed. The programmers were ignorant of the ways of this World and they had no time to learn. From her association with Wiz, Moira was better equipped to deal with them than anyone else in the Citadel—even if she frequently didn't understand them. So Moira became 'liaison, staff support and den mother' with her own box on the table of organization charcoaled on the wall of Bullpen.

For the first time since she had come to the Capital, Moira had a job that kept her busy and fulfilled. Most of the time it also kept her mind off Wiz.

She did not go into the Bullpen at night, but her days were filled with obtaining materials the team needed, making sure there was sufficient ink and parchment available, and now with the new spell seeing that food would be ready for them when they emerged at dawn. She also served as go-between to smooth matters between the team and the Mighty and the Citadel's people.

Thus she was the one the Master of Dragons cornered later that morning and berated because one of those execrable new wizards had the fornicating stupidity to blunder out into the execrable aerie just as the execrable morning patrols were taking off. This execrable woman nearly caused a dragon fight, disrupted operations and delayed launching half the patrols by nearly a day-tenth. If these execrable aliens couldn't stay in their places he would go to the execrable Council and get an execrable spell to put a fornicating wall of fire across the fornicating door to the fornicating aerie.

"Begging My Lady's pardon, of course," the man said when he paused for breath.

Moira agreed with him, soothed him, promised him it would never happen again and sent him away still grumbling but more or less content.

After he left, she sat in the tiny room at the keep she

used for an office and scowled at the wall. From the Master's description she recognized that the offender was Judith, but what in the World had she been doing in the aerie? Everyone knew dragons were difficult, chancy creatures whose handling had to be left to experts. Even if someone didn't know that, it was obvious that a fire-breathing monster with an eighty-foot wingspan was not something to be approached as casually as a pony. These people from Wiz's world might be strange and more than a touch fey, but they were intelligent and they did not appear suicidal.

*Well, speculation gets me nothing,* she thought, rising from her desk. *The thing to do is find Judith and have a talk with her.*

*That and give orders to the guardsmen that the team is not to be allowed free run of the castle,* she added as she went out the door.

It took Moira the better part of an hour to find the miscreant. She was standing on the parapet looking so utterly miserable that Moira's carefully prepared scolding died in her throat.

"My Lady, are you all right?"

"Oh, hello Moira," Judith sniffed. "No, I'm fine."

"Forgive me, but you seem upset."

Judith smiled wanly. "I was just thinking that you should be very careful what you wish for because you may get it."

"My Lady?"

Judith turned toward her and Moira could see she had been crying.

"You heard what happened this morning? When I went to see the dragons?"

"That was not wise, My lady. Dragons are dangerous."

"Yeah. Dangerous, nasty-tempered, foul-smelling beasts." She took a sobbing breath. "Up close they're not even pretty."

"I am sorry if they frightened you, My Lady."

"No, they didn't exactly frighten me." She smiled through her tears. "I probably scared the dragons worse than they scared me. I guess I'm really mourning the death of my dreams."

She sniffed again and smiled with one corner of her mouth. "Funny isn't it? I'm thirty-three years old and I've still got dreams. Or I did until I came here. I believe in romance. Not so much the boy-girl kind as, well— romance."

"Romance?" Moira asked, puzzled.

"Yeah. Castles, dragons, knights in shining armor. All that stuff. And then one day they all come true. And you know what? They're all about as romantic as a Cupertino car wash."

Moira thought about it for a minute.

"Why should it be otherwise? People are people in your World or mine. As best I can see they all have the same wants and needs."

"Yeah, but it was supposed to be different! Does that make any sense?" Judith asked miserably.

"In a way," Moira said. "I am not what you call a romantic person, but I think I understand somewhat.

"You know they tell the story of Wiz and I throughout the North." A quick smile. "We are heroes, you see. Figures of romance.

"But what we did was not terribly heroic and it wasn't at all romantic. Mostly I was very frightened and cold. Wiz was too angry that I had been stolen to be heroic. We both did the best we could and by fortune it worked out well."

"So what you're saying is there is no romance in the world, in any world?"

"No, but I think there is another element, one that comes between the doing and the hearing. That is what turns something frightening or wearying or utterly miserable into a romance. I think that element is in the mind of the teller."

She paused and looked out over the battlements to the fleecy clouds. "I think you confuse what is outside with what is within you. The dragons, or the freeways, those are the external things. It is not the deeds or the things that make a romance, it is what you do with them inside yourself.

"My lady, do you remember the day you arrived, when the dragon cavalry swept over the keep? You made us see them in a way we had never seen them before. I think that is the real secret of romance. Not places or people, but the ability to look at the World and see the romance that is there."

Judith quirked one side of her face up into a smile. "You may be right. I sure don't seem to be having much luck finding that quality outside of me."

"But you have it inside, Lady. That is better than not having it at all."

"I guess you're right," Judith said, fumbling a well-used handkerchief from her gown's sleeve. "Thanks."

"You are mor than welcome, My lady. Just stay out of the aeries, please."

As the days dragged on Wiz came to know his pursuers well enough that they developed distinct personalities. There was the fat one who hated to exercise and who searched perfunctorily and never a place that was hard to reach or might be dangerous. There was the one who was addicted to laying in ambush, but whose fondness for onions and persistent flatulence gave him away. There was the lean one with the long arms who seemed to delight in rooftops and other high places.

And then there was Seklos. Seklos of the keen nose, who never seemed to rest and who searched relentlessly, who poked into every nook and cranny and who checked everything.

This couldn't go on. He would slip sooner or later. So far only more luck than any mortal deserved had kept him alive and free. But that couldn't last.

Meanwhile, the longer this murderous game of hide-and-seek went on, the more likely it was that there would be a war. It wasn't just his life that was on the line here—*although that is a major consideration,* he thought, it was the fate of the entire World.

Well, if he couldn't run forever and he had to survive, there was only one thing to do. He didn't want to fight the Dark League, but they would not rest until he was dead. He had no way out so he had to fight them to the death.

*Yeah, but whose death?* He shook the thought off and began to consider methods of fighting back.

This place was odd, Wiz thought. It was a tower in the shadow of what had obviously been a major palace. But the tower was squat and ill-proportioned with doorways big enough to drive a truck through.

The peculiar proportions were emphasized by the fact that the top was missing, blasted away during his attack on the city. But it was sound up to the fourth level, which was where Wiz was standing now.

The room was large and roughly circular, with a single large French door that led out onto a tiny balcony overlooking the street below. It gave a wonderful view of the city, but aside from that seemed useless.

So did the contents of the room. It had either been stripped or hadn't had anything in it to begin with. Just a few stone benches around the walls and some miscellaneous trash on the floor.

He was about to leave when he heard voices outside. Someone was coming up the street below and it could only be wizards of the Dark League.

Normally Wiz would have run away, but his new resolve made him step out on the balcony to check out the situation.

The situation could not have been better. Laying on the balcony were several large blocks of stone which must have fallen when the top of the tower went. Coming up the narrow street were two wizards of the Dark League and one of them was Seklos!

Wiz picked up one of the blocks of stone and rested it on the carved stone railing. Then he watched the wizards get closer and closer and smiled.

". . . dragging me all the way up here," the other wizard said as they came closer. Wiz recognized him as the cautious one.

"Because this is where he must be," Seklos said. "Fool, do you not see that the quicker we catch this most troublesome bird, the sooner we can leave this place?"

Wiz put both hands on the block and held his breath.

"But why me?" the other wizard asked.

He never got his answer. At that moment they came under the balcony and Wiz shoved the rock over the edge.

Wiz watched with a sinking heart as the stone smashed into the pavement and shattered a good arm's length behind his intended victim. He scuttled back from the edge dislodging a shower of pebbles in the process.

Seklos' companion gaped at the shattered rock on the pavement behind them. "Dangerous place." He looked up at the tower nervously. "The stones are loose."

Seklos looked up at the parapet. "I do not believe in such accidents." He turned to his companion. "Go, spread the word that this area is to be cordoned off and searched most carefully. I think we may be near our Sparrow."

As he pounded down the stairs, Wiz realized he had made a serious mistake. There was only one door to the tower and that was just around the corner from where the wizards had been standing. If he didn't get out the door before Seklos came looking for him . . .

Too late! He was still nearly a flight from the bottom when Seklos came through the door and into the tower. As quietly as he could, Wiz backed up the stairs.

Seklos came on, staff in hand, ready to strike at the slightest sound or movement. Wiz moved back up the spiraling stairs ahead of him. There was no time to open a door and no room to squeeze past his pursuer. The only place he could go was back into the room where he had thrown the rock.

*That'll still work,* he thought, fighting down the panic rising inside him. *He can't see me and as soon as he comes into the room I'll be able to slip around him and get down the stairs.* Moving as quietly as he could, he eased through the door and made for the far end, next to the window.

Seklos strode into the room and sniffed the air. His head swung this way and that like a hunting dog tracing a scent. Wiz stood stock still, afraid to breathe. Two more steps and he would be far enough in that he could get behind him and out the door.

Seklos took a single cautious step into the room and scanned from side to side. The wizard stopped short. "What . . ." Then his face split in an evil smile.

"A cloak of invisibility? Clever Sparrow. Oh, very clever indeed. But did they not tell you never to stand in a sunbeam wearing a tarncape?" He raised his hand and flicked his wrist in the direction of the window. Wiz had a glimpse of something silvery flying through the air. Instinctively he dove and rolled.

Behind him the stone wall exploded into flame. Wiz hugged the floor and squinted his eyes shut to block out the heat.

*Dust!* Wiz thought frantically. *The dust gave me away!* Seklos must have seen his outline in the sunlit dust motes. He raised his head and saw Seklos blocking the doorway, his staff extended in front of him. Behind him a wall of luminous blue blocked the doorway.

In desperation, Wiz hefted the halberd. He knew he couldn't get in under the staff with the shorter weapon, so he threw it at the wizard, sidearm so it spun horizontally.

As soon as it left Wiz's hands the halberd became visible. Seklos dodged it easily, swaying to one side like a snake. His face lit with unholy glee as he watched it sail past him.

"So you confirm your presence. Thank you, Sparrow. And now you cannot hide. Your cloak cannot save you." The wizard extended his staff and waved it from side to side like a blind man while he fumbled in his sleeve.

On tiptoe Wiz backed away from the questing staff. No good to try to get around him. Frantically he looked for someplace to hide.

The only possible place was under one of the benches. Wiz squeezed beneath the nearest one, face to the wall in a vain attempt to muffle his breathing. He clinched his eyes tight and waited to feel the lethal staff tip in the center of his back.

"Come out, little Sparrow," the hateful, hate-filled voice crooned. "Come out and face your end."

There was a hideous roar followed by a ringing scream cut short in mid-cry. Then there was a thrashing and horrible crunching noise. Wiz forced himself further back into the crevice.

Then all was silence. No sound from Seklos, no sound of anything else. As quietly as he could Wiz twisted around and looked out.

At first he thought it had suddenly turned to night. All he saw from beneath the bench was blackness. And then the blackness moved. The enormous black body hopped ponderously to one side, the huge head turned. Wiz went weak from sheer terror.

The thing looked at Wiz with burning red eyes and then turned away. It lumbered through the last dying vestiges of the blue fire and out the door. Wiz heard it make its way down the corridor.

It took a long time for Wiz to get his heart back under control. The monster had destroyed the wizard and it looked right at him, but it hadn't touched him. The way

the thing looked at him Wiz knew it had to have seen
him. But it hadn't made a move to harm him. Somehow
Wiz did not think it was because the monster was a
friend.

Wiz had never seen the huge black creature, but he
recognized it from descriptions. It was Bale-Zur, the
slaying demon which had brought Toth-Set-Ra to power
in the Dark League and then destroyed him when Wiz
attacked the City of Night.

There was something about that. Something he had
learned. He cudgeled his brains, trying to recall that
almost-remembered bit of knowledge. Something he saw?
No, something someone told him. Before he used his
new magic to travel to the City of Night and rescue
Moira. Something someone told him about demons, or
dragons, or . . .

Of course! True names. Humans weren't the only
creatures with true names. Fully mature dragons had
them. And so did some kinds of demons because it was
only by knowing their true names that they could be
controlled. That was how Bale-Zur found his prey. Unlike
other demons, the great slaying demon did not need to
know a thing's true name to destroy it. All it needed was
for the being's true name to have been spoken somewhere in the World at some time.

And of all mortals in the world, William Irving Zumwalt was the only one safe from Bale-Zur. No one had
ever spoken his full name—his true name—anywhere in
this World.

Licking his lips, he stepped over the gruesome remains
of the wizard. As he did so he kicked something that
rolled across the floor.

Wiz was almost afraid to look down for fear his foot
had touched some body part. But it was only a silvery
sphere about the size of a baseball that had been
clutched in what was left of Seklos' hand.

*Seklos must have grabbed it when Bale-Zur attacked*

*him,* Wiz thought. Overcoming his revulsion, he bent down and picked up the sphere. He couldn't be sure but it looked like the thing that the wizard had thrown at him, the one that spread fire on the stones.

He forced himself to look at what was left of Seklos and realized his left sleeve was lumpy. Swallowing his gorge, Wiz reached into the blood-sodden sleeve and fished out two more of the spheres. He could have done it faster except he kept his eyes closed through the whole process.

The three spheres gave him weapons, his first real weapons that might be effective against the wizards of the Dark League.

*The wizards . . . !* Seklos had sent his companion for help. Wiz stuffed the balls into his pouch, grabbed his halberd and dashed down the stairs. There were three wizards not more than a hundred yards up the street when he emerged from the building. Without hesitating, Wiz ran around the corner, leaving the black robes to wonder at the sound of footsteps with no sign of the runner.

Several blocks away, Wiz sank back against the wall of an empty storeroom and listened for any sound of pursuit.

The situation got worse and worse. His cloak of invisibility's spell had some loopholes. Wiz had no doubt at all that there were counter-spells that would render it useless.

Wiz forced himself to calm down and think. Through all the hunger and cold and terror, he had to *think*.

He had to summon help somehow and if he expected to live long enough for that he had to defeat or neutralize the Dark League. Two problems and both of them looked insoluble.

But maybe—just maybe—one problem could solve another again.

He needed magic to get out of here. If not magic to

walk the Wizard's Way, then a burst of magic to attract the Watchers who stood guard over the whole of the World.

But it didn't have to be a burst of *his* magic.

Wiz looked at the three spheres in his lap and a plan began to form in his mind.


Dzhir Kar rested his pink scarred forehead in his one good hand and ground his teeth in frustration.

The Sparrow had slipped through his grasp again. They had been within a hairsbreadth of him this time, he knew it. Yet that damnable little bird had fluttered through his clutches once more.

And now Seklos was gone. Seklos the tireless, the indefatigable. Seklos who hated this Sparrow almost as much as he did. Torn apart by something in the upper city while the entire contingent of the Dark League came running to his rescue.

That hadn't been lost on the rest of his band. They had seen what had happened to Seklos and the sight had done nothing for their ardor in the search. Now most of them wanted to leave the City of Night and abandon the search. Only his overwhelming skill at magic and the loss of the natural leader of any opposition to him kept them here.

Still his demon lay coiled in an alcove of the chamber. Occasionally it would raise its head and the tendrils along its fanged mouth would quiver as the Sparrow considered using magic, but so far there was no magic from this most alien of wizards, nothing the demon could home in on.

It was enough, Dzhir Kar thought, to make a wizard cry.

# Twenty
## FORCING A FIGHT

*Never give a sucker an even break.*
— W. C. Fields

*Especially not if he's a big, mean sucker.*
— the collected sayings of Wiz Zumwalt

Wiz tiptoed down the corridor, convinced that the sound of his heart must be giving him away at every beat. Over and over he repeated to himself the route out of this maze.

It was unfamiliar ground to him. This was the one part of the City of Night he had been striving to avoid ever since he was kidnapped. This was the path to the lair of the Dark League.

There were no guards and no sign of magic protecting this place, which only made Wiz more nervous.

Finally he turned a corner and saw a brightly lighted doorway not thirty feet ahead. There were two black robes standing in front of it talking. Through the open door he could see others moving around.

Wiz stepped back around the corner and for the first time in weeks, removed his cloak of invisibility. Taking one of Seklos's fire globes in his hand he turned the corner again and, before the wizards could react, threw the ball straight at them.

His aim with the ball was no better than his aim with the rock. About two-thirds of the way down the corridor the ball broke against the wall and a sheet of flame erupted between him and the wizards. A lightning bolt lanced through the flames and struck near him. Wiz turned and ran with the shouts of the wizards ringing in his ear.

*The tricky part is going to be making sure that everyone arrives when they are supposed to,* he thought as he dodged down the corridor. Another bolt of lightning crashed into the stone behind Wiz, knocking off chips and tainting the air with the tang of ozone.

*That and staying alive.* Wiz ran faster and threw the tarncape around his shoulders.

"*What was that?*" Dzhir Kar roared, rising from his desk. From his place in an alcove off the workroom, Pryddian cringed back.

One of the wizards burst into the room, hair and beard singed and smoking holes in his robe. "Dread Master, the Sparrow has attacked us?"

"Then after him. After him! Everyone!" Dzhir Kar was hopping up and down in fury. "Catch him and bring him to me."

The wizards piled out of the workroom in a rush. Dzhir Kar paused long enough to look over at his demon, still coiled with its eyes closed. He grasped his staff with his good hand and hobbled after his wizards.

"Dread Master?" Pryddian spoke tentatively.

Dzhir Kar gestured and a wall of heatless blue fire sprang into being across the door to Pryddian's alcove. The apprentice cringed back away from the deadly flame.

"Stay there until we return," he croaked and hobbled out.

It turned out to be nearly as hard to keep the hunt going as it had been to avoid it entirely. By alternately

showing and concealing himself, Wiz was able to keep
his pursuers after him. Once or twice he almost had to
shout at them to bring them back on the track. At first
he worried about being too obvious. Then he saw that
the wizards were so eager to catch him that nothing could
make them pause to consider his motives.

He had to wait for several minutes outside the gate
near the strange tower before he was spotted by a wizard.
Then three of them came around the corner at once and
let fly at him with a flurry of lightning bolts as he dodged
through.

"This way, Dread Master, this way," the wizards
chorused a few moments later when Dzhir Kar came up,
using his staff as a crutch.

"He did not go beyond this place," another assured
him. "We came from all point of the compass."

Dzhir Kar peered through the gate at the courtyard
beyond. The square was windowless with walls perhaps
four times the height of a man. A single door gaped on
the opposite side of them from the gateway.

"Trapped!" Dzhir Kar crowed. "There is no way out
of that building. We have him now. Spread out, brothers.
Spread out fingertip to fingertip and we will hunt down
our Sparrow." He picked up a handful of windblown dust
from the marble paving and threw it into the air before
him.

"Use the dust. It will show his form."

The wizards quickly formed a ragged line. Two paces
apart they advanced across the court, tossing dust into
the air as they went.

Lying on his belly on the roof of the building Wiz
watched them come. It had taken him the better part
of the night to chop and pry a hole in the roof so he
would have this vantage point and escape route. Now
all he could do was watch and wait—and be ready to
run if his plan went awry.

The line of wizards was half-way across the square

when the shadows in the building began to move. As one man they stopped, forewarned by their magical senses. The line wavered as some of them stepped back, away from the darkened doorway where something was clearly stirring. Wiz held his breath.

And into the square came the demon Bale-Zur.

Normal mortals would have fled. But wizards need courage beyond ordinary men and women. Besides, they knew it would be futile to run.

A score of wizards threw back their sleeves and raised their staffs almost in unison. Suddenly it was Hell out for the Fourth of July in the square.

Magics flashed and roared across the square. Spells crackled through the air to bounce off the demon like many-hued lightnings. Balls of green and purple and blinding white fire flew this way and that across the square.

None of it mattered. Bale-Zur did not even flinch as he came across the marble flagging with a hopping, toad-like gait. A wizard screamed as the creature reached out with great rending claws.

Crippled as he was, Dzhir Kar could not run. He stood his ground to the end, flinging spells at the demon until the clawed hand reached down and scooped him up to the rending, blood-stained jaws.

The last few wizards tried to run, but it made no difference. In spite of his clumsy gait Bale-Zur was far faster than any human. Their screams mingled with the demon's roars as he crushed the life out of them. Wiz clapped his hands to his ears and turned away from the scene in the court below him.

Then all was silent. There were no more cries, no more roars, no more crash and flash of magic. Suddenly the only sound was the icy wind playing over the stone-work and making weird little whistling noises as it stirred the dust below.

Once again the warty head swiveled and again Wiz

stared into eyes as red as the fires of Hell. Then the eyes slid over him and the huge toadlike demon turned away. Soundlessly it half-dragged, half-hopped out of the square, heedless of the black-robed bodies it crushed beneath its great clawed feet.

"Odd," the Watcher said, staring back into her crystal.

"What?" the wizard asked.

"There in the City of Night, a sudden flare of magic."

"Is it the Sparrow?" the other asked eagerly.

"No, it is not the new magic." She shrugged. "Perhaps just a remnant of the Dark League's power."

The other nodded. The Watchers were used to strange things happening in the ruined city. As long as they were not too powerful they were nothing to worry about or to be passed up the chain of command.

Still, the Mighty were frantic to find Wiz and this was an unusual occurrence. The shift commander looked up. "What have we got near the City of Night?"

"No assets in place right now," the patrol commander called back from the other side of the pit. "There is a squadron of dragon cavalry that could swing further south and be there in two day-tenths."

"Then send them south," the shift commander told her. "Have them search over the City of Night carefully." The patrol commander nodded and turned back to her crystal.

"Should we also inform Bal-Simba, Lord?" asked the deputy commander.

"No. No point in that. This may be nothing after all."

With the flash and pulse of repeated magics still ringing in his ears, Wiz made his way to the large open space in the center of the city.

The forces unleashed as the wizards fought for their lives against Bale-Zur would provide a beacon, a magical flare big enough to be seen by the Watchers back at the

Capital. Now all he had to do was mark his chosen vantage point and scan the skies for the dragon patrols which were sure to come south to investigate the magical maelstrom he had touched off. There was food and water in his pack for several days, and two more of the fire globes to make a final signal to guide the rescuers in. He had even taken the precaution of gathering up several long pieces of white fabric to use as marker panels. They would stand out vividly against the dark sand.

Carefully he laid down the white cloth taken from the chests in the shape of a large X. He anchored the pieces with handfuls of the fine black volcanic sand that floored the square. That done, he stood up, stretched and leaned over backwards to ease his aching back muscles.

Wiz looked up, squinting into the pale sun. The walls ran straight up and smooth for perhaps thirty feet. Above that they moved out in a series of steps. Like ranks of bleachers.

*Like ranks of bleacher seats . . .* Wiz looked around with a new comprehension. The black sand beneath his feet, the unclimbable walls, the seats above suddenly all made sense. An arena. He was standing in an arena. The central tower must have something to do with the events held here.

Wiz shuddered. Knowing what the Dark League had been he didn't want to think about what those events must have been like.

*Well, that's over and done with,* he told himself. *Arena or not, it's still the best place in the city to watch for help.*

He looked over the tower speculatively. It was a squat oval with slanting sides perhaps four stories tall. The top was mostly flat with a large square block, man high, in the middle. In use the tower would have been as impossible to scale as the arena walls, but the earthquakes that had accompanied his attack on the City of Night had caused one section of the tower to collapse, leaving a crude stairway of large stone blocks up to the top.

Wiz hefted his pack, picked up his halberd and started across the sands to the tower.

There was a scuffling sound from the far end of the arena. Wiz turned and saw several lean wolf-like shapes almost as dark as the sand emerge from one of the doors.

With a sinking feeling, Wiz realized he wasn't out of the woods yet.

*Now what in the World did those sods back at the Capital want?* The Dragon Leader thought.

He and his patrol had been on the wing for nearly twelve hours already. Men and dragons alike were tired and even with heating spells they were chilled beyond numbness. The flight would have to stop to rest the dragons on the way back as it was. If they continued south to pass over the City of Night they might have to set down on the Southern Continent itself. The Dragon Leader didn't like that at all. The Dark League might be gone, but there were still things on that continent he did not wish to meet on the ground with half a dozen exhausted men and dragons.

Still, orders were orders. He rose in his saddle against the restraining straps and signaled his men to turn their patrol line south toward the ruined city.

*One quick pass,* he promised himself. *One quick pass and then it's north and home!*

A weird warbling howl broke the windy stillness of the ruined city.

*Dire Beasts!*

Wiz had only seen the wolflike creatures once before, by moonlight on the night he and Moira had been chased through the forest by the forces of the Dark League. He had had only a glimpse then and the sight had left him with nightmares for months. Now he counted a half dozen of the great wolflike creatures slinking out into the open space.

Frantically Wiz scrambled up the broken stone on the side of the tower. The blocks were six and seven feet high and sometimes he had to stand on tiptoe or jump to reach the next one. Once his fingers slipped off the smooth surface and he landed painfully on the block he had just left. Another time he jumped back as a block teetered dangerously when he grasped it.

He reached the top panting and gasping. Then he rolled over flat on his belly and peered down into the arena. The dire Beasts had congregated below, looking up the way Wiz had come. One or two of them broke off from the pack and slunk around the base of the tower, as if looking for another way up.

He half-formed a spell in his mind, but he felt the familiar dread quivering and knew that the demon had survived its creators.

Now the ones that had split came racing back. The entire pack put their noses together and whined and growled at each other, looking up occasionally toward Wiz. Finally the huddle broke and very tentatively one of the Dire Beasts began to climb.

The things were much better climbers than wolves were, but not as good as a man. Only the one collapsed section of the tower gave access to the platform where Wiz lay.

Wiz put his pack aside and picked up his halberd. He was armed and his enemies had to climb up a steep grade to reach him one at a time. Somehow Wiz doubted that was enough to make it a fair fight.

The dark coastline ahead looked about half as attractive as Hell with the fires out.

Not all the fires on the southern continent were out. The volcano that towered above the City of Night was trailing a thin smear of dirty smoke from its top. Rising along its flank, the City of Night was a disordered jumble.

Dragon Leader made his decision. They would come

in fast, swooping from altitude to gain speed. One single fast pass over the ruined city and they would be away for an island in the Freshened Sea where they could rest for a few hours. Signaling his men to spread out in a patrol line, Dragon Leader urged his weary mount to climb higher in preparation for the sweep.

"Got something here," the rider on the far left of the patrol line reported. Dragon Leader pressed his mount's flank with his knees to bring him around to check.

As soon as he glided over the courtyard he saw what had attracted the rider's attention.

Scattered around were several dark-robed bodies, some crushed and dismembered. The walls and paving of the court were streaked and discolored from the aftereffects of powerful spells. One section of the wall had melted and run like candle wax under the magical impact.

*Looks like they dueled among themselves,* Dragon leader thought. *That explains the magic the Watchers sensed.* He looked down at the crumpled dark forms and shrugged mentally. *Whatever it was, it doesn't involve us.* He spoke into his communications crystal. "Echelon right and climb for altitude. We need to reach the island before dark."

Now there were four Dire Beasts climbing the broken rock toward him. Wiz bit his lip and watched them come. He fished into his pouch and pulled out one of the fire globes. Animals were supposed to be afraid of fire. Perhaps this would frighten them off.

Lying flat on the stones, Wiz tossed the fire globe over the side. There was a satisfying "whoosh" and leap of flames. After a second, he stuck his head over the edge to see the effect.

He nearly lost his nose for his pains. Not only hadn't the fire daunted the beast, the first one was almost to the top. Powerful jaws with two sets of fangs snapped shut so close Wiz could smell the stench of the thing's breath. He jerked his head back and rolled away. Then he realized he had to keep the thing off the platform at all costs.

Too late. The wolf thing had gained the platform with all four feet. Hackles up and back fur stiffened into a mane, the Dire Beast advanced on him. Wiz fumbled in his pouch and came up with the second fire ball.

The globe flew straight and true to shatter at the beast's feet. Instantly the animal was engulfed in an inferno. With a howl of agony, it threw itself from the stone platform. It made a blazing fireball all the way to the blackened sand. It struck with a "thump" and lay still.

For a moment the Dire Beasts hung back. Then one of them howled and they charged up the crumbling stone again.

In the back of his mind, Wiz realized he had just thrown away his last hope of signaling should help arrive.

Dragon Leader had just crossed the beach out over the Freshened Sea when his wingman broke in on the communications frequency.

"Smoke behind us."

Dragon Leader twisted in his saddle. A thin black curl of smoke was rising in the distance, back over the city.

He hesitated. Should they turn south again to check it out? It was probably an accidental fire or a new volcanic vent. Their orders had been to search for magic. Certainly it was not magic, he told himself. Therefore it was none of his business.

The welfare of his troop was his business and that demanded he get them to a safe resting place as soon as possible. The other members of the flight craned their necks to see and he could feel them waiting for orders.

"Not our pigeon," Dragon Leader said finally into the communications crystal. "Hold your course." The rest of the troop relaxed. He felt his wingman start to say something and he braced for a challenge to the order, but the challenge never came.

They had flown north for three more wing beats when he sensed a change in the formation. He looked back and saw his wingman sliding in.

The formation had opened out, as it always did on long patrols. Now the wingman was closing in to the precise Number Two position, tucked in tight to his leader's right, exactly as he had been taught in riding school. In spite of the long hours they had been in the air, the younger man was sitting bolt upright in his saddle and he was ostentatiously checking his weapons and equipment in exactly the manner prescribed when leaving a combat zone.

*Every maneuver, every patrol, you will perform as if it were the real thing! . . . by the checklist, mister!*

He felt his subordinate's eyes boring into him and he knew every other man in the flight was watching as well. Dragon Leader had seen nearly thirty winters and suddenly he felt all of them.

"Shit!" he muttered to himself. But he sat up straighter and tightened the straps holding him to the saddle. Then he pressed his knees into his weary mount's side and with a wave of his arm turned his squadron south again over the City of Night.

Wiz thrust desperately at the snarling face just a few inches below him. The creature snaked its head to the side to avoid the thrust and snapped at the halberd head. Claws scrabbled against rough stone as the Dire Beast got first one foot and then another up on the stone ledge. Wiz chopped down at a leg, but the animal yanked it back and the blade struck sparks from the basalt. The head lunged forward and the jaws snapped like a pistol shot. Wiz was forced to give ground as the creature got all four feet on the stone. Behind the first, Wiz could see the head of a second Dire Beast climbing the same path.

Unbidden, Donal's words came back to him. *Put your back to the wall and die like a man.*

Halberd in both hands, Wiz edged away from the snarling monster, back towards the wall. Hackles up, the creature advanced slowly across the rock.

Wiz bumped into the wall and nearly stumbled. He pressed his back against the cold, rough stone and raised the broken halberd. The two Dire Beasts split up and circled to either side of him. Wiz took a deep, gasping breath and squinted into the pale sun, trying to keep track of both creatures at once.

A shadow fell over his face. Above him he heard the sound of wings. Dragon wings.

*What in the . . . ?*

Dragon leader scanned the scene below. Down in the arena there were about a half dozen wolves or something attacking what looked like a lone man.

There was even a checklist for cases like this. It called for two dragons to drop low to investigate while the others stayed overhead flying a complex figure eight pattern. Dragon riders knew from bitter experience that there were things beyond the borders of men which were masters of illusion and used that power to lure men and dragons to their deaths.

Dragon Leader watched as the speck on the ground retreated before the two larger, darker specks that split up to come at him from either side. The checklist called for him to spread his formation out while the two scouts descended in broad circles, looking for signs of an ambush. Already the two dragon riders on the rear of the formation were drifting out and getting ready to spiral down on his command.

The tiny figure moved back against the central pylon and raised a weapon of some sort above its head. The attackers were now on either side of him, ready for the final killing lunge.

*Bugger the checklist!* Dragon Leader winged his mount over and signaled the rest of the squadron to follow. In a compact mass a dozen dragons hurtled down on the arena.

The Dire Beasts were so intent on their prey they had no warning. The first they knew of the dragons overhead was when a fusillade of missiles tore into their pack.

Suddenly two of the beasts were down with iron arrows in them. One of them bit weakly at the bolt that skewered through its flank and the other one was already still. Three more arrows vibrated in the sand where they had missed their targets.

The dragons swept low into the arena, their wingtips almost brushing the dark sand and the wind of their passage, raising clouds of sand behind them as their riders pulled them into steep turns.

The Dire Beasts on the rock hesitated, torn between the nearness of their prey and the threat from the air. Finally a gout of dragon fire decided for them and they broke away, leaping down the crumbled stone and sprinting across the arena pursued by arrows and bursts of fire.

One of the dragons settled onto the ledge behind Wiz. As the animal folded its wings, the rider swung off and walked stiffly to where he stood.

The man was dirty, disheveled and his eyes were rimmed red from fatigue and hours of squinting into the wind. Still he was the loveliest sight Wiz had ever seen.

"Lord, we have been scouring the World for you!"

"Just get me out of here," Wiz said weakly.

# PART IV:
# RUN TIME

# Twenty-One
## BED REST

*Sleep? Isn't that a completely inadequate substitute for caffeine?*

—programmers' saying

A hospital looks like a hospital anywhere you go. At least this one smelled of sweet herbs and fresh cut hay instead of stinking of disinfectant.

Wiz was in no shape to appreciate it. He was asleep when they carried him in and he was still asleep when Moira and Bal-Simba came to see him.

Moira bit her lip to keep from crying when Bronwyn and Bal-Simba ushered her into his room. They had cleaned him up, but he was thin and drawn with new lines etched about his mouth and eyes. He looked as if he had aged a decade in the weeks he had been gone. He was still and unresponsive and for a terrible moment she thought he was dying.

But Bronwyn touched her arm when she moved toward the bedside. "It would be best if you did not wake him, Lady," the healer said.

"What is wrong with him?"

"Shock, fatigue and starvation mostly. There was some sickness in his lungs but we cleared that up."

"What happened to him?"

"We are not certain," Bal-Simba told her. "He was kidnapped to the City of Night by what is left of the Dark League, but aside from that he has told us very little." He frowned. "He was not in very good shape when we found him."

"Best we leave now," Bronwyn said softly. "He needs to sleep for as long as he can."

"May I stay, Lady?" Moira asked. "I'd like to be here when he awakes."

"It is likely to be a long vigil. He will doubtless sleep the night through and perhaps a good portion of tomorrow."

"Please, Lady?"

Bronwyn sighed. "Very well. But leave him strictly alone."

Moira nodded and settled herself in a chair next to the bed.

Pryddian hunched into the corner to get out of the freezing wind. The stones were like ice against his back and the chill crept closer around him. Overhead the clouds rolled low and slate gray, driven and torn to streamers. He felt a freezing drop on his face and realized it was starting to snow.

He had to find shelter. But there was no shelter to be seen. Behind him was the pitch black mouth of the tunnel he had stumbled from. The buildings on either side of the street had collapsed in heaps and the roadway was full of rubble.

Pryddian was not sure what day it was. At least one had passed since he had been left imprisoned in the workroom, but was it just one or had there been more?

He had been content to wait for the wizards' return— until the lights went out, the wall of fire vanished and the heating spell failed leaving him alone with the demon in icy darkness. It took him a few minutes in the absolute dark to nerve himself to try the door and it took him hours more to blunder out into the wan cold day.

Pryddian shivered as he considered his options. The wizards had not returned from their confrontation with the Sparrow. That meant they were either dead or they had forgotten him in their victory. Remembering the way the light globes had flickered and failed and how the heat cut off suddenly, Pryddian did not think the Dark League had won.

He shivered uncontrollably and his breath puffed white. Now what? He could not walk the Wizard's Way unaided; he did not know how. He could not sail the Freshened Sea back; he was not a sailor and there were no boats left in the City of Night. He did not even have a communications crystal to call the Council and beg for rescue.

Come to that, he could not find his way back to the Dark League's workroom, not through that maze of darkened tunnels. Despair, cold and cruel as the wind, knifed through him as he realized he was probably doomed to dwell alone in the City of Night for the rest of his life. He did not allow himself to think about how long that might be.

He felt more snowflakes on his face, stinging now as the rising wind drove them against his exposed skin. *No point in standing here.* Somewhere in the city there had to be something to eat and a place out of the cold.

Cautious as a mouse, Pryddian, ex-apprentice of both the Council of the North and the Dark League, picked his way down the ruined street in search of food and warmth.

Bronwyn was right. Wiz slept like a log the night through, not even turning. Moira watched and dozed as best she could in the chair, waking every time Wiz so much as sighed.

The middle of the following morning he began to stir. Moira moved to his bedside as his eyes fluttered open.

"Moira?" Wiz said weakly.

"Hush," she said as she caressed his forehead. Instinctively he reached up to clasp her to him.

"Feeling better, are we?" said a brisk voice from the door. Wiz and Moira broke their clinch with a start and turned to see Bronwyn stride into the room with Arianne trailing her.

The healer ran a practiced eye over Wiz, checked his pulse and poked and prodded him a bit and then nodded in satisfaction.

"Will I ever play the piano again, Doc?"

"You mean will you recover? Of course you will. But that is what I need to speak to you about.

"There is nothing wrong with you that time and rest and a little careful nursing will not cure." She looked over at Moira. "Now I could use a healing spell to cure you this afternoon. It would be better if you were left to heal naturally but they tell me the North needs you on your feet as quickly as possible." She frowned her professional disapproval, but Arianne nodded.

"Yeah," Wiz shifted and sat up in bed, "there's a lot I've got to do."

Bronwyn sighed. "Very well, then. I will keep you here overnight just to be sure, though. After that get what rest you can and try to conserve your strength."

She turned to Moira. "Lady, you are bonded to this one. Will you assist me?"

Moira nodded. "Willingly."

Bronwyn took a position on the right side of the bed and Moira stood on the left. Each of them took one of Wiz's hands, and Bronwyn began to chant and gesture with her wand. She tapped Wiz's temples, his throat, his chest and his groin with the wand, then laid it aside and clasped Moira's free hand. Now Moira took up the chant in a minor key.

As they watched, the color flowed back into Wiz's skin and the lines in his face smoothed out. Wiz's mouth formed a little o of surprise as he felt the strength flow back into him.

Bronwyn released her grip, sighed and sagged into a chair.

Wiz shook his head. "Whoooeeee. That is really something."

"Just be careful not to overtax yourself," Bronwyn said from her chair. "Healing spells extract their price."

"I think I know the first one. I'm starved."

"Indeed," Arianne said. "I will see to it. And what will you do afterwards?"

"First I need to talk to Bal-Simba. We're in big trouble.

"And then," he said deliberately, "I'm going to eat a little crow."

Arianne nodded and left. Bronwyn stayed for a few minutes more, resting in the chair and then examining Wiz again before repeating her admonition that he get all the rest he could.

"Bal-Simba or no, I am keeping you one more night," she told him. Then she too left.

Finally Wiz and Moira were alone.

Moira rested her hand on Wiz's shoulder and he clasped it tightly in both of his.

"God, I missed you," he said.

"And I missed you," she told him, putting her other hand on top of his.

"We've got to talk, you know," he said at last.

"I know. I came back from Heart's Ease to talk to you and you were gone."

"Yeah, I thought about you in the City of Night a lot. When I could.

"Moira, I'm sorry," Wiz said. "I let myself get so wrapped up in my own problems that I shut you out."

"And I crowded you too closely because I had nothing of my own here."

He smiled up at her. "We'll just have to try to do better, won't we?"

"We shall both have to try."

"Darling, do me a favor will you? If I start acting like a jerk again, punch me in the ribs. Hard."

Moira took his hand in hers. "I think I can manage that."

He reached up, pulled her down to him and kissed her again.

"In fact I will do better than that," she said with an amused glint in her sea-green eyes. "If you *ever* ignore me again, or treat me like a piece of furniture, I will make you very sorry indeed." Moira made a quick little motion with her hand and the air in front of her sparkled with shards of the rainbow. "And believe me, My Lord, I am just the witch who can do it."

Wiz looked at her openmouthed. "You wouldn't do that to me, would you?"

Moira smiled sweetly. "Try me."

There was a discreet knock at the door. They turned and saw a servant carrying a covered tray.

"Your, ah, dinner, Lord," the man said with an odd expression as he laid the tray on the table beside Wiz's bed. He removed the warming cover and withdrew.

Sitting on the plate, neatly trussed and roasted, was a small bird. The odor from the platter had unappetizing overtones.

Wiz looked at it dubiously. Then he poked at it with his knife. Then he looked up at Moira.

"Crow, right?"

Her eyes sparkled. "Well, Lord, you did say . . ."

"I know," Wiz sighed. "I know." Deliberately he cut a slice of the breast, put it into his mouth and chewed a couple of times.

"You know," he said at last. "I think I finally understand that expression."

Wiz was dozing again when he got his next visitor.

"Wiz?" a familiar voice said gently. At first he thought he was dreaming. There was no way he could be hearing . . .

"Wiz?"

"*Jerry!*" Wiz sat bolt upright in bed. "How the hell . . ."

"Relax, I volunteered," his friend told him. "We've got over a dozen people here; programmers, systems analysts, documentation specialists. We've been working on your spell compiler and magic operating system. We call it WIZ-DOS. You're famous, boy."

Wiz shook his head. "I . . . I don't know what to say . . . except God, it's good to see you!"

"I missed you too. ZetaSoft wasn't the same after you left. Look, I know you're supposed to be resting, but there are a couple of things that have been driving us nuts."

Without waiting for an answer he spread four scrolls out on the bed.

"Okay, now here . . ."

"Just what do you think you're doing?"

They both looked up to see Bronwyn standing in the door, hands on hips and fire in her eye.

"This is a friend of mine," Wiz told her. "I was just helping him . . ."

"You are helping nothing!" Bronwyn said, advancing into the room. "You risk relapse My Lord! Especially with the healing spell. You are supposed to be resting and rest you shall." She turned to Jerry. "As for you, you will take your magics and you will go back where you came from." She gestured as if exorcising a demon. "Begone"

"Look, I need to talk . . ."

"Out," Bronwyn ordered.

"But this will only take . . ."

"Out!" She made shooing motions. "Tomorrow he will be released and he can work himself to death as he pleases. But he will have a good night's sleep before he begins."

"Tomorrow, okay?" Jerry grabbed the scrolls and left.

Later in the afternoon Bal-Simba came to visit him.

"They tell me you are recovered," the huge black wizard said as he entered the room.

"They want me to stay here overnight just in case, but I'm fine."

"Arianne said you wanted to talk to me."

"Yeah. We've got a very serious problem." He outlined his conversation with Duke Aelric and what he had seen on his travels through the Wild Wood.

Bal-Simba nodded gravely at the end of it. "I have talked to Aelric and I already know much of it. Besides there have been some incidents." He told Wiz about the disappearing villages.

"So it's already started," Wiz said heavily. "Shit! I should have gotten back sooner."

"Little enough you could have done about that, Sparrow. Now, what of Duke Aelric?"

"He thinks we can make some kind of deal. But we're going to have to work fast."

"What would he require?"

Wiz looked uncomfortable. "It's not him, exactly. The way he explained it to me, there are so many factions and kinds of non-mortals that we can't just sit down and bargain. What we've got to do is remove the threat in their eyes so their coalition falls apart. Then maybe we can come to an agreement with the elves."

"And what would this take?"

"Hey, I don't know, I'm just the messenger boy."

"Hardly," rumbled Bal-Simba. "It was obviously your idea. Further, the elves, or at least Duke Aelric, are willing to treat with you."

*Yeah*, Wiz thought, *only one of them keeps trying to kill me.* "You make it sound like I'm ambassador to the elves or something."

"Very nearly, Sparrow. You have had more success dealing with them than any living mortal."

"Great. Another job I don't want and I'm no good at."

Bal-Simba sighed. "Sparrow, we would be much further along if you would stop prejudging what you are or are not capable of. You can do a great deal more than you suppose if you put your mind to it. Now I ask you again, what will it take to avert a war?"

Wiz thought. "At the very least we're going to have to fix things so they don't feel threatened. That means we're going to have to do something about **demon_debug**."

"That falls within the purview of you and the team from your world," Bal-Simba said. "What else?"

"Well, we're going to have to stop this mad dash into the Wild Wood. We may be able to work out some kind of homesteading arrangement later, but for right now we need to keep people from going further."

Bal-Simba stroked his chin and the little bones of his necklace clicked against each other. "As easy to sweep back the sea, I fear."

"Can't you order them to stop?"

The giant wizard smiled wryly. "Sparrow, even at the height of our power the Council never had that kind of hold over the people. Were we to issue such an order it would be ignored and there are not enough guardsmen to post at every forest road and trail."

"You've got to do something."

"We can only try."

"I understand you've got a whole team of programmers here," Wiz said to change the subject.

"Almost a score of them, recruited from the Valley of Quartz."

"You mean Silicon Valley."

"That is what I said, is it not? In any event they have been working on your system of magic and making excellent progress—or so they tell me." He chuckled. "Meanwhile they have been, ah, enlivening things here to no end."

"I dunno," Wiz said. "You make me feel superfluous. I've been gone and you and Moira have been doing all

the work. All I managed to do was get myself kidnapped
and chased all over the City of Night."

"Hardly. Aside from wiping out the remnants of the
Dark League, you were the one who approached Duke
Aelric with the notion of a treaty."

"You could have done that."

Bal-Simba shook his head. "No, Sparrow, I could not.
In the first place he never would have talked to me. In
the second place I would not have had the courage to
do something so insanely dangerous."

"Oh," said Wiz in a very small voice.

"Well, I do not wish to tire you, so we will leave these
matters for the morrow."

"Fine. I'm pretty bushed. I'm going to get a snack and
go back to sleep."

Bal-Simba made no move to leave.

"Is there something else?"

"There are questions we must answer and soon," he
said at last. "Some things yet unclear about what happened to you."

"For instance?"

"Was your kidnapping connected with the attempts on
your life?"

"No. That was someone else. I think I can take care
of that."

"Ahh, I see," he said and then hesitated again. "I
understand Ebrion is dead."

"Yeah. I was there when it happened."

The wizard looked closely at him. "Was he involved
in your kidnapping?"

Wiz opened his mouth and then stopped. Telling
Bal-Simba what had happened would definitely dis-
credit Ebrion's faction—the people who had been
trouble ever since he arrived at the Capital. But
discrediting them wouldn't make them go away. They'd
still be here and they'd be even angrier and more
frustrated.

*Always leave your opponent a line of retreat—unless you want a fight to the death.*

Wiz realized Bal-Simba was watching him intently.

"Would it do any good if I said Ebrion was involved?" he said at last. "I mean in the long run?"

The giant black wizard considered. "In the long run? No, not really."

"Then let's say he died trying to save me and leave it at that."

"Sparrow, you never cease to amaze me," Bal-Simba rumbled. "You grow constantly in wisdom."

Wiz snorted. "Too schoon ve get old und too late schmart." Then he sobered. "I just hope it really isn't too late. I made a royal mess of things this time."

"Things are in an, ah, 'interesting' state," Bal-Simba agreed. "But certainly not beyond hope."

# Twenty-Two
## MENDING FENCES

*Good client relations are the key to a successful project.*
*—consultants' saying*

The Mighty in the Capital gathered in the chantry the next morning in no very good mood. They knew that Wiz had been kidnapped by magic and they knew Ebrion was dead. Some of them, guiltily remembering old conversations and half-dropped hints, suspected very strongly the two events were not unconnected. Most of them didn't know enough to suspect, but they had an uneasy feeling that someone's head was on the block.

As the blue-robed men and women took their seats in the carved throne-like chairs around the room they murmured and muttered among themselves. Bal-Simba had commanded this meeting, but obviously the Sparrow was the one who would do the talking.

Wiz stood up as soon as Bal-Simba called them to order.

"This isn't easy for me to say," Wiz looked out over the assembled group. "But you were right and I was wrong. I am sorry. No matter how my magic compiler turns out, humans are still going to need your wisdom and your sense of restraint. I was so wrapped up in the technical details I couldn't see that.

"My blindness has had very serious consequences. Now I can only hope to undo the damage I have done."

He took a deep breath and went on. "I can't change the past, none of us can. But we can put it aside and go on from there. I'm asking you to work with me, both with the problems we have right now and in the long run.

"I hope that we can work together in spite of what happened in the past. We need each other." He paused. "At least, I need you. Thank you for listening." With that he stepped away from the podium to a smattering of applause.

"What of Ebrion?" someone called from the back of the room. Suddenly there was dead silence. The Mighty froze where they were and everyone looked at Wiz.

Wiz licked his lips. "I am sorry to say Ebrion is dead. He was a good man and he always acted in the way he believed was right. He was killed trying to protect me."

There was an almost audible sigh from the assembled wizards.

Several of the Mighty crowded around afterwards. The first to reach him was Malus. "Well, my boy," Malus said. "Well, well." Then the fat little wizard hugged Wiz to him.

"The fault was hardly yours alone, Lord," Juvian said, stepping up to him. "We have had our blindnesses." Several of the others pressed forward to offer their support as well, and for several minutes Wiz, Moira and the wizards stood making strained small talk.

"If you will excuse me, My Lords," Wiz said at last, "I have to meet with the programming team this afternoon and I want to get something to eat before then."

Malus followed them out. "I wanted you to see something," he said once they were alone in the corridor. "Your friend Karl has been teaching us while you were gone." He shook his head. "It is hard, very hard, this new magic of yours, but I have been practicing and, well . . . **greeting exe.**"

Suddenly, written between them in glowing green letters six inches high was:

HELLO  WORLD

"It is my first spell with the new magic," Malus said shyly. "How do you like it?"

Wiz grinned, Moira hugged the tubby little wizard and kissed him on the cheek.

"I think that's wonderful, My Lord," she said, "and I'm sure Wiz does too."

"It's great," Wiz agreed. It's one of the best presents I could have had. Thank you, Malus."

"That speech has to be the hardest thing I ever did," Wiz said as they made their way back to their chamber.

Moira squeezed his hand more tightly. "Perhaps it was also the bravest."

He put his arm around her waist and kissed her. Then he opened the door and ushered her back into their apartment.

"The place looks bare with all my notes and stuff gone," he said, looking over at the table beneath the window.

"They went to a good home," Moira told him. Personally she thought it was a great improvement, but she wasn't going to say so now.

"What have we got to eat? I'm starved and it smells wonderful."

Moira brought the dishes out of the cupboard where they had been magically kept warm. "I had luncheon sent up from the kitchens. Beef barley soup, roast beef, potatoes and bread and cheese."

"Heaven."

Wiz ate ravenously, enough for three normal men. Moira contented herself with a cup of soup and watched him pack the food away.

"Well," he said pushing away from the table at last, "that was wonderful, but I need to go meet the programmers."

Moira shook out her mane of copper-colored hair. "I was hoping you could spend some time with me this afternoon," she said softly.

"I'd like to darling, but I've got to get up to speed on this."

Moira put her arms around his neck. "Won't it keep for a while?"

"Look, I really do need to get to the team meeting." Moira melted against him and pressed her lips to his for a long, slow kiss.

"Of course," he said as the kiss ended, "I could always tell them I was held captive by a wicked witch."

Moira opened her green eyes wide. "Wicked, My Lord?"

Wiz pulled her to him. "Darling, when you get going you're the wickedest witch that ever was."

As always the Council of the North met in the morning. However this time Wiz was sitting in the center of the long wooden table, next to Bal-Simba and he was anything but bored with the proceedings.

" . . . so that's it," he concluded. "Unless we can curb the invasion of the Wild Wood and stop people from using **demon_debug** we are going to have a war."

For once there were no objections from Honorious, no sniping from Juvian and no clarifications from Agricolus. Every man and woman at the table looked grave.

Juvian, who oversaw the Council's dealings with the hedge witches, pursed his lips. "All easier said than done, I fear. The villagers prefer **demon_debug** because it is so effective against magic."

"**ddt** is just as effective and a lot less harmful to the environment. We've got to get them to use it instead of **demon_debug**."

The sorcerer rubbed a pudgy hand over a jowl. "That will not be easy, Lord. We do not have the authority we once had."

"They'll listen to you if they ever want another bit of magic out of me," Wiz said firmly. "Look, this has got to stop. Unless magic is actively dangerous it is not to be destroyed."

Juvian shook his head. "I do not know, Lord."

"Just tell them that if they don't stop, I'll come there and start throwing lightning bolts."

"If you wish it we will, of course, but I do not know if they will listen to us."

"We have got to *make* them listen."

"We will do our best Lord, but it will be difficult."

"Okay," Wiz sighed, "what about limiting migration then?"

"That is not merely difficult, that is impossible," Honorious said. "The farms are too small and the soil is too poor. On that the peasants will not listen at all."

"We don't have to freeze our boundaries exactly where we are. The part of the Wild Wood closest to the Fringe was human territory once anyway. But we can't have uncontrolled expansion."

"Then tell us how to prevent such expansion, Lord."

"If we don't prevent it we'll be at war."

The old wizard sighed heavily. "Then, Lord, my advice is to prepare for war. For the people will not obey us on this."

All up and down the table the wizards looked even grimmer. But none of them disagreed with Honorious or offered an alternative.

# Twenty-Three
## BRAINSTORM TIME

*At some point in the project you're going to have to break down and finally define the problem.*

—programmers' saying

"Okay," Larry Fox said, "what about corned_beef?"

Wiz had spent most of the previous afternoon and a good part of the morning meeting the team and reviewing what they had done. Now he was beginning to tackle the problems Jerry had dumped in his lap—literally— two days before. All the stalls in the Bull Pen were taken so they had wedged a table in down by the whiteboard and tea urn. He and Larry had spent hours going over obscure bits of code and untangling particularly strange demons.

"corned_beef is a hashing routine, obviously," Wiz told him between bites of his third sandwich of the afternoon. "It's a fast way to search for a demon—a routine—by name."

"But where's the rest of it? We figured out that it was doing a hashed look up, but we couldn't see how you searched the entries."

"Mmmf," said Wiz around his mouthful of sandwich. He shook his head and swallowed hard. "It's a perfect hash. One item per entry, always." He took another big bite of sandwich. "You take the first characters of the demon's name, multiply that by a magic number. That gives you the number that serves as a subscript to the array. If you pick your numbers right you always get a unique entry for each item."

"That's weird!"

Wiz shrugged. "It works."

"One more question. Why do you divide by 65,353?"

"Because you've got to divide by a prime number, preferably one at least twice as large as the number of entries you want in the hash table. 65,353 is a Mersinne Prime and it was the largest prime I could remember."

Larry frowned. "Are you sure 65,353 is prime? I don't think it is."

Wiz shrugged and took another bite. "It worked."

"Okay," Larry said, "I'll clear the rest of these changes with Jerry or Karl and get right to work on them."

"No need for that. I intended to fix those other points anyway and it's in the language specification."

Larry hesitated. "I'd still better clear them."

Wiz started to object and then stopped. It really wasn't his project any more, he realized. The original specification might be his, but even that had been modified in the process of development. Now it was a team project and Jerry Andrews was the team leader. It hurt to recognize that, but fighting it would only damage the project.

"Fine," he sighed. "Let me know what Jerry wants to do about it."

The next afternoon the entire team gathered in the Bull Pen. One of the long trestle tables had been cleared and stools and benches were pulled up around it. Wiz sat at one end of the table with Moira and Jerry by his side. In the center was the new version of the Dragon Book, with the small red dragon curled peacefully asleep atop it.

"The news from the Council isn't good," Wiz told them. "I was hoping they could solve their immediate problems by traditional methods once they understood what the problem was. They've been pushing for us to wave a magic wand," he smiled wryly at the phrase, "and make them go away. Well, as of this morning, it is definite. There is simply no way they can do it. We've got to come up with a magical means to head off a war."

"Not much to ask, is it?" Nancy said.

"Okay," Wiz said. "We've got two problems here. One of them is the hacked version of that protection spell. The second one is we've got to keep people from penetrating further into the Wild Wood until we get things straightened out."

"What's the main problem?" Judith asked.

"The spell, I think. That's what seems to be doing the most damage right now. We've got to either neutralize it or keep people from using it."

"Can you not neutralize their magic as you did at the City of Night?" Moira asked.

"The worms? That's too non-specific." He shook his head. "No, we can't afford to soak up all the available magic. That would leave the humans right back where they were before we started. We need something more subtle."

"But we have to have it quickly," the redheaded witch said. "We cannot afford to waste time in pursuit of the 'elegance' you keep talking about."

"So we're gonna need something quick and dirty." He held up a hand. "But not *too* dirty. Does anyone have any ideas?"

"Sounds like a job for a virus," Nancy said.

"Naw, as soon as they see the program is infected, they'll switch back to the old one."

"A birthday virus!" Danny shouted suddenly.

"A what?" Wiz asked.

"A virus that doesn't trigger until a specific event occurs. We set the magic event far enough in the future

that the program will have had time to spread everywhere. Then it triggers," he waved his hands, "poof! The
spell doesn't work anymore."

"You know," Jerry said suspiciously, "you talk like
you've had a lot of experience at this."

The other shrugged. "It's, you know, been a special
interest of mine."

Jerry snorted. "When we get back, remind me never
to use any software you had anything to do with."

Wiz ignored the byplay. "Okay, what keeps them from
going back to the old spell?"

There was silence down the table.

"We can't just wipe it out of their memories, can we?"
Jerry sighed.

"Even if we could, there are sure to be written copies
around. When the new program self-destructs, they'll just
go back to the old one."

"Can we come up with a spell to attach itself to
**demon_debug** and destroy it?"

Wiz thought hard. "I did something like that against
the Dark League. The problem is, when it destroyed the
spell it took out everything for about thirty yards around
in a humongous blast. We don't want to kill them and
it would be a big job to weaken the effect."

"Aw, they'd get the message after the first couple of
explosions," Danny said.

"No," Wiz said firmly.

"Well . . ." The young programmer's face lit up. "Hey
wait a minute! Suppose they get the idea the spell's no
good?"

"The problem is that it *is* good against magic. Too
good."

Danny smiled an evil smile. "Not if we're the ones
making the magic."

Wiz looked at Danny and then at Jerry. "Now that's
got possibilities. Suppose we cook up something
**demon_debug** *doesn't* work against?"

"Yeah," Jerry said slowly. "Something that will convince them they don't ever want to mess with **demon_debug** again. Danny, stick around after the meeting, will you? I think I know how we can put that arcade-game mind of yours to work."

Wiz made a check mark on the slate in front of him. "Okay, that gives us a handle on one problem. Now for the other one, keeping humans out of the Wild Wood."

"I don't suppose we can just make a law?" Jerry asked hopefully.

Moira snorted and shook her head so violently her copper curls flew in front of her face.

"That is what the Council has been trying. The hunger for land is deep in our farmers and the soil within the Fringe is thin and poor." She reached up and brushed a strand of hair off her upper lip. —Besides, I think you misread the relation between the Mighty and the people. The Mighty are guardians and protectors, not governors."

"And right now the Council's influence with the people is at an all-time low," Wiz said grimly. *Thanks in part to my meddling.*

"So we're gong to need a barrier," Judith said. "A wall."

"They would climb a simple wall," Moira told her. "Or else batter breaches in it."

"What about your basic wall of fire?" Karl asked.

"How do you keep from burning down the Wild Wood?"

"We could do a line of death," someone else suggested.

"We don't want to kill them, just keep them in," Wiz said.

"An electrified fence?"

"That's a thought."

"Yeah," Danny said, "with mine fields and guard towers!"

"That is *not* a thought," Wiz said firmly.

Again everyone at the table fell silent. The little red dragon whuffed in his sleep and scuffled the papers beneath him with tiny running motions as he chased a dream mouse.

"Okay," Cindy said slowly. "What about making them not *want* to go beyond a certain point?"

"A geas?" Moira shook her head. "You cannot lay geas on an entire people, including ones you have never seen."

"But **ddt** does essentially that for magical creatures," Cindy said.

"That isn't a geas," Wiz told her. That's a repulsion spell. Different animal."

"Well, how about a repulsion spell then?"

"Repulsion spells attach to specific objects," Moira explained. "You would have to put the spell on every rock, every tree and every finger-length of soil along the line."

"That's not a problem—in theory," Jerry said. "We can write a program that will do it. It would take a lot of demons . . . No, wait a minute! We could use the principle of similarity. Mark the line on a map."

"Yeah, fine," said Nancy. "Where are we going to get a map accurate enough to make a spell like that stick? Have you seen what these people call a map?"

"Okay so we make our own map," Wiz said.

"How are we going to do that?" asked Karl. "You can't just sketch it from dragon back."

"If we have to mark everything individually, it will take years to get the barrier up," Jerry said. "I don't think we've got years."

"We will be fortunate if we have weeks," Moira told him

"Wait a minute!" Wiz put in. "We can use a modified version of my searching spell. Generate thousands of mapping units. We'll have our data in a couple of days."

"Searching spell? You mean that R-squared D-squared thing?"

"No, the three-layer search system. You've used it, haven't you?"

"That is the spell I was telling you about, Lord," Moira said to Jerry. "The one we could not find."

Wiz frowned. "There was a copy in my notes. Well, it doesn't matter. It won't take long to rewrite it and I'd want to translate it to run under the latest version of the compiler anyway."

Wiz made another mark on his slate.

"That's it then. Okay people, split into your teams and let's get cracking. We've got a lot of work to do here."

"Are you sure this will work?" Bal-Simba asked dubiously as Wiz, Jerry and Moira showed him the team's latest creation.

"It will if they try to use **demon_debug** on it," Wiz assured him. "The basic spell is a modification of the one I used to create the watchers against the Dark League."

"And it will harm no one?" the giant black sorcerer pressed.

"It can't do physical damage to anyone, Lord," Jerry said confidently. Of course, what it can do to their mental state . . .

"Amazing," Bal-Simba said as he studied the creature on the table before him. "Where did you get the idea for these things?"

"Where I get all my best ideas," Wiz said jauntily. "I stole it."

# Twenty-Four
## DEMONS GO HOME

*Customer support is an art, not a science.*
                         *—marketing saying*
*So are most other forms of torture.*
                         *—programmers' response*

"Lady, Lady come quickly!" Mayor Andrew pounded frantically on the door and looked fearfully over his shoulder toward the village square. "We are beset!"

"Unnugh?" Alaina rolled over in her bed and tried to shake the mead fumes from her head. She threw the dirty bedclothes aside and stumbled to the door, cursing as she banged into an overturned stool.

"Not so loud," she grumbled, fumbling with the bar. "Not so bleeding loud." She threw open the door and glared at Andrew. "Now what is it?"

In answer he pointed back into the village. Pale translucent shapes floated here and there over the houses, flitting down the streets and hovering before windows. Now and again a bone-chilling shriek broke the night's silence.

Alaina gathered herself. "Magic, eh? Well we'll see about that." She snatched a grubby cloak from the hook beside the door and threw it over her night dress. Barefoot and with her hair in disarray she marched toward the square with the mayor trailing close behind.

One of the ghostly shapes floated down out of the night sky at her, gibbering as it came. Alaina stopped short and flung her arm up to it.

"**demon_debug BEGONE**," she commanded in a cracked voice. "**exe!**"

The pale form stopped in mid-flight, shuddered and dropped to the earth, coalescing and changing form as it did so. By the time it reached the ground it was a small green man-like thing with a bald head, pointed ears and a wide mouth. In the flickering light of the mayor's torch, Alaina could see that the little creature was bright green.

It blinked once, extended a foot-long tongue and licked one of its eyebrows, like a cat grooming itself. Then it smiled up at her nastily.

"Ya know, Lady," the little green man said with a distinct Brooklyn accent, "ya really shouldnna have done that."

"I tell you we are overrun with these things!" Alaina screamed into the communications crystal. "They are everywhere."

One of the little green men sat on top of the image formed above the crystal, his legs dangling down in front, as if he were sitting on top of a television instead of in mid-air. She brushed at him like shooing a fly, but her hand passed through the little man's legs. He stuck out a foot-long pink tongue and gave the hedge witch an especially juicy raspberry.

From where he sat in the Council's great hall, Wiz couldn't see the little green man. But Alaina's gestures told him clearly what must be happening.

"How long have you had this problem?" he asked sympathetically.

"Since last night. These things are driving us mad and

when I call for help, you make me wait for near a day-tenth before anyone will speak to me. Nothing but that terrible music in the background while I wait."

Alaina put her head in her hands. The day had been the worst of her life. In laying the banshees she had created dozens of the little green men. Now they were all over the village, getting into everything, making rude and obnoxious comments to everyone and not giving anyone a moment's peace.

Worse, there was nothing you could do to them. Magic didn't seem to work and physical objects passed completely through them. Mayor Andrew was nursing a broken hand after trying to hit one of the little creatures that happened to be standing in front of a post. He was so angry at Alaina he wouldn't even come to her for healing.

"I am sorry about the wait," Wiz told her. "We are very busy here and none of our service representatives, ah wizards, were immediately available." Out of the corner of his eye, Wiz could see all the communications positions in the great hall filled with wizards talking to people just as he was. But this one was special. Part of the reason Alaina had to wait was he wanted to handle this village himself. "Now, about these little green men. How did they appear?"

"First there was a plague of banshees and when I tried to exorcise them, we got—this." She waved her hand helplessly. "Oh, I would rather the banshees," she moaned.

"We have not been able to re-create your problem here," Wiz told her. "There is nothing in **ddt** that could produce an effect like that."

"I didn't use **ddt**, I used **demon_debug**," Alaina said.

Wiz frowned and pursed his lips. "Well, as you know, **demon_debug** was not our spell. We cannot be responsible for the consequences if users attempt to apply spells with unauthorized modifications."

Alaina moaned again.

"However," Wiz went on, "we have encountered this problem before. The spell you used was not thoroughly tested before release and contained some serious bugs that interact destructively with certain kinds of magic. In fact, we find it actually attracts those kinds of magic. You were quite fortunate, you know."

"Fortunate?" Alaina asked miserably. Now three of the little green menaces were dancing a jig between her and Wiz's image. They were accompanying themselves with their own singing and none of them had the slightest sense of pitch or rhythm.

"Fortunate," Wiz said solemnly. "It might have been dragons."

"Eh?" said Alaina, straining to hear over the cater-wauling.

"*I said it might have been dragons,*" Wiz shouted.

Now the green creatures had split up. Two of them were playing nose flutes which droned together like out-of-tune bagpipes while the third took center stage to perform a solo—and extremely rude—version of the Highland fling.

"*Help us, Lord,*" Alaina shouted hoarsely over the racket of the demons. Wiz winced and muted the sound from his crystal.

"As it happens we do have a beta version of **ddt** Release 2.0. It should be very effective against these secondary demons." He pursed his lips severely. "However I would strongly suggest that you do not use any unauthorized spells from now on. The incompatibility problems are likely to become much more severe."

"Anything," Alaina said fervently. "Anything at all. I'll burn every copy of **demon_debug** I can get my hands on. Just rid us of these monsters!"

"I'll get a messenger off with **ddt** Release 2.0 right away," Wiz told the hedge witch. "And remember, no unauthorized spells."

He left Alaina blubbering thanks as the image faded.

"That'll hold her," he said as he turned away from the now-dead crystal to Moira. "What's the matter?" he asked as he caught her look.

"Wiz, this is cruel."

"What they did to that rock creature was ten times worse," Wiz said. "At least these demons won't hurt them and they'll vanish at a touch of Release 2.0. Besides, I want to make sure that new spell gets spread to every part of the human inhabited world—and that no one tries to use **demon_debug** again."

"Still, you make them suffer needlessly."

Wiz rose and held her close. "Not needlessly. If we don't stop them there won't be any magical beings at all left anywhere inside the Fringe."

"And would that be such a bad thing?"

He took her arms. "You don't mean that. Magic is just as much a part of this World as humans are. You don't handle something by destroying it. You come to terms with it and learn to use it."

Moira sighed and Wiz felt her relax in his grip. "Oh, you are right, of course. But I wish there were some other way."

"So do I," Wiz said. I don't like this either." *Except in certain selected cases.*

"Well, what do you think?" Jerry asked the group gathered around the long table in the Bull Pen.

Moira gave a little gasp. "It is beautiful."

"It should be accurate enough to do the job," Wiz said judiciously as he looked over the map.

The little red dragon wandered over, sniffed at the map, decided it wasn't good enough to eat or interesting enough to play with, and returned to his nap on top of the nearby books.

He was the only one in the room who was not impressed. It was a very special map. The parchment it was drawn on was made from the skin of a wild ox from the Wild Wood. The inks used in the drawing were made of pigments taken from the wood itself. Black from the oak galls, browns and full reds from the earth of the Wild Wood and the blues and the greens from minerals taken from its rocks. The pens and brushes used to draw the map were also made from Wild Wood products. Hairs from the tails of forest martens and squirrels, pens from the quills of forest birds and elder bushes. Even the water to mix the inks and the pumice to pounce the skin had come from the Wild Wood.

Unlike any other map ever seen in the World it was also accurate and to scale, thanks to modified versions of Wiz's searching demons and an Emac Jerry had hacked to do the cartography.

The effect was breathtaking. The mountains seemed to rise up out of the parchment and the brooks and rivers appeared to flow in their beds. Even the forests seemed to be alive.

They all admired the map silently for a moment. Then Jerry picked up the wand that lay beside the map. It was made of ebony and ivory and was about the size and shape of a conductor's baton.

"I still feel silly waving a magic wand around," he said to no one in particular.

"Just think of it as a funny looking mouse," Wiz advised.

"Okay, phase two." Jerry took the wand and drew it along the line on the map. Where the wand passed a trail of glowing green remained.

There was a stirring in the air, but nothing else changed.

"That's it?" Judith asked.

"That's it," Jerry said. "You wanted lightning bolts maybe?"

"Is it permanent?" Moira asked.

"Until it's reversed," Jerry said. "But we can reverse it any time."

"This will work until the Council can come up with some kind of policy they can enforce," Wiz said. "It also establishes our good intentions with the elves and the other non-mortals. As long as the barrier's in place I don't think we will have a war."

Einrich topped the rise and stopped. The path ahead of him lay clear, but he could not go that way. His ox whuffed and stamped nervously, catching his master's indecision.

The peasant scanned the forest. The trees here were no different than the ones in the valley behind them. The same huge old giants sheltering an undergrowth of ferns. But it was different and he could not go that way.

The trail ran on ahead as it ran behind, winding between the big trees, skirting logs and avoiding the thickly grown patches where a tree had fallen and saplings and busy new growth competed for the light. But he could not follow the trail on.

Einrich frowned and without knowing quite why, turned back. The valley behind was far enough.

# *Twenty-Five*
## PROJECT'S END

*Programming is like pinball. The reward for doing it well is
the opportunity to do it again.*

—programmers' saying

" . . . and a fifty percent bonus for successful completion of contract," the clerk said, adding a second, smaller stack of golden cartwheels to the stack already on the table. "Sign here please." Karl bent down and marked the leather-bound ledger next to his name. Behind him the other programmers were lined up to receive their pay.

"Hey, I like this," one of them said. "No invoicing, no hassles with the bookkeeping department and nobody trying to hang onto the money a few days more to improve their cash flow. Why can't all assignments be like this?"

"Speak for yourself. When I get home I'm going to hit the hot tub for about two days solid."

"I'm for a Big Mac first," someone else said. "No, make that six Big Macs."

At the side of the room Bal-Simba smiled. "I am almost sorry to see them go. They have certainly enlivened this place."

"Um, yes," said Malus, who was standing between Bal-

607

Simba and Wiz. He didn't say it with a lot of conviction. "Uh, they are *all* going back, aren't they?"

Wiz shook his head. "No. I learned my lesson. Jerry's going to stay behind on a long-term contract to help with the programming. He isn't the teacher that Karl is, but he's a lot better than I am. In another year or so he can leave and we'll be able to use our own people."

"Oh," said Malus. "But just one, you say?"

"Just one."

Moira, who was standing behind them, grinned at the byplay and turned her attention back to the programmers. They were all glad to be going, she saw. The work had been interesting, but the job was done. Now it was time to move on to other things.

Moira felt a pang. She would miss them, with their strange jokes and their casual insanities and their odd, warped way of looking at the universe. She would miss the camaraderie she had shared with them and even their cheerful way of working themselves into blind exhaustion to meet their goals.

But much as she liked them, they were not of her World. Malus was right. They did not belong here and it would be hard on everyone if they stayed.

Still, it hurt to say goodbye.

"Lady?" a voice said softly. Moira turned and saw it was Judith. She had changed from the long dress and girdle she had worn around the keep and back into her slacks and unicorn T-shirt, the first time she had worn that outfit since arrival.

"I wanted to thank you before we left."

"Thank me?" Moira said blankly.

"For your advice. You know, up on the battlements that day. About romance and where you can find it."

Moira bobbed a curtsey. "I am glad it pleased you, My Lady."

Judith made a little face. "I don't know that it pleased me, but it helped. You were right. If I want to see the romance in the world I am going to have to stop looking for someone else to create it for me." She smiled wryly. "If I can't count on anyone else to make my dreams real I'll have to do it myself."

"How will you do that?"

"I'm going to write a fantasy trilogy," said Judith. "It's going to be full of romance and color and heroics."

"And dragons?"

Judith grinned. "Oh yes. Lots of dragons."

"Well, you'll have the money to do it," Nancy said as she and Mike joined them. "If you're not extravagant you can live for a while on what this job paid, even at Bay Area prices."

"Are you planning to live at ease on your new wealth?" Moira asked.

"Nope," Mike said. "We're going to open a shop specializing in real-time programming and process control," Mike said.

"Yeah," Nancy added. "After this gig *anything* is gonna be easy." She looked over at Judith. "We were hoping to get you to join us, but I guess not."

"Oh, all this talking about leaving reminds me," Moira said. "Will you excuse me, My Ladies, My Lord?"

"You will be here to see us off, won't you?"

"Oh yes," Moira said. "But there is one other detail that must be attended to. Please excuse me." She grasped Judith's hands in hers. "And good luck."

"My Lords, Ladies, may I have your attention for a moment?"

Heads turned toward the dais where Moira was standing alone. "While you are all gathered here, and before you depart, there is one other denizen of our World we wish you to meet."

She gestured toward the side of the stage and a demon lurched out from behind the curtains. Nearly everyone in the room, programmers and wizards alike, gasped.

It was twelve feet tall, horned and fanged, with a barbed tail sticking out from underneath the jacket of its pin-striped suit. Its forest green skin contrasted vividly with its dark purple shirt and its stark white tie. Under one arm it carried a violin case big enough to hold a bull fiddle.

Moira smiled sweetly. I am certain you all remember the non-disclosure agreement you signed when you took this job?"

The programmers gulped and nodded.

"This is Guido," Moira said. "He is our contract enforcer."

Guido favored the group with a smile that showed all three rows of dagger-like teeth.

Nobody said anything.

"Naturally we will insist on strict observance of the non-disclosure clause," Moira said and smiled sweetly again.

"Can that thing reach us when we get home?" Karl whispered to Jerry.

"You want to find out?"

Karl thought a minute. "No, not really."

Neither of them said anything as the demon clumped back behind the curtain.

"Boy, that's one way to get everyone's attention," Karl said.

Jerry scanned the room, counting people with his forefinger. "Not everyone. Danny's missing."

"The little twerp's probably late as usual."

"Hey, Fox," Jerry called across the room. "Where's Danny?"

Larry shrugged. "I dunno. He collected his money and split."

"Well, if he doesn't get back here soon he's going to miss the bus. Damn! I'd better go find him."

Moira had come up to Jerry at the end of the exchange. "No, My Lord, you stay here. I will go find him."

Danny turned out to be in the first place Moira checked, which was his room. He was wearing an open-throated collarless shirt, light leather jerkin and trousers tucked into high soft boots. He was stuffing his belongings into a leather traveler's pack. June stood next to him, so close he nearly bumped into her every time he turned to take more things form the cupboard.

"That is hardly appropriate for your world," Moira said, eyeing his clothing.

"I'm not going back," Danny said defiantly. "I'm going to stay here." June stood close and squeezed his hand hard.

Moira looked hard at June. She had a definite glow about her that meant only one thing to the hedge witch's trained eye.

"You are pregnant!" she said accusingly.

June smiled shyly and nodded.

"You see," Danny said triumphantly. "I can't go back."

*Fortuna!* Moira thought, *didn't the little ninny have enough sense to take precautions?*

"You cannot stay, either. How to you plan to support yourself—and your family?"

"I'm staying," he said gruffly. "Here at the keep or someplace else, but there's nothing back there for me. And I can work. It's not like I'm lazy or anything.

"Look," he went on, almost pleading. "Wiz is going to need help, right? I mean like there's still a shitload of stuff to do. Well, I can help him."

Moira realized she was completely out of her depth.

"I think we had better talk to Wiz about this," she said finally. "I don't think he is going to like it."

Wiz didn't like it. He scowled through the whole recitation, or as much as you can scowl while you're eating an apple. When Danny finally ran down he continued to scowl and kept on eating. Then he tossed the core of that apple away, selected another one from the bowl and took a hefty bite out of it while he tried to think. Danny stood silent and held one of June's hands in both of his, as if he were afraid she would vanish if he let go.

"Won't there be trouble if you don't go back?" Wiz asked at last.

Danny shook his head vigorously. "Nah. My dad doesn't want anything to do with me since I dropped out of school and my mom's remarried. I'm over eighteen, so what could they do anyway?"

"You realize that if you don't go back now it may be a long time before you get another chance?"

"I don't want to go back. I want to say here with June."

Wiz thought for about as long as it took him to finish the apple.

"Leave us alone for a few minutes, will you?"

The couple left the room, still joined at the fingers.

"What do you think?" Wiz asked as soon as the door closed behind them.

Jerry shrugged. "I don't know how much help he'd be, but I don't think it would be a problem to have him around. He's got more sense than most hackers his age." He caught the look in Moira's eye. "Programming sense," he amended.

"Moira?"

"I doubt it will last. Both are children in more than just years and neither has a strong family upbringing. Still, they deserve the chance to try and I am not sure what June would do if they were parted forcibly." She looked at Wiz. "It has to be your decision, Lord. Ultimately you would be the one responsible for him."

Wiz grabbed another apple from the bowl and took two bites. "I'd just as soon he went back. He's got potential, but sometimes he's so obnoxious I want to kick his ass from one end of the castle to the other." He sighed. "On the other hand, I don't like playing the ogre by separating them and he sure can't take her back to

Cupertino." He stood silent for a moment, chewing reflectively.

"Okay, if we can paper this over so he's not missed, I guess he can stay." He looked sharply at Moira. "What's wrong?"

"Wrong?"

"You've got that look in your eye."

"Oh, nothing," Moira said. "It is just that I got an odd feeling . . ." She shook herself. "No, nothing at all."

Wiz knew better than to pursue that. "All right, bring them back in here."

"Okay," Wiz said as he faced the pair. "You can stay. If," he waggled a finger at Danny. "*If* we can arrange this so you won't be missed. You can't just drop out of sight."

"That's easy," Danny said. "I'll write my mom a letter telling her I've taken a long-term contract overseas." He grinned. "That's even true. Then I'll throw in a couple of more letters to be mailed on her birthday and stuff. That way she won't worry and we'll just gradually lose touch."

Wiz wondered what Danny's mother would make of getting letters on parchment, but he decided not to ask.

"All right. Get those letters written and get them back here before it is time to leave. We'll see they get sent."

"I hope I'm not going to regret this," Wiz said after the pair raced out of the room.

"I wouldn't lay you odds," Jerry told him.

Again the programmers—less two—gathered in a tight knot inside the circle inscribed on the chantry floor. As the sundial's shadow shortened, they chattered among themselves and called goodbyes to the friends who had come to see them off. Wiz, Moira and Jerry stood on the dais next to Bal-Simba and waved back until the shadow reached its mark and the wizard motioned them to silence.

Once again the six-part chant welled up and the air shimmered and twisted about the group in the center of the room. The voices grew stronger and the people grew fainter until at last there was nothing but emptiness where they had been. The chant itself died away and nothing was left but the echoes.

In unison the wizards dropped their arms and at Bal-Simba's dismissal stepped away from their places. As the others filed out of the chantry the huge black wizard stepped down from the dais and ritually defaced the circle with his staff.

Wiz, Moira and Jerry remained for a couple of minutes more, looking at the place where their friends had been.

"Well, come on," Wiz said finally. "We've got a full day ahead of us tomorrow."

"How do you feel?" Moira asked Wiz as they walked hand in hand back to their apartment.

"Tired, hungry and very glad it's over." He frowned and sighed. "Only it isn't over. We're going to have to arrange some sort of meeting with the non-mortals to work out a treaty, and we've got a pile of work to do on the software."

They came to the door and paused. "But at least it's over for today and yes, I'm very glad of that." He bent his head down to kiss her and she responded enthusiastically.

"But first, food," he said as he pushed open the door to their rooms with his foot. "What's for dinner?"

Moira smiled mysteriously. "Something very special."

"Special or not, I hope there's a lot of it. I'm starved again."

"Sit down and I will bring it to you."

Wiz plopped himself down at the table and poured out a large glass of fruit juice from the pitcher sitting on it. He tasted it and then added several dollops of honey.

"Here it is," Moira said as she came through the door with a large flat box in her hands.

"Pizza!" Wiz said lovingly, caressing the cardboard as she set it on the table. "A real pizza from Little Italy!"

"I got it when I visited your world," Moira told him. "I have kept it hot and fresh by magic since we returned."

Wiz opened the box and breathed deeply. "Pepperoni, sausage and mushrooms. With extra cheese! This is wonderful."

"Best of all, the cooks say that now that they know what a pizza is supposed to be, they can make them."

"Wonderful," Wiz said, concentrating on separating a slice of pizza without losing the toppings.

"I thought you would be pleased."

"Oh, you have your compensations, wench," he said mock-loftily as he lifted the steaming slice to his mouth.

Moira smiled sweetly, waited until just the right moment and jabbed her elbow into his ribs—hard.

And Wiz Zumwalt—mightiest sorcerer in all the World, conqueror of demons, twice victor over the Dark League and keeper of the World's balance—tried to breath tomato sauce through his nose.